W9-CEU-217

THE
SATANIC
VERSES

ALSO BY SALMAN RUSHDIE

FICTION

Grimus
Midnight's Children
Shame
Haroun and the Sea of Stories
East, West
The Moor's Last Sigh
The Ground Beneath Her Feet

NONFICTION

The Jaguar Smile
Imaginary Homelands
The Wizard of Oz

SCREENPLAY

Midnight's Children

ANTHOLOGY

Mirrorwork (*co-editor*)

SALMAN RUSHDIE

THE SATANIC VERSES

A Novel

PICADOR USA

HENRY HOLT AND COMPANY

NEW YORK

THE SATANIC VERSES. Copyright © 1988 by Salman Rushdie. All rights
reserved. Printed in the United States of America. No part of
this book may be used or reproduced in any manner whatsoever
without written permission except in the case of brief quotations
embodied in critical articles or reviews. For information, address:
Picador USA, 175 Fifth Avenue, New York, N.Y. 10010.

Picador® is a U.S. registered trademark and is used by
Henry Holt and Company under license from Pan Books Limited.

For information on Picador USA Reading Group Guides, as well
as ordering, please contact the Trade Marketing department at
St. Martin's Press.
Phone: 1-800-221-7945 extension 763
Fax: 212-677-7456
E-mail: trademarketing@stmartins.com

Designed by Kathryn Parise

Library of Congress Cataloging-in-Publication Data

Rushdie, Salman.
    The satanic verses : a novel / Salman Rushdie.
        p.   cm.
    ISBN 0-312-27082-8
    I. Title.
PR6068.U757S27385   1997
823'.914—dc21   97-795
                                                            CIP

First published in the United States by Viking

First Picador USA Edition: December 2000

10 9 8 7 6 5 4 3 2 1

*Dedicated to the individuals
and organizations who have supported this publication.*

Satan, being thus confined to a vagabond, wandering, unsettled condition, is without any certain abode; for though he has, in consequence of his angelic nature, a kind of empire in the liquid waste or air, yet this is certainly part of his punishment, that he is . . . without any fixed place, or space, allowed him to rest the sole of his foot upon.

Daniel Defoe, *The History of the Devil*

CONTENTS

PART I

THE
ANGEL GIBREEL

1

'To be born again,' sang Gibreel Farishta tumbling from the heavens, 'first you have to die. Ho ji! Ho ji! To land upon the bosomy earth, first one needs to fly. Tat-taa! Taka-thun! How to ever smile again, if first you won't cry? How to win the darling's love, mister, without a sigh? Baba, if you want to get born again . . .' Just before dawn one winter's morning, New Year's Day or thereabouts, two real, full-grown, living men fell from a great height, twenty-nine thousand and two feet, towards the English Channel, without benefit of parachutes or wings, out of a clear sky.

'I tell you, you must die, I tell you, I tell you,' and thusly and so beneath a moon of alabaster until a loud cry crossed the night, 'To the devil with your tunes,' the words hanging crystalline in the iced white night, 'in the movies you only mimed to playback singers, so spare me these infernal noises now.'

Gibreel, the tuneless soloist, had been cavorting in moonlight as he sang his impromptu gazal, swimming in air, butterfly-stroke, breast-stroke, bunching himself into a ball, spreadeagling himself against the almost-infinity of the almost-dawn, adopting heraldic postures, rampant, couchant, pitting levity against gravity. Now he rolled happily towards the sardonic voice. 'Ohé, Salad baba, it's you, too good. What-ho, old Chumch.' At which the other, a fastidious shadow falling headfirst in a grey suit with all the jacket buttons done up, arms by his sides, taking for granted the improbability of the bowler hat on his head, pulled a nickname-hater's face. 'Hey, Spoono,' Gibreel yelled, eliciting a second inverted wince, 'Proper London, bhai! Here we come! Those bastards down there won't know what hit them. Meteor or lightning or vengeance of God. Out of thin air, baby. *Dharrraaammm!* Wham, na? What an entrance, yaar. I swear: splat.'

Out of thin air: a big bang, followed by falling stars. A universal beginning, a miniature echo of the birth of time . . . the jumbo jet *Bostan*, Flight AI-420, blew apart without any warning, high above the great, rotting, beautiful, snow-white, illuminated city, Mahagonny, Babylon, Alphaville. But Gibreel has already named it, I mustn't interfere: Proper London, capital of Vilayet, winked blinked nodded in the night. While at Himalayan height a brief and premature sun burst into the powdery January air, a blip vanished from radar screens, and the thin air was full of bodies, descending from the Everest of the catastrophe to the milky paleness of the sea.

Who am I?

Who else is there?

The aircraft cracked in half, a seed-pod giving up its spores, an egg yielding its mystery. Two actors, prancing Gibreel and buttony, pursed Mr Saladin Chamcha, fell like titbits of tobacco from a broken old cigar. Above, behind, below them in the void there hung reclining seats, stereophonic headsets, drinks trolleys, motion discomfort receptacles, disembarkation cards, duty-free video games, braided caps, paper cups, blankets, oxygen masks. Also – for there had been more than a few migrants aboard, yes, quite a quantity of wives who had been grilled by reasonable, doing-their-job officials about the length of and distinguishing moles upon their husbands' genitalia, a sufficiency of children upon whose legitimacy the British Government had cast its ever-reasonable doubts – mingling with the remnants of the plane, equally fragmented, equally absurd, there floated the debris of the soul, broken memo-

ries, sloughed-off selves, severed mother-tongues, violated priva-
cies, untranslatable jokes, extinguished futures, lost loves, the forgotten meaning of hollow, booming words, *land, belonging, home.*
Knocked a little silly by the blast, Gibreel and Saladin plummeted
like bundles dropped by some carelessly open-beaked stork, and
because Chamcha was going down head first, in the recommended position for babies entering the birth canal, he commenced to feel a low irritation at the other's refusal to fall in plain
fashion. Saladin nosedived while Farishta embraced air, hugging it
with his arms and legs, a flailing, overwrought actor without techniques of restraint. Below, cloud-covered, awaiting their entrance,
the slow congealed currents of the English Sleeve, the appointed
zone of their watery reincarnation.

'O, my shoes are Japanese,' Gibreel sang, translating the old
song into English in semi-conscious deference to the uprushing
host-nation, 'These trousers English, if you please. On my head,
red Russian hat; my heart's Indian for all that.' The clouds were
bubbling up towards them, and perhaps it was on account of that
great mystification of cumulus and cumulo-nimbus, the mighty
rolling thunderheads standing like hammers in the dawn, or perhaps it was the singing (the one busy performing, the other booing
the performance), or their blast-delirium that spared them full
foreknowledge of the imminent . . . but for whatever reason, the
two men, Gibreelsaladin Farishtachamcha, condemned to this
endless but also ending angelicdevilish fall, did not become aware
of the moment at which the processes of their transmutation
began.

Mutation?

Yessir, but not random. Up there in air-space, in that soft,
imperceptible field which had been made possible by the century
and which, thereafter, made the century possible, becoming one
of its defining locations, the place of movement and of war, the
planet-shrinker and power-vacuum, most insecure and transitory
of zones, illusory, discontinuous, metamorphic, – because when
you throw everything up in the air anything becomes possible –

wayupthere, at any rate, changes took place in delirious actors that would have gladdened the heart of old Mr Lamarck: under extreme environmental pressure, characteristics were acquired.

What characteristics which? Slow down; you think Creation happens in a rush? So then, neither does revelation . . . take a look at the pair of them. Notice anything unusual? Just two brown men, falling hard, nothing so new about that, you may think; climbed too high, got above themselves, flew too close to the sun, is that it?

That's not it. Listen:

Mr Saladin Chamcha, appalled by the noises emanating from Gibreel Farishta's mouth, fought back with verses of his own. What Farishta heard wafting across the improbable night sky was an old song, too, lyrics by Mr James Thomson, seventeen-hundred to seventeen-forty-eight. '. . . at Heaven's command,' Chamcha carolled through lips turned jingoistically redwhiteblue by the cold, 'aroooose from out the aaaazure main.' Farishta, horrified, sang louder and louder of Japanese shoes, Russian hats, inviolately subcontinental hearts, but could not still Saladin's wild recital: 'And guardian aaaaangels sung the strain.'

Let's face it: it was impossible for them to have heard one another, much less conversed and also competed thus in song. Accelerating towards the planet, atmosphere roaring around them, how could they? But let's face this, too: they did.

Downdown they hurtled, and the winter cold frosting their eyelashes and threatening to freeze their hearts was on the point of waking them from their delirious daydream, they were about to become aware of the miracle of the singing, the rain of limbs and babies of which they were a part, and the terror of the destiny rushing at them from below, when they hit, were drenched and instantly iced by, the degree-zero boiling of the clouds.

They were in what appeared to be a long, vertical tunnel. Chamcha, prim, rigid, and still upside-down, saw Gibreel Farishta in his purple bush-shirt come swimming towards him across that cloud-walled funnel, and would have shouted, 'Keep away, get away from me,' except that something prevented him, the beginning of a little fluttery screamy thing in his intestines, so instead of uttering words of rejection he opened his arms and Farishta swam into them until they were embracing head-to-tail, and the force of their collision sent them tumbling end over end, performing their geminate cartwheels all the way down and along the hole that went to Wonderland; while pushing their way out of the white came a succession of cloudforms, ceaselessly metamorphosing, gods into bulls, women into spiders, men into wolves. Hybrid cloud-creatures pressed in upon them, gigantic flowers with human breasts dangling from fleshy stalks, winged cats, centaurs, and Chamcha in his semi-consciousness was seized by the notion that he, too, had acquired the quality of cloudiness, becoming metamorphic, hybrid, as if he were growing into the person whose head nestled now between his legs and whose legs were wrapped around his long, patrician neck.

This person had, however, no time for such 'high falutions'; was, indeed, incapable of faluting at all; having just seen, emerging from the swirl of cloud, the figure of a glamorous woman of a certain age, wearing a brocade sari in green and gold, with a diamond in her nose and lacquer defending her high-coiled hair against the pressure of the wind at these altitudes, as she sat, equably, upon a flying carpet. 'Rekha Merchant,' Gibreel greeted her. 'You couldn't find your way to heaven or what?' Insensitive words to speak to a dead woman! But his concussed, plummeting condition may be offered in mitigation . . . Chamcha, clutching his legs, made an uncomprehending query: 'What the hell?'

'You don't see her?' Gibreel shouted. 'You don't see her god-damn Bokhara rug?'

No, no, Gibbo, her voice whispered in his ears, don't expect him to confirm. I am strictly for your eyes only, maybe you are going crazy, what do you think, you namaqool, you piece of pig excrement, my love. With death comes honesty, my beloved, so I can call you by your true names.

Cloudy Rekha murmured sour nothings, but Gibreel cried again to Chamcha: 'Spoono? You see her or you don't?'

Saladin Chamcha saw nothing, heard nothing, said nothing.

Gibreel faced her alone. 'You shouldn't have done it,' he admonished her. 'No, sir. A sin. A suchmuch thing.'

O, you can lecture me now, she laughed. You are the one with the high moral tone, that's a good one. It was you who left me, her voice reminded his ear, seeming to nibble at the lobe. It was you, O moon of my delight, who hid behind a cloud. And I in darkness, blinded, lost, for love.

He became afraid. 'What do you want? No, don't tell, just go.'

When you were sick I could not see you, in case of scandal, you knew I could not, that I stayed away for your sake, but afterwards you punished, you used it as your excuse to leave, your cloud to hide behind. That, and also her, the icewoman. Bastard. Now that I am dead I have forgotten how to forgive. I curse you, my Gibreel, may your life be hell. Hell, because that's where you sent me, damn you, where you came from, devil, where you're going, sucker, enjoy the bloody dip. Rekha's curse; and after that, verses in a language he did not understand, all harshnesses and sibilance, in which he thought he made out, but maybe not, the repeated name *Al-Lat*.

He clutched at Chamcha; they burst through the bottom of the clouds.

Speed, the sensation of speed, returned, whistling its fearful note. The roof of cloud fled upwards, the water-floor zoomed closer, their eyes opened. A scream, that same scream that had fluttered in his guts when Gibreel swam across the sky, burst from Chamcha's lips; a shaft of sunlight pierced his open mouth and set it free. But they had fallen through the transformations of the clouds, Chamcha and Farishta, and there was a fluidity, an indistinctness, at the edges of them, and as the sunlight hit Chamcha it released more than noise:

'Fly,' Chamcha shrieked at Gibreel. 'Start flying, now.' And added, without knowing its source, the second command: 'And sing.'

How does newness come into the world? How is it born?

Of what fusions, translations, conjoinings is it made?

How does it survive, extreme and dangerous as it is? What

compromises, what deals, what betrayals of its secret nature must it make to stave off the wrecking crew, the exterminating angel, the guillotine?

Is birth always a fall?

Do angels have wings? Can men fly?

When Mr Saladin Chamcha fell out of the clouds over the English Channel he felt his heart being gripped by a force so implacable that he understood it was impossible for him to die. Afterwards, when his feet were once more firmly planted on the ground, he would begin to doubt this, to ascribe the implausibilities of his transit to the scrambling of his perceptions by the blast, and to attribute his survival, his and Gibreel's, to blind, dumb luck. But at the time he had no doubt; what had taken him over was the will to live, unadulterated, irresistible, pure, and the first thing it did was to inform him that it wanted nothing to do with his pathetic personality, that half-reconstructed affair of mimicry and voices, it intended to bypass all that, and he found himself surrendering to it, yes, go on, as if he were a bystander in his own mind, in his own body, because it began in the very centre of his body and spread outwards, turning his blood to iron, changing his flesh to steel, except that it also felt like a fist that enveloped him from outside, holding him in a way that was both unbearably tight and intolerably gentle; until finally it had conquered him totally and could work his mouth, his fingers, whatever it chose, and once it was sure of its dominion it spread outward from his body and grabbed Gibreel Farishta by the balls.

'Fly,' it commanded Gibreel. 'Sing.'

Chamcha held on to Gibreel while the other began, slowly at first and then with increasing rapidity and force, to flap his arms. Harder and harder he flapped, and as he flapped a song burst out of him, and like the song of the spectre of Rekha Merchant it was sung in a language he did not know to a tune he had never heard. Gibreel never repudiated the miracle; unlike Chamcha, who tried to reason it out of existence, he never stopped saying that the gazal had been celestial, that without the song the flapping would have been for nothing, and without the flapping it was a sure thing that they would have hit the waves like rocks or what and simply burst into pieces on making contact with the taut drum of the sea. Whereas instead they began to slow down. The more emphatically Gibreel flapped and sang, sang and flapped, the more pronounced the deceleration, until finally the two of them were floating down to the Channel like scraps of paper in a breeze.

They were the only survivors of the wreck, the only ones who fell from *Bostan* and lived. They were found washed up on a beach. The more voluble of the two, the one in the purple shirt, swore in his wild ramblings that they had walked upon the water, that the waves had borne them gently in to shore; but the other, to whose head a soggy bowler hat clung as if by magic, denied this. 'God, we were lucky,' he said. 'How lucky can you get?'

I know the truth, obviously. I watched the whole thing. As to omnipresence and -potence, I'm making no claims at present, but I can manage this much, I hope. Chamcha willed it and Farishta did what was willed.

Which was the miracle worker?

Of what type – angelic, satanic – was Farishta's song?

Who am I?

Let's put it this way: who has the best tunes?

These were the first words Gibreel Farishta said when he awoke on the snowbound English beach with the improbability of a starfish by his ear: 'Born again, Spoono, you and me. Happy birthday, mister; happy birthday to you.'

Whereupon Saladin Chamcha coughed, spluttered, opened his eyes, and, as befitted a new-born babe, burst into foolish tears.

2

Reincarnation was always a big topic with Gibreel, for fifteen years the biggest star in the history of the Indian movies, even before he 'miraculously' defeated the Phantom Bug that everyone had begun to believe would terminate his contracts. So maybe someone should have been able to forecast, only nobody did, that when he was up and about again he would sotospeak succeed where the germs had failed and walk out of his old life forever within a week of his fortieth birthday, vanishing, poof!, like a trick, *into thin air.*

The first people to notice his absence were the four members of his film-studio wheelchair-team. Long before his illness he had formed the habit of being transported from set to set on the great D. W. Rama lot by this group of speedy, trusted athletes, because a man who makes up to eleven movies 'sy-multaneous' needs to conserve his energies. Guided by a complex coding system of slashes, circles and dots which Gibreel remembered from his childhood among the fabled lunch-runners of Bombay (of which more later), the chair-men zoomed him from role to role, delivering him as punctually and unerringly as once his father had delivered lunch. And after each take Gibreel would skip back into the chair and be navigated at high speed towards the next set, to be re-costumed, made up and handed his lines. 'A career in the

Bombay talkies,' he told his loyal crew, 'is more like a wheelchair race with one-two pit stops along the route.'

After the illness, the Ghostly Germ, the Mystery Malaise, the Bug, he had returned to work, easing himself in, only seven pictures at a time . . . and then, justlikethat, he wasn't there. The wheelchair stood empty among the silenced sound-stages; his absence revealed the tawdry shamming of the sets. Wheelchairmen, one to four, made excuses for the missing star when movie executives descended upon them in wrath; Ji, he must be sick, he has always been famous for his punctual, no, why to criticize, maharaj, great artists must from time to time be permitted their temperament, na, and for their protestations they became the first casualties of Farishta's unexplained hey-presto, being fired, four three two one, ekdumjaldi, ejected from studio gates so that a wheelchair lay abandoned and gathering dust beneath the painted coco-palms around a sawdust beach.

Where was Gibreel? Movie producers, left in seven lurches, panicked expensively. See, there, at the Willingdon Club golf links – only nine holes nowadays, skyscrapers having sprouted out of the other nine like giant weeds, or, let's say, like tombstones marking the sites where the torn corpse of the old city lay – there, right there, upper-echelon executives, missing the simplest putts; and, look above, tufts of anguished hair, torn from senior heads, wafting down from high-level windows. The agitation of the producers was easy to understand, because in those days of declining audiences and the creation of historical soap operas and contemporary crusading housewives by the television network, there was but a single name which, when set above a picture's title, could still offer a sure-fire, cent-per-cent guarantee of an Ultrahit, a Smashation, and the owner of said name had departed, up, down or sideways, but certainly and unarguably vamoosed . . .

All over the city, after telephones, motorcyclists, cops, frogmen and trawlers dragging the harbour for his body had laboured mightily but to no avail, epitaphs began to be spoken in memory of the darkened star. On one of Rama Studios' seven impotent stages, Miss Pimple Billimoria, the latest chilli-and-spices bombshell – *she's no flibberti-gibberti mamzell, but a whir-stir-get-lost-sir bundla dynamite* – clad in temple-dancer veiled undress and positioned beneath writhing cardboard representations of copulating Tantric figures from the Chandela period, – and perceiving that her major scene was not to be, her big break lay in pieces – offered up a spiteful farewell before an audience of sound recordists and electricians smoking their cynical beedis. Attended by a dumbly distressed ayah, all elbows, Pimple attempted scorn. 'God, what a stroke of luck, for Pete's sake,' she cried. 'I mean today it was the love scene, chhi chhi, I was just dying inside, thinking how to go near to that fatmouth with his breath of rotting cockroach dung.' Bell-heavy anklets jingled as she stamped. 'Damn good for him the movies don't smell, or he wouldn't get one job as a leper even.' Here Pimple's soliloquy climaxed in such a torrent of obscenities that the beedi-smokers sat up for the first time and commenced animatedly to compare Pimple's vocabulary with that of the infamous bandit queen Phoolan Devi whose oaths could melt rifle barrels and turn journalists' pencils to rubber in a trice.

Exit Pimple, weeping, censored, a scrap on a cutting-room floor. Rhinestones fell from her navel as she went, mirroring her tears . . . in the matter of Farishta's halitosis she was not, however, altogether wrong; if anything, she had a little understated the case. Gibreel's exhalations, those ochre clouds of sulphur and brimstone, had always given him – when taken together with his pronounced widow's peak and crowblack hair – an air more saturnine than haloed, in spite of his archangelic name. It was said after he disappeared that he ought to have been easy to find, all it took was a halfway decent nose . . . and one week after he took off, an exit more tragic than Pimple Billimoria's did much to intensify the devilish odour that was beginning to attach itself to that forsolong sweet-smelling name. You could say that he had stepped out of the screen into the world, and in life, unlike the cinema, people know it if you stink.

We are creatures of air, Our roots in dreams And clouds, reborn In flight. Goodbye. The enigmatic note discovered by the police in

Gibreel Farishta's penthouse, located on the top floor of the Everest Vilas skyscraper on Malabar Hill, the highest home in the highest building on the highest ground in the city, one of those double-vista apartments from which you could look this way across the evening necklace of Marine Drive or that way out to Scandal Point and the sea, permitted the newspaper headlines to prolong their cacophonies. FARISHTA DIVES UNDERGROUND, opined *Blitz* in somewhat macabre fashion, while Busybee in *The Daily* preferred GIBREEL FLIES COOP. Many photographs were published of that fabled residence in which French interior decorators bearing letters of commendation from Reza Pahlevi for the work they had done at Persepolis had spent a million dollars re-creating at this exalted altitude the effect of a Bedouin tent. Another illusion unmade by his absence; GIBREEL STRIKES CAMP, the headlines yelled, but had he gone up or down or sideways? No one knew. In that metropolis of tongues and whispers, not even the sharpest ears heard anything reliable. But Mrs Rekha Merchant, reading all the papers, listening to all the radio broadcasts, staying glued to the Doordarshan TV programmes, gleaned something from Farishta's message, heard a note that eluded everyone else, and took her two daughters and one son for a walk on the roof of her high-rise home. Its name was Everest Vilas.

His neighbour; as a matter of fact, from the apartment directly beneath his own. His neighbour and his friend; why should I say any more? Of course the scandal-pointed malice-magazines of the city filled their columns with hint innuendo and nudge, but that's no reason for sinking to their level. Why tarnish her reputation now?

Who was she? Rich, certainly, but then Everest Vilas was not exactly a tenement in Kurla, eh? Married, yessir, thirteen years, with a husband big in ball-bearings. Independent, her carpet and antique showrooms thriving at their prime Colaba sites. She called her carpets *klims* and *kleens* and the ancient artefacts were *antiqueues.* Yes, and she was beautiful, beautiful in the hard, glossy manner of those rarefied occupants of the city's sky-homes, her bones skin posture all bearing witness to her long divorce from the impoverished, heavy, pullulating earth. Everyone agreed she had a strong personality, drank *like a fish* from Lalique crystal and hung her hat *shameless* on a Chola Natraj and knew what she wanted and how to get it, fast. The husband was a mouse with money and a good squash wrist. Rekha Merchant read Gibreel Farishta's farewell note in the newspapers, wrote a letter of her own, gathered her children, summoned the elevator, and rose heavenward (one storey) to meet her chosen fate.

'Many years ago,' her letter read, 'I married out of cowardice. Now, finally, I'm doing something brave.' She left a newspaper on her bed with Gibreel's message circled in red and heavily underscored – three harsh lines, one of them ripping the page in fury. So naturally the bitch-journals went to town and it was all LOVELY'S LOVELORN LEAP, and BROKEN-HEARTED BEAUTY TAKES LAST DIVE. But:

Perhaps she, too, had the rebirth bug, and Gibreel, not understanding the terrible power of metaphor, had recommended flight. *To be born again, first you have to* and she was a creature of the sky, she drank Lalique champagne, she lived on Everest, and one of her fellow-Olympians had flown; and if he could, then she, too, could be winged, and rooted in dreams.

She didn't make it. The lala who was employed as gatekeeper of the Everest Vilas compound offered the world his blunt testimony. 'I was walking, here here, in the compound only, when there came a thud, *tharaap*. I turned. It was the body of the oldest daughter. Her skull was completely crushed. I looked up and saw the boy falling, and after him the younger girl. What to say, they almost hit me where I stood. I put my hand on my mouth and came to them. The young girl was whining softly. Then I looked up a further time and the Begum was coming. Her sari was floating out like a big balloon and all her hair was loose. I took my eyes away from her because she was falling and it was not respectful to look up inside her clothes.'

Rekha and her children fell from Everest; no survivors. The whispers blamed Gibreel. Let's leave it at that for the moment.

Oh: don't forget: he saw her after she died. He saw her several times. It was a long time before people understood how sick the great man was. Gibreel, the star. Gibreel, who vanquished the Nameless Ailment. Gibreel, who feared sleep.

After he departed the ubiquitous images of his face began to rot. On the gigantic, luridly coloured hoardings from which he had watched over the populace, his lazy eyelids started flaking and crumbling, drooping further and further until his irises looked like two moons sliced by clouds, or by the soft knives of his long lashes. Finally the eyelids fell off, giving a wild, bulging look to his painted eyes. Outside the picture palaces of Bombay, mammoth cardboard effigies of Gibreel were seen to decay and list. Dangling limply on their sustaining scaffolds, they lost arms, withered, snapped at the neck. His portraits on the covers of movie magazines acquired the pallor of death, a nullity about the eye, a hollowness. At last his images simply faded off the printed page, so that the shiny covers of *Celebrity* and *Society* and *Illustrated Weekly* went blank at the bookstalls and their publishers fired the printers and blamed the quality of the ink. Even on the silver screen itself, high above his worshippers in the dark, that supposedly immortal physiognomy began to putrefy, blister and bleach; projectors jammed unaccountably every time he passed through the gate, his films ground to a halt, and the lamp-heat of the malfunctioning projectors burned his celluloid memory away: a star gone supernova, with the consuming fire spreading outwards, as was fitting, from his lips.

It was the death of God. Or something very like it; for had not that outsize face, suspended over its devotees in the artificial cinematic night, shone like that of some supernal Entity that had its being at least halfway between the mortal and the divine? More than halfway, many would have argued, for Gibreel had spent the greater part of his unique career incarnating, with absolute conviction, the countless deities of the subcontinent in the popular genre movies known as 'theologicals'. It was part of the magic of his persona that he succeeded in crossing religious boundaries without giving offence. Blue-skinned as Krishna he danced, flute in hand, amongst the beauteous gopis and their udder-heavy cows; with upturned palms, serene, he meditated (as Gautama) upon humanity's suffering beneath a studio-rickety bodhi-tree. On those infrequent occasions when he descended from the heavens he never went too far, playing, for example, both the Grand Mughal and his famously wily minister in the classic *Akbar and Birbal.* For over a decade and a half he had represented, to hundreds of millions of believers in that country in which, to this day, the human population outnumbers the divine by less than three to one, the most acceptable, and instantly recognizable, face of the Supreme. For many of his fans, the boundary separating the performer and his roles had longago ceased to exist.

The fans, yes, and? How about Gibreel?

That face. In real life, reduced to life-size, set amongst ordinary mortals, it stood revealed as oddly un-starry. Those low-slung eyelids could give him an exhausted look. There was, too, something coarse about the nose, the mouth was too well fleshed to be strong, the ears were long-lobed like young, knurled jackfruit. The most profane of faces, the most sensual of faces. In which, of late, it had been possible to make out the seams mined by his recent, near-fatal illness. And yet, in spite of profanity and debilitation, this was a face inextricably mixed up with holiness, perfection, grace: God stuff. No accounting for tastes, that's all. At any rate, you'll agree that for such an actor (for any actor, maybe, even for Chamcha, but most of all for him) to have a bee in his bonnet about *avatars,* like much-metamorphosed Vishnu, was not so very surprising. Rebirth: that's God stuff, too.

Or, but, thenagain . . . not always. There are secular reincarnations, too. Gibreel Farishta had been born Ismail Najmuddin in Poona, British Poona at the empire's fag-end, long before the Pune of Rajneesh etc. (Pune, Vadodara, Mumbai; even towns can take stage names nowadays.) Ismail after the child involved in the sacrifice of Ibrahim, and Najmuddin, *star of the faith;* he'd given up quite a name when he took the angel's.

Afterwards, when the aircraft *Bostan* was in the grip of the hijackers, and the passengers, fearing for their futures, were regressing into their pasts, Gibreel confided to Saladin Chamcha that his choice of pseudonym had been his way of making a homage to the memory of his dead mother, 'my mummyji, Spoono, my one and only Mamo, because who else was it who started the whole angel business, her personal angel, she called me, *farishta,* because apparently I was too damn sweet, believe it or not, I was good as goddamn gold.'

Poona couldn't hold him; he was taken in his infancy to the bitch-city, his first migration; his father got a job amongst the fleet-footed inspirers of future wheelchair quartets, the lunch-porters or dabbawallas of Bombay. And Ismail the farishta followed, at thirteen, in his father's footsteps.

Gibreel, captive aboard AI-420, sank into forgivable rhapsodies, fixing Chamcha with his glittering eye, explicating the mysteries of the runners' coding system, black swastika red circle yellow slash dot, running in his mind's eye the entire relay from home to office desk, that improbable system by which two thousand dabbawallas delivered, each day, over one hundred thousand lunch-pails, and on a bad day, Spoono, maybe fifteen got mislaid, we were illiterate, mostly, but the signs were our secret tongue.

Bostan circled London, gunmen patrolling the gangways, and the lights in the passenger cabins had been switched off, but Gibreel's energy illuminated the gloom. On the grubby movie screen on which, earlier in the journey, the inflight inevitability of Walter Matthau had stumbled lugubriously into the aerial ubiquity of Goldie Hawn, there were shadows moving, projected by the nostalgia of the hostages, and the most sharply defined of them was this spindly adolescent, Ismail Najmuddin, mummy's angel in a Gandhi cap, running tiffins across the town. The young dabba-walla skipped nimbly through the shadow-crowd, because he was used to such conditions, think, Spoono, picture, thirty-forty tiffins in a long wooden tray on your head, and when the local train stops you have maybe one minute to push on or off, and then running in the streets, flat out, yaar, with the trucks buses scooters cycles and what-all, one-two, one-two, lunch, lunch, the dabbas must get through, and in the monsoon running down the railway line when the train broke down, or waist-deep in water in some flooded street, and there were gangs, Salad baba, truly, organized gangs of dabba-stealers, it's a hungry city, baby, what to tell you, but we could handle them, we were everywhere, knew everything, what thieves could escape our eyes and ears, we never went to any policia, we looked after our own.

At night father and son would return exhausted to their shack by the airport runway at Santacruz and when Ismail's mother saw him approaching, illuminated by the green red yellow of the departing jet-planes, she would say that simply to lay eyes on him made all her dreams come true, which was the first indication that there was something peculiar about Gibreel, because from the beginning, it seemed, he could fulfil people's most secret desires without having any idea of how he did it. His father Najmuddin Senior never seemed to mind that his wife had eyes only for her son, that the boy's feet received nightly pressings while the father's went unstroked. A son is a blessing and a blessing requires the gratitude of the blest.

Naima Najmuddin died. A bus hit her and that was that, Gibreel wasn't around to answer her prayers for life. Neither father nor son ever spoke of grief. Silently, as though it were customary and expected, they buried their sadness beneath extra work, engaging in an inarticulate contest, who could carry the most dabbas on his head, who could acquire the most new contracts per month, who could run faster, as though the greater labour would indicate the greater love. When he saw his father at night, the knotted veins bulging in his neck and at his temples, Ismail Najmuddin would understand how much the older man had resented him, and how important it was for the father to defeat the son and regain, thereby, his usurped primacy in the affections of his dead wife. Once he realized this, the youth eased off, but his father's zeal remained unrelenting, and pretty soon he was getting promotion, no longer a mere runner but one of the organizing muqaddams. When Gibreel was nineteen, Najmuddin Senior became a member of the lunch-runners' guild, the Bombay

Tiffin Carriers' Association, and when Gibreel was twenty, his father was dead, stopped in his tracks by a stroke that almost blew him apart. 'He just ran himself into the ground,' said the guild's General Secretary, Babasaheb Mhatre himself. 'That poor bastard, he just ran out of steam.' But the orphan knew better. He knew that his father had finally run hard enough and long enough to wear down the frontiers between the worlds, he had run clear out of his skin and into the arms of his wife, to whom he had proved, once and for all, the superiority of his love. Some migrants are happy to depart.

Babasaheb Mhatre sat in a blue office behind a green door above a labyrinthine bazaar, an awesome figure, buddha-fat, one of the great moving forces of the metropolis, possessing the occult gift of remaining absolutely still, never shifting from his room, and yet being everywhere important and meeting everyone who mattered in Bombay. The day after young Ismail's father ran across the border to see Naima, the Babasaheb summoned the young man into his presence. 'So? Upset or what?' The reply, with downcast eyes: ji, thank you, Babaji, I am okay. 'Shut your face,' said Babasaheb Mhatre. 'From today you live with me.' Butbut, Babaji . . . 'But me no buts. Already I have informed my good-wife. I have spoken.' Please excuse Babaji but how what why? 'I have *spoken*.'

Gibreel Farishta was never told why the Babasaheb had decided to take pity on him and pluck him from the futurelessness of the streets, but after a while he began to have an idea. Mrs Mhatre was a thin woman, like a pencil beside the rubbery Babasaheb, but she was filled so full of mother-love that she should have been fat like a potato. When the Baba came home she put sweets into his mouth with her own hands, and at nights the newcomer to the household could hear the great General Secretary of the BTCA protesting, Let me go, wife, I can undress myself. At breakfast she spoon-fed Mhatre with large helpings of malt, and before he went to work she brushed his hair. They were a childless couple, and young Najmuddin understood that the Babasaheb wanted him to share the load. Oddly enough, however, the Begum did not treat the young man as a child. 'You see, he is a grown fellow,' she told her husband when poor Mhatre pleaded, 'Give the boy the blasted spoon of malt.' Yes, a grown fellow, 'we must make a man of him, husband, no babying for him.' 'Then damn it to hell,' the Babasaheb exploded, 'why do you do it to me?' Mrs Mhatre burst into tears. 'But you are everything to me,' she wept, 'you are my father, my lover, my baby too. You are my lord and my suckling child. If I displease you then I have no life.'

Babasaheb Mhatre, accepting defeat, swallowed the tablespoon of malt.

He was a kindly man, which he disguised with insults and noise. To console the orphaned youth he would speak to him, in the blue office, about the philosophy of rebirth, convincing him that his parents were already being scheduled for re-entry some-where, unless of course their lives had been so holy that they had attained the final grace. So it was Mhatre who started Farishta off on the whole reincarnation business, and not just reincarnation. The Babasaheb was an amateur psychic, a tapper of table-legs and a bringer of spirits into glasses. 'But I gave that up,' he told his protégé, with many suitably melodramatic inflections, gestures, frowns, 'after I got the fright of my bloody life.'

Once (Mhatre recounted) the glass had been visited by the most co-operative of spirits, such a too-friendly fellow, see, so I thought to ask him some big questions. *Is there a God,* and that glass which had been running round like a mouse or so just stopped dead, middle of table, not a twitch, completely phutt, kaput. So, then, okay, I said, if you won't answer that try this one instead, and I came right out with it, *Is there a Devil.* After that the glass – baprebap! – began to shake – catch your ears! – slowslow at first, then faster-faster, like a jelly, until it jumped! – ai-hai! – up from the table, into the air, fell down on its side, and – o-ho! – into a thousand and one pieces, smashed. Believe don't believe, Babasaheb Mhatre told his charge, but thenandthere I learned my lesson: don't meddle, Mhatre, in what you do not comprehend.

This story had a profound effect on the consciousness of the young listener, because even before his mother's death he had become convinced of the existence of the supernatural world. Sometimes when he looked around him, especially in the afternoon heat when the air turned glutinous, the visible world, its features and inhabitants and things, seemed to be sticking up through the atmosphere like a profusion of hot icebergs, and he had the idea that everything continued down below the surface of the soupy air: people, motor-cars, dogs, movie billboards, trees, nine-tenths of their reality concealed from his eyes. He would blink, and the illusion would fade, but the sense of it never left him. He grew up believing in God, angels, demons, afreets, djinns, as matter-of-factly as if they were bullock-carts or lamp-posts, and it struck him as a failure in his own sight that he had never seen a ghost. He would dream of discovering a magic optometrist from whom he would purchase a pair of green-tinged spectacles which would correct his regrettable myopia, and after that he would be able to see through the dense, blinding air to the fabulous world beneath.

From his mother Naima Najmuddin he heard a great many stories of the Prophet, and if inaccuracies had crept into her versions he wasn't interested in knowing what they were. 'What a man!' he thought. 'What angel would not wish to speak to him?' Sometimes, though, he caught himself in the act of forming blasphemous thoughts, for example when without meaning to, as he drifted off to sleep in his cot at the Mhatre residence, his somnolent fancy began to compare his own condition with that of the Prophet at the time when, having been orphaned and short of funds, he made a great success of his job as the business manager of the wealthy widow Khadija, and ended up marrying her as well. As he slipped into sleep he saw himself sitting on a rose-strewn dais, simpering shyly beneath the sari-pallu which he had placed demurely over his face, while his new husband, Babasaheb Mhatre, reached lovingly towards him to remove the fabric, and gaze at his features in a mirror placed in his lap. This dream of marrying the Babasaheb brought him awake, flushing hotly for shame, and after that he began to worry about the impurity in his make-up that could create such terrible visions.

Mostly, however, his religious faith was a low-key thing, a part of him that required no more special attention than any other. When Babasaheb Mhatre took him into his home it confirmed to the young man that he was not alone in the world, that something was taking care of him, so he was not entirely surprised when the Babasaheb called him into the blue office on the morning of his twenty-first birthday and sacked him without even being prepared to listen to an appeal.

'You're fired,' Mhatre emphasized, beaming. 'Cashiered, had your chips. Dis-*miss*.'

'But, uncle,'

'Shut your face.'

Then the Babasaheb gave the orphan the greatest present of his life, informing him that a meeting had been arranged for him at the studios of the legendary film magnate Mr D. W. Rama; an audition. 'It is for appearance only,' the Babasaheb said. 'Rama is my good friend and we have discussed. A small part to begin, then it is up to you. Now get out of my sight and stop pulling such humble faces, it does not suit.'

'But, uncle,'

'Boy like you is too damn goodlooking to carry tiffins on his head all his life. Get gone now, go, be a homosexual movie actor. I fired you five minutes back.'

'But, uncle,'

'I have spoken. Thank your lucky stars.'

He became Gibreel Farishta, but for four years he did not become a star, serving his apprenticeship in a succession of minor knock-about comic parts. He remained calm, unhurried, as though he could see the future, and his apparent lack of ambition made him something of an outsider in that most self-seeking of industries. He was thought to be stupid or arrogant or both. And throughout the four wilderness years he failed to kiss a single woman on the mouth.

On-screen, he played the fall guy, the idiot who loves the beauty and can't see that she wouldn't go for him in a thousand years, the funny uncle, the poor relation, the village idiot, the servant, the incompetent crook, none of them the type of part that ever rates a love scene. Women kicked him, slapped him, teased him, laughed at him, but never, on celluloid, looked at him or sang to him or danced around him with cinematic love in their eyes. Off-screen, he lived alone in two empty rooms near the studios and tried to imagine what women looked like without clothes on. To get his mind off the subject of love and desire, he studied, becoming an omnivorous autodidact, devouring the metamorphic myths of Greece and Rome, the avatars of Jupiter, the boy who became a flower, the spider-woman, Circe, everything; and the theosophy of Annie Besant, and unified field theory, and the incident of the Satanic verses in the early career of the Prophet, and the politics of Muhammad's harem after his return to Mecca in triumph; and the surrealism of the newspapers, in which butterflies could fly into young girls' mouths, asking to be consumed, and children were born with no faces, and young boys dreamed in impossible detail of earlier incarnations, for instance in a golden fortress filled with precious stones. He filled himself up with God knows what, but he could not deny, in the small hours of his insomniac nights, that he was full of something that had never been used, that he did not know how to begin to use, that is, love. In his dreams he was tormented by women of unbearable sweetness and beauty, so he preferred to stay awake and force himself to rehearse some part of his general knowledge in order to blot out the tragic feeling of being endowed with a larger-than-usual capacity for love, without a single person on earth to offer it to.

His big break arrived with the coming of the theological movies. Once the formula of making films based on the puranas, and adding the usual mixture of songs, dances, funny uncles etc., had paid off, every god in the pantheon got his or her chance to be a star. When D. W. Rama scheduled a production based on the story of Ganesh, none of the leading box-office names of the time were willing to spend an entire movie concealed inside an elephant's head. Gibreel jumped at the chance. That was his first hit,

Ganpati Baba, and suddenly he was a superstar, but only with the trunk and ears on. After six movies playing the elephant-headed god he was permitted to remove the thick, pendulous, grey mask and put on, instead, a long, hairy tail, in order to play Hanuman the monkey king in a sequence of adventure movies that owed more to a certain cheap television series emanating from Hong Kong than it did to the Ramayana. This series proved so popular that monkey-tails became de rigueur for the city's young bucks at the kind of parties frequented by convent girls known as 'firecrackers' because of their readiness to go off with a bang.

After Hanuman there was no stopping Gibreel, and his phenomenal success deepened his belief in a guardian angel. But it also led to a more regrettable development.

(I see that I must, after all, spill poor Rekha's beans.)

Even before he replaced false head with fake tail he had become irresistibly attractive to women. The seductions of his fame had grown so great that several of these young ladies asked him if he would keep the Ganesh-mask on while they made love, but he refused out of respect for the dignity of the god. Owing to the innocence of his upbringing he could not at that time differentiate between quantity and quality and accordingly felt the need to make up for lost time. He had so many sexual partners that it was not uncommon for him to forget their names even before they had left his room. Not only did he become a philanderer of the worst type, but he also learned the arts of dissimulation, because a man who plays gods must be above reproach. So skilfully did he conceal his life of scandal and debauch that his old patron, Babasaheb Mhatre, lying on his deathbed a decade after he sent a young dabbawalla out into the world of illusion, black-money and lust, begged him to get married to prove he was a man. 'God-sake, mister,' the Babasaheb pleaded, 'when I told you back then to go and be a homo I never thought you would take me seriously, there is a limit to respecting one's elders, after all.' Gibreel threw up his hands and swore that he was no such disgraceful thing, and that when the right girl came along he would of course undergo nuptials with a will. 'What you waiting? Some goddess from heaven? Greta Garbo, Gracekali, who?' cried the old man, coughing blood, but Gibreel left him with the enigma of a smile that allowed him to die without having his mind set entirely at rest.

The avalanche of sex in which Gibreel Farishta was trapped managed to bury his greatest talent so deep that it might easily have been lost forever, his talent, that is, for loving genuinely, deeply and without holding back, the rare and delicate gift which he had never been able to employ. By the time of his illness he had all but forgotten the anguish he used to experience owing to his longing for love, which had twisted and turned in him like a sorcerer's knife. Now, at the end of each gymnastic night, he slept easily and long, as if he had never been plagued by dream-women, as if he had never hoped to lose his heart.

'Your trouble,' Rekha Merchant told him when she material-ized out of the clouds, 'is everybody always forgave you, God knows why, you always got let off, you got away with murder. Nobody ever held you responsible for what you did.' He couldn't argue. 'God's gift,' she screamed at him, 'God knows where you thought you were from, jumped-up type from the gutter, God knows what diseases you brought.'

But that was what women did, he thought in those days, they were the vessels into which he could pour himself, and when he moved on, they would understand that it was his nature, and for-give. And it was true that nobody blamed him for leaving, for his thousand and one pieces of thoughtlessness, how many abortions, Rekha demanded in the cloud-hole, how many broken hearts. In all those years he was the beneficiary of the infinite generosity of women, but he was its victim, too, because their forgiveness made possible the deepest and sweetest corruption of all, namely the idea that he was doing nothing wrong.

Rekha: she entered his life when he bought the penthouse at Everest Vilas and she offered, as a neighbour and businesswoman, to show him her carpets and antiques. Her husband was at a world-wide congress of ball-bearings manufacturers in Gothen-burg, Sweden, and in his absence she invited Gibreel into her apartment of stone lattices from Jaisalmer and carved wooden handrails from Keralan palaces and a stone Mughal chhatri or cupola turned into a whirlpool bath; while she poured him French champagne she leaned against marbled walls and felt the cool veins of the stone against her back. When he sipped the champagne she teased him, surely gods should not partake of alcohol, and he answered with a line he had once read in an interview with the Aga Khan, O, you know, this champagne is only for outward show, the moment it touches my lips it turns to water. After that it didn't take long for her to touch his lips and deliquesce into his arms. By the time her children returned from school with the ayah she was immaculately dressed and coiffed, and sat with him in the drawing-room, revealing the secrets of the carpet business, confessing that art silk stood for artificial not artistic, telling him not to be fooled by her brochure in which a rug was seductively described as being made of wool plucked from the throats of baby lambs, which means, you see, only *low-grade wool*, advertising, what to do, this is how it is.

He did not love her, was not faithful to her, forgot her birthdays, failed to return her phone calls, turned up when it was most inconvenient owing to the presence in her home of dinner guests from the world of the ball-bearing, and like everyone else she forgave him. But her forgiveness was not the silent, mousy let-off he got from the others. Rekha complained like crazy, she gave him hell, she bawled him out and cursed him for a useless lafanga and haramzada and salah and even, in extremis, for being guilty of the impossible feat of fucking the sister he did not have. She spared him nothing, accusing him of being a creature of surfaces, like a movie screen, and then she went ahead and forgave him anyway and allowed him to unhook her blouse. Gibreel could not resist the operatic forgiveness of Rekha Merchant, which was all the more moving on account of the flaw in her own position, her infidelity to the ball-bearing king, which Gibreel forbore to mention, taking his verbal beatings like a man. So that whereas the pardons he got from the rest of his women left him cold and he forgot them the moment they were uttered, he kept coming back to Rekha, so that she could abuse him and then console him as only she knew how.

Then he almost died.

He was filming at Kanya Kumari, standing on the very tip of Asia, taking part in a fight scene set at the point on Cape Comorin where it seems that three oceans are truly smashing into one another. Three sets of waves rolled in from the west east south and collided in a mighty clapping of watery hands just as Gibreel took a punch on the jaw, perfect timing, and he passed out on the spot, falling backwards into tri-oceanic spume. He did not get up.

To begin with everybody blamed the giant English stunt-man Eustace Brown, who had delivered the punch. He protested vehemently. Was he not the same fellow who had performed opposite Chief Minister N. T. Rama Rao in his many theological movie roles? Had he not perfected the art of making the old man look good in combat without hurting him? Had he ever complained that NTR never pulled *his* punches, so that he, Eustace, invariably ended up black and blue, having been beaten stupid by a little old guy whom he could've eaten for breakfast, on *toast*, and had he ever, even once, lost his temper? Well, then? How could anyone think he would hurt the immortal Gibreel? – They fired him anyway and the police put him in the lock-up, just in case.

But it was not the punch that had flattened Gibreel. After the star had been flown into Bombay's Breach Candy Hospital in an Air Force jet made available for the purpose; after exhaustive tests had come up with almost nothing; and while he lay unconscious, dying, with a blood-count that had fallen from his normal fifteen to a murderous four point two, a hospital spokesman faced the national press on Breach Candy's wide white steps. 'It is a freak mystery,' he gave out. 'Call it, if you so please, an act of God.'

Gibreel Farishta had begun to haemorrhage all over his insides for no apparent reason, and was quite simply bleeding to death inside his skin. At the worst moment the blood began to seep out through his rectum and penis, and it seemed that at any moment it might burst torrentially through his nose and ears and out of the corners of his eyes. For seven days he bled, and received transfusions, and every clotting agent known to medical science, including a concentrated form of rat poison, and although the treatment resulted in a marginal improvement the doctors gave him up for lost.

The whole of India was at Gibreel's bedside. His condition was the lead item on every radio bulletin, it was the subject of hourly news-flashes on the national television network, and the crowd that gathered in Warden Road was so large that the police had to disperse it with lathi-charges and tear-gas, which they used even though every one of the half-million mourners was already tearful and wailing. The Prime Minister cancelled her appointments and flew to visit him. Her son the airline pilot sat in Farishta's bedroom, holding the actor's hand. A mood of apprehension settled over the nation, because if God had unleashed such an act of retribution against his most celebrated incarnation, what did he have in store for the rest of the country? If Gibreel died, could India be far behind? In the mosques and temples of the nation, packed congregations prayed, not only for the life of the dying actor, but for the future, for themselves.

Who did not visit Gibreel in hospital? Who never wrote, made no telephone call, despatched no flowers, sent in no tiffins of delicious home cooking? While many lovers shamelessly sent him get-well cards and lamb pasandas, who, loving him most of all, kept herself to herself, unsuspected by her ball-bearing of a husband? Rekha Merchant placed iron around her heart, and went through the motions of her daily life, playing with her children, chit-chatting with her husband, acting as his hostess when required, and never, not once, revealed the bleak devastation of her soul.

He recovered.

The recovery was as mysterious as the illness, and as rapid. It, too, was called (by hospital, journalists, friends) an act of the Supreme. A national holiday was declared; fireworks were set off up and down the land. But when Gibreel regained his strength, it became clear that he had changed, and to a startling degree, because he had lost his faith.

On the day he was discharged from hospital he went under police escort through the immense crowd that had gathered to celebrate its own deliverance as well as his, climbed into his Mercedes and told the driver to give all the pursuing vehicles the slip, which took seven hours and fifty-one minutes, and by the end of the manoeuvre he had worked out what had to be done. He got out of the limousine at the Taj hotel and without looking left or right went directly into the great dining-room with its buffet table groaning under the weight of forbidden foods, and he loaded his plate with all of it, the pork sausages from Wiltshire and the cured York hams and the rashers of bacon from godknowswhere; with the gammon steaks of his unbelief and the pig's trotters of secularism; and then, standing there in the middle of the hall, while photographers popped up from nowhere, he began to eat as fast as possible, stuffing the dead pigs into his face so rapidly that bacon rashers hung out of the sides of his mouth.

During his illness he had spent every minute of consciousness calling upon God, every second of every minute. Ya Allah whose servant lies bleeding do not abandon me now after watching over me so long. Ya Allah show me some sign, some small mark of your favour, that I may find in myself the strength to cure my ills. O God most beneficent most merciful, be with me in this my time of need, my most grievous need. Then it occurred to him that he was being punished, and for a time that made it possible to suffer the pain, but after a time he got angry. Enough, God, his unspoken words demanded, why must I die when I have not killed, are you vengeance or are you love? The anger with God carried him through another day, but then it faded, and in its place there came a terrible emptiness, an isolation, as he realized he was talking to *thin air*, that there was nobody there at all, and then he felt more foolish than ever in his life, and he began to plead into the emptiness, ya Allah, just be there, damn it, just be. But he felt nothing, nothing nothing, and then one day he found that he no longer needed there to be anything to feel. On that day of metamorphosis the illness changed and his recovery began. And to prove to himself the non-existence of God, he now stood in the dining-hall of the city's most famous hotel, with pigs falling out of his face.

He looked up from his plate to find a woman watching him. Her hair was so fair that it was almost white, and her skin possessed the colour and translucency of mountain ice. She laughed at him and turned away.

'Don't you get it?' he shouted after her, spewing sausage fragments from the corners of his mouth. 'No thunderbolt. That's the point.'

She came back to stand in front of him. 'You're alive,' she told him. 'You got your life back. *That's* the point.'

He told Rekha: the moment she turned around and started walking back I fell in love with her. Alleluia Cone, climber of mountains, vanquisher of Everest, blonde yahudan, ice queen. Her challenge, *change your life, or did you get it back for nothing,* I couldn't resist.

'You and your reincarnation junk,' Rekha cajoled him. 'Such a nonsense head. You come out of hospital, back through death's door, and it goes to your head, crazy boy, at once you must have some escapade thing, and there she is, hey presto, the blonde mame. Don't think I don't know what you're like, Gibbo, so what now, you want me to forgive you or what?'

No need, he said. He left Rekha's apartment (its mistress wept, face-down, on the floor); and never entered it again.

Three days after he met her with his mouth full of unclean meat Allie got into an aeroplane and left. Three days out of time behind a do-not-disturb sign, but in the end they agreed that the world was real, what was possible was possible and what was impossible was im-, brief encounter, ships that pass, love in a transit lounge. After she left, Gibreel rested, tried to shut his ears to her challenge, resolved to get his life back to normal. Just because he'd lost his belief it didn't mean he couldn't do his job, and in spite of the scandal of the ham-eating photographs, the first scandal ever to attach itself to his name, he signed movie contracts and went back to work.

And then, one morning, a wheelchair stood empty and he had gone. A bearded passenger, one Ismail Najmuddin, boarded Flight AI-420 to London. The 747 was named after one of the gardens of Paradise, not Gulistan but *Bostan*. 'To be born again,' Gibreel Farishta said to Saladin Chamcha much later, 'first you have to die. Me, I only half-expired, but I did it on two occasions, hospital and plane, so it adds up, it counts. And now, Spoono my friend, here I stand before you in Proper London, Vilayet, regenerated, a new man with a new life. Spoono, is this not a bloody fine thing?'

Why did he leave?

Because of her, the challenge of her, the newness, the fierceness of the two of them together, the inexorability of an impossible thing that was insisting on its right to become.

And, or, maybe: because after he ate the pigs the retribution began, a nocturnal retribution, a punishment of dreams.

3

Once the flight to London had taken off, thanks to his magic trick of crossing two pairs of fingers on each hand and rotating his thumbs, the narrow, fortyish fellow who sat in a non-smoking window seat watching the city of his birth fall away from him like old snakeskin allowed a relieved expression to pass briefly across his face. This face was handsome in a somewhat sour, patrician fashion, with long, thick, downturned lips like those of a disgusted turbot, and thin eyebrows arching sharply over eyes that watched the world with a kind of alert contempt. Mr Saladin Chamcha had constructed this face with care – it had taken him several years to get it just right – and for many more years now he had thought of it simply as *his own* – indeed, he had forgotten what he had looked like before it. Furthermore, he had shaped himself a voice to go with the face, a voice whose languid, almost lazy vowels contrasted disconcertingly with the sawn-off abruptness of the consonants. The combination of face and voice was a potent one; but, during his recent visit to his home town, his first such visit in fifteen years (the exact period, I should observe, of Gibreel Farishta's film stardom), there had been strange and worrying developments. It was unfortunately the case that his voice (the first to go) and, subsequently, his face itself, had begun to let him down.

It started – Chamcha, allowing fingers and thumbs to relax and hoping, in some embarrassment, that his last remaining superstition had gone unobserved by his fellow-passengers, closed his eyes and remembered with a delicate shudder of horror – on his flight east some weeks ago. He had fallen into a torpid sleep, high above the desert sands of the Persian Gulf, and been visited in a dream by a bizarre stranger, a man with a glass skin, who rapped his knuckles mournfully against the thin, brittle membrane covering his entire body and begged Saladin to help him, to release him from the prison of his skin. Chamcha picked up a stone and began to batter at the glass. At once a latticework of blood oozed up through the cracked surface of the stranger's body, and when Chamcha tried to pick off the broken shards the other began to scream, because chunks of his flesh were coming away with the glass. At this point an air stewardess bent over the sleeping Chamcha and demanded, with the pitiless hospitality of her tribe: *Something to drink, sir? A drink?,* and Saladin, emerging from the dream, found his speech unaccountably metamorphosed into the Bombay lilt he had so diligently (and so long ago!) unmade. 'Achha, means what?' he mumbled. 'Alcoholic beverage or what?' And, when the stewardess reassured him, whatever you wish, sir, all beverages are gratis, he heard, once again, his traitor voice: 'So, okay, bibi, give one whiskysoda only.'

What a nasty surprise! He had come awake with a jolt, and sat stiffly in his chair, ignoring alcohol and peanuts. How had the past bubbled up, in transmogrified vowels and vocab? What next? Would he take to putting coconut-oil in his hair? Would he take to squeezing his nostrils between thumb and forefinger, blowing noisily and drawing forth a glutinous silver arc of muck? Would he become a devotee of professional wrestling? What further, diabolic humiliations were in store? He should have known it was a mistake to *go home,* after so long, how could it be other than a regression; it was an unnatural journey; a denial of time; a revolt against history; the whole thing was bound to be a disaster.

I'm not myself, he thought as a faint fluttering feeling began in the vicinity of his heart. But what does that mean, anyway, he added bitterly. After all, 'les acteurs ne sont pas des gens', as the great ham Frederick had explained in *Les Enfants du Paradis*. Masks beneath masks until suddenly the bare bloodless skull.

The seatbelt light came on, the captain's voice warned of air turbulence, they dropped in and out of air pockets. The desert lurched about beneath them and the migrant labourer who had boarded at Qatar clutched at his giant transistor radio and began to retch. Chamcha noticed that the man had not fastened his belt, and pulled himself together, bringing his voice back to its haughtiest English pitch. 'Look here, why don't you . . .' he indicated, but the sick man, between bursts of heaving into the paper bag which Saladin had handed him just in time, shook his head, shrugged, replied: 'Sahib, for what? If Allah wishes me to die, I shall die. If he does not, I shall not. Then of what use is the safety?'

Damn you, India, Saladin Chamcha cursed silently, sinking back into his seat. To hell with you, I escaped your clutches long ago, you won't get your hooks into me again, you cannot drag me back.

Once upon a time – *it was and it was not so,* as the old stories used to say, *it happened and it never did* – maybe, then, or maybe not, a ten-year-old boy from Scandal Point in Bombay found a wallet lying in the street outside his home. He was on the way home from school, having just descended from the school bus on which he had been obliged to sit squashed between the adhesive sweatiness of boys in shorts and be deafened by their noise, and because even in those days he was a person who recoiled from raucousness, jostling and the perspiration of strangers he was feeling faintly nauseated by the long, bumpy ride home. However, when he saw the black leather billfold lying at his feet, the nausea vanished, and he bent down excitedly and grabbed, – opened, – and found, to his delight, that it was full of cash, – and not merely rupees, but real money, negotiable on black markets and international exchanges, – pounds! Pounds sterling, from Proper London in the fabled country of Vilayet across the black water and far away. Dazzled by the thick wad of foreign currency, the boy raised his eyes to make sure he had not been observed, and for a moment it seemed to him that a rainbow had arched down to him from the heavens, a rainbow like an angel's breath, like an answered prayer, coming to an end in the very spot on which he stood. His fingers trembled as they reached into the wallet, towards the fabulous hoard.

'Give it.' It seemed to him in later life that his father had been spying on him throughout his childhood, and even though Changez Chamchawala was a big man, a giant even, to say nothing of his wealth and public standing, he still always had the lightness of foot and also the inclination to sneak up behind his son and spoil whatever he was doing, whipping the young Salahuddin's bedsheet off at night to reveal the shameful penis in the clutching, red hand. And he could smell money from a hundred and one miles away, even through the stink of chemicals and fertilizer that always hung around him owing to his being the country's largest manufacturer of agricultural sprays and fluids and artificial dung. Changez Chamchawala, philanthropist, philanderer, living legend, leading light of the nationalist movement, sprang from the gateway of his home to pluck a bulging wallet from his son's frustrated hand. 'Tch tch,' he admonished, pocketing the pounds sterling, 'you should not pick things up from the street. The ground is dirty, and money is dirtier, anyway.'

On a shelf of Changez Chamchawala's teak-lined study, beside a ten-volume set of the Richard Burton translation of the *Arabian Nights*, which was being slowly devoured by mildew and bookworm owing to the deep-seated prejudice against books which led Changez to own thousands of the pernicious things in order to humiliate them by leaving them to rot unread, there stood a magic lamp, a brightly polished copper-and-brass avatar of Aladdin's very own genie-container: a lamp begging to be rubbed. But Changez neither rubbed it nor permitted it to be rubbed by, for example, his son. 'One day,' he assured the boy, 'you'll have it for yourself. Then rub and rub as much as you like and see what doesn't come to you. Just now, but, it is mine.' The promise of the magic lamp infected Master Salahuddin with the notion that one day his troubles would end and his innermost desires would be gratified, and all he had to do was wait it out; but then there was the incident of the wallet, when the magic of a rainbow had worked for him, not for his father but for him, and Changez Chamchawala had stolen the crock of gold. After that the son became convinced that his father would smother all his hopes unless he got away, and from that moment he became desperate to leave, to escape, to place oceans between the great man and himself.

Salahuddin Chamchawala had understood by his thirteenth year that he was destined for that cool Vilayet full of the crisp promises of pounds sterling at which the magic billfold had hinted, and he grew increasingly impatient of that Bombay of dust, vulgarity, policemen in shorts, transvestites, movie fanzines, pavement sleepers and the rumoured singing whores of Grant Road who had begun as devotees of the Yellamma cult in Karnataka but ended up here as dancers in the more prosaic temples of the flesh. He was fed up of textile factories and local trains and all the confusion and superabundance of the place, and longed for that dream-Vilayet of poise and moderation that had come to obsess him by night and day. His favourite playground rhymes were those that yearned for foreign cities: kitchy-con kitchy-ki kitchy-con stanty-eye kitchy-ople kitchy-cople kitchy-Con-stanti-nople. And his favourite game was the version of grandmother's footsteps in which, when he was *it*, he would turn his back on upcreeping playmates to gabble out, like a mantra, like a spell, the six letters of his dream-city, *ellowen deeowen*. In his secret heart, he crept silently up on London, letter by letter, just as his friends crept up to him. *Ellowen deeowen London*.

The mutation of Salahuddin Chamchawala into Saladin Chamcha began, it will be seen, in old Bombay, long before he got close enough to hear the lions of Trafalgar roar. When the England cricket team played India at the Brabourne Stadium,

he prayed for an England victory, for the game's creators to defeat
the local upstarts, for the proper order of things to be maintained.
(But the games were invariably drawn, owing to the featherbed
somnolence of the Brabourne Stadium wicket; the great issue,
creator versus imitator, colonizer against colonized, had perforce
to remain unresolved.)

In his thirteenth year he was old enough to play on the rocks at
Scandal Point without having to be watched over by his ayah,
Kasturba. And one day (it was so, it was not so), he strolled out of
the house, that ample, crumbling, salt-caked building in the Parsi
style, all columns and shutters and little balconies, and through the
garden that was his father's pride and joy and which in a certain
evening light could give the impression of being infinite (and
which was also enigmatic, an unsolved riddle, because nobody,
not his father, not the gardener, could tell him the names of most
of the plants and trees), and out through the main gateway, a
grandiose folly, a reproduction of the Roman triumphal arch of
Septimius Severus, and across the wild insanity of the street, and
over the sea wall, and so at last on to the broad expanse of shiny
black rocks with their little shrimpy pools. Christian girls giggled
in frocks, men with furled umbrellas stood silent and fixed upon
the blue horizon. In a hollow of black stone Salahuddin saw a man
in a dhoti bending over a pool. Their eyes met, and the man
beckoned him with a single finger which he then laid across his
lips. *Shh,* and the mystery of rock-pools drew the boy towards the
stranger. He was a creature of bone. Spectacles framed in what
might have been ivory. His finger curling, curling, like a baited
hook, come. When Salahuddin came down the other grasped
him, put a hand around his mouth and forced his young hand
between old and fleshless legs, to feel the fleshbone there. The
dhoti open to the winds. Salahuddin had never known how to
fight; he did what he was forced to do, and then the other simply
turned away from him and let him go.

After that Salahuddin never went to the rocks at Scandal Point;
nor did he tell anyone what had happened, knowing the neur-
asthenic crises it would unleash in his mother and suspecting that

his father would say it was his own fault. It seemed to him that everything loathsome, everything he had come to revile about his home town, had come together in the stranger's bony embrace, and now that he had escaped that evil skeleton he must also escape Bombay, or die. He began to concentrate fiercely upon this idea, to fix his will upon it at all times, eating shitting sleeping, convincing himself that he could make the miracle happen even without his father's lamp to help him out. He dreamed of flying out of his bedroom window to discover that there, below him, was – not Bombay – but Proper London itself, Bigben Nelsonscolumn Lordstavern Bloodytower Queen. But as he floated out over the great metropolis he felt himself beginning to lose height, and no matter how hard he struggled kicked swam-in-air he continued to spiral slowly downwards to earth, then faster, then faster still, until he was screaming headfirst down towards the city, Saintpauls, Puddinglane, Threadneedlestreet, zeroing in on London like a bomb.

When the impossible happened, and his father, out of the blue, offered him an English education, *to get me out of the way,* he thought, *otherwise why, it's obvious, but don't look a gift horse andsoforth,* his mother Nasreen Chamchawala refused to cry, and volunteered, instead, the benefit of her advice. 'Don't go dirty like those English,' she warned him. 'They wipe their bee tee ems with paper only. Also, they get into each other's dirty bathwater.' These vile slanders proved to Salahuddin that his mother was doing her damnedest to prevent him from leaving, and in spite of their mutual love he replied, 'It is inconceivable, Ammi, what you say. England is a great civilization, what are you talking, bunk.'

She smiled her little nervy smile and did not argue. And, later, stood dry-eyed beneath the triumphal arch of a gateway and would not go to Santacruz airport to see him off. Her only child. She heaped garlands around his neck until he grew dizzy with the cloying perfumes of mother-love.

Nasreen Chamchawala was the slightest, most fragile of

women, her bones like tinkas, like minute slivers of wood. To make up for her physical insignificance she took at an early age to dressing with a certain outrageous, excessive verve. Her sari-patterns were dazzling, even garish: lemon silk adorned with huge brocade diamonds, dizzy black-and-white Op Art swirls, gigantic lipstick kisses on a bright white ground. People forgave her her lurid taste because she wore the blinding garments with such innocence; because the voice emanating from that textile cacophony was so tiny and hesitant and proper. And because of her soirées.

Each Friday of her married life, Nasreen would fill the halls of the Chamchawala residence, those usually tenebrous chambers like great hollow burial vaults, with bright light and brittle friends. When Salahuddin was a little boy he had insisted on playing doorman, and would greet the jewelled and lacquered guests with great gravity, permitting them to pat him on the head and call him *cuteso* and *chweetie-pie*. On Fridays the house was full of noise; there were musicians, singers, dancers, the latest Western hits as heard on Radio Ceylon, raucous puppet-shows in which painted clay rajahs rode puppet-stallions, decapitating enemy marionettes with imprecations and wooden swords. During the rest of the week, however, Nasreen would stalk the house warily, a pigeon of a woman walking on tiptoed feet through the gloom, as if she were afraid to disturb the shadowed silence; and her son, walking in her footsteps, also learned to lighten his footfall lest he rouse whatever goblin or afreet might be lying in wait.

But: Nasreen Chamchawala's caution failed to save her life. The horror seized and murdered her when she believed herself most safe, clad in a sari covered in cheap newspaper photos and head-lines, bathed in chandelier-light, surrounded by her friends.

By then five and a half years had passed since young Salahuddin, garlanded and warned, boarded a Douglas DC-8 and journeyed into the west. Ahead of him, England; beside him, his father,

Changez Chamchawala; below him, home and beauty. Like Nasreen, the future Saladin had never found it easy to cry.

On that first aeroplane he read science fiction tales of inter-planetary migration: Asimov's *Foundation*, Ray Bradbury's *Martian Chronicles*. He imagined the DC-8 was the mother ship, bearing the Chosen, the Elect of God and man, across unthinkable distances, travelling for generations, breeding eugenically, that their seed might one day take root somewhere in a brave new world beneath a yellow sun. He corrected himself: not the mother but the father ship, because there he was, after all, the great man, Abbu, Dad. Thirteen-year-old Salahuddin, setting aside recent doubts and grievances, entered once again his childish adoration of his father, because he had, had, had worshipped him, he was a great father until you started growing a mind of your own, and then to argue with him was called a betrayal of his love, but never mind that now, *I accuse him of becoming my supreme being, so that what happened was like a loss of faith* . . . yes, the father ship, an air-craft was not a flying womb but a metal phallus, and the passengers were spermatozoa waiting to be spilt.

Five and a half hours of time zones; turn your watch upside down in Bombay and you see the time in London. *My father,* Chamcha would think, years later, in the midst of his bitterness. *I accuse him of inverting Time.*

How far did they fly? Five and a half thousand as the crow. Or: from Indianness to Englishness, an immeasurable distance. Or, not very far at all, because they rose from one great city, fell to another. The distance between cities is always small; a villager, travelling a hundred miles to town, traverses emptier, darker, more terrifying space.

What Changez Chamchawala did when the aeroplane took off: trying not to let his son see him doing it, he crossed two pairs of fingers on each hand, and rotated both his thumbs.

And when they were installed in a hotel within a few feet of the ancient location of the Tyburn tree, Changez said to his son:

'Take. This belongs to you.' And held out, at arm's length, a black billfold about whose identity there could be no mistake. 'You are a man now. Take.'

The return of the confiscated wallet, complete with all its currency, proved to be one of Changez Chamchawala's little traps. Salahuddin had been deceived by these all his life. Whenever his father wanted to punish him, he would offer him a present, a bar of imported chocolate or a tin of Kraft cheese, and would then grab him when he came to get it. 'Donkey,' Changez scorned his infant son. 'Always, always, the carrot leads you to my stick.'

Salahuddin in London took the proffered wallet, accepting the gift of manhood; whereupon his father said: 'Now that you are a man, it is for you to look after your old father while we are in London town. You pay all the bills.'

January, 1961. A year you could turn upside down and it would still, unlike your watch, tell the same time. It was winter; but when Salahuddin Chamchawala began to shiver in his hotel room, it was because he was scared halfway out of his wits; his crock of gold had turned, suddenly, into a sorcerer's curse.

Those two weeks in London before he went to his boarding school turned into a nightmare of cash-tills and calculations, because Changez had meant exactly what he said and never put his hand into his own pocket once. Salahuddin had to buy his own clothes, such as a double-breasted blue serge mackintosh and seven blue-and-white striped Van Heusen shirts with detachable semi-stiff collars which Changez made him wear every day, to get used to the studs, and Salahuddin felt as if a blunt knife were being pushed in just beneath his newly broken Adam's-apple; and he had to make sure there would be enough for the hotel room, and everything, so that he was too nervous to ask his father if they could go to a movie, not even one, not even *The Pure Hell of St Trinians*, or to eat out, not a single Chinese meal, and in later years he would remember nothing of his first fortnight in his beloved Ellowen Deeowen except pounds shillings pence, like the disciple of the philosopher-king Chanakya who asked the great man what he meant by saying one could live in the world and also not live in it, and who was told to carry a brim-full pitcher of water through a holiday crowd without spilling a drop, on pain of death, so that when he returned he was unable to describe the day's festivities, having been like a blind man, seeing only the jug on his head.

Changez Chamchawala became very still in those days, seeming not to care if he ate or drank or did any damn thing, he was happy sitting in the hotel room watching television, especially when the Flintstones were on, because, he told his son, that Wilma bibi reminded him of Nasreen. Salahuddin tried to prove he was a man by fasting right along with his father, trying to outlast him, but he never managed it, and when the pangs got too strong he went out of the hotel to the cheap joint nearby where you could buy take-away roast chickens that hung greasily in the window, turning slowly on their spits. When he brought the chicken into the hotel lobby he became embarrassed, not wanting the staff to see, so he stuffed it inside double-breasted serge and went up in the lift reeking of spit-roast, his mackintosh bulging, his face turning red. Chicken-breasted beneath the gaze of dowagers and liftwallahs he felt the birth of that implacable rage which would burn within him, undiminished, for over a quarter of a century; which would boil away his childhood father-worship and make him a secular man, who would do his best, thereafter, to live without a god of any type; which would fuel, perhaps, his determination to become the thing his father was-not-could-never-be, that is, a goodand-proper Englishman. Yes, an English, even if his mother had been right all along, even if there was only paper in the toilets and tepid, used water full of mud and soap to step into after taking exercise, even if it meant a lifetime spent amongst winter-naked trees whose fingers clutched despairingly at the few, pale hours of watery, filtered light. On winter nights he, who had never slept beneath more than a sheet, lay beneath mountains of wool and felt like a figure in an ancient myth, condemned by the gods to have a boulder pressing down upon his chest; but never mind, he would be English, even if his classmates giggled at his voice and excluded him from their secrets, because these exclusions only increased his determination, and that was when he began to act, to find masks that these fellows would recognize, paleface masks, clown-masks, until he fooled them into thinking he was *okay*, he was *people-like-us*. He fooled them the way a sensitive human being can persuade gorillas to accept him into their family, to fondle and caress and stuff bananas in his mouth.

(After he had settled up the last bill, and the wallet he had once found at a rainbow's end was empty, his father said to him: 'See now. You pay your way. I've made a man of you.' But what man? That's what fathers never know. Not in advance; not until it's too late.)

One day soon after he started at the school he came down to breakfast to find a kipper on his plate. He sat there staring at it, not knowing where to begin. Then he cut into it, and got a mouthful of tiny bones. And after extracting them all, another mouthful, more bones. His fellow-pupils watched him suffer in silence; not one of them said, here, let me show you, you eat it in this way. It took him ninety minutes to eat the fish and he was not permitted to rise from the table until it was done. By that time he was shaking, and if he had been able to cry he would have done so. Then the thought occurred to him that he had been taught an important lesson. England was a peculiar-tasting smoked fish full of spikes and bones, and nobody would ever tell him how to eat it. He discovered that he was a bloody-minded person. 'I'll show them all,' he swore. 'You see if I don't.' The eaten kipper was his first victory, the first step in his conquest of England.

William the Conqueror, it is said, began by eating a mouthful of English sand.

Five years later he was back home after leaving school, waiting until the English university term began, and his transmutation into a Vilayeti was well advanced. 'See how well he complains,' Nasreen teased him in front of his father. 'About everything he has such big-big criticisms, the fans are fixed too loosely to the roof and will fall to slice our heads off in our sleep, he says, and the food is too fattening, why we don't cook some things without frying, he wants to know, the top-floor balconies are unsafe and the paint is peeled, why can't we take pride in our surroundings, isn't it, and the garden is overgrown, we are just junglee people, he thinks so, and look how coarse our movies are, now he doesn't enjoy, and so much disease you can't even drink water from the tap, my god, he really got an education, husband, our little Sallu, England-returned, and talking so fine and all.'

They were walking on the lawn in the evening, watching the sun dive into the sea, wandering in the shade of those great spreading trees, some snaky some bearded, which Salahuddin (who now called himself Saladin after the fashion of the English school, but would remain Chamchawala for a while yet, until a theatrical agent shortened his name for commercial reasons) had begun to be able to name, jackfruit, banyan, jacaranda, flame of the forest, plane. Small chhooi-mooi touch-me-not plants grew at the foot of the tree of his own life, the walnut-tree that Changez had planted with his own hands on the day of the coming of the son. Father and son at the birth-tree were both awkward, unable to respond properly to Nasreen's gentle fun. Saladin had been seized by the melancholy notion that the garden had been a better place before he knew its names, that something had been lost which he would never be able to regain. And Changez Chamchawala found that he could no longer look his son in the eye, because the bitterness he saw came close to freezing his heart. When he spoke, turning roughly away from the eighteen-year-old walnut in which, at times during their long separations, he had imagined his only son's soul to reside, the words came out incorrectly and made him sound like the rigid, cold figure he had hoped he would never become, and feared he could not avoid.

'Tell your son,' Changez boomed at Nasreen, 'that if he went abroad to learn contempt for his own kind, then his own kind can feel nothing but scorn for him. What is he? A fauntleroy, a grand panjandrum? Is this my fate: to lose a son and find a freak?'

'Whatever I am, father dear,' Saladin told the older man, 'I owe it all to you.'

It was their last family chat. All that summer feelings continued to run high, for all Nasreen's attempts at mediation, *you must apologize to your father, darling, poor man is suffering like the devil but his pride won't let him hug you.* Even the ayah Kasturba and the old bearer Vallabh, her husband, attempted to mediate but neither father nor son would bend. 'Same material is the problem,' Kasturba told Nasreen. 'Daddy and sonny, same material, same to same.'

When the war with Pakistan began that September Nasreen decided, with a kind of defiance, that she would not cancel her Friday parties, 'to show that Hindus-Muslims can love as well as hate,' she pointed out. Changez saw a look in her eyes and did not attempt to argue, but set the servants to putting blackout curtains over all the windows instead. That night, for the last time, Saladin Chamchawala played his old role of doorman, dressed up in an English dinner-jacket, and when the guests came – the same old guests, dusted with the grey powders of age but otherwise the same – they bestowed upon him the same old pats and kisses, the nostalgic benedictions of his youth. 'Look how grown,' they were saying. 'Just a darling, what to say.' They were all trying to hide their fear of the war, *danger of air-raids,* the radio said, and when they ruffled Saladin's hair their hands were a little too shaky, or alternatively a little too rough.

Late that evening the sirens sang and the guests ran for cover, hiding under beds, in cupboards, anywhere. Nasreen Chamchawala found herself alone by a food-laden table, and attempted to reassure the company by standing there in her newsprint sari, munching a piece of fish as if nothing were the matter. So it was that when she started choking on the fishbone of her death there was nobody to help her, they were all crouching in corners with their eyes shut; even Saladin, conqueror of kippers, Saladin of the

England-returned upper lip, had lost his nerve. Nasreen Chamchawala fell, twitched, gasped, died, and when the all-clear
sounded the guests emerged sheepishly to find their hostess extinct
in the middle of the dining-room, stolen away by the exterminating angel, khali-pili khalaas, as Bombay-talk has it, finished off
for no reason, gone for good.

Less than a year after the death of Nasreen Chamchawala from her
inability to triumph over fishbones in the manner of her foreign-
educated son, Changez married again without a word of warning
to anyone. Saladin in his English college received a letter from his
father commanding him, in the irritatingly orotund and obsoles-
cent phraseology that Changez always used in correspondence, to
be happy. 'Rejoice,' the letter said, 'for what is lost is reborn.' The
explanation for this somewhat cryptic sentence came lower down
in the aerogramme, and when Saladin learned that his new stepmother was also called Nasreen, something went wrong in his
head, and he wrote his father a letter full of cruelty and anger,
whose violence was of the type that exists only between fathers and
sons, and which differs from that between daughters and mothers
in that there lurks behind it the possibility of actual, jaw-breaking
fisticuffs. Changez wrote back by return of post; a brief letter, four
lines of archaic abuse, cad rotter bounder scoundrel varlet whore-
son rogue. 'Kindly consider all family connections irreparably
sundered,' it concluded. 'Consequences your responsibility.'

After a year of silence, Saladin received a further communication, a letter of forgiveness that was in all particulars harder to take
than the earlier, excommunicatory thunderbolt. 'When you
become a father, O my son,' Changez Chamchawala confided,
'then shall you know those moments – ah! Too sweet! – when,
for love, one dandles the bonny babe upon one's knee; whereupon, without warning or provocation, the blessed creature – may
I be frank? – it *wets* one. Perhaps for a moment one feels the gorge
rising, a tide of anger swells within the blood – but then it dies

away, as quickly as it came. For do we not, as adults, understand that the little one is not to blame? He knows not what he does.'

Deeply offended at being compared to a urinating baby, Saladin maintained what he hoped was a dignified silence. By the time of his graduation he had acquired a British passport, because he had arrived in the country just before the laws tightened up, so he was able to inform Changez in a brief note that he intended to settle down in London and look for work as an actor. Changez Chamchawala's reply came by express mail. 'Might as well be a confounded gigolo. It's my belief some devil has got into you and turned your wits. You who have been given so much: do you not feel you owe anything to anyone? To your country? To the memory of your dear mother? To your own mind? Will you spend your life jiggling and preening under bright lights, kissing blonde women under the gaze of strangers who have paid to watch your shame? You are no son of mine, but a *ghoul, a hoosh,* a demon up from hell. An actor! Answer me this: what am I to tell my friends?'

And beneath a signature, the pathetic, petulant postscript. 'Now that you have your own bad djinni, do not think you will inherit the magic lamp.'

After that, Changez Chamchawala wrote to his son at irregular intervals, and in every letter he returned to the theme of demons and possession: 'A man untrue to himself becomes a two-legged lie, and such beasts are Shaitan's best work,' he wrote, and also, in more sentimental vein: 'I have your soul kept safe, my son, here in this walnut-tree. The devil has only your body. When you are free of him, return and claim your immortal spirit. It flourishes in the garden.'

The handwriting in these letters altered over the years, changing from the florid confidence that had made it instantly identifiable and becoming narrower, undecorated, purified. Eventually the letters stopped, but Saladin heard from other sources that his father's preoccupation with the supernatural had continued to deepen, until finally he had become a recluse, perhaps in order to escape this world in which demons could steal his own son's body, a world unsafe for a man of true religious faith.

His father's transformation disconcerted Saladin, even at such a great distance. His parents had been Muslims in the lackadaisical, light manner of Bombayites; Changez Chamchawala had seemed far more godlike to his infant son than any Allah. That this father, this profane deity (albeit now discredited), had dropped to his knees in his old age and started bowing towards Mecca was hard for his godless son to accept.

'I blame that witch,' he told himself, falling for rhetorical purposes into the same language of spells and goblins that his father had commenced to employ. 'That Nasreen Two. Is it I who have been the subject of devilment, am I the one possessed? It's not my handwriting that changed.'

The letters didn't come any more. Years passed; and then Saladin Chamcha, actor, self-made man, returned to Bombay with the Prospero Players, to interpret the role of the Indian doctor in *The Millionairess* by George Bernard Shaw. On stage, he tailored his voice to the requirements of the part, but those long-suppressed locutions, those discarded vowels and consonants, began to leak out of his mouth out of the theatre as well. His voice was betraying him; and he discovered his component parts to be capable of other treasons, too.

A man who sets out to make himself up is taking on the Creator's role, according to one way of seeing things; he's unnatural, a blasphemer, an abomination of abominations. From another angle, you could see pathos in him, heroism in his struggle, in his willingness to risk: not all mutants survive. Or, consider him sociopolitically: most migrants learn, and can become disguises. Our own false descriptions to counter the falsehoods invented about us, concealing for reasons of security our secret selves.

A man who invents himself needs someone to believe in him, to prove he's managed it. Playing God again, you could say. Or you could come down a few notches, and think of Tinkerbell; fairies don't exist if children don't clap their hands. Or you might simply say: it's just like being a man.

Not only the need to be believed in, but to believe in another. You've got it: Love.

Saladin Chamcha met Pamela Lovelace five and a half days before the end of the 1960s, when women still wore bandannas in their hair. She stood at the centre of a room full of Trotskyist actresses and fixed him with eyes so bright, so bright. He monopolized her all evening and she never stopped smiling and she left with another man. He went home to dream of her eyes and smile, the slenderness of her, her skin. He pursued her for two years. England yields her treasures with reluctance. He was astonished by his own perseverance, and understood that she had become the custodian of his destiny, that if she did not relent then his entire attempt at metamorphosis would fail. 'Let me,' he begged her, wrestling politely on her white rug that left him, at his midnight bus stops, covered in guilty fluff. 'Believe me. I'm the one.'

One night, *out of the blue,* she let him, she said she believed. He married her before she could change her mind, but never learned to read her thoughts. When she was unhappy she would lock herself in the bedroom until she felt better. 'It's none of your business,' she told him. 'I don't want anybody to see me when I'm like that.' He used to call her a clam. 'Open up,' he hammered on all the locked doors of their lives together, basement first, then maisonette, then mansion. 'I love you, let me in.' He needed her so badly, to reassure himself of his own existence, that he never comprehended the desperation in her dazzling, permanent smile, the terror in the brightness with which she faced the world, or the reasons why she hid when she couldn't manage to beam. Only when it was too late did she tell him that her parents had committed suicide together when she had just begun to menstruate, over their heads in gambling debts, leaving her with the aristocratic bellow of a voice that marked her out as a golden girl, a woman to envy, whereas in fact she was abandoned, lost, her parents couldn't even be bothered to wait and watch her grow up, that's how much *she* was loved, so of course she had no confidence at all, and every moment she spent in the world was full of panic, so she smiled and smiled and maybe once a week she locked the door and shook and felt like a husk, like an empty peanut-shell, a monkey without a nut.

They never managed to have children; she blamed herself. After ten years Saladin discovered that there was something the matter with some of his own chromosomes, two sticks too long, or too short, he couldn't remember. His genetic inheritance; apparently he was lucky to exist, lucky not to be some sort of deformed freak. Was it his mother or his father from whom? The doctors couldn't say; he blamed, it's easy to guess which one, after all, it wouldn't do to think badly of the dead.

They hadn't been getting along lately.

He told himself that afterwards, but not during.

Afterwards, he told himself, we were on the rocks, maybe it was the missing babies, maybe we just grew away from each other, maybe this, maybe that.

During, he looked away from all the strain, all the scratchiness, all the fights that never got going, he closed his eyes and waited until her smile came back. He allowed himself to believe in that smile, that brilliant counterfeit of joy.

He tried to invent a happy future for them, to make it come true by making it up and then believing in it. On his way to India he was thinking how lucky he was to have her, I'm lucky yes I am don't argue I'm the luckiest bastard in the world. And: how wonderful it was to have before him the stretching, shady avenue of years, the prospect of growing old in the presence of her gentleness.

He had worked so hard and come so close to convincing himself of the truth of these paltry fictions that when he went to bed with Zeeny Vakil within forty-eight hours of arriving in Bombay, the first thing he did, even before they made love, was to faint, to pass out cold, because the messages reaching his brain were in such serious disagreement with one another, as if his right eye saw the world moving to the left while his left eye saw it sliding to the right.

Zeeny was the first Indian woman he had ever made love to. She barged into his dressing-room after the first night of *The Million-airess*, with her operatic arms and her gravel voice, as if it hadn't been years. *Years*. 'Yaar, what a disappointment, I swear, I sat through the whole thing just to hear you singing 'Goodness Gracious Me' like Peter Sellers or what, I thought, let's find out if the guy learned to hit a note, you remember when you did Elvis impersonations with your squash racket, darling, too hilarious, completely cracked. But what is this? Song is not in drama. The hell. Listen, can you escape from all these palefaces and come out with us wogs? Maybe you forgot what that is like.'

He remembered her as a stick-figure of a teenager in a lopsided Quant hairstyle and an equal-but-oppositely lopsided smile. A rash, bad girl. Once for the hell of it she walked into a notorious adda, a dive, on Falkland Road, and sat there smoking a cigarette and drinking Coke until the pimps who ran the joint threatened to cut her face, no freelances permitted. She stared them down, finished her cigarette, left. Fearless. Maybe crazy. Now in her middle thirties she was a qualified doctor with a consultancy at Breach Candy Hospital, who worked with the city's homeless, who had gone to Bhopal the moment the news broke of the invisible American cloud that ate people's eyes and lungs. She was an art critic whose book on the confining myth of authenticity, that folkloristic straitjacket which she sought to replace by an ethic of historically validated eclecticism, for was not the entire national culture based on the principle of borrowing whatever clothes seemed to fit, Aryan, Mughal, British, take-the-best-and-leave-the-rest? – had created a predictable stink, especially because of its title. She had called it *The Only Good Indian*. 'Meaning, is a dead,' she told Chamcha when she gave him a copy. 'Why should there

be a good, right way of being a wog? That's Hindu fundamen-
talism. Actually, we're all bad Indians. Some worse than others.'

She had come into the fullness of her beauty, long hair left
loose, and she was no stick-figure these days. Five hours after she
entered his dressing-room they were in bed, and he passed out.
When he awoke she explained 'I slipped you a mickey finn.' He
never worked out whether or not she had been telling the truth.

Zeenat Vakil made Saladin her project. 'The reclamation of,'
she explained. 'Mister, we're going to get you back.' At times he
thought she intended to achieve this by eating him alive. She
made love like a cannibal and he was her long pork. 'Did you
know,' he asked her, 'of the well-established connection between
vegetarianism and the man-eating impulse?' Zeeny, lunching on
his naked thigh, shook her head. 'In certain extreme cases,' he
went on, 'too much vegetable consumption can release into the
system biochemicals that induce cannibal fantasies.' She looked up
and smiled her slanting smile. Zeeny, the beautiful vampire.
'Come off it,' she said. 'We are a nation of vegetarians, and ours is
a peaceful, mystical culture, everybody knows.'

He, for his part, was required to handle with care. The first
time he touched her breasts she spouted hot astounding tears the
colour and consistency of buffalo milk. She had watched her
mother die like a bird being carved for dinner, first the left breast
then the right, and still the cancer had spread. Her fear of
repeating her mother's death placed her chest off limits. Fearless Zeeny's secret terror. She had never had a child but her eyes
wept milk.

After their first lovemaking she started right in on him, the tears
forgotten now. 'You know what you are, I'll tell you. A deserter
is what, more English than, your Angrez accent wrapped around
you like a flag, and don't think it's so perfect, it slips, baba, like a
false moustache.'

'There's something strange going on,' he wanted to say, 'my
voice,' but he didn't know how to put it, and held his tongue.

'People like you,' she snorted, kissing his shoulder. 'You come back after so long and think godknowswhat of yourselves. Well, baby, we got a lower opinion of you.' Her smile was brighter than Pamela's. 'I see,' he said to her, 'Zeeny, you didn't lose your Binaca smile.'

Binaca. Where had that come from, the long forgotten tooth-paste advertisement? And the vowel sounds, distinctly unreliable. Watch out, Chamcha, look out for your shadow. That black fellow creeping up behind.

On the second night she arrived at the theatre with two friends in tow, a young Marxist film-maker called George Miranda, a shambling whale of a man with rolled-up kurta sleeves, a flapping waistcoat bearing ancient stains, and a surprisingly military moustache with waxed points; and Bhupen Gandhi, poet and journalist, who had gone prematurely grey but whose face was baby-innocent until he unleashed his sly, giggling laugh. 'Come on, Salad baba,' Zeeny announced. 'We're going to show you the town.' She turned to her companions. 'These *Asians* from foreign got no shame,' she declared. 'Saladin, like a bloody lettuce, I ask you.'

'There was a TV reporter here some days back,' George Miranda said. 'Pink hair. She said her name was Kerleeda. I couldn't work it out.'

'Listen, George is too unworldly,' Zeeny interrupted. 'He doesn't know what freaks you guys turn into. That Miss Singh, outrageous. I told her, the name's Khalida, dearie, rhymes with Dalda, that's a cooking medium. But she couldn't say it. Her own name. Take me to your kerleader. You types got no culture. Just wogs now. Ain't it the truth?' she added, suddenly gay and round-eyed, afraid she'd gone too far. 'Stop bullying him, Zeenat,' Bhupen Gandhi said in his quiet voice. And George, awkwardly, mumbled: 'No offence, man. Joke-shoke.'

Chamcha decided to grin and then fight back. 'Zeeny,' he said, 'the earth is full of Indians, you know that, we get everywhere, we become tinkers in Australia and our heads end up in Idi Amin's fridge. Columbus was right, maybe; the world's made up of Indies, East, West, North. Damn it, you should be proud of us, our enterprise, the way we push against frontiers. Only thing is, we're not Indian like you. You better get used to us. What was the name of that book you wrote?'

'Listen,' Zeeny put her arm through his. 'Listen to my Salad. Suddenly he wants to be Indian after spending his life trying to turn white. All is not lost, you see. Something in there still alive.' And Chamcha felt himself flushing, felt the confusion mounting. India; it jumbled things up.

'For Pete's sake,' she added, knifing him with a kiss. '*Chamcha*. I mean, fuck it. You name yourself Mister Toady and you expect us not to laugh.'

In Zeeny's beaten-up Hindustan, a car built for a servant culture, the back seat better upholstered than the front, he felt the night closing in on him like a crowd. India, measuring him against her forgotten immensity, her sheer presence, the old despised disorder. An Amazonic hijra got up like an Indian Wonder Woman, complete with silver trident, held up the traffic with one imperious arm, sauntered in front of them. Chamcha stared into herhis glaring eyes. Gibreel Farishta, the movie star who had unaccountably vanished from view, rotted on the hoardings. Rubble, litter, noise. Cigarette advertisements smoking past: SCISSORS – FOR THE MAN OF ACTION, SATISFACTION. And, more improbably: PANAMA – PART OF THE GREAT INDIAN SCENE.

'Where are we going?' The night had acquired the quality of green neon strip-lighting. Zeeny parked the car. 'You're lost,' she accused him. 'What do you know about Bombay? Your own city, only it never was. To you, it's a dream of childhood. Growing up on Scandal Point is like living on the moon. No bustees there, no sirree, only servants' quarters. Did Shiv Sena elements come there to make communal trouble? Were your neighbours starving in the textile strike? Did Datta Samant stage a rally in front of your bungalows? How old were you when you met a trade unionist? How old the first time you got on a local train instead of a car with

driver? That wasn't Bombay, darling, excuse me. That was Wonderland, Peristan, Never-Never, Oz.'

'And you?' Saladin reminded her. 'Where were you back then?'

'Same place,' she said fiercely. 'With all the other bloody
Munchkins.'

Back streets. A Jain temple was being re-painted and all the
saints were in plastic bags to protect them from the drips. A pavement magazine vendor displayed newspapers full of horror: a
railway disaster. Bhupen Gandhi began to speak in his mild
whisper. After the accident, he said, the surviving passengers swam
to the shore (the train had plunged off a bridge) and were met by
local villagers, who pushed them under the water until they
drowned and then looted their bodies.

'Shut your face,' Zeeny shouted at him. 'Why are you telling
him such things? Already he thinks we're savages, a lower form.'

A shop was selling sandalwood to burn in a nearby Krishna
temple and sets of enamelled pink-and-white Krishna-eyes that
saw everything. 'Too damn much to see,' Bhupen said. 'That is
fact of matter.'

In a crowded dhaba that George had started frequenting when he
was making contact, for movie purposes, with the dadas or bosses
who ran the city's flesh trade, dark rum was consumed at aluminium tables and George and Bhupen started, a little boozily, to
quarrel. Zeeny drank Thums Up Cola and denounced her friends
to Chamcha. 'Drinking problems, both of them, broke as old pots,
they both mistreat their wives, sit in dives, waste their stinking
lives. No wonder I fell for you, sugar, when the local product is so
low grade you get to like goods from foreign.'

George had gone with Zeeny to Bhopal and was becoming
noisy on the subject of the catastrophe, interpreting it ideologically. 'What is Amrika for us?' he demanded. 'It's not a real place.
Power in its purest form, disembodied, invisible. We can't see it
but it screws us totally, no escape.' He compared the Union Car-
bide company to the Trojan Horse. 'We invited the bastards in.' It

was like the story of the forty thieves, he said. Hiding in their amphoras and waiting for the night. 'We had no Ali Baba, misfortunately,' he cried. 'Who did we have? Mr Rajiv G.'

At this point Bhupen Gandhi stood up abruptly, unsteadily, and began, as though possessed, as though a spirit were upon him, to *testify*. 'For me,' he said, 'the issue cannot be foreign intervention. We always forgive ourselves by blaming outsiders, America, Pakistan, any damn place. Excuse me, George, but for me it all goes back to Assam, we have to start with that.' The massacre of the innocents. Photographs of children's corpses, arranged neatly in lines like soldiers on parade. They had been clubbed to death, pelted with stones, their necks cut in half by knives. Those neat ranks of death, Chamcha remembered. As if only horror could sting India into orderliness.

Bhupen spoke for twenty-nine minutes without hesitations or pauses. 'We are all guilty of Assam,' he said. 'Each person of us. Unless and until we face it, that the children's deaths were our fault, we cannot call ourselves a civilized people.' He drank rum quickly as he spoke, and his voice got louder, and his body began to lean dangerously, but although the room fell silent nobody moved towards him, nobody tried to stop him talking, nobody called him a drunk. In the middle of a sentence, *everyday blindings, or shootings, or corruptions, who do we think we,* he sat down heavily and stared into his glass.

Now a young man stood up in a far corner of the joint and argued back. Assam had to be understood politically, he cried, there were economic reasons, and yet another fellow came to his feet to reply, cash matters do not explain why a grown man clubs a little girl to death, and then another fellow said, if you think that, you have never been hungry, salah, how bloody romantic to suppose economics cannot make men into beasts. Chamcha clutched at his glass as the noise level rose, and the air seemed to thicken, gold teeth flashed in his face, shoulders rubbed against his, elbows nudged, the air was turning into soup, and in his chest the irregular palpitations had begun. George grabbed him by the wrist and dragged him out into the street. 'You okay, man? You were turning green.' Saladin nodded his thanks, gasped in lungfuls of the night, calmed down. 'Rum and exhaustion,' he said. 'I have the peculiar habit of getting my nerves after the show. Quite often I get wobbly. Should have known.' Zeeny was looking at him, and there was more in her eyes than sympathy. A glittering look, triumphant, hard. *Something got through to you,* her expression gloated. *About bloody time.*

After you recover from typhoid, Chamcha reflected, you remain immune to the disease for ten years or so. But nothing is forever; eventually the antibodies vanish from your blood. He had to accept the fact that his blood no longer contained the immunizing agents that would have enabled him to suffer India's reality. Rum, heart palpitations, a sickness of the spirit. Time for bed.

She wouldn't take him to her place. Always and only the hotel, with the gold-medallioned young Arabs strutting in the midnight corridors holding bottles of contraband whisky. He lay on the bed with his shoes on, his collar and tie loose, his right arm flung across his eyes; she, in the hotel's white bathrobe, bent over him and kissed his chin. 'I'll tell you what happened to you tonight,' she said. 'You could say we cracked your shell.'

He sat up, angry. 'Well, this is what's inside,' he blazed at her. 'An Indian translated into English-medium. When I attempt Hindustani these days, people look polite. This is me.' Caught in the aspic of his adopted language, he had begun to hear, in India's Babel, an ominous warning: don't come back again. When you have stepped through the looking-glass you step back at your peril. The mirror may cut you to shreds.

'I was so proud of Bhupen tonight,' Zeeny said, getting into bed. 'In how many countries could you go into some bar and start up a debate like that? The passion, the seriousness, the respect. You keep your civilization, Toadji; I like this one plenty fine.'

'Give up on me,' he begged her. 'I don't like people dropping in to see me without warning, I have forgotten the rules of seven-tiles and kabaddi, I can't recite my prayers, I don't know what should happen at a nikah ceremony, and in this city where I grew up I get lost if I'm on my own. This isn't home. It makes me giddy because it feels like home and is not. It makes my heart tremble and my head spin.'

'You're a stupid,' she shouted at him. 'A stupid. Change back! Damn fool! Of course you can.' She was a vortex, a siren, tempting him back to his old self. But it was a dead self, a shadow, a ghost, and he would not become a phantom. There was a return ticket to London in his wallet, and he was going to use it.

'You never married,' he said when they both lay sleepless in the small hours. Zeeny snorted. 'You've really been gone too long. Can't you see me? I'm a blackie.' Arching her back and throwing off the sheet to show off her lavishness. When the bandit queen Phoolan Devi came out of the ravines to surrender and be photographed, the newspapers at once uncreated their own myth of her *legendary beauty*. She became *plain, a common creature, unappetizing* where she had been *toothsome*. Dark skin in north India. 'I don't buy it,' Saladin said. 'You don't expect me to believe that.'

She laughed. 'Good, you're not a complete idiot yet. Who needs to marry? I had work to do.'

And after a pause, she threw his question back at him. *So, then. And you?*

Not only married, but rich. 'So tell, na. How you live, you and the mame.' In a five-storey mansion in Notting Hill. He had started feeling insecure there of late, because the most recent batch of burglars had taken not only the usual video and stereo but also the wolfhound guard dog. It was not possible, he had begun to feel, to live in a place where the criminal elements kidnapped the animals. Pamela told him it was an old local custom. In the Olden Days, she said (history, for Pamela, was divided into the Ancient Era, the Dark Ages, the Olden Days, the British Empire, the Modern Age and the Present), petnapping was good business. The poor would steal the canines of the rich, train them to forget their names, and sell them back to their grieving, helpless owners in shops on Portobello Road. Pamela's local history was always detailed and frequently unreliable. 'But, my God,' Zeeny Vakil said, 'you must sell up pronto and move. I know those English, all the same, riff-raff and nawabs. You can't fight their bloody traditions.'

My wife, Pamela Lovelace, frail as porcelain, graceful as gazelles, he remembered. *I put down roots in the women I love.* The banalities of infidelity. He put them away and talked about his work.

When Zeeny Vakil found out how Saladin Chamcha made his money, she let fly a series of shrieks that made one of the medallioned Arabs knock at the door to make sure everything was all right. He saw a beautiful woman sitting up in bed with what looked like buffalo milk running down her face and dripping off the point of her chin, and, apologizing to Chamcha for the intrusion, he withdrew hastily, *sorry, sport, hey, you're some lucky guy.*

'You poor potato,' Zeeny gasped between peals of laughter. 'Those Angrez bastards. They really screwed you up.'

So now his work was funny. 'I have a gift for accents,' he said haughtily. 'Why I shouldn't employ?'

' *"Why I should not employ?"* ' she mimicked him, kicking her legs in the air. 'Mister actor, your moustache just slipped again.'

Oh my God.

What's happening to me?

What the devil?

Help.

Because he did have that gift, truly he did, he was the Man of a Thousand Voices and a Voice. If you wanted to know how your ketchup bottle should talk in its television commercial, if you were unsure as to the ideal voice for your packet of garlic-flavoured crisps, he was your very man. He made carpets speak in warehouse advertisements, he did celebrity impersonations, baked beans, frozen peas. On the radio he could convince an audience that he was Russian, Chinese, Sicilian, the President of the United States. Once, in a radio play for thirty-seven voices, he interpreted every single part under a variety of pseudonyms and nobody ever worked it out. With his female equivalent, Mimi Mamoulian, he ruled the airwaves of Britain. They had such a large slice of the voiceover racket that, as Mimi said, 'People better not mention the Monopolies Commission around us, not even in fun.' Her range was astonishing; she could do any age, anywhere in the world, any point on the vocal register, angelic Juliet to fiendish Mae West. 'We should get married sometime, when you're free,' Mimi once suggested to him. 'You and me, we could be the United Nations.'

'You're Jewish,' he pointed out. 'I was brought up to have views on Jews.'

'So I'm Jewish,' she shrugged. 'You're the one who's circumcised. Nobody's perfect.'

Mimi was tiny with tight dark curls and looked like a Michelin poster. In Bombay, Zeenat Vakil stretched and yawned and drove other women from his thoughts. 'Too much,' she laughed at him. 'They pay you to imitate them, as long as they don't have to look at you. Your voice becomes famous but they hide your face. Got any ideas why? Warts on your nose, cross-eyes, what? Anything come to mind, baby? You goddamn lettuce brain, I swear.'

It was true, he thought. Saladin and Mimi were legends of a sort, but crippled legends, dark stars. The gravitational field of their abilities drew work towards them, but they remained invisible, shedding bodies to put on voices. On the radio, Mimi could become the Botticelli Venus, she could be Olympia, Monroe, any damn woman she pleased. She didn't give a damn about the way she looked; she had become her voice, she was worth a mint, and three young women were hopelessly in love with her. Also, she bought property. 'Neurotic behaviour,' she would confess unashamedly. 'Excessive need for rooting owing to upheavals of Armenian-Jewish history. Some desperation owing to advancing years and small polyps detected in the throat. Property is so soothing, I do recommend it.' She owned a Norfolk vicarage, a farmhouse in Normandy, a Tuscan bell-tower, a sea-coast in Bohemia. 'All haunted,' she explained. 'Clanks, howls, blood on the rugs, women in nighties, the works. Nobody gives up land without a fight.'

Nobody except me, Chamcha thought, a melancholy clutching at him as he lay beside Zeenat Vakil. Maybe I'm a ghost already. But at least a ghost with an airline ticket, success, money, wife. A shade, but living in the tangible, material world. With *assets*. Yes, sir.

Zeeny stroked the hairs curling over his ears. 'Sometimes, when you're quiet,' she murmured, 'when you aren't doing funny voices or acting grand, and when you forget people are watching, you look just like a blank. You know? An empty slate, nobody home. It makes me mad, sometimes, I want to slap you. To sting you back into life. But I also get sad about it. Such a fool, you, the big star whose face is the wrong colour for their colour TVs, who has to travel to wogland with some two-bit company, playing the babu part on top of it, just to get into a play. They kick you around and still you stay, you love them, bloody slave mentality, I swear. Chamcha,' she grabbed his shoulders and shook him, sitting astride him with her forbidden breasts a few inches from his face, 'Salad baba, whatever you call yourself, for Pete's sake *come home*.'

His big break, the one that could soon make money lose its meaning, had started small: children's television, a thing called *The Aliens Show*, by *The Munsters* out of *Star Wars* by way of *Sesame Street*. It was a situation comedy about a group of extraterrestrials ranging from cute to psycho, from animal to vegetable, and also mineral, because it featured an artistic space-rock that could quarry itself for its raw material, and then regenerate itself in time for the next week's episode; this rock was named Pygmalien, and owing to the stunted sense of humour of the show's producers there was also a coarse, belching creature like a puking cactus that came from a desert planet at the end of time: this was Matilda, the Australien, and there were the three grotesquely pneumatic, singing space sirens known as the Alien Korns, maybe because you could lie down among them, and there was a team of Venusian hip-hoppers and subway spray-painters and soul-brothers who called themselves the Alien Nation, and under a bed in the spaceship that was the programme's main location there lived Bugsy the giant dung-beetle from the Crab Nebula who had run away from his father, and in a fish-tank you could find Brains the super-intelligent giant abalone who liked eating Chinese, and then there was Ridley, the most terrifying of the regular cast, who looked like a Francis Bacon painting of a mouthful of teeth waving at the end of a sightless pod, and who had an obsession with the actress Sigourney Weaver. The stars of the show, its Kermit and Miss Piggy, were the very fashionable, slinkily attired, stunningly hair-styled duo, Maxim and Mamma Alien, who yearned to be – what else? – television personalities. They were played by Saladin Chamcha and Mimi Mamoulian, and they changed their voices along with their clothes, to say nothing of their hair, which could go from purple to vermilion between shots, which could stand diagonally three feet up from their heads or vanish altogether; or their features and limbs, because they were capable of changing all of them, switching legs, arms, noses, ears, eyes, and every switch conjured up a different accent from their legendary, protean gul-lets. What made the show a hit was its use of the latest computer-generated imagery. The backgrounds were all simulated: spaceship, other-world landscapes, intergalactic game-show stu-dios; and the actors, too, were processed through machines, obliged to spend four hours every day being buried under the latest in prosthetic make-up which – once the video-computers had gone to work – made them look just like simulations, too. Maxim Alien, space playboy, and Mamma, undefeated galactic wrestling champion and universal all-comers pasta queen, were overnight sensations. Prime-time beckoned; America, Eurovision, the world.

As *The Aliens Show* got bigger it began to attract political criti-cism. Conservatives attacked it for being too frightening, too sexually explicit (Ridley could become positively erect when he thought too hard about Miss Weaver), too *weird*. Radical com-mentators began to attack its stereotyping, its reinforcement of the idea of aliens-as-freaks, its lack of positive images. Chamcha came under pressure to quit the show; refused; became a target.

'Trouble waiting when I go home,' he told Zeeny. 'The damn show isn't an allegory. It's an entertainment. It aims to please.'

'To please whom?' she wanted to know. 'Besides, even now they only let you on the air after they cover your face with rubber and give you a red wig. Big deal deluxe, say I.'

'The point is,' she said when they awoke the next morning, 'Salad darling, you really are good looking, no quesch. Skin like milk, England returned. Now that Gibreel has done a bunk, you could be next in line. I'm serious, yaar. They need a new face. Come home and you could be the next, bigger than Bachchan was, bigger than Farishta. Your face isn't as funny as theirs.'

When he was young, he told her, each phase of his life, each self he tried on, had seemed reassuringly temporary. Its imperfections didn't matter, because he could easily replace one moment by the next, one Saladin by another. Now, however, change had begun to feel painful; the arteries of the possible had begun to harden. 'It isn't easy to tell you this, but I'm married now, and not just to wife but life.' *The accent slippage again.* 'I really came to Bombay for one reason, and it wasn't the play. He's in his late seventies now, and I won't have many more chances. He hasn't been to the show; Muhammad must go to the mountain.'

My father, Changez Chamchawala, owner of a magic lamp. 'Changez Chamchawala, are you kidding, don't think you can leave me behind,' she clapped her hands. 'I want to check out the hair and toenails.' His father, the famous recluse. Bombay was a culture of re-makes. Its architecture mimicked the skyscraper, its cinema endlessly re-invented *The Magnificent Seven* and *Love Story*, obliging all its heroes to save at least one village from murderous dacoits and all its heroines to die of leukaemia at least once in their careers, preferably at the start. Its millionaires, too, had taken to importing their lives. Changez's invisibility was an Indian dream of the crorepati penthoused wretch of Las Vegas; but a dream was not a photograph, after all, and Zeeny wanted to see with her own eyes. 'He makes faces at people if he's in a bad mood,' Saladin warned her. 'Nobody believes it till it happens, but it's true. Such faces! Gargoyles. Also, he's a prude and he'll call you a tart and anyway I'll probably have a fight with him, it's on the cards.'

What Saladin Chamcha had come to India for: forgiveness. That was his business in his old home town. But whether to give or to receive, he was not able to say.

Bizarre aspects of the present circumstances of Mr Changez Chamchawala: with his new wife, Nasreen the Second, he lived for five days every week in a high-walled compound nicknamed the Red Fort in the Pali Hill district beloved of movie stars; but every weekend he returned without his wife to the old house at Scandal Point, to spend his days of rest in the lost world of the past, in the company of the first, and dead, Nasreen. Furthermore: it was said that his second wife refused to set foot in the old place. 'Or isn't allowed to,' Zeeny hypothesized in the back of the black-glass-windowed Mercedes limousine which Changez had sent to collect his son. As Saladin finished filling in the background, Zeenat Vakil whistled appreciatively. 'Cra*zee*.'

The Chamchawala fertilizer business, Changez's empire of dung, was to be investigated for tax fraud and import duty evasion by a Government commission, but Zeeny wasn't interested in that. 'Now,' she said, 'I'll get to find out what you're really like.'

Scandal Point unfurled before them. Saladin felt the past rush in like a tide, drowning him, filling his lungs with its revenant saltiness. *I'm not myself today,* he thought. The heart flutters. Life damages the living. None of us are ourselves. None of us are *like this*.

These days there were steel gates, operated by remote control from within, sealing the crumbling triumphal arch. They opened with a slow whirring sound to admit Saladin into that place of lost time. When he saw the walnut-tree in which his father had claimed that his soul was kept, his hands began to shake. He hid behind the neutrality of facts. 'In Kashmir,' he told Zeeny, 'your birth-tree is a financial investment of a sort. When a child comes of age, the grown walnut is comparable to a matured insurance policy; it's a valuable tree, it can be sold, to pay for weddings, or a start in life. The adult chops down his childhood to help his grown-up self. The unsentimentality is appealing, don't you think?'

The car had stopped under the entrance porch. Zeeny fell silent as the two of them climbed the six stairs to the front door, where they were greeted by a composed and ancient bearer in white, brass-buttoned livery, whose shock of white hair Chamcha suddenly recognized, by translating it back into black, as the mane of that same Vallabh who had presided over the house as its major-domo in the Olden Days. 'My God, Vallabhbhai,' he managed, and embraced the old man. The servant smiled a difficult smile. 'I grow so old, baba, I was thinking you would not recognize.' He led them down the crystal-heavy corridors of the mansion and Saladin realized that the lack of change was excessive, and plainly deliberate. It was true, Vallabh explained to him, that when the Begum died Changez Sahib had sworn that the house would be her memorial. As a result nothing had changed since the day she died, paintings, furniture, soap-dishes, the red-glass figures of fighting bulls and china ballerinas from Dresden, all left in their exact positions, the same magazines on the same tables, the same crumpled balls of paper in the wastebaskets, as though the house had died, too, and been embalmed. 'Mummified,' Zeeny said, voicing the unspeakable as usual. 'God, but it's spooky, no?' It was at this point, while Vallabh the bearer was opening the double doors leading into the blue drawing-room, that Saladin Chamcha saw his mother's ghost.

He let out a loud cry and Zeeny whirled on her heel. 'There,' he pointed towards the far, darkened end of the hallway, 'no question, that blasted newsprint sari, the big headlines, the one she wore the day she, she,' but now Vallabh had begun to flap his arms like a weak, flightless bird, you see, baba, it was only Kasturba, you have not forgotten, my wife, only my wife. *My ayah Kasturba with whom I played in rock-pools. Until I grew up and went without her and in a hollow a man with ivory glasses.* 'Please, baba, nothing to be cross, only when the Begum died Changez Sahib donated to my wife some few garments, you do not object? Your mother was a so-generous woman, when alive she always gave with an open hand.' Chamcha, recovering his equilibrium, was feeling foolish. 'For God's sake, Vallabh,' he muttered. 'For God's sake. Obviously I don't object.' An old stiffness re-entered Vallabh; the right to free speech of the old retainer permitted him to reprove, 'Excuse, baba, but you should not blaspheme.'

'See how he's sweating,' Zeeny stage-whispered. 'He looks scared stiff.' Kasturba entered the room, and although her reunion with Chamcha was warm enough there was still a wrongness in the air. Vallabh left to bring beer and Thums Up, and when Kasturba also excused herself, Zeeny at once said: 'Something fishy. She walks like she owns the dump. The way she holds herself. And the old man was afraid. Those two are up to something, I bet.' Chamcha tried to be reasonable. 'They stay here alone most of the time, probably sleep in the master bedroom and eat off the good plates, it must get to feeling like their place.' But he was thinking how strikingly, in that old sari, his ayah Kasturba had come to resemble his mother.

'Stayed away so long,' his father's voice spoke behind him, 'that now you can't tell a living ayah from your departed ma.'

Saladin turned around to take in the melancholy sight of a father who had shrivelled like an old apple, but who insisted nevertheless on wearing the expensive Italian suits of his opulently fleshy years. Now that he had lost both Popeye-forearms and Bluto-belly, he seemed to be roaming about inside his clothes like a man in search of something he had not quite managed to identify. He stood in the doorway looking at his son, his nose and lips curled, by the withering sorcery of the years, into a feeble simulacrum of his former ogre-face. Chamcha had barely begun to understand that his father was no longer capable of frightening anybody, that his spell had been broken and he was just an old geezer heading for the grave; while Zeeny had noted with some disappointment that Changez Chamchawala's hair was conservatively short, and since he was wearing highly polished Oxford lace-ups it didn't seem likely that the eleven-inch toenail story was true either; when the ayah Kasturba returned, smoking a cigarette, and strolled past the three of them, father son mistress, towards a blue velour-covered button-backed Chesterfield sofa, upon which she arranged her body as sensually as any movie starlet, even though she was a woman well advanced in years.

No sooner had Kasturba completed her shocking entrance than Changez skipped past his son and planted himself beside the erstwhile ayah. Zeeny Vakil, her eyes sparkling with scandal-points of light, hissed at Chamcha: 'Close your mouth, dear. It looks bad.' And in the doorway, the bearer Vallabh, pushing a drinks trolley, watched unemotionally while his employer of many long years placed an arm around his uncomplaining wife.

When the progenitor, the creator is revealed as satanic, the child will frequently grow prim. Chamcha heard himself inquire: 'And my stepmother, father dear? She is keeping well?'

The old man addressed Zeeny. 'He is not such a goody with you, I hope so. Or what a sad time you must have.' Then to his son in harsher tones. 'You have an interest in my wife these days? But she has none in you. She won't meet you now. Why should she forgive? You are no son to her. Or, maybe, by now, to me.'

I did not come to fight him. Look, the old goat. I mustn't fight. But this, this is intolerable. 'In my mother's house,' Chamcha cried melodramatically, losing his battle with himself. 'The state thinks your business is corrupt, and here is the corruption of your soul. Look what you've done to them. Vallabh and Kasturba. With your money. How much did it take? To poison their lives. You're a sick man.' He stood before his father, blazing with righteous rage.

Vallabh the bearer, unexpectedly, intervened. 'Baba, with respect, excuse me but what do you know? You have left and gone and now you come to judge us.' Saladin felt the floor giving way beneath his feet; he was staring into the inferno. 'It is true he pays us,' Vallabh went on. 'For our work, and also for what you see. For this.' Changez Chamchawala tightened his grip on the ayah's unresisting shoulders.

'How much?' Chamcha shouted. 'Vallabh, how much did you two men decide upon? How much to prostitute your wife?'

'What a fool,' Kasturba said contemptuously. 'England-educated and what-all, but still with a head full of hay. You come talking so big-big, *in your mother's house* etcetera, but maybe you didn't love her so much. But we loved her, we all. We three. And in this manner we may keep her spirit alive.'

'It is pooja, you could say,' came Vallabh's quiet voice. 'An act of worship.'

'And you,' Changez Chamchawala spoke as softly as his servant, 'you come here to this temple. With your unbelief. Mister, you've got a nerve.'

And finally, the treason of Zeenat Vakil. 'Come off it, Salad,' she said, moving to sit on the arm of the Chesterfield next to the old man. 'Why be such a sourpuss? You're no angel, baby, and these people seem to have worked things out okay.'

Saladin's mouth opened and shut. Changez patted Zeeny on the knee. 'He came to accuse, dear. He came to avenge his youth, but we have turned the tables and he is confused. Now we must let him have his chance, and you must referee. I will not be sentenced by him, but I will accept the worst from you.'

The bastard. Old bastard. He wanted me off-balance, and here I am, knocked sideways. I won't speak, why should I, not like this, the humiliation. 'There was,' said Saladin Chamcha, 'a wallet of pounds, and there was a roasted chicken.'

⌘

Of what did the son accuse the father? Of everything: espionage on child-self, rainbow-pot-stealing, exile. Of turning him into what he might not have become. Of making-a-man of. Of what-will-I-tell-my-friends. Of irreparable sunderings and offensive forgiveness. Of succumbing to Allah-worship with new wife and also to blasphemous worship of late spouse. Above all, of magiclampism, of being an open-sesamist. Everything had come easily to him, charm, women, wealth, power, position. Rub, poof, genie, wish, at once master, hey presto. He was a father who had promised, and then withheld, a magic lamp.

Changez, Zeeny, Vallabh, Kasturba remained motionless and silent until Saladin Chamcha came to a flushed, embarrassed halt. 'Such violence of the spirit after so long,' Changez said after a silence. 'So sad. A quarter of a century and still the son begrudges the peccadilloes of the past. O my son. You must stop carrying me around like a parrot on your shoulder. What am I? Finished. I'm not your Old Man of the Sea. Face it, mister: I don't explain you any more.'

Through a window Saladin Chamcha caught sight of a forty-year-old walnut-tree. 'Cut it down,' he said to his father. 'Cut it, sell it, send me the cash.'

Chamchawala rose to his feet, and extended his right hand. Zeeny, also rising, took it like a dancer accepting a bouquet; at once, Vallabh and Kasturba diminished into servants, as if a clock had silently chimed pumpkin-time. 'Your book,' he said to Zeeny. 'I have something you'd like to see.'

The two of them left the room; impotent Saladin, after a moment's floundering, stamped petulantly in their wake. 'Sour-puss,' Zeeny called gaily over her shoulder. 'Come on, snap out of it, grow up.'

The Chamchawala art collection, housed here at Scandal Point, included a large group of the legendary *Hamza-nama* cloths, members of that sixteenth-century sequence depicting scenes from the life of a hero who may or may not have been the same Hamza as the famous one, Muhammad's uncle whose liver was eaten by the Meccan woman Hind as he lay dead on the battlefield of Uhud. 'I like these pictures,' Changez Chamchawala told Zeeny, 'because the hero is permitted to fail. See how often he has to be rescued from his troubles.' The pictures also provided eloquent proof of Zeeny Vakil's thesis about the eclectic, hybridized nature of the

Indian artistic tradition. The Mughals had brought artists from every part of India to work on the paintings; individual identity was submerged to create a many-headed, many-brushed Over-artist who, literally, *was* Indian painting. One hand would draw the mosaic floors, a second the figures, a third would paint the Chinese-looking cloudy skies. On the backs of the cloths were the stories that accompanied the scenes. The pictures would be shown like a movie: held up while someone read out the hero's tale. In the *Hamza-nama* you could see the Persian miniature fusing with Kannada and Keralan painting styles, you could see Hindu and Muslim philosophy forming their characteristically late-Mughal synthesis.

A giant was trapped in a pit and his human tormentors were spearing him in the forehead. A man sliced vertically from the top of his head to his groin still held his sword as he fell. Everywhere, bubbling spillages of blood. Saladin Chamcha took a grip on himself. 'The savagery,' he said loudly in his English voice. 'The sheer barbaric love of pain.'

Changez Chamchawala ignored his son, had eyes only for Zeeny; who gazed straight back into his own. 'Ours is a government of philistines, young lady, don't you agree? I have offered this whole collection free gratis, did you know? Let them only house it properly, let them build a place. Condition of cloths is not A-1, you see . . . they won't do it. No interest. Meanwhile I get offers every month from Amrika. Offers of what-what size! You wouldn't believe. I don't sell. Our heritage, my dear, every day the USA is taking it away. Ravi Varma paintings, Chandela bronzes, Jaisalmer lattices. We sell ourselves, isn't it? They drop their wallets on the ground and we kneel at their feet. Our Nandi bulls end up in some gazebo in Texas. But you know all this. You know India is a free country today.' He stopped, but Zeeny waited; there was more to come. It came: 'One day I will also take the dollars. Not for the money. For the pleasure of being a whore. Of becoming nothing. Less than nothing.' And now, at last, the real storm, the words behind the words, *less than nothing*. 'When I die,' Changez Chamchawala said to Zeeny, 'what will I be? A pair of emptied shoes. That is my fate, that he has made for me. This actor. This pretender. He has made himself into an imitator of non-existing men. I have nobody to follow me, to give what I have made. This is his revenge: he steals from me my posterity.' He smiled, patted her hand, released her into the care of his son. 'I have told her,' he said to Saladin. 'You are still carrying your take-away chicken. I have told her my complaint. Now she must judge. That was the arrangement.'

Zeenat Vakil walked up to the old man in his outsize suit, put her hands on his cheeks, and kissed him on the lips.

After Zeenat betrayed him in the house of his father's perversions, Saladin Chamcha refused to see her or answer the messages she left at the hotel desk. *The Millionairess* came to the end of its run; the tour was over. Time to go home. After the closing-night party Chamcha headed for bed. In the elevator a young and clearly honeymooning couple were listening to music on headphones. The young man murmured to his wife: 'Listen, tell me. Do I still seem a stranger to you sometimes?' The girl, smiling fondly, shook her head, *can't hear,* removed the headphones. He repeated, gravely: 'A stranger, to you, don't I still sometimes seem?' She, with unfaltering smile, laid her cheek for an instant on his high scrawny shoulder. 'Yes, once or twice,' she said, and put the headphones on again. He did the same, seeming fully satisfied by her answer. Their bodies took on, once again, the rhythms of the playback music. Chamcha got out of the lift. Zeeny was sitting on the floor with her back against his door.

Inside the room, she poured herself a large whisky and soda. 'Behaving like a baby,' she said. 'You should be ashamed.'

That afternoon he had received a package from his father. Inside it was a small piece of wood and a large number of notes, not rupees but sterling pounds: the ashes, so to speak, of a walnut-tree. He was full of inchoate feeling and because Zeenat had turned up she became the target. 'You think I love you?' he said, speaking with deliberate viciousness. 'You think I'll stay with you? I'm a married man.'

'I didn't want you to stay for me,' she said. 'For some reason, I wanted it for you.'

A few days earlier, he had been to see an Indian dramatization of a story by Sartre on the subject of shame. In the original, a husband suspects his wife of infidelity and sets a trap to catch her out. He pretends to leave on a business trip, but returns a few hours later to spy on her. He is kneeling to look through the keyhole of their front door. Then he feels a presence behind him, turns without rising, and there she is, looking down at him with revulsion and disgust. This tableau, he kneeling, she looking down, is the Sartrean archetype. But in the Indian version the kneeling husband felt no presence behind him; was surprised by the wife; stood to face her on equal terms; blustered and shouted; until she wept, he embraced her, and they were reconciled.

'You say I should be ashamed,' Chamcha said bitterly to Zeenat. 'You, who are without shame. As a matter of fact, this may be a national characteristic. I begin to suspect that Indians lack the necessary moral refinement for a true sense of tragedy, and therefore cannot really understand the idea of shame.'

Zeenat Vakil finished her whisky. 'Okay, you don't have to say any more.' She held up her hands. 'I surrender. I'm going. Mr Saladin Chamcha. I thought you were still alive, only just, but still breathing, but I was wrong. Turns out you were dead all the time.'

And one more thing before going milk-eyed through the door. 'Don't let people get too close to you, Mr Saladin. Let people through your defences and the bastards go and knife you in the heart.'

After that there had been nothing to stay for. The aeroplane lifted and banked over the city. Somewhere below him, his father was dressing up a servant as his dead wife. The new traffic scheme had jammed the city centre solid. Politicians were trying to build careers by going on padyatras, pilgrimages on foot across the country. There were graffiti that read: *Advice to politicos. Only step to take: padyatra to hell.* Or, sometimes: *to Assam.*

Actors were getting mixed up in politics: MGR, N. T. Rama Rao, Bachchan. Durga Khote complained that an actors' association was a 'red front'. Saladin Chamcha, on Flight 420, closed his eyes; and felt, with deep relief, the tell-tale shiftings and settlings in his throat which indicated that his voice had begun of its own accord to revert to its reliable, English self.

The first disturbing thing that happened to Mr Chamcha on that flight was that he recognized, among his fellow-passengers, the woman of his dreams.

4

The dream-woman had been shorter and less graceful than the real one, but the instant Chamcha saw her walking calmly up and down the aisles of *Bostan* he remembered the nightmare. After Zeenat Vakil's departure he had fallen into a troubled sleep, and the premonition had come to him: the vision of a woman bomber with an almost inaudibly soft, Canadian-accented voice whose depth and melody made it sound like an ocean heard from a long way away. The dream-woman had been so loaded down with explosives that she was not so much the bomber as the bomb; the woman walking the aisles held a baby that seemed to be sleeping noiselessly, a baby so skilfully swaddled and held so close to the breast that Chamcha could not see so much as a lock of new-born hair. Under the influence of the remembered dream he conceived the notion that the baby was in fact a bundle of dynamite sticks, or some sort of ticking device, and he was on the verge of crying out when he came to his senses and admonished himself severely. This was precisely the type of superstitious flummery he was leaving behind. He was a neat man in a buttoned suit heading for London and an ordered, contented life. He was a member of the real world.

He travelled alone, shunning the company of the other

members of the Prospero Players troupe, who had scattered around the economy class cabin wearing Fancy-a-Donald T-shirts and trying to wiggle their necks in the manner of natyam dancers and looking absurd in Benarsi saris and drinking too much cheap airline champagne and importuning the scorn-laden stewardesses who, being Indian, understood that actors were cheap-type persons; and behaving, in short, with normal thespian impropriety. The woman holding the baby had a way of looking through the paleface players, of turning them into wisps of smoke, heat-mirages, ghosts. For a man like Saladin Chamcha the debasing of Englishness by the English was a thing too painful to contemplate. He turned to his newspaper in which a Bombay 'rail roko' demonstration was being broken up by police lathi-charges. The newspaper's reporter suffered a broken arm; his camera, too, was smashed. The police had issued a 'note'. *Neither the reporter nor any other person was assaulted intentionally.* Chamcha drifted into airline sleep. The city of lost histories, felled trees and unintentional assaults faded from his thoughts. When he opened his eyes a little later he had his second surprise of that macabre journey. A man was passing him on the way to the toilet. He was bearded and wore cheap tinted spectacles, but Chamcha recognized him anyway: here, travelling incognito in the economy class of Flight AI-420, was the vanished superstar, the living legend, Gibreel Farishta himself.

'Sleep okay?' He realized the question was addressed to him, and turned away from the apparition of the great movie actor to stare at the equally extraordinary sight sitting next to him, an improbable American in baseball cap, metal-rim spectacles and a neon-green bush-shirt across which there writhed the intertwined and luminous golden forms of a pair of Chinese dragons. Chamcha had edited this entity out of his field of vision in an attempt to wrap himself in a cocoon of privacy, but privacy was no longer possible.

'Eugene Dumsday at your service,' the dragon man stuck out a huge red hand. 'At yours, and at that of the Christian guard.'

Sleep-fuddled Chamcha shook his head. 'You are a military man?'

'Ha! Ha! Yes, sir, you could say. A humble foot soldier, sir, in the army of Guard Almighty.' Oh, *almighty* guard, why didn't you say. 'I am a man of science, sir, and it has been my mission, my mission and let me add my privilege, to visit your great nation to do battle with the most pernicious devilment ever got folks' brains by the balls.'

'I don't follow.'

Dumsday lowered his voice. 'I'm talking monkey-crap here, sir. Darwinism. The evolutionary heresy of Mr Charles Darwin.' His tones made it plain that the name of anguished, God-ridden Darwin was as distasteful as that of any other forktail fiend, Beelzebub, Asmodeus or Lucifer himself. 'I have been warning your fellow-men,' Dumsday confided, 'against Mr Darwin and his works. With the assistance of my personal fifty-seven-slide presentation. I spoke most recently, sir, at the World Understanding Day banquet of the Rotary Club, Cochin, Kerala. I spoke of my own country, of its young people. I see them lost, sir. The young people of America: I see them in their despair, turning to narcotics, even, for I'm a plain-speaking man, to pre-marital sexual relations. And I said this then and I say it now to you. If I believed my great-granddaddy was a chimpanzee, why, I'd be pretty depressed myself.'

Gibreel Farishta was seated across the way, staring out of the window. The inflight movie was starting up, and the aircraft lights were being dimmed. The woman with the baby was still on her feet, walking up and down, perhaps to keep the baby quiet. 'How did it go down?' Chamcha asked, sensing that some contribution from him was being required.

A hesitancy came over his neighbour. 'I believe there was a glitch in the sound system,' he said finally. 'That would be my best guess. I can't see how those good people would've set to talking amongst themselves if they hadn't've thought I was through.'

Chamcha felt a little abashed. He had been thinking that in a

country of fervent believers the notion that science was the enemy
of God would have an easy appeal; but the boredom of the
Rotarians of Cochin had shown him up. In the flickering light of
the inflight movie, Dumsday continued, in his voice of an innocent ox, to tell stories against himself without the faintest indication of knowing what he was doing. He had been accosted, at the
end of a cruise around the magnificent natural harbour of Cochin,
to which Vasco da Gama had come in search of spices and so set
in motion the whole ambiguous history of east-and-west, by an
urchin full of pssts and hey-mister-okays. 'Hi there, yes! You
want hashish, sahib? Hey, misteramerica. Yes, unclesam, you want
opium, best quality, top price? Okay, you want *cocaine*?'

Saladin began, helplessly, to giggle. The incident struck him as
Darwin's revenge: if Dumsday held poor, Victorian, starchy
Charles responsible for American drug culture, how delicious that
he should himself be seen, across the globe, as representing the
very ethic he battled so fervently against. Dumsday fixed him with
a look of pained reproof. It was a hard fate to be an American
abroad, and not to suspect why you were so disliked.

After the involuntary giggle had escaped Saladin's lips,
Dumsday sank into a sullen, injured drowse, leaving Chamcha to
his own thoughts. Should the inflight movie be thought of as a
particularly vile, random mutation of the form, one that would
eventually be extinguished by natural selection, or were they the
future of the cinema? A future of screwball caper movies eternally
starring Shelley Long and Chevy Chase was too hideous to con-
template; it was a vision of Hell . . . Chamcha was drifting back
into sleep when the cabin lights came on; the movie stopped; and
the illusion of the cinema was replaced by one of watching the
television news, as four armed, shouting figures came running
down the aisles.

The passengers were held on the hijacked aircraft for one hundred
and eleven days, marooned on a shimmering runway around

which there crashed the great sand-waves of the desert, because
once the four hijackers, three men one woman, had forced the
pilot to land nobody could make up their minds what to do with
them. They had come down not at an international airport but at
the absurd folly of a jumbo-sized landing strip which had been
built for the pleasure of the local sheikh at his favourite desert
oasis, to which there now also led a six-lane highway very popular
among single young men and women, who would cruise along its
vast emptiness in slow cars ogling one another through the windows . . . once 420 had landed here, however, the highway was
full of armoured cars, troop transports, limousines waving flags.
And while diplomats haggled over the airliner's fate, to storm or
not to storm, while they tried to decide whether to concede or to
stand firm at the expense of other people's lives, a great stillness
settled around the airliner and it wasn't long before the mirages
began.

   In the beginning there had been a constant flow of events, the
hijacking quartet full of electricity, jumpy, trigger-happy. These
are the worst moments, Chamcha thought while children
screamed and fear spread like a stain, here's where we could all go
west. Then they were in control, three men one woman, all tall,
none of them masked, all handsome, they were actors, too, they
were stars now, shootingstars or falling, and they had their own
stage-names. Dara Singh Buta Singh Man Singh. The woman was
Tavleen. The woman in the dream had been anonymous, as if
Chamcha's sleeping fancy had no time for pseudonyms; but, like
her, Tavleen spoke with a Canadian accent, smooth-edged, with
those give-away rounded O's. After the plane landed at the oasis
of Al-Zamzam it became plain to the passengers, who were
observing their captors with the obsessive attention paid to a cobra
by a transfixed mongoose, that there was something posturing in
the beauty of the three men, some amateurish love of risk and
death in them that made them appear frequently at the open doors
of the airplane and flaunt their bodies at the professional snipers
who must have been hiding amid the palm-trees of the oasis. The

woman held herself aloof from such silliness and seemed to be restraining herself from scolding her three colleagues. She seemed insensible to her own beauty, which made her the most dangerous of the four. It struck Saladin Chamcha that the young men were too squeamish, too narcissistic, to want blood on their hands. They would find it difficult to kill; they were here to be on television. But Tavleen was here on business. He kept his eyes on her. The men do not *know*, he thought. They want to behave the way they have seen hijackers behaving in the movies and on TV; they are reality aping a crude image of itself, they are worms swallowing their tails. But she, the woman, *knows* . . . while Dara, Buta, Man Singh strutted and pranced, she became quiet, her eyes turned inwards, and she scared the passengers stiff.

What did they want? Nothing new. An independent homeland, religious freedom, release of political detainees, justice, ransom money, a safe-conduct to a country of their choice. Many of the passengers came to sympathize with them, even though they were under constant threat of execution. If you live in the twentieth century you do not find it hard to see yourself in those, more desperate than yourself, who seek to shape it to their will.

After they landed the hijackers released all but fifty of the passengers, having decided that fifty was the largest number they could comfortably supervise. Women, children, Sikhs were all released. It turned out that Saladin Chamcha was the only member of the Prospero Players who was not given his freedom; he found himself succumbing to the perverse logic of the situation, and instead of feeling upset at having been retained he was glad to have seen the back of his badly behaved colleagues; good riddance to bad rubbish, he thought.

The creationist scientist Eugene Dumsday was unable to bear the realization that the hijackers did not intend to release him. He rose to his feet, swaying at his great height like a skyscraper in a hurricane, and began shouting hysterical incoherences. A stream of dribble ran out of the corner of his mouth; he licked at it feverishly with his tongue. *Now just hold hard here, busters, now goddamn it enough is ENOUGH, whaddya wheredya get the idea you can* and so forth, in the grip of his waking nightmare he drivelled on and on until one of the four, obviously it was the woman, came up, swung her rifle butt and broke his flapping jaw. And worse: because slobbering Dumsday had been licking his lips as his jaw slammed shut, the tip of his tongue sheared off and landed in Saladin Chamcha's lap; followed in quick time by its former owner. Eugene Dumsday fell tongueless and insensate into the actor's arms.

Eugene Dumsday gained his freedom by losing his tongue; the persuader succeeded in persuading his captors by surrendering his instrument of persuasion. They didn't want to look after a wounded man, risk of gangrene and so on, and so he joined the exodus from the plane. In those first wild hours Saladin Chamcha's mind kept throwing up questions of detail, are those automatic rifles or sub-machine guns, how did they smuggle all that metal on board, in which parts of the body is it possible to be shot and still survive, how scared they must be, the four of them, how full of their own deaths . . . once Dumsday had gone, he had expected to sit alone, but a man came and sat in the creationist's old seat, saying you don't mind, yaar, in such circs a guy needs company. It was the movie star, Gibreel.

After the first nervous days on the ground, during which the three turbaned young hijackers went perilously close to the edges of insanity, screaming into the desert night *you bastards, come and get us,* or, alternatively, *o god o god they're going to send in the fucking commandos, the motherfucking Americans, yaar, the sister-fucking British,* – moments during which the remaining hostages closed their eyes and prayed, because they were always most afraid when the hijackers showed signs of weakness, – everything settled down into what began to feel like normality. Twice a day a solitary vehicle carried food and drink to *Bostan* and left it on the tarmac. The hostages had to bring in the cartons while the hijackers watched them from the safety of the plane. Apart from this daily visit there was no contact with the outside world. The radio had gone dead. It was as if the incident had been forgotten, as if it were so embarrassing that it had simply been erased from the record. 'The bastards are leaving us to rot,' screamed Man Singh, and the hostages joined in with a will. 'Hijras! Chootias! Shits!'

They were wrapped in heat and silence and now the spectres began to shimmer out of the corners of their eyes. The most highly strung of the hostages, a young man with a goatee beard and close-cropped curly hair, awoke at dawn, shrieking with fear because he had seen a skeleton riding a camel across the dunes. Other hostages saw coloured globes hanging in the sky, or heard the beating of gigantic wings. The three male hijackers fell into a deep, fatalistic gloom. One day Tavleen summoned them to a conference at the far end of the plane; the hostages heard angry voices. 'She's telling them they have to issue an ultimatum,' Gibreel Farishta said to Chamcha. 'One of us has to die, or such.' But when the men returned Tavleen wasn't with them and the dejection in their eyes was tinged, now, with shame. 'They lost their guts,' Gibreel whispered. 'No can do. Now what is left for our Tavleen bibi? Zero. Story funtoosh.'

What she did:

In order to prove to her captives, and also to her fellow-captors, that the idea of failure, or surrender, would never weaken her resolve, she emerged from her momentary retreat in the first-class cocktail lounge to stand before them like a stewardess demonstrating safety procedures. But instead of putting on a lifejacket and holding up blow-tube whistle etcetera, she quickly lifted the loose black djellabah that was her only garment and stood before them stark naked, so that they could all see the arsenal of her body, the grenades like extra breasts nestling in her cleavage, the gelignite taped around her thighs, just the way it had been in Chamcha's dream. Then she slipped her robe back on and spoke in her faint oceanic voice. 'When a great idea comes into the world, a great cause, certain crucial questions are asked of it,' she murmured. 'History asks us: what manner of cause are we? Are we uncompromising, absolute, strong, or will we show ourselves to be timeservers, who compromise, trim and yield?' Her body had provided her answer.

The days continued to pass. The enclosed, boiling circumstances of his captivity, at once intimate and distant, made Saladin Chamcha want to argue with the woman, unbendingness can also be monomania, he wanted to say, it can be tyranny, and also it can be brittle, whereas what is flexible can also be humane, and strong enough to last. But he didn't say anything, of course, he fell into the torpor of the days. Gibreel Farishta discovered in the seat pocket in front of him a pamphlet written by the departed Dumsday. By this time Chamcha had noticed the determination with which the movie star resisted the onset of sleep, so it wasn't surprising to see him reciting and memorizing the lines of the creationist's leaflet, while his already heavy eyelids drooped lower and lower until he forced them to open wide again. The leaflet argued that even the scientists were busily re-inventing God, that once they had proved the existence of a single unified force of which electromagnetism, gravity and the strong and weak forces of the new physics were all merely aspects, avatars, one might say, or angels, then what would we have but the oldest thing of all, a supreme entity controlling all creation . . . 'You see, what our friend says is, if you have to choose between some type of disembodied force-field and the actual living God, which one would you go for? Good point, na? You can't pray to an electric current. No point asking a wave-form for the key to Paradise.' He closed his eyes, then snapped them open again. 'All bloody bunk,' he said fiercely. 'Makes me sick.'

After the first days Chamcha no longer noticed Gibreel's bad breath, because nobody in that world of sweat and apprehension was smelling any better. But his face was impossible to ignore, as the great purple welts of his wakefulness spread outwards like oil-slicks from his eyes. Then at last his resistance ended and he collapsed on to Saladin's shoulder and slept for four days without waking once.

When he returned to his senses he found that Chamcha, with

the help of the mouse-like, goateed hostage, a certain Jalandri, had moved him to an empty row of seats in the centre block. He went to the toilet to urinate for eleven minutes and returned with a look of real terror in his eyes. He sat down by Chamcha again, but wouldn't say a word. Two nights later, Chamcha heard him fighting, once again, against the onset of sleep. Or, as it turned out: of dreams.

'Tenth highest peak in the world,' Chamcha heard him mutter, 'is Xixabangma Feng, eight oh one three metres. Annapurna ninth, eighty seventy-eight.' Or he would begin at the other end: 'One, Chomolungma, eight eight four eight. Two, K2, eighty-six eleven. Kanchenjunga, eighty-five ninety-eight, Makalu, Dhaulagiri, Manaslu. Nanga Parbat, metres eight thousand one hundred and twenty-six.'

'You count eight thousand metre peaks to fall asleep?' Chamcha asked him. Bigger than sheep, but not so numerous.

Gibreel Farishta glared at him; then bowed his head; came to a decision. 'Not to sleep, my friend. To stay awake.'

That was when Saladin Chamcha found out why Gibreel Farishta had begun to fear sleep. Everybody needs somebody to talk to and Gibreel had spoken to nobody about what had happened after he ate the unclean pigs. The dreams had begun that very night. In these visions he was always present, not as himself but as his name-sake, and I don't mean interpreting a role, Spoono, I am him, he is me, I am the bloody archangel, Gibreel himself, large as bloody life.

Spoono. Like Zeenat Vakil, Gibreel had reacted with mirth to Saladin's abbreviated name. 'Bhai, wow. I'm tickled, truly. Tickled pink. So if you are an English *chamcha* these days, let it be. Mr Sally Spoon. It will be our little joke.' Gibreel Farishta had a way of failing to notice when he made people angry. *Spoon, Spoono, my old Chumch:* Saladin hated them all. But could do nothing. Except hate.

Maybe it was because of the nicknames, maybe not, but Saladin found Gibreel's revelations pathetic, anticlimactic, what was so strange if his dreams characterized him as the angel, dreams do every damn thing, did it really display more than a banal kind of egomania? But Gibreel was sweating from fear: 'Point is, Spoono,' he pleaded, 'every time I go to sleep the dream starts up from where it stopped. Same dream in the same place. As if somebody just paused the video while I went out of the room. Or, or. As if he's the guy who's awake and this is the bloody nightmare. His bloody dream: us. Here. All of it.' Chamcha stared at him. 'Crazy, right,' he said. 'Who knows if angels even sleep, never mind dream. I sound crazy. Am I right or what?'

'Yes. You sound crazy.'

'Then what the hell,' he wailed, 'is going on in my head?'

The longer he spent without going to sleep the more talkative he became, he began to regale the hostages, the hijackers, as well as the dilapidated crew of Flight 420, those formerly scornful stewardesses and shining flight-deck personnel who were now looking mournfully moth-eaten in a corner of the plane and even losing their earlier enthusiasm for endless games of rummy, – with his increasingly eccentric reincarnation theories, comparing their sojourn on that airstrip by the oasis of Al-Zamzam to a second period of gestation, telling everybody that they were all dead to the world and in the process of being regenerated, made anew. This idea seemed to cheer him up somewhat, even though it made many of the hostages want to string him up, and he leapt up on to a seat to explain that the day of their release would be the day of their rebirth, a piece of optimism that calmed his audience down. 'Strange but true!' he cried. 'That will be day zero, and because we will all share the birthday we will all be exactly the same age from that day on, for the rest of our lives. How do you call it when fifty kids come out of the same mother? God knows. Fiftuplets. Damn!'

Reincarnation, for frenzied Gibreel, was a term beneath whose shield many notions gathered a-babeling: phoenix-from-ashes, the resurrection of Christ, the transmigration, at the instant of death, of the soul of the Dalai Lama into the body of a new-born child . . . such matters got mixed up with the avatars of Vishnu, the metamorphoses of Jupiter, who had imitated Vishnu by adopting the form of a bull; and so on, including of course the progress of human beings through successive cycles of life, now as cockroaches, now as kings, towards the bliss of no-more-returns. *To be born again, first you have to die.* Chamcha did not bother to protest that in most of the examples Gibreel provided in his soliloquies, metamorphosis had not required a death; the new flesh had been entered into through other gates. Gibreel in full flight, his arms waving like imperious wings, brooked no interruptions. 'The old must die, you get my message, or the new cannot be whatnot.'

Sometimes these tirades would end in tears. Farishta in his exhaustion-beyond-exhaustion would lose control and place his sobbing head on Chamcha's shoulder, while Saladin – prolonged captivity erodes certain reluctances among the captives – would stroke his face and kiss the top of his head, *There, there, there.* On other occasions Chamcha's irritation would get the better of him. The seventh time that Farishta quoted the old Gramsci chestnut, Saladin shouted out in frustration, maybe that's what's happening to you, loudmouth, your old self is dying and that dream-angel of yours is trying to be born into your flesh.

'You want to hear something really crazy?' Gibreel after a hundred and one days offered Chamcha more confidences. 'You want to know why I'm here?' And told him anyway: 'For a woman. Yes, boss. For the bloody love of my bloody life. With whom I have spent a sum total of days three point five. Doesn't that prove I really am cracked? QED, Spoono, old Chumch.'

And: 'How to explain it to you? Three and a half days of it, how long do you need to know that the best thing has happened, the deepest thing, the has-to-be-it? I swear: when I kissed her there were mother-fucking sparks, yaar, believe don't believe, she said it was static electricity in the carpet but I've kissed chicks in hotel rooms before and this was a definite first, a definite one-and-only. Bloody electric shocks, man, I had to jump back with pain.'

He had no words to express her, his woman of mountain ice, to express how it had been in that moment when his life had been in pieces at his feet and she had become its meaning. 'You don't see,' he gave up. 'Maybe you never met a person for whom you'd cross the world, for whom you'd leave everything, walk out and take a plane. She climbed Everest, man. Twenty-nine thousand and two feet, or maybe twenty-nine one four one. Straight to the top. You think I can't get on a jumbo-jet for a woman like that?'

The harder Gibreel Farishta tried to explain his obsession with the mountain-climber Alleluia Cone, the more Saladin tried to conjure up the memory of Pamela, but she wouldn't come. At first it would be Zeeny who visited him, her shade, and then after a time there was nobody at all. Gibreel's passion began to drive Chamcha wild with anger and frustration, but Farishta didn't notice it, slapped him on the back, *cheer up, Spoono, won't be long now.*

On the hundred and tenth day Tavleen walked up to the little goateed hostage, Jalandri, and motioned with her finger. Our patience has been exhausted, she announced, we have sent repeated ultimatums with no response, it is time for the first sacrifice. She used that word: sacrifice. She looked straight into Jalandri's eyes and pronounced his death sentence. 'You first. Apostate traitor bastard.' She ordered the crew to prepare for take-off, she wasn't going to risk a storming of the plane after the execution, and with the point of her gun she pushed Jalandri towards the open door at the front, while he screamed and begged for mercy. 'She's got sharp eyes,' Gibreel said to Chamcha. 'He's a cut-sird.' Jalandri had become the first target because of his decision to give up the turban and cut his hair, which made him a traitor to his faith, a shorn Sirdarji. *Cut-Sird.* A seven-letter condemnation; no appeal.

Jalandri had fallen to his knees, stains were spreading on the seat of his trousers, she was dragging him to the door by his hair. Nobody moved. Dara Buta Man Singh turned away from the tableau. He was kneeling with his back to the open door; she made him turn round, shot him in the back of the head, and he toppled out on to the tarmac. Tavleen shut the door.

Man Singh, youngest and jumpiest of the quartet, screamed at her: 'Now where do we go? In any damn place they'll send the commandos in for sure. We're gone geese now.'

'Martyrdom is a privilege,' she said softly. 'We shall be like stars; like the sun.'

Sand gave way to snow. Europe in winter, beneath its white, transforming carpet, its ghost-white shining up through the night. The Alps, France, the coastline of England, white cliffs rising to whitened meadowlands. Mr Saladin Chamcha jammed on an anticipatory bowler hat. The world had rediscovered Flight AI-420, the Boeing 747 *Bostan*. Radar tracked it; radio messages crackled. *Do you want permission to land?* But no permission was requested. *Bostan* circled over England's shore like a gigantic seabird. Gull. Albatross. Fuel indicators dipped: towards zero.

When the fight broke out, it took all the passengers by surprise, because this time the three male hijackers didn't argue with Tavleen, there were no fierce whispers about the *fuel* about *what the fuck you're doing* but just a mute stand-off, they wouldn't even talk to one another, as if they had given up hope, and then it was Man Singh who cracked and went for her. The hostages watched the fight to the death, unable to feel involved, because a curious detachment from reality had come over the aircraft, a kind of inconsequential casualness, a fatalism, one might say. They fell to the floor and her knife went up through his stomach. That was all, the brevity of it adding to its seeming unimportance. Then in the instant when she rose up it was as if everybody awoke, it became clear to them all that she really meant business, she was going through with it, all the way, she was holding in her hand the wire that connected all the pins of all the grenades beneath her gown, all those fatal breasts, and although at that moment Buta and Dara rushed at her she pulled the wire anyway, and the walls came tumbling down.

No, not death: birth.

PART II

MAHOUND

Gibreel when he submits to the inevitable, when he slides heavy-lidded towards visions of his angeling, passes his loving mother who has a different name for him, Shaitan, she calls him, just like Shaitan, same to same, because he has been fooling around with the tiffins to be carried into the city for the office workers' lunch, mischeevious imp, she slices the air with her hand, rascal has been putting Muslim meat compartments into Hindu non-veg tiffin-carriers, customers are up in arms. Little devil, she scolds, but then folds him in her arms, my little farishta, boys will be boys, and he falls past her into sleep, growing bigger as he falls and the falling begins to feel like flight, his mother's voice wafts distantly up to him, baba, look how you grew, enor-mouse, wah-wah, applause. He is gigantic, wingless, standing with his feet upon the horizon and his arms around the sun. In the early dreams he sees beginnings, Shaitan cast down from the sky, making a grab for a branch of the highest Thing, the lote-tree of the uttermost end that stands beneath the Throne, Shaitan missing, plummeting, splat. But he lived on, was not couldn't be dead, sang from hellbelow his soft seductive verses. O the sweet songs that he knew. With his daughters as his fiendish backing group, yes, the three of them, Lat Manat Uzza, motherless girls laughing with their Abba, giggling behind their hands at Gibreel, what a trick we got in store for you, they giggle, for you and for that businessman on the hill. But before the businessman there are other stories, here he is, Archangel Gibreel, revealing the spring of Zamzam to Hagar the Egyptian so that, abandoned by the prophet Ibrahim with their child in the desert, she might drink the cool spring waters and so live. And later, after the Jurhum filled up Zamzam with mud and golden gazelles, so that it was lost for a time, here he is again, pointing it out to that one, Muttalib of the scarlet tents, father of the child with the silver hair who fathered, in turn, the businessman. The businessman: here he comes.

Sometimes when he sleeps Gibreel becomes aware, without the dream, of himself sleeping, of himself dreaming his own awareness of his dream, and then a panic begins, O God, he cries out, O all-good allahgod, I've had my bloody chips, me. Got bugs in the brain, full mad, a looney tune and a gone baboon. Just as he, the businessman, felt when he first saw the archangel: thought he was cracked, wanted to throw himself down from a rock, from a high rock, from a rock on which there grew a stunted lote-tree, a rock as high as the roof of the world.

He's coming: making his way up Cone Mountain to the cave. Happy birthday: he's forty-four today. But though the city behind and below him throngs with festival, up he climbs, alone. No new birthday suit for him, neatly pressed and folded at the foot of his bed. A man of ascetic tastes. (What strange manner of businessman is this?)

Question: What is the opposite of faith?

Not disbelief. Too final, certain, closed. Itself a kind of belief. Doubt.

The human condition, but what of the angelic? Halfway between Allahgod and homosap, did they ever doubt? They did: challenging God's will one day they hid muttering beneath the Throne, daring to ask forbidden things: antiquestions. Is it right that. Could it not be argued. Freedom, the old antiquest. He calmed them down, naturally, employing management skills à la god. Flattered them: you will be the instruments of my will on earth, of the salvationdamnation of man, all the usual etcetera.

And hey presto, end of protest, on with the haloes, back to work. Angels are easily pacified; turn them into instruments and they'll play your harpy tune. Human beings are tougher nuts, can doubt anything, even the evidence of their own eyes. Of behind-their-own eyes. Of what, as they sink heavy-lidded, transpires behind closed peepers . . . angels, they don't have much in the way of a will. To will is to disagree; not to submit; to dissent.

I know; devil talk. Shaitan interrupting Gibreel.

Me?

The businessman: looks as he should, high forehead, eaglenose, broad in the shoulders, narrow in the hip. Average height, brooding, dressed in two pieces of plain cloth, each four ells in length, one draped around his body, the other over his shoulder. Large eyes; long lashes like a girl's. His strides can seem too long for his legs, but he's a light-footed man. Orphans learn to be moving targets, develop a rapid walk, quick reactions, hold-your-tongue caution. Up through the thorn-bushes and opobalsam trees he comes, scrabbling on boulders, this is a fit man, no soft-bellied usurer he. And yes, to state it again: takes an odd sort of business wallah to cut off into the wilds, up Mount Cone, some-times for a month at a stretch, just to be alone.

His name: a dream-name, changed by the vision. Pronounced correctly, it means he-for-whom-thanks-should-be-given, but he won't answer to that here; nor, though he's well aware of what they call him, to his nickname in Jahilia down below – *he-who-goes-up-and-down-old-Coney*. Here he is neither Mahomet nor MoeHammered; has adopted, instead, the demon-tag the farangis hung around his neck. To turn insults into strengths, whigs, tories, Blacks all chose to wear with pride the names they were given in scorn; likewise, our mountain-climbing, prophet-motivated soli-tary is to be the medieval baby-frightener, the Devil's synonym: Mahound.

That's him. Mahound the businessman, climbing his hot mountain in the Hijaz. The mirage of a city shines below him in the sun.

❧

The city of Jahilia is built entirely of sand, its structures formed of the desert whence it rises. It is a sight to wonder at: walled, four-gated, the whole of it a miracle worked by its citizens, who have learned the trick of transforming the fine white dune-sand of those forsaken parts, – the very stuff of inconstancy, – the quintessence of unsettlement, shifting, treachery, lack-of-form, – and have turned it, by alchemy, into the fabric of their newly invented permanence. These people are a mere three or four generations removed from their nomadic past, when they were as rootless as the dunes, or rather rooted in the knowledge that the journeying itself was home.

– Whereas the migrant can do without the journey altogether; it's no more than a necessary evil; the point is to arrive. –

Quite recently, then, and like the shrewd businessmen they were, the Jahilians settled down at the intersection-point of the routes of the great caravans, and yoked the dunes to their will. Now the sand serves the mighty urban merchants. Beaten into cobbles, it paves Jahilia's tortuous streets; by night, golden flames blaze out from braziers of burnished sand. There is glass in the windows, in the long, slitlike windows set in the infinitely high sand-walls of the merchant palaces; in the alleys of Jahilia, donkey-carts roll forward on smooth silicon wheels. I, in my wickedness, sometimes imagine the coming of a great wave, a high wall of foaming water roaring across the desert, a liquid catastrophe full of snapping boats and drowning arms, a tidal wave that would reduce these vain sandcastles to the nothingness, to the grains from which they came. But there are no waves here. Water is the enemy in Jahilia. Carried in earthen pots, it must never be spilled (the penal code deals fiercely with offenders), for where it drops the city erodes alarmingly. Holes appear in roads, houses tilt and sway. The water-carriers of Jahilia are loathed necessities, pariahs who cannot be ignored and therefore can never be forgiven. It never rains in Jahilia; there are no fountains in the silicon gardens. A few palms stand in enclosed courtyards, their roots travelling far and wide below the earth in search of moisture. The city's water comes from underground streams and springs, one such being the fabled Zamzam, at the heart of the concentric sand-city, next to the House of the Black Stone. Here, at Zamzam, is a beheshti, a despised water-carrier, drawing up the vital, dangerous fluid. He has a name: Khalid.

A city of businessmen, Jahilia. The name of the tribe is *Shark*.

In this city, the businessman-turned-prophet, Mahound, is founding one of the world's great religions; and has arrived, on this day, his birthday, at the crisis of his life. There is a voice whispering in his ear: *What kind of idea are you? Man-or-mouse?*

We know that voice. We've heard it once before.

While Mahound climbs Coney, Jahilia celebrates a different anniversary. In ancient time the patriarch Ibrahim came into this valley with Hagar and Ismail, their son. Here, in this waterless wilderness, he abandoned her. She asked him, can this be God's will? He replied, it is. And left, the bastard. From the beginning men used God to justify the unjustifiable. He moves in mysterious ways: men say. Small wonder, then, that women have turned to me. – But I'll keep to the point; Hagar wasn't a witch. She was trusting: *then surely He will not let me perish.* After Ibrahim left her, she fed the baby at her breast until her milk ran out. Then she climbed two hills, first Safa then Marwah, running from one to the other in her desperation, trying to sight a tent, a camel, a human being. She saw nothing. That was when he came to her, Gibreel, and showed her the waters of Zamzam. So Hagar survived; but why now do the pilgrims congregate? To celebrate her survival? No, no. They are celebrating the honour done the valley by the visit of, you've guessed it, Ibrahim. In that loving consort's name, they gather, worship and, above all, spend.

Jahilia today is all perfume. The scents of Araby, of *Arabia Odorifera*, hang in the air: balsam, cassia, cinnamon, frankincense, myrrh. The pilgrims drink the wine of the date-palm and wander in the great fair of the feast of Ibrahim. And, among them, one wanders whose furrowed brow sets him apart from the cheerful crowd: a tall man in loose white robes, he'd stand almost a full head higher than Mahound. His beard is shaped close to his slanting, high-boned face; his gait contains the lilt, the deadly elegance of power. What's he called? – The vision yields his name eventually; it, too, is changed by the dream. Here he is, Karim Abu Simbel, Grandee of Jahilia, husband to the ferocious, beautiful Hind. Head of the ruling council of the city, rich beyond numbering, owner of the lucrative temples at the city gates, wealthy in camels, comptroller of caravans, his wife the greatest beauty in the land: what could shake the certainties of such a man? And yet, for Abu Simbel, too, a crisis is approaching. A name gnaws at him, and you can guess what it is, Mahound Mahound Mahound.

O the splendour of the fairgounds of Jahilia! Here in vast scented tents are arrays of spices, of senna leaves, of fragrant woods; here the perfume vendors can be found, competing for the pilgrims' noses, and for their wallets, too. Abu Simbel pushes his way through the crowds. Merchants, Jewish, Monophysite, Nabataean, buy and sell pieces of silver and gold, weighing them, biting coins with knowing teeth. There is linen from Egypt and silk from China; from Basra, arms and grain. There is gambling, and drinking, and dance. There are slaves for sale, Nubian, Anatolian, Aethiop. The four factions of the tribe of Shark control separate zones of the fair, the scents and spices in the Scarlet Tents, while in the Black Tents the cloth and leather. The Silver-Haired grouping is in charge of precious metals and swords. Entertainment – dice, belly-dancers, palm-wine, the smoking of hashish and afeem – is the prerogative of the fourth quarter of the tribe, the Owners of the Dappled Camels, who also run the slave trade. Abu Simbel looks into a dance tent. Pilgrims sit clutching moneybags in their left hands; every so often a coin is moved from bag to right-hand palm. The dancers shake and sweat, and their eyes never leave the pilgrims' fingertips; when the coin transfer ceases, the dance also ends. The great man makes a face and lets the tentflap fall.

Jahilia has been built in a series of rough circles, its houses spreading outwards from the House of the Black Stone, approximately in order of wealth and rank. Abu Simbel's palace is in the first circle, the innermost ring; he makes his way down one of the rambling, windy radial roads, past the city's many seers who, in return for pilgrim money, are chirping, cooing, hissing, possessed variously by djinnis of birds, beasts, snakes. A sorceress, failing for a moment to look up, squats in his path: 'Want to capture a girlie's heart, my dear? Want an enemy under your thumb? Try me out; try my little knots!' And raises, dangles a knotty rope, ensnarer of human lives – but, seeing now to whom she speaks, lets fall her disappointed arm and slinks away, mumbling, into sand.

Everywhere, noise and elbows. Poets stand on boxes and declaim while pilgrims throw coins at their feet. Some bards speak rajaz verses, their four-syllable metre suggested, according to legend, by the walking pace of the camel; others speak the qasidah, poems of wayward mistresses, desert adventure, the hunting of the onager. In a day or so it will be time for the annual poetry competition, after which the seven best verses will be nailed up on the walls of the House of the Black Stone. The poets are getting into shape for their big day; Abu Simbel laughs at minstrels singing vicious satires, vitriolic odes commissioned by one chief against another, by one tribe against its neighbour. And nods in recognition as one of the poets falls into step beside him, a sharp narrow youth with frenzied fingers. This young lampoonist already has the most feared tongue in all Jahilia, but to Abu Simbel he is almost deferential. 'Why so preoccupied, Grandee? If you were not losing your hair I'd tell you to let it down.' Abu Simbel grins his sloping grin. 'Such a reputation,' he muses. 'Such fame, even before your milk-teeth have fallen out. Look out or we'll have to draw those teeth for you.' He is teasing, speaking lightly, but even this lightness is laced with menace, because of the extent of his power. The boy is unabashed. Matching Abu Simbel stride for stride, he replies: 'For every one you pull out, a stronger one will grow, biting deeper, drawing hotter spurts of blood.' The Grandee, vaguely, nods. 'You like the taste of blood,' he says. The boy shrugs. 'A poet's work,' he answers. 'To name the unnam-able, to point at frauds, to take sides, start arguments, shape the world and stop it from going to sleep.' And if rivers of blood flow from the cuts his verses inflict, then they will nourish him. He is the satirist, Baal.

A curtained litter passes by; some fine lady of the city, out to see the fair, borne on the shoulders of eight Anatolian slaves. Abu Simbel takes the young Baal by the elbow, under the pretext of steering him out of the road; murmurs, 'I hoped to find you; if you will, a word.' Baal marvels at the skill of the Grandee. Searching for a man, he can make his quarry think he has hunted the hunter. Abu Simbel's grip tightens; by the elbow, he steers his companion towards the holy of holies at the centre of the town.

'I have a commission for you,' the Grandee says. 'A literary matter. I know my limitations; the skills of rhymed malice, the arts of metrical slander, are quite beyond my powers. You understand.'

But Baal, the proud, arrogant fellow, stiffens, stands on his dig-nity. 'It isn't right for the artist to become the servant of the state.' Simbel's voice falls lower, acquires silkier rhythms. 'Ah, yes. Whereas to place yourself at the disposal of assassins is an entirely honourable thing.' A cult of the dead has been raging in Jahilia. When a man dies, paid mourners beat themselves, scratch their breasts, tear hair. A hamstrung camel is left on the grave to die. And if the man has been murdered his closest relative takes ascetic vows and pursues the murderer until the blood has been avenged by blood; whereupon it is customary to compose a poem of cele-bration, but few revengers are gifted in rhyme. Many poets make a living by writing assassination songs, and there is general agree-ment that the finest of these blood-praising versifiers is the preco-cious polemicist, Baal. Whose professional pride prevents him from being bruised, now, by the Grandee's little taunt. 'That is a cultural matter,' he replies. Abu Simbel sinks deeper still into silki-ness. 'Maybe so,' he whispers at the gates of the House of the Black Stone, 'but, Baal, concede: don't I have some small claim upon you? We both serve, or so I thought, the same mistress.'

Now the blood leaves Baal's cheeks; his confidence cracks, falls from him like a shell. The Grandee, seemingly oblivious to the alteration, sweeps the satirist forward into the House.

They say in Jahilia that this valley is the navel of the earth; that the planet, when it was being made, went spinning round this point. Adam came here and saw a miracle: four emerald pillars bearing aloft a giant glowing ruby, and beneath this canopy a huge white stone, also glowing with its own light, like a vision of his soul. He built strong walls around the vision to bind it forever to the earth. This was the first House. It was rebuilt many times – once by Ibrahim, after Hagar's and Ismail's angel-assisted survival – and gradually the countless touchings of the white stone by the pilgrims of the centuries darkened its colour to black. Then the time of the idols began; by the time of Mahound, three hundred and sixty stone gods clustered around God's own stone.

What would old Adam have thought? His own sons are here now: the colossus of Hubal, sent by the Amalekites from Hit, stands above the treasury well, Hubal the shepherd, the waxing crescent moon; also, glowering, dangerous Kain. He is the waning crescent, blacksmith and musician; he, too, has his devotees.

Hubal and Kain look down on Grandee and poet as they stroll. And the Nabataean proto-Dionysus, He-Of-Shara; the morning star, Astarte, and saturnine Nakruh. Here is the sun god, Manaf! Look, there flaps the giant Nasr, the god in eagle-form! See Quzah, who holds the rainbow . . . is this not a glut of gods, a stone flood, to feed the glutton hunger of the pilgrims, to quench their unholy thirst. The deities, to entice the travellers, come – like the pilgrims – from far and wide. The idols, too, are delegates to a kind of international fair.

There is a god here called Allah (means simply, the god). Ask the Jahilians and they'll acknowledge that this fellow has some sort of overall authority, but he isn't very popular: an all-rounder in an age of specialist statues.

Abu Simbel and newly perspiring Baal have arrived at the shrines, placed side by side, of the three best-beloved goddesses in Jahilia. They bow before all three: Uzza of the radiant visage, goddess of beauty and love; dark, obscure Manat, her face averted, her purposes mysterious, sifting sand between her fingers – she's in charge of destiny – she's Fate; and lastly the highest of the three, the mother-goddess, whom the Greeks called Lato. Ilat, they call her here, or, more frequently, Al-Lat. *The goddess*. Even her name makes her Allah's opposite and equal. Lat the omnipotent. His face showing sudden relief, Baal flings himself to the ground and prostrates himself before her. Abu Simbel stays on his feet.

The family of the Grandee, Abu Simbel – or, to be more precise, of his wife Hind – controls the famous temple of Lat at the city's southern gate. (They also draw the revenues from the Manat temple at the east gate, and the temple of Uzza in the north.) These concessions are the foundations of the Grandee's wealth, so he is of course, Baal understands, the servant of Lat. And the satirist's devotion to this goddess is well known throughout Jahilia. So that was all he meant! Trembling with relief, Baal remains prostrate, giving thanks to his patron Lady. Who looks upon him benignly; but a goddesses's expression is not to be relied upon. Baal has made a serious mistake.

Without warning, the Grandee kicks the poet in the kidney. Attacked just when he has decided he's safe, Baal squeals, rolls over, and Abu Simbel follows him, continuing to kick. There is the sound of a cracking rib. 'Runt,' the Grandee remarks, his voice remaining low and good natured. 'High-voiced pimp with small testicles. Did you think that the master of Lat's temple would claim comradeship with you just because of your adolescent passion for her?' And more kicks, regular, methodical. Baal weeps at Abu Simbel's feet. The House of the Black Stone is far from empty, but who would come between the Grandee and his wrath? Abruptly, Baal's tormentor squats down, grabs the poet by the hair, jerks his head up, whispers into his ear: 'Baal, she wasn't the mistress I meant,' and then Baal lets out a howl of hideous self-pity, because he knows his life is about to end, to end when he has so much still to achieve, the poor guy. The Grandee's lips brush his ear. 'Shit of a frightened camel,' Abu Simbel breathes, 'I know you fuck my wife.' He observes, with interest, that Baal has acquired a prominent erection, an ironic monument to his fear.

Abu Simbel, the cuckolded Grandee, stands up, commands, 'On your feet', and Baal, bewildered, follows him outside.

The graves of Ismail and his mother Hagar the Egyptian lie by the north-west face of the House of the Black Stone, in an enclosure surrounded by a low wall. Abu Simbel approaches this area, halts a little way off. In the enclosure is a small group of men. The water-carrier Khalid is there, and some sort of bum from Persia by the outlandish name of Salman, and to complete this trinity of scum there is the slave Bilal, the one Mahound freed, an enormous black monster, this one, with a voice to match his size. The three idlers sit on the enclosure wall. 'That bunch of riff-raff,' Abu Simbel says. 'Those are your targets. Write about them; and their leader, too.' Baal, for all his terror, cannot conceal his disbelief. 'Grandee, those *goons* – those fucking *clowns*? You don't have to worry about them. What do you think? That Mahound's one God will bankrupt your temples? Three-sixty versus one, and the one wins? Can't happen.' He giggles, close to hysteria. Abu Simbel remains calm: 'Keep your insults for your verses.' Giggling Baal can't stop. 'A revolution of water-carriers, immigrants and slaves . . . wow, Grandee. I'm really scared.' Abu Simbel looks carefully at the tittering poet. 'Yes,' he answers, 'that's right, you should be afraid. Get writing, please, and I expect these verses to be your masterpieces.' Baal crumples, whines. 'But they are a waste of my, my small talent . . .' He sees that he has said too much.

'Do as you're told,' are Abu Simbel's last words to him. 'You have no choice.'

The Grandee lolls in his bedroom while concubines attend to his needs. Coconut-oil for his thinning hair, wine for his palate, tongues for his delight. *The boy was right. Why do I fear Mahound?* He begins, idly, to count the concubines, gives up at fifteen with a flap of his hand. *The boy. Hind will go on seeing him, obviously; what chance does he have against her will?* It is a weakness in him, he knows, that he sees too much, tolerates too much. He has his appetites, why should she not have hers? As long as she is discreet; and as long as he knows. He must know; knowledge is his narcotic, his addiction. He cannot tolerate what he does not know and for that reason, if for no other, Mahound is his enemy, Mahound with his raggle-taggle gang, the boy was right to laugh. He, the Grandee, laughs less easily. Like his opponent he is a cautious man, he walks on the balls of his feet. He remembers the big one, the slave, Bilal: how his master asked him, outside the Lat temple, to enumerate the gods. 'One,' he answered in that huge musical voice. Blasphemy, punishable by death. They stretched him out in the fairground with a boulder on his chest. *How many did you say?* One, he repeated, one. A second boulder was added to the first. *One one one.* Mahound paid his owner a large price and set him free.

No, Abu Simbel reflects, the boy Baal was wrong, these men are worth our time. Why do I fear Mahound? For that: one one one, his terrifying singularity. Whereas I am always divided, always two or three or fifteen. I can even see his point of view; he is as wealthy and successful as any of us, as any of the councillors, but because he lacks the right sort of family connections, we haven't offered him a place amongst our group. Excluded by his orphaning from the mercantile elite, he feels he has been cheated, he has not had his due. He always was an ambitious fellow. Ambitious, but also solitary. You don't rise to the top by climbing up a hill all by yourself. Unless, maybe, you meet an angel there . . . yes, that's it. I see what he's up to. He wouldn't understand me, though. *What kind of idea am I?* I bend. I sway. I calculate the odds, trim my sails, manipulate, survive. That is why I won't accuse Hind of adultery. We are a good pair, ice and fire. Her family shield, the fabled red lion, the many-toothed manticore. Let her play with her satirist; between us it was never sex. I'll finish him when she's finished with. Here's a great lie, thinks the

Grandee of Jahilia drifting into sleep: the pen is mightier than the sword.

The fortunes of the city of Jahilia were built on the supremacy of sand over water. In the old days it had been thought safer to transport goods across the desert than over the seas, where monsoons could strike at any time. In those days before meteorology such matters were impossible to predict. For this reason the caravanserais prospered. The produce of the world came up from Zafar to Sheba, and thence to Jahilia and the oasis of Yathrib and on to Midian where Moses lived; thence to Aqabah and Egypt. From Jahilia other trails began: to the east and north-east, towards Mesopotamia and the great Persian empire. To Petra and to Palmyra, where once Solomon loved the Queen of Sheba. Those were fatted days. But now the fleets plying the waters around the peninsula have grown hardier, their crews more skilful, their navigational instruments more accurate. The camel trains are losing business to the boats. Desert-ship and sea-ship, the old rivalry, sees a tilt in the balance of power. Jahilia's rulers fret, but there is little they can do. Sometimes Abu Simbel suspects that only the pilgrimage stands between the city and its ruin. The council searches the world for statues of alien gods, to attract new pilgrims to the city of sand; but in this, too, they have competitors. Down in Sheba a great temple has been built, a shrine to rival the House of the Black Stone. Many pilgrims have been tempted south, and the numbers at the Jahilia fairgrounds are falling.

At the recommendation of Abu Simbel, the rulers of Jahilia have added to their religious practices the tempting spices of profanity. The city has become famous for its licentiousness, as a gambling den, a whorehouse, a place of bawdy songs and wild, loud music. On one occasion some members of the tribe of Shark went too far in their greed for pilgrim money. The gatekeepers at the House began demanding bribes from weary voyagers; four of them, piqued at receiving no more than a pittance, pushed two travellers to their deaths down the great, steep flight of stairs. This practice backfired, discouraging return visits ... Today, female pilgrims are often kidnapped for ransom, or sold into concubinage. Gangs of young Sharks patrol the city, keeping their own kind of law. It is said that Abu Simbel meets secretly with the gang-leaders and organizes them all. This is the world into which Mahound has brought his message: one one one. Amid such multiplicity, it sounds like a dangerous word.

The Grandee sits up and at once concubines approach to resume their oilings and smoothings. He waves them away, claps his hands. The eunuch enters. 'Send a messenger to the house of the kahin Mahound,' Abu Simbel commands. *We will set him a little test. A fair contest: three against one.*

Water-carrier immigrant slave: Mahound's three disciples are washing at the well of Zamzam. In the sand-city, their obsession with water makes them freakish. Ablutions, always ablutions, the legs up to the knees, the arms down to the elbows, the head down to the neck. Dry-torsoed, wet-limbed and damp-headed, what eccentrics they look! Splish, splosh, washing and praying. On their knees, pushing arms, legs, heads back into the ubiquitous sand, and then beginning again the cycle of water and prayer. These are easy targets for Baal's pen. Their water-loving is a treason of a sort; the people of Jahilia accept the omnipotence of sand. It lodges between their fingers and toes, cakes their lashes and hair, clogs their pores. They open themselves to the desert: come, sand, wash us in aridity. That is the Jahilian way from the highest citizen to the lowest of the low. They are people of silicon, and water-lovers have come among them.

Baal circles them from a safe distance – Bilal is not a man to trifle with – and yells gibes. 'If Mahound's ideas were worth anything, do you think they'd only be popular with trash like you?' Salman restrains Bilal: 'We should be honoured that the mighty Baal has chosen to attack us,' he smiles, and Bilal relaxes, subsides.

Khalid the water-carrier is jumpy, and when he sees the heavy figure of Mahound's uncle Hamza approaching he runs towards him anxiously. Hamza at sixty is still the city's most renowned fighter and lion-hunter. Though the truth is less glorious than the eulogies: Hamza has many times been defeated in combat, saved by friends or lucky chances, rescued from lions' jaws. He has the money to keep such items out of the news. And age, and survival, bestow a sort of validation upon a martial legend. Bilal and Salman, forgetting Baal, follow Khalid. All three are nervous, young.

He's still not home, Hamza reports. And Khalid, worried: But it's been hours, what is that bastard doing to him, torture, thumb-screws, whips? Salman, once again, is the calmest: That isn't Simbel's style, he says, it's something sneaky, depend upon it. And Bilal bellows loyally: Sneaky or not, I have faith in him, in the Prophet. He won't break. Hamza offers only a gentle rebuke: Oh, Bilal, how many times must he tell you? Keep your faith for God. The Messenger is only a man. The tension bursts out of Khalid: he squares up to old Hamza, demands, Are you saying that the Mes-senger is weak? You may be his uncle ... Hamza clouts the water-carrier on the side of the head. Don't let him see your fear, he says, not even when you're scared half to death.

The four of them are washing once more when Mahound arrives; they cluster around him, whowhatwhy. Hamza stands back. 'Nephew, this is no damn good,' he snaps in his soldier's bark. 'When you come down from Coney there's a brightness on you. Today it's something dark.'

Mahound sits on the edge of the well and grins. 'I've been offered a deal.' *By Abu Simbel?* Khalid shouts. *Unthinkable. Refuse.* Faithful Bilal admonishes him: Do not lecture the Messenger. Of course, he has refused. Salman the Persian asks: What sort of deal. Mahound smiles again. 'At least one of you wants to know.'

'It's a small matter,' he begins again. 'A grain of sand. Abu Simbel asks Allah to grant him one little favour.' Hamza sees the exhaustion in him. As if he had been wrestling with a demon.

The water-carrier is shouting: 'Nothing! Not a jot!' Hamza shuts him up.

'If our great God could find it in his heart to concede – he used that word, *concede* – that three, only three of the three hundred and sixty idols in the house are worthy of worship . . .'

'There is no god but God!' Bilal shouts. And his fellows join in: 'Ya Allah!' Mahound looks angry. 'Will the faithful hear the Messenger?' They fall silent, scuffing their feet in the dust.

'He asks for Allah's approval of Lat, Uzza and Manat. In return, he gives his guarantee that we will be tolerated, even officially recognized; as a mark of which, I am to be elected to the council of Jahilia. That's the offer.'

Salman the Persian says: 'It's a trap. If you go up Coney and come down with such a Message, he'll ask, how could you make Gibreel provide just the right revelation? He'll be able to call you a charlatan, a fake.' Mahound shakes his head. 'You know, Salman, that I have learned how to *listen*. This *listening* is not of the ordinary kind; it's also a kind of asking. Often, when Gibreel comes, it's as if he knows what's in my heart. It feels to me, most times, as if he comes from within my heart: from within my deepest places, from my soul.'

'Or it's a different trap,' Salman persists. 'How long have we been reciting the creed you brought us? There is no god but God. What are we if we abandon it now? This weakens us, renders us absurd. We cease to be dangerous. Nobody will ever take us seriously again.'

Mahound laughs, genuinely amused. 'Maybe you haven't been here long enough,' he says kindly. 'Haven't you noticed? The people do not take us seriously. Never more than fifty in the audience when I speak, and half of those are tourists. Don't you read the lampoons that Baal pins up all over town?' He recites:

> *Messenger, do please lend a*
> *careful ear. Your monophilia,*
> *your one one one, ain't for Jahilia.*
> *Return to sender.*

'They mock us everywhere, and you call us dangerous,' he cried.

Now Hamza looks worried. 'You never worried about their opinions before. Why now? Why after speaking to Simbel?'

Mahound shakes his head. 'Sometimes I think I must make it easier for the people to believe.'

An uneasy silence covers the disciples; they exchange looks, shift their weight. Mahound cries out again. 'You all know what has been happening. Our failure to win converts. The people will not give up their gods. They will not, not.' He stands up, strides away from them, washes by himself on the far side of the Zamzam well, kneels to pray.

'The people are sunk in darkness,' says Bilal, unhappily. 'But they will see. They will hear. God is one.' Misery infects the four of them; even Hamza is brought low. Mahound has been shaken, and his followers quake.

He stands, bows, sighs, comes round to rejoin them. 'Listen to me, all of you,' he says, putting one arm around Bilal's shoulders, the other around his uncle's. 'Listen: it is an interesting offer.'

Unembraced Khalid interrupts bitterly: 'It is a *tempting* deal.' The others look horrified. Hamza speaks very gently to the water-carrier. 'Wasn't it you, Khalid, who wanted to fight me just now because you wrongly assumed that, when I called the Messenger a man, I was really calling him a weakling? Now what? Is it my turn to challenge you to a fight?'

Mahound begs for peace. 'If we quarrel, there's no hope.' He tries to raise the discussion to the theological level. 'It is not suggested that Allah accept the three as his equals. Not even Lat. Only that they be given some sort of intermediary, lesser status.'

'Like devils,' Bilal bursts out.

'No,' Salman the Persian gets the point. 'Like archangels. The Grandee's a clever man.'

'Angels and devils,' Mahound says. 'Shaitan and Gibreel. We all, already, accept their existence, halfway between God and man. Abu Simbel asks that we admit just three more to this great company. Just three, and, he indicates, all Jahilia's souls will be ours.'

'And the House will be cleansed of statues?' Salman asks.

Mahound replies that this was not specified. Salman shakes his head. 'This is being done to destroy you.' And Bilal adds: 'God cannot be four.' And Khalid, close to tears: 'Messenger, what are you saying? Lat, Manat, Uzza – they're all *females*! For pity's sake! Are we to have goddesses now? Those old cranes, herons, hags?'

Misery strain fatigue, etched deeply into the Prophet's face. Which Hamza, like a soldier on a battlefield comforting a wounded friend, cups between his hands. 'We can't sort this out for you, nephew,' he says. 'Climb the mountain. Go ask Gibreel.'

Gibreel: the dreamer, whose point of view is sometimes that of the camera and at other moments, spectator. When he's a camera the pee oh vee is always on the move, he hates static shots, so he's floating up on a high crane looking down at the foreshortened figures of the actors, or he's swooping down to stand invisibly between them, turning slowly on his heel to achieve a three-hundred-and-sixty-degree pan, or maybe he'll try a dolly shot, tracking along beside Baal and Abu Simbel as they walk, or hand-held with the help of a steadicam he'll probe the secrets of the Grandee's bedchamber. But mostly he sits up on Mount Cone like a paying customer in the dress circle, and Jahilia is his silver screen. He watches and weighs up the action like any movie fan, enjoys the fights infidelities moral crises, but there aren't enough girls for a real hit, man, and where are the goddamn songs? They should have built up that fairground scene, maybe a cameo role for Pimple Billimoria in a show-tent, wiggling her famous bazooms.

And then, without warning, Hamza says to Mahound: 'Go ask Gibreel,' and he, the dreamer, feels his heart leaping in alarm, who, me? *I'm* supposed to know the answers here? I'm sitting here watching this picture and now this actor points his finger out at me, who ever heard the like, who asks the bloody audience of a 'theological' to solve the bloody plot? – But as the dream shifts, it's always changing form, he, Gibreel, is no longer a mere spectator but the central player, the star. With his old weakness for taking too many roles: yes, yes, he's not just playing the archangel but also him, the businessman, the Messenger, Mahound, coming up the mountain when he comes. Nifty cutting is required to pull off this double role, the two of them can never be seen in the same shot, each must speak to empty air, to the imagined incarnation of the other, and trust to technology to create the missing vision, with scissors and Scotch tape or, more exotically, with the help of a travelling mat. Not to be confused ha ha with any magic carpet.

He has understood: that he is afraid of the other, the businessman, isn't it crazy? The archangel quaking before the mortal man. It's true, but: the kind of fear you feel when you're on a film set for the very first time and there, about to make his entrance, is one of the living legends of the cinema; you think, I'll disgrace myself, I'll dry, I'll corpse, you want like mad to be *worthy*. You will be sucked along in the slipstream of his genius, he can make you look good, like a high flier, but you will know if you aren't pulling your weight and even worse so will he . . . Gibreel's fear, the fear of the self his dream creates, makes him struggle against Mahound's arrival, to try and put it off, but he's coming now, no quesch, and the archangel holds his breath.

Those dreams of being pushed out on stage when you've no business being there, you don't know the story haven't learned any lines, but there's a full house watching, watching: feels like that. Or the true story of the white actress playing a black woman in Shakespeare. She went on stage and then realized she still had her glasses on, eek, but she had forgotten to blacken her hands so she couldn't reach up to take the specs off, double eek: like that also. *Mahound comes to me for revelation, asking me to choose between monotheist and henotheist alternatives, and I'm just some idiot actor having a bhaenchud nightmare, what the fuck do I know, yaar, what to tell you, help. Help.*

To reach Mount Cone from Jahilia one must walk into dark ravines where the sand is not white, not the pure sand filtered long ago through the bodies of sea-cucumbers, but black and dour, sucking light from the sun. Coney crouches over you like an imaginary beast. You ascend along its spine. Leaving behind the last trees, white-flowered with thick, milky leaves, you climb among the boulders, which get larger as you get higher, until they resemble huge walls and start blotting out the sun. The lizards are blue as shadows. Then you are on the peak, Jahilia behind you, the featureless desert ahead. You descend on the desert side, and about five hundred feet down you reach the cave, which is high enough to stand upright in, and whose floor is covered in miraculous albino sand. As you climb you hear the desert doves calling your name, and the rocks greet you, too, in your own language, crying *Mahound, Mahound.* When you reach the cave you are tired, you lie down, you fall asleep.

But when he has rested he enters a different sort of sleep, a sort of not-sleep, the condition that he calls his *listening*, and he feels a dragging pain in the gut, like something trying to be born, and now Gibreel, who has been hovering-above-looking-down, feels a confusion, *whom am I*, in these moments it begins to seem that the archangel is actually *inside the Prophet*, I am the dragging in the gut, I am the angel being extruded from the sleeper's navel, I emerge, Gibreel Farishta, while my other self, Mahound, lies *listening*, entranced, I am bound to him, navel to navel, by a shining cord of light, not possible to say which of us is dreaming the other. We flow in both directions along the umbilical cord.

Today, as well as the overwhelming intensity of Mahound, Gibreel feels his despair: his doubts. Also, that he is in great need, but Gibreel still doesn't know his lines . . . he listens to the listening-which-is-also-an-asking. Mahound *asks*: They were shown miracles but they didn't believe. They saw you come to me, in full view of the city, and open my breast, they saw you wash my heart in the waters of Zamzam and replace it inside my body. Many of them saw this, but still they worship stones. And when you came at night and flew me to Jerusalem and I hovered above the holy city, didn't I return and describe it exactly as it is, accurate down to the last detail? So that there could be no doubting the miracle, and still they went to Lat. Haven't I already done my best to make things simple for them? When you carried me up to the Throne itself, and Allah laid upon the faithful the great burden of forty prayers a day. On the return journey I met Moses and he said, the burden is too heavy, go back and plead for less. Four times I went back, four times Moses said, still too many, go back again. But by the fourth time Allah had reduced the duty to five prayers and I refused to return. I felt ashamed to beg any more. In his bounty he asks for five instead of forty, and still they love Manat, they want Uzza. What can I do? What shall I recite?

Gibreel remains silent, empty of answers, for Pete's sake, bhai, don't go asking me. Mahound's anguish is awful. He *asks*: is it possible that they *are* angels? Lat, Manat, Uzza . . . can I call them angelic? Gibreel, have you got sisters? Are these the daughters of God? And he castigates himself, O my vanity, I am an arrogant man, is this weakness, is it just a dream of power? Must I betray myself for a seat on the council? Is this sensible and wise or is it hollow and self-loving? I don't even know if the Grandee is sincere. Does he know? Perhaps not even he. I am weak and he's strong, the offer gives him many ways of ruining me. But I, too, have much to gain. The souls of the city, of the world, surely they are worth three angels? Is Allah so unbending that he will not embrace three more to save the human race? – I don't know anything. – Should God be proud or humble, majestic or simple, yielding or un-? *What kind of idea is he? What kind am I?*

Halfway into sleep, or halfway back to wakefulness, Gibreel Farishta is often filled with resentment by the non-appearance, in his persecuting visions, of the One who is supposed to have the answers, *He* never turns up, the one who kept away when I was dying, when I needed needed him. The one it's all about, Allah Ishvar God. Absent as ever while we writhe and suffer in his name.

The Supreme Being keeps away; what keeps returning is this scene, the entranced Prophet, the extrusion, the cord of light, and then Gibreel in his dual role is both above-looking-down and below-staring-up. And both of them scared out of their minds by the transcendence of it. Gibreel feels paralysed by the presence of the Prophet, by his greatness, thinks I can't make a sound I'd seem such a goddamn fool. Hamza's advice: never show your fear: archangels need such advice as well as water-carriers. An archangel must look composed, what would the Prophet think if God's Exalted began to gibber with stage fright?

It happens: revelation. Like this: Mahound, still in his notsleep, becomes rigid, veins bulge in his neck, he clutches at his centre. No, no, nothing like an epileptic fit, it can't be explained away that easily; what epileptic fit ever caused day to turn to night, caused clouds to mass overhead, caused the air to thicken into soup while an angel hung, scared silly, in the sky above the sufferer, held up like a kite on a golden thread? The dragging again the dragging and now the miracle starts in his my our guts, he is straining with all his might at something, forcing something, and Gibreel begins to feel that strength that force, here it is *at my own jaw* working it, opening shutting; and the power, starting within Mahound, reaching up to *my vocal cords* and the voice comes.

Not my voice I'd never know such words I'm no classy speaker never was never will be but this isn't my voice it's a Voice.

Mahound's eyes open wide, he's seeing some kind of vision, staring at it, oh, that's right, Gibreel remembers, me. He's seeing me. My lips moving, being moved by. What, whom? Don't know, can't say. Nevertheless, here they are, coming out of my mouth, up my throat, past my teeth: the Words.

Being God's postman is no fun, yaar.

Butbutbut: God isn't in this picture.

God knows whose postman I've been.

In Jahilia they are waiting for Mahound by the well. Khalid the water-carrier, as ever the most impatient, runs off to the city gate to keep a look-out. Hamza, like all old soldiers accustomed to keeping his own company, squats down in the dust and plays a game with pebbles. There is no sense of urgency; sometimes he is away for days, even weeks. And today the city is all but deserted; everybody has gone to the great tents at the fairground to hear the poets compete. In the silence, there is only the noise of Hamza's pebbles, and the gurgles of a pair of rock-doves, visitors from Mount Cone. Then they hear the running feet.

Khalid arrives, out of breath, looking unhappy. The Messenger has returned, but he isn't coming to Zamzam. Now they are all on their feet, perplexed by this departure from established practice. Those who have been waiting with palm-fronds and steles ask Hamza: Then there will be no Message? But Khalid, still catching his breath, shakes his head. 'I think there will be. He looks the way he does when the Word has been given. But he didn't speak to me and walked towards the fairground instead.'

Hamza takes command, forestalling discussion, and leads the way. The disciples – about twenty have gathered – follow him to the fleshpots of the city, wearing expressions of pious disgust. Hamza alone seems to be looking forward to the fair.

Outside the tents of the Owners of the Dappled Camels they find Mahound, standing with his eyes closed, steeling himself to the task. They ask anxious questions; he doesn't answer. After a few moments, he enters the poetry tent.

Inside the tent, the audience reacts to the arrival of the unpopular Prophet and his wretched followers with derision. But as Mahound walks forward, his eyes firmly closed, the boos and catcalls die away and a silence falls. Mahound does not open his eyes for an instant, but his steps are sure, and he reaches the stage without stumblings or collisions. He climbs the few steps up into the light; still his eyes stay shut. The assembled lyric poets, composers of assassination eulogies, narrative versifiers and satirists – Baal is here, of course – gaze with amusement, but also with a little unease, at the sleepwalking Mahound. In the crowd his disciples jostle for room. The scribes fight to be near him, to take down whatever he might say.

The Grandee Abu Simbel rests against bolsters on a silken carpet positioned beside the stage. With him, resplendent in golden Egyptian neckwear, is his wife Hind, that famous Grecian profile with the black hair that is as long as her body. Abu Simbel rises and calls to Mahound, 'Welcome.' He is all urbanity. 'Welcome, Mahound, the seer, the kahin.' It's a public declaration of respect, and it impresses the assembled crowd. The Prophet's disciples are no longer shoved aside, but allowed to pass. Bewildered, half-pleased, they come to the front. Mahound speaks without opening his eyes.

'This is a gathering of many poets,' he says clearly, 'and I cannot claim to be one of them. But I am the Messenger, and I bring verses from a greater One than any here assembled.'

The audience is losing patience. Religion is for the temple; Jahilians and pilgrims alike are here for entertainment. Silence the fellow! Throw him out! – But Abu Simbel speaks again. 'If your God has really spoken to you,' he says, 'then all the world must hear it.' And in an instant the silence in the great tent is complete.

'The Star,' Mahound cries out, and the scribes begin to write.

'In the name of Allah, the Compassionate, the Merciful!

'By the Pleiades when they set: Your companion is not in error; neither is he deviating.

'Nor does he speak from his own desires. It is a revelation that has been revealed: one mighty in power has taught him.

'He stood on the high horizon: the lord of strength. Then he came close, closer than the length of two bows, and revealed to his servant that which is revealed.

'The servant's heart was true when seeing what he saw. Do you, then, dare to question what was seen?

"I saw him also at the lote-tree of the uttermost end, near which lies the Garden of Repose. When that tree was covered by its covering, my eye was not averted, neither did my gaze wander; and I saw some of the greatest signs of the Lord.'

At this point, without any trace of hesitation or doubt, he recites two further verses.

'Have you thought upon Lat and Uzza, and Manat, the third, the other?' – After the first verse, Hind gets to her feet; the Grandee of Jahilia is already standing very straight. And Mahound, with silenced eyes, recites: 'They are the exalted birds, and their intercession is desired indeed.'

As the noise – shouts, cheers, scandal, cries of devotion to the goddess Al-Lat – swells and bursts within the marquee, the already astonished congregation beholds the doubly sensational spectacle of the Grandee Abu Simbel placing his thumbs upon the lobes of his ears, fanning out the fingers of both hands and uttering in a loud voice the formula: 'Allahu Akbar.' After which he falls to his knees and presses a deliberate forehead to the ground. His wife, Hind, immediately follows his lead.

The water-carrier Khalid has remained by the open tent-flap throughout these events. Now he stares in horror as everyone gathered there, both the crowd in the tent and the overflow of men and women outside it, begins to kneel, row by row, the movement rippling outwards from Hind and the Grandee as though they were pebbles thrown into a lake; until the entire gathering, outside the tent as well as in, kneels bottom-in-air before the shuteye Prophet who has recognized the patron deities of the town. The Messenger himself remains standing, as if loth to join the assembly in its devotions. Bursting into tears, the water-carrier flees into the empty heart of the city of the sands. His teardrops, as he runs, burn holes in the earth, as if they contain some harsh corrosive acid.

Mahound remains motionless. No trace of moisture can be detected on the lashes of his unopened eyes.

On that night of the desolating triumph of the businessman in the tent of the unbelievers, there take place certain murders for which the first lady of Jahilia will wait years to take her terrible revenge.

The Prophet's uncle Hamza has been walking home alone, his

head bowed and grey in the twilight of that melancholy victory, when he hears a roar and looks up, to see a gigantic scarlet lion poised to leap at him from the high battlements of the city. He knows this beast, this fable. *The iridescence of its scarlet hide blends into the shimmering brightness of the desert sands. Through its nostrils it exhales the horror of the lonely places of the earth. It spits out pestilence, and when armies venture into the desert, it consumes them utterly.* Through the blue last light of evening he shouts at the beast, preparing, unarmed as he is, to meet his death. 'Jump, you bastard, manticore. I've strangled big cats with my bare hands, in my time.' When I was younger. When I was young.

There is laughter behind him, and distant laughter echoing, or so it seems, from the battlements. He looks around him; the manticore has vanished from the ramparts. He is surrounded by a group of Jahilians in fancy dress, returning from the fair and giggling. 'Now that these mystics have embraced our Lat, they are seeing new gods round every corner, no?' Hamza, understanding that the night will be full of terrors, returns home and calls for his battle sword. 'More than anything in the world,' he growls at the papery valet who has served him in war and peace for forty-four years, 'I hate admitting that my enemies have a point. Damn sight better to kill the bastards, I've always thought. Neatest bloody solution.' The sword has remained sheathed in its leather scabbard since the day of his conversion by his nephew, but tonight, he confides to the valet, 'The lion is loose. Peace will have to wait.'

It is the last night of the festival of Ibrahim. Jahilia is masquerade and madness. The oiled fatty bodies of the wrestlers have completed their writhings and the seven poems have been nailed to the walls of the House of the Black Stone. Now singing whores replace the poets, and dancing whores, also with oiled bodies, are at work as well; night-wrestling replaces the daytime variety. The courtesans dance and sing in golden, bird-beaked masks, and the gold is reflected in their clients' shining eyes. Gold, gold everywhere, in the palms of the profiteering Jahilians and their libidinous guests, in the flaming sand-braziers, in the glowing walls of the night city. Hamza walks dolorously through the streets of gold, past pilgrims who lie unconscious while cutpurses earn their living. He hears the wine-blurred carousing through every golden-gleaming doorway, and feels the song and howling laughter and coin-chinkings hurting him like mortal insults. But he doesn't find what he's looking for, not here, so he moves away from the illuminated revelry of gold and begins to stalk the shadows, hunting the apparition of the lion.

And finds, after hours of searching, what he knew would be waiting, in a dark corner of the city's outer walls, the thing of his vision, the red manticore with the triple row of teeth. The manticore has blue eyes and a mannish face and its voice is half-trumpet and half-flute. It is fast as the wind, its nails are corkscrew talons and its tail hurls poisoned quills. It loves to feed on human flesh . . . a brawl is taking place. Knives hissing in the silence, at times the clash of metal against metal. Hamza recognizes the men under attack: Khalid, Salman, Bilal. A lion himself now, Hamza draws his sword, roars the silence into shreds, runs forward as fast as sixty-year-old legs will go. His friends' assailants are unrecognizable behind their masks.

It has been a night of masks. Walking the debauched Jahilian streets, his heart full of bile, Hamza has seen men and women in the guise of eagles, jackals, horses, gryphons, salamanders, warthogs, rocs; welling up from the murk of the alleys have come two-headed amphisbaenae and the winged bulls known as Assyrian sphinxes. Djinns, houris, demons populate the city on this night of phantasmagoria and lust. But only now, in this dark place, does he see the red masks he's been looking for. The manlion masks: he rushes towards his fate.

In the grip of a self-destructive unhappiness the three disciples had started drinking, and owing to their unfamiliarity with alcohol they were soon not just intoxicated but stupid-drunk. They stood in a small piazza and started abusing the passers-by, and after a while the water-carrier Khalid brandished his waterskin, boasting.

He could destroy the city, he carried the ultimate weapon. Water: it would cleanse Jahilia the filthy, wash it away, so that a new start could be made from the purified white sand. That was when the lion-men started chasing them, and after a long pursuit they were cornered, the booziness draining out of them on account of their fear, they were staring into the red masks of death when Hamza arrived just in time.

. . . Gibreel floats above the city watching the fight. It's quickly over once Hamza gets to the scene. Two masked assailants run away, two lie dead. Bilal, Khalid and Salman have been cut, but not too badly. Graver than their wounds is the news behind the lion-masks of the dead. 'Hind's brothers,' Hamza recognizes. 'Things are finishing for us now.'

Slayers of manticores, water-terrorists, the followers of Mahound sit and weep in the shadow of the city wall.

As for him, Prophet Messenger Businessman: his eyes are open now. He paces the inner courtyard of his house, his wife's house, and will not go in to her. She is almost seventy and feels these days more like a mother than a. She, the rich woman, who employed him to manage her caravans long ago. His management skills were the first things she liked about him. And after a time, they were in love. It isn't easy to be a brilliant, successful woman in a city where the gods are female but the females are merely goods. Men had either been afraid of her, or had thought her so strong that she didn't need their consideration. He hadn't been afraid, and had given her the feeling of constancy she needed. While he, the orphan, found in her many women in one: mother sister lover sibyl friend. When he thought himself crazy she was the one who believed in his visions. 'It is the archangel,' she told him, 'not some fog out of your head. It is Gibreel, and you are the Messenger of God.'

He can't won't see her now. She watches him through a stone-latticed window. He can't stop walking, moves around the court-yard in a random sequence of unconscious geometries, his footsteps tracing out a series of ellipses, trapeziums, rhomboids, ovals, rings. While she remembers how he would return from the caravan trails full of stories heard at wayside oases. A prophet, Isa, born to a woman named Maryam, born of no man under a palm-tree in the desert. Stories that made his eyes shine, then fade into a distantness. She recalls his excitability: the passion with which he'd argue, all night if necessary, that the old nomadic times had been better than this city of gold where people exposed their baby daughters in the wilderness. In the old tribes even the poorest orphan would be cared for. God is in the desert, he'd say, not here in this miscarriage of a place. And she'd reply, Nobody's arguing, my love, it's late, and tomorrow there are the accounts.

She has long ears; has already heard what he said about Lat, Uzza, Manat. So what? In the old days he wanted to protect the baby daughters of Jahilia; why shouldn't he take the daughters of Allah under his wing as well? But after asking herself this question she shakes her head and leans heavily on the cool wall beside her stone-screened window. While below her, her husband walks in pentagons, parallelograms, six-pointed stars, and then in abstract and increasingly labyrinthine patterns for which there are no names, as though unable to find a simple line.

When she looks into the courtyard some moments later, however, he has gone.

The Prophet wakes between silk sheets, with a bursting headache, in a room he has never seen. Outside the window the sun is near its savage zenith, and silhouetted against the whiteness is a tall figure in a black hooded cloak, singing softly in a strong, low voice. The song is one that the women of Jahilia chorus as they drum the men to war.

> *Advance and we embrace you,*
> *embrace you, embrace you,*
> *advance and we embrace you*
> *and soft carpets spread.*

Turn back and we desert you,
we leave you, desert you,
retreat and we'll not love you,
not in love's bed.

He recognizes Hind's voice, sits up, and finds himself naked beneath the creamy sheet. He calls to her: 'Was I attacked?' Hind turns to him, smiling her Hind smile. 'Attacked?' she mimics him, and claps her hands for breakfast. Minions enter, bring, serve, remove, scurry off. Mahound is helped into a silken robe of black and gold; Hind, exaggeratedly, averts her eyes. 'My head,' he asks again. 'Was I struck?' She stands at the window, her head hung low, playing the demure maid. 'Oh, Messenger, Messenger,' she mocks him. 'What an ungallant Messenger it is. Couldn't you have come to my room consciously, of your own will? No, of course not, I repel you, I'm sure.' He will not play her game. 'Am I a prisoner?' he asks, and again she laughs at him. 'Don't be a fool.' And then, shrugging, relents: 'I was walking the city streets last night, masked, to see the festivities, and what should I stumble over but your unconscious body? Like a drunk in the gutter, Mahound. I sent my servants for a litter and brought you home. Say thank you.'

'Thank you.'

'I don't think you were recognized,' she says. 'Or you'd be dead, maybe. You know how the city was last night. People overdo it. My own brothers haven't come home yet.'

It comes back to him now, his wild anguished walk in the corrupt city, staring at the souls he had supposedly saved, looking at the simurgh-effigies, the devil-masks, the behemoths and hippogriffs. The fatigue of that long day on which he climbed down from Mount Cone, walked to the town, underwent the strain of the events in the poetry marquee, – and afterwards, the anger of the disciples, the doubt, – the whole of it had overwhelmed him. 'I fainted,' he remembers.

She comes and sits close to him on the bed, extends a finger, finds the gap in his robe, strokes his chest. 'Fainted,' she murmurs. 'That's weakness, Mahound. Are you becoming weak?'

She places the stroking finger over his lips before he can reply. 'Don't say anything, Mahound. I am the Grandee's wife, and neither of us is your friend. My husband, however, is a weak man. In Jahilia they think he's cunning, but I know better. He knows I take lovers and he does nothing about it, because the temples are in my family's care. Lat's, Uzza's, Manat's. The − shall I call them *mosques?* − of your new angels.' She offers him melon cubes from a dish, tries to feed him with her fingers. He will not let her put the fruit into his mouth, takes the pieces with his own hand, eats. She goes on. 'My last lover was the boy, Baal.' She sees the rage on his face. 'Yes,' she says contentedly. 'I heard he had got under your skin. But he doesn't matter. Neither he nor Abu Simbel is your equal. But I am.'

'I must go,' he says. 'Soon enough,' she replies, returning to the window. At the perimeter of the city they are packing away the tents, the long camel-trains are preparing to depart, convoys of carts are already heading away across the desert; the carnival is over. She turns to him again.

'I am your equal,' she repeats, 'and also your opposite. I don't want you to become weak. You shouldn't have done what you did.'

'But you will profit,' Mahound replies bitterly. 'There's no threat now to your temple revenues.'

'You miss the point,' she says softly, coming closer to him, bringing her face very close to his. 'If you are for Allah, I am for Al-Lat. And she doesn't believe your God when he recognizes her. Her opposition to him is implacable, irrevocable, engulfing. The war between us cannot end in truce. And what a truce! Yours is a patronizing, condescending lord. Al-Lat hasn't the slightest wish to be his daughter. She is his equal, as I am yours. Ask Baal: he knows her. As he knows me.'

'So the Grandee will betray his pledge,' Mahound says.

'Who knows?' scoffs Hind. 'He doesn't even know himself. He

has to work out the odds. Weak, as I told you. But you know I'm telling the truth. Between Allah and the Three there can be no peace. I don't want it. I want the fight. To the death; that is the kind of idea I am. What kind are you?'

'You are sand and I am water,' Mahound says. 'Water washes sand away.'

'And the desert soaks up water,' Hind answers him. 'Look around you.'

Soon after his departure the wounded men arrive at the Grandee's palace, having screwed up their courage to inform Hind that old Hamza has killed her brothers. But by then the Messenger is nowhere to be found; is heading, once again, slowly towards Mount Cone.

Gibreel, when he's tired, wants to murder his mother for giving him such a damn fool nickname, *angel*, what a word, he begs *what? whom?* to be spared the dream-city of crumbling sandcastles and lions with three-tiered teeth, no more heart-washing of prophets or instructions to recite or promises of paradise, let there be an end to revelations, finito, khattam-shud. What he longs for: black, dreamless sleep. Mother-fucking dreams, cause of all the trouble in the human race, movies, too, if I was God I'd cut the imagination right out of people and then maybe poor bastards like me could get a good night's rest. Fighting against sleep, he forces his eyes to stay open, unblinking, until the visual purple fades off the retinas and sends him blind, but he's only human, in the end he falls down the rabbit-hole and there he is again, in Wonderland, up the mountain, and the businessman is waking up, and once again his wanting, his need, goes to work, not on my jaws and voice this time, but on my whole body; he diminishes me to his own size and pulls me in towards him, his gravitational field is unbelievable, as powerful as a goddamn megastar . . . and then Gibreel and the Prophet are wrestling, both naked, rolling over and over, in the cave of the fine white sand that rises around them like a veil. *As if he's learning me, searching me, as if I'm the one under-going the test.*

In a cave five hundred feet below the summit of Mount Cone, Mahound wrestles the archangel, hurling him from side to side, and let me tell you he's getting in *everywhere*, his tongue in my ear his fist around my balls, there was never a person with such a rage in him, he has to has to know he has to K N O W and I have nothing to tell him, he's twice as physically fit as I am and four times as knowledgeable, minimum, we may both have taught ourselves by listening a lot but as is plaintosee he's even a better listener than me; so we roll kick scratch, he's getting cut up quite a bit but of course my skin stays smooth as a baby, you can't snag an angel on a bloody thorn-bush, you can't bruise him on a rock. And they have an audience, there are djinns and afreets and all sorts of spooks sitting on the boulders to watch the fight, and in the sky are the three winged creatures, looking like herons or swans or just women depending on the tricks of the light . . . Mahound finishes it. He throws the fight.

After they had wrestled for hours or even weeks Mahound was pinned down beneath the angel, it's what he wanted, it was his will filling me up and giving me the strength to hold him down, because archangels can't lose such fights, it wouldn't be right, it's only devils who get beaten in such circs, so the moment I got on top he started weeping for joy and then he did his old trick, forcing my mouth open and making the voice, the Voice, pour out of me once again, made it pour all over him, like sick.

At the end of his wrestling match with the Archangel Gibreel, the Prophet Mahound falls into his customary, exhausted, post-revelatory sleep, but on this occasion he revives more quickly than usual. When he comes to his senses in that high wilderness there is nobody to be seen, no winged creatures crouch on rocks, and he jumps to his feet, filled with the urgency of his news. 'It was the Devil,' he says aloud to the empty air, making it true by giving it voice. 'The last time, it was Shaitan.' This is what he has *heard* in his *listening*, that he has been tricked, that the Devil came to him in the guise of the archangel, so that the verses he memorized, the ones he recited in the poetry tent, were not the real thing but its diabolic opposite, not godly, but satanic. He returns to the city as quickly as he can, to expunge the foul verses that reek of brimstone and sulphur, to strike them from the record for ever and ever, so that they will survive in just one or two unreliable collections of old traditions and orthodox interpreters will try and unwrite their story, but Gibreel, hovering-watching from his highest camera angle, knows one small detail, just one tiny thing that's a bit of a problem here, namely that *it was me both times, baba, me first and second also me.* From my mouth, both the statement and the repudiation, verses and converses, universes and reverses, the whole thing, and we all know how my mouth got worked.

'First it was the Devil,' Mahound mutters as he rushes to Jahilia. 'But this time, the angel, no question. He wrestled me to the ground.'

The disciples stop him in the ravines near the foot of Mount Cone to warn him of the fury of Hind, who is wearing white mourning garments and has loosened her black hair, letting it fly about her like a storm, or trail in the dust, erasing her footsteps so that she seems like an incarnation of the spirit of vengeance itself. They have all fled the city, and Hamza, too, is lying low; but the word is that Abu Simbel has not, as yet, acceded to his wife's pleas for the blood that washes away blood. He is still calculating the odds in the matter of Mahound and the goddesses . . . Mahound, against his followers' advice, returns to Jahilia, going straight to the House of the Black Stone. The disciples follow him in spite of their fear. A crowd gathers in the hope of further scandal or dismemberment or some such entertainment. Mahound does not disappoint them.

He stands in front of the statues of the Three and announces the abrogation of the verses which Shaitan whispered in his ear. These verses are banished from the true recitation, *al-qur'an*. New verses are thundered in their place.

'Shall He have daughters and you sons?' Mahound recites. 'That would be a fine division!

'These are but names you have dreamed of, you and your fathers. Allah vests no authority in them.'

He leaves the dumbfounded House before it occurs to anybody to pick up, or throw, the first stone.

After the repudiation of the Satanic verses, the Prophet Mahound returns home to find a kind of punishment awaiting him. A kind of vengeance – whose? Light or dark? Goodguy badguy? – wrought, as is not unusual, upon the innocent. The Prophet's wife, seventy years old, sits by the foot of a stone-latticed window, sits upright with her back to the wall, dead.

Mahound in the grip of his misery keeps himself to himself, hardly says a word for weeks. The Grandee of Jahilia institutes a policy of persecution that advances too slowly for Hind. The name of the new religion is *Submission*; now Abu Simbel decrees that its adherents must submit to being sequestered in the most wretched, hovel-filled quarter of the city; to a curfew; to a ban on employment. And there are many physical assaults, women spat upon in shops, the manhandling of the faithful by the gangs of young turks whom the Grandee secretly controls, fire thrown at night through a window to land amongst unwary sleepers. And, by one of the familiar paradoxes of history, the numbers of the faithful multiply, like a crop that miraculously flourishes as conditions of soil and climate grow worse and worse.

An offer is received, from the citizens of the oasis-settlement of Yathrib to the north: Yathrib will shelter those-who-submit, if they wish to leave Jahilia. Hamza is of the opinion that they must go. 'You'll never finish your Message here, nephew, take my word. Hind won't be happy till she's ripped out your tongue, to say nothing of my balls, excuse me.' Mahound, alone and full of echoes in the house of his bereavement, gives his consent, and the faithful depart to make their plans. Khalid the water-carrier hangs back and the hollow-eyed Prophet waits for him to speak. Awkwardly, he says: 'Messenger, I doubted you. But you were wiser than we knew. First we said, Mahound will never compromise, and you compromised. Then we said, Mahound has betrayed us, but you were bringing us a deeper truth. You brought us the Devil himself, so that we could witness the workings of the Evil One, and his overthrow by the Right. You have enriched our faith. I am sorry for what I thought.'

Mahound moves away from the sunlight falling through the window. 'Yes.' Bitterness, cynicism. 'It was a wonderful thing I did. Deeper truth. Bringing you the Devil. Yes, that sounds like me.'

From the peak of Mount Cone, Gibreel watches the faithful escaping Jahilia, leaving the city of aridity for the place of cool palms and water, water, water. In small groups, almost empty-handed, they move across the empire of the sun, on this first day of the first year at the new beginning of Time, which has itself been born again, as the old dies behind them and the new waits ahead. And one day Mahound himself slips away. When his escape is discovered, Baal composes a valedictory ode:

> *What kind of idea*
> *does 'Submission' seem today?*
> *One full of fear.*
> *An idea that runs away.*

Mahound has reached his oasis; Gibreel is not so lucky. Often, now, he finds himself alone on the summit of Mount Cone, washed by the cold, falling stars, and then they fall upon him from the night sky, the three winged creatures, Lat Uzza Manat, flapping around his head, clawing at his eyes, biting, whipping him with their hair, their wings. He puts up his hands to protect himself, but their revenge is tireless, continuing whenever he rests, whenever he drops his guard. He struggles against them, but they are faster, nimbler, winged.

He has no devil to repudiate. Dreaming, he cannot wish them away.

PART III

Ellowen Deeowen

1

I know what a ghost is, the old woman affirmed silently. Her name was Rosa Diamond; she was eighty-eight years old; and she was squinting beakily through her salt-caked bedroom windows, watching the full moon's sea. And I know what it isn't, too, she nodded further, it isn't a scarification or a flapping sheet, so pooh and pish to all *that* bunkum. What's a ghost? Unfinished business, is what. – At which the old lady, six feet tall, straight-backed, her hair hacked short as any man's, jerked the corners of her mouth downwards in a satisfied, tragedy-mask pout, – pulled a knitted blue shawl tight around bony shoulders, – and closed, for a moment, her sleepless eyes, to pray for the past's return. Come on, you Norman ships, she begged: let's have you, Willie-the-Conk.

Nine hundred years ago all this was under water, this portioned shore, this private beach, its shingle rising steeply towards the little row of flaky-paint villas with their peeling boathouses crammed full of deckchairs, empty picture frames, ancient tuckboxes stuffed with bundles of letters tied up in ribbons, mothballed silk-and-lace lingerie, the tearstained reading matter of once-young girls, lacrosse sticks, stamp albums, and all the buried treasure-chests of memories and lost time. The coastline had changed, had moved a mile or more out to sea, leaving the first Norman castle stranded far from water, lapped now by marshy land that afflicted with all manner of dank and boggy agues the poor who lived there on their whatstheword *estates*. She, the old lady, saw the castle as the ruin of a fish betrayed by an antique ebbing tide, as a sea-monster petrified by time. Nine hundred years! Nine centuries past, the Norman fleet had sailed right through this Englishwoman's home. On clear nights when the moon was full, she waited for its shining, revenant ghost.

Best place to see 'em come, she reassured herself, grandstand view. Repetition had become a comfort in her antiquity; the well-worn phrases, *unfinished business*, *grandstand view*, made her feel solid, unchanging, sempiternal, instead of the creature of cracks and absences she knew herself to be. – When the full moon sets, the dark before the dawn, that's their moment. Billow of sail, flash of oars, and the Conqueror himself at the flagship's prow, sailing up the beach between the barnacled wooden breakwaters and a few inverted sculls. – O, I've seen things in my time, always had the gift, the phantom-sight. – The Conqueror in his pointy metal-nosed hat, passing through her front door, gliding betwixt the cakestands and antimacassared sofas, like an echo resounding faintly through that house of remembrances and yearnings; then falling silent; *as the grave*.

– Once as a girl on Battle Hill, she was fond of recounting, always in the same time-polished words, – once as a solitary child, I found myself, quite suddenly and with no sense of strangeness, in the middle of a war. Longbows, maces, pikes. The flaxen-Saxon boys, cut down in their sweet youth. Harold Arroweye and William with his mouth full of sand. Yes, always the gift, the phantom-sight. – The story of the day on which the child Rosa had seen a vision of the battle of Hastings had become, for the old woman, one of the defining landmarks of her being, though it had been told so often that nobody, not even the teller, could confidently swear that it was true. *I long for them sometimes*, ran Rosa's practised thoughts. *Les beaux jours: the dear, dead days*. She closed, once more, her reminiscent eyes. When she opened them, she saw, down by the water's edge, no denying it, something beginning to move.

What she said aloud in her excitement: 'I don't believe it!' – 'It isn't true!' – 'He's never *here*!' – On unsteady feet, with bumping chest, Rosa went for her hat, cloak, stick. While, on the winter seashore, Gibreel Farishta awoke with a mouth full of, no, not sand.

Snow.

Ptui!

Gibreel spat; leapt up, as if propelled by expectorated slush; wished Chamcha – as has been reported – many happy returns of the day; and commenced to beat the snow from sodden purple sleeves. 'God, yaar,' he shouted, hopping from foot to foot, 'no wonder these people grow hearts of bloody ice.'

Then, however, the pure delight of being surrounded by such a quantity of snow quite overcame his first cynicism – for he was a tropical man – and he started capering about, saturnine and soggy, making snowballs and hurling them at his prone companion, envisioning a snowman, and singing a wild, swooping rendition of the carol 'Jingle Bells.' The first hint of light was in the sky, and on this cosy sea-coast danced Lucifer, the morning's star.

His breath, it should be mentioned, had somehow or other wholly ceased to smell . . .

'Come on, baby,' cried invincible Gibreel, in whose behaviour the reader may, not unreasonably, perceive the delirious, dislocating effects of his recent fall. 'Rise 'n' shine! Let's take this place by storm!' Turning his back on the sea, blotting out the bad memory in order to make room for the next things, passionate as always for newness, he would have planted (had he owned one) a flag, to claim in the name of whoknowswho this white country, his new-found land. 'Spoono,' he pleaded, 'shift, baba, or are you bloody dead?' Which being uttered brought the speaker to (or at least towards) his senses. He bent over the other's prostrate form, did not dare to touch. 'Not now, old Chumch,' he urged. 'Not when we came so far.'

Saladin: was not dead, but weeping. The tears of shock freezing on his face. And all his body cased in a fine skin of ice, smooth as glass, like a bad dream come true. In the miasmic semi-consciousness induced by his low body temperature he was possessed by the nightmare-fear of cracking, of seeing his blood bubbling up from the ice-breaks, of his flesh coming away with the shards. He was full of questions, did we truly, I mean, with your hands flapping, and then the waters, you don't mean to tell me they *actually*, like in the movies, when Charlton Heston stretched out his staff, so that we could, across the ocean-floor, it never happened, couldn't have, but if not then how, or did we in some way under-water, escorted by the mermaids, the sea passing through us as if we were fish or ghosts, was that the truth, yes or no, I need to have to . . . but when his eyes opened the questions acquired the indistinct-ness of dreams, so that he could no longer grasp them, their tails flicked before him and vanished like submarine fins. He was looking up at the sky, and noticed that it was the wrong colour entirely, blood-orange flecked with green, and the snow was blue as ink. He blinked hard but the colours refused to change, giving rise to the notion that he had fallen out of the sky into some wrong-ness, some other place, not England or perhaps not-England, some counterfeit zone, rotten borough, altered state. Maybe, he consid-ered briefly: Hell? No, no, he reassured himself as unconsciousness threatened, that can't be it, not yet, you aren't dead yet; but dying.

Well then: a transit lounge.

He began to shiver; the vibration grew so intense that it occurred to him that he might break up under the stress, like a, like a, plane.

Then nothing existed. He was in a void, and if he were to sur-vive he would have to construct everything from scratch, would have to invent the ground beneath his feet before he could take a step, only there was no need now to worry about such matters, because here in front of him was the inevitable: the tall, bony figure of Death, in a wide-brimmed straw hat, with a dark cloak flapping in the breeze. Death, leaning on a silver-headed cane, wearing olive-green Wellington boots.

'What do you imagine yourselves to be doing here?' Death wanted to know. 'This is private property. There's a sign.' Said in a woman's voice that was somewhat tremulous and more than somewhat thrilled.

A few moments later, Death bent over him – *to kiss me*, he panicked silently. *To suck the breath from my body.* He made small, futile movements of protest.

'He's alive all right,' Death remarked to, who was it, Gibreel. 'But, my dear. His breath: what a *pong*. When did he last clean his teeth?'

One man's breath was sweetened, while another's, by an equal and opposite mystery, was soured. What did they expect? Falling like that out of the sky: did they imagine there would be no side-effects? Higher Powers had taken an interest, it should have been obvious to them both, and such Powers (I am, of course, speaking of myself) have a mischievous, almost a wanton attitude to tumbling flies. And another thing, let's be clear: great falls change people. You think *they* fell a long way? In the matter of tumbles, I yield pride of place to no personage, whether mortal or im-. From clouds to ashes, down the chimney you might say, from heavenlight to hellfire . . . under the stress of a long plunge, I was saying, mutations are to be expected, not all of them random. Unnatural selections. Not much of a price to pay for survival, for being reborn, for becoming *new*, and at their age at that.

What? I should enumerate the changes?

Good breath/bad breath.

And around the edges of Gibreel Farishta's head, as he stood with his back to the dawn, it seemed to Rosa Diamond that she discerned a faint, but distinctly golden, *glow*.

And were those bumps, at Chamcha's temples, under his sodden and still-in-place bowler hat?

And, and, and.

When she laid eyes on the bizarre, satyrical figure of Gibreel Farishta prancing and dionysiac in the snow, Rosa Diamond did not think of *say it* angels. Sighting him from her window, through salt-cloudy glass and age-clouded eyes, she felt her heart kick out, twice, so painfully that she feared it might stop; because in that indistinct form she seemed to discern the incarnation of her soul's most deeply buried desire. She forgot the Norman invaders as if they had never been, and struggled down a slope of treacherous pebbles, too quickly for the safety of her not-quite-nonagenarian limbs, so that she could pretend to scold the impossible stranger for trespassing on her land.

Usually she was implacable in defence of her beloved fragment of the coast, and when summer weekenders strayed above the high tide line she descended upon them *like a wolf on the fold*, her phrase for it, to explain and to demand: – This is my garden, do you see. – And if they grew brazen, – getoutofitsillyoldmoo, itsthesoddingbeach, – she would return home to bring out a long green garden hose and turn it remorselessly upon their tartan blankets and plastic cricket bats and bottles of sun-tan lotion, she would smash their children's sandcastles and soak their liversausage sandwiches, smiling sweetly all the while: *You won't mind if I just water my lawn?* . . . O, she was a One, known in the village, they couldn't lock her away in any old folks' home, sent her whole family packing when they dared to suggest it, never darken her doorstep, she told them, cut the whole lot off without a penny or a by your leave. All on her own now, she was, never a visitor from week to blessed week, not even Dora Shufflebotham who went in and did for her all those years, Dora passed over September last, may she rest, still it's a wonder at her age how the old trout manages, all those stairs, she may be a bit of a bee but give the devil her due, there's many's'd go barmy being that alone.

For Gibreel there was neither a hosepipe nor the *sharp end* of her tongue. Rosa uttered token words of reproof, held her nostrils while examining the fallen and newly sulphurous Saladin (who had not, at this point, removed his bowler hat), and then, with an access of shyness which she greeted with nostalgic astonishment, stammered an invitation, yyou bbetter bring your ffriend in out of the cccold, and stamped back up the shingle to put the kettle on, grateful to the bite of the winter air for reddening her cheeks and *saving*, in the old comforting phrase, *her blushes*.

As a young man Saladin Chamcha had possessed a face of quite exceptional innocence, a face that did not seem ever to have encountered disillusion or evil, with skin as soft and smooth as a princess's palm. It had served him well in his dealings with women, and had, in point of fact, been one of the first reasons his future wife Pamela Lovelace had given for falling in love with him. 'So round and cherubic,' she marvelled, cupping her hands under his chin. 'Like a rubber ball.'

He was offended. 'I've got bones,' he protested. 'Bone *structure*.'

'Somewhere in there,' she conceded. 'Everybody does.'

After that he was haunted for a time by the notion that he looked like a featureless jellyfish, and it was in large part to assuage this feeling that he set about developing the narrow, haughty demeanour that was now second nature to him. It was, therefore, a matter of some consequence when, on arising from a long slumber racked by a series of intolerable dreams, prominent among which were images of Zeeny Vakil, transformed into a mermaid, singing to him from an iceberg in tones of agonizing sweetness, lamenting her inability to join him on dry land, calling him, calling; – but when he went to her she shut him up fast in the heart of her ice-mountain, and her song changed to one of triumph and revenge . . . it was, I say, a serious matter when Saladin Chamcha woke up, looked into a mirror framed in blue-and-gold Japonaiserie lacquer, and found that old cherubic face staring out at him once again; while, at his temples, he observed a brace of fearfully discoloured swellings, indications that he must have suffered, at some point in his recent adventures, a couple of mighty blows.

Looking into the mirror at his altered face, Chamcha attempted to remind himself of himself. I am a real man, he told the mirror, with a real history and a planned-out future. I am a man to whom certain things are of importance: rigour, self-discipline, reason, the pursuit of what is noble without recourse to that old crutch, God. The ideal of beauty, the possibility of exaltation, the mind. I am: a married man. But in spite of his litany, perverse thoughts insisted on visiting him. As for instance: that the world did not exist beyond that beach down there, and, now, this house. That if he weren't careful, if he rushed matters, he would fall off the edge, into clouds. Things had to be *made*. Or again: that if he were to telephone his home, right now, as he should, if he were to inform his loving wife that he was not dead, not blown to bits in mid-air but right here, on solid ground, if he were to do this eminently sensible thing, the person who answered the phone would not recognize his name. Or thirdly: that the sound of footsteps ringing in his ears, distant footsteps, but coming closer, was not some temporary tinnitus caused by his fall, but the noise of some approaching doom, drawing closer, letter by letter, ellowen, dee-owen, London. *Here I am, in Grandmother's house. Her big eyes, hands, teeth.*

There was a telephone extension on his bedside table. There, he admonished himself. Pick it up, dial, and your equilibrium will be restored. Such maunderings: they aren't like you, not worthy of you. Think of her grief; call her now.

It was night-time. He didn't know the hour. There wasn't a clock in the room and his wristwatch had disappeared somewhere along the line. Should he shouldn't he? – He dialled the nine numbers. A man's voice answered on the fourth ring.

'What the hell?' Sleepy, unidentifiable, familiar.

'Sorry,' Saladin Chamcha said. 'Excuse, please. Wrong number.'

Staring at the telephone, he found himself remembering a drama production seen in Bombay, based on an English original, a story by, by, he couldn't put his finger on the name, Tennyson? No, no. Somerset Maugham? – To hell with it. – In the original and now authorless text, a man, long thought dead, returns after an absence of many years, like a living phantom, to his former haunts. He visits his former home at night, surreptitiously, and looks in through an open window. He finds that his wife, believing herself widowed, has re-married. On the window-sill he

sees a child's toy. He spends a period of time standing in the darkness, wrestling with his feelings; then picks the toy off the ledge;
and departs forever, without making his presence known. In the
Indian version, the story had been rather different. The wife had
married her husband's best friend. The returning husband arrived
at the door and marched in, expecting nothing. Seeing his wife
and his old friend sitting together, he failed to understand that
they were married. He thanked his friend for comforting his wife;
but he was home now, and so all was well. The married couple
did not know how to tell him the truth; it was, finally, a servant
who gave the game away. The husband, whose long absence was
apparently due to a bout of amnesia, reacted to the news of the
marriage by announcing that he, too, must surely have re-married
at some point during his long absence from home; unfortunately,
however, now that the memory of his former life had returned he
had forgotten what had happened during the years of his disappearance. He went off to ask the police to trace his new wife,
even though he could remember nothing about her, not her eyes,
not the simple fact of her existence.

The curtain fell.

Saladin Chamcha, alone in an unknown bedroom in unfamiliar
red-and-white striped pyjamas, lay face downwards on a narrow
bed and wept. 'Damn all Indians,' he cried into the muffling bedclothes, his fists punching at frilly-edged pillowcases from Harrods
in Buenos Aires so fiercely that the fifty-year-old fabric was ripped
to shreds. '*What the hell.* The vulgarity of it, the *sod it sod it* indeli-
cacy. *What the hell.* That bastard, those bastards, their lack of *bastard* taste.'

It was at this moment that the police arrived to arrest him.

On the night after she had taken the two of them in from the
beach, Rosa Diamond stood once again at the nocturnal window
of her old woman's insomnia, contemplating the nine-hundred-
year-old sea. The smelly one had been sleeping ever since they
put him to bed, with hot-water bottles packed in tightly around

him, best thing for him, let him get his strength. She had put them upstairs, Chamcha in the spare room and Gibreel in her late husband's old study, and as she watched the great shining plain of the sea she could hear him moving up there, amid the ornithological prints and bird-call whistles of the former Henry Diamond, the bolas and bullwhip and aerial photographs of the Los Alamos estancia far away and long ago, a man's footsteps in that room, how reassuring they felt. Farishta was pacing up and down, avoiding sleep, for reasons of his own. And below his footfall Rosa, looking up at the ceiling, called him in a whisper by a long-unspoken name. Martin she said. His last name the same as that of his country's deadliest snake, the viper. The víbora, *de la Cruz*.

At once she saw the shapes moving on the beach, as if the forbidden name had conjured up the dead. Not again, she thought, and went for her opera-glasses. She returned to find the beach full of shadows, and this time she was afraid, because whereas the Norman fleet came sailing, when it came, proudly and openly and without recourse to subterfuge, these shades were sneaky, emitting stifled imprecations and alarming, muted yaps and barks, they seemed headless, crouching, arms and legs a-dangle like giant, unshelled crabs. Scuttling, sidelong, heavy boots crunching on shingle. Lots of them. She saw them reach her boathouse on which the fading image of an eyepatched pirate grinned and brandished a cutlass, and that was too much, *I'm not having it,* she decided, and, stumbling downstairs for warm clothing, she fetched the chosen weapon of her retribution: a long coil of green garden hose. At her front door she called out in a clear voice. 'I can see you quite plainly. Come out, come out, whoever you are.'

They switched on seven suns and blinded her, and then she panicked, illuminated by the seven blue-white floodlights around which, like fireflies or satellites, there buzzed a host of smaller lights: lanterns torches cigarettes. Her head was spinning, and for a moment she lost her ability to distinguish between *then* and *now*, in her consternation she began to say Put out that light, don't you know there's a blackout, you'll be having Jerry down on us if you carry on so. 'I'm raving,' she realized disgustedly, and banged the tip of her stick into her doormat. Whereupon, as if by magic, policemen materialized in the dazzling circle of light.

It turned out that somebody had reported a suspicious person on the beach, remember when they used to come in fishing-boats, the illegals, and thanks to that single anonymous telephone call there were now fifty-seven uniformed constables combing the beach, their flashlights swinging crazily in the dark, constables from as far away as Hastings Eastbourne Bexhill-upon-Sea, even a deputation from Brighton because nobody wanted to miss the fun, the thrill of the chase. Fifty-seven beachcombers were accompanied by thirteen dogs, all sniffing the sea air and lifting excited legs. While up at the house away from the great posse of men and dogs, Rosa Diamond found herself gazing at the five constables guarding the exits, front door, ground-floor windows, scullery door, in case the putative miscreant attempted an alleged escape; and at the three men in plain clothes, plain coats and plain hats with faces to match; and in front of the lot of them, not daring to look her in the eye, young Inspector Lime, shuffling his feet and rubbing his nose and looking older and more bloodshot than his forty years. She tapped him on the chest with the end of her stick, *at this time of night, Frank, what's the meaning of,* but he wasn't going to allow her to boss him around, not tonight, not with the men from the immigration watching his every move, so he drew himself up and pulled in his chins.

'Begging your pardon, Mrs D. – certain allegations, – information laid before us, – reason to believe, – merit investigation, – necessary to search your, – a warrant has been obtained.'

'Don't be absurd, Frank dear,' Rosa began to say, but just then the three men with the plain faces drew themselves up and seemed to stiffen, each of them with one leg slightly raised, like pointer dogs; the first began to emit an unusual hiss of what sounded like pleasure, while a soft moan escaped from the lips of the second, and the third commenced to roll his eyes in an oddly contented way. Then they all pointed past Rosa Diamond, into her floodlit hallway, where Mr Saladin Chamcha stood, his left hand holding up his pyjamas because a button had come off when

he hurled himself on to his bed. With his right hand he was rubbing at an eye.

'Bingo,' said the hissing man, while the moaner clasped his
hands beneath his chin to indicate that all his prayers had been
answered, and the roller of eyes shouldered past Rosa Diamond,
without standing on ceremony, except that he did mutter,
'Madam, pardon *me*.'

Then there was a flood, and Rosa was jammed into a corner of
her own sitting-room by that bobbing sea of police helmets, so
that she could no longer make out Saladin Chamcha or hear what
he was saying. She never heard him explain about the detonation
of the *Bostan* – there's been a mistake, he cried, I'm not one of
your fishing-boat sneakers-in, not one of your ugando-kenyattas,
me. The policemen began to grin, I see, sir, at thirty thousand
feet, and then you swam ashore. You have the right to remain
silent, they tittered, but quite soon they burst out into uproarious
guffaws, we've got a right one here and no mistake. But Rosa
couldn't make out Saladin's protests, the laughing policemen got
in the way, you've got to believe me, I'm a British, he was saying,
with right of abode, too, but when he couldn't produce a passport
or any other identifying document they began to weep with
mirth, the tears streaming down even the blank faces of the plain-
clothes men from the immigration service. Of course, don't tell
me, they giggled, they fell out of your jacket during your tumble,
or did the mermaids pick your pocket in the sea? Rosa couldn't
see, in that laughter-heaving surge of men and dogs, what uniformed arms might be doing to Chamcha's arms, or fists to his
stomach, or boots to his shins; nor could she be sure if it was his
voice crying out or just the howling of the dogs. But she did,
finally, hear his voice rise in a last, despairing shout: 'Don't any of
you watch TV? Don't you see? I'm Maxim. Maxim Alien.'

'So you are,' said the popeyed officer. 'And I am Kermit the
Frog.'

What Saladin Chamcha never said, not even when it was clear
that something had gone badly wrong: 'Here is a London
number,' he neglected to inform the arresting policemen. 'At the

other end of the line you will find, to vouch for me, for the truth of what I'm saying, my lovely, white, English wife.' No, sir. *What the hell.*

Rosa Diamond gathered her strength. 'Just one moment, Frank Lime,' she sang out. 'You look here,' but the three plain men had begun their bizarre routine of hiss moan roll-eye once again, and in the sudden silence of that room the eye-roller pointed a trembling finger at Chamcha and said, 'Lady, if it's proof you're after, you couldn't do better than *those*.'

Saladin Chamcha, following the line of Popeye's pointing finger, raised his hands to his forehead, and then he knew that he had woken into the most fearsome of nightmares, a nightmare that had only just begun, because there at his temples, growing longer by the moment, and sharp enough to draw blood, were two new, goaty, unarguable horns.

Before the army of policemen took Saladin Chamcha away into his new life, there was one more unexpected occurrence. Gibreel Farishta, seeing the blaze of lights and hearing the delirious laughter of the law-enforcement officers, came downstairs in a maroon smoking jacket and jodhpurs, chosen from Henry Diamond's wardrobe. Smelling faintly of mothballs, he stood on the first-floor landing and observed the proceedings without comment. He stood there unnoticed until Chamcha, handcuffed and on his way out to the Black Maria, barefoot, still clutching his pyjamas, caught sight of him and cried out, 'Gibreel, for the love of God tell them what's what.'

Hisser Moaner Popeye turned eagerly towards Gibreel. 'And who might this be?' inquired Inspector Lime. 'Another sky-diver?'

But the words died on his lips, because at that moment the floodlights were switched off, the order to do so having been given when Chamcha was handcuffed and taken in charge, and in the aftermath of the seven suns it became clear to everyone there that a pale, golden light was emanating from the direction of the man in the smoking jacket, was in fact streaming softly outwards from a point immediately behind his head. Inspector Lime never referred to that light again, and if he had been asked about it would have denied ever having seen such a thing, a halo, in the late twentieth century, pull the other one.

But at any rate, when Gibreel asked, 'What do these men want?', every man there was seized by the desire to answer his question in literal, detailed terms, to reveal their secrets, as if he were, as if, but no, ridiculous, they would shake their heads for weeks, until they had all persuaded themselves that they had done as they did for purely logical reasons, he was Mrs Diamond's old friend, the two of them had found the rogue Chamcha half-drowned on the beach and taken him in for humanitarian reasons, no call to harass either Rosa or Mr Farishta any further, a more reputable looking gentleman you couldn't wish to see, in his smoking jacket and his, his, well, eccentricity never was a crime, anyhow.

'Gibreel,' said Saladin Chamcha, 'help.'

But Gibreel's eye had been caught by Rosa Diamond. He looked at her, and could not look away. Then he nodded, and went back upstairs. No attempt was made to stop him.

When Chamcha reached the Black Maria, he saw the traitor, Gibreel Farishta, looking down at him from the little balcony outside Rosa's bedroom, and there wasn't any light shining around the bastard's head.

2

Kan ma kan/Fi qadim azzaman ... It was so, it was not, in a
long time long forgot, that there lived in the silver-land of
Argentina a certain Don Enrique Diamond, who knew much
about birds and little about women, and his wife, Rosa, who
knew nothing about men but a good deal about love. One day it
so happened that when the señora was out riding, sitting
sidesaddle and wearing a hat with a feather in it, she arrived at the
Diamond estancia's great stone gates, which stood insanely in the
middle of the empty pampas, to find an ostrich running at her as
hard as it could, running for its life, with all the tricks and varia-
tions it could think of; for the ostrich is a crafty bird, difficult to
catch. A little way behind the ostrich was a cloud of dust full of
the noises of hunting men, and when the ostrich was within six
feet of her the cloud sent bolas to wrap around its legs and bring it
crashing to the ground at her grey mare's feet. The man who dismounted to kill the bird never took his eyes off Rosa's face. He
took a silver-hafted knife from a scabbard at his belt and plunged it
into the bird's throat, all the way up to the hilt, and he did it
without once looking at the dying ostrich, staring into Rosa Diamond's eyes while he knelt on the wide yellow earth. His name
was Martín de la Cruz.

After Chamcha had been taken away, Gibreel Farishta often wondered about his own behaviour. In that dreamlike moment when he had been trapped by the eyes of the old Englishwoman it had seemed to him that his will was no longer his own to command, that somebody else's needs were in charge. Owing to the bewildering nature of recent events, and also to his determination to stay awake as much as possible, it was a few days before he connected what was going on to the world behind his eyelids, and only then did he understand that he had to get away, because the universe of his nightmares had begun to leak into his waking life, and if he was not careful he would never manage to begin again, to be reborn with her, through her, Alleluia, who had seen the roof of the world.

He was shocked to realize that he had made no attempt to contact Allie at all; or to help Chamcha in his time of need. Nor had he been at all perturbed by the appearance on Saladin's head of a pair of fine new horns, a thing that should surely have occasioned some concern. He had been in some sort of trance, and when he asked the old dame what she thought of it all she smiled weirdly and told him that there was nothing new under the sun, she had seen things, the apparitions of men with horned helmets, in an ancient land like England there was no room for new stories, every blade of turf had already been walked over a hundred thousand times. For long periods of the day her talk became rambling and confused, but at other times she insisted on cooking him huge heavy meals, shepherd's pies, rhubarb crumble with thick custard, thick-gravied hotpots, all manner of weighty soups. And at all times she wore an air of inexplicable contentment, as if his presence had satisfied her in some deep, unlooked-for way. He went shopping in the village with her; people stared; she ignored them, waving her imperious stick. The days passed. Gibreel did not leave.

'Blasted English mame,' he told himself. 'Some type of extinct species. What the hell am I doing here?' But stayed, held by unseen chains. While she, at every opportunity, sang an old song, in Spanish, he couldn't understand a word. Some sorcery there? Some ancient Morgan Le Fay singing a young Merlin into her crystal cave? Gibreel headed for the door; Rosa piped up; he stopped in his tracks. 'Why not, after all,' he shrugged. 'The old woman needs company. Faded grandeur, I swear! Look what she's come to here. Anyhow, I need the rest. Gather my forces. Just a coupla days.'

In the evenings they would sit in that drawing-room stuffed with silver ornaments, including on the wall a certain silver-hafted knife, beneath the plaster bust of Henry Diamond that stared down from the top of the corner cabinet, and when the grandfather clock struck six he would pour two glasses of sherry and she would begin to talk, but not before she said, as predictably as clockwork, *Grandfather is always four minutes late, for good manners, he doesn't like to be too punctual.* Then she began without bothering with onceuponatime, and whether it was all true or all false he could see the fierce energy that was going into the telling, the last desperate reserves of her will that she was putting into her story, *the only bright time I can remember,* she told him, so that he perceived that this memory-jumbled rag-bag of material was in fact the very heart of her, her self-portrait, the way she looked in the mirror when nobody else was in the room, and that the silver land of the past was her preferred abode, not this dilapidated house in which she was constantly bumping into things, – knocking over coffee-tables, bruising herself on doorknobs – bursting into tears, and crying out: *Everything shrinks.*

When she sailed to Argentina in 1935 as the bride of the Anglo-Argentine Don Enrique of Los Alamos, he pointed to the ocean and said, that's the pampa. You can't tell how big it is by looking at it. You have to travel through it, the unchangingness, day after day. In some parts the wind is strong as a fist, but it's completely silent, it'll knock you flat but you'll never hear a thing. No trees is why: not an ombú, not a poplar, nada. And you have to watch out for ombú leaves, by the way. Deadly poison. The wind won't kill you but the leaf-juice can. She clapped her hands like a child: Honestly, Henry, silent winds, poisonous leaves. You make it sound like a fairy-story. Henry, fairhaired, soft-bodied, wide-eyed and ponderous, looked appalled. *Oh, no,* he said. *It's not so bad as that.*

She arrived in that immensity, beneath that infinite blue vault of sky, because Henry popped the question and she gave the only answer that a forty-year-old spinster could. But when she arrived she asked herself a bigger question: of what was she capable in all that space? What did she have the courage for, how could she *expand?* To be good or bad, she told herself: but to be *new.* Our neighbour Doctor Jorge Babington, she told Gibreel, never liked me, you know, he would tell me tales of the British in South America, always such gay blades, he said contemptuously, spies and brigands and looters. *Are you such exotics in your cold England?* he asked her, and answered his own question, *señora, I don't think so. Crammed into that coffin of an island, you must find wider horizons to express these secret selves.*

Rosa Diamond's secret was a capacity for love so great that it soon became plain that her poor prosaic Henry would never fulfil it, because whatever romance there was in that jellied frame was reserved for birds. Marsh hawks, screamers, snipe. In a small rowing boat on the local lagunas he spent his happiest days amid the bulrushes with his field-glasses to his eyes. Once on the train to Buenos Aires he embarrassed Rosa by demonstrating his favourite bird-calls in the dining-car, cupping his hands around his mouth: sleepyhead bird, vanduria ibis, trupial. Why can't you love me this way, she wanted to ask. But never did, because for Henry she was a good sort, and passion was an eccentricity of other races. She became the generalissimo of the homestead, and tried to stifle her wicked longings. At night she took to walking out into the pampa and lying on her back to look at the galaxy above, and sometimes, under the influence of that bright flow of beauty, she would begin to tremble all over, to shudder with a deep delight, and to hum an unknown tune, and this star-music was as close as she came to joy.

Gibreel Farishta: felt her stories winding round him like a web, holding him in that lost world where *fifty sat down to dinner every day, what men they were, our gauchos, nothing servile there, very fierce and proud, very. Pure carnivores; you can see it in the pictures.* During the long nights of their insomnia she told him about the heat-haze that would come over the pampa so that the few trees stood out like islands and a rider looked like a mythological being, galloping across the surface of the ocean. *It was like the ghost of the sea.* She told him campfire stories, for example about the atheist gaucho who disproved Paradise, when his mother died, by calling upon her spirit to return, every night for seven nights. On the eighth night he announced that she had obviously not heard him, or she would certainly have come to console her beloved son; therefore, death must be the end. She snared him in descriptions of the days when the Perón people came in their white suits and slicked down hair and the peons chased them off, she told him how the railroads were built by the Anglos to service their estancias, and the dams, too, the story, for example, of her friend Claudette, 'a real heartbreaker, my dear, married an engineer chap name of Granger, disappointed half the Hurlingham. Off they went to some dam he was building, and next thing they heard, the rebels were coming to blow it up. Granger went with the men to guard the dam, leaving Claudette alone with the maid, and wouldn't you know, a few hours later, the maid came running, señora, ees one hombre at the door, ees as beeg as a house. What else? A rebel captain. – 'And your spouse, madame?' – 'Waiting for you at the dam, as he should be.' – 'Then since he has not seen fit to protect you, the revolution will.' And he left guards outside the house, my dear, quite a thing. But in the fighting both men were killed, husband and captain and Claudette insisted on a joint funeral, watched the two coffins going side by side into the ground, mourned for them both. After that we knew she was a dangerous lot, *trop fatale*, eh? What? *Trop* jolly *fatale*.' In the tall story of the beautiful Claudette, Gibreel heard the music of Rosa's own longings. At such moments he would catch sight of her looking at him from the corners of her eyes, and he would feel a tugging in the region of his navel, as if something were trying to come out. Then she looked away, and the sensation faded. Perhaps it was only a side-effect of stress.

He asked her one night if she had seen the horns growing on Chamcha's head, but she went deaf and, instead of answering, told him how she would sit on a camp stool by the galpón or bull-pen at Los Alamos and the prize bulls would come up and lay their horned heads in her lap. One afternoon a girl named Aurora del Sol, who was the fiancée of Martín de la Cruz, let fall a saucy remark: I thought they only did that in the laps of virgins, she stage-whispered to her giggling friends, and Rosa turned to her sweetly and replied, Then perhaps, my dear, you would like to try? From that time Aurora del Sol, the best dancer at the estancia and the most desirable of all the peon women, became the deadly enemy of the too-tall, too-bony woman from over the sea.

'You look just like him,' Rosa Diamond said as they stood at her night-time window, side by side, looking out to sea. 'His double. Martín de la Cruz.' At the mention of the cowboy's name Gibreel felt so violent a pain in his navel, a pulling pain, as if somebody had stuck a hook in his stomach, that a cry escaped his lips. Rosa Diamond appeared not to hear. 'Look,' she cried happily, 'over there.'

Running along the midnight beach in the direction of the Martello tower and the holiday camp, – running along the water's edge so that the incoming tide washed away its footprints, – swerving and feinting, running for its life, there came a full-grown, large-as-life ostrich. Down the beach it fled, and Gibreel's eyes followed it in wonder, until he could no longer make it out in the dark.

The next thing that happened took place in the village. They had gone into town to collect a cake and a bottle of champagne, because Rosa had remembered that it was her eighty-ninth birthday. Her family had been expelled from her life, so there had been no cards or telephone calls. Gibreel insisted that they should hold some sort of celebration, and showed her the secret inside his shirt, a fat money-belt full of pounds sterling acquired on the black market before leaving Bombay. 'Also credit cards galore,' he said. 'I am no indigent fellow. Come, let us go. My treat.' He was now so deeply in thrall to Rosa's narrative sorcery that he hardly remembered from day to day that he had a life to go to, a woman to surprise by the simple fact of his being alive, or any such thing. Trailing behind her meekly, he carried Mrs Diamond's shopping-bags.

He was loafing around on a street corner while Rosa chatted to the baker when he felt, once again, that dragging hook in his stomach, and he fell against a lamp-post and gasped for air. He heard a clip-clopping noise, and then around the corner came an archaic pony-trap, full of young people in what seemed at first sight to be fancy dress: the men in tight black trousers studded at the calf with silver buttons, their white shirts open almost to the waist; the women in wide skirts of frills and layers and bright colours, scarlet, emerald, gold. They were singing in a foreign language and their gaiety made the street look dim and tawdry, but Gibreel realized that something weird was afoot, because nobody else in the street took the slightest notice of the pony-trap. Then Rosa emerged from the baker's with the cake-box dangling by its ribbon from the index finger of her left hand, and exclaimed: 'Oh, there they are, arriving for the dance. We always had dances, you know, they like it, it's in their blood.' And, after a pause: 'That was the dance at which he killed the vulture.'

That was the dance at which a certain Juan Julia, nicknamed The Vulture on account of his cadaverous appearance, drank too much and insulted the honour of Aurora del Sol, and didn't stop until Martín had no option but to fight, *hey Martín, why you enjoy fucking with this one, I thought she was pretty dull*. 'Let us go away from the dancing,' Martín said, and in the darkness, silhouetted against the fairy-lights hung from the trees around the dance-floor, the two men wrapped ponchas around their forearms, drew their knives, circled, fought. Juan died. Martín de la Cruz picked up the dead man's hat and threw it at the feet of Aurora del Sol. She picked up the hat and watched him walk away.

Rosa Diamond at eighty-nine in a long silver sheath dress with a cigarette holder in one gloved hand and a silver turban on her head drank gin-and-sin from a green glass triangle and told stories of the good old days. 'I want to dance,' she announced suddenly. 'It's my birthday and I haven't danced once.'

The exertions of that night on which Rosa and Gibreel danced until dawn proved too much for the old lady, who collapsed into bed the next day with a low fever that induced ever more delirious apparitions: Gibreel saw Martín de la Cruz and Aurora del Sol dancing flamenco on the tiled and gabled roof of the Diamond house, and Peronistas in white suits stood on the boathouse to address a gathering of peons about the future: 'Under Perón these lands will be expropriated and distributed among the people. The British railroads also will become the property of the state. Let's chuck them out, these brigands, these privateers . . .' The plaster bust of Henry Diamond hung in mid-air, observing the scene, and a white-suited agitator pointed a finger at him and cried, That's him, your oppressor; there is the enemy. Gibreel's stomach ached so badly that he feared for his life, but at the very moment that his rational mind was considering the possibility of an ulcer or appendicitis, the rest of his brain whispered the truth, which was that he was being held prisoner and manipulated by the force of Rosa's will, just as the Angel Gibreel had been obliged to speak by the overwhelming need of the Prophet, Mahound.

'She's dying,' he realized. 'Not long to go, either.' Tossing in her bed in the fever's grip Rosa Diamond muttered about ombú poison and the enmity of her neighbour Doctor Babington, who asked Henry, is your wife perhaps quiet enough for the pastoral life, and who gave her (as a present for recovering from typhus) a copy of Amerigo Vespucci's account of his voyages. 'The man was a notorious fantasist, of course,' Babington smiled, 'but fantasy can be stronger than fact; after all, he had continents named after him.' As she grew weaker she poured more and more of her remaining strength into her own dream of Argentina, and Gibreel's navel felt as if it had been set on fire. He lay slumped in an armchair at her bedside and the apparitions multiplied by the hour. Woodwind music filled the air, and, most wonderful of all, a small white island appeared just off the shore, bobbing on the waves like a raft; it was white as snow, with white sand sloping up to a clump of albino trees, which were white, chalk-white, paper-white, to the very tips of their leaves.

After the arrival of the white island Gibreel was overcome by a deep lethargy. Slumped in an armchair in the bedroom of the dying woman, his eyelids drooping, he felt the weight of his body increase until all movement became impossible. Then he was in another bedroom, in tight black trousers, with silver buttons along the calves and a heavy silver buckle at the waist. *You sent for me, Don Enrique,* he was saying to the soft, heavy man with a face like a white plaster bust, but he knew who had asked for him, and he never took his eyes from her face, even when he saw the colour rising from the white frill around her neck.

Henry Diamond had refused to permit the authorities to become involved in the matter of Martín de la Cruz, *these people are my responsibility,* he told Rosa, *it is a question of honour.* Instead he had gone to some lengths to demonstrate his continuing trust in the killer, de la Cruz, for example by making him the captain of the estancia polo team. But Don Enrique was never really the same once Martín had killed the Vulture. He was more and more easily exhausted, and became listless, uninterested even in birds. Things began to come apart at Los Alamos, imperceptibly at first, then more obviously. The men in the white suits returned and were not chased away. When Rosa Diamond contracted typhus, there were many at the estancia who took it for an allegory of the old estate's decline.

What am I doing here, Gibreel thought in great alarm, as he stood before Don Enrique in the rancher's study, while Doña Rosa blushed in the background, *this is someone else's place.* – Great confidence in you, Henry was saying, not in English but Gibreel could still understand. – My wife is to undertake a motor tour, for her convalescence, and you will accompany . . . Responsibilities at

Los Alamos prevent me from going along. *Now I must speak, what to say,* but when his mouth opened the alien words emerged, it will be my honour, Don Enrique, click of heels, swivel, exit.

Rosa Diamond in her eighty-nine-year-old weakness had begun to dream her story of stories, which she had guarded for more than half a century, and Gibreel was on a horse behind her Hispano-Suiza, driving from estancia to estancia, through a wood of arayana trees, beneath the high cordillera, arriving at grotesque homesteads built in the style of Scottish castles or Indian palaces, visiting the land of Mr Cadwallader Evans, he of the seven wives who were happy enough to have only one night of duty each per week, and the territory of the notorious MacSween who had become enamoured of the ideas arriving in Argentina from Germany, and had started flying, from his estancia's flagpole, a red flag at whose heart a crooked black cross danced in a white circle. It was on the MacSween estancia that they came across the lagoon, and Rosa saw for the first time the white island of her fate, and insisted on rowing out for a picnic luncheon, accompanied neither by maid nor by chauffeur, taking only Martín de la Cruz to row the boat and to spread a scarlet cloth upon the white sand and to serve her with meat and wine.

As white as snow and as red as blood and as black as ebony. As she reclined in black skirt and white blouse, lying upon scarlet which itself lay over white, while he (also wearing black and white) poured red wine into the glass in her white-gloved hand, – and then, to his own astonishment, *bloody goddamn,* as he caught at her hand and began to kiss, – something happened, the scene grew blurred, one minute they were lying on the scarlet cloth, rolling all over it so that cheeses and cold cuts and salads and pâtés were crushed beneath the weight of their desire, and when they returned to the Hispano-Suiza it was impossible to conceal anything from chauffeur or maid on account of the foodstains all over their clothes, – while the next minute she was recoiling from him, not cruelly but in sadness, drawing her hand away and making a tiny gesture of the head, *no,* and he stood, bowed, retreated, leaving her with virtue and lunch intact, – the two possibilities kept alternating, while dying Rosa tossed on her bed, did-she-didn't-she, making the last version of the story of her life, unable to decide what she wanted to be true.

'I'm going crazy,' Gibreel thought. 'She's dying, but I'm losing my mind.' The moon was out, and Rosa's breathing was the only sound in the room: snoring as she breathed in and exhaling heavily, with small grunting noises. Gibreel tried to rise from his chair, and found he could not. Even in these intervals between the visions his body remained impossibly heavy. As if a boulder had been placed upon his chest. And the images, when they came, continued to be confused, so that at one moment he was in a hayloft at Los Alamos, making love to her while she murmured his name, over and over, *Martin of the Cross,* – and the next moment she was ignoring him in broad daylight beneath the watching eyes of a certain Aurora del Sol, – so that it was not possible to distinguish memory from wishes, or guilty reconstructions from confessional truths, – because even on her deathbed Rosa Diamond did not know how to look her history in the eye.

Moonlight streamed into the room. As it struck Rosa's face it appeared to pass right through her, and indeed Gibreel was beginning to be able to make out the pattern of the lace embroidery on her pillowcase. Then he saw Don Enrique and his friend, the puritanical and disapproving Dr Babington, standing on the balcony, as solid as you could wish. It occurred to him that as the apparitions increased in clarity Rosa grew fainter and fainter, fading away, exchanging places, one might say, with the ghosts. And because he had also understood that the manifestations depended on him, his stomach-ache, his stone-like weightiness, he began to fear for his own life as well.

'You wanted me to falsify Juan Julia's death certificate,' Dr Babington was saying. 'I did so out of our old friendship. But it was wrong to do so; and I see the result before me. You have sheltered a killer and it is, perhaps, your conscience that is eating you away. Go home, Enrique. Go home, and take that wife of yours, before something worse happens.'

'I am home,' Henry Diamond said. 'And I take exception to your mention of my wife.'

'Wherever the English settle, they never leave England,' Dr Babington said as he faded into the moonlight. 'Unless, like Doña Rosa, they fall in love.'

A cloud passed across the moonlight, and now that the balcony was empty Gibreel Farishta finally managed to force himself out of the chair and on to his feet. Walking was like dragging a ball and chain across the floor, but he reached the window. In every direction, and as far as he could see, there were giant thistles waving in the breeze. Where the sea had been there was now an ocean of thistles, extending as far as the horizon, thistles as high as a full-grown man. He heard the disembodied voice of Dr Babington mutter in his ear: 'The first plague of thistles for fifty years. The past, it seems, returns.' He saw a woman running through the thick, rippling growth, barefoot, with loose dark hair. 'She did it,' Rosa's voice said clearly behind him. 'After betraying him with the Vulture and making him into a murderer. He wouldn't look at her after that. Oh, she did it all right. Very dangerous one, that one. Very.' Gibreel lost sight of Aurora del Sol in the thistles; one mirage obscured another.

He felt something grab him from behind, spin him around and fling him flat on his back. There was nobody to be seen, but Rosa Diamond was sitting bolt upright in bed, staring at him wide-eyed, making him understand that she had given up hope of clinging on to life, and needed him to help her complete the last revelation. As with the businessman of his dreams, he felt helpless, ignorant . . . she seemed to know, however, how to draw the images from him. Linking the two of them, navel to navel, he saw a shining cord.

Now he was by a pond in the infinity of the thistles, allowing his horse to drink, and she came riding up on her mare. Now he was embracing her, loosening her garments and her hair, and now they were making love. Now she was whispering, how can you like me, I am so much older than you, and he spoke comforting words.

Now she rose, dressed, rode away, while he remained there, his body languid and warm, failing to notice the moment when a woman's hand stole out of the thistles and took hold of his silver-hafted knife . . .

No! No! No, this way!

Now she rode up to him by the pond, and the moment she dismounted, looking nervously at him, he fell upon her, he told her he couldn't bear her rejections any longer, they fell to the ground together, she screamed, he tore at her clothes, and her hands, clawing at his body, came upon the handle of a knife . . .

No! No, never, no! This way: here!

Now the two of them were making love, tenderly, with many slow caresses; and now a third rider entered the clearing by the pool, and the lovers rushed apart; now Don Enrique drew his small pistol and aimed at his rival's heart, –

– and he felt Aurora stabbing him in the heart, over and over, this is for Juan, and this is for abandoning me, and this is for your grand English whore, –

– and he felt his victim's knife entering his heart, as Rosa stabbed him, once, twice, and again, –

– and after Henry's bullet had killed him the Englishman took the dead man's knife and stabbed him, many times, in the bleeding wound.

Gibreel, screaming loudly, lost consciousness at this point.

When he regained his senses the old woman in the bed was speaking to herself, so softly that he could barely make out the words. 'The pampero came, the south-west wind, flattening the thistles. That's when they found him, or was it before.' The last of the story. How Aurora del Sol spat in Rosa Diamond's face at the funeral of Martín de la Cruz. How it was arranged that nobody was to be charged for the murder, on condition that Don Enrique took Doña Rosa and returned to England with all speed. How they boarded the train at the Los Alamos station and the men in white suits stood on the platform, wearing borsalino hats, making sure they really left. How, once the train had started moving, Rosa Diamond opened the holdall on the seat beside her, and said defiantly, *I brought something. A little souvenir.* And unwrapped a cloth bundle to reveal a gaucho's silver-hafted knife.

'Henry died the first winter home. Then nothing happened. The war. The end.' She paused. 'To diminish into this, after being in that vastness. It isn't to be borne.' And, after a further silence: 'Everything shrinks.'

There was a change in the moonlight, and Gibreel felt a weight lifting from him, so rapidly that he thought he might float up towards the ceiling. Rosa Diamond lay still, eyes closed, her arms resting on the patchwork counterpane. She looked: *normal*. Gibreel realized that there was nothing to prevent him from walking out of the door.

He made his way downstairs carefully, his legs still a little unsteady; found the heavy gabardine overcoat that had once belonged to Henry Diamond, and the grey felt trilby inside which Don Enrique's name had been sewn by his wife's own hand; and left, without looking back. The moment he got outside a wind snatched his hat and sent it skipping down the beach. He chased it, caught it, jammed it back on. *London shareef, here I come.* He had the city in his pocket: Geographers' London, the whole dog-eared metropolis, A to Z.

'What to do?' he was thinking. 'Phone or not phone? No, just turn up, ring the bell and say, baby, your wish came true, from sea bed to your bed, takes more than a plane crash to keep me away from you. – Okay, maybe not quite, but words to that effect. – Yes. Surprise is the best policy. Allie Bibi, boo to you.'

Then he heard the singing. It was coming from the old boathouse with the one-eyed pirate painted on the outside, and the song was foreign, but familiar: a song that Rosa Diamond had often hummed, and the voice, too, was familiar, although a little different, less quavery; *younger*. The boathouse door was unaccountably unlocked, and banging in the wind. He went towards the song.

'Take your coat off,' she said. She was dressed as she had been on the day of the white island: black skirt and boots, white silk blouse, hatless. He spread the coat on the boathouse floor, its bright scarlet lining glowing in the confined, moonlit space. She lay down amid the random clutter of an English life, cricket stumps, a yellowed lampshade, chipped vases, a folding table, trunks; and extended an arm towards him. He lay down by her side.

'How can you like me?' she murmured. 'I am so much older than you.'

3

When they pulled his pyjamas down in the windowless police van and he saw the thick, tightly curled dark hair covering his thighs, Saladin Chamcha broke down for the second time that night; this time, however, he began to giggle hysterically, infected, perhaps, by the continuing hilarity of his captors. The three immigration officers were in particularly high spirits, and it was one of these – the popeyed fellow whose name, it transpired, was Stein – who had 'debagged' Saladin with a merry cry of, 'Opening time, Packy; let's see what you're made of!' Red-and-white stripes were dragged off the protesting Chamcha, who was reclining on the floor of the van with two stout policemen holding each arm and a fifth constable's boot placed firmly upon his chest, and whose protests went unheard in the general mirthful din. His horns kept banging against things, the wheel-arch, the uncarpeted floor or a policeman's shin – on these last occasions he was soundly buffeted about the face by the understandably irate law-enforcement officer – and he was, in sum, in as miserably low spirits as he could recall. Nevertheless, when he saw what lay beneath his borrowed pyjamas, he could not prevent that disbelieving giggle from escaping past his teeth.

His thighs had grown uncommonly wide and powerful, as well as hairy. Below the knee the hairiness came to a halt, and his legs narrowed into tough, bony, almost fleshless calves, terminating in a pair of shiny, cloven hoofs, such as one might find on any billy-goat. Saladin was also taken aback by the sight of his phallus, greatly enlarged and embarrassingly erect, an organ that he had the greatest difficulty in acknowledging as his own. 'What's this, then?' joked Novak – the former 'Hisser' – giving it a playful tweak. 'Fancy one of us, maybe?' Whereupon the 'moaning' im-migration officer, Joe Bruno, slapped his thigh, dug Novak in the ribs, and shouted, 'Nah, that ain't it. Seems like we really got his goat.' 'I get it,' Novak shouted back, as his fist accidentally punched Saladin in his newly enlarged testicles. 'Hey! Hey!' howled Stein, with tears in his eyes. 'Listen, here's an even better . . . no wonder he's so fucking *horny*.'

At which the three of them, repeating many times 'Got his goat . . . horny . . .' fell into one another's arms and howled with delight. Chamcha wanted to speak, but was afraid that he would find his voice mutated into goat-bleats, and, besides, the policeman's boot had begun to press harder than ever on his chest, and it was hard to form any words. What puzzled Chamcha was that a circumstance which struck him as utterly bewildering and unprecedented – that is, his metamorphosis into this supernatural imp – was being treated by the others as if it were the most banal and familiar matter they could imagine. 'This isn't England,' he thought, not for the first or last time. How could it be, after all; where in all that moderate and common-sensical land was there room for such a police van in whose interior such events as these might plausibly transpire? He was being forced towards the con-clusion that he had indeed died in the exploding aeroplane and that everything that followed had been some sort of after-life. If that were the case, his long-standing rejection of the Eternal was beginning to look pretty foolish. – But where, in all this, was any sign of a Supreme Being, whether benevolent or malign? Why did Purgatory, or Hell, or whatever this place might be, look so much like that Sussex of rewards and fairies which every schoolboy knew? – Perhaps, it occurred to him, he had not actually perished in the *Bostan* disaster, but was lying gravely ill in some hospital ward, plagued by delirious dreams? This explanation appealed to him, not least because it unmade the meaning of a certain late-night telephone call, and a man's voice that he was trying, unsuccessfully, to forget ... He felt a sharp kick land on his ribs, painful and realistic enough to make him doubt the truth of all such hallucination-theories. He returned his attention to the actual, to this present comprising a sealed police van containing three immigration officers and five policemen that was, for the moment at any rate, all the universe he possessed. It was a universe of fear.

Novak and the rest had snapped out of their happy mood. 'Animal,' Stein cursed him as he administered a series of kicks, and Bruno joined in: 'You're all the same. Can't expect animals to observe civilized standards. Eh?' And Novak took up the thread: 'We're talking about fucking personal hygiene here, you little fuck.'

Chamcha was mystified. Then he noticed that a large number of soft, pellety objects had appeared on the floor of the Black Maria. He felt consumed by bitterness and shame. It seemed that even his natural processes were goatish now. The humiliation of it! He was – had gone to some lengths to become – a sophisticated man! Such degradations might be all very well for riff-raff from villages in Sylhet or the bicycle-repair shops of Gujranwala, but he was cut from different cloth! 'My good fellows,' he began, attempting a tone of authority that was pretty difficult to bring off from that undignified position on his back with his hoofy legs wide apart and a soft tumble of his own excrement all about him, 'my good fellows, you had best understand your mistake before it's too late.'

Novak cupped a hand behind an ear. 'What's that? What was that noise?' he inquired, looking about him, and Stein said, 'Search me.' 'Tell you what it sounded like,' Joe Bruno volunteered, and with his hands around his mouth he bellowed: 'Maa-aa-aa!' Then the three of them all laughed once more, so that Saladin had no way of telling if they were simply insulting him or if his vocal cords had truly been infected, as he feared, by this macabre demoniasis that had overcome him without the slightest warning. He had begun to shiver again. The night was extremely cold.

The officer, Stein, who appeared to be the leader of the trinity, or at least the primus inter pares, returned abruptly to the subject of the pellety refuse rolling around the floor of the moving van. 'In this country,' he informed Saladin, 'we clean up our messes.'

The policemen stopped holding him down and pulled him into a kneeling position. 'That's right,' said Novak, 'clean it up.' Joe Bruno placed a large hand behind Chamcha's neck and pushed his head down towards the pellet-littered floor. 'Off you go,' he said, in a conversational voice. 'Sooner you start, sooner you'll polish it off.'

Even as he was performing (having no option) the latest and basest ritual of his unwarranted humiliation, – or, to put it another way, as the circumstances of his miraculously spared life grew ever more infernal and outré – Saladin Chamcha began to notice that the three immigration officers no longer looked or acted nearly as strangely as at first. For one thing, they no longer resembled one another in the slightest. Officer Stein, whom his colleagues called 'Mack' or 'Jockey', turned out to be a large, burly man with a thick roller-coaster of a nose; his accent, it now transpired, was exaggeratedly Scottish. 'Tha's the ticket,' he remarked approvingly as Chamcha munched miserably on. 'An actor, was it? I'm partial to watchin' a guid man perform.'

This observation prompted Officer Novak – that is, 'Kim' – who had acquired an alarmingly pallid colouring, an ascetically bony face that reminded one of medieval icons, and a frown suggesting some deep inner torment, to burst into a short peroration about his favourite television soap-opera stars and game-show hosts, while Officer Bruno, who struck Chamcha as having grown exceedingly handsome all of a sudden, his hair shiny with styling gel and centrally divided, his blond beard contrasting dramatically with the darker hair on his head, – Bruno, the youngest of the three, asked lasciviously, what about watchin' girls, then, that's my game. This new notion set the three of them off into all manner of half-completed anecdotes pregnant with suggestions of a certain type, but when the five policemen attempted to join in they joined ranks, grew stern, and put the constables in their places. 'Little children,' Mr Stein admonished them, 'should be seen an' no hearrud.'

By this time Chamcha was gagging violently on his meal, forcing himself not to vomit, knowing that such an error would only prolong his misery. He was crawling about on the floor of the van, seeking out the pellets of his torture as they rolled from side to side, and the policemen, needing an outlet for the frustration engendered by the immigration officer's rebuke, began to abuse Saladin roundly and pull the hair on his rump to increase both his discomfort and his discomfiture. Then the five policemen defiantly started up their own version of the immigration officers' conversation, and set to analysing the merits of divers movie stars, darts players, professional wrestlers and the like; but because they had been put into a bad humour by the loftiness of 'Jockey' Stein, they were unable to maintain the abstract and intellectual tone of their superiors, and fell to quarrelling over the relative merits of the Tottenham Hotspur 'double' team of the early 1960s and the mighty Liverpool side of the present day, – in which the Liverpool supporters incensed the Spurs fans by alleging that the great Danny Blanchflower was a 'luxury' player, a cream puff, flower by name, pansy by nature; – whereupon the offended claque responded by shouting that in the case of Liverpool it was the supporters who were the bum-boys, the Spurs mob could take them apart with their arms tied behind their backs. Of course all the constables were familiar with the techniques of football hooligans, having spent many Saturdays with their backs to the game watching the spectators in the various stadiums up and down the country, and as their argument grew heated they reached the point of wishing to demonstrate, to their opposing colleagues, exactly what they meant by 'tearing apart', bollocking', 'bottling' and the like. The angry factions glared at one another and then, all together, they turned to gaze upon the person of Saladin Chamcha.

Well, the ruckus in that police van grew noisier and noisier, – and it's true to say that Chamcha was partly to blame, because he had started squealing like a pig, – and the young bobbies were thumping and gouging various parts of his anatomy, using him both as a guinea-pig and a safety-valve, remaining careful, in spite of their excitation, to confine their blows to his softer, more fleshy parts, to minimize the risk of breakages and bruises; and when Jockey, Kim and Joey saw what their juniors were getting up to, they chose to be tolerant, because boys would have their fun.

Besides, all this talk of watching had brought Stein, Bruno and Novak round to an examination of weightier matters, and now, with solemn faces and judicious voices, they were speaking of the need, in this day and age, for an increase in observation, not merely in the sense of 'spectating', but in that of 'watchfulness', and 'surveillance'. The young constables' experience was extremely relevant, Stein intoned: watch the crowd, not the game. 'Eternal vigilance is the price o' liberty,' he proclaimed.

'Eek,' cried Chamcha, unable to avoid interrupting. 'Aargh, unnhh, owoo.'

After a time a curious mood of detachment fell upon Saladin. He no longer had any idea of how long they had been travelling in the Black Maria of his hard fall from grace, nor could he have hazarded a guess as to the proximity of their ultimate destination, even though the tinnitus in his ears was growing gradually louder, those phantasmal grandmother's footsteps, ellowen, deeowen, London. The blows raining down on him now felt as soft as a lover's caresses; the grotesque sight of his own metamorphosed body no longer appalled him; even the last pellets of goat-excrement failed to stir his much-abused stomach. Numbly, he crouched down in his little world, trying to make himself smaller and smaller, in the hope that he might eventually disappear altogether, and so regain his freedom.

The talk of surveillance techniques had reunited immigration officers and policemen, healing the breach caused by Jockey Stein's words of puritanical reproof. Chamcha, the insect on the floor of the van, heard, as if through a telephone scrambler, the faraway voices of his captors speaking eagerly of the need for more video equipment at public events and of the benefits of computerized information, and, in what appeared to be a complete contradiction, of the efficacy of placing too rich a mixture in the nosebags of police horses on the night before a big match, because when equine stomach-upsets led to the marchers being showered with shit it always provoked them into violence, *an' then we can really get amongst them, can't we just.* Unable to find a way of making this universe of soap operas, matchoftheday, cloaks and daggers cohere into any recognizable whole, Chamcha closed his ears to the chatter and listened to the footsteps in his ears.

Then the penny dropped.

'Ask the Computer!'

Three immigration officers and five policemen fell silent as the foul-smelling creature sat up and hollered at them. 'What's he on about?' asked the youngest policeman – one of the Tottenham supporters, as it happened – doubtfully. 'Shall I fetch him another whack?'

'My name is Salahuddin Chamchawala, professional name Saladin Chamcha,' the demi-goat gibbered. 'I am a member of Actors' Equity, the Automobile Association and the Garrick Club. My car registration number is suchandsuch. Ask the Computer. Please.'

'Who're you trying to kid?' inquired one of the Liverpool fans, but he, too, sounded uncertain. 'Look at yourself. You're a fucking Packy billy. Sally-who? – What kind of name is that for an Englishman?'

Chamcha found a scrap of anger from somewhere. 'And what about them?' he demanded, jerking his head at the immigration officers. 'They don't sound so Anglo-Saxon to me.'

For a moment it seemed that they might all fall upon him and tear him limb from limb for such temerity, but at length the skull-faced Officer Novak merely slapped his face a few times while replying, 'I'm from Weybridge, you cunt. Get it straight: *Wey*-bridge, where the fucking *Beatles* used to live.'

Stein said: 'Better check him out.' Three and a half minutes later the Black Maria came to a halt and three immigration officers, five constables and one police driver held a crisis conference – *here's a pretty effing pickle* – and Chamcha noted that in their new mood all nine had begun to look alike, rendered equal and identical by their tension and fear. Nor was it long before he understood that the call to the Police National Computer, which had promptly identified him as a British Citizen first class, had not improved his situation, but had placed him, if anything, in greater danger than before.

– We could say, – one of the nine suggested, – that he was lying unconscious on the beach. – Won't work, – came the reply, on account of the old lady and the other geezer. – Then he resisted arrest and turned nasty and in the ensuing altercation he kind of fainted. – Or the old bag was ga-ga, made no sense to any of us, and the other guy wossname never spoke up, and as for this bugger, you only have to clock the bleeder, looks like the very devil, what were we supposed to think? – And then he went and passed out on us, so what could we do, in all fairness, I ask you, your honour, but bring him in to the medical facility at the Detention Centre, for proper care followed by observation and questioning, using our reason-to-believe guidelines; what do you reckon on something of that nature? – It's nine against one, but the old biddy and the second bloke make it a bit of a bastard. – Look, we can fix the tale later, first thing like I keep saying is to get him unconscious. – Right.

Chamcha woke up in a hospital bed with green slime coming up from his lungs. His bones felt as if somebody had put them in the icebox for a long while. He began to cough, and when the fit ended nineteen and a half minutes later he fell back into a shallow, sickly sleep without having taken in any aspect of his present whereabouts. When he surfaced again a friendly woman's face was looking down at him, smiling reassuringly. 'You goin to be fine,' she said, patting him on the shoulder. 'A lickle pneumonia is all you got.' She introduced herself as his physiotherapist, Hyacinth Phillips. And added, 'I never judge a person by appearances. No, sir. Don't you go thinking I do.'

With that, she rolled him over on to his side, placed a small cardboard box by his lips, hitched up her white housecoat, kicked off her shoes, and leaped athletically on to the bed to sit astride him, for all the world as if he were a horse that she meant to ride right through the screens surrounding his bed and out into goodness knew what manner of transmogrified landscape. 'Doctor's orders,' she explained. 'Thirty-minute sessions, twice a day.' Without further preamble, she began pummelling him briskly about the middle body, with lightly clenched, but evidently expert, fists.

For poor Saladin, fresh from his beating in the police van, this new assault was the last straw. He began to struggle beneath her pounding fists, crying loudly, 'Let me out of here; has anybody informed my wife?' The effort of shouting out induced a second coughing spasm that lasted seventeen and three-quarter minutes and earned him a telling off from the physiotherapist, Hyacinth. 'You wastin my time,' she said. 'I should be done with your right lung by now and instead I hardly get started. You go behave or not?' She had remained on the bed, straddling him, bouncing up and down as his body convulsed, like a rodeo rider hanging on for the nine-second bell. He subsided in defeat, and allowed her to beat the green fluid out of his inflamed lungs. When she finished he was obliged to admit that he felt a good deal better. She removed the little box which was now half-full of slime and said cheerily, 'You be standin up firm in no time,' and then, colouring in confusion, apologized, 'Excuse *me*,' and fled without remembering to pull back the encircling screens.

'Time to take stock of the situation,' he told himself. A quick physical examination informed him that his new, mutant condition had remained unchanged. This cast his spirits down, and he realized that he had been half-hoping that the nightmare would have ended while he slept. He was dressed in a new pair of alien pyjamas, this time of an undifferentiated pale green colour, which matched both the fabric of the screens and what he could see of the walls and ceiling of that cryptic and anonymous ward. His legs still ended in those distressing hoofs, and the horns on his head were as sharp as before . . . he was distracted from this morose inventory by a man's voice from nearby, crying out in heart-rending distress: 'Oh, if ever a body suffered . . . !'

'What on earth?' Chamcha thought, and determined to investigate. But now he was becoming aware of many other sounds, as unsettling as the first. It seemed to him that he could hear all sorts of animal noises: the snorting of bulls, the chattering of monkeys, even the pretty-polly mimic-squawks of parrots or talking budgerigars. Then, from another direction, he heard a woman grunting and shrieking, at what sounded like the end of a painful labour; followed by the yowling of a new-born baby. However, the woman's cries did not subside when the baby's began; if anything, they redoubled in their intensity, and perhaps fifteen minutes later Chamcha distinctly heard a second infant's voice joining the first. Still the woman's birth-agony refused to end, and at intervals ranging from fifteen to thirty minutes for what seemed like an endless time she continued to add new babies to the already improbable numbers marching, like conquering armies, from her womb.

His nose informed him that the sanatorium, or whatever the place called itself, was also beginning to stink to the heavens; jungle and farmyard odours mingled with a rich aroma similar to that of exotic spices sizzling in clarified butter – coriander, turmeric, cinnamon, cardamoms, cloves. 'This is too much,' he thought firmly. 'Time to get a few things sorted out.' He swung his legs out of bed, tried to stand up, and promptly fell to the floor, being utterly unaccustomed to his new legs. It took him around an hour to overcome this problem – learning to walk by holding on to the bed and stumbling around it until his confidence grew. At length, and not a little unsteadily, he made his way to the nearest screen; whereupon the face of the immigration officer Stein appeared, Cheshire-Cat-like, between two of the screens to his left, followed rapidly by the rest of the fellow, who drew the screens together behind him with suspicious rapidity.

'Doing all right?' Stein asked, his smile remaining wide.

'When can I see the doctor? When can I go to the toilet? When can I leave?' Chamcha asked in a rush. Stein answered equably: the doctor would be round presently; Nurse Phillips would bring him a bedpan; he could leave as soon as he was well. 'Damn decent of you to come down with the lung thing,' Stein added, with the gratitude of an author whose character had unexpectedly solved a ticklish technical problem. 'Makes the story much more convincing. Seems you were that sick, you did pass out on us after all. Nine of us remember it well. Thanks.' Chamcha could not find any words. 'And another thing,' Stein went on. 'The old burd, Mrs Diamond. Turns out to be dead in her bed, cold as mutton, and the other gentleman vanished clear away. The possibility of foul play has no as yet been eliminated.'

'In conclusion,' he said before disappearing forever from Saladin's new life, 'I suggest, Mr Citizen Saladin, that you dinna trouble with a complaint. You'll forgive me for speaking plain, but with your wee horns and your great hoofs you wouldna look the most reliable of witnesses. Good day to you now.'

Saladin Chamcha closed his eyes and when he opened them his tormentor had turned into the nurse and physiotherapist, Hyacinth Phillips. 'Why you wan go walking?' she asked. 'Whatever your heart desires, you jus ask me, Hyacinth, and we'll see what we can fix.'

'Ssst.'

That night, in the greeny light of the mysterious institution, Saladin was awakened by a hiss out of an Indian bazaar.

'Ssst. You, Beelzebub. Wake up.'

Standing in front of him was a figure so impossible that Chamcha wanted to bury his head under the sheets; yet could not, for was not he himself . . . ? 'That's right,' the creature said. 'You see, you're not alone.'

It had an entirely human body, but its head was that of a ferocious tiger, with three rows of teeth. 'The night guards often doze off,' it explained. 'That's how we manage to get to talk.'

Just then a voice from one of the other beds — each bed, as Chamcha now knew, was protected by its own ring of screens — wailed loudly: 'Oh, if ever a body suffered!' and the man-tiger, or manticore, as it called itself, gave an exasperated growl. 'That Moaner Lisa,' it exclaimed. 'All they did to him was make him blind.'

'Who did what?' Chamcha was confused.

'The point is,' the manticore continued, 'are you going to put up with it?'

Saladin was still puzzled. The other seemed to be suggesting that these mutations were the responsibility of — of whom? How could they be? — 'I don't see,' he ventured, 'who can be blamed . . .'

The manticore ground its three rows of teeth in evident frustration. 'There's a woman over that way,' it said, 'who is now mostly water-buffalo. There are businessmen from Nigeria who have grown sturdy tails. There is a group of holidaymakers from Senegal who were doing no more than changing planes when they were turned into slippery snakes. I myself am in the rag trade; for some years now I have been a highly paid male model, based in Bombay, wearing a wide range of suitings and shirtings also. But who will employ me now?' he burst into sudden and unexpected tears. 'There, there,' said Saladin Chamcha, automatically. 'Everything will be all right, I'm sure of it. Have courage.'

The creature composed itself. 'The point is,' it said fiercely, 'some of us aren't going to stand for it. We're going to bust out of here before they turn us into anything worse. Every night I feel a different piece of me beginning to change. I've started, for example, to break wind continually . . . I beg your pardon . . . you see what I mean? By the way, try these,' he slipped Chamcha a packet of extra-strength peppermints. 'They'll help your breath. I've bribed one of the guards to bring in a supply.'

'But how do they do it?' Chamcha wanted to know.

'They describe us,' the other whispered solemnly. 'That's all. They have the power of description, and we succumb to the pictures they construct.'

'It's hard to believe,' Chamcha argued. 'I've lived here for many years and it never happened before . . .' His words dried up because he saw the manticore looking at him through narrow, distrustful eyes. 'Many years?' it asked. 'How could that be? – Maybe you're an informer? – Yes, that's it, a spy?'

Just then a wail came from a far corner of the ward. 'Lemme go,' a woman's voice howled. 'O Jesus I want to go. Jesus Mary I gotta go, lemme go, O God, O Jesus God.' A very lecherous-looking wolf put its head through Saladin's screens and spoke urgently to the manticore. 'The guards'll be here soon,' it hissed. 'It's her again, Glass Bertha.'

'Glass . . . ?' Saladin began. 'Her skin turned to glass,' the manticore explained impatiently, not knowing that he was bringing Chamcha's worst dream to life. 'And the bastards smashed it up for her. Now she can't even walk to the toilet.'

A new voice hissed out across the greeny night. 'For God's sake, woman. Go in the fucking bedpan.'

The wolf was pulling the manticore away. 'Is he with us or not?' it wanted to know. The manticore shrugged. 'He can't make up his mind,' it answered. 'Can't believe his own eyes, that's his trouble.'

They fled, hearing the approaching crunch of the guards' heavy boots.

The next day there was no sign of a doctor, or of Pamela, and Chamcha in his utter bewilderment woke and slept as if the two conditions no longer required to be thought of as opposites, but as states that flowed into and out of one another to create a kind of unending delirium of the senses . . . he found himself dreaming of the Queen, of making tender love to the Monarch. She was the body of Britain, the avatar of the State, and he had chosen her, joined with her; she was his Beloved, the moon of his delight.

Hyacinth came at the appointed times to ride and pummel him, and he submitted without any fuss. But when she finished she whispered into his ear: 'You in with the rest?' and he understood that she was involved in the great conspiracy, too. 'If you are,' he heard himself saying, 'then you can count me in.' She nodded, looking pleased. Chamcha felt a warmth filling him up, and he began to wonder about taking hold of one of the physiotherapist's exceedingly dainty, albeit powerful, little fists; but just then a shout came from the direction of the blind man: 'My stick, I've lost my stick.'

'Poor old bugger,' said Hyacinth, and hopping off Chamcha she darted across to the sightless fellow, picked up the fallen stick, restored it to its owner, and came back to Saladin. 'Now,' she said. 'I'll see you this pm; okay, no problems?'

He wanted her to stay, but she acted brisk. 'I'm a busy woman, Mr Chamcha. Things to do, people to see.'

When she had gone he lay back and smiled for the first time in a long while. It did not occur to him that his metamorphosis must be continuing, because he was actually entertaining romantic notions about a black woman; and before he had time to think such complex thoughts, the blind man next door began, once again, to speak.

'I have noticed you,' Chamcha heard him say, 'I have noticed you, and come to appreciate your kindness and understanding.' Saladin realized that he was making a formal speech of thanks to the empty space where he clearly believed the physiotherapist was still standing. 'I am not a man who forgets a kindness. One day, perhaps, I may be able to repay it, but for the moment, please know that it is remembered, and fondly, too . . .' Chamcha did not have the courage to call out, *she isn't there, old man, she left some time back*. He listened unhappily until at length the blind man asked the thin air a question: 'I hope, perhaps, you may also remember me? A little? On occasion?' Then came a silence; a dry laugh; the sound of a man sitting down, heavily, all of a sudden. And finally, after an unbearable pause, bathos: 'Oh,' the soliloquist bellowed, 'oh, if ever a body suffered . . . !'

We strive for the heights but our natures betray us, Chamcha thought; clowns in search of crowns. The bitterness overcame him. *Once I was lighter, happier, warm. Now the black water is in my veins*.

Still no Pamela. *What the hell*. That night, he told the manticore and the wolf that he was with them, all the way.

The great escape took place some nights later, when Saladin's lungs had been all but emptied of slime by the ministrations of Miss Hyacinth Phillips. It turned out to be a well-organized affair on a pretty large scale, involving not only the inmates of the sanatorium but also the *detenus*, as the manticore called them, held behind wire fences in the Detention Centre nearby. Not being one of the grand strategists of the escape, Chamcha simply waited by his bed as instructed until Hyacinth brought him word, and then they ran out of that ward of nightmares into the clarity of a cold, moonlit sky, past several bound, gagged men: their former guards. There were many shadowy figures running through the glowing night, and Chamcha glimpsed beings he could never have imagined, men and women who were also partially plants, or giant insects, or even, on occasion, built partly of brick or stone; there were men with rhinoceros horns instead of noses and women with necks as long as any giraffe. The monsters ran quickly, silently, to the edge of the Detention Centre compound, where the manticore and other sharp-toothed mutants were waiting by the large holes they had bitten into the fabric of the containing fence, and then they were out, free, going their separate ways, without hope, but also without shame. Saladin Chamcha and Hyacinth Phillips ran side by side, his goat-hoofs clip-clopping on the hard pavements: *east* she told him, as he heard his own footsteps replace the tinnitus in his ears, east east east they ran, taking the low roads to London town.

4

Jumpy Joshi had become Pamela Chamcha's lover by what she afterwards called 'sheer chance' on the night she learned of her husband's death in the *Bostan* explosion, so that the sound of his old college friend Saladin's voice speaking from beyond the grave in the middle of the night, uttering the five gnomic words *sorry, excuse please, wrong number*, – speaking, moreover, less than two hours after Jumpy and Pamela had made, with the assistance of two bottles of whisky, the two-backed beast, – put him in a tight spot. 'Who was *that*?' Pamela, still mostly asleep, with a blackout mask over her eyes, rolled over to inquire, and he decided to reply, 'Just a breather, don't worry about it,' which was all very well, except then he had to do the worrying all by himself, sitting up in bed, naked, and sucking, for comfort, as he had all his life, the thumb on his right hand.

He was a small person with wire coathanger shoulders and an enormous capacity for nervous agitation, evidenced by his pale, sunken-eyed face; his thinning hair – still entirely black and curly – which had been ruffled so often by his frenzied hands that it no longer took the slightest notice of brushes or combs, but stuck out every which way and gave its owner the perpetual air of having just woken up, late, and in a hurry; and his endearingly high, shy and self-deprecating, but also hiccoughy and over-excited, giggle;

all of which had helped turn his name, Jamshed, into this *Jumpy* that everybody, even first-time acquaintances, now automatically used; everybody, that, is, except Pamela Chamcha. Saladin's wife, he thought, sucking away feverishly. – Or widow? – Or, God help me, wife, after all. He found himself resenting Chamcha. A return from a watery grave: so operatic an event, in this day and age, seemed almost indecent, an act of bad faith.

He had rushed over to Pamela's place the moment he heard the news, and found her dry-eyed and composed. She led him into her clutter-lover's study on whose walls watercolours of rose-gardens hung between clenched-fist posters reading *Partido Socialista*, photographs of friends and a cluster of African masks, and as he picked his way across the floor between ashtrays and the *Voice* newspaper and feminist science-fiction novels she said, flatly, 'The surprising thing is that when they told me I thought, well, shrug, his death will actually make a pretty small hole in my life.' Jumpy, who was close to tears, and bursting with memories, stopped in his tracks and flapped his arms, looking, in his great shapeless black coat, and with his pallid, terror-stricken face, like a vampire caught in the unexpected and hideous light of day. Then he saw the empty whisky bottles. Pamela had started drinking, she said, some hours back, and since then she had been going at it steadily, rhythmically, with the dedication of a long-distance runner. He sat down beside her on her low, squashy sofa-bed, and offered to act as a pacemaker. 'Whatever you want,' she said, and passed him the bottle.

Now, sitting up in bed with a thumb instead of a bottle, his secret and his hangover banging equally painfully inside his head (he had never been a drinking or a secretive man), Jumpy felt tears coming on once again, and decided to get up and walk himself around. Where he went was upstairs, to what Saladin had insisted on calling his 'den', a large loft-space with skylights and windows looking down on an expanse of communal gardens dotted with comfortable trees, oak, larch, even the last of the elms, a survivor of the plague years. *First the elms, now us,* Jumpy reflected. *Maybe the trees were a warning.* He shook himself to banish such small-hour morbidities, and perched on the edge of his friend's mahogany desk. Once at a college party he had perched, just so, on a table soggy with spilled wine and beer next to an emaciated girl in black lace minidress, purple feather boa and eyelids like silver helmets, unable to pluck up the courage to say hello. Finally he did turn to her and stutter out some banality or other; she gave him a look of absolute contempt and said without moving her black-lacquer lips, *conversation's dead, man.* He had been pretty upset, so upset that he blurted out, *tell me, why are all the girls in this town so rude?,* and she answered, without pausing to think, *because most of the boys are like you.* A few moments later Chamcha came up, reeking of patchouli, wearing a white kurta, everybody's god-damn cartoon of the mysteries of the East, and the girl left with him five minutes later. The bastard, Jumpy Joshi thought as the old bitterness surged back, he had no shame, he was ready to be anything they wanted to buy, that read-your-palm bedspread-jacket Hare-Krishna dharma-bum, you wouldn't have caught me dead. That stopped him, that word right there. Dead. Face it, Jamshed, the girls never went for you, that's the truth, and the rest is envy. Well, maybe so, he half-conceded, and then again. Maybe dead, he added, and then again, maybe not.

Chamcha's room struck the sleepless intruder as contrived, and therefore sad: the caricature of an actor's room full of signed photographs of colleagues, handbills, framed programmes, pro-duction stills, citations, awards, volumes of movie-star memoirs, a room bought off the peg, by the yard, an imitation of life, a mask's mask. Novelty items on every surface: ashtrays in the shape of pianos, china pierrots peeping out from behind a shelf of books. And everywhere, on the walls, in the movie posters, in the glow of the lamp borne by bronze Eros, in the mirror shaped like a heart, oozing up through the blood-red carpet, dripping from the ceiling, Saladin's need for love. In the theatre everybody gets kissed and everybody is darling. The actor's life offers, on a daily basis, the simulacrum of love; a mask can be satisfied, or at least consoled, by the echo of what it seeks. The desperation there was in him, Jumpy recognized, he'd do anything, put on any damn-fool costume, change into any shape, if it earned him a loving word. Saladin, who wasn't by any means unsuccessful with women, see above. The poor stumblebum. Even Pamela, with all her beauty and brightness, hadn't been enough.

It was clear he'd been getting to be a long way from enough for her. Somewhere around the bottom of the second whisky bottle she leaned her head on his shoulder and said boozily, 'You can't imagine the relief of being with someone with whom I don't have to have a fight every time I express an opinion. Someone on the side of the goddamn angels.' He waited; after a pause, there was more. 'Him and his Royal Family, you wouldn't believe. Cricket, the Houses of Parliament, the Queen. The place never stopped being a picture postcard to him. You couldn't get him to look at what was really real.' She closed her eyes and allowed her hand, by accident, to rest on his. 'He was a real Saladin,' Jumpy said. 'A man with a holy land to conquer, his England, the one he believed in. You were part of it, too.' She rolled away from him and stretched out on top of magazines, crumpled balls of waste paper, mess. 'Part of it? I was bloody Britannia. Warm beer, mince pies, common-sense and me. But I'm really real, too, J.J.; I really am.' She reached over to him, pulled him across to where her mouth was waiting, kissed him with a great un-Pamela-like slurp. 'See what I mean?' Yes, he saw.

'You should have heard him on the Falklands war,' she said later, disengaging herself and fiddling with her hair. ' "Pamela, suppose you heard a noise downstairs in the middle of the night and went to investigate and found a huge man in the living-room with a shotgun, and he said, Go back upstairs, what would you do?" I'd go upstairs, I said. "Well, it's like that. Intruders in the home. It won't do." ' Jumpy noticed her fists had clenched and her knuckles were bone-white. 'I said, if you must use these blasted cosy metaphors, then get them right. What's it *like* is if two people claim they own a house, and one of them is squatting the place, and *then* the other turns up with the shotgun. That's what it's *like*.' 'That's what's really real,' Jumpy nodded, seriously. 'Right,' she slapped his knee. 'That's really right, Mr Real Jam . . . it's really like that. Actually. Another drink.'

She leaned over to the tape deck and pushed a button. Jesus, Jumpy thought, *Boney M?* Give me a break. For all her tough, race-professional attitudes, the lady still had a lot to learn about music. Here it came, boomchickaboom. Then, without warning, he was crying, provoked into real tears by counterfeit emotion, by a disco-beat imitation of pain. It was the one hundred and thirty-seventh psalm, 'Super flumina'. King David calling out across the centuries. How shall we sing the Lord's song in a strange land.

'I had to learn the psalms at school,' Pamela Chamcha said, sitting on the floor, her head leaning against the sofa-bed, her eyes shut tight. *By the river of Babylon, where we sat down, oh oh we wept . . .* she stopped the tape, leaned back again, began to recite. 'If I forget thee, O Jerusalem, let my right hand forget its cunning; if I do not remember thee, let my tongue cleave to the roof of my mouth; yea, if I prefer not Jerusalem in my mirth.'

Later, asleep in bed, she dreamed of her convent school, of matins and evensong, of the chanting of psalms, when Jumpy rushed in and shook her awake, shouting, 'It's no good, I've got to tell you. He isn't dead. Saladin: he's bloody well alive.'

She came wide awake at once, plunging her hands into her thick, curly, hennaed hair, in which the first strands of white were just beginning to be noticeable; she knelt on the bed, naked, with her hands in her hair, unable to move, until Jumpy had finished speaking, and then, without warning, she began to hit out at him, punching him on the chest and arms and shoulders and even his face, as hard as she could hit. He sat down on the bed beside her, looking ridiculous in her frilly dressing-gown, while she beat him; he allowed his body to go loose, to receive the blows, to submit. When she ran out of punches her body was covered in perspiration and he thought she might have broken one of his arms. She sat down beside him, panting, and they were silent.

Her dog entered the bedroom, looking worried, and padded over to offer her his paw, and to lick at her left leg. Jumpy stirred, cautiously. 'I thought he got stolen,' he said eventually. Pamela jerked her head for *yes, but.* 'The thieves got in touch. I paid the ransom. He now answers to the name of Glenn. That's okay; I could never pronounce Sher Khan properly, anyway.'

After a while, Jumpy found that he wanted to talk. 'What you did, just now,' he began.

'Oh, God.'

'No. It's like a thing I once did. Maybe the most sensible thing I ever did.' In the summer of 1967, he had bullied the 'apolitical' twenty-year-old Saladin along on an anti-war demonstration. 'Once in your life, Mister Snoot, I'm going to drag you down to my level.' Harold Wilson was coming to town, and because of the Labour Government's support of US involvement in Vietnam, a mass protest had been planned. Chamcha went along, 'out of curiosity,' he said. 'I want to see how allegedly intelligent people turn themselves into a mob.'

That day it rained an ocean. The demonstrators in Market Square were soaked through. Jumpy and Chamcha, swept along by the crowd, found themselves pushed up against the steps of the town hall; *grandstand view*, Chamcha said with heavy irony. Next to them stood two students disguised as Russian assassins, in black fedoras, greatcoats and dark glasses, carrying shoeboxes filled with ink-dipped tomatoes and labelled in large block letters, *bombs*. Shortly before the Prime Minister's arrival, one of them tapped a policeman on the shoulder and said: 'Excuse, please. When Mr Wilson, self-styled Prime Meenster, comes in long car, kindly request to wind down weendow so my friend can throw with him the bombs. The policeman answered, 'Ho, ho, sir. Very good. Now I'll tell you what. You can throw eggs at him, sir, 'cause that's all right with me. And you can throw tomatoes at him, sir, like what you've got there in that box, painted black, labelled *bombs*, 'cause that's all right with me. You throw anything hard at him, sir, and my mate here'll get you with his gun.' O days of innocence when the world was young . . . when the car arrived there was a surge in the crowd and Chamcha and Jumpy were separated. Then Jumpy appeared, climbed on to the bonnet of Harold Wilson's limousine, and began to jump up and down on the bonnet, creating large dents, leaping like a wild man to the rhythm of the crowd's chanting: *We shall fight, we shall win, long live Ho Chi Minh.*

'Saladin started yelling at me to get off, partly because the crowd was full of Special Branch types converging on the limo, but mainly because he was so damn embarrassed.' But he kept leaping, up higher and down harder, drenched to the bone, long hair flying: Jumpy the jumper, leaping into the mythology of those antique years. And Wilson and Marcia cowered in the back seat. *Ho! Ho! Ho Chi Minh!* At the last possible moment Jumpy took a deep breath, and dived head-first into a sea of wet and friendly faces; and vanished. They never caught him: fuzz pigs filth. 'Saladin wouldn't speak to me for over a week,' Jumpy remembered. 'And when he did, all he said was, "I hope you realize those cops could have shot you to pieces, but they didn't."'

They were still sitting side by side on the edge of the bed. Jumpy touched Pamela on the forearm. 'I just mean I know how it feels. Wham, bam. It felt incredible. It felt necessary.'

'Oh, my God,' she said, turning to him. 'Oh, my God, I'm sorry, but yes, it did.'

In the morning it took an hour to get through to the airline on account of the volume of calls still being generated by the catastrophe, and then another twenty-five minutes of insistence – *but he telephoned, it was his voice* – while at the other end of the phone a woman's voice, professionally trained to deal with human beings in crisis, understood how she felt and sympathized with her in this awful moment and remained very patient, but clearly didn't believe a word she said. *I'm sorry, madam, I don't mean to be brutal, but the plane broke up in mid-air at thirty thousand feet.* By the end of the call Pamela Chamcha, normally the most controlled of women, who locked herself in a bathroom when she wanted to cry, was shrieking down the line, for God's sake, woman, will you shut up with your little good-samaritan speeches and listen to what I'm saying? Finally she slammed down the receiver and rounded on Jumpy Joshi, who saw the expression in her eyes and spilled the coffee he had been bringing her because his limbs began to tremble in fright. 'You fucking creep,' she cursed him. "Still alive, is he? I suppose he flew down from the sky on fucking *wings* and headed straight for the nearest phone booth to change out of his fucking Superman costume and ring the little wife.' They were in the kitchen and Jumpy noticed a group of kitchen knives attached to a magnetic strip on the wall next to Pamela's left arm. He opened his mouth to speak, but she wouldn't let him. 'Get out before I do something,' she said. 'I can't believe I fell for it. You and voices on the phone: I should have fucking known.'

In the early 1970s Jumpy had run a travelling disco out of the back of his yellow mini-van. He called it Finn's Thumb in honour of the legendary sleeping giant of Ireland, Finn MacCool, another sucker, as Chamcha used to say. One day Saladin had played a practical joke on Jumpy, by ringing him up, putting on a vaguely Mediterranean accent, and requesting the services of the musical Thumb on the island of Skorpios, on behalf of Mrs Jacqueline Kennedy Onassis, offering a fee of ten thousand dollars and transportation to Greece, in a private aircraft, for up to six persons. This was a terrible thing to do to a man as innocent and upright as Jamshed Joshi. 'I need an hour to think,' he had said, and then fallen into an agony of the soul. When Saladin rang back an hour later and heard that Jumpy was turning down Mrs Onassis's offer for political reasons, he understood that his friend was in training to be a saint, and it was no good trying to pull his leg. 'Mrs Onassis will be broken in the heart for sure,' he had concluded, and Jumpy had worriedly replied, 'Please tell her it's nothing personal, as a matter of fact personally I admire her a great deal.'

We have all known one another too long, Pamela thought as Jumpy left. We can hurt each other with memories two decades old.

❧

On the subject of mistakes with voices, she thought as she drove much too fast down the M4 that afternoon in the old MG hardtop from which she got a degree of pleasure that was, as she had always cheerfully confessed, 'quite ideologically unsound', – on that subject, I really ought to be more charitable.

Pamela Chamcha, née Lovelace, was the possessor of a voice for which, in many ways, the rest of her life had been an effort to compensate. It was a voice composed of tweeds, headscarves, summer pudding, hockey-sticks, thatched houses, saddle-soap, house-parties, nuns, family pews, large dogs and philistinism, and in spite of all her attempts to reduce its volume it was loud as a dinner-jacketed drunk throwing bread rolls in a Club. It had been the tragedy of her younger days that thanks to this voice she had been endlessly pursued by the gentlemen farmers and debs' delights and somethings in the city whom she despised with all her heart, while the greenies and peacemarchers and world-changers with whom she instinctively felt at home treated her with deep suspicion, bordering on resentment. How could one be *on the side of the angels* when one sounded like a no-goodnik every time one moved one's lips? Accelerating past Reading, Pamela gritted her teeth. One of the reasons she had decided to *admit it* end her marriage before fate did it for her was that she had woken up one day and realized that Chamcha was not in love with her at all, but with that voice stinking of Yorkshire pudding and hearts of oak, that hearty, rubicund voice of ye olde dream-England which he so desperately wanted to inhabit. It had been a marriage of crossed purposes, each of them rushing towards the very thing from which the other was in flight.

No survivors. And in the middle of the night, Jumpy the idiot and his stupid false alarm. She was so shaken up by it that she hadn't even got round to being shaken up by having gone to bed with Jumpy and made love in what *admit it* had been a pretty satisfying fashion, *spare me your nonchalance,* she rebuked herself, *when did you last have so much fun.* She had a lot to deal with and so here she was, dealing with it by running away as fast as she could go. A few days of pampering oneself in an expensive country hotel and the world may begin to seem less like a fucking hellhole. Therapy by luxury: okayokay, she allowed, I know: I'm *reverting to class*. Fuck it; watch me go. If you've got any objections, blow them out of your ass. Arse. Ass.

One hundred miles an hour past Swindon, and the weather turned nasty. Sudden, dark clouds, lightning, heavy rain; she kept her foot on the accelerator. *No survivors*. People were always dying on her, leaving her with a mouth full of words and nobody to spit them at. Her father the classical scholar who could make puns in ancient Greek and from whom she inherited the Voice, her legacy and curse; and her mother who pined for him during the War, when he was a Pathfinder pilot, obliged to fly home from Germany one hundred and eleven times in a slow aeroplane through a night which his own flares had just illuminated for the benefit of the bombers, – and who vowed, when he returned with the noise of the ack-ack in his ears, that she would never leave him, – and so followed him everywhere, into the slow hollow of depression from which he never really emerged, – and into debt, because he didn't have the face for poker and used her money when he ran out of his own, – and at last to the top of a tall building, where they found their way at last. Pamela never forgave them, especially for making it impossible for her to tell them of her unforgiveness. To get her own back, she set about rejecting everything of them that remained within her. Her brains, for example: she refused to go to college. And because she could not shake off her voice, she made it speak ideas which her conservative suicides of parents would have anathematized. She married an Indian. And, because he turned out to be too much like them, would have left him. Had decided to leave. When, once again, she was cheated by a death.

She was overtaking a frozen-food road train, blinded by the spray kicked up by its wheels, when she hit the expanse of water that had been waiting for her in a slight declivity, and then the MG was aquaplaning at terrifying speed, swerving out of the fast lane and spinning round so that she saw the headlights of the road train staring at her like the eyes of the exterminating angel, Azrael. 'Curtains,' she thought; but her car swung and skidded out of the path of the juggernaut, slewing right across all three lanes of the motorway, all of them miraculously empty, and coming to rest with rather less of a thump than one might have expected against the crash barrier at the edge of the hard shoulder, after spinning through a further one hundred and eighty degrees to face, once again, into the west, where with all the corny timing of real life, the sun was breaking up the storm.

The fact of being alive compensated for what life did to one. That night, in an oak-panelled dining-room decorated with medieval flags, Pamela Chamcha in her most dazzling gown ate venison and drank a bottle of Château Talbot at a table heavy with silver and crystal, celebrating a new beginning, an escape from the jaws of, a fresh start, to be born again first you have to: well, almost, anyway. Under the lascivious eyes of Americans and salesmen she ate and drank alone, retiring early to a princess's bedroom in a stone tower to take a long bath and watch old movies on television. In the aftermath of her brush with death she felt the past dropping away from her: her adolescence, for example, in the care of her wicked uncle Harry Higham, who lived in a seventeenth-century manor house once owned by a distant relative, Matthew Hopkins, the Witchfinder-General, who had named it *Gremlins* in, no doubt, a macabre attempt at humour. Remembering Mr Justice Higham in order to forget him, she murmured to the absent Jumpy that she, too, had her Vietnam story. After the first big Grosvenor Square demonstration at which many people threw marbles under the feet of charging police horses, there occurred the one and only instance in British law in which the marble was deemed to be a lethal weapon, and young persons were jailed, even deported, for possessing the small glass spheres. The presiding judge in the case of the Grosvenor Marbles was this same Henry (thereafter known as 'Hang'em') Higham, and to be his

niece had been a further burden for a young woman already
weighed down by her right-wing voice. Now, warm in bed in
her temporary castle, Pamela Chamcha rid herself of this old
demon, *goodbye, Hang'em, I've no more time for you*; and of her
parents' ghosts; and prepared to be free of the most recent ghost
of all.

Sipping cognac, Pamela watched vampires on TV and allowed
herself to take pleasure in, well, in herself. Had she not invented
herself in her own image? I am that I am, she toasted herself in
Napoleon brandy. I work in a community relations council in the
borough of Brickhall, London, NEI; deputy community relations
officer and damn good at it, ifisaysomyself. Cheers! We just
elected our first black Chair and all the votes cast against him were
white. Down the hatch! Last week a respected Asian street trader,
for whom MPs of all parties had interceded, was deported after
eighteen years in Britain because, fifteen years ago, he posted a
certain form forty-eight hours late. Chin-chin! Next week in
Brickhall Magistrates' Court the police will be trying to fit up a
fifty-year-old Nigerian woman, accusing her of assault, having
previously beaten her senseless. Skol! This is my head: see it?
What I call my job: bashing my head against Brickhall.

Saladin was dead and she was alive.

She drank to that. There were things I was waiting to tell you,
Saladin. Some big things: about the new high-rise office building
in Brickhall High Street, across from McDonald's; – they built it
to be perfectly sound-proof, but the workers were so disturbed by
the silence that now they play tapes of white noise on the tannoy
system. – You'd have liked that, eh? – And about this Parsi
woman I know, Bapsy, that's her name, she lived in Germany for
a while and fell in love with a Turk. – Trouble was, the only language they had in common was German; now Bapsy has forgotten
almost all she knew, while his gets better and better; he writes her
increasingly poetic letters and she can hardly reply in nursery
rhyme. – Love dying, because of an inequality of language, what
do you think of that? – Love dying. There's a subject for us, eh?
Saladin? What do you say?

And a couple of tiny little things. There's a killer on the loose in my patch, specializes in killing old women; so don't worry, I'm safe. Plenty older than me.

One more thing: I'm leaving you. It's over. We're through.

I could never say anything to you, not really, not the least thing. If I said you were putting on weight you'd yell for an hour, as if it would change what you saw in the mirror, what the tightness of your own trousers was telling you. You interrupted me in public. People noticed it, what you thought of me. I forgave you, that was my fault; I could see the centre of you, that question so frightful that you had to protect it with all that posturing certainty. That empty space.

Goodbye, Saladin. She drained her glass and set it down beside her. The returning rain knocked at her leaded windows; she drew her curtains shut and turned out the light.

Lying there, drifting towards sleep, she thought of the last thing she needed to tell her late husband. 'In bed,' the words came, 'you never seemed interested in me; not in my pleasure, what I needed, not really ever. I came to think you wanted, not a lover. A servant.' There. Now rest in peace.

She dreamed of him, his face, filling the dream. 'Things are ending,' he told her. 'This civilization; things are closing in on it. It has been quite a culture, brilliant and foul, cannibal and Christian, the glory of the world. We should celebrate it while we can; until night falls.'

She didn't agree, not even in the dream, but she knew, as she dreamed, that there was no point telling him now.

After Pamela Chamcha threw him out, Jumpy Joshi went over to Mr Sufyan's Shaandaar Café in Brickhall High Street and sat there trying to decide if he was a fool. It was early in the day, so the place was almost empty, apart from a fat lady buying a box of pista barfi and jalebis, a couple of bachelor garment workers drinking chaloo chai and an elderly Polish woman from the old days when it was the Jews who ran the sweatshops round here, who sat all day in a corner with two vegetable samosas, one puri and a glass of milk, announcing to everyone who came in that she was only there because 'it was next best to kosher and today you must do the best you can'. Jumpy sat down with his coffee beneath the lurid painting of a bare-breasted myth-woman with several heads and wisps of clouds obscuring her nipples, done life-size in salmon pink, neon-green and gold, and because the rush hadn't started yet Mr Sufyan noticed he was down in the dumps.

'Hey, Saint Jumpy,' he sang out, 'why you bringing your bad weather into my place? This country isn't full enough of clouds?'

Jumpy blushed as Sufyan bounced over to him, his little white cap of devotion pinned in place as usual, the moustache-less beard hennaed red after its owner's recent pilgrimage to Mecca. Muhammad Sufyan was a burly, thick-forearmed fellow with a belly on him, as godly and as unfanatic a believer as you could meet, and Joshi thought of him as a sort of elder relative. 'Listen, Uncle,' he said when the café proprietor was standing over him, 'you think I'm a real idiot or what?'

'You ever make any money?' Sufyan asked.

'Not me, Uncle.'

'Ever do any business? Import-export? Off-licence? Corner shop?'

'I never understood figures.'

'And where your family members are?'

'I've got no family, Uncle. There's only me.'

'Then you must be praying to God continually for guidance in your loneliness?'

'You know me, Uncle. I don't pray.'

'No question about it,' Sufyan concluded. 'You're an even bigger fool than you know.'

'Thanks, Uncle,' Jumpy said, finishing his coffee. 'You've been a great help.'

Sufyan, knowing that the affection in his teasing was cheering the other man up in spite of his long face, called across to the light-skinned, blue-eyed Asian man who had just come in wearing a snappy check overcoat with extra-wide lapels. 'You,

Hanif Johnson,' he called out, 'come here and solve a mystery.' Johnson, a smart lawyer and local boy made good, who maintained an office above the Shaandaar Café, tore himself away from Sufyan's two beautiful daughters and headed over to Jumpy's table. 'You explain this fellow,' Sufyan said. 'Beats me. Doesn't drink, thinks of money like a disease, owns maybe two shirts and no VCR, forty years old and isn't married, works for two pice in the sports centre teaching martial arts and what-all, lives on air, behaves like a rishi or pir but doesn't have any faith, going nowhere but looks like he knows some secret. All this and a college education, you work it out.'

Hanif Johnson punched Jumpy on the shoulder. 'He hears voices,' he said. Sufyan threw up his hands in mock amazement. 'Voices, oop-baba! Voices from where? Telephone? Sky? Sony Walkman hidden in his coat?'

'Inner voices,' Hanif said solemnly. 'Upstairs on his desk there's a piece of paper with some verses written on it. And a title: *The River of Blood.*'

Jumpy jumped, knocking over his empty cup. 'I'll kill you,' he shouted at Hanif, who skipped quickly across the room, singing out, 'We got a poet in our midst, Sufyan Sahib. Treat with respect. Handle with care. He says a street is a river and we are the flow; humanity is a river of blood, that's the poet's point. Also the individual human being,' he broke off to run around to the far side of an eight-seater table as Jumpy came after him, blushing furiously, flapping his arms. 'In our very bodies, does the river of blood not flow?' *Like the Roman,* the ferrety Enoch Powell had said, *I seem to see the river Tiber foaming with much blood.* Reclaim the metaphor, Jumpy Joshi had told himself. Turn it; make it a thing we can use. 'This is like rape,' he pleaded with Hanif. 'For God's sake, stop.'

'Voices that one hears are outside, but,' the café proprietor was musing. 'Joan of Arc, na. Or that what's his name with the cat: Turn-again Whittington. But with such voices one becomes great, or rich at least. This one however is not great, and poor.'

'Enough.' Jumpy held both arms above his head, grinning without really wanting to. 'I surrender.'

For three days after that, in spite of all the efforts of Mr Sufyan, Mrs Sufyan, their daughters Mishal and Anahita, and the lawyer Hanif Johnson, Jumpy Joshi was not really himself, 'More a Dumpy than a Jumpy,' as Sufyan said. He went about his business, at the youth clubs, at the offices of the film co-operative to which he belonged, and in the streets, distributing leaflets, selling certain newspapers, hanging out; but his step was heavy as he went his way. Then, on the fourth evening, the telephone rang behind the counter of the Shaandaar Café.

'Mr Jamshed Joshi,' Anahita Sufyan carolled, doing her imitation of an upper-class English accent. 'Will Mr Joshi please come to the instrument? There is a personal call.'

Her father took one look at the joy bursting out on Jumpy's face and murmured softly to his wife, 'Mrs, the voice this boy is wanting to hear is not inner by any manner of means.'

The impossible thing came between Pamela and Jamshed after they had spent seven days making love to one another with inexhaustible enthusiasm, infinite tenderness and such freshness of spirit that you'd have thought the procedure had only just been invented. For seven days they remained undressed with the central heating turned high, and pretended to be tropical lovers in some hot bright country to the south. Jamshed, who had always been clumsy with women, told Pamela that he had not felt so wonderful since the day in his eighteenth year when he had finally learned how to ride a bicycle. The moment the words were out he became afraid that he had spoiled everything, that this comparison of the great love of his life to the rickety bike of his student days would be taken for the insult it undeniably was; but he needn't have worried, because Pamela kissed him on the mouth and thanked him for saying the most beautiful thing any man had ever said to any woman. At this point he understood that he could do no wrong, and for the first time in his life he began to feel genuinely safe, safe as houses, safe as a human being who is loved; and so did Pamela Chamcha.

On the seventh night they were awakened from dreamless sleep by the unmistakable sound of somebody trying to break into the house. 'I've got a hockey-stick under my bed,' Pamela whispered, terrified. 'Give it to me,' Jumpy, who was equally scared, hissed back. 'I'm coming with you,' quaked Pamela, and Jumpy quavered, 'Oh, no you don't.' In the end they both crept downstairs, each wearing one of Pamela's frilly dressing-gowns, each with a hand on the hockey-stick that neither felt brave enough to use. Suppose it's a man with a shotgun, Pamela found herself thinking, a man with a shotgun saying, Go back upstairs . . . They reached the foot of the stairs. Somebody turned on the lights.

Pamela and Jumpy screamed in unison, dropped the hockey-stick and ran upstairs as fast as they could go; while down in the front hall, standing brightly illuminated by the front door with the glass panel it had smashed in order to turn the knob of the tongue-and-groove lock (Pamela in the throes of her passion had forgotten to use the security locks), was a figure out of a nightmare or a late-night TV movie, a figure covered in mud and ice and blood, the hairiest creature you ever saw, with the shanks and hoofs of a giant goat, a man's torso covered in goat's hair, human arms, and a horned but otherwise human head covered in muck and grime and the beginnings of a beard. Alone and unobserved, the impossible thing pitched forward on to the floor and lay still.

Upstairs, at the very top of the house, that is to say in Saladin's 'den', Mrs Pamela Chamcha was writhing in her lover's arms, crying her heart out, and bawling at the top of her voice: 'It isn't true. My husband exploded. No survivors. Do you hear me? I am the widow Chamcha whose spouse is beastly dead.'

5

M r Gibreel Farishta on the railway train to London was once
again seized as who would not be by the fear that God had
decided to punish him for his loss of faith by driving him insane.
He had seated himself by the window in a first-class non-smoking
compartment, with his back to the engine because unfortunately
another fellow was already in the other place, and jamming his
trilby down on his head he sat with his fists deep in scarlet-lined
gabardine and panicked. The terror of losing his mind to a
paradox, of being unmade by what he no longer believed existed,
of turning in his madness into the avatar of a chimerical archangel,
was so big in him that it was impossible to look at it for long; yet
how else was he to account for the miracles, metamorphoses and
apparitions of recent days? 'It's a straight choice,' he trembled
silently. 'It's A, I'm off my head, or B, baba, somebody went and
changed the rules.'

Now, however, there had the comforting cocoon of this
railway compartment in which the miraculous was reassuringly
absent, the arm-rests were frayed, the reading light over his
shoulder didn't work, the mirror was missing from its frame, and
then there were the regulations: the little circular red-and-white
signs forbidding smoking, the stickers penalizing the improper use
of the chain, the arrows indicating the points to which – and not

beyond! – it was permitted to open the little sliding windows. Gibreel paid a visit to the toilet and here, too, a small series of prohibitions and instructions gladdened his heart. By the time the conductor arrived with the authority of his crescent-cutting ticket-punch, Gibreel had been somewhat soothed by these manifestations of law, and began to perk up and invent rationalizations. He had had a lucky escape from death, a subsequent delirium of some sort, and now, restored to himself, could expect the threads of his old life – that is, his old new life, the new life he had planned before the er interruption – to be picked up again. As the train carried him further and further away from the twilight zone of his arrival and subsequent mysterious captivity, bearing him along the happy predictability of parallel metal lines, he felt the pull of the great city beginning to work its magic on him, and his old gift of hope reasserted itself, his talent for embracing renewal, for blinding himself to past hardships so that the future could come into view. He sprang up from his seat and thumped down on the opposite side of the compartment, with his face symbolically towards London, even though it meant giving up the window. What did he care for windows? All the London he wanted was right there, in his mind's eye. He spoke her name aloud: 'Alleluia.'

'Alleluia, brother,' the compartment's only other occupant affirmed. 'Hosanna, my good sir, and amen.'

'Although I must add, sir, that my beliefs are strictly non-denominational,' the stranger continued. 'Had you said "La-ilaha", I would gladly have responded with a full-throated "illallah".'

Gibreel realized that his move across the compartment and his inadvertent taking of Allie's unusual name had been mistaken by his companion for overtures both social and theological. 'John Maslama,' the fellow cried, snapping a card out of a little crocodile-skin case and pressing it upon Gibreel. 'Personally, I follow my own variant of the universal faith invented by the Emperor Akbar. God, I would say, is something akin to the Music of the Spheres.'

It was plain that Mr Maslama was bursting with words, and that, now that he had popped, there was nothing for it but to sit it out, to permit the torrent to run its orotund course. As the fellow had the build of a prize-fighter, it seemed inadvisable to irritate him. In his eyes Farishta spotted the glint of the True Believer, a light which, until recently, he had seen in his own shaving-mirror every day.

'I have done well for myself, sir,' Maslama was boasting in his well-modulated Oxford drawl. 'For a brown man, exceptionally well, considering the quiddity of the circumstances in which we live; as I hope you will allow.' With a small but eloquent sweep of his thick ham of a hand, he indicated the opulence of his attire: the bespoke tailoring of his three-piece pin-stripe, the gold watch with its fob and chain, the Italian shoes, the crested silk tie, the jewelled links at his starched white cuffs. Above this costume of an English milord there stood a head of startling size, covered with thick, slicked-down hair, and sprouting implausibly luxuriant eyebrows beneath which blazed the ferocious eyes of which Gibreel had already taken careful note. 'Pretty fancy,' Gibreel now conceded, some response being clearly required. Maslama nodded. 'I have always tended,' he admitted, 'towards the ornate.'

He had made what he called his *first pile* producing advertising jingles, 'that ol' devil music', leading women into lingerie and lipgloss and men into temptation. Now he owned record stores all over town, a successful nightclub called Hot Wax, and a store full of gleaming musical instruments that was his special pride and joy. He was an Indian from Guyana, 'but there's nothing left in that place, sir. People are leaving it faster than planes can fly.' He had made good in quick time, 'by the grace of God Almighty. I'm a regular Sunday man, sir; I confess to a weakness for the English Hymnal, and I sing to raise the roof.'

The autobiography was concluded with a brief mention of the existence of a wife and some dozen children. Gibreel offered his congratulations and hoped for silence, but now Maslama dropped his bombshell. 'You don't need to tell me about yourself,' he said jovially. 'Naturally I know who you are, even if one does not

expect to see such a personage on the Eastbourne–Victoria line.'
He winked leeringly and placed a finger alongside his nose.
'Mum's the word. I respect a man's privacy, no question about it;
no question at all.'

'I? Who am I?' Gibreel was startled into absurdity. The other
nodded weightily, his eyebrows waving like soft antlers. 'The
prize question, in my opinion. These are problematic times, sir,
for a moral man. When a man is unsure of his essence, how may
he know if he be good or bad? But you are finding me tedious. I
answer my own questions by my faith in It, sir,' – here Maslama
pointed to the ceiling of the railway compartment – 'and of course
you are not in the least confused about your identity, for you are
the famous, the may I say legendary Mr Gibreel Farishta, star of
screen and, increasingly, I'm sorry to add, of pirate video; my
twelve children, one wife and I are all long-standing, unreserved
admirers of your divine heroics.' He grabbed, and pumped
Gibreel's right hand.

'Tending as I do towards the pantheistic view,' Maslama thundered on, 'my own sympathy for your work arises out of your
willingness to portray deities of every conceivable water. You,
sire, are a rainbow coalition of the celestial; a walking United
Nations of gods! You are, in short, the future. Permit me to salute
you.' He was beginning to give off the unmistakable odour of the
genuine crazy, and even though he had not yet said or done anything beyond the merely idiosyncratic, Gibreel was getting
alarmed and measuring the distance to the door with anxious little
glances. 'I incline, sir,' Maslama was saying, 'towards the opinion
that whatever name one calls It by is no more than a code; a
cypher, Mr Farishta, behind which the true name lies concealed.'

Gibreel remained silent, and Maslama, making no attempt to
hide his disappointment, was obliged to speak for him. 'What is
that true name, I hear you inquire,' he said, and then Gibreel
knew he was right; the man was a full-fledged lunatic, and his
autobiography was very likely as much of a concoction as his
'faith'. Fictions were walking around wherever he went, Gibreel
reflected, fictions masquerading as real human beings. 'I have

brought him upon me,' he accused himself. 'By fearing for my own sanity I have brought forth, from God knows what dark recess, this voluble and maybe dangerous nut.'

'You don't know it!' Maslama yelled suddenly, jumping to his feet. 'Charlatan! Poser! Fake! You claim to be the screen immortal, avatar of a hundred and one gods, and you haven't a *foggy*! How is it possible that I, a poor boy made good from Bartica on the Essequibo, can know such things while Gibreel Farishta does not? Phoney! Phooey to you!'

Gibreel got to his feet, but the other was filling almost all the available standing room, and he, Gibreel, had to lean over awkwardly to one side to escape Maslama's windmilling arms, one of which knocked off his grey trilby. At once Maslama's mouth fell open. He seemed to shrink several inches, and after a few frozen moments, he fell to his knees with a thud.

What's he doing down there, Gibreel wondered, picking up my hat? But the madman was begging for forgiveness. 'I never doubted you would come,' he was saying. 'Pardon my clumsy rage.' The train entered a tunnel, and Gibreel saw that they were surrounded by a warm golden light that was coming from a point just behind his head. In the glass of the sliding door, he saw the reflection of the halo around his hair.

Maslama was struggling with his shoelaces. 'All my life, sir, I knew I had been chosen,' he was saying in a voice as humble as it had earlier been menacing. 'Even as a child in Bartica, I knew.' He pulled off his right shoe and began to roll down his sock. 'I was given,' he said, 'a sign.' The sock was removed, revealing what looked to be a perfectly ordinary, if outsize, foot. Then Gibreel counted and counted again, from one to six. 'The same on the other foot,' Maslama said proudly. 'I never doubted the meaning for a minute.' He was the self-appointed helpmate of the Lord, the sixth toe on the foot of the Universal Thing. Something was badly amiss with the spiritual life of the planet, thought Gibreel Farishta. Too many demons inside people claiming to believe in God.

The train emerged from the tunnel. Gibreel took a decision.

'Stand, six-toed John,' he intoned in his best Hindi movie manner. 'Maslama, arise.'

The other scrambled to his feet and stood pulling at his fingers, his head bowed. 'What I want to know, sir,' he mumbled, 'is, which is it to be? Annihilation or salvation? Why have you returned?'

Gibreel thought rapidly. 'It is for judging,' he finally answered. 'Facts in the case must be sifted, due weight given pro and contra. Here it is the human race that is the undertrial, and it is a defendant with a rotten record: a history-sheeter, a bad egg. Careful evaluations must be made. For the present, verdict is reserved; will be promulgated in due course. In the meantime, my presence must remain a secret, for vital security reasons.' He put his hat back on his head, feeling pleased with himself.

Maslama was nodding furiously. 'You can depend on me,' he promised. 'I'm a man who respects a person's privacy. Mum' – for the second time! – 'is the word.'

Gibreel fled the compartment with the lunatic's hymns in hot pursuit. As he rushed to the far end of the train Maslama's paeans remained faintly audible behind him. 'Alleluia! Alleluia!' Apparently his new disciple had launched into selections from Handel's *Messiah*.

However: Gibreel wasn't followed, and there was, fortunately, a first-class carriage at the rear of the train, too. This one was of open-plan design, with comfortable orange seats arranged in fours around tables, and Gibreel settled down by a window, staring towards London, with his chest thumping and his hat jammed down on his head. He was trying to come to terms with the undeniable fact of the halo, and failing to do so, because what with the derangement of John Maslama behind him and the excitement of Alleluia Cone ahead it was hard to get his thoughts straight. Then to his despair Mrs Rekha Merchant floated up alongside his window, sitting on her flying Bokhara, evidently impervious to the snowstorm that was building up out there and making England look like a television set after the day's programmes end. She gave him a little wave and he felt hope ebbing from him. Retribution on a levitating rug: he closed his eyes and concentrated on trying not to shake.

'I know what a ghost is,' Allie Cone said to a classroom of teenage girls whose faces were illuminated by the soft inner light of worship. 'In the high Himalayas it is often the case that climbers find themselves being accompanied by the ghosts of those who failed in the attempt, or the sadder, but also prouder, ghosts of those who succeeded in reaching the summit, only to perish on the way down.'

Outside, in the Fields, the snow was settling on the high, bare trees, and on the flat expanse of the park. Between the low, dark snow-clouds and the white-carpeted city the light was a dirty yellow colour, a narrow, foggy light that dulled the heart and made it impossible to dream. Up *there*, Allie remembered, up there at eight thousand metres, the light was of such clarity that it seemed to resonate, to sing, like music. Here on the flat earth the light, too, was flat and earthbound. Here nothing flew, the sedge was withered, and no birds sang. Soon it would be dark.

'Ms Cone?' The girls' hands, waving in the air, drew her back into the classroom. 'Ghosts, miss? Straight up?' 'You're pulling our legs, right?' Scepticism wrestled with adoration in their faces. She knew the question they really wanted to ask, and probably would not: the question of the miracle of her skin. She had heard them whispering excitedly as she entered the classroom, 's true, look how *pale*, 's incredible. Alleluia Cone, whose iciness could resist the heat of the eight-thousand-metre sun. Allie the snow maiden, the icequeen. *Miss, how come you never get a tan?* When she went up Everest with the triumphant Collingwood expedition, the papers called them Snow White and the Seven Dwarfs, though she was no Disneyish cutie, her full lips pale rather than rose-red, her hair ice-blonde instead of black, her eyes not innocently wide but narrowed, out of habit, against the high snowglare. A memory of Gibreel Farishta welled up, catching her unawares: Gibreel at some point during their three and a half days, booming with his usual foot-in-mouth lack of restraint, 'Baby, you're no iceberg, whatever they say. You're a passionate lady, bibi. Hot, like a kachori.' He had pretended to blow on scalded fingertips, and shook his hand for emphasis: *O, too hot. O, throw water.* Gibreel Farishta. She controlled herself: Hi, ho, it's off to work.

'Ghosts,' she repeated firmly. 'On the Everest climb, after I came through the ice-fall, I saw a man sitting on an outcrop in the lotus position, with his eyes shut and a tartan tam-o'-shanter on his head, chanting the old mantra: om mani padmé hum.' She had guessed at once, from his archaic clothing and surprising behaviour, that this was the spectre of Maurice Wilson, the yogi who had prepared for a solo ascent of Everest, back in 1934, by starving himself for three weeks in order to cement so deep a union between his body and soul that the mountain would be too weak to tear them apart. He had gone up in a light aircraft as high as it would take him, crash-landed deliberately in a snowfield, headed upwards, and never returned. Wilson opened his eyes as Allie approached, and nodded lightly in greeting. He strolled beside her for the rest of that day, or hung in the air while she worked her way up a face. Once he belly-flopped into the snow of a sharp incline and glided upwards as if he were riding on an invisible anti-gravity toboggan. Allie had found herself behaving quite naturally, as if she'd just bumped into an old acquaintance, for reasons afterwards obscure to her.

Wilson chattered on a fair bit – 'Don't get a lot of company these days, one way and another' – and expressed, among other things, his deep irritation at having had his body discovered by the Chinese expedition of 1960. 'Little yellow buggers actually had the gall, the sheer face, to film my corpse.' Alleluia Cone was struck by the bright, yellow-and-black tartan of his immaculate knickerbockers. All this she told the girls at Brickhall Fields Girls' School, who had written so many letters pleading for her to address them that she had not been able to refuse. 'You've got to,' they pleaded in writing. 'You even live here.' From the window of the classroom she could see her flat across the park, just visible through the thickening fall of snow.

What she did not tell the class was this: as Maurice Wilson's ghost described, in patient detail, his own ascent, and also his posthumous discoveries, for example the slow, circuitous, infinitely delicate and invariably unproductive mating ritual of the yeti, which he had witnessed recently on the South Col, – so it occurred to her that her vision of the eccentric of 1934, the first human being ever to attempt to scale Everest on his own, a sort of abominable snowman himself, had been no accident, but a kind of signpost, a declaration of kinship. A prophecy of the future, perhaps, for it was at that moment that her secret dream was born, the impossible thing: the dream of the unaccompanied climb. It was possible, also, that Maurice Wilson was the angel of her death.

'I wanted to talk about ghosts,' she was saying, 'because most mountaineers, when they come down from the peaks, grow embarrassed and leave these stories out of their accounts. But they do exist, I have to admit it, even though I'm the type who's always kept her feet on solid ground.'

That was a laugh. Her feet. Even before the ascent of Everest she had begun to suffer from shooting pains, and was informed by her general practitioner, a no-nonsense Bombay woman called Dr Mistry, that she was suffering from fallen arches. 'In common parlance, flat feet.' Her arches, always weak, had been further weakened by years of wearing sneakers and other unsuitable shoes. Dr Mistry couldn't recommend much: toe-clenching exercises, running upstairs barefoot, sensible footwear. 'You're young enough,' she said. 'If you take care, you'll live. If not, you'll be a cripple at forty.' When Gibreel – damn it! – heard that she had climbed Everest with spears in her feet he took to calling her his silkie. He had read a Bumper Book of fairy-tales in which he found the story of the sea-woman who left the ocean and took on human form for the sake of the man she loved. She had feet instead of fins, but every step she took was an agony, as if she were walking over broken glass; yet she went on walking, forward, away from the sea and over land. You did it for a bloody mountain, he said. Would you do it for a man?

She had concealed her foot-ache from her fellow-mountaineers because the lure of Everest had been so overwhelming. But these days the pain was still there, and growing, if anything, worse. Chance, a congenital weakness, was proving to be her footbinder. Adventure's end, Allie thought; betrayed by my feet. The image of footbinding stayed with her. *Goddamn Chinese,* she mused, echoing Wilson's ghost.

'Life is so easy for some people,' she had wept into Gibreel Farishta's arms. 'Why don't *their* blasted feet give out?' He had kissed her forehead. 'For you, it may always be a struggle,' he said. 'You want it too damn much.'

The class was waiting for her, growing impatient with all this talk of phantoms. They wanted *the* story, her story. They wanted to stand on the mountain-top. *Do you know how it feels,* she wanted to ask them, *to have the whole of your life concentrated into one moment, a few hours long? Do you know what it's like when the only direction is down?* 'I was in the second pair with Sherpa Pemba,' she said. 'The weather was perfect, perfect. So clear you felt you could look right through the sky into whatever lay beyond. The first pair must have reached the summit by now, I said to Pemba. Conditions are holding and we can go. Pemba grew very serious, quite a change, because he was one of the expedition clowns. He had never been to the summit before, either. At that stage I had no plans to go without oxygen, but when I saw that Pemba intended it, I thought, okay, me too. It was a stupid whim, unprofessional, really, but I suddenly wanted to be a woman sitting on top of that bastard mountain, a human being, not a breathing machine. Pemba said, Allie Bibi, don't do, but I just started up. In a while we passed the others coming down and I could see the wonderful thing in their eyes. They were so high, possessed of such an exaltation, that they didn't even notice I wasn't wearing the oxygen equipment. Be careful, they shouted over to us, Look out for the angels. Pemba had fallen into a good breathing pattern and I fell into step with it, breathing in with his in, out with his out. I could

feel something lifting off the top of my head and I was grinning,
just grinning from ear to ear, and when Pemba looked my way I
could see he was doing the same. It looked like a grimace, like
pain, but it was just foolish joy.' She was a woman who had been
brought to transcendence, to the miracles of the soul, by the hard
physical labour of hauling herself up an icebound height of rock.
'At that moment,' she told the girls, who were climbing beside
her every step of the way, 'I believed it all: that the universe has a
sound, that you can lift a veil and see the face of God, everything.
I saw the Himalayas stretching below me and that was God's face,
too. Pemba must have seen something in my expression that
bothered him because he called across, Look out, Allie Bibi, the
height. I recall sort of floating over the last overhang and up to the
top, and then we were there, with the ground falling away on
every side. Such light; the universe purified into light. I wanted to
tear off my clothes and let it soak into my skin.' Not a titter from
the class; they were dancing naked with her on the roof of the
world. 'Then the visions began, the rainbows looping and dancing
in the sky, the radiance pouring down like a waterfall from the
sun, and there were angels, the others hadn't been joking. I saw
them and so did Sherpa Pemba. We were on our knees by then.
His pupils looked pure white and so did mine, I'm sure. We
would probably have died there, I'm sure, snow-blind and
mountain-foolish, but then I heard a noise, a loud, sharp report,
like a gun. That snapped me out of it. I had to yell at Pem until
he, too, shook himself and we started down. The weather was
changing rapidly; a blizzard was on the way. The air was heavy
now, heaviness instead of that light, that lightness. We just made it
to the meeting point and the four of us piled into the little tent at
Camp Six, twenty-seven thousand feet. You don't talk much up
there. We all had our Everests to re-climb, over and over, all
night. But at some point I asked: 'What was that noise? Did
anyone fire a gun?' They looked at me as if I was touched. Who'd
do such a damnfool thing at this altitude, they said, and anyway,
Allie, you know damn well there isn't a gun anywhere on the
mountain. They were right, of course, but I heard it, I know that

much: wham bam, shot and echo. That's it,' she ended abruptly. 'The end. Story of my life.' She picked up a silver-headed cane and prepared to depart. The teacher, Mrs Bury, came forward to utter the usual platitudes. But the girls were not to be denied. 'So what was it, then, Allie?' they insisted; and she, looking suddenly ten years older than her thirty-three, shrugged. 'Can't say,' she told them. 'Maybe it was Maurice Wilson's ghost.'

She left the classroom, leaning heavily on her stick.

The city – Proper London, yaar, no bloody *less!* – was dressed in white, like a mourner at a funeral. – Whose bloody funeral, mister, Gibreel Farishta asked himself wildly, not mine, I bloody *hope* and *trust*. When the train pulled into Victoria station he plunged out without waiting for it to come to a complete halt, turned his ankle and went sprawling beneath the baggage trolleys and sneers of the waiting Londoners, clinging, as he fell, on to his increasingly battered hat. Rekha Merchant was nowhere to be seen, and seizing the moment Gibreel ran through the scattering crowd like a man possessed, only to find her by the ticket barrier, floating patiently on her carpet, invisible to all eyes but his own, three feet off the ground.

'What do you want,' he burst out, 'what's your business with me?' 'To watch you fall,' she instantly replied. 'Look around,' she added, 'I've already made you look like a pretty big fool.'

People were clearing a space around Gibreel, the wild man in an outsize overcoat and trampy hat, *that man's talking to himself,* a child's voice said, and its mother answered *shh, dear, it's wicked to mock the afflicted.* Welcome to London. Gibreel Farishta rushed towards the stairs leading down towards the Tube. Rekha on her carpet let him go.

But when he arrived in a great rush at the northbound platform of the Victoria Line he saw her again. This time she was a colour photograph in a 48-sheet advertising poster on the wall across the track, advertising the merits of the international direct-dialling system. *Send your voice on a magic-carpet ride to India,* she advised. *No djinns or lamps required.* He gave a loud cry, once again causing his fellow-travellers to doubt his sanity, and fled over to the south-bound platform, where a train was just pulling in. He leapt aboard, and there was Rekha Merchant facing him with her carpet rolled up and lying across her knees. The doors closed behind him with a bang.

That day Gibreel Farishta fled in every direction around the Underground of the city of London and Rekha Merchant found him wherever he went; she sat beside him on the endless up-escalator at Oxford Circus and in the tightly packed elevators of Tufnell Park she rubbed up against him from behind in a manner that she would have thought quite outrageous during her lifetime. On the outer reaches of the Metropolitan Line she hurled the phantoms of her children from the tops of claw-like trees, and when he came up for air outside the Bank of England she flung herself histrionically from the apex of its neo-classical pediment. And even though he did not have any idea of the true shape of that most protean and chameleon of cities he grew convinced that it kept changing shape as he ran around beneath it, so that the stations on the Underground changed lines and followed one another in apparently random sequence. More than once he emerged, suffocating, from that subterranean world in which the laws of space and time had ceased to operate, and tried to hail a taxi; not one was willing to stop, however, so he was obliged to plunge back into that hellish maze, that labyrinth without a solution, and continue his epic flight. At last, exhausted beyond hope, he surrendered to the fatal logic of his insanity and got out arbitrarily at what he conceded must be the last, meaningless station of his prolonged and futile journey in search of the chimera of renewal. He came out into the heartbreaking indifference of a litter-blown street by a lorry-infested roundabout. Darkness had already fallen as he walked unsteadily, using the last reserves of his optimism, into an unknown park made spectral by the ectoplasmic quality of the tungsten lamps. As he sank to his knees in the isolation of the winter night he saw the figure of a woman moving slowly towards him across the snow-shrouded grass, and surmised that it must be his nemesis, Rekha Merchant, coming to deliver her death-kiss, to drag him down into a deeper underworld than the one in which she had broken his wounded spirit. He no longer cared, and by the time the woman reached him he had fallen forward on to his forearms, his coat dangling loosely about him and giving him the look of a large, dying beetle who was wearing, for obscure reasons, a dirty grey trilby hat.

As if from a great distance he heard a shocked cry escape the woman's lips, a gasp in which disbelief, joy and a strange resentment were all mixed up, and just before his senses left him he understood that Rekha had permitted him, for the time being, to reach the illusion of a safe haven, so that her triumph over him could be the sweeter when it came at the last.

'You're alive,' the woman said, repeating the first words she had ever spoken to his face. 'You got your life back. That's the point.'

Smiling, he fell asleep at Allie's flat feet in the falling snow.

PART IV

AYESHA

Even the serial visions have migrated now; they know the city better than he. And in the aftermath of Rosa and Rekha the dream-worlds of his archangelic other self begin to seem as tangible as the shifting realities he inhabits while he's awake. This, for instance, has started coming: a mansion block built in the Dutch style in a part of London which he will subsequently identify as Kensington, to which the dream flies him at high speed past Barkers department store and the small grey house with double bay windows where Thackeray wrote *Vanity Fair* and the square with the convent where the little girls in uniform are always going in, but never come out, and the house where Talleyrand lived in his old age when after a thousand and one chameleon changes of allegiance and principle he took on the outward form of the French ambassador to London, and arrives at a seven-storey corner block with green wrought-iron balconies up to the fourth, and now the dream rushes him up the outer wall of the house and on the fourth floor it pushes aside the heavy curtains at the living-room window and finally there he sits, unsleeping as usual, eyes wide in the dim yellow light, staring into the future, the bearded and turbaned Imam.

Who is he? An exile. Which must not be confused with, allowed to run into, all the other words that people throw around:

émigré, expatriate, refugee, immigrant, silence, cunning. Exile is a dream of glorious return. Exile is a vision of revolution: Elba, not St Helena. It is an endless paradox: looking forward by always looking back. The exile is a ball hurled high into the air. He hangs there, frozen in time, translated into a photograph; denied motion, suspended impossibly above his native earth, he awaits the inevitable moment at which the photograph must begin to move, and the earth reclaim its own. These are the things the Imam thinks. His home is a rented flat. It is a waiting-room, a photograph, air.

The thick wallpaper, olive stripes on a cream ground, has faded a little, enough to emphasize the brighter rectangles and ovals that indicate where pictures used to hang. The Imam is the enemy of images. When he moved in the pictures slid noiselessly from the walls and slunk from the room, removing themselves from the rage of his unspoken disapproval. Some representations, however, are permitted to remain. On the mantelpiece he keeps a small group of postcards bearing conventional images of his homeland, which he calls simply Desh: a mountain looming over a city; a picturesque village scene beneath a mighty tree; a mosque. But in his bedroom, on the wall facing the hard cot where he lies, there hangs a more potent icon, the portrait of a woman of exceptional face, famous for her profile of a Grecian statue and the black hair that is as long as she is high. A powerful woman, his enemy, his other: he keeps her close. Just as, far away in the palaces of her omnipotence she will be clutching his portrait beneath her royal cloak or hiding it in a locket at her throat. She is the Empress, and her name is – what else? – Ayesha. On this island, the exiled Imam, and at home in Desh, She. They plot each other's deaths.

The curtains, thick golden velvet, are kept shut all day, because otherwise the evil thing might creep into the apartment: foreignness, Abroad, the alien nation. The harsh fact that he is here and not There, upon which all his thoughts are fixed. On those rare occasions when the Imam goes out to take the Kensington air, at the centre of a square formed by eight young men in sunglasses and bulging suits, he folds his hands before him and fixes his gaze upon them, so that no element or particle of this hated city, – this sink of iniquities which humiliates him by giving him sanctuary, so that he must be beholden to it in spite of the lustfulness, greed and vanity of its ways, – can lodge itself, like a dust-speck, in his eyes. When he leaves this loathed exile to return in triumph to that other city beneath the postcard-mountain, it will be a point of pride to be able to say that he remained in complete ignorance of the Sodom in which he had been obliged to wait; ignorant, and therefore unsullied, unaltered, pure.

And another reason for the drawn curtains is that of course there are eyes and ears around him, not all of them friendly. The orange buildings are not neutral. Somewhere across the street there will be zoom lenses, video equipment, jumbo mikes; and always the risk of snipers. Above and below and beside the Imam are the safe apartments occupied by his guards, who stroll the Kensington streets disguised as women in shrouds and silvery beaks; but it is as well to be too careful. Paranoia, for the exile, is a prerequisite of survival.

A fable, which he heard from one of his favourites, the American convert, formerly a successful singer, now known as Bilal X. In a certain nightclub to which the Imam is in the habit of sending his lieutenants to listen in to certain other persons belonging to certain opposed factions, Bilal met a young man from Desh, also a singer of sorts, so they fell to talking. It turned out that this Mahmood was a badly scared individual. He had recently *shacked up* with a gori, a long red woman with a big figure, and then it turned out that the previous lover of his beloved Renata was the exiled boss of the SAVAK torture organization of the Shah of Iran. The number one Grand Panjandrum himself, not some minor sadist with a talent for extracting toenails or setting fire to eyelids, but the great haramzada in person. The day after Mahmood and Renata moved into their new apartment a letter arrived for Mahmood. *Okay, shit-eater, you're fucking my woman, I just wanted to say hello.* The next day a second letter arrived. *By the way, prick, I forgot to mention, here is your new telephone number.* At that point Mahmood and Renata had asked for an ex-directory listing but had not as yet been given their new number by the telephone company. When it came through two days later and was exactly the same as the one on the letter, Mahmood's hair fell out all at once. Then, seeing it lying on the pillow, he joined his hands together in front of Renata and begged, 'Baby, I love you, but you're too hot for me, please go somewhere, far far.' When the Imam was told this story he shook his head and said, that whore, who will touch her now, in spite of her lust-creating body? She put a stain on herself worse than leprosy; thus do human beings mutilate themselves. But the true moral of the fable was the need for eternal vigilance. London was a city in which the ex-boss of SAVAK had great connections in the telephone company and the Shah's ex-chef ran a thriving restaurant in Hounslow. Such a welcoming city, such a refuge, they take all types. Keep the curtains drawn.

Floors three to five of this block of mansion flats are, for the moment, all the homeland the Imam possesses. Here there are rifles and short-wave radios and rooms in which the sharp young men in suits sit and speak urgently into several telephones. There is no alcohol here, nor are playing cards or dice anywhere in evidence, and the only woman is the one hanging on the old man's bedroom wall. In this surrogate homeland, which the insomniac saint thinks of as his waiting-room or transit lounge, the central heating is at full blast night and day, and the windows are tightly shut. The exile cannot forget, and must therefore simulate, the dry heat of Desh, the once and future land where even the moon is hot and dripping like a fresh, buttered chapati. O that longed-for part of the world where the sun and moon are male but their hot sweet light is named with female names. At night the exile parts his curtains and the alien moonlight sidles into the room, its coldness striking his eyeballs like a nail. He winces, narrows his eyes. Loose-robed, frowning, ominous, awake: this is the Imam.

Exile is a soulless country. In exile, the furniture is ugly, expensive, all bought at the same time in the same store and in too much of a hurry: shiny silver sofas with fins like old Buicks DeSotos Oldsmobiles, glass-fronted bookcases containing not books but clippings files. In exile the shower goes scalding hot whenever anybody turns on a kitchen tap, so that when the Imam goes to bathe his entire retinue must remember not to fill a kettle or rinse a dirty plate, and when the Imam goes to the toilet his disciples leap scalded from the shower. In exile no food is ever cooked; the dark-spectacled bodyguards go out for take-away. In exile all attempts to put down roots look like treason: they are admissions of defeat.

The Imam is the centre of a wheel.

Movement radiates from him, around the clock. His son, Khalid, enters his sanctum bearing a glass of water, holding it in his right hand with his left palm under the glass. The Imam drinks water constantly, one glass every five minutes, to keep himself clean; the water itself is cleansed of impurities, before he sips, in an American filtration machine. All the young men surrounding him are well aware of his famous Monograph on Water, whose purity, the Imam believes, communicates itself to the drinker, its thinness and simplicity, the ascetic pleasures of its taste. 'The Empress,' he points out, 'drinks wine.' Burgundies, clarets, hocks mingle their intoxicating corruptions within that body both fair and foul. The sin is enough to condemn her for all time without hope of redemption. The picture on his bedroom wall shows the Empress Ayesha holding, in both hands, a human skull filled with a dark red fluid. The Empress drinks blood, but the Imam is a water man. 'Not for nothing do the peoples of our hot lands offer it reverence,' the Monograph proclaims. 'Water, preserver of life. No civilized individual can refuse it to another. A grandmother, be her limbs ever so arthritically stiff, will rise at once and go to the tap if a small child should come to her and ask, pani, nani. Beware all those who blaspheme against it. Who pollutes it, dilutes his soul.'

The Imam has often vented his rage upon the memory of the late Aga Khan, as a result of being shown the text of an interview in which the head of the Ismailis was observed drinking vintage champagne. *O, sir, this champagne is only for outward show. The instant it touches my lips, it turns to water.* Fiend, the Imam is wont to thunder. Apostate, blasphemer, fraud. When the future comes such individuals will be judged, he tells his men. Water will have its day and blood will flow like wine. Such is the miraculous nature of the future of exiles: what is first uttered in the impotence of an overheated apartment becomes the fate of nations. Who has not dreamed this dream, of being a king for a day? – But the Imam dreams of more than a day; feels, emanating from his fingertips, the arachnid strings with which he will control the movement of history.

No: not history.

His is a stranger dream.

His son, water-carrying Khalid, bows before his father like a pilgrim at a shrine, informs him that the guard on duty outside the sanctum is Salman Farsi. Bilal is at the radio transmitter, broadcasting the day's message, on the agreed frequency, to Desh.

The Imam is a massive stillness, an immobility. He is living stone. His great gnarled hands, granite-grey, rest heavily on the wings of his high-backed chair. His head, looking too large for the body beneath, lolls ponderously on the surprisingly scrawny neck that can be glimpsed through the grey-black wisps of beard. The Imam's eyes are clouded; his lips do not move. He is pure force, an elemental being; he moves without motion, acts without doing, speaks without uttering a sound. He is the conjurer and history is his trick.

No, not history: something stranger.

The explanation of this conundrum is to be heard, at this very moment, on certain surreptitious radio waves, on which the voice of the American convert Bilal is singing the Imam's holy song. Bilal the muezzin: his voice enters a ham radio in Kensington and emerges in dreamed-of Desh, transmuted into the thunderous speech of the Imam himself. Beginning with ritual abuse of the Empress, with lists of her crimes, murders, bribes, sexual relations with lizards, and so on, he proceeds eventually to issue in ringing tones the Imam's nightly call to his people to rise up against the evil of her State. 'We will make a revolution,' the Imam proclaims through him, 'that is a revolt not only against a tyrant, but against history.' For there is an enemy beyond Ayesha, and it is History herself. History is the blood-wine that must no longer be drunk. History the intoxicant, the creation and possession of the Devil, of the great Shaitan, the greatest of the lies — progress, science, rights — against which the Imam has set his face. History is a deviation from the Path, knowledge is a delusion, because the sum of knowledge was complete on the day Al-Lah finished his revelation to Mahound. 'We will unmake the veil of history,' Bilal declaims into the listening night, 'and when it is unravelled, we will see Paradise standing there, in all its glory and light.' The Imam chose Bilal for this task on account of the beauty of his voice, which in its previous incarnation succeeded in climbing the Everest of the hit parade, not once but a dozen times, to the very top. The voice is rich and authoritative, a voice in the habit of being listened to; well-nourished, highly trained, the voice of American confidence, a weapon of the West turned against its makers, whose might upholds the Empress and her tyranny. In the early days Bilal X protested at such a description of his voice. He, too, belonged to an oppressed people, he insisted, so that it was unjust to equate him with the Yankee imperialists. The Imam answered, not without gentleness: Bilal, your suffering is ours as well. But to be raised in the house of power is to learn its ways, to soak them up, through that very skin that is the cause of your oppression. The habit of power, its timbre, its posture, its way of being with others. It is a disease, Bilal, infecting all who come too near it. If the powerful trample over you, you are infected by the soles of their feet.

Bilal continues to address the darkness. 'Death to the tyranny of the Empress Ayesha, of calendars, of America, of time! We seek the eternity, the timelessness, of God. His still waters, not her flowing wines.' Burn the books and trust the Book; shred the papers and hear the Word, as it was revealed by the Angel Gibreel to the Messenger Mahound and explicated by your interpreter and Imam. 'Ameen,' Bilal said, concluding the night's proceedings.

While, in his sanctum, the Imam sends a message of his own: and summons, conjures up, the archangel, Gibreel.

He sees himself in the dream: no angel to look at, just a man in his ordinary street clothes, Henry Diamond's posthumous hand-me-downs: gabardine and trilby over outsize trousers held up by braces, a fisherman's woollen pullover, billowy white shirt. This dream-Gibreel, so like the waking one, stands quaking in the sanctum of the Imam, whose eyes are white as clouds.

Gibreel speaks querulously, to hide his fear.

'Why insist on archangels? Those days, you should know, are gone.'

The Imam closes his eyes, sighs. The carpet extrudes long hairy tendrils, which wrap themselves around Gibreel, holding him fast.

'You don't need me,' Gibreel emphasizes. 'The revelation is complete. Let me go.'

The other shakes his head, and speaks, except that his lips do not move, and it is Bilal's voice that fills Gibreel's ears, even though the broadcaster is nowhere to be seen, *tonight's the night,* the voice says, *and you must fly me to Jerusalem.*

Then the apartment dissolves and they are standing on the roof beside the water-tank, because the Imam, when he wishes to move, can remain still and move the world around him. His beard is blowing in the wind. It is longer now; if it were not for the wind that catches at it as if it were a flowing chiffon scarf, it would touch the ground by his feet; he has red eyes, and his voice hangs around him in the sky. *Take me.* Gibreel argues, Seems you can do it easily by yourself: but the Imam, in a single movement of astonishing rapidity, slings his beard over his shoulder, hoists up his skirts to reveal two spindly legs with an almost monstrous covering of hair, and leaps high into the night air, twirls himself about, and settles on Gibreel's shoulders, clutching on to him with fingernails that have grown into long, curved claws. Gibreel feels himself rising into the sky, bearing the old man of the sea, the

Imam with hair that grows longer by the minute, streaming in every direction, his eyebrows like pennants in the wind.

Jerusalem, he wonders, which way is that? – And then, it's a slippery word, Jerusalem, it can be an idea as well as a place: a goal, an exaltation. Where is the Imam's Jerusalem? 'The fall of the harlot,' the disembodied voice resounds in his ears. 'Her crash, the Babylonian whore.'

They zoom through the night. The moon is heating up, beginning to bubble like cheese under a grill; he, Gibreel, sees pieces of it falling off from time to time, moon-drips that hiss and bubble on the sizzling griddle of the sky. Land appears below them. The heat grows intense.

It is an immense landscape, reddish, with flat-topped trees. They fly over mountains that are also flat-topped; even the stones, here, are flattened by the heat. Then they come to a high mountain of almost perfectly conical dimensions, a mountain that also sits postcarded on a mantelpiece far away; and in the shadow of the mountain, a city, sprawling at its feet like a supplicant, and on the mountain's lower slopes, a palace, the palace, her place: the Empress, whom radio messages have unmade. This is a revolution of radio hams.

Gibreel, with the Imam riding him like a carpet, swoops lower, and in the steaming night it looks as if the streets are alive, they seem to be writhing, like snakes; while in front of the palace of the Empress's defeat a new hill seems to be growing, *while we watch, baba, what's going on here?* The Imam's voice hangs in the sky: 'Come down. I will show you Love.'

They are at rooftop-level when Gibreel realizes that the streets are swarming with people. Human beings, packed so densely into those snaking paths that they have blended into a larger, composite entity, relentless, serpentine. The people move slowly, at an even pace, down alleys into lanes, down lanes into side streets, down side streets into highways, all of them converging upon the grand avenue, twelve lanes wide and lined with giant eucalyptus trees, that leads to the palace gates. The avenue is packed with humanity; it is the central organ of the new, many-headed being. Seventy abreast, the people walk gravely towards the Empress's gates. In front of which her household guards are waiting in three ranks, lying, kneeling and standing, with machine-guns at the ready. The people are walking up the slope towards the guns; seventy at a time, they come into range; the guns babble, and they die, and then the next seventy climb over the bodies of the dead, the guns giggle once again, and the hill of the dead grows higher. Those behind it commence, in their turn, to climb. In the dark doorways of the city there are mothers with covered heads, pushing their beloved sons into the parade, *go, be a martyr, do the needful, die.* 'You see how they love me,' says the disembodied voice. 'No tyranny on earth can withstand the power of this slow, walking love.'

'This isn't love,' Gibreel, weeping, replies. 'It's hate. She has driven them into your arms.' The explanation sounds thin, superficial.

'They love me,' the Imam's voice says, 'because I am water. I am fertility and she is decay. They love me for my habit of smashing clocks. Human beings who turn away from God lose love, and certainty, and also the sense of His boundless time, that encompasses past, present and future; the timeless time, that has no need to move. We long for the eternal, and I am eternity. She is nothing: a tick, or tock. She looks in her mirror every day and is terrorized by the idea of age, of time passing. Thus she is the prisoner of her own nature; she, too, is in the chains of Time. After the revolution there will be no clocks; we'll smash the lot. The word *clock* will be expunged from our dictionaries. After the revolution there will be no birthdays. We shall all be born again, all of us the same unchanging age in the eye of Almighty God.'

He falls silent, now, because below us the great moment has come: the people have reached the guns. Which are silenced in their turn, as the endless serpent of the people, the gigantic python of the risen masses, embraces the guards, suffocating them, and silences the lethal chuckling of their weapons. The Imam sighs heavily. 'Done.'

The lights of the palace are extinguished as the people walk towards it, at the same measured pace as before. Then, from within the darkened palace, there rises a hideous sound, beginning as a high, thin, piercing wail, then deepening into a howl, an ululation loud enough to fill every cranny of the city with its rage. Then the golden dome of the palace bursts open like an egg, and rising from it, glowing with blackness, is a mythological apparition with vast black wings, her hair streaming loose, as long and black as the Imam's is long and white: Al-Lat, Gibreel understands, bursting out of Ayesha's shell.

'Kill her,' the Imam commands.

Gibreel sets him down on the palace's ceremonial balcony, his arms outstretched to encompass the joy of the people, a sound that drowns even the howls of the goddess and rises up like a song. And then he is being propelled into the air, having no option, he is a marionette going to war; and she, seeing him coming, turns, crouches in air, and, moaning dreadfully, comes at him with all her might. Gibreel understands that the Imam, fighting by proxy as usual, will sacrifice him as readily as he did the hill of corpses at the palace gate, that he is a suicide soldier in the service of the cleric's cause. I am weak, he thinks, I am no match for her, but she, too, has been weakened by her defeat. The Imam's strength moves Gibreel, places thunderbolts in his hands, and the battle is joined; he hurls lightning spears into her feet and she plunges comets into his groin, *we are killing each other,* he thinks, *we will die and there will be two new constellations in space: Al-Lat, and Gibreel.* Like exhausted warriors on a corpse-littered field, they totter and slash. Both are failing fast.

She falls.

Down she tumbles, Al-Lat queen of the night; crashes upside-down to earth, crushing her head to bits; and lies, a headless black angel, with her wings ripped off, by a little wicket gate in the palace gardens, all in a crumpled heap. – And Gibreel, looking away from her in horror, sees the Imam grown monstrous, lying in the palace forecourt with his mouth yawning open at the gates; as the people march through the gates he swallows them whole.

The body of Al-Lat has shrivelled on the grass, leaving behind only a dark stain; and now every clock in the capital city of Desh begins to chime, and goes on unceasingly, beyond twelve, beyond twenty-four, beyond one thousand and one, announcing the end of Time, the hour that is beyond measuring, the hour of the exile's return, of the victory of water over wine, of the commencement of the Untime of the Imam.

When the nocturnal story changes, when, without warning, the progress of events in Jahilia and Yathrib gives way to the struggle of Imam and Empress, Gibreel briefly hopes that the curse has ended, that his dreams have been restored to the random eccentricity of ordinary life; but then, as the new story, too, falls into the old pattern, continuing each time he drops off from the precise point at which it was interrupted, and as his own image, translated into an avatar of the archangel, re-enters the frame, so his hope dies, and he succumbs once more to the inexorable. Things have reached the point at which some of his night-sagas seem more bearable than others, and after the apocalypse of the Imam he feels almost pleased when the next narrative begins, extending his internal repertory, because at least it suggests that the deity whom he, Gibreel, has tried unsuccessfully to kill can be a God of love, as well as one of vengeance, power, duty, rules and hate; and it is, too, a nostalgic sort of tale, of a lost homeland; it feels like a return to the past . . . what story is this? Coming right up. To begin at the beginning: On the morning of his fortieth birthday, in a room full of butterflies, Mirza Saeed Akhtar watched his sleeping wife . . .

On the fateful morning of his fortieth birthday, in a room full of butterflies, the zamindar Mirza Saeed Akhtar watched over his sleeping wife, and felt his heart fill up to the bursting-point with love. He had awoken early for once, rising before dawn with a

bad dream souring his mouth, his recurring dream of the end of
the world, in which the catastrophe was invariably his fault. He
had been reading Nietzsche the night before – 'the pitiless end of
that small, overextended species called Man' – and had fallen
asleep with the book resting face downwards on his chest. Waking
to the rustle of butterfly wings in the cool, shadowy bedroom, he
was angry with himself for being so foolish in his choice of bedside reading matter. He was, however, wide awake now. Getting
up quietly, he slipped his feet into chappals and strolled idly along
the verandas of the great mansion, still in darkness on account of
their lowered blinds, and the butterflies bobbed like courtiers at
his back. In the far distance, someone was playing a flute. Mirza
Saeed drew up the chick blinds and fastened their cords. The gardens were deep in mist, through which the butterfly clouds were
swirling, one mist intersecting another. This remote region had
always been renowned for its lepidoptera, for these miraculous
squadrons that filled the air by day and night, butterflies with the
gift of chameleons, whose wings changed colour as they settled on
vermilion flowers, ochre curtains, obsidian goblets or amber
finger-rings. In the zamindar's mansion, and also in the nearby village, the miracle of the butterflies had become so familiar as to
seem mundane, but in fact they had only returned nineteen years
ago, as the servant women would recall. They had been the
familiar spirits, or so the legend ran, of a local saint, the holy
woman known only as Bibiji, who had lived to the age of two
hundred and forty-two and whose grave, until its location was
forgotten, had the property of curing impotence and warts. Since
the death of Bibiji one hundred and twenty years ago the butterflies had vanished into the same realm of the legendary as Bibiji
herself, so that when they came back exactly one hundred and one
years after their departure it looked, at first, like an omen of some
imminent, wonderful thing. After Bibiji's death – it should
quickly be said – the village had continued to prosper, the potato
crops remained plentiful, but there had been a gap in many hearts,
even though the villagers of the present had no memory of the

time of the old saint. So the return of the butterflies lifted many spirits, but when the expected wonders failed to materialize the locals sank back, little by little, into the insufficiency of the day-to-day. The name of the zamindar's mansion, *Peristan*, may have had its origins in the magical creatures' fairy wings, and the village's name, *Titlipur*, certainly did. But names, once they are in common use, quickly become mere sounds, their etymology being buried, like so many of the earth's marvels, beneath the dust of habit. The human inhabitants of Titlipur, and its butterfly hordes, moved amongst one another with a kind of mutual disdain. The villagers and the zamindar's family had long ago abandoned the attempt to exclude the butterflies from their homes, so that now whenever a trunk was opened, a batch of wings would fly out of it like Pandora's imps, changing colour as they rose; there were butterflies under the closed lids of the thunderboxes in the toilets of Peristan, and inside every wardrobe, and between the pages of books. When you awoke you found the butterflies sleeping on your cheeks.

The commonplace eventually becomes invisible, and Mirza Saeed had not really noticed the butterflies for a number of years. On the morning of his fortieth birthday, however, as the first light of dawn touched the house and the butterflies began instantly to glow, the beauty of the moment took his breath away. He ran at once to the bedroom in the zenana wing in which his wife Mishal lay sleeping, veiled in a mosquito-net. The magic butterflies were resting on her exposed toes, and a mosquito had evidently found its way inside as well, because there was a line of little bites along the raised edge of her collar-bone. He wanted to lift the net, crawl inside and kiss the bites until they faded away. How inflamed they looked! How, when she awoke, they would itch! But he held himself back, preferring to enjoy the innocence of her sleeping form. She had soft, red-brown hair, white white skin, and her eyes, behind the closed lids, were silky grey. Her father was a director of the state bank, so it had been an irresistible match, an arranged marriage which restored the fortunes of the Mirza's ancient, decaying family and then ripened, over time and in spite of their failure to have children, into a union of real love. Full of emotion, Mirza Saeed watched Mishal sleep and chased the last shreds of his nightmare from his mind. 'How can the world be done for,' he reasoned contentedly to himself, 'if it can offer up such instances of perfection as this lovely dawn?'

Continuing down the line of these happy thoughts, he formulated a silent speech to his resting wife. 'Mishal, I'm forty years old and as contented as a forty-day babe. I see now that I've been falling deeper and deeper into our love over the years, and now I swim, like some fish, in that warm sea.' How much she gave him, he marvelled; how much he needed her! Their marriage transcended mere sensuality, was so intimate that a separation was unthinkable. 'Growing old beside you,' he told her while she slept, 'will be, Mishal, a privilege.' He permitted himself the sentimentality of blowing a kiss in her direction and then tiptoeing from the room. Out once more on the main veranda of his private quarters on the mansion's upper storey, he glanced across to the gardens, which were coming into view as the dawn lifted the mist, and saw the sight that would destroy his peace of mind forever, smashing it beyond hope of repair at the very instant in which he had become certain of its invulnerability to the ravages of fate.

A young woman was squatting on the lawn, holding out her left palm. Butterflies were settling on this surface while, with her right hand, she picked them up and put them in her mouth. Slowly, methodically, she breakfasted on the acquiescent wings.

Her lips, cheeks, chin were heavily stained by the many different colours that had rubbed off the dying butterflies.

When Mirza Saeed Akhtar saw the young woman eating her gossamer breakfast on his lawn, he felt a surge of lust so powerful that he instantly felt ashamed. 'It's impossible,' he scolded himself, 'I am not an animal, after all.' The young woman wore a saffron yellow sari wrapped around her nakedness, after the fashion of the poor women of that region, and as she stooped over the butterflies the sari, hanging loosely forwards, bared her small breasts to the gaze of the transfixed zamindar. Mirza Saeed stretched out his hands to grip the balcony railing, and the slight movement of his white kurta must have caught her eye, because she lifted her head quickly and looked right into his face.

And did not immediately look down again. Nor did she get up and run away, as he had half expected.

What she did: waited for a few seconds, as though to see if he intended to speak. When he did not, she simply resumed her strange meal without taking her eyes from his face. The strangest aspect of it was that the butterflies seemed to be funnelling downwards from the brightening air, going willingly towards her outstretched palms and their own deaths. She held them by the wingtips, threw her head back and flicked them into her mouth with the tip of her narrow tongue. Once she kept her mouth open, the dark lips parted defiantly, and Mirza Saeed trembled to see the butterfly fluttering within the dark cavern of its death, yet making no attempt to escape. When she was satisfied that he had seen this, she brought her lips together and began to chew. They remained thus, peasant woman below, landowner above, until her eyes unexpectedly rolled upwards in their sockets and she fell heavily, twitching violently, on to her left side.

After a few seconds of transfixed panic, the Mirza shouted, 'Ohé, house! Ohé, wake up, emergency!' At the same time he ran towards the stately mahogany staircase from England, brought here from some unimaginable Warwickshire, some fantastic location in which, in a damp and lightless priory, King Charles I had ascended these same steps, before losing his head, in the seventeenth century of another system of time. Down these stairs hurtled Mirza Saeed Akhtar, last of his line, trampling over the ghostly impressions of beheaded feet as he sped towards the lawn.

The girl was having convulsions, crushing butterflies beneath her rolling, kicking body. Mirza Saeed got to her first, although the servants and Mishal, awakened by his cry, were not far behind. He grasped the girl by the jaw and forced it open, inserting a nearby twig, which she at once bit in half. Blood trickled from her cut mouth, and he feared for her tongue, but the sickness left her just then, she became calm, and slept. Mishal had her carried to her own bedroom, and now Mirza Saeed was obliged to gaze on a second sleeping beauty in that bed, and was stricken for a second time by what seemed too rich and deep a sensation to be called by the crude name, *lust*. He found that he was at once sickened by his own impure designs and also elated by the feelings that were coursing within him, fresh feelings whose newness excited him greatly. Mishal came to stand beside her husband. 'Do you know her?' Saeed asked, and she nodded. 'An orphan girl. She makes small enamel animals and sells them at the trunk road. She has had the falling sickness since she was very little.' Mirza Saeed was awed, not for the first time, by his wife's gift of involvement with other human beings. He himself could hardly recognize more than a handful of the villagers, but she knew each person's pet names, family histories and incomes. They even told her their dreams, although few of them dreamed more than once a month on account of being too poor to afford such luxuries. The over-flowing fondness he had felt at dawn returned, and he placed his arm around her shoulders. She leaned her head against him and said softly: 'Happy birthday.' He kissed the top of her hair. They stood embracing, watching the sleeping girl. Ayesha: his wife told him the name.

After the orphan girl Ayesha arrived at puberty and became, on account of her distracted beauty and her air of staring into another world, the object of many young men's desires, it began to be said that she was looking for a lover from heaven, because she thought herself too good for mortal men. Her rejected suitors complained that in practical terms she had no business acting so choosy, in the first place because she was an orphan, and in the second, because she was possessed by the demon of epilepsy, who would certainly put off any heavenly spirits who might otherwise have been inter-ested. Some embittered youths went so far as to suggest that as

Ayesha's defects would prevent her from ever finding a husband she might as well start taking lovers, so as not to waste that beauty, which ought in all fairness to have been given to a less problematic individual. In spite of these attempts by the young men of Titlipur to turn her into their whore, Ayesha remained chaste, her defence being a look of such fierce concentration on patches of air immediately above people's left shoulders that it was regularly mistaken for contempt. Then people heard about her new habit of swallowing butterflies and they revised their opinion of her, convinced that she was touched in the head and therefore dangerous to lie with in case the demons crossed over into her lovers. After this the lustful males of her village left her alone in her hovel, alone with her toy animals and her peculiar fluttering diet. One young man, however, took to sitting a little distance from her doorway, facing discreetly in the opposite direction, as if he were on guard, even though she no longer had any need of protectors. He was a former untouchable from the neighbouring village of Chatnapatna who had been converted to Islam and taken the name of Osman. Ayesha never acknowledged Osman's presence, nor did he ask for such acknowledgement. The leafy branches of the village waved over their heads in the breeze.

The village of Titlipur had grown up in the shade of an immense banyan-tree, a single monarch that ruled, with its multiple roots, over an area more than half a mile in diameter. By now the growth of tree into village and village into tree had become so intricate that it was impossible to differentiate between the two. Certain districts of the tree had become well-known lovers' nooks; others were chicken runs. Some of the poorer labourers had constructed rough-and-ready shelters in the angles of stout branches, and actually lived inside the dense foliage. There were branches that were used as pathways across the village, and children's swings made out of the tree's beards, and in places where the tree stooped low down towards the earth its leaves formed roofs for many a hutment that seemed to hang from the greenery like the nest of a weaver bird. When the village panchayat assembled, it sat on the mightiest branch of all. The vil-

lagers had grown accustomed to referring to the tree by the name
of the village, and to the village simply as 'the tree'. The banyan's
non-human inhabitants – honey ants, squirrels, owls – were
accorded the respect due to fellow-citizens. Only the butterflies
were ignored, like hopes long since shown to be false.

It was a Muslim village, which was why the convert Osman had
come here with his clown's outfit and his 'boom-boom' bullock
after he had embraced the faith in an act of desperation, hoping
that changing to a Muslim name would do him more good than
earlier re-namings, for example when untouchables were renamed 'children of God.' As a child of God in Chatnapatna he
had not been permitted to draw water from the town well,
because the touch of an outcaste would have polluted the drinking
water . . . Landless and, like Ayesha, an orphan, Osman earned his
living as a clown. His bullock wore bright red paper cones over its
horns and much tinselly drapery over its nose and back. He went
from village to village performing an act, at marriages and other
celebrations, in which the bullock was his essential partner and
foil, nodding in answer to his questions, one nod for no, twice
for yes.

'Isn't this a nice village we've come to?' Osman would ask.

Boom, the bullock disagreed.

'It isn't? Oh yes it is. Look: aren't the people good?'

Boom.

'What? Then it's a village full of sinners?'

Boom, boom.

'Baapu-ré! Then, will everybody go to hell?'

Boom, boom.

'But, bhaijan. Is there any hope for them?'

Boom, boom, the bullock offered salvation. Excitedly, Osman
bent down, placing his ear by the bullock's mouth. 'Tell, quickly.
What should they do to be saved?' At this point the bullock
plucked Osman's cap off his head and carried it around the crowd,
asking for money, and Osman would nod, happily: Boom, boom.

Osman the convert and his boom-boom bullock were well
liked in Titlipur, but the young man only wanted the approval of

one person, and she would not give it. He had admitted to her
that his conversion to Islam had been largely tactical, 'Just so I
could get a drink, bibi, what's a man to do?' She had been out-
raged by his confession, informed him that he was no Muslim at
all, his soul was in peril and he could go back to Chatnapatna and
die of thirst for all she cared. Her face coloured, as she spoke, with
an unaccountably strong disappointment in him, and it was the
vehemence of this disappointment that gave him the optimism to
remain squatting a dozen paces from her home, day after day, but
she continued to stalk past him, nose in air, without so much as a
good morning or hope-you're-well.

Once a week, the potato carts of Titlipur trundled down the
rutted, narrow, four-hour track to Chatnapatna, which stood at
the point at which the track met the grand trunk road. In Chatnapatna stood the high, gleaming aluminium silos of the potato
wholesalers, but this had nothing to do with Ayesha's regular visits
to the town. She would hitch a ride on a potato cart, clutching a
little sackcloth bundle, to take her toys to market. Chatnapatna
was known throughout the region for its kiddies' knick-knacks,
carved wooden toys and enamelled figurines. Osman and his bullock stood at the edge of the banyan-tree, watching her bounce
about on top of the potato sacks until she had diminished to a dot.

In Chatnapatna she made her way to the premises of Sri
Srinivas, owner of the biggest toy factory in town. On its walls
were the political graffiti of the day: *Vote for Hand.* Or, more
politely: *Please vote for CP(M).* Above these exhortations was the
proud announcement: *Srinivas's Toy Univas. Our Moto: Sincerity &
Creativity.* Srinivas was inside: a large jelly of a man, his head a
hairless sun, a fiftyish fellow whom a lifetime of selling toys had
failed to sour. Ayesha owed him her livelihood. He had been so
taken with the artistry of her whittling that he had agreed to buy
as many as she could produce. But in spite of his habitual bonhomie his expression darkened when Ayesha undid her bundle to
show him two dozen figures of a young man in a clown hat,
accompanied by a decorated bullock that could dip its tinselled

head. Understanding that Ayesha had forgiven Osman his conversion, Sri Srinivas cried, 'That man is a traitor to his birth, as you
well know. What kind of a person will change gods as easily as his
dhotis? God knows what got into you, daughter, but I don't want
these dolls.' On the wall behind his desk hung a framed certificate
which read, in elaborately curlicued print: *This is to certify that MR
SRI S. SRINIVAS is an Expert on the Geological History of the Planet
Earth, having flown through Grand Canyon with SCENIC AIR-
LINES*. Srinivas closed his eyes and folded his arms, an
unlaughing Buddha with the indisputable authority of one who
had flown. 'That boy is a devil,' he said with finality, and Ayesha
folded the dolls into her piece of sackcloth and turned to leave,
without arguing. Srinivas's eyes flew open. 'Damn you,' he
shouted, 'aren't you going to give me a hard time? You think I
don't know you need the money? Why you did such a damn
stupid thing? What are you going to do now? Just go and make
some FP dolls, double quick, and I will buy at best rate plus,
because I am generous to a fault.' Mr Srinivas's personal invention
was the Family Planning doll, a socially responsible variant of the
old Russian-doll notion. Inside a suited-and-booted Abba-doll
was a demure, sari-clad Amma, and inside her a daughter containing a son. Two children are plenty: that was the message of the
dolls. 'Make quickly quickly,' Srinivas called after the departing
Ayesha. 'FP dolls have high turnover.' Ayesha turned, and smiled.
'Don't worry about me, Srinivasji,' she said, and left.

Ayesha the orphan was nineteen years old when she began her
walk back to Titlipur along the rutted potato track, but by the
time she turned up in her village some forty-eight hours later she
had attained a kind of agelessness, because her hair had turned as
white as snow while her skin had regained the luminous perfection of a new-born child's, and although she was completely
naked the butterflies had settled upon her body in such thick
swarms that she seemed to be wearing a dress of the most delicate
material in the universe. The clown Osman was practising routines with the boom-boom bullock near the track, because even

though he had been worried sick by her extended absence, and had spent the whole of the previous night searching for her, it was still necessary to earn a living. When he laid eyes on her, that young man who had never respected God because of having been born untouchable was filled with holy terror, and did not dare to approach the girl with whom he was so helplessly in love.

She went into her hut and slept for a day and a night without waking up. Then she went to see the village headman, Sarpanch Muhammad Din, and informed him matter-of-factly that the Archangel Gibreel had appeared to her in a vision and had lain down beside her to rest. 'Greatness has come among us,' she informed the alarmed Sarpanch, who had until then been more concerned with potato quotas than transcendence. 'Everything will be required of us, and everything will be given to us also.'

In another part of the tree, the Sarpanch's wife Khadija was consoling a weeping clown, who was finding it hard to accept that he had lost his beloved Ayesha to a higher being, for when an archangel lies with a woman she is lost to men forever. Khadija was old and forgetful and frequently clumsy when she tried to be loving, and she gave Osman cold comfort: 'The sun always sets when there is fear of tigers,' she quoted the old saying: bad news always comes all at once.

Soon after the story of the miracle got out, the girl Ayesha was summoned to the big house, and in the following days she spent long hours closeted with the zamindar's wife, Begum Mishal Akhtar, whose mother had also arrived on a visit, and fallen for the archangel's white-haired wife.

The dreamer, dreaming, wants (but is unable) to protest: I never laid a finger on her, what do you think this is, some kind of wet dream or what? Damn me if I know from where that girl was getting her information/inspiration. Not from this quarter, that's for sure.

This happened: she was walking back to her village, but then she seemed to grow weary all of a sudden, and went off the path to lie in the shade of a tamarind-tree and rest. The moment her eyes closed he was there beside her, dreaming Gibreel in coat and hat, sweltering in the heat. She looked at him but he couldn't say what she saw, wings maybe, haloes, the works. Then he was lying there and finding he could not get up, his limbs had become heavier than iron bars, it seemed as if his body might be crushed by its own weight into the earth. When she finished looking at him she nodded, gravely, as if he had spoken, and then she took off her scrap of a sari and stretched out beside him, nude. Then in the dream he fell asleep, out cold as if somebody pulled out the plug, and when dreamed himself awake again she was standing in front of him with that loose white hair and the butterflies clothing her: transformed. She was still nodding, with a rapt expression on her face, receiving a message from somewhere that she called Gibreel. Then she left him lying there and returned to the village to make her entrance.

So now I have a dream-wife, the dreamer becomes conscious enough to think. What the hell to do with her? – But it isn't up to him. Ayesha and Mishal Akhtar are together in the big house.

Ever since his birthday Mirza Saeed had been full of passionate desires, 'as if life really does begin at forty', his wife marvelled. Their marriage became so energetic that the servants had to change the bedsheets three times per day. Mishal hoped secretly that this heightening of her husband's libido would lead her to conceive, because she was of the firm opinion that enthusiasm mattered, whatever doctors might say to the contrary, and that the years of taking her temperature every morning before getting out of bed, and then plotting the results on graph paper in order to establish her pattern of ovulation, had actually dissuaded the babies from being born, partly because it was difficult to be properly ardent when science got into bed along with you, and partly, too, in her view, because no self-respecting foetus would wish to enter the womb of so mechanically programmed a mother. Mishal still prayed for a child, although she no longer mentioned the fact to Saeed so as to spare him the sense of having failed her in this respect. Eyes shut, feigning sleep, she would call on God for a sign, and when Saeed became so loving, so frequently, she wondered if maybe this might not be it. As a result, his strange request that from now on, whenever they came to stay at Peristan, she should adopt the 'old ways' and retreat into purdah, was not treated by her with the contempt it deserved. In the city, where they kept a large and hospitable house, the zamindar and his wife were known as one of the most 'modern' and 'go-go' couples on the scene; they collected contemporary art and threw wild parties and invited friends round for fumbles in the dark on sofas while watching soft-porno VCRs. So when Mirza Saeed said, 'Would it not be sort of delicious, Mishu, if we tailored our behaviour to fit this old house,' she should have laughed in his face. Instead she replied, 'What you like, Saeed,' because he gave her to understand that it was a sort of erotic game. He even hinted that his passion for her had become so overwhelming that he might need to express it at any moment, and if she were out in the open at the time it might embarrass the staff; certainly her presence would make it impossible for him to concentrate on any of his tasks, and besides, in the city, 'we will still be completely up-to-date'. From this she understood that the city was full of distractions for the Mirza, so that the chances of conceiving were greatest right here in Titlipur. She resolved to stay put. This was when she invited her mother to come and stay, because if she were to confine herself to the zenana she would need company. Mrs Qureishi arrived wobbling with plump fury, determined to scold her son-in-law until he gave up this purdah foolishness, but Mishal amazed her mother by begging: 'Please don't.' Mrs Qureishi, the wife of the state bank director, was quite a sophisticate herself. 'In fact, all your teenage, Mishu, you were the grey goose and I was the hipster. I thought you dragged yourself out of that ditch but I see he pushed you back in there again.' The financier's wife had always been of the opinion that her son-in-law was a secret cheapskate, an opinion which had survived intact in spite of being starved of any scrap of supporting evidence. Ignoring her daughter's veto, she sought out Mirza Saeed in the formal garden and launched into him, wobbling, as was her wont, for emphasis. 'What type of life are you living?' she demanded. 'My daughter is not for locking up, but for taking out! What is all your fortune for, if you keep it also under lock and key? My son, unlock both wallet and wife! Take her away, renew your love, on some enjoyable *outing*!' Mirza Saeed opened his mouth, found no reply, shut it again. Dazzled by her own oratory, which had given rise, quite on the spur of the moment, to the idea of a holiday, Mrs Qureishi warmed to her theme. 'Just get set, and go!' she urged. 'Go, man, go! Go away with her, or will you lock her up until she goes away,' – here she jabbed an ominous finger at the sky – *'forever?'*

Guiltily, Mirza Saeed promised to consider the idea.

'What are you waiting for?' she cried in triumph. 'You big softo? You . . . you *Hamlet?'*

His mother-in-law's attack brought on one of the periodic bouts of self-reproach which had been plaguing Mirza Saeed ever since he persuaded Mishal to take the veil. To console himself he settled down to read Tagore's story *Ghare-Baire* in which a zamindar persuades his wife to come *out* of purdah, whereupon he takes up with a firebrand politico involved in the 'swadeshi' campaign, and the zamindar winds up dead. The novel cheered him up momentarily, but then his suspicions returned. Had he been sincere in the reasons he gave his wife, or was he simply finding a way of leaving the coast clear for his pursuit of the madonna of the butterflies, the epileptic, Ayesha? 'Some coast,' he thought, remembering Mrs Qureishi with her eyes of an accusative hawk, 'some clear.' His mother-in-law's presence, he argued to himself, was further proof of his bona fides. Had he not positively encouraged Mishal to send for her, even though he knew perfectly well that the old fatty couldn't stand him and would suspect him of every damn slyness under the sun? 'Would I have been so keen for her to come if I was planning on hanky panky?' he asked himself. But the nagging inner voices continued: All this recent sexology, this renewed interest in your lady wife, is simple transference. Really, you are longing for your peasant floozy to come and flooze with you.'

Guilt had the effect of making the zamindar feel entirely worthless. His mother-in-law's insults came to seem, in his unhappiness, like the literal truth. 'Softo,' she called him, and sitting in his study, surrounded by bookcases in which worms were munching contentedly upon priceless Sanskrit texts such as were not to be found even in the national archives, and also, less upliftingly, on the complete works of Percy Westerman, G. A. Henty and Dornford Yates, Mirza Saeed admitted, yes, spot on, I am soft. The house was seven generations old and for seven generations the softening had been going on. He walked down the corridor in which his ancestors hung in baleful, gilded frames, and contemplated the mirror which he kept hanging in the last space as a reminder that one day he, too, must step up on to this wall. He was a man without sharp corners or rough edges; even his elbows were covered by little pads of flesh. In the mirror he saw the thin moustache, the weak chin, the lips stained by paan. Cheeks, nose, forehead: all soft, soft, soft. 'Who would see anything in a type like me?' he cried, and when he realized that he had been so agitated that he had spoken aloud he knew he must be in love, that he was sick as a dog with love, and that the object of his affections was no longer his loving wife.

'Then what a damn, shallow, tricksy and self-deceiving fellow I am,' he sighed to himself, 'to change so much, so fast. I deserve to be finished off without ceremony.' But he was not the type to fall on his sword. Instead, he strolled a while around the corridors of Peristan, and pretty soon the house worked its magic and restored him to something like a good mood once again.

The house: in spite of its faery name, it was a solid, rather prosy building, rendered exotic only by being in the wrong country. It had been built seven generations ago by a certain Perowne, an English architect much favoured by the colonial authorities, whose only style was that of the neo-classical English country house. In those days the great zamindars were crazy for European architecture. Saeed's great-great-great-great-grandfather had hired the fellow five minutes after meeting him at the Viceroy's reception, to indicate publicly that not all Indian Muslims had supported the action of the Meerut soldiers or been in sympathy with the subsequent uprisings, no, not by any means; – and then given him carte blanche; – so here Peristan now stood, in the middle of near-tropical potato fields and beside the great banyan-tree, covered in bougainvillaea creeper, with snakes in the kitchens and butterfly skeletons in the cupboards. Some said its name owed more to the Englishman's than to anything more fanciful: it was a mere contraction of *Perownistan*.

After seven generations it was at last beginning to look as if it belonged in this landscape of bullock carts and palm-trees and high, clear, star-heavy skies. Even the stained-glass window looking down on the staircase of King Charles the Headless had been, in an indefinable manner, naturalized. Very few of these old zamindar houses had survived the egalitarian depredations of the present, and accordingly there hung over Peristan something of the musty air of a museum, even though – or perhaps because – Mirza Saeed took great pride in the old place and had spent lavishly to keep it in trim. He slept under a high canopy of worked and beaten brass in a ship-like bed that had been occupied by three Viceroys. In the grand salon he liked to sit with Mishal and Mrs Qureishi in the unusual three-way love seat. At one end of this room a colossal Shiraz carpet stood rolled up, on wooden blocks, awaiting the glamorous reception which would merit its unfurling, and which never came. In the dining-room there were stout classical columns with ornate Corinthian tops, and there were peacocks, both real and stone, strolling on the main steps to the house, and Venetian chandeliers tinkling in the hall. The original punkahs were still in full working order, all their operating cords travelling by way of pulleys and holes in walls and floors to a little, airless boot-room where the punkah-wallah sat and tugged the lot together, trapped in the irony of the foetid air of that tiny windowless room while he despatched cool breezes to all other parts of the house. The servants, too, went back seven generations and had therefore lost the art of complaining. The old ways ruled: even the Titlipur sweet-vendor was required to seek the zamindar's approval before commencing to sell any innovative sweetmeat he might have invented. Life in Peristan was as soft as it was hard under the tree; but, even into such cushioned existences, heavy blows can fall.

The discovery that his wife was spending most of her time closeted with Ayesha filled the Mirza with an insupportable irritation, an eczema of the spirit that maddened him because there was no way of scratching it. Mishal was hoping that the archangel, Ayesha's husband, would grant her a baby, but because she couldn't tell that to her husband she grew sullen and shrugged petulantly when he asked her why she wasted so much time with the village's craziest girl. Mishal's new reticence worsened the itch in Mirza Saeed's heart, and made him jealous, too, although he wasn't sure if he was jealous of Ayesha, or Mishal. He noticed for the first time that the mistress of the butterflies had eyes of the same lustrous grey shade as his wife, and for some reason this made him cross, too, as if it proved that the women were ganging up on him, whispering God knew what secrets; maybe they were chittering and chattering about *him*! This zenana business seemed to have backfired; even that old jelly Mrs Qureishi had been taken in by Ayesha. Quite a threesome, thought Mirza Saeed; when mumbo-jumbo gets in through your door, good sense leaves by the window.

As for Ayesha: when she encountered the Mirza on the balcony, or in the garden as he wandered reading Urdu love-poetry, she was invariably deferential and shy; but her good behaviour, coupled with the total absence of any spark of erotic interest, drove Saeed further and further into the helplessness of his despair. So it was that when, one day, he spied Ayesha entering his wife's quarters and heard, a few minutes later, his mother-in-law's voice rise in a melodramatic shriek, he was seized by a mood of mulish vengefulness and deliberately waited a full three minutes before going to investigate. He found Mrs Qureishi tearing her hair and sobbing like a movie queen, while Mishal and Ayesha sat cross-legged on the bed, facing each other, grey eyes staring into grey, and Mishal's face was cradled between Ayesha's outstretched palms.

It turned out that the archangel had informed Ayesha that the zamindar's wife was dying of cancer, that her breasts were full of the malign nodules of death, and that she had no more than a few months to live. The location of the cancer had proved to Mishal the cruelty of God, because only a vicious deity would place death in the breast of a woman whose only dream was to suckle new life. When Saeed entered, Ayesha had been whispering urgently to Mishal: 'You mustn't think that way. God will save you. This is a test of faith.'

Mrs Qureishi told Mirza Saeed the bad news with many shrieks and howls, and for the confused zamindar it was the last straw. He flew into a temper and started yelling loudly and trembling as if he might at any moment start smashing up the furniture in the room and its occupants as well.

'To hell with your spook cancer,' he screamed at Ayesha in his exasperation. 'You have come into my house with your craziness and angels and dripped poison into my family's ears. Get out of here with your visions and your invisible spouse. This is the modern world, and it is medical doctors and not ghosts in potato fields who tell us when we are ill. You have created this bloody hullabaloo for nothing. Get out and never come on to my land again.'

Ayesha heard him out without removing her eyes or hands from Mishal. When Saeed stopped for breath, clenching and unclenching his fists, she said softly to his wife: 'Everything will be required of us, and everything will be given.' When he heard this formula, which people all over the village were beginning to parrot as if they knew what it meant, Mirza Saeed Akhtar went briefly out of his mind, raised his hand and knocked Ayesha senseless. She fell to the floor, bleeding from the mouth, a tooth loosened by his fist, and as she lay there Mrs Qureishi hurled abuse at her son-in-law. 'O God, I have put my daughter in the care of a killer. O God, a woman hitter. Go on, hit me also, get some practice. Defiler of saints, blasphemer, devil, unclean.' Saeed left the room without saying a word.

The next day Mishal Akhtar insisted on returning to the city for a complete medical check-up. Saeed took a stand. 'If you want to indulge in superstition, go, but don't expect me to come along. It's eight hours' drive each way; so, to hell with it.' Mishal left that afternoon with her mother and the driver, and as a result Mirza Saeed was not where he should have been, that is, at his wife's side, when the results of the tests were communicated to her: positive, inoperable, too far advanced, the claws of the cancer dug in deeply throughout her chest. A few months, six if she was lucky, and before that, coming soon, the pain. Mishal returned to Peristan and went straight to her rooms in the zenana, where she wrote her husband a formal note on lavender stationery, telling him of the doctor's diagnosis. When he read her death sentence, written in her own hand, he wanted very badly to burst into tears, but his eyes remained obstinately dry. He had had no time for the Supreme Being for many years, but now a couple of Ayesha's phrases popped back into his mind. *God will save you. Everything will be given.* A bitter, superstitious notion occurred to him: 'It is a curse,' he thought. 'Because I lusted after Ayesha, she has murdered my wife.'

When he went to the zenana, Mishal refused to see him, but her mother, barring the doorway, handed Saeed a second note on scented blue notepaper, 'I want to see Ayesha,' it read. 'Kindly permit this.' Bowing his head, Mirza Saeed gave his assent, and crept away in shame.

With Mahound, there is always a struggle; with the Imam, slavery; but with this girl, there is nothing. Gibreel is inert, usually asleep in the dream as he is in life. She comes upon him under a tree, or in a ditch, hears what he isn't saying, takes what she needs, and leaves. What does he know about cancer, for example? Not a solitary thing.

All around him, he thinks as he half-dreams, half-wakes, are people hearing voices, being seduced by words. But not his; never his original material. – Then whose? Who is whispering in their ears, enabling them to move mountains, halt clocks, diagnose disease?

He can't work it out.

The day after Mishal Akhtar's return to Titlipur, the girl Ayesha, whom people were beginning to call a kahin, a pir, disappeared completely for a week. Her hapless admirer, Osman the clown, who had been following her at a distance along the dusty potato track to Chatnapatna, told the villagers that a breeze got up and blew dust into his eyes; when he got it out again she had 'just gone'. Usually, when Osman and his bullock started telling their tall tales about djinnis and magic lamps and open-sesames, the villagers looked tolerant and teased him, okay, Osman, save it for those idiots in Chatnapatna; they may fall for that stuff but here in Titlipur we know which way is up and that palaces do not appear unless a thousand and one labourers build them, nor do they disappear unless the same workers knock them down. On this occasion, however, nobody laughed at the clown, because where Ayesha was concerned the villagers were willing to believe anything. They had grown convinced that the snow-haired girl was the true successor to old Bibiji, because had the butterflies not reappeared in the year of her birth, and did they not follow her around like a cloak? Ayesha was the vindication of the long-soured hope engendered by the butterflies' return, and the evidence that great things were still possible in this life, even for the weakest and poorest in the land.

'The angel has taken her away,' marvelled the Sarpanch's wife

Khadija, and Osman burst into tears. 'But no, it is a wonderful thing,' old Khadija uncomprehendingly explained. The villagers teased the Sarpanch: 'How you got to be village headman with such a tactless spouse, beats us.'

'You chose me,' he dourly replied.

On the seventh day after her disappearance Ayesha was sighted walking towards the village, naked again and dressed in golden butterflies, her silver hair streaming behind her in the breeze. She went directly to the home of Sarpanch Muhammad Din and asked that the Titlipur panchayat be convened for an immediate emergency meeting. 'The greatest event in the history of the tree has come upon us,' she confided. Muhammad Din, unable to refuse her, fixed the time of the meeting for that evening, after dark.

That night the panchayat members took their places on the usual branch of the tree, while Ayesha the kahin stood before them on the ground. 'I have flown with the angel into the highest heights,' she said. 'Yes, even to the lote-tree of the uttermost end. The archangel, Gibreel: he has brought us a message which is also a command. Everything is required of us, and everything will be given.'

Nothing in the life of the Sarpanch Muhammad Din had prepared him for the choice he was about to face. 'What does the angel ask, Ayesha, daughter?' he asked, fighting to steady his voice.

'It is the angel's will that all of us, every man, and woman and child in the village, begin at once to prepare for a pilgrimage. We are commanded to walk from this place to Mecca Sharif, to kiss the Black Stone in the Ka'aba at the centre of the Haram Sharif, the sacred mosque. There we must surely go.'

Now the panchayat's quintet began to debate heatedly. There were the crops to consider, and the impossibility of abandoning their homes en masse. 'It is not to be conceived of, child,' the Sarpanch told her. 'It is well known that Allah excuses haj and umra to those who are genuinely unable to go for reasons of poverty or health.' But Ayesha remained silent and the elders continued to argue. Then it was as if her silence infected everyone else and for a long moment, in which the question was settled – although by what means nobody ever managed to comprehend – there were no words spoken at all.

It was Osman the clown who spoke up at last, Osman the convert, for whom his new faith had been no more than a drink of water. 'It's almost two hundred miles from here to the sea,' he cried. 'There are old ladies here, and babies. However can we go?'

'God will give us the strength,' Ayesha serenely replied.

'Hasn't it occurred to you,' Osman shouted, refusing to give up, 'that there's a mighty ocean between us and Mecca Sharif? How will we ever cross? We have no money for the pilgrim boats. Maybe the angel will grow us wings, so we can fly?'

Many villagers rounded angrily upon the blasphemer Osman. 'Be quiet now,' Sarpanch Muhammad Din rebuked him. 'You haven't been long in our faith or our village. Keep your trap shut and learn our ways.'

Osman, however, answered cheekily, 'So this is how you welcome new settlers. Not as equals, but as people who must do as they are told.' A knot of red-faced men began to tighten around Osman, but before anything else could happen the kahin Ayesha changed the mood entirely by answering the clown's questions.

'This, too, the angel has explained,' she said quietly. 'We will walk two hundred miles, and when we reach the shores of the sea, we will put our feet into the foam, and the waters will open for us. The waves shall be parted, and we shall walk across the ocean-floor to Mecca.'

The next morning Mirza Saeed Akhtar awoke in a house that had fallen unusually silent, and when he called for the servants there was no reply. The stillness had spread into the potato fields, too; but under the broad, spreading roof of the Titlipur tree all was hustle and bustle. The panchayat had voted unanimously to obey the command of the Archangel Gibreel, and the villagers had begun to prepare for departure. At first the Sarpanch had wanted the carpenter Isa to construct litters that could be pulled by oxen and on which the old and infirm could ride, but that idea had been knocked on the head by his own wife, who told him, 'You don't listen, Sarpanch sahibji! Didn't the angel say we must walk? Well then, that is what we must do.' Only the youngest of infants were to be excused the foot-pilgrimage, and they would be carried (it had been decided) on the backs of all the adults, in rotation. The villagers had pooled all their resources, and heaps of potatoes, lentils, rice, bitter gourds, chillies, aubergines and other vegetables were piling up next to the panchayat bough. The weight of the provisions was to be evenly divided between the walkers. Cooking utensils, too, were being gathered together, and whatever bedding could be found. Beasts of burden were to be taken, and a couple of carts carrying live chickens and such, but in general the pilgrims were under the Sarpanch's instructions to keep personal belongings to a minimum. Preparations had been under way since before dawn, so that by the time an incensed Mirza Saeed strode into the village, things were well advanced. For forty-five minutes the zamindar slowed things up by making angry speeches and shaking individual villagers by the shoulders, but then, fortunately, he gave up and left, so that the work could be continued at its former, rapid pace. As the Mirza departed he smacked his head repeatedly and called people names, such as *loonies, simpletons,* very bad words, but he had always been a godless man, the weak end of a strong line, and he had to be left to find his own fate; there was no arguing with men like him.

By sunset the villagers were ready to depart, and the Sarpanch told everyone to rise for prayers in the small hours so that they could leave immediately afterwards and thus avoid the worst heat of the day. That night, lying down on his mat beside old Khadija, he murmured, 'At last. I've always wanted to see the Ka'aba, to circle it before I die.' She reached out from her mat to take his hand. 'I, too, have hoped for it, against hope,' she said. 'We'll walk through the waters together.'

Mirza Saeed, driven into an impotent frenzy by the spectacle of the packing village, burst in on his wife without ceremony. 'You should see what's going on, Mishu,' he exclaimed, gesticulating absurdly. 'The whole of Titlipur has taken leave of its brains, and is off to the seaside. What is to happen to their homes, their fields? There is ruination in store. Must be political agitators involved. Someone has been bribing someone. – Do you think if I offered cash they would stay here like sane persons?' His voice dried. Ayesha was in the room.

'You bitch,' he cursed her. She was sitting cross-legged on the bed while Mishal and her mother squatted on the floor, sorting through their belongings and working out how little they could manage with on the pilgrimage.

'You're not going,' Mirza Saeed ranted. 'I forbid it, the devil alone knows what germ this whore has infected the villagers with, but you are my wife and I refuse to let you embark upon this suicidal venture.'

'Good words,' Mishal laughed bitterly. 'Saeed, good choice of words. You know I can't live but you talk about suicide. Saeed, a thing is happening here, and you with your imported European atheism don't know what it is. Or maybe you would if you looked beneath your English suitings and tried to locate your heart.'

'It's incredible,' Saeed cried. 'Mishal, Mishu, is this you? All of a sudden you've turned into this God-bothered type from ancient history?'

Mrs Qureishi said, 'Go away, son. No room for unbelievers here. The angel has told Ayesha that when Mishal completes the pilgrimage to Mecca her cancer will have disappeared. Everything is required and everything will be given.'

Mirza Saeed Akhtar put his palms against a wall of his wife's bedroom and pressed his forehead against the plaster. After a long pause he said: 'If it is a question of performing umra then for God's sake let's go to town and catch a plane. We can be in Mecca within a couple of days.'

Mishal answered, 'We are commanded to walk.'

Saeed lost control of himself. 'Mishal? Mishal?' he shrieked. 'Commanded? Archangels, Mishu? *Gibreel?* God with a long beard and angels with wings? Heaven and hell, Mishal? The Devil with a pointy tail and cloven hoofs? How far are you going with this? Do women have souls, what do you say? Or the other way: do souls have gender? Is God black or white? When the waters of the ocean part, where will the extra water go? Will it stand up sideways like walls? Mishal? Answer me. Are there miracles? Do you believe in Paradise? Will I be forgiven my sins?' He began to cry, and fell on to his knees, with his forehead still pressed against the wall. His dying wife came up and embraced him from behind. 'Go with the pilgrimage, then,' he said, dully. 'But at least take the Mercedes station wagon. It's got air-conditioning and you can take the icebox full of Cokes.'

'No,' she said, gently. 'We'll go like everybody else. We're pilgrims, Saeed. This isn't a picnic at the beach.'

'I don't know what to do,' Mirza Saeed Akhtar wept. 'Mishu, I can't handle this by myself.'

Ayesha spoke from the bed. 'Mirza sahib, come with us,' she said. 'Your ideas are finished with. Come and save your soul.'

Saeed stood up, red-eyed. 'A bloody outing you wanted,' he said viciously to Mrs Qureishi. 'That chicken certainly came home to roost. Your outing will finish off the lot of us, seven generations, the whole bang shoot.'

Mishal leaned her cheek against his back. 'Come with us, Saeed. Just come.'

He turned to face Ayesha. 'There is no God,' he said firmly.

'There is no God but God, and Muhammad is His Prophet,' she replied.

'The mystical experience is a subjective, not an objective truth,' he went on. 'The waters will not open.'

'The sea will part at the angel's command,' Ayesha answered.

'You are leading these people into certain disaster.'

'I am taking them into the bosom of God.'

'I don't believe in you,' Mirza Saeed insisted. 'But I'm going to come, and will try to end this insanity with every step I take.'

'God chooses many means,' Ayesha rejoiced, 'many roads by which the doubtful may be brought into his certainty.'

'Go to hell,' shouted Mirza Saeed Akhtar, and ran, scattering butterflies, from the room.

'Who is the madder,' Osman the clown whispered into his bullock's ear as he groomed it in its small byre, 'the madwoman, or the fool who loves the madwoman?' The bullock didn't reply. 'Maybe we should have stayed untouchable,' Osman continued. 'A compulsory ocean sounds worse than a forbidden well.' And the bullock nodded, twice for yes, boom, boom.

PART V

❧

A City Visible
but Unseen

❧

1

'*O*nce *I'm an owl, what is the spell or antidote for turning me back into myself?*' Mr Muhammad Sufyan, prop. Shaandaar Café and landlord of the rooming-house above, mentor to the variegated, transient and particoloured inhabitants of both, seen-it-all type, least doctrinaire of hajis and most unashamed of VCR addicts, ex-schoolteacher, self-taught in classical texts of many cultures, dismissed from post in Dhaka owing to cultural differences with certain generals in the old days when Bangladesh was merely an East Wing, and therefore, in his own words, 'not so much an immig as an emig runt' – this last a good-natured allusion to his lack of inches, for though he was a wide man, thick of arm and waist, he stood no more than sixty-one inches off the ground, blinked in his bedroom doorway, awakened by Jumpy Joshi's urgent midnight knock, polished his half-rimmed spectacles on the edge of Bengali-style kurta (drawstrings tied at the neck in a neat bow), squeezed lids tightly shut open shut over myopic eyes, replaced glasses, opened eyes, stroked moustacheless hennaed beard, sucked teeth, and responded to the now-indisputable horns on the brow of the shivering fellow whom Jumpy, like the cat, appeared to have dragged in, with the above impromptu quip, stolen, with commendable mental alacrity for one aroused from his slumbers, from Lucius Apuleius of Madaura, Moroccan priest,

251

A D 120–180 approx., colonial of an earlier Empire, a person who denied the accusation of having bewitched a rich widow yet confessed, somewhat perversely, that at an early stage in his career he had been transformed, by witchcraft, into (not an owl, but) an ass. 'Yes, yes,' Sufyan continued, stepping out into the passage and blowing a white mist of winter breath into his cupped hands, 'Poor misfortunate, but no point wallowing. Constructive attitude must be adopted. I will wake my wife.'

Chamcha was beard-fuzz and grime. He wore a blanket like a toga below which there protruded the comic deformity of goats' hoofs, while above it could be seen the sad comedy of a sheepskin jacket borrowed from Jumpy, its collar turned up, so that sheepish curls nestled only inches from pointy billy-goat horns. He seemed incapable of speech, sluggish of body, dull of eye; even though Jumpy attempted to encourage him – 'There, you see, we'll have this well sorted in a flash' – he, Saladin, remained the most limp and passive of – what? – let us say: satyrs. Sufyan, meanwhile, offered further Apuleian sympathy. 'In the case of the ass, reverse metamorphosis required personal intervention of goddess Isis,' he beamed. 'But old times are for old fogies. In your instance, young mister, first step would possibly be a bowl of good hot soup.'

At this point his kindly tones were quite drowned by the intervention of a second voice, raised high in operatic terror; moments after which, his small form was being jostled and shoved by the mountainous, fleshy figure of a woman, who seemed unable to decide whether to push him out of her way or keep him before her as a protective shield. Crouching behind Sufyan, this new being extended a trembling arm at whose end was a quivering, pudgy, scarlet-nailed index finger. 'That over there,' she howled. 'What thing is come upon us?'

'It is a friend of Joshi's,' Sufyan said mildly, and continued, turning to Chamcha, 'Please forgive, – the unexpectedness et cet, isn't it? – Anyhow, may I present my Mrs; – my Begum Sahiba, – Hind.'

'What friend? How friend?' the croucher said. 'Ya Allah, eyes aren't next to your nose?'

The passageway, – bare-board floor, torn floral paper on the walls, – was starting to fill up with sleepy residents. Prominent among whom were two teenage girls, one spike-haired, the other pony-tailed, and both relishing the opportunity to demonstrate their skills (learned from Jumpy) in the martial arts of karate and Wing Chun: Sufyan's daughters, Mishal (seventeen) and fifteen-year-old Anahita, leapt from their bedroom in fighting gear, Bruce Lee pajamas worn loosely over T-shirts bearing the image of the new Madonna; – caught sight of unhappy Saladin; – and shook their heads in wide-eyed delight.

'Radical,' said Mishal, approvingly. And her sister nodded assent: 'Crucial. Fucking *A*.' Her mother did not, however, reproach her for her language; Hind's mind was elsewhere, and she wailed louder than ever: 'Look at this husband of mine. What sort of haji is this? Here is Shaitan himself walking in through our door, and I am made to offer him hot chicken yakhni, cooked by my own right hand.'

Useless, now, for Jumpy Joshi to plead with Hind for tolerance, to attempt explanations and demand solidarity. 'If he's not the devil on earth,' the heaving-chested lady pointed out unanswerably, 'from where that plague-breath comes that he's breathing? From, maybe, the Perfumed Garden?'

'Not Gulistan, but Bostan,' said Chamcha, suddenly. 'A I Flight 420.' On hearing his voice, however, Hind squealed frightfully, and plunged past him, heading for the kitchen.

'Mister,' Mishal said to Saladin as her mother fled downstairs, 'anyone who scares her that way has got to be seriously *bad*.'

'Wicked,' Anahita agreed. 'Welcome aboard.'

This Hind, now so firmly entrenched in exclamatory mode, had once been – strangebuttrue! – the most blushing of brides, the soul of gentleness, the very incarnation of tolerant good humour. As the wife of the erudite schoolteacher of Dhaka, she had entered into her duties with a will, the perfect helpmeet, bringing her husband cardamom-scented tea when he stayed up late marking examination papers, ingratiating herself with the school principal at the termly Staff Families Outing, struggling with the novels of Bibhutibhushan Banerji and the metaphysics of Tagore in an attempt to be more worthy of a spouse who could quote effortlessly from Rig-Veda as well as Quran-Sharif, from the military accounts of Julius Caesar as well as the Revelations of St John the Divine. In those days she had admired his pluralistic openness of mind, and struggled, in her kitchen, towards a parallel eclecticism, learning to cook the dosas and uttapams of South India as well as the soft meatballs of Kashmir. Gradually her espousal of the cause of gastronomic pluralism grew into a grand passion, and while secularist Sufyan swallowed the multiple cultures of the subcontinent – 'and let us not pretend that Western culture is not present; after these centuries, how could it not also be part of our heritage?' – his wife cooked, and ate in increasing quantities, its food. As she devoured the highly spiced dishes of Hyderabad and the high-faluting yoghurt sauces of Lucknow her body began to alter, because all that food had to find a home somewhere, and she began to resemble the wide rolling land mass itself, the subcontinent without frontiers, because food passes across any boundary you care to mention.

Mr Muhammad Sufyan, however, gained no weight: not a *tola*, not an *ounce*.

His refusal to fatten was the beginning of the trouble. When she reproached him – "You don't like my cooking? For whom I'm doing it all and blowing up like a balloon?' – he answered, mildly, looking up at her (she was the taller of the two) over the top of half-rimmed specs: 'Restraint is also part of our traditions, Begum. Eating two mouthfuls less than one's hunger: self-denial, the ascetic path.' What a man: all the answers, but you couldn't get him to give you a decent fight.

Restraint was not for Hind. Maybe, if Sufyan had ever complained; if just once he'd said, *I thought I was marrying one woman but these days you're big enough for two;* if he'd ever given her the incentive! – then maybe she'd have desisted, why not, of course she would; so it was his fault, for having no aggression, what kind of a male was it who didn't know how to insult his fat lady wife? – In truth, it was entirely possible that Hind would have failed to control her eating binges even if Sufyan had come up with the required imprecations and entreaties; but, since he did not, she munched on, content to dump the whole blame for her figure on him.

As a matter of fact, once she had started blaming him for things, she found that there were a number of other matters she could hold against him; and found, too, her tongue, so that the school-teacher's humble apartment resounded regularly to the kinds of tickings-off he was too much of a mouse to hand out to his pupils. Above all, he was berated for his excessively high principles, thanks to which, Hind told him, she knew he would never permit her to become a rich man's wife; – for what could one say about a man who, finding that his bank had inadvertently credited his salary to his account twice in the same month, promptly *drew the institution's notice* to the error and handed back the cash?; – what hope was there for a teacher who, when approached by the wealthiest of the schoolchildren's parents, flatly refused to con-template accepting the usual remunerations in return for services rendered when marking the little fellows' examination papers?

'But all of that I could forgive,' she would mutter darkly at him, leaving unspoken the rest of the sentence, which was *if it hadn't been for your two real offences: your sexual, and political, crimes.*

Ever since their marriage, the two of them had performed the sexual act infrequently, in total darkness, pin-drop silence and almost complete immobility. It would not have occurred to Hind to wiggle or wobble, and since Sufyan appeared to get through it all with an absolute minimum of motion, she took it – had always taken it – that the two of them were of the same mind on this matter, viz., that it was a dirty business, not to be discussed before or after, and not to be drawn attention to during, either. That the children took their time in coming she took as God's punishment for He only knew what misdeeds of her earlier life; that they both turned out to be girls she refused to blame on Allah, preferring, instead, to blame the weakling seed implanted in her by her unmanly spouse, an attitude she did not refrain from expressing, with great emphasis, and to the horror of the midwife, at the very moment of little Anahita's birth. 'Another girl,' she gasped in disgust. 'Well, considering who made the baby, I should think myself lucky it's not a cockroach, or a mouse.' After this second daughter she told Sufyan that enough was enough, and ordered him to move his bed into the hall. He accepted without any argument her refusal to have more children; but then she discovered that the lecher thought he could still, from time to time, enter her darkened room and enact that strange rite of silence and near-motionlessness to which she had only submitted in the name of reproduction. 'What do you think,' she shouted at him the first time he tried it, 'I do this thing for *fun*?'

Once he had got it through his thick skull that she meant business, no more hanky-panky, no sir, she was a decent woman, not a lust-crazed libertine, he began to stay out late at night. It was during this period – she had thought, mistakenly, that he was visiting prostitutes – that he became involved with politics, and not just any old politics, either, oh no, Mister Brainbox had to go and join the devils themselves, the Communist Party, no less, so much for those principles of his; demons, that's what they were, worse by far than whores. It was because of this dabbling in the occult that she had to pack up her bags at such short notice and leave for England with two small babies in tow; because of this ideological witchcraft that she had had to endure all the privations and humiliations of the process of immigration; and on account of this diabolism of his that she was stuck forever in this England and would never see her village again. 'England,' she once said to him, 'is your revenge upon me for preventing you from performing your obscene acts upon my body.' He had not given an answer; and silence denotes assent.

And what was it that made them a living in this Vilayet of her exile, this Yuké of her sex-obsessed husband's vindictiveness? What? His book learning? His *Gitanjali*, *Eclogues*, or that play *Othello* that he explained was really Attallah or Attaullah except the writer couldn't spell, what sort of writer was that, anyway?

It was: her cooking. 'Shaandaar,' it was praised. 'Outstanding, brilliant, delicious.' People came from all over London to eat her samosas, her Bombay chaat, her gulab jamans straight from Paradise. What was there for Sufyan to do? Take the money, serve the tea, run from here to there, behave like a servant for all his education. O, yes, of course, the customers liked his personality, he always had an appealing character, but when you're running an eatery it isn't the conversation they pay for on the bill. Jalebis, barfi, Special of the Day. How life had turned out! She was the mistress now.

Victory!

And yet it was also a fact that she, cook and breadwinner, chiefest architect of the success of the Shaandaar Café, which had finally enabled them to buy the whole four-storey building and start renting out its rooms, – she was the one around whom there hung, like bad breath, the miasma of defeat. While Sufyan twinkled on, she looked extinguished, like a lightbulb with a broken filament, like a fizzled star, like a flame. – Why? – Why, when Sufyan, who had been deprived of vocation, pupils and respect, bounded about like a young lamb, and even began to put on weight, fattening up in Proper London as he had never done back home; why, when power had been removed from his hands and delivered into hers, did she act – as her husband put it – the 'sad sack', the 'glum chum' and the 'moochy pooch'? Simple: not in spite of, but on account of. Everything she valued had been upset by the change; had in this process of translation, been lost.

Her language: obliged, now, to emit these alien sounds that made her tongue feel tired, was she not entitled to moan? Her familiar place: what matter that they had lived, in Dhaka, in a teacher's humble flat, and now, owing to entrepreneurial good sense, savings and skill with spices, occupied this four-storey terraced house? Where now was the city she knew? Where the village of her youth and the green waterways of home? The customs around which she had built her life were lost, too, or at least were hard to find. Nobody in this Vilayet had time for the slow courtesies of life back home, or for the many observances of faith.

Furthermore: was she not forced to put up with a husband of no
account, whereas before she could bask in his dignified position?
Where was the pride in being made to work for her living, for his
living, whereas before she could sit at home in much-befitting
pomp? – And she knew, how could she not, the sadness beneath
his bonhomie, and that, too, was a defeat; never before had she
felt so inadequate as a wife, for what kind of a Mrs is it that cannot
cheer up her man, but must observe the counterfeit of happiness
and make do, as if it were the genuine McCoy? – Plus also: they
had come into a demon city in which anything could happen,
your windows shattered in the middle of the night without any
cause, you were knocked over in the street by invisible hands, in
the shops you heard such abuse you felt like your ears would drop
off but when you turned in the direction of the words you saw
only empty air and smiling faces, and every day you heard about
this boy, that girl, beaten up by ghosts. – Yes, a land of phantom
imps, how to explain; best thing was to stay home, not go out for
so much as to post a letter, stay in, lock the door, say your prayers,
and the goblins would (maybe) stay away. – Reasons for defeat?
Baba, who could count them? Not only was she a shopkeeper's
wife and a kitchen slave, but even her own people could not be
relied on; – there were men she thought of as respectable types,
sharif, giving telephone divorces to wives back home and running
off with some haramzadi female, and girls killed for dowry (some
things could be brought through the foreign customs without
duty); – and worst of all, the poison of this devil-island had
infected her baby girls, who were growing up refusing to speak
their mother-tongue, even though they understood every word,
they did it just to hurt; and why else had Mishal cut off all her hair
and put rainbows into it; and every day it was fight, quarrel, disobey, – and worst of all, there was not one new thing about her
complaints, this is how it was for women like her, so now she was
no longer just one, just herself, just Hind wife of teacher Sufyan;
she had sunk into the anonymity, the characterless plurality, of
being merely one-of-the-women-like-her. This was history's

lesson: nothing for women-like-her to do but suffer, remember, and die.

What she did: to deny her husband's weakness, she treated him, for the most part, like a lord, like a monarch, for in her lost world her glory had lain in his; to deny the ghosts outside the café, she stayed indoors, sending others out for kitchen provisions and household necessities, and also for the endless supply of Bengali and Hindi movies on VCR through which (along with her ever-increasing hoard of Indian movie magazines) she could stay in touch with events in the 'real world', such as the bizarre disappearance of the incomparable Gibreel Farishta and the subsequent tragic announcement of his death in an airline accident; and to give her feelings of defeated, exhausted despair some outlet, she shouted at her daughters. The elder of whom, to get her own back, hacked off her hair and permitted her nipples to poke through shirts worn provocatively tight.

The arrival of a fully developed devil, a horned goat-man, was, in the light of the foregoing, something very like the last, or at any rate the penultimate, straw.

Shaandaar residents gathered in the night-kitchen for an impromptu crisis summit. While Hind hurled imprecations into chicken soup, Sufyan placed Chamcha at a table, drawing up, for the poor fellow's use, an aluminium chair with a blue plastic seat, and initiated the night's proceedings. The theories of Lamarck, I am pleased to report, were quoted by the exiled schoolteacher, who spoke in his best didactic voice. When Jumpy had recounted the unlikely story of Chamcha's fall from the sky – the protagonist himself being too immersed in chicken soup and misery to speak for himself – Sufyan, sucking teeth, made reference to the last edition of *The Origin of Species*. 'In which even great Charles accepted the notion of mutation in extremis, to ensure survival of species; so what if his followers – always more Darwinian than man himself! – repudiated, posthumously, such Lamarckian heresy, insisting on natural selection and nothing but, – however, I am bound to admit, such theory is not extended to survival of individual specimen but only to species as a whole; – in addition, regarding nature of mutation, problem is to comprehend actual utility of the change.'

'Da-ad,' Anahita Sufyan, eyes lifting to heaven, cheek lying ho-hum against palm, interrupted these cogitations. 'Give over. Point is, how'd he turn into such a, such a,' – admiringly – 'freak?'

Upon which, the devil himself, looking up from chicken soup, cried out, 'No, I'm not. I'm not a freak, O no, certainly I am not.' His voice, seeming to rise from an unfathomable abyss of grief, touched and alarmed the younger girl, who rushed over to where he sat, and, impetuously caressing a shoulder of the unhappy beast, said, in an attempt to make amends: 'Of course you aren't, I'm sorry, of course I don't think you're a freak; it's just that you look like one.'

Saladin Chamcha burst into tears.

Mrs Sufyan, meanwhile, had been horrified by the sight of her younger daughter actually laying hands on the creature, and turning to the gallery of nightgowned residents she waved a soup-ladle at them and pleaded for support. 'How to tolerate? – Honour, safety of young girls cannot be assured. – That in my own house, such a thing . . . !'

Mishal Sufyan lost patience. 'Jesus, Mum.'

'Jesus?'

'Dju think it's temporary?' Mishal, turning her back on scandal-ized Hind, inquired of Sufyan and Jumpy. 'Some sort of posses-sion thing – could we maybe get it you know *exorcized*?' Omens, shinings, ghoulies, nightmares on Elm Street, stood excitedly in her eyes, and her father, as much the VCR aficionado as any teenager, appeared to consider the possibility seriously. 'In *Der Steppenwolf*,' he began, but Jumpy wasn't having any more of that. 'The central requirement,' he announced, 'is to take an ideologi-cal view of the situation.'

That silenced everyone.

'Objectively,' he said, with a small self-deprecating smile, 'what has happened here? A: Wrongful arrest, intimidation, violence. Two: Illegal detention, unknown medical experimentation in hospital,' – murmurs of assent here, as memories of intra-vaginal inspections, Depo-Provera scandals, unauthorized post-partum sterilizations, and, further back, the knowledge of Third World drug-dumping arose in every person present to give substance to the speaker's insinuations, – because what you believe depends on what you've seen, – not only what is visible, but what you are prepared to look in the face, – and anyhow, something had to explain horns and hoofs; in those policed medical wards, anything could happen – 'And thirdly,' Jumpy continued, 'psychological breakdown, loss of sense of self, inability to cope. We've seen it all before.'

Nobody argued, not even Hind; there were some truths from which it was impossible to dissent. 'Ideologically,' Jumpy said, 'I refuse to accept the position of victim. Certainly, he has been victim*ized*, but we know that all abuse of power is in part the responsibility of the abused; our passiveness colludes with, permits such crimes.' Whereupon, having scolded the gathering into shamefaced submission, he requested Sufyan to make available the small attic room that was presently unoccupied, and Sufyan, in his turn, was rendered entirely unable, by feelings of solidarity and guilt, to ask for a single p in rent. Hind did, it is true, mumble: 'Now I know the world is mad, when a devil becomes my house guest,' but she did so under her breath, and nobody except her elder daughter Mishal heard what she said.

Sufyan, taking his cue from his younger daughter, went up to where Chamcha, huddled in his blanket, was drinking enormous quantities of Hind's unrivalled chicken yakhni, squatted down, and placed an arm around the still-shivering unfortunate. 'Best place for you is here,' he said, speaking as if to a simpleton or small child. 'Where else would you go to heal your disfigurements and recover your normal health? Where else but here, with us, among your own people, your own kind?'

Only when Saladin Chamcha was alone in the attic room at the very end of his strength did he answer Sufyan's rhetorical question. 'I'm not your kind,' he said distinctly into the night. 'You're not my people. I've spent half my life trying to get away from you.'

His heart began to misbehave, to kick and stumble as if it, too, wanted to metamorphose into some new, diabolic form, to substitute the complex unpredictability of tabla improvisations for its old metronomic beat. Lying sleepless in a narrow bed, snagging his horns in bedsheets and pillowcases as he tossed and turned, he suffered the renewal of coronary eccentricity with a kind of fatalistic acceptance: if everything else, then why not this, too? Badoomboom, went the heart, and his torso jerked. *Watch it or I'll really let you have it. Doomboombadoom.* Yet: this was Hell, all right. The city of London, transformed into Jahannum, Gehenna, Muspellheim.

Do devils suffer in Hell? Aren't they the ones with the pitchforks?

Water began to drip steadily through the dormer window. Outside, in the treacherous city, a thaw had come, giving the streets the unreliable consistency of wet cardboard. Slow masses of whiteness slid from sloping, grey-slate roofs. The footprints of delivery vans corrugated the slush. First light; and the dawn chorus began, chattering of road-drills, chirrup of burglar alarms, trumpeting of wheeled creatures clashing at corners, the deep whirr of a large olive-green garbage eater, screaming radio-voices from a wooden painter's cradle clinging to the upper storey of a Free House, roar of the great wakening juggernauts rushing awesomely down this long but narrow pathway. From beneath the earth came tremors denoting the passage of huge subterranean worms that devoured and regurgitated human beings, and from the skies the thrum of choppers and the screech of higher, gleaming birds.

The sun rose, unwrapping the misty city like a gift. Saladin Chamcha slept.

Which afforded him no respite: but returned him, rather, to that other night-street down which, in the company of the physiotherapist Hyacinth Phillips, he had fled towards his destiny, clip-clop, on unsteady hoofs; and reminded him that, as captivity receded and the city drew nearer, Hyacinth's face and body had seemed to change. He saw the gap opening and widening between her central upper incisors, and the way her hair knotted and plaited itself into medusas, and the strange triangularity of her profile, which sloped outwards from her hairline to the tip of her nose, swung about and headed in an unbroken line inwards to her neck. He saw in the yellow light that her skin was growing darker by the minute, and her teeth more prominent, and her body as long as a child's stick-figure drawing. At the same time she was casting him glances of an ever more explicit lechery, and grasping his hand in fingers so bony and inescapable that it was as though a skeleton had seized him and was trying to drag him down into a grave; he could smell the freshly dug earth, the cloying scent of it, on her breath, on her lips . . . revulsion seized him. How could he ever have thought her attractive, even desired her, even gone so far as to fantasize, while she straddled him and pummelled fluid from his lungs, that they were lovers in the violent throes of sexual congress? . . . The city thickened around them like a forest; the buildings twined together and grew as matted as her hair. 'No light can get in here,' she whispered to him. 'It's black; all black.' She made as if to lie down and pull him towards her, towards the earth, but he shouted, 'Quick, the church,' and plunged into an unprepossessing box-like building, seeking more than one kind of sanctuary. Inside, however, the pews were full of Hyacinths, young and old, Hyacinths wearing shapeless blue two-piece suits, false pearls, and little pill-box hats decked out with bits of gauze, Hyacinths wearing virginal white nightgowns, every imaginable form of Hyacinth, all singing loudly, *Fix me, Jesus;* until they saw Chamcha, quit their spiritualling, and commenced to bawl in a most unspiritual manner, *Satan, the Goat, the Goat,* and suchlike stuff. Now it became clear that the Hyacinth with whom he'd entered was looking at him with new eyes, just the way he'd looked at her in the street; that she, too, had started seeing something that made her feel pretty sick; and when he saw the disgust on that hideously pointy and clouded face he just let rip. *'Hubshees,'* he cursed them in, for some reason, his discarded mother-tongue. Troublemakers and savages, he called them. 'I feel sorry for you,' he pronounced. 'Every morning you have to look at yourself in the mirror and see, staring back, the darkness: the stain, the proof that you're the lowest of the low.' They rounded upon him then, that congregation of Hyacinths, his own Hyacinth now lost among them, indistinguishable, no longer an individual but a woman-like-them, and he was being beaten frightfully, emitting a piteous bleating noise, running in circles, looking for a way out; until he realized that his assailants' fear was greater than their wrath, and he rose up to his full height, spread his arms, and screamed devil-sounds at them, sending them scurrying for cover, cowering behind pews, as he strode bloody but unbowed from the battlefield.

Dreams put things in their own way; but Chamcha, coming briefly awake as his heartbeat skipped into a new burst of syncopations, was bitterly aware that the nightmare had not been so very far from the truth; the spirit, at least, was right. – That was the last of Hyacinth, he thought, and faded away again. – To find himself shivering in the hall of his own home while, on a higher plane, Jumpy Joshi argued fiercely with Pamela. *With my wife.*

And when dream-Pamela, echoing the real one word for word, had rejected her husband a hundred and one times, *he doesn't exist, it, such things are not so,* it was Jamshed the virtuous who, setting aside love and desire, helped. Leaving behind a weeping Pamela – *Don't you dare bring that back here,* she shouted from the top floor – from Saladin's den – Jumpy, wrapping Chamcha in sheepskin and blanket, led enfeebled through the shadows to the Shaandaar Café, promising with empty kindness: 'It'll be all right. You'll see. It'll all be fine.'

When Saladin Chamcha awoke, the memory of these words

filled him with a bitter anger. Where's Farishta, he found himself thinking. That bastard: I bet he's doing okay. – It was a thought to which he would return, with extraordinary results; for the moment, however, he had other fish to fry.

I am the incarnation of evil, he thought. He had to face it. However it had happened, it could not be denied. I am *no longer myself*, or not only. I am the embodiment of wrong, of what-we-hate, of sin.

Why? Why me?

What evil had he done – what vile thing could he, would he do?

For what was he – he couldn't avoid the notion – being punished? And, come to that, *by whom*? (I held my tongue.)

Had he not pursued his own idea of *the good*, sought to become that which he most admired, dedicated himself with a will bordering on obsession to the conquest of Englishness? Had he not worked hard, avoided trouble, striven to become new? Assiduity, fastidiousness, moderation, restraint, self-reliance, probity, family life: what did these add up to if not a moral code? Was it his fault that Pamela and he were childless? Were genetics his responsibility? Could it be, in this inverted age, that he was being victimized by – the fates, he agreed with himself to call the persecuting agency – precisely *because of* his pursuit of 'the good'? – That nowadays such a pursuit was considered wrong-headed, even evil? – Then how cruel these fates were, to instigate his rejection by the very world he had so determinedly courted; how desolating, to be cast from the gates of the city one believed oneself to have taken long ago! – What mean small-mindedness was this, to cast him back into the bosom of *his people*, from whom he'd felt so distant for so long! – Here thoughts of Zeeny Vakil welled up, and guiltily, nervously, he forced them down again.

His heart kicked him violently, and he sat up, doubled over, gasped for breath. *Calm down, or it's curtains. No place for such stressful cogitations: not any more.* He took deep breaths; lay back; emptied his mind. The traitor in his chest resumed normal service.

No more of that, Saladin Chamcha told himself firmly. No more of thinking myself evil. Appearances deceive; the cover is not the best guide to the book. Devil, Goat, Shaitan? Not I.

Not I: another.

Who?

Mishal and Anahita arrived with breakfast on a tray and excitement all over their faces. Chamcha devoured cornflakes and Nescafé while the girls, after a few moments of shyness, gabbled at him, simultaneously, non-stop. 'Well, you've set the place buzzing and no mistake.' – 'You haven't gone and changed back in the night or anything?' – 'Listen, it's not a trick, is it? I mean, it's not make-up or something theatrical? – I mean, Jumpy says you're an actor, and I only thought, – I mean,' and here young Anahita dried up, because Chamcha, spewing cornflakes, howled angrily: 'Make-up? Theatrical? *Trick?*'

'No offence,' Mishal said anxiously on her sister's behalf. 'It's just we've been thinking, know what I mean, and well it'd just be awful if you weren't, but you are, 'course you are, so that's all right,' she finished hastily as Chamcha glared at her again. – 'Thing is,' Anahita resumed, and then, faltering, 'Mean to say, well, we just think it's great.' – 'You, she means,' Mishal corrected. 'We think you're, you know.' – 'Brilliant,' Anahita said and dazzled the bewildered Chamcha with a smile. 'Magic. You know. *Extreme.*'

'We didn't sleep all night,' Mishal said. 'We've got ideas.'

'What we reckoned,' Anahita trembled with the thrill of it, 'as you've turned into, – what you are, – then maybe, well, probably, actually, even if you haven't tried it out, it could be, you could . . .' And the older girl finished the thought: 'You could've developed – you know – *powers.*'

'We thought, anyway,' Anahita added, weakly, seeing the clouds gathering on Chamcha's brow. And, backing towards the door, added: 'But we're probably wrong. – Yeh. We're wrong all right. Enjoy your meal.' – Mishal, before she fled, took a small bottle full of green fluid out of a pocket of her red-and-black-check donkey jacket, put it on the floor by the door, and delivered the following parting shot. 'O, excuse me, but Mum says, can you use this, it's mouthwash, for your breath.'

That Mishal and Anahita should adore the disfiguration which he loathed with all his heart convinced him that 'his people' were as crazily wrong-headed as he'd long suspected. That the two of them should respond to his bitterness – when, on his second attic morning, they brought him a masala dosa instead of packet cereal complete with toy silver spacemen, and he cried out, ungratefully: 'Now I'm supposed to eat this filthy foreign food?' – with expressions of sympathy, made matters even worse. 'Sawful muck,' Mishal agreed with him. 'No bangers in here, worse luck.' Conscious of having insulted their hospitality, he tried to explain that he thought of himself, nowadays, as, well, British . . . 'What about us?' Anahita wanted to know. 'What do you think we are?' – And Mishal confided: 'Bangladesh in't nothing to me. Just some place Dad and Mum keep banging on about.' – And Anahita, conclusively: 'Bungleditch.' – With a satisfied nod. – 'What I call it, anyhow.'

But they weren't British, he wanted to tell them: not *really*, not in any way he could recognize. And yet his old certainties were slipping away by the moment, along with his old life . . . 'Where's the telephone?' he demanded. 'I've got to make some calls.'

It was in the hall; Anahita, raiding her savings, lent him the coins. His head wrapped in a borrowed turban, his body concealed in borrowed trousers (Jumpy's) and Mishal's shoes, Chamcha dialled the past.

'Chamcha,' said the voice of Mimi Mamoulian. 'You're dead.'

This happened while he was away: Mimi blacked out and lost her teeth. 'A whiteout is what it was,' she told him, speaking more harshly than usual because of difficulty with her jaw. 'A reason why? Don't ask. Who can ask for reason in these times? What's your number?' she added as the pips went. 'I'll call you right back.' But it was a full five minutes before she did. 'I took a leak. You have a reason why you're alive? Why the waters parted for you and the other guy but closed over the rest? Don't tell me you were worthier. People don't buy that nowadays, not even you, Chamcha. I was walking down Oxford Street looking for crocodile shoes when it happened: out cold in mid-stride and I fell forward like a tree, landed on the point of my chin and all the teeth fell out on the sidewalk in front of the man doing find-the-lady. People can be thoughtful, Chamcha. When I came to I found my teeth in a little pile next to my face. I opened my eyes and saw the little bastards staring at me, wasn't that nice? First thing I thought, thank God, I've got the money. I had them stitched back in, privately of course, great job, better than before. So I've been taking a break for a while. The voiceover business is in bad shape, let me tell you, what with you dying and my teeth, we just have no sense of responsibility. Standards have been low-ered, Chamcha. Turn on the TV, listen to radio, you should hear how corny the pizza commercials, the beer ads with the Cherman accents from Central Casting, the Martians eating potato powder and sounding like they came from the Moon. They fired us from *The Aliens Show*. Get well soon. Incidentally, you might say the same for me.'

So he had lost work as well as wife, home, a grip on life. 'It's not just the dentals that go wrong,' Mimi powered on. 'The fucking plosives scare me stupid. I keep thinking I'll spray the old bones on the street again. Age, Chamcha: it's all humiliations. You get born, you get beaten up and bruised all over and finally you break and they shovel you into an urn. Anyway, if I never work again I'll die comfortable. Did you know I'm with Billy Battuta now? That's right, how could you, you've been swim-ming. Yeah, I gave up waiting for you so I cradlesnatched one of your ethnic co-persons. You can take it as a compliment. Now I gots to run. Nice talking to the dead, Chamcha. Next time dive from the low board. Toodle oo.'

I am by nature an inward man, he said silently into the discon-nected phone. I have struggled, in my fashion, to find my way towards an appreciation of the high things, towards a small measure of fineness. On good days I felt it was within my grasp, somewhere within me, somewhere within. But it eluded me. I have become embroiled, in things, in the world and its messes, and I cannot resist. The grotesque has me, as before the quotidian had me, in its thrall. The sea gave me up; the land drags me down.

He was sliding down a grey slope, the black water lapping at his heart. Why did rebirth, the second chance granted to Gibreel Farishta and himself, feel so much, in his case, like a perpetual ending? He had been reborn into the knowledge of death; and the inescapability of change, of things-never-the-same, of no-way-back, made him afraid. When you lose the past you're naked in front of contemptuous Azraeel, the death-angel. Hold on if you can, he told himself. Cling to yesterdays. Leave your nail-marks in the grey slope as you slide.

Billy Battuta: that worthless piece of shit. Playboy Pakistani, turned an unremarkable holiday business – *Battuta's Travels* – into a fleet of supertankers. A con-man, basically, famous for his romances with leading ladies of the Hindi screen and, according to gossip, for his predilection for white women with enormous breasts and plenty of rump, whom he 'treated badly', as the euphemism had it, and 'rewarded handsomely'. What did Mimi want with bad Billy, his sexual instruments and his Maserati Biturbo? For boys like Battuta, white women – never mind fat, Jewish, non-deferential white women – were for fucking and throwing over. What one hates in whites – love of brown sugar – one must also hate when it turns up, inverted, in black. Bigotry is not only a function of power.

Mimi telephoned the next evening from New York. Anahita called him to the phone in her best damnyankee tones, and he struggled into his disguise. When he got there she had rung off, but she rang back. 'Nobody pays transatlantic prices for hanging on.' 'Mimi,' he said, with desperation patent in his voice, 'you didn't say you were leaving.' 'You didn't even tell me your damn address,' she responded. 'So we both have secrets.' He wanted to say, Mimi, come home, you're going to get kicked. 'I introduced him to the family,' she said, too jokily. 'You can imagine. Yassir Arafat meets the Begins. Never mind. We'll all live.' He wanted to say, Mimi, you're all I've got. He managed, however, only to piss her off. 'I wanted to warn you about Billy,' was what he said.

She went icy. 'Chamcha, listen up. I'll discuss this with you one time because behind all your bullshit you do maybe care for me a little. So comprehend, please, that I am an intelligent female. I have read *Finnegans Wake* and am conversant with postmodernist critiques of the West, e.g. that we have here a society capable only of pastiche: a "flattened" world. When I become the voice of a bottle of bubble bath, I am entering Flatland knowingly, under-standing what I'm doing and why. Viz., I am earning cash. And as an intelligent woman, able to do fifteen minutes on Stoicism and more on Japanese cinema, I say to you, Chamcha, that I am fully aware of Billy boy's rep. Don't teach me about exploitation. We had exploitation when you-plural were running round in skins. Try being Jewish, female and ugly sometime. You'll beg to be black. Excuse my French: brown.'

'You concede, then, that he's exploiting you,' Chamcha inter-posed, but the torrent swept him away. 'What's the fuckin' diff?' she trilled in her Tweetie Pie voice. 'Billy's a funny boy, a natural scam artist, one of the greats. Who knows for how long this is? I'll tell you some notions I do not require: patriotism, God and love. Definitely not wanted on the voyage. I like Billy because he knows the score.'

'Mimi,' he said, 'something's happened to me,' but she was still protesting too much and missed it. He put the receiver down without giving her his address.

She rang him once more, a few weeks later, and by now the unspoken precedents had been set; she didn't ask for, he didn't give his whereabouts, and it was plain to them both that an age had ended, they had drifted apart, it was time to wave goodbye. It was still all Billy with Mimi: his plans to make Hindi movies in England and America, importing the top stars, Vinod Khanna, Sridevi, to cavort in front of Bradford Town Hall and the Golden Gate Bridge – 'it's some sort of tax dodge, obviously,' Mimi carolled gaily. In fact, things were heating up for Billy; Chamcha had seen his name in the papers, coupled with the terms *fraud squad* and *tax evasion*, but once a scam man, always a ditto, Mimi said. 'So he says to me, do you want a mink? I say, Billy, don't buy me things, but he says, who's talking about buying? Have a mink. It's business.' They had been in New York again, and Billy had hired a stretched Mercedes limousine 'and a stretched chauffeur also'. Arriving at the furriers, they looked like an oil sheikh and his moll. Mimi tried on the five figure numbers, waiting for Billy's lead. At length he said, You like that one? It's nice. Billy, she whispered, it's *forty thousand*, but he was already smooth-talking the assistant: it was Friday afternoon, the banks were closed, would the store take a cheque. 'Well, by now they *know* he's an oil sheikh, so they say yes, we leave with the coat, and he takes me into another store right around the block, points to the coat, and says, I just bought this for forty thousand dollars, here's the receipt, will you give me thirty for it, I need the cash, big weekend ahead.' – Mimi and Billy had been kept waiting while the second store rang the first, where all the alarm bells went off in the manager's brain, and five minutes later the police arrived, arrested Billy for passing a dud cheque, and he and Mimi spent the weekend in jail. On Monday morning the banks opened and it turned out that Billy's account was in credit to the tune of forty-two thousand, one hundred and seventeen dollars, so the cheque had been good all the time. He informed the furriers of his intention to sue them for two million dollars damages, defamation of character, open and shut case, and within forty-eight hours they settled out of court for $250,000 on the nail. 'Don't you love him?' Mimi asked Chamcha. 'The boy's a genius. I mean, this was *class*.'

I am a man, Chamcha realized, who does not know the score, living in an amoral, survivalist, get-away-with-it-world. Mishal and Anahita Sufyan, who still accountably treated him like a kind of soul-mate, in spite of all his attempts to dissuade them, were beings who plainly admired such creatures as moonlighters, shop-lifters, filchers: scam artists in general. He corrected himself: not admired, that wasn't it. Neither girl would ever steal a pin. But they saw such persons as representatives of the gestalt, of how-it-was. As an experiment he told them the story of Billy Battuta and the mink coat. Their eyes shone, and at the end they applauded and giggled with delight: wickedness unpunished made them laugh. Thus, Chamcha realized, people must once have applauded and giggled at the deeds of earlier outlaws, Dick Turpin, Ned Kelly, Phoolan Devi, and of course that other Billy: William Bonney, also a Kid.

'Scrapheap Youths' Criminal Idols,' Mishal read his mind and then, laughing at his disapproval, translated it into yellowpress headlines, while arranging her long, and, Chamcha realized, astonishing body into similarly exaggerated cheesecake postures. Pouting outrageously, fully aware of having stirred him, she prettily added: 'Kissy kissy?'

Her younger sister, not to be outdone, attempted to copy Mishal's pose, with less effective results. Abandoning the attempt with some annoyance, she spoke sulkily. 'Trouble is, we've got good prospects, us. Family business, no brothers, bob's your uncle. This place makes a packet, dunnit? Well then.' The Shaandaar rooming-house was categorized as a Bed and Breakfast establishment, of the type that borough councils were using more and more owing to the crisis in public housing, lodging five-person families in single rooms, turning blind eyes to health and safety regulations, and claiming 'temporary accommodation' allowances from the central government. 'Ten quid per night per person,' Anahita informed Chamcha in his attic. 'Three hundred and fifty nicker per room per week, it comes to, as often as not. Six occupied rooms: you work it out. Right now, we're losing three hundred pounds a month on this attic, so I hope you feel really bad.' For that kind of money, it struck Chamcha, you could rent pretty reasonable family-sized apartments in the private sector. But that wouldn't be classified as temporary accommodation; no central funding for such solutions. Which would also be opposed by local politicians committed to fighting the 'cuts'. *La lutte continue;* meanwhile, Hind and her daughters raked in the cash, unworldly Sufyan went to Mecca and came home to dispense homely wisdom, kindliness and smiles. And behind six doors that opened a crack every time Chamcha went to make a phone call or use the toilet, maybe thirty temporary human beings, with little hope of being declared permanent.

The real world.

'You needn't look so fish-faced and holy, anyway,' Mishal Sufyan pointed out. 'Look where all your law abiding got you.'

'Your universe is shrinking.' A busy man, Hal Valance, creator of *The Aliens Show* and sole owner of the property, took exactly seventeen seconds to congratulate Chamcha on being alive before beginning to explain why this fact did not affect the show's decision to dispense with his services. Valance had started out in advertising and his vocabulary had never recovered from the blow. Chamcha could keep up, however. All those years in the voiceover business taught you a little bad language. In marketing parlance, *a universe* was the total potential market for a given product or service: the chocolate universe, the slimming universe. The dental universe was everybody with teeth; the others were the denture cosmos. 'I'm talking,' Valance breathed down the phone in his best Deep Throat voice, 'about the ethnic universe.'

My people again: Chamcha, disguised in turban and the rest of his ill-fitting drag, hung on a telephone in a passageway while the eyes of impermanent women and children gleamed through barely opened doors; and wondered what his people had done to him now. 'No capeesh,' he said, remembering Valance's fondness for Italian-American argot – this was, after all, the author of the fast food slogan *Getta pizza da action*. On this occasion, however, Valance wasn't playing. 'Audience surveys show,' he breathed, 'that ethnics don't watch ethnic shows. They don't want 'em, Chamcha. They want fucking *Dynasty*, like everyone else. Your profile's wrong, if you follow: with you in the show it's just

too damn racial. *The Aliens Show* is too big an idea to be held back
by the racial dimension. The merchandising possibilities alone, but
I don't have to tell you this.'

Chamcha saw himself reflected in the small cracked mirror
above the phone box. He looked like a marooned genie in search
of a magic lamp. 'It's a point of view,' he answered Valance,
knowing argument to be useless. With Hal, all explanations were
post facto rationalizations. He was strictly a seat-of-the-pants man,
who took for his motto the advice given by Deep Throat to Bob
Woodward: *Follow the money.* He had the phrase set in large sans-
serif type and pinned up in his office over a still from *All the President's Men*: Hal Holbrook (another Hal!) in the car park, standing
in the shadows. Follow the money: it explained, as he was fond of
saying, his five wives, all independently wealthy, from each of
whom he had received a handsome divorce settlement. He was
presently married to a wasted child maybe one-third his age, with
waist-length auburn hair and a spectral look that would have made
her a great beauty a quarter of a century earlier. 'This one doesn't
have a bean; she's taking me for all I've got and when she's taken
it she'll bugger off,' Valance had told Chamcha once, in happier
days. 'What the hell. I'm human, too. This time it's love.' More
cradlesnatching. No escape from it in these times. Chamcha on
the telephone found he couldn't remember the infant's name.
'You know my motto,' Valance was saying. 'Yes,' Chamcha said
neutrally. 'It's the right line for the product.' The product, you
bastard, being you.

By the time he met Hal Valance (how many years ago? Five,
maybe six), over lunch at the White Tower, the man was already
a monster: pure, self-created image, a set of attributes plastered
thickly over a body that was, in Hal's own words, 'in training to
be Orson Welles'. He smoked absurd, caricature cigars, refusing
all Cuban brands, however, on account of his uncompromisingly
capitalistic stance. He owned a Union Jack waistcoat and insisted
on flying the flag over his agency and also above the door of his
Highgate home; was prone to dress up as Maurice Chevalier and
sing, at major presentations, to his amazed clients, with the help of

straw boater and silver-headed cane; claimed to own the first
Loire château to be fitted with telex and fax machines; and made
much of his 'intimate' association with the Prime Minister he
referred to affectionately as 'Mrs Torture'. The personification of
philistine triumphalism, midatlantic-accented Hal was one of the
glories of the age, the creative half of the city's hottest agency, the
Valance & Lang Partnership. Like Billy Battuta he liked big cars
driven by big chauffeurs. It was said that once, while being driven
at high speed down a Cornish lane in order to 'heat up' a particularly glacial seven-foot Finnish model, there had been an accident:
no injuries, but when the other driver emerged furiously from his
wrecked vehicle he turned out to be even larger than Hal's
minder. As this colossus bore down on him, Hal lowered his
push-button window and breathed, with a sweet smile: 'I strongly
advise you to turn around and walk swiftly away; because, sir, if
you do not do so within the next fifteen seconds, I am going to
have you killed.' Other advertising geniuses were famous for their
work: Mary Wells for her pink Braniff planes, David Ogilvy for
his eyepatch, Jerry della Femina for 'From those wonderful folks
who gave you Pearl Harbor'. Valance, whose agency went in for
cheap and cheerful vulgarity, all bums and honky-tonk, was
renowned in the business for this (probably apocryphal) 'I'm
going to have you killed', a turn of phrase which proved, to those
in the know, that the guy really was a genius. Chamcha had long
suspected he'd made up the story, with its perfect ad-land compo-
nents – Scandinavian icequeen, two thugs, expensive cars, Valance
in the Blofeld role and 007 nowhere on the scene – and put it
about himself, knowing it to be good for business.

The lunch was by way of thanking Chamcha for his part in a
recent, smash-hit campaign for Slimbix diet foods. Saladin had
been the voice of a cutesy cartoon blob: *Hi, I'm Cal, and I'm one
sad calorie.* Four courses and plenty of champagne as a reward for
persuading people to starve. *How's a poor calorie to earn a salary?
Thanks to Slimbix, I'm out of work.* Chamcha hadn't known what to
expect from Valance. What he got was, at least, unvarnished.
'You've done well,' Hal congratulated him, 'for a person of the

tinted persuasion.' And proceeded, without taking his eyes off
Chamcha's face: 'Let me tell you some facts. Within the last three
months, we re-shot a peanut-butter poster because it researched
better without the black kid in the background. We re-recorded a
building society jingle because T'Chairman thought the singer
sounded black, even though he was white as a sodding sheet, and
even though, the year before, we'd used a black boy who, luckily
for him, didn't suffer from an excess of soul. We were told by a
major airline that we couldn't use any blacks in their ads, even
though they were actually employees of the airline. A black actor
came to audition for me and he was wearing a Racial Equality
button badge, a black hand shaking a white one. I said this: don't
think you're getting special treatment from me, chum. You
follow me? You follow what I'm telling you?' It's a goddamn
audition, Saladin realized. 'I've never felt I belonged to a race,' he
replied. Which was perhaps why, when Hal Valance set up his
production company, Chamcha was on his 'A list'; and why,
eventually, Maxim Alien came his way.

When *The Aliens Show* started coming in for stick from black
radicals, they gave Chamcha a nickname. On account of his
private-school education and closeness to the hated Valance, he
was known as 'Brown Uncle Tom'.

Apparently the political pressure on the show had increased in
Chamcha's absence, orchestrated by a certain Dr Uhuru Simba.
'Doctor of what, beats me,' Valance deepthroated down the
phone. 'Our ah researchers haven't come up with anything yet.'
Mass pickets, an embarrassing appearance on *Right to Reply*. 'The
guy's built like a fucking tank.' Chamcha envisaged the pair of
them, Valance and Simba, as one another's antitheses. It seemed
that the protests had succeeded: Valance was 'de-politicizing' the
show, by firing Chamcha and putting a huge blond Teuton with
pectorals and a quiff inside the prosthetic make-up and computer-
generated imagery. A latex-and-Quantel Schwarzenegger, a synthetic, hip-talking version of Rutger Hauer in *Blade Runner*. The
Jews were out, too: instead of Mimi, the new show would have a
voluptuous shiksa doll. 'I sent word to Dr Simba: stick that up

your fucking pee aitch dee. No reply has been received. He'll
have to work harder than that if he's going to take over *this* little
country. I,' Hal Valance announced, 'love this fucking country.
That's why I'm going to sell it to the whole goddamn world,
Japan, America, fucking Argentina. I'm going to sell the arse off
it. That's what I've been selling all my fucking life: the fucking
nation. The *flag*.' He didn't hear what he was saying. When he got
going on this stuff, he went puce and often wept. He had done
just that at the White Tower, that first time, while stuffing himself
full of Greek food. The date came back to Chamcha now: just
after the Falklands war. People had a tendency to swear loyalty
oaths in those days, to hum 'Pomp and Circumstance' on the
buses. So when Valance, over a large balloon of Armagnac, started
up – 'I'll tell you why I love this country' – Chamcha, pro-
Falklands himself, thought he knew what was coming next. But
Valance began to describe the research programme of a British
aerospace company, a client of his, which had just revolutionized
the construction of missile guidance systems by studying the flight
pattern of the common housefly. 'Inflight course corrections,' he
whispered theatrically. 'Traditionally done in the line of flight:
adjust the angle up a bit, down a touch, left or right a nadge. Scientists studying high-speed film of the humble fly, however, have
discovered that the little buggers always, but always, make corrections *in right angles*.' He demonstrated with his hand stretched out,
palm flat, fingers together. 'Bzzt! Bzzt! The bastards actually fly
vertically up, down or sideways. Much more accurate. Much
more fuel efficient. Try to do it with an engine that depends on
nose-to-tail airflow, and what happens? The sodding thing can't
breathe, stalls, falls out of the sky, lands on your fucking allies. Bad
karma. You follow. You follow what I'm saying. So these guys,
they invent an engine with three-way airflow: nose to tail, plus
top to bottom, plus side to side. And bingo: a missile that flies like
a goddamn fly, and can hit a fifty p coin travelling at a ground
speed of one hundred miles an hour at a distance of three miles.
What I love about this country is that: its genius. Greatest inventors in the world. It's beautiful: am I right or am I right?' He had

been deadly serious. Chamcha answered: 'You're right.' 'You're damn right I'm right,' he confirmed.

They met for the last time just before Chamcha took off for Bombay: Sunday lunch at the flag-waving Highgate mansion. Rosewood panelling, a terrace with stone urns, a view down a wooded hill. Valance complaining about a new development that would louse up the scenery. Lunch was predictably jingoistic: *rosbif, boudin Yorkshire, choux de bruxelles*. Baby, the nymphet wife, didn't join them, but ate hot pastrami on rye while shooting pool in a nearby room. Servants, a thunderous Burgundy, more Armagnac, cigars. The self-made man's paradise, Chamcha reflected, and recognized the envy in the thought.

After lunch, a surprise. Valance led him into a room in which there stood two clavichords of great delicacy and lightness. 'I make 'em,' his host confessed. 'To relax. Baby wants me to make her a fucking guitar.' Hal Valance's talent as a cabinet-maker was undeniable, and somehow at odds with the rest of the man. 'My father was in the trade,' he admitted under Chamcha's probing, and Saladin understood that he had been granted a privileged glimpse into the only piece that remained of Valance's original self, the Harold that derived from history and blood and not from his own frenetic brain.

When they left the secret chamber of the clavichords, the familiar Hal Valance instantly reappeared. Leaning on the balustrade of his terrace, he confided: 'The thing that's so amazing about her is the size of what she's trying to do.' Her? Baby? Chamcha was confused. 'I'm talking about you-know-who,' Valance explained helpfully. 'Torture. Maggie the Bitch.' Oh. 'She's radical all right. What she wants – what she actually thinks she can fucking *achieve* – is literally to invent a whole goddamn new middle class in this country. Get rid of the old woolly incompetent buggers from fucking Surrey and Hampshire, and bring in the new. People without background, without history. Hungry people. People who really *want*, and who know that with her, they can bloody well *get*. Nobody's ever tried to replace a whole fucking *class* before, and the amazing thing is she might just do it if they don't get her first. The old class. The dead men. You follow what I'm saying.' 'I think so,' Chamcha lied. 'And it's not just the businessmen,' Valance said slurrily. 'The intellectuals, too. Out with the whole faggoty crew. In with the hungry guys with the wrong education. New professors, new painters, the lot. It's a bloody revolution. Newness coming into this country that's stuffed full of fucking old *corpses*. It's going to be something to see. It already is.'

Baby wandered out to meet them, looking bored. 'Time you were off, Chamcha,' her husband commanded. 'On Sunday afternoons we go to bed and watch pornography on video. It's a whole new world, Saladin. Everybody has to join sometime.'

No compromises. You're in or you're dead. It hadn't been Chamcha's way; not his, nor that of the England he had idolized and come to conquer. He should have understood then and there: he was being given, had been given, fair warning.

And now the coup de grâce. 'No hard feelings,' Valance was murmuring into his ear. 'See you around, eh? Okay, right.'

'Hal,' he made himself object, 'I've got a contract.'

Like a goat to the slaughter. The voice in his ear was now openly amused. 'Don't be silly,' it told him. 'Of course you haven't. Read the small print. Get a *lawyer* to read the small print. Take me to court. Do what you have to do. It's nothing to me. Don't you get it? You're history.'

Dialling tone.

Abandoned by one alien England, marooned within another, Mr Saladin Chamcha in his great dejection received news of an old companion who was evidently enjoying better fortunes. The shriek of his landlady − '*Tini bénché achén!*' − warned him that something was up. Hind was billowing along the corridors of the Shaandaar B and B, waving, it turned out, a current copy of the imported Indian fanzine *Ciné-Blitz*. Doors opened; temporary beings popped out, looking puzzled and alarmed. Mishal Sufyan emerged from her room with yards of midriff showing between shortie tank-top and 501s. From the office he maintained across the hall, Hanif Johnson emerged in the incongruity of a sharp three-piece suit, was hit by the midriff and covered his face. 'Lord have mercy,' he prayed. Mishal ignored him and yelled after her mother: 'What's up? Who's alive?'

'Shameless from somewhere,' Hind shouted back along the passage, 'cover your nakedness.'

'Fuck off,' Mishal muttered under her breath, fixing mutinous eyes on Hanif Johnson. 'What about the michelins sticking out between her sari and her choli, I want to know.' Down at the other end of the passage, Hind could be seen in the half-light, thrusting *Ciné-Blitz* at the tenants, repeating, he's alive. With all the fervour of those Greeks who, after the disappearance of the politician Lambrakis, covered the country with the whitewashed letter Z. *Zi: he lives.*

'Who?' Mishal demanded again.

'*Gibreel,*' came the cry of impermanent children. '*Farishta bénché achén.*' Hind, disappearing downstairs, did not observe her elder daughter returning to her room, – leaving the door ajar; – and being followed, when he was sure the coast was clear, by the well-known lawyer Hanif Johnson, suited and booted, who maintained this office to keep in touch with the grass roots, who was also doing well in a smart uptown practice, who was well connected with the local Labour Party and was accused by the sitting MP of scheming to take his place when reselection came around.

When was Mishal Sufyan's eighteenth birthday? – Not for a few weeks yet. And where was her sister, her roommate, sidekick, shadow, echo and foil? Where was the potential chaperone? She was: out.

But to continue:

The news from *Ciné-Blitz* was that a new, London-based film production outfit headed by the whiz-kid tycoon Billy Battuta, whose interest in cinema was well known, had entered into an association with the reputable, independent Indian producer Mr S. S. Sisodia for the purpose of producing a comeback vehicle for the legendary Gibreel, now exclusively revealed to have escaped the jaws of death for a second time. 'It is true I was booked on the plane under the name of Najmuddin,' the star was quoted as saying. 'I know that when the investigating sleuths identified this as my incognito – in fact, my real name – it caused great grief back home, and for this I do sincerely apologize to my fans. You see, the truth is, that grace of God I somehow missed the flight, and as I had wished in any case to go to ground, excuse, please, no pun intended, I permitted the fiction of my demise to stand uncorrected and took a later flight. Such luck: truly, an angel must have been watching over me.' After a time of reflection, however, he had concluded that it was wrong to deprive his public, in this unsportsmanlike and hurtful way, of the true data and also his presence on the screen. 'Therefore I have accepted this project with full commitment and joy.' The film was to be – what else – a theological, but of a new type. It would be set in an imaginary and fabulous city made of sand, and would recount the story of the encounter between a prophet and an archangel; also the temptation of the prophet, and his choice of the path of purity and not that of base compromise. 'It is a film,' the producer, Sisodia, informed *Ciné-Blitz*, 'about how newness enters the world.' – But would it not be seen as blasphemous, a crime against . . . – 'Certainly not,' Billy Battuta insisted. 'Fiction is fiction; facts are facts. Our purpose is not to make some farrago like that movie *The Message* in which, whenever Prophet Muhammad (on whose name be peace!) was heard to speak, you saw only the head of his camel, moving its mouth. *That* – excuse me for pointing out – had no class. We are making a high-taste, quality picture. A moral tale: like – what do you call them? – fables.'

'Like a dream,' Mr Sisodia said.

When the news was brought to Chamcha's attic later that day by Anahita and Mishal Sufyan, he flew into the vilest rage either of them had ever witnessed, a fury under whose fearful influence his voice rose so high that it seemed to tear, as if his throat had grown knives and ripped his cries to shreds; his pestilential breath all but blasted them from the room, and with arms raised high and goat-legs dancing he looked, at last, like the very devil whose image he had become. 'Liar,' he shrieked at the absent Gibreel.

'Traitor, deserter, scum. Missed the plane, did you? – Then whose head, in my own lap, with my own hands . . . ? – who received caresses, spoke of nightmares, and fell at last singing from the sky?'

'There, there,' pleaded terrified Mishal. 'Calm down. You'll have Mum up here in a minute.'

Saladin subsided, a pathetic goaty heap once again, no threat to anyone. 'It's not true,' he wailed. 'What happened, happened to us both.'

'Course it did,' Anahita encouraged him. 'Nobody believes those movie magazines, anyway. They'll say anything, them.'

Sisters backed out of the room, holding their breath, leaving Chamcha to his misery, failing to observe something quite remarkable. For which they must not be blamed; Chamcha's antics were sufficient to have distracted the keenest eyes. It should also, in fairness, be stated that Saladin failed to notice the change himself.

What happened? This: during Chamcha's brief but violent outburst against Gibreel, the horns on his head (which, one may as well point out, had grown several inches while he languished in the attic of the Shaandaar B and B) definitely, unmistakably, – by about three-quarters of an inch, – *diminished*.

In the interest of the strictest accuracy, one should add that, lower down his transformed body, – inside borrowed pantaloons (delicacy forbids the publication of explicit details), – something else, let us leave it at that, got a little smaller, too.

Be that as it may: it transpired that the optimism of the report in the imported movie magazine had been ill founded, because within days of its publication the local papers carried news of Billy Battuta's arrest, in a midtown New York sushi bar, along with a female companion, Mildred Mamoulian, described as an actress, forty years of age. The story was that he had approached numbers of society matrons, 'movers and shakers', asking for 'very substantial' sums of money which he had claimed to need in order to buy his freedom from a sect of devil worshippers. Once a confidence man, always a confidence man: it was what Mimi Mamoulian would no doubt have described as a beautiful sting. Penetrating the heart of American religiosity, pleading to be saved – 'when you sell your soul you can't expect to buy back cheap' – Billy had banked, the investigators alleged, 'six figure sums'. The world community of the faithful longed, in the late 1980s, for *direct contact with the supernal*, and Billy, claiming to have raised (and therefore to need rescuing from) infernal fiends, was on to a winner, especially as the Devil he offered was so democratically responsive to the dictates of the Almighty Dollar. What Billy offered the West Side matrons in return for their fat cheques was verification: yes, there is a Devil; I've seen him with my own eyes – God, it was frightful! – and if Lucifer existed, so must Gabriel; if Hellfire had been seen to burn, then somewhere, over the rainbow, Paradise must surely shine. Mimi Mamoulian had, it was alleged, played a full part in the deceptions, weeping and pleading for all she was worth. They were undone by overconfidence, spotted at Takesushi (whooping it up and cracking jokes with the chef) by a Mrs Aileen Struwelpeter who had, only the previous afternoon, handed the then-distraught and terrified couple a five-thousand-dollar cheque. Mrs Struwelpeter was not without influence in the New York Police Department, and the boys in blue arrived before Mimi had finished her tempura. They both went quietly. Mimi was wearing, in the newspaper photographs, what Chamcha guessed was a forty-thousand-dollar mink coat, and an expression on her face that could only be read one way.

The hell with you all.

Nothing further was heard, for some while, about Farishta's film.

It was so, it was not, that as Saladin Chamcha's incarceration in the body of a devil and the attic of the Shaandaar B and B lengthened into weeks and months, it became impossible not to notice that his condition was worsening steadily. His horns (notwithstanding their single, momentary and unobserved diminution) had grown both thicker and longer, twirling themselves into fanciful arabesques, wreathing his head in a turban of darkening bone. He

had grown a thick, long beard, a disorienting development in one
whose round, moony face had never boasted much hair before;
indeed, he was growing hairier all over his body, and had even
sprouted, from the base of his spine, a fine tail that lengthened by
the day and had already obliged him to abandon the wearing of
trousers; he tucked the new limb, instead, inside baggy salwar
pantaloons filched by Anahita Sufyan from her mother's gener-
ously tailored collection. The distress engendered in him by his
continuing metamorphosis into some species of bottled djinn will
readily be imagined. Even his appetites were altering. Always fussy
about his food, he was appalled to find his palate coarsening, so
that all foodstuffs began to taste much the same, and on occasion
he would find himself nibbling absently at his bedsheets or old
newspapers, and come to his senses with a start, guilty and shamefaced at this further evidence of his progress away from manhood
and towards – yes – goatishness. Increasing quantities of green
mouthwash were required to keep his breath within acceptable
limits. It really was too grievous to be borne.

His presence in the house was a continual thorn in the side of
Hind, in whom regret for the lost income mingled with the remnants of her initial terror, although it's true to say that the soothing
processes of habituation had worked their sorceries on her,
helping her to see Saladin's condition as some kind of Elephant
Man illness, a thing to feel disgusted by but not necessarily to fear.
'Let him keep out of my way and I'll keep out of his,' she told her
daughters. 'And you, the children of my despair, why you spend
your time sitting up there with a sick person while your youth is
flying by, who can say, but in this Vilayet it seems everything I
used to know is a lie, such as the idea that young girls should help
their mothers, think of marriage, attend to studies, and not go sitting with goats, whose throats, on Big Eid, it is our old custom to
slit.'

Her husband remained solicitous, however, even after the
strange incident that took place when he ascended to the attic and
suggested to Saladin that the girls might not have been so wrong,
that perhaps the, how could one put it, possession of his body

could be terminated by the intercession of a mullah? At the mention of a priest Chamcha reared up on his feet, raising both arms above his head, and somehow or other the room filled up with dense and sulphurous smoke while a high-pitched vibrato screech with a kind of tearing quality pierced Sufyan's hearing like a spike. The smoke cleared quickly enough, because Chamcha flung open a window and fanned feverishly at the fumes, while apologizing to Sufyan in tones of acute embarrassment: 'I really can't say what came over me, – but at times I fear I am changing into something, – something one must call *bad*.'

Sufyan, kindly fellow that he was, went over to where Chamcha sat clutching at his horns, patted him on the shoulder, and tried to bring what good cheer he could. 'Question of mutability of the essence of the self,' he began, awkwardly, 'has long been subject of profound debate. For example, great Lucretius tells us, in *De Rerum Natura*, this following thing: *quodcumque suis mutatum finibus exit, continuo hoc mors est illius quod fuit ante.* Which being translated, forgive my clumsiness, is "Whatever by its changing goes out of its frontiers," – that is, bursts its banks, – or, maybe, breaks out of its limitations, – so to speak, disregards its own rules, but that is too free, I am thinking . . . "that thing", at any rate, Lucretius holds, "by doing so brings immediate death to its old self". However,' up went the ex-schoolmaster's finger, 'poet Ovid, in the *Metamorphoses*, takes diametrically opposed view. He avers thus: "As yielding wax" – heated, you see, possibly for the sealing of documents or such, – "is stamped with new designs And changes shape and seems not still the same, Yet is indeed the same, even so our souls," – you hear, good sir? Our spirits! Our immortal essences! – "Are still the same forever, but adopt In their migrations ever-varying forms." '

He was hopping, now, from foot to foot, full of the thrill of the old words. 'For me it is always Ovid over Lucretius,' he stated. 'Your soul, my good poor dear sir, is the same. Only in its migration it has adopted this presently varying form.'

'This is pretty cold comfort,' Chamcha managed a trace of his old dryness. 'Either I accept Lucretius and conclude that some demonic and irreversible mutation is taking place in my inmost depths, or I go with Ovid and concede that everything now emerging is no more than a manifestation of what was already there.'

'I have put my argument badly,' Sufyan miserably apologized. 'I meant only to reassure.'

'What consolation can there be,' Chamcha answered with bitter rhetoric, his irony crumbling beneath the weight of his unhappiness, 'for a man whose old friend and rescuer is also the nightly lover of his wife, thus encouraging – as your old books would doubtless affirm – the growth of cuckold's horns?'

The old friend, Jumpy Joshi, was unable for a single moment of his waking hours to rid himself of the knowledge that, for the first time in as long as he could remember, he had lost the will to lead his life according to his own standards of morality. At the sports centre where he taught martial arts techniques to ever-greater numbers of students, emphasizing the spiritual aspects of the disciplines, much to their amusement ('Ah so, Grasshopper,' his star pupil Mishal Sufyan would tease him, 'when honolable fascist swine jump at you flom dark alleyway, offer him teaching of Buddha before you kick him in honolable balls'), – he began to display such *passionate intensity* that his pupils, realizing that some inner anguish was being expressed, grew alarmed. When Mishal asked him about it at the end of a session that had left them both bruised and panting for breath, in which the two of them, teacher and star, had hurled themselves at one another like the hungriest of lovers, he threw her question back at her with an uncharacteristic lack of openness. 'Talk about pot and kettle,' he said. 'Question of mote and beam.' They were standing by the vending machines. She shrugged. 'Okay,' she said. 'I confess, but keep the secret.' He reached for his Coke: 'What secret?' Innocent Jumpy. Mishal whispered in his ear: 'I'm getting laid. By your friend: Mister Hanif Johnson, Bar At Law.'

He was shocked, which irritated her. 'O, come *on*. It's not like I'm *fifteen*.' He replied, weakly, 'If your mother ever,' and once again she was impatient. 'If you want to know,' petulantly, 'the one I'm worried about is Anahita. She wants whatever I've got. And she, by the way, really is fifteen.' Jumpy noticed that he'd knocked over his paper-cup and there was Coke on his shoes. 'Out with it,' Mishal was insisting. 'I owned up. Your turn.' But Jumpy couldn't say; was still shaking his head about Hanif. 'It'd be the finish of him,' he said. That did it. Mishal put her nose in the air. 'O, I get it,' she said. 'Not good enough for him, you reckon.' And over her departing shoulder: 'Here, Grasshopper. Don't holy men ever fuck?'

Not so holy. He wasn't cut out for sainthood, any more than the David Carradine character in the old *Kung Fu* programmes: like Grasshopper, like Jumpy. Every day he wore himself out trying to stay away from the big house in Notting Hill, and every evening he ended up at Pamela's door, thumb in mouth, biting the skin around the edges of the nail, fending off the dog and his own guilt, heading without wasting any time for the bedroom. Where they would fall upon one another, mouths searching out the places in which they had chosen, or learned, to begin: first his lips around her nipples, then hers moving along his lower thumb.

She had come to love in him this quality of impatience, because it was followed by a patience such as she had never experienced, the patience of a man who had never been 'attractive' and was therefore prepared to value what was offered, or so she had thought at first; but then she learned to appreciate his conscious-ness of and solicitude for her own internal tensions, his sense of the difficulty with which her slender, bony, small-breasted body found, learned and finally surrendered to a rhythm, his knowledge of time. She loved in him, too, his overcoming of himself; loved, knowing it to be a wrong reason, his willingness to overcome his scruples so that they might be together: loved the desire in him that rode over all that had been imperative in him. Loved it, without being willing to see, in this love, the beginning of an end.

Near the end of their lovemaking, she became noisy. 'Yow!' she shouted, all the aristocracy in her voice crowding into the meaningless syllables of her abandonment. 'Whoop! Hi! *Hah.*'

She was still drinking heavily, scotch bourbon rye, a stripe of redness spreading across the centre of her face. Under the influence of alcohol her right eye narrowed to half the size of the left, and she began, to his horror, to disgust him. No discussion of her boozing was permitted, however: the one time he tried he found himself on the street with his shoes clutched in his right hand and his overcoat over his left arm. Even after that he came back: and she opened the door and went straight upstairs as though nothing had happened. Pamela's taboos: jokes about her background, mentions of whisky-bottle 'dead soldiers', and any suggestion that her late husband, the actor Saladin Chamcha, was still alive, living across town in a bed and breakfast joint, in the shape of a supernatural beast.

These days, Jumpy – who had, at first, badgered her incessantly about Saladin, telling her she should go ahead and divorce him, but this pretence of widowhood was intolerable: what about the man's assets, his rights to a share of the property, and so forth? Surely she would not leave him destitute? – no longer protested about her unreasonable behaviour. 'I've got a confirmed report of his death,' she told him on the only occasion on which she was prepared to say anything at all. 'And what have you got? A billygoat, a circus freak, nothing to do with me.' And this, too, like her drinking, had begun to come between them. Jumpy's martial arts sessions increased in vehemence as these problems loomed larger in his mind.

Ironically, while Pamela refused point-blank to face the facts about her estranged husband, she had become embroiled, through her job at the community relations committee, in an investigation into allegations of the spread of witchcraft among the officers at the local police station. Various stations did from time to time gain the reputation of being 'out of control' – Notting Hill, Kentish Town, Islington – but witchcraft? Jumpy was sceptical. 'The trouble with you,' Pamela told him in her loftiest shooting-stick voice, 'is that you still think of normality as being normal. My God: look at what's happening in this country. A few bent coppers taking their clothes off and drinking urine out of helmets isn't so weird. Call it working-class Freemasonry, if you want. I've got black people coming in every day, scared out of their heads, talking about obeah, chicken entrails, the lot. The goddamn bastards are *enjoying* this: scare the coons with their own ooga booga and have a few naughty nights into the bargain. Unlikely? Bloody *wake up*.' Witchfinding, it seemed, ran in the family: from Matthew Hopkins to Pamela Lovelace. In Pamela's voice, speaking at public meetings, on local radio, even on regional news programmes on television, could be heard all the zeal and authority of the old Witchfinder-General, and it was only on account of that voice of a twentieth-century Gloriana that her campaign was not laughed instantly into extinction. *New Broomstick Needed to Sweep Out Witches*. There was talk of an official inquiry. What drove Jumpy wild, however, was Pamela's refusal to connect her arguments in the question of the occult policemen to the matter of her own husband: because, after all, the transformation of Saladin Chamcha had precisely to do with the idea that normality was no longer composed (if it had ever been) of banal, 'normal' elements. 'Nothing to do with it,' she said flatly when he tried to make the point: imperious, he thought, as any hanging judge.

After Mishal Sufyan told him about her illegal sexual relations with Hanif Johnson, Jumpy on his way over to Pamela Chamcha's had to stifle a number of bigoted thoughts, such as *if his father hadn't been white he'd never have done it*; Hanif, he raged, that immature bastard who probably cut notches in his cock to keep count of his conquests, this Johnson with aspirations to represent his people who couldn't wait until they were of age before he started shafting them! . . . couldn't he see that Mishal with her omniscient body was just a, just a, child? – *No she wasn't*. – Damn him, then, damn him for (and here Jumpy shocked himself) being the first.

Jumpy en route to his mistress tried to convince himself that his resentments of Hanif, *his friend Hanif*, were primarily – how to put it? – *linguistic*. Hanif was in perfect control of the languages that mattered: sociological, socialistic, black-radical, anti-anti-anti-racist, demagogic, oratorical, sermonic: the vocabularies of power. *But you bastard you rummage in my drawers and laugh at my stupid poems. The real language problem: how to bend it shape it, how to let it be our freedom, how to repossess its poisoned wells, how to master the river of words of time of blood: about all that you haven't got a clue.* How hard that struggle, how inevitable the defeat. *Nobody's going to elect me to anything. No power-base, no constituency: just the battle with the words.* But he, Jumpy, also had to admit that his envy of Hanif was as much as anything rooted in the other's greater control of the languages of desire. Mishal Sufyan was quite something, an elongated, tubular beauty, but he wouldn't have known how, even if he'd thought of, he'd never have dared. Language is courage: the ability to conceive a thought, to speak it, and by doing so to make it true.

When Pamela Chamcha answered the door he found that her hair had gone snow-white overnight, and that her response to this inexplicable calamity had been to shave her head right down to the scalp and then conceal it inside an absurd burgundy turban which she refused to remove.

'It just happened,' she said. 'One must not rule out the possibility that I have been bewitched.'

He wasn't standing for that. 'Or the notion of a reaction, however delayed, to the news of your husband's altered, but extant, state.'

She swung to face him, halfway up the stairs to the bedroom, and pointed dramatically towards the open sitting-room door. 'In that case,' she triumphed, 'why did it also happen to the dog?'

He might have told her, that night, that he wanted to end it, that his conscience no longer permitted, – he might have been willing to face her rage, and to live with the paradox that a decision could be simultaneously conscientious and immoral (because cruel, unilateral, selfish); but when he entered the bedroom she grabbed his face with both hands, and watching closely to see how he took the news she confessed to having lied about contraceptive precautions. She was pregnant. It turned out she was better at making unilateral decisions than he, and had simply taken from him the child Saladin Chamcha had been unable to provide. 'I wanted it,' she cried defiantly, and at close range. 'And now I'm going to have it.'

Her selfishness had pre-empted his. He discovered that he felt relieved; absolved of the responsibility for making and acting upon moral choices, – because how could he leave her now? – he put such notions out of his head and allowed her, gently but with unmistakable intent, to push him backwards on to the bed.

Whether the slowly transmogrifying Saladin Chamcha was turning into some sort of science-fiction or horror-video *mutey*, some random mutation shortly to be naturally selected out of existence, – or whether he was evolving into an avatar of the Master of Hell, – or whatever was the case, the fact is (and it will be as well in the present matter to proceed cautiously, stepping from established fact to established fact, leaping to no conclusion until our yellowbrick lane of things-incontrovertibly-so has led us to within an inch or two of our destination) that the two daughters of Haji Sufyan had taken him under their wing, caring for the Beast as only Beauties can; and that, as time passed, he came to be extremely fond of the pair of them himself. For a long while Mishal and Anahita struck him as inseparable, fist and shadow, shot and echo, the younger girl seeking always to emulate her tall, feisty sibling, practising karate kicks and Wing Chun forearm smashes in flattering imitation of Mishal's uncompromising ways. More recently, however, he had noted the growth of a saddening hostility between the sisters. One evening at his

attic window Mishal was pointing out some of the Street's characters, – there, a Sikh ancient shocked by a racial attack into
complete silence; he had not spoken, it was said, for nigh on
seven years, before which he had been one of the city's few
'black' justices of the peace . . . now, however, he pronounced
no sentences, and was accompanied everywhere by a crotchety
wife who treated him with dismissive exasperation, *O, ignore him,
he never says a dicky bird*; – and over there, a perfectly ordinary-
looking 'accountant type' (Mishal's term) on his way home with
briefcase and box of sweetmeats; this one was known in the
Street to have developed the strange need to rearrange his sitting-
room furniture for half an hour each evening, placing chairs in
rows interrupted by an aisle and pretending to be the conductor of
a single-decker bus on its way to Bangladesh, an obsessive fantasy
in which all his family were obliged to participate, *and after half an
hour precisely he snaps out of it, and the rest of the time he's the dullest
guy you could meet*; – and after some moments of this, fifteen-year-
old Anahita broke in spitefully: 'What she means is, you're not
the only casualty, round here the freaks are two a penny, you
only have to look.'

Mishal had developed the habit of talking about the Street as if
it were a mythological battleground and she, on high at
Chamcha's attic window, the recording angel and the exterminator, too. From her Chamcha learned the fables of the new
Kurus and Pandavas, the white racists and black 'self-help' or vigilante posses starring in this modern *Mahabharata*, or, more accu-
rately, *Mahavilayet*. Up there, under the railway bridge, the
National Front used to do battle with the fearless radicals of the
Socialist Workers Party, 'every Sunday from closing time to
opening time,' she sneered, 'leaving us lot to clear up the
wreckage the rest of the sodding week.' – Down that alley was
where the Brickhall Three were done over by the police and then
fitted up, verballed, framed; up that side-street he'd find the scene
of the murder of the Jamaican, Ulysses E. Lee, and in that public
house the stain on the carpet marking where Jatinder Singh Mehta

breathed his last. 'Thatcherism has its effect,' she declaimed, while Chamcha, who no longer had the will or the words to argue with her, to speak of justice and the rule of law, watched Anahita's mounting rage. – 'No pitched battles these days,' Mishal elucidated. 'The emphasis is on small-scale enterprises and the cult of the individual, right? In other words, five or six white bastards murdering us, one individual at a time.' These days the posses roamed the nocturnal Street, ready for aggravation. 'It's our turf,' said Mishal Sufyan of that Street without a blade of grass in sight. 'Let 'em come and get it if they can.'

'Look at her,' Anahita burst out. 'So ladylike, in'she? So refined. Imagine what Mum'd say if she knew.' – 'If she knew what, you little grass – ?' But Anahita wasn't to be cowed: 'O, yes,' she wailed. 'O, yes, we know, don't think we don't. How she goes to the bhangra beat shows on Sunday mornings and changes in the ladies into those tarty-farty clothes – who she wiggles with and jiggles with at the Hot Wax daytime disco that she thinks I never heard of before – what went on at that bluesdance she crept off to with Mister You-know-who Cocky-bugger – some big sister,' she produced her grandstand finish, 'she'll probably wind up dead of wossname *ignorance*.' Meaning, as Chamcha and Mishal well knew, – those cinema commercials, expressionist tombstones rising from earth and sea, had left the residue of their slogan well implanted, no doubt of that – *Aids*.

Mishal fell upon her sister, pulling her hair, – Anahita, in pain, was nevertheless able to get in another dig, 'Least I didn't cut my hair into any weirdo pincushion, must be a nutter who fancies *that*,' and the two departed, leaving Chamcha to wonder at Anahita's sudden and absolute espousal of her mother's ethic of femininity. *Trouble brewing,* he concluded.

Trouble came: soon enough.

More and more, when he was alone, he felt the slow heaviness pushing him down, until he fell out of consciousness, running down like a wind-up toy, and in those passages of stasis that always ended just before the arrival of visitors his body would emit alarming noises, the howlings of infernal wahwah pedals, the snare-drum cracking of satanic bones. These were the periods in which, little by little, he grew. And as he grew, so too did the rumours of his presence; you can't keep a devil locked up in the attic and expect to keep it to yourself forever.

How the news got out (for the people in the know remained tight-lipped, the Sufyans because they feared loss of business, the temporary beings because their feelings of evanescence had rendered them unable, for the moment, to act, – and all parties because of the fear of the arrival of the police, never exactly reluctant to enter such establishments, bump accidentally into a little furniture and step by chance on a few arms legs necks): he began to appear to the locals in their dreams. The mullahs at the Jamme Masjid which used to be the Machzikel HaDath synagogue which had in its turn replaced the Huguenots' Calvinist church; – and Dr Uhuru Simba the man-mountain in African pill-box hat and red-yellow-black poncho who had led the successful protest against *The Aliens Show* and whom Mishal Sufyan hated more than any other black man on account of his tendency to punch uppity women in the mouth, herself for example, in public, at a meeting, plenty of witnesses, but it didn't stop the Doctor, *he's a crazy bastard, that one,* she told Chamcha when she pointed him out from the attic one day, *capable of anything; he could've killed me, and all because I told everybody he wasn't no African, I knew him when he was plain Sylvester Roberts from down New Cross way; fucking witch doctor, if you ask me;* – and Mishal herself, and Jumpy, and Hanif; – and the Bus Conductor, too, they all dreamed him, rising up in the Street like Apocalypse and burning the town like toast. And in every one of the thousand and one dreams he, Saladin Chamcha, gigantic of limb and horn-turbaned of head, was singing, in a voice so diabolically ghastly and guttural that it proved impossible to identify the verses, even though the dreams turned out to have the terrifying quality of being serial, each one following on from the one the night before, and so on, night after night, until even the Silent Man, that former justice of the peace who had not spoken since the night in an Indian restaurant when a young drunk stuck a knife under his nose, threatened to cut him, and then committed the far more shocking offence of spitting all over his food, – until this mild gentleman astounded his wife by sitting upright in his sleep, ducking his neck forwards like a pigeon's, clapping the insides of his wrists together beside his right ear, and roaring out a song at the top of his voice, which sounded so alien and full of static that she couldn't make out a word.

Very quickly, because nothing takes a long time any more, the image of the dream-devil started catching on, becoming popular, it should be said, only amongst what Hal Valance had described as the *tinted persuasion*. While non-tint neo-Georgians dreamed of a sulphurous enemy crushing their perfectly restored residences beneath his smoking heel, nocturnal browns-and-blacks found themselves cheering, in their sleep, this what-else-after-all-but-black-man, maybe a little twisted up by fate class race history, all that, but getting off his behind, bad and mad, to kick a little ass.

At first these dreams were private matters, but pretty soon they started leaking into the waking hours, as Asian retailers and manu-facturers of button-badges sweatshirts posters understood the power of the dream, and then all of a sudden he was everywhere, on the chests of young girls and in the windows protected against bricks by metal grilles, he was a defiance and a warning. Sympathy for the Devil: a new lease of life for an old tune. The kids in the Street started wearing rubber devil-horns on their heads, the way they used to wear pink-and-green balls jiggling on the ends of stiff wires a few years previously, when they preferred to imitate spacemen. The symbol of the Goatman, his fist raised in might, began to crop up on banners at political demonstrations, Save the Six, Free the Four, Eat the Heinz Fifty-Seven. *Pleasechu meechu,* the radios sang, *hopeyu guessma nayym.* Police community relations officers pointed to the 'growing devil-cult among young blacks and Asians' as a 'deplorable tendency', using this 'Satanist revival'

to fight back against the allegations of Ms Pamela Chamcha and
the local CRC: 'Who are the witches now?' 'Chamcha,' Mishal
said excitedly, 'you're a hero. I mean, people can really identify
with you. It's an image white society has rejected for so long that
we can really take it, you know, occupy it, inhabit it, reclaim it
and make it our own. It's time you considered action.'

'Go away,' cried Saladin, in his bewilderment. 'This isn't what I
wanted. This is not what I meant, at all.'

'You're growing out of the attic, anyhow,' rejoined Mishal,
miffed. 'It won't be big enough for you in not too long a while.'

Things were certainly coming to a head.

'Another old lady get slice las' night,' announced Hanif Johnson,
affecting a Trinidadian accent in the way he had. 'No mo soshaal
security for she.' Anahita Sufyan, on duty behind the counter of
the Shaandaar Café, banged cups and plates. 'I don't know why
you do that,' she complained. 'Sends me spare.' Hanif ignored
her, sat down beside Jumpy, who muttered absently: 'What're
they saying?' – Approaching fatherhood was weighing on Jumpy
Joshi, but Hanif slapped him on the back. 'The ol' poetry not goin
great, bra,' he commiserated. 'Look like that river of blood get
coagulate.' A look from Jumpy changed his tune. 'They sayin
what they say,' he answered. 'Look out for coloureds cruisin in
cars. Now if she was black, man, it'd be "No grounds fi suspec
racial motive." I tell you,' he went on, dropping the accent,
'sometimes the level of aggression bubbling just under the skin of
this town gets me really scared. It's not just the damn Granny
Ripper. It's everywhere. You bump into a guy's newspaper in a
rush-hour train and you can get your face broken. Everybody's so
goddamn *angry*, seems like to me. Including, old friend, you,' he
finished, noticing. Jumpy stood, excused himself, and walked out
without an explanation. Hanif spread his arms, gave Anahita his
most winsome smile: 'What'd I do?'

Anahita smiled back sweetly. 'Dju ever think, Hanif, that
maybe people don't like you very much?'

When it became known that the Granny Ripper had struck again, suggestions that the solution to the hideous killings of old women by a 'human fiend', – who invariably arranged his victims' internal organs neatly around their corpses, one lung by each ear, and the heart, for obvious reasons, in the mouth, – would most likely be found by investigating the new occultism among the city's blacks which was giving the authorities so much cause for concern, – began to be heard with growing frequency. The detention and interrogation of 'tints' intensified accordingly, as did the incidence of snap raids on establishments 'suspected of harbouring underground occultist cells'. What was happening, although nobody admitted it or even, at first, understood, was that everyone, black brown white, had started thinking of the dream-figure as *real*, as a being who had crossed the frontier, evading the normal controls, and was now roaming loose about the city. Illegal migrant, outlaw king, foul criminal or race-hero, Saladin Chamcha was getting to be true. Stories rushed across the city in every direction: a physiotherapist sold a shaggy-dog tale to the Sundays, was not believed, but *no smoke without fire*, people said; it was a precarious state of affairs, and it couldn't be long before the raid on the Shaandaar Café that would send the whole thing higher than the sky. Priests became involved, adding another unstable element – the linkage between the term *black* and the sin *blasphemy* – to the mix. In his attic, slowly, Saladin Chamcha grew.

He chose Lucretius over Ovid. The inconstant soul, the muta-bility of everything, *das Ich*, every last speck. A being going through life can become so other to himself as to *be another*, dis-crete, severed from history. He thought, at times, of Zeeny Vakil on that other planet, Bombay, at the far rim of the galaxy: Zeeny, eclecticism, hybridity. The optimism of those ideas! The certainty on which they rested: of will, of choice! But, Zeeny mine, life just happens to you: like an accident. No: it happens to you as a result of your condition. Not choice, but – at best – process, and, at worst, shocking, total change. Newness: he had sought a different kind, but this was what he got.

Bitterness, too, and hatred, all these coarse things. He would enter into his new self; he would be what he had become: loud, stenchy, hideous, outsize, grotesque, inhuman, powerful. He had the sense of being able to stretch out a little finger and topple church spires with the force growing in him, the anger, the anger, the anger. *Powers.*

He was looking for someone to blame. He, too, dreamed; and in his dreams, a shape, a face, was floating closer, ghostly still, unclear, but one day soon he would be able to call it by its name.

I am, he accepted, *that I am.*

Submission.

His cocooned life at the Shaandaar B and B blew apart the evening Hanif Johnson came in shouting that they had arrested Uhuru Simba for the Granny Ripper murders, and the word was they were going to lay the Black Magic thing on him too, he was going to be the voodoo-priest baron-samedi fall guy, and the reprisals – beatings-up, attacks on property, the usual – were already beginning. 'Lock your doors,' Hanif told Sufyan and Hind. 'There's a bad night ahead.'

Hanif was standing slap in the centre of the café, confident of the effect of the news he was bringing, so when Hind came across to him and hit him in the face with all her strength he was so unprepared for the blow that he actually fainted, more from surprise than pain. He was revived by Jumpy, who threw a glass of water at him the way he had been taught to do by the movies, but by then Hind was hurling his office equipment down into the street from upstairs; typewriter ribbons and red ribbons, too, the sort used for securing legal documents, made festive streamers in the air. Anahita Sufyan, unable any more to resist the demonic proddings of her jealousy, had told Hind about Mishal's relations with the up-and-coming lawyer-politico, and after that there had been no holding Hind, all the years of her humiliation had come pouring out of her, it wasn't enough that she was stuck in this country full of jews and strangers who lumped her in with the negroes, it wasn't enough that her husband was a weakling who performed the Haj but couldn't be bothered with godliness in his own home, but this had to happen to her also; she went at Mishal with a kitchen knife and her daughter responded by unleashing a painful series of kicks and jabs, self-defence only, otherwise it would have been matricide for sure. – Hanif regained consciousness and Haji Sufyan looked down on him, moving his hands in small helpless circles by his sides, weeping openly, unable to find consolation in learning, because whereas for most Muslims a journey to Mecca was the great blessing, in his case it had turned out to be the beginning of a curse; – 'Go,' he said, 'Hanif, my friend, get out,' – but Hanif wasn't going without having his say, *I've kept my mouth shut for too long,* he cried, *you people who call yourself so moral while you make fortunes off the misery of your own race,* whereupon it became clear that Haji Sufyan had never known of the prices being charged by his wife, who had not told him, swearing her daughters to secrecy with terrible and binding oaths, knowing that if he discovered he'd find a way of giving the money back so that they could go on rotting in poverty; – and he, the twinkling familiar spirit of the Shaandaar Café, after that lost all love of life. – And now Mishal arrived in the café, O the shame of a family's inner life being enacted thus, like a cheap drama, before the eyes of paying customers, – although in point of fact the last tea-drinker was hurrying from the scene as fast as her old legs would carry her. Mishal was carrying bags. 'I'm leaving, too,' she announced. 'Try and stop me. It's only eleven days.'

When Hind saw her elder daughter on the verge of walking out of her life forever, she understood the price one pays for harbouring the Prince of Darkness under one's roof. She begged her husband to see reason, to realize that his good-hearted generosity had brought them into this hell, and that if only that devil, Chamcha, could be removed from the premises, then maybe they could become once again the happy and industrious family of old. As she finished speaking, however, the house above her head began to rumble and shake, and there was the noise of something coming down the stairs, growling and – or so it seemed – singing, in a voice so vilely hoarse that it was impossible to understand the words.

It was Mishal who went up to meet him in the end, Mishal with Hanif Johnson holding her hand, while the treacherous Anahita watched from the foot of the stairs. Chamcha had grown to a height of over eight feet, and from his nostrils there emerged smoke of two different colours, yellow from the left, and from the right, black. He was no longer wearing clothes. His bodily hair had grown thick and long, his tail was swishing angrily, his eyes were a pale but luminous red, and he had succeeded in terrifying the entire temporary population of the bed and breakfast establishment to the point of incoherence. Mishal, however, was not too scared to talk. 'Where do you think you're going?' she asked him. 'You think you'd last five minutes out there, looking like you do?' Chamcha paused, looked himself over, observed the sizeable erection emerging from his loins, and shrugged. 'I am *considering action*,' he told her, using her own phrase, although in that voice of lava and thunder it didn't seem to belong to her any more. 'There is a person I wish to find.'

'Hold your horses,' Mishal told him. 'We'll work something out.'

What is to be found here, one mile from the Shaandaar, here where the beat meets the street, at Club Hot Wax, formerly the Blak-An-Tan? On this star-crossed and moonless night, let us follow the figures – some strutting, decked out, hot-to-trot, others surreptitious, shadow-hugging, shy – converging from all quarters of the neighbourhood to dive, abruptly, underground, and through this unmarked door. What's within? Lights, fluids, powders, bodies shaking themselves, singly, in pairs, in threes, moving towards possibilities. But what, then, are these other figures, obscure in the on-off rainbow brilliance of the *space*, these forms frozen in their attitudes amid the frenzied dancers? What are these that hip-hop and hindi-pop but never move an inch? – 'You lookin good, Hot Wax posse!' Our host speaks: ranter, toaster, deejay nonpareil – the prancing Pinkwalla, his suit of lights blushing to the beat. – Truly, he is exceptional, a seven-foot albino, his hair the palest rose, the whites of his eyes likewise, his features unmistakably Indian, the haughty nose, long thin lips, a face from a *Hamza-nama* cloth. An Indian who has never seen India, East-India-man from the West Indies, white black man. A star.

Still the motionless figures dance between the shimmying of sisters, the jouncing and bouncing of youth. What are they? – Why, waxworks, nothing more. – Who are they? – History. See, here is Mary Seacole, who did as much in the Crimea as another magic-lamping Lady, but, being dark, could scarce be seen for the flame of Florence's candle; – and, over there!, one Abdul Karim, aka The Munshi, whom Queen Victoria sought to promote, but who was done down by colour-barring ministers. They're all here, dancing motionlessly in hot wax: the black clown of Septimius Severus, to the right; to the left, George IV's barber dancing with the slave, Grace Jones. Ukawsaw Gronniosaw, the African prince who was sold for six feet of cloth, dances according to his ancient fashion with the slave's son Ignatius Sancho, who became in 1782 the first African writer to be published in England. – The migrants of the past, as much the living dancers' ancestors as their own flesh and blood, gyrate stilly while Pinkwalla rants toasts raps up on the stage, *Now-mi-feel-indignation-when-dem-talk-immigration-when-dem-make-insinuation-we-no-part-a-de-nation-an-mi-make-proclamation-a-de-true-situation-how-we-make-contribution-since-de-Rome-Occupation*, and from a different part of the crowded room, bathed in evil green light, wax villains cower and grimace: Mosley, Powell, Edward Long, all the local avatars of Legree. And now a murmur begins in the belly of the Club, mounting, becoming a single word, chanted over and over: 'Meltdown,' the customers demand. 'Meltdown, meltdown, melt.'

Pinkwalla takes his cue from the crowd, *So-it-meltdown-time-when-de-men-of-crime-gonna-get-in-line-for-some-hell-fire-fryin*, after which he turns to the crowd, arms wide, feet with the beat, to ask, *Who's-it-gonna-be? Who-you-wanna-see?* Names are shouted, compete, coalesce, until the assembled company is united once more, chanting a single word. Pinkwalla claps his hands. Curtains part behind him, allowing female attendants in shiny pink shorts and singlets to wheel out a fearsome cabinet: man-sized, glass-fronted, internally-illuminated – the microwave oven, complete with Hot Seat, known to Club regulars as: Hell's Kitchen. 'All *right*,' cries Pinkwalla. 'Now we really cookin.'

Attendants move towards the tableau of hate-figures, pounce upon the night's sacrificial offering, the one most often selected, if truth be told; at least three times a week. Her permawaved coiffure, her pearls, her suit of blue. *Maggie-maggie-maggie,* bays the crowd. *Burn-burn-burn.* The doll, – the *guy*, – is strapped into the Hot Seat. Pinkwalla throws the switch. And O how prettily she melts, from the inside out, crumpling into formlessness. Then she is a puddle, and the crowd sighs its ecstasy: *done.* 'The fire this time,' Pinkwalla tells them. Music regains the night.

When Pinkwalla the deejay saw what was climbing under cover of darkness into the back of his panel van, which his friends Hanif and Mishal had persuaded him to bring round the back of the Shaandaar, the fear of obeah filled his heart; but there was also the contrary exhilaration of realizing that the potent hero of his many dreams was a flesh-and-blood actuality. He stood across the street, shivering under a lamp-post though it wasn't particularly cold, and stayed there for half an hour while Mishal and Hanif spoke urgently to him, *he needs somewhere to go, we have to think about his future.* Then he shrugged, walked over to the van, and started up the engine. Hanif sat beside him in the cab; Mishal travelled with Saladin, hidden from view.

It was almost four in the morning when they bedded Chamcha down in the empty, locked-up nightclub. Pinkwalla – his real name, Sewsunker, was never used – had unearthed a couple of sleeping-bags from a back room, and they sufficed. Hanif Johnson, saying goodnight to the fearsome entity of whom his lover Mishal seemed entirely unafraid, tried to talk to him seriously, 'You've got to realize how important you could be for us, there's more at stake here than your personal needs,' but mutant Saladin only snorted, yellow and black, and Hanif backed quickly away. When he was alone with the waxworks Chamcha was able to fix his thoughts once again on the face that had finally coalesced in his mind's eye, radiant, the light streaming out around him from a point just behind his head, Mister Perfecto, portrayer of gods, who always landed on his feet, was always forgiven his sins, loved, praised, adored . . . the face he had been trying to identify in his dreams, Mr Gibreel Farishta, transformed into the simulacrum of an angel as surely as he was the Devil's mirror-self.

Who should the Devil blame but the Archangel, Gibreel?

The creature on the sleeping-bags opened its eyes; smoke began to issue from its pores. The face on every one of the waxwork dummies was the same now, Gibreel's face with its widow's peak and its long thin saturnine good looks. The creature bared its teeth and let out a long, foul breath, and the waxworks dissolved into puddles and empty clothes, all of them, every one. The creature lay back, satisfied. And fixed its mind upon its foe.

Whereupon it felt within itself the most inexplicable sensations of compression, suction, withdrawal; it was racked by terrible, squeezing pains, and emitted piercing squeals that nobody, not even Mishal who was staying with Hanif in Pinkwalla's apartment above the Club, dared to investigate. The pains mounted in intensity, and the creature thrashed and tossed around the dance-floor, wailing most piteously; until, at length, granted respite, it fell asleep.

When Mishal, Hanif and Pinkwalla ventured into the clubroom several hours later, they observed a scene of frightful devastation, tables sent flying, chairs broken in half, and, of course, every waxwork – good and evil – Topsy and Legree – melted like tigers into butter; and at the centre of the carnage, sleeping like a baby, no mythological creature at all, no iconic Thing of horns and hellsbreath, but Mr Saladin Chamcha himself, apparently restored to his old shape, mother-naked but of entirely human aspect and proportions, *humanized* – is there any option but to conclude? – by the fearsome concentration of his hate.

He opened his eyes; which still glowed pale and red.

2

Alleluia Cone, coming down from Everest, saw a city of ice to the west of Camp Six, across the Rock Band, glittering in the sunlight below the massif of Cho Oyu. *Shangri-La,* she momentarily thought; however, this was no green vale of immortality but a metropolis of gigantic ice-needles, thin, sharp and cold. Her attention was distracted by Sherpa Pemba warning her to maintain her concentration, and the city had gone when she looked back. She was still at twenty-seven thousand feet, but the apparition of the impossible city threw her back across space and time to the Bayswater study of old dark wooden furniture and heavy velvet curtains in which her father Otto Cone, the art historian and biographer of Picabia, had spoken to her in her fourteenth and his final year of 'the most dangerous of all the lies we are fed in our lives', which was, in his opinion, the idea of the continuum. 'Anybody ever tries to tell you how this most beautiful and most evil of planets is somehow homogeneous, composed only of reconcilable elements, that it all *adds up*, you get on the phone to the straitjacket tailor,' he advised her, managing to give the impression of having visited more planets than one before coming to his conclusions. 'The world is incompatible, just never forget it: gaga. Ghosts, Nazis, saints, all alive at the same time; in one spot, blissful happiness, while down the road, the inferno.

You can't ask for a wilder place.' Ice cities on the roof of the world wouldn't have fazed Otto. Like his wife Alicja, Allie's mother, he was a Polish émigré, a survivor of a wartime prison camp whose name was never mentioned throughout Allie's childhood. 'He wanted to make it as if it had not been,' Alicja told her daughter later. 'He was unrealistic in many ways. But a good man; the best I knew.' She smiled an inward smile as she spoke, tolerating him in memory as she had not always managed to during his life, when he was frequently appalling. For example: he developed a hatred of communism which drove him to embarrassing extremes of behaviour, notably at Christmas, when this Jewish man insisted on celebrating with his Jewish family and others what he described as 'an English rite', as a mark of respect to their new 'host nation' – and then spoiled it all (in his wife's eyes) by bursting into the salon where the assembled company was relaxing in the glow of log fire, Christmas tree lights and brandy, got up in pantomime Chinee, with droopy moustaches and all, crying: 'Father Christmas is dead! I have killed him! I am The Mao: no presents for anyone! Hee! Hee! Hee!' Allie on Everest, remembering, winced – her mother's wince, she realized, transferred to her frosted face.

The incompatibility of life's elements: in a tent at Camp Four, 27,600 feet, the idea which seemed at times to be her father's daemon sounded banal, emptied of meaning, of *atmosphere*, by the altitude. 'Everest silences you,' she confessed to Gibreel Farishta in a bed above which parachute silk formed a canopy of hollow Himalayas. 'When you come down, nothing seems worth saying, nothing at all. You find the nothingness wrapping you up, like a sound. Non-being. You can't keep it up, of course. The world rushes in soon enough. What shuts you up is, I think, the sight you've had of perfection: why speak if you can't manage perfect thoughts, perfect sentences? It feels like a betrayal of what you've been through. But it fades; you accept that certain compromises, closures, are required if you're to continue.' They spent most of their time in bed during their first weeks together: the appetite of each for the other seemingly inexhaustible, they made love six or

seven times a day. 'You opened me up,' she told him. 'You with
the ham in your mouth. It was exactly as if you were speaking to
me, as if I could read your thoughts. Not as if,' she amended. 'I
did read them, right?' He nodded: it was true. 'I read your
thoughts and the right words just came out of my mouth,' she
marvelled. 'Just flowed out. Bingo: love. In the beginning was the
word.'

Her mother took a fatalistic view of this dramatic turn of events
in Allie's life, the return of a lover from beyond the grave. 'I'll tell
you what I honestly thought when you gave me the news,' she
said over lunchtime soup and kreplach at the Whitechapel
Bloom's. 'I thought, oh dear, it's grand passion; poor Allie has to
go through this now, the unfortunate child.' Alicja's strategy was
to keep her emotions strictly under control. She was a tall, ample
woman with a sensual mouth but, as she put it, 'I've never been a
noise-maker.' She was frank with Allie about her sexual passivity,
and revealed that Otto had been, 'Let's say, otherwise inclined.
He had a weakness for grand passion, but it always made him so
miserable I could not get worked up about it.' She had been reassured by her knowledge that the women with whom her little,
bald, jumpy husband consorted were 'her type', big and buxom,
'except they were brassy, too: they did what he wanted, shouting
things out to spur him on, pretending for all they were worth; it
was his enthusiasm they responded to, I think, and maybe his
chequebook, too. He was of the old school and gave generous
gifts.'

Otto had called Alleluia his 'pearl without price', and dreamed
for her a great future, as maybe a concert pianist or, failing that, a
Muse. 'Your sister, frankly, is a disappointment to me,' he said
three weeks before his death in that study of Great Books and
Picabian bric-à-brac – a stuffed monkey which he claimed was a
'first draft' of the notorious *Portrait of Cézanne, Portrait of Rem-
brandt, Portrait of Renoir*, numerous mechanical contraptions
including sexual stimulators that delivered small electric shocks,
and a first edition of Jarry's *Ubu Roi*. 'Elena has wants where she
should have thoughts.' He Anglicized the name – Yelyena into

Ellaynah – just as it had been his idea to reduce 'Alleluia' to Allie and bowdlerize himself, Cohen from Warsaw, into Cone. Echoes of the past distressed him; he read no Polish literature, turning his back on Herbert, on Miłosz, on 'younger fellows' like Baranczak, because for him the language was irredeemably polluted by history. 'I am English now,' he would say proudly in his thick East European accent. 'Silly mid-off! Pish-Tush! Widow of Windsor! Bugger all.' In spite of his reticences he seemed content enough being a pantomime member of the English gentry. In retrospect, though, it looked likely that he'd been only too aware of the fragility of the performance, keeping the heavy drapes almost permanently drawn in case the inconsistency of things caused him to see monsters out there, or moonscapes instead of the familiar Moscow Road.

'He was strictly a melting-pot man,' Alicja said while attacking a large helping of tsimmis. 'When he changed our name I told him, Otto, it isn't required, this isn't America, it's London W-two; but he wanted to wipe the slate clean, even his Jewishness, excuse me but I know. The fights with the Board of Deputies! All very civilized, parliamentary language throughout, but bareknuckle stuff none the less.' After his death she went straight back to Cohen, the synagogue, Chanukah and Bloom's. 'No more imitation of life,' she munched, and waved a sudden, distracted fork. 'That picture. I was crazy for it. Lana Turner, am I right? And Mahalia Jackson singing in a church.'

Otto Cone as a man of seventy-plus jumped into an empty liftshaft and died. Now there was a subject which Alicja, who would readily discuss most taboo matters, refused to touch upon: why does a survivor of the camps live forty years and then complete the job the monsters didn't get done? Does great evil eventually triumph, no matter how strenuously it is resisted? Does it leave a sliver of ice in the blood, working its way through until it hits the heart? Or, worse: can a man's death be incompatible with his life? Allie, whose first response on learning of her father's death had been fury, flung such questions as these at her mother. Who, stonefaced beneath a wide black hat, said only: 'You have inherited his lack of restraint, my dear.'

After Otto's death Alicja ditched the elegant high style of dress and gesture which had been her offering on the altar of his lust for integration, her attempt to be his Cecil Beaton grande dame. 'Phoo,' she confided in Allie, 'what a relief, my dear, to be shapeless for a change.' She now wore her grey hair in a straggly bun, put on a succession of identical floral-print supermarket dresses, abandoned make-up, got herself a painful set of false teeth, planted vegetables in what Otto had insisted should be an English floral garden (neat flowerbeds around the central, symbolic tree, a 'chimeran graft' of laburnum and broom) and gave, instead of dinners full of cerebral chat, a series of lunches – heavy stews and a minimum of three outrageous puddings – at which dissident Hungarian poets told convoluted jokes to Gurdjieffian mystics, or (if things didn't quite work out) the guests sat on cushions on the floor, staring gloomily at their loaded plates, and something very like total silence reigned for what felt like weeks. Allie eventually turned away from these Sunday afternoon rituals, sulking in her room until she was old enough to move out, with Alicja's ready assent, and from the path chosen for her by the father whose betrayal of his own act of survival had angered her so much. She turned towards action; and found she had mountains to climb.

Alicja Cohen, who had found Allie's change of course perfectly comprehensible, even laudable, and rooted for her all the way, could not (she admitted over coffee) quite see her daughter's point in the matter of Gibreel Farishta, the revenant Indian movie star. 'To hear you talk, dear, the man's not in your league,' she said, using a phrase she believed to be synonymous with *not your type*, and which she would have been horrified to hear described as a racial, or religious, slur: which was inevitably the sense in which her daughter understood it. 'That's just fine by me,' Allie riposted with spirit, and rose. 'The fact is, I don't even *like* my league.'

Her feet ached, obliging her to limp, rather than storm, from the restaurant. 'Grand passion,' she could hear her mother behind her back announcing loudly to the room at large. 'The gift of tongues; means a girl can babble out any blasted thing.'

Certain aspects of her education had been unaccountably neglected. One Sunday not long after her father's death she was buying the Sunday papers from the corner kiosk when the vendor announced: 'It's the last week this week. Twenty-three years I've been on this corner and the Pakis have finally driven me out of business.' She heard the word *p-a-c-h-y*, and had a bizarre vision of elephants lumbering down the Moscow Road, flattening Sunday news vendors. 'What's a pachy?' she foolishly asked and the reply was stinging: 'A brown Jew.' She went on thinking of the proprietors of the local 'CTN' (confectioner-tobacconist-newsagent) as *pachyderms* for quite a while: as people set apart – rendered objectionable – by the nature of their skin. She told Gibreel this story, too. 'Oh,' he responded, crushingly, 'an elephant joke.' He wasn't an easy man.

But there he was in her bed, this big vulgar fellow for whom she could open as she had never opened before; he could reach right into her chest and caress her heart. Not for many years had she entered the sexual arena with such celerity, and never before had so swift a liaison remained wholly untainted by regret or self-disgust. His extended silence (she took it for that until she learned that his name was on the *Bostan*'s passenger list) had been sharply painful, suggesting a difference in his estimation of their encounter; but to have been mistaken about his desire, about such an abandoned, hurtling thing, was surely impossible? The news of his death accordingly provoked a double response: on the one hand, there was a kind of grateful, relieved joy to be had from the knowledge that he had been racing across the world to surprise her, that he had given up his entire life in order to construct a new one with her; while, on the other, there was the hollow grief of being deprived of him in the very moment of knowing that she truly had been loved. Later, she became aware of a further, less generous, reaction. What had he thought he was doing, planning to arrive without a word of warning on her doorstep, assuming that she'd be waiting with open arms, an unencumbered life, and no doubt a large enough apartment for them both? It was the kind of behaviour one would expect of a spoiled movie actor who expects his desires simply to fall like ripe fruits into his lap . . . in short, she had felt invaded, or potentially invaded. But then she had rebuked herself, pushing such notions back down into the pit where they belonged, because after all Gibreel had paid heavily for his presumption, if presumption it was. A dead lover deserves the benefit of the doubt.

Then there he lay at her feet, unconscious in the snow, taking her breath away with the impossibility of his being there at all, leading her momentarily to wonder if he might not be another in the series of visual aberrations – she preferred the neutral phrase to the more loaded *visions* – by which she'd been plagued ever since her decision to scorn oxygen cylinders and conquer Chomolungma on lung power alone. The effort of raising him, slinging his arm around her shoulders and half-carrying him to her flat – more than half, if the truth be told – fully persuaded her that he was no chimera, but heavy flesh and blood. Her feet stung her all the way home, and the pain reawakened all the resentments she'd stifled when she thought him dead. What was she supposed to do with him now, the lummox, sprawled out across her bed? God, but she'd forgotten what a sprawler the man was, how during the night he colonized your side of the bed and denuded you entirely of bedclothes. But other sentiments, too, had re-emerged, and these won the day; for here he was, sleeping beneath her protection, the abandoned hope: at long last, love.

He slept almost round the clock for a week, waking up only to satisfy the minimum requirements of hunger and hygiene, saying almost nothing. His sleep was tormented: he thrashed about the bed, and words occasionally escaped his lips: *Jahilia, Al-Lat, Hind.* In his waking moments he appeared to wish to resist sleep, but it claimed him, waves of it rolling over him and drowning him while he, almost piteously, waved a feeble arm. She was unable to guess what traumatic events might have given rise to such behaviour, and, feeling a little alarmed, telephoned her mother. Alicja arrived to inspect the sleeping Gibreel, pursed her lips, and pronounced: 'He's a man possessed.' She had receded more and more into a kind of Singer Brothers dybbukery, and her mysticism never failed to exasperate her pragmatic, mountain-climbing daughter. 'Use maybe a suction pump on his ear,' Alicja recommended. 'That's the exit these creatures prefer.' Allie shepherded her mother out of the door. 'Thanks a lot,' she said. 'I'll let you know.'

On the seventh day he came wide awake, eyes popping open like a doll's, and instantly reached for her. The crudity of the approach made her laugh almost as much as its unexpectedness, but once again there was that feeling of naturalness, of rightness; she grinned, 'Okay, you asked for it,' and slipped out of the baggy, elasticated maroon pantaloons and loose jacket – she disliked clothes that revealed the contours of her body – and that was the beginning of the sexual marathon that left them both sore, happy and exhausted when it finally ground to a halt.

He told her: he fell from the sky and lived. She took a deep breath and believed him, because of her father's faith in the myriad and contradictory possibilities of life, and because, too, of what the mountain had taught her. 'Okay,' she said, exhaling. 'I'll buy it. Just don't tell my mother, all right?' The universe was a place of wonders, and only habituation, the anaesthesia of the everyday, dulled our sight. She had read, a couple of days back, that as part of their natural processes of combustion, the stars in the skies crushed carbon into diamonds. The idea of the stars raining diamonds into the void: that sounded like a miracle, too. If that could happen, so could this. Babies fell out of zillionth-floor windows and bounced. There was a scene about that in François Truffaut's movie *L'Argent du Poche* . . . She focused her thoughts. 'Sometimes,' she decided to say, 'wonderful things happen to me, too.'

She told him then what she had never told any living being: about the visions on Everest, the angels and the ice-city. 'It wasn't only on Everest, either,' she said, and continued after a hesitation. When she got back to London, she went for a walk along the Embankment to try and get him, as well as the mountain, out of her blood. It was early in the morning and there was the ghost of a mist and the thick snow made everything vague. Then the icebergs came.

There were ten of them, moving in stately single file upriver. The mist was thicker around them, so it wasn't until they sailed right up to her that she understood their shapes, the precisely miniaturized configurations of the ten highest mountains in the world, in ascending order, with her mountain, *the* mountain bringing up the rear. She was trying to work out how the icebergs had managed to pass under the bridges across the river when the mist thickened, and then, a few instants later, dissolved entirely, taking the icebergs with it. 'But they were there,' she insisted to Gibreel. 'Nanga Parbat, Dhaulagiri, Xixabangma Feng.' He didn't argue. 'If you say it, then I know it truly was so.'

An iceberg is water striving to be land; a mountain, especially a Himalaya, especially Everest, is land's attempt to metamorphose into sky; it is grounded flight, the earth mutated — nearly — into air, and become, in the true sense, exalted. Long before she ever encountered the mountain, Allie was aware of its brooding presence in her soul. Her apartment was full of Himalayas. Representations of Everest in cork, in plastic, in tile, stone, acrylics, brick jostled for space; there was even one sculpted entirely out of ice, a tiny berg which she kept in the freezer and brought out from time to time to show off to friends. Why so many? *Because* — no other possible answer — *they were there.* 'Look,' she said, stretching out a hand without leaving the bed and picking up, from her bedside table, her newest acquisition, a simple Everest in weathered pine. 'A gift from the sherpas of Namche Bazar.' Gibreel took it, turned it in his hands. Pemba had offered it to her shyly when they said goodbye, insisting it was from all the sherpas as a group, although it was evident that he'd whittled it himself. It was a detailed model, complete with the ice fall and the Hillary Step that is the last great obstacle on the way to the top, and the route they had taken to the summit was scored deeply into the wood. When Gibreel turned it upside down he found a message, scratched into the base in painstaking English. *To Ali Bibi. We were luck. Not to try again.*

What Allie did not tell Gibreel was that the sherpa's prohibition had scared her, convincing her that if she ever set her foot again upon the goddess-mountain, she would surely die, because it is not permitted to mortals to look more than once upon the face of the divine; but the mountain was diabolic as well as transcendent, or, rather, its diabolism and its transcendence were one, so that even the contemplation of Pemba's ban made her feel a pang of need so deep that it made her groan aloud, as if in sexual ecstasy or despair. 'The Himalayas,' she told Gibreel so as not to say what was really on her mind, 'are emotional peaks as well as physical ones: like opera. That's what makes them so awesome. Nothing but the giddiest heights. A hard trick to pull off, though.' Allie had a way of switching from the concrete to the abstract, a trope so casually achieved as to leave the listener half-wondering if she knew the difference between the two; or, very often, unsure as to whether, finally, such a difference could be said to exist.

Allie kept to herself the knowledge that she must placate the mountain or die, that in spite of the flat feet which made any serious mountaineering out of the question she was still infected by Everest, and that in her heart of hearts she kept hidden an impossible scheme, the fatal vision of Maurice Wilson, never achieved to this day. That is: the solo ascent.

What she did not confess: that she had seen Maurice Wilson since her return to London, sitting among the chimneypots, a beckoning goblin in plus-fours and tam-o'-shanter hat. – Nor did Gibreel Farishta tell her about his pursuit by the spectre of Rekha Merchant. There were still closed doors between them for all their physical intimacy: each kept secret a dangerous ghost. – And Gibreel, on hearing of Allie's other visions, concealed a great agitation behind his neutral words – *if you say it, then I know* – an agitation born of this further evidence that the world of dreams was leaking into that of the waking hours, that the seals dividing

the two were breaking, and that at any moment the two firma-
ments could be joined, – that is to say, the end of all things was
near. One morning Allie, awaking from spent and dreamless sleep,
found him immersed in her long-unopened copy of Blake's *Marriage of Heaven and Hell*, in which her younger self, disrespectful of
books, had made a number of marks: underlinings, ticks in the
margins, exclamations, multiple queries. Seeing that she had
awoken, he read out a selection of these passages with a wicked
grin. 'From the Proverbs of Hell,' he began. *'The lust of the goat is
the bounty of God.'* She blushed furiously. 'And what is more,' he
continued, *'The ancient tradition that the world will be consumed in fire
at the end of six thousand years is true, as I have heard from Hell.* Then,
lower down the page: *This will come to pass by an improvement of sensual enjoyment.* Tell me, who is this? I found her pressed in the
pages.' He handed her a dead woman's photograph: her sister,
Elena, buried here and forgotten. Another addict of visions; and a
casualty of the habit. 'We don't talk about her much.' She was
kneeling unclothed on the bed, her pale hair hiding her face. 'Put
her back where you found her.'

*I saw no God, nor heard any, in a finite organical perception; but my
senses discover'd the infinite in every thing.* He riffled on through the
book, and replaced Elena Cone next to the image of the Regenerated Man, sitting naked and splay-legged on a hill with the sun
shining out of his rear end. *I have always found that Angels have the
vanity to speak of themselves as the only wise.* Allie put her hands up
and covered her face. Gibreel tried to cheer her up. 'You have
written in the flyleaf: "Creation of world acc. Archbish. Usher,
4004 BC. Estim'd date of apocalypse, ∴, 1996." So time for
improvement of sensual enjoyment still remains.' She shook her
head: stop. He stopped. 'Tell me,' he said, putting away the book.

Elena at twenty had taken London by storm. Her feral six-foot
body winking through a golden chain-mail Rabanne. She had
always carried herself with uncanny assurance, proclaiming her
ownership of the earth. The city was her medium, she could swim

in it like a fish. She was dead at twenty-one, drowned in a bathtub of cold water, her body full of psychotropic drugs. Can one drown in one's element, Allie had wondered long ago. If fish can drown in water, can human beings suffocate in air? In those days Allie, eighteen-nineteen, had envied Elena her certainties. What was *her* element? In what periodic table of the spirit could it be found? – Now, flat-footed, Himalayan veteran, she mourned its loss. When you have earned the high horizon it isn't easy to go back into your box, into a narrow island, an eternity of anticlimax. But her feet were traitors and the mountain would kill.

Mythological Elena, the cover girl, wrapped in couture plastics, had been sure of her immortality. Allie, visiting her in her World's End *crashpad*, refused a proffered sugar-lump, mumbled something about brain damage, feeling inadequate, as usual in Elena's company. Her sister's face, the eyes too wide apart, the chin too sharp, the effect overwhelming, stared mockingly back. 'No shortage of brain cells,' Elena said. 'You can spare a few.' The spare capacity of the brain was Elena's capital. She spent her cells like money, searching for her own heights; trying, in the idiom of the day, to fly. Death, like life, came to her coated in sugar.

She had tried to 'improve' the younger Alleluia. 'Hey, you're a great looking kid, why hide it in those dungarees? I mean, God, darling, you've got all the equipment in there.' One night she dressed Allie up, in an olive-green item composed of frills and absences that barely covered her body-stockinged groin: *sugaring me like candy*, was Allie's puritanical thought, *my own sister putting me on display in the shop-window, thanks a lot*. They went to a gaming club full of ecstatic lordlings, and Allie had left fast when Elena's attention was elsewhere. A week later, ashamed of herself for being such a coward, for rejecting her sister's attempt at intimacy, she sat on a beanbag at World's End and confessed to Elena that she was no longer a virgin. Whereupon her elder sister slapped her in the mouth and called her ancient names: tramp, slut, tart. 'Elena Cone never allows a man to lay a *finger*,' she yelled, revealing her ability to think of herself as a third person, 'not a goddamn finger*nail*. I know what I'm worth, darling, I know how the mystery dies the moment they put their willies in, I should have known you'd turn out to be a whore. Some fucking communist, I suppose,' she wound down. She had inherited her father's prejudices in such matters. Allie, as Elena knew, had not.

They hadn't met much after that, Elena remaining until her death the virgin queen of the city – the post-mortem confirmed her as *virgo intacta* – while Allie gave up wearing underwear, took odd jobs on small, angry magazines, and because her sister was untouchable she became the other thing, every sexual act a slap in her sibling's glowering, whitelipped face. Three abortions in two years and the belated knowledge that her days on the contraceptive pill had put her, as far as cancer was concerned, in one of the highest-risk categories of all.

She heard about her sister's end from a newsstand billboard, MODEL'S 'ACID BATH' DEATH. You're not even safe from puns when you die, was her first reaction. Then she found she was unable to weep.

'I kept seeing her in magazines for months,' she told Gibreel. 'On account of the glossies' long lead times.' Elena's corpse danced across Moroccan deserts, clad only in diaphanous veils; or it was sighted in the Sea of Shadows on the moon, naked except for spaceman's helmet and half a dozen silk ties knotted around breasts and groin. Allie took to drawing moustaches on the pictures, to the outrage of newsagents; she ripped her late sister out of the journals of her zombie-like undeath and crumpled her up. Haunted by Elena's periodical ghost, Allie reflected on the dangers of attempting to *fly*; what flaming falls, what macabre hells were reserved for such Icarus types! She came to think of Elena as a soul in torment, to believe that this captivity in an immobile world of girlie calendars in which she wore black breasts of moulded plastic, three sizes larger than her own; of pseudo-erotic snarls; of advertising messages printed across her navel, was no less than Elena's personal hell. Allie began to see the scream in her sister's eyes, the anguish of being trapped forever in those fashion spreads. Elena was being tortured by demons, consumed in fires, and she couldn't even move . . . after a time Allie had to avoid the shops in which her sister could be found staring from the racks. She lost the ability to open magazines, and hid all the pictures of Elena she owned. 'Goodbye, Yel,' she told her sister's memory, using her old nursery name. 'I've got to look away from you.'

'But I turned out to be like her, after all.' Mountains had begun to sing to her; whereupon she, too, had risked brain cells in search of exaltation. Eminent physicians expert in the problems facing mountaineers had frequently proved, beyond reasonable doubt, that human beings could not survive without breathing apparatus much above eight thousand metres. The eyes would haemorrhage beyond hope of repair, and the brain, too, would start to explode, losing cells by the billion, too many and too fast, resulting in the permanent damage known as High Altitude Deterioration, fol-lowed in quick time by death. Blind corpses would remain pre-served in the permafrost of those highest slopes. But Allie and Sherpa Pemba went up and came down to tell the tale. Cells from the brain's deposit boxes replaced the current-account casualties. Nor did her eyes blow out. Why had the scientists been wrong? 'Prejudice, mostly,' Allie said, lying curled around Gibreel beneath parachute silk. 'They can't quantify the will, so they leave it out of their calculations. But it's will that gets you up Everest, will and anger, and it can bend any law of nature you care to mention, at least in the short term, gravity not excluded. If you don't push your luck, anyway.'

There had been some damage. She had been suffering unac-countable lapses of memory: small, unpredictable things. Once at the fishmonger's she had forgotten the word *fish*. Another morning she found herself in her bathroom picking up a tooth-brush blankly, quite unable to work out its purpose. And one morning, waking up beside the sleeping Gibreel, she had been on the verge of shaking him awake to demand, 'Who the hell are you? How did you get in my bed?' – when, just in time, the memory returned. 'I'm hoping it's temporary,' she told him. But kept to herself, even now, the appearances of Maurice Wilson's ghost on the rooftops surrounding the Fields, waving his inviting arm.

꧁

She was a competent woman, formidable in many ways: very much the professional sportswoman of the 1980s, a client of the giant MacMurray public relations agency, sponsored to the gills. Nowadays she, too, appeared in advertisements, promoting her own range of outdoor products and leisurewear, aimed at holiday-makers and amateurs more than pro climbers, to maximize what Hal Valance would have called the universe. She was the golden girl from the roof of the world, the survivor of 'my Teutonic two-some', as Otto Cone had been fond of calling his daughters. *Once again, Yel, I follow in your footsteps.* To be an attractive woman in a sport dominated by, well, hairy men was to be saleable, and the 'icequeen' image didn't hurt either. There was money in it, and now that she was old enough to compromise her old, fiery ideals with no more than a shrug and a laugh, she was ready to make it, ready, even, to appear on TV talk-shows to fend off, with risqué hints, the inevitable and unchanging questions about life with the boys at twenty-odd thousand feet. Such high-profile capers sat uneasily alongside the view of herself to which she still fiercely clung: the idea that she was a natural solitary, the most private of women, and that the demands of her business life were ripping her in half. She had her first fight with Gibreel over this, because he said, in his unvarnished way: 'I guess it's okay to run from the cameras as long as you know they're chasing after you. But suppose they stop? My guess is you'd turn and run the other way.' Later, when they'd made up, she teased him with her growing stardom (since she became the first sexually attractive blonde to conquer Everest, the noise had increased considerably, she received photographs of gorgeous hunks in the mail, also invita-tions to high life soirées and a quantity of insane abuse): 'I could be in movies myself now that you've retired. Who knows? Maybe I will.' To which he responded, shocking her by the force of his words, 'Over my goddamn dead body.'

In spite of her pragmatic willingness to enter the polluted waters of the real and swim in the general direction of the current, she never lost the sense that some awful disaster was lurking just around the corner – a legacy, this, of her father's and sister's sudden deaths. This hairs-on-neck prickliness had made her a cautious climber, a 'real percentage man', as the lads would have it, and as admired friends died on various mountains her caution increased. Away from mountaineering, it gave her, at times, an unrelaxed look, a jumpiness; she acquired the heavily defended air of a fortress preparing for an inevitable assault. This added to her reputation as a frosty berg of a woman; people kept their distance, and, to hear her tell it, she accepted loneliness as the price of solitude. – But there were more contradictions here, for she had, after all, only recently thrown caution overboard when she chose to make the final assault on Everest without oxygen. 'Aside from all the other implications,' the agency assured her in its formal letter of congratulations, 'this humanizes you, it shows you've got that what-the-hell streak, and that's a positive new dimension.' They were working on it. In the meantime, Allie thought, smiling at Gibreel in tired encouragement as he slipped down towards her lower depths, There's now you. Almost a total stranger and here you've gone and moved right in. God, I even carried you across the threshold, near as makes no difference. Can't blame you for accepting the lift.

He wasn't housetrained. Used to servants, he left clothes, crumbs, used tea-bags where they fell. Worse: he *dropped* them, actually let them fall where they would need picking up; perfectly, richly unconscious of what he was doing, he went on proving to himself that he, the poor boy from the streets, no longer needed to tidy up after himself. It wasn't the only thing about him that drove her crazy. She'd pour glasses of wine; he'd drink his fast and then, when she wasn't looking, grab hers, placating her with an angelic-faced, ultra-innocent 'Plenty more, isn't it?' His bad behaviour around the house. He liked to fart. He complained – actually complained, after she'd literally scooped him out of the snow! – about the smallness of the accommodations. 'Every time I take two steps my face hits a wall.' He was rude to telephone callers, *really* rude, without bothering to find

out who they were: automatically, the way film stars were in
Bombay when, by some chance, there wasn't a flunkey available
to protect them from such intrusions. After Alicja had weathered
one such volley of obscene abuse, she said (when her daughter
finally got on the end of the phone): 'Excuse me for mentioning,
darling, but your boyfriend is in my opinion a case.'

'A case, mother?' This drew out Alicja's grandest voice. She
was still capable of grandeur, had a gift for it, in spite of her post-
Otto decision to disguise herself as a bag-lady. 'A case,' she
announced, taking into consideration the fact that Gibreel was an
Indian import, 'of cashew and monkey nuts.'

Allie didn't argue with her mother, being by no means certain
that she could continue to live with Gibreel, even if he had
crossed the earth, even if he had fallen from the sky. The long
term was hard to predict; even the medium term looked cloudy.
For the moment, she concentrated on trying to get to know this
man who had just assumed, right off, that he was the great love of
her life, with a lack of doubt that meant he was either right or off
his head. There were plenty of difficult moments. She didn't
know what he knew, what she could take for granted: she tried,
once, referring to Nabokov's doomed chess-player Luzhin, who
came to feel that in life as in chess there were certain combinations
that would inevitably arise to defeat him, as a way of explaining by
analogy her own (in fact somewhat different) sense of impending
catastrophe (which had to do not with recurring patterns but with
the inescapability of the unforeseeable), but he fixed her with a
hurt stare that told her he'd never heard of the writer, let alone
The Defence. Conversely, he surprised her by asking, out of the
blue, 'Why Picabia?' Adding that it was peculiar, was it not, for
Otto Cohen, a veteran of the terror camps, to go in for all that
neo-Fascistic love of machinery, brute power, dehumanization
glorified. 'Anybody who's spent any time with machines at all,' he
added, 'and baby, that's us all, knows first and foremost there's
only one thing certain about them, computer or bicycle. They go
wrong.' Where did you find out about, she began, and faltered
because she didn't like the patronizing note she was striking, but

he answered without vanity. The first time he'd heard about Marinetti, he said, he'd got the wrong end of the stick and thought Futurism was something to do with puppets. 'Marionettes, kathputli, at that time I was keen to use advanced puppetry techniques in a picture, maybe to depict demons or other supernormal beings. So I got a book.' *I got a book:* Gibreel the autodidact made it sound like an injection. To a girl from a house that revered books – her father had made them all kiss any volume that fell by chance to the floor – and who had reacted by treating them badly, ripping out pages she wanted or didn't like, scribbling and scratching at them to show them who was boss, Gibreel's form of irreverence, non-abusive, taking books for what they offered without feeling the need to genuflect or destroy, was something new; and, she accepted, pleasing. She learned from him. He, however, seemed impervious to any wisdom she might wish to impart, about, for example, the correct place in which to dispose of dirty socks. When she attempted to suggest he 'did his share', he went into a profound, injured sulk, expecting to be cajoled back into a good humour. Which, to her disgust, she found herself willing, for the moment at any rate, to do.

The worst thing about him, she tentatively concluded, was his genius for thinking himself slighted, belittled, under attack. It became almost impossible to mention anything to him, no matter how reasonable, no matter how gently put. 'Go, go eat air,' he'd shout, and retire into the tent of his wounded pride. – And the most seductive thing about him was the way he knew instinctively what she wanted, how when he chose he could become the agent of her secret heart. As a result, their sex was literally electric. That first tiny spark, on the occasion of their inaugural kiss, wasn't any one-off. It went on happening, and sometimes while they made love she was convinced she could hear the crackle of electricity all around them; she felt, at times, her hair standing on end. 'It reminds me of the electric dildo in my father's study,' she told Gibreel, and they laughed. 'Am I the love of your life?' she asked quickly, and he answered, just as quickly: 'Of course.'

She admitted to him early on that the rumours about her unat tainability, even frigidity, had some basis in fact. 'After Yel died, I took on that side of her as well.' She hadn't needed, any more, to hurl lovers into her sister's face. 'Plus I really wasn't enjoying it any more. It was mostly revolutionary socialists at the time, making do with me while they dreamed about the heroic women they'd seen on their three-week trips to Cuba. Never touched *them*, of course; the combat fatigues and ideological purity scared them silly. They came home humming "Guantanamera" and rang me up.' She opted out. 'I thought, let the best minds of my generation soliloquize about power over some other poor woman's body, I'm off.' She began climbing mountains, she used to say when she began, 'because I knew they'd never follow me up there. But then I thought, bullshit. I didn't do it for them; I did it for me.'

For an hour every evening she would run barefoot up and down the stairs to the street, on her toes, for the sake of her fallen arches. Then she'd collapse into a heap of cushions, looking enraged, and he'd flap helplessly around, usually ending up pouring her a stiff drink: Irish whiskey, mostly. She had begun drinking a fair bit as the reality of her foot problem sank in. ('For Christ's sake keep the feet quiet,' a voice from the PR agency told her surreally on the phone. 'If they get out it's finito, curtains, sayonara, go home, goodnight.') On their twenty-first night together, when she had worked her way through five doubles of Jameson's, she said: 'Why I really went up there. Don't laugh: to escape from good and evil.' He didn't laugh. 'Are mountains above morality, in your estimation?' he asked seriously. 'This's what I learned in the revolution,' she went on. 'This thing: information got abolished sometime in the twentieth century, can't say just when; stands to reason, that's part of the information that got abolsh, abo*lished*. Since then we've been living in a fairy-story. Got me? Everything happens by magic. Us fairies haven't a fucking notion what's going on. So how do we know if it's right or wrong? We don't even know what it *is*. So what I thought was, you can either break your heart trying to work it all out, or you can go sit on a mountain, because that's where all the truth went, believe it or not, it just upped and ran away from these cities where even the stuff under our feet is all made up, a lie, and it hid up there in the thin thin air where the liars don't dare come after it in case their brains explode. It's up there all right. I've been there. Ask me.' She fell asleep; he carried her to the bed.

After the news of his death in the plane crash reached her, she had tormented herself by inventing him: by speculating, that is to say, about her lost lover. He had been the first man she'd slept with in more than five years: no small figure in her life. She had turned away from her sexuality, her instincts having warned her that to do otherwise might be to be absorbed by it; that it was for her, would always be, a big subject, a whole dark continent to map, and she wasn't prepared to go that way, be that explorer, chart those shores: not any more, or, maybe, not yet. But she'd never shaken off the feeling of being damaged by her ignorance of Love, of what it might be like to be wholly possessed by that archetypal, capitalized djinn, the yearning towards, the blurring of the boundaries of the self, the unbuttoning, until you were open from your adam's-apple to your crotch: just words, because she didn't know the thing. Suppose he had come to me, she dreamed. I could have learned him, step by step, climbed him to the very summit. Denied mountains by my weak-boned feet, I'd have looked for the mountain in him: establishing base camp, sussing out routes, negotiating ice-falls, crevasses, overhangs. I'd have assaulted the peak and seen the angels dance. O, but he's dead, and at the bottom of the sea.

Then she found him. – And maybe he'd invented her, too, a little bit, invented someone worth rushing out of one's old life to love. – Nothing so remarkable in that. Happens often enough; and the two inventors go on, rubbing the rough edges off one another, adjusting their inventions, moulding imagination to actuality, learning how to be together: or not. It works out or it doesn't. But to suppose that Gibreel Farishta and Alleluia Cone could have gone along so familiar a path is to make the mistake of thinking their relationship ordinary. It wasn't; didn't have so much as a shot at ordinariness.

It was a relationship with serious flaws.

('The modern city,' Otto Cone on his hobbyhorse had lectured his bored family at table, 'is the locus classicus of incompatible realities. Lives that have no business mingling with one another sit side by side upon the omnibus. One universe, on a zebra crossing, is caught for an instant, blinking like a rabbit, in the headlamps of a motor-vehicle in which an entirely alien and contradictory continuum is to be found. And as long as that's all, they pass in the night, jostling on Tube stations, raising their hats in some hotel corridor, it's not so bad. But if they meet! It's uranium and plutonium, each makes the other decompose, boom.' – 'As a matter of fact, dearest,' Alicja said dryly, 'I often feel a little incompatible myself.')

The flaws in the grand passion of Alleluia Cone and Gibreel Farishta were as follows: her secret fear of her secret desire, that is, love; – owing to which she was wont to retreat from, even hit violently out at, the very person whose devotion she sought most; – and the deeper the intimacy, the harder she kicked; – so that the other, having been brought to a place of absolute trust, and having lowered all his defences, received the full force of the blow, and was devastated; – which, indeed, is what befell Gibreel Farishta, when after three weeks of the most ecstatic lovemaking either of them had ever known he was told without ceremony that he had better find himself somewhere to live, pretty sharpish, because she, Allie, required more elbow-room than was presently available; –

– and his overweening possessiveness and jealousy, of which he himself had been wholly unaware, owing to his never previously having thought of a woman as a treasure that had to be guarded at all costs against the piratical hordes who would naturally be trying to purloin her; – and of which more will be said almost instantly; –

– and the fatal flaw, namely, Gibreel Farishta's imminent realization – or, if you will, *insane idea*, – that he truly was nothing less than an archangel in human form, and not just any archangel, but the Angel of the Recitation, the most exalted (now that Shaitan had fallen) of them all.

They had spent their days in such isolation, wrapped up in the sheets of their desires, that his wild, uncontrollable jealousy, which, as Iago warned, 'doth mock the meat it feeds on', did not instantly come to light. It first manifested itself in the absurd matter of the trio of cartoons which Allie had hung in a group by her front door, mounted in cream and framed in old gold, all bearing the same message, scrawled across the lower right-hand corner of the cream mounts: *To A., in hopes, from Brunel.* When Gibreel noticed these inscriptions he demanded an explanation, pointing furiously at the cartoons with fully extended arm, while with his free hand he clutched a bedsheet around him (he was attired in this informal manner because he'd decided the time was ripe for him to make a full inspection of the premises, *can't spend one's whole life on one's back, or even yours,* he'd said); Allie, forgivably, laughed. 'You look like Brutus, all murder and dignity,' she teased him. 'The picture of an honourable man.' He shocked her by shouting violently: 'Tell me at once who the bastard is.'

'You can't be serious,' she said. Jack Brunel worked as an animator, was in his late fifties and had known her father. She had never had the faintest interest in him, but he had taken to courting her by the strangulated, wordless method of sending her, from time to time, these graphic gifts.

'Why you didn't throw them in the wpb?' Gibreel howled. Allie, still not fully understanding the size of his rage, continued lightly. She had kept the pictures because she liked them. The first was an old *Punch* cartoon in which Leonardo da Vinci stood in his atelier, surrounded by pupils, and hurled the Mona Lisa like a frisbee across the room. *'Mark my words,'* he said in the caption, *'one day men shall fly to Padua in such as these.'* In the second frame there was a page from *Toff,* a British boys' comic dating from World War II. It had been thought necessary in a time when so many children became evacuees to create, by way of explanation, a comic-strip version of events in the adult world. Here, therefore, was one of the weekly encounters between the home team –

the Toff (an appalling monocled child in Etonian bum-freezer and pin-striped trousers) and cloth-capped, scuff-kneed Bert – and the dastardly foe, Hawful Hadolf and the Nastiparts (a bunch of thuggish fiends, each of whom had one extremely nasty part, e.g. a steel hook instead of a hand, feet like claws, teeth that could bite through your arm). The British team invariably came out on top. Gibreel, glancing at the framed comic, was scornful. 'You bloody *Angrez*. You really think like this; this is what the war was really like for you.' Allie decided not to mention her father, or to tell Gibreel that one of the *Toff* artists, a virulently anti-Nazi Berlin man named Wolf, had been arrested one day and led away for internment along with all the other Germans in Britain, and, according to Brunel, his colleagues hadn't lifted a finger to save him. 'Heartlessness,' Jack had reflected. 'Only thing a cartoonist really needs. What an artist Disney would have been if he hadn't had a heart. It was his fatal flaw.' Brunel ran a small animation studio named Scarecrow Productions, after the character in *The Wizard of Oz*.

The third frame contained the last drawing from one of the films of the great Japanese animator Yoji Kuri, whose uniquely cynical output perfectly exemplified Brunel's unsentimental view of the cartoonist's art. In this film, a man fell off a skyscraper; a fire engine rushed to the scene and positioned itself beneath the falling man. The roof slid back, permitting a huge steel spike to emerge, and, in the still on Allie's wall, the man arrived head first and the spike rammed into his brain. 'Sick,' Gibreel Farishta pronounced.

These lavish gifts having failed to get results, Brunel was obliged to break cover and show up in person. He presented himself at Allie's apartment one night, unannounced and already considerably the worse for alcohol, and produced a bottle of dark rum from his battered briefcase. At three the next morning he had drunk the rum but showed no signs of leaving. Allie, going ostentatiously off to the bathroom to brush her teeth, returned to find the animator standing stark naked in the centre of her living-room rug, revealing a surprisingly shapely body covered by an inordinate amount of thick grey hair. When he saw her he spread his arms and cried: 'Take me! Do what you will!' She made him dress, as kindly as she could, and put him and his briefcase gently out of the door. He never returned.

Allie told Gibreel the story, in an open, giggling manner that suggested she was entirely unprepared for the storm it would unleash. It is possible, however (things had been rather strained between them in recent days) that her innocent air was a little disingenuous, that she was almost hoping for him to begin the bad behaviour, so that what followed would be his responsibility, not hers . . . at any rate, Gibreel blew sky-high, accusing Allie of having falsified the story's ending, suggesting that poor Brunel was still waiting by his telephone and that she intended to ring him the moment his, Farishta's, back was turned. Ravings, in short, jealousy of the past, the worst kind of all. As this terrible emotion took charge of him, he found himself improvising a whole series of lovers for her, imagining them to be waiting around every corner. She had used the Brunel story to taunt him, he shouted, it was a deliberate and cruel threat. 'You want men down on their knees,' he screamed, every scrap of his self-control long gone. 'Me, I do not kneel.'

'That's it,' she said. 'Out.'

His anger redoubled. Clutching his toga around him, he stalked into the bedroom to dress, putting on the only clothes he possessed, including the scarlet-lined gabardine overcoat and grey felt trilby of Don Enrique Diamond; Allie stood in the doorway and watched. 'Don't think I'm coming back,' he yelled, knowing his rage was more than sufficient to get him out of the door, waiting for her to begin to calm him down, to speak softly, to give him a way of staying. But she shrugged and walked away, and it was then, at that precise moment of his greatest wrath, that the boundaries of the earth broke, he heard a noise like the bursting of a dam, and as the spirits of the world of dreams flooded through the breach into the universe of the quotidian, Gibreel Farishta saw God.

For Blake's Isaiah, God had simply been an immanence, an

incorporeal indignation; but Gibreel's vision of the Supreme
Being was not abstract in the least. He saw, sitting on the bed, a
man of about the same age as himself, of medium height, fairly
heavily built, with salt-and-pepper beard cropped close to the line
of the jaw. What struck him most was that the apparition was
balding, seemed to suffer from dandruff and wore glasses. This was
not the Almighty he had expected. 'Who are you?' he asked with
interest. (Of no interest to him now was Alleluia Cone, who had
stopped in her tracks on hearing him begin to talk to himself, and
who was now observing him with an expression of genuine
panic.)

'Ooparvala,' the apparition answered. 'The Fellow Upstairs.'

'How do I know you're not the other One,' Gibreel asked
craftily, 'Neechayvala, the Guy from Underneath?'

A daring question, eliciting a snappish reply. This Deity might
look like a myopic scrivener, but It could certainly mobilize
the traditional apparatus of divine rage. Clouds massed outside the
window; wind and thunder shook the room. Trees fell in the
Fields. 'We're losing patience with you, Gibreel Farishta. You've
doubted Us just about long enough.' Gibreel hung his head,
blasted by the wrath of God. 'We are not obliged to explain Our
nature to you,' the dressing-down continued. 'Whether We be
multiform, plural, representing the union-by-hybridization of
such opposites as *Oopar* and *Neechay*, or whether We be pure,
stark, extreme, will not be resolved here.' The disarranged bed on
which his Visitor had rested Its posterior (which, Gibreel now
observed, was glowing faintly, like the rest of the Person) was
granted a highly disapproving glance. 'The point is, there will be
no more dilly-dallying. You wanted clear signs of Our existence?
We sent Revelation to fill your dreams: in which not only Our
nature, but yours also, was clarified. But you fought against it,
struggling against the very sleep in which We were awakening
you. Your fear of the truth has finally obliged Us to expose Our-
self, at some personal inconvenience, in this woman's residence at
an advanced hour of the night. It is time, now, to shape up. Did

We pluck you from the skies so that you could boff and spat with some (no doubt remarkable) flatfoot blonde? There's work to be done.'

'I am ready,' Gibreel said humbly. 'I was just going, anyway.'

'Look,' Allie Cone was saying, 'Gibreel, goddamn it, never mind the fight. Listen: I love you.'

There were only the two of them in the apartment now. 'I have to go,' Gibreel said, quietly. She hung upon his arm. 'Truly, I don't think you're really well.' He stood upon his dignity. 'Having commanded my exit, you no longer have jurisdiction *re* my health.' He made his escape. Alleluia, trying to follow him, was afflicted by such piercing pains in both feet that, having no option, she fell weeping to the floor: like an actress in a masala movie; or Rekha Merchant on the day Gibreel walked out on her for the last time. Like, anyhow, a character in a story of a kind in which she could never have imagined she belonged.

The meteorological turbulence engendered by God's anger with his servant had given way to a clear, balmy night presided over by a fat and creamy moon. Only the fallen trees remained to bear witness to the might of the now-departed Being. Gibreel, trilby jammed down on his head, money-belt firmly around his waist, hands deep in gabardine – the right hand feeling, in there, the shape of a paperback book – was giving silent thanks for his escape. Certain now of his archangelic status, he banished from his thoughts all remorse for his time of doubting, replacing it with a new resolve: to bring this metropolis of the ungodly, this latter-day 'Ad or Thamoud, back to the knowledge of God, to shower upon it the blessings of the Recitation, the sacred Word. He felt his old self drop from him, and dismissed it with a shrug, but chose to retain, for the time being, his human scale. This was not the time to grow until he filled the sky from horizon to horizon – though that, too, would surely come before long.

The city's streets coiled around him, writhing like serpents. London had grown unstable once again, revealing its true, capricious, tormented nature, its anguish of a city that had lost its sense of itself and wallowed, accordingly, in the impotence of its selfish, angry present of masks and parodies, stifled and twisted by the insupportable, unrejected burden of its past, staring into the bleakness of its impoverished future. He wandered its streets through that night, and the next day, and the next night, and on until the light and dark ceased to matter. He no longer seemed to need food or rest, but only to move constantly through that tortured metropolis whose fabric was now utterly transformed, the houses in the rich quarters being built of solidified fear, the government buildings partly of vainglory and partly of scorn, and the residences of the poor of confusion and material dreams. When you looked through an angel's eyes you saw essences instead of surfaces, you saw the decay of the soul blistering and bubbling on the skins of people in the street, you saw the generosity of certain spirits resting on their shoulders in the form of birds. As he roamed the metamorphosed city he saw bat-winged imps sitting on the corners of buildings made of deceits and glimpsed goblins oozing wormily through the broken tilework of public urinals for men. As once the thirteenth-century German monk Richalmus would shut his eyes and instantly see clouds of minuscule demons surrounding every man and woman on earth, dancing like dustspecks in the sunlight, so now Gibreel with open eyes and by the light of the moon as well as the sun detected everywhere the presence of his adversary, his – to give the old word back its original meaning – *shaitan*.

Long before the Flood, he remembered – now that he had reassumed the role of archangel, the full range of archangelic memory and wisdom was apparently being restored to him, little by little – a number of angels (the names Semjaza and Azazel came first to mind) had been flung out of Heaven because they had been *lusting after the daughters of men*, who in due course gave birth to an evil race of giants. He began to understand the degree of the danger from which he had been saved when he departed from the vicinity of Alleluia Cone. O most false of creatures! O princess of the powers of the air! – When the Prophet, on whose name be peace, had first received the wahi, the Revelation, had he not feared for his sanity? – And who had offered him the reassuring certainty he needed? – Why, Khadija, his wife. She it was who convinced him that he was not some raving crazy but the Messenger of God. – Whereas what had Alleluia done for him? *You're not yourself. I don't think you're really well.* – O bringer of tribulation, creatrix of strife, of soreness of the heart! Siren, temptress, fiend in human form! That snowlike body with its pale, pale hair: how she had used it to fog his soul, and how hard he had found it, in the weakness of his flesh, to resist . . . enmeshed by her in the web of a love so complex as to be beyond comprehension, he had come to the very edge of the ultimate Fall. How beneficent, then, the Over-Entity had been to him! – He saw now that the choice was simple: the infernal love of the daughters of men, or the celestial adoration of God. He had found it possible to choose the latter; in the nick of time.

He drew out of the right-hand pocket of his overcoat the book that had been there ever since his departure from Rosa's house a millennium ago: the book of the city he had come to save, Proper London, capital of Vilayet, laid out for his benefit in exhaustive detail, the whole bang shoot. He would redeem this city: Geographers' London, all the way from A to Z.

On a street corner in a part of town once known for its population of artists, radicals and men in search of prostitutes, and now given over to advertising personnel and minor film producers, the Archangel Gibreel chanced to see a lost soul. It was young, male, tall, and of extreme beauty, with a strikingly aquiline nose and longish black hair oiled down and parted in the centre; its teeth were made of gold. The lost soul stood at the very edge of the pavement, its back to the road, leaning forwards at a slight angle and clutching, in its right hand, something it evidently held very dear. Its behaviour was striking: first it would stare fiercely at the thing it held in its hand, and then look around, whipping its head from right to left, scrutinizing with blazing concentration the faces of the passers-by. Reluctant to approach too quickly, Gibreel on a first pass saw that the object the lost soul was clutching was a small passport-sized photograph. On his second pass he went right up to the stranger and offered his help. The other eyed him suspiciously, then thrust the photograph under his nose. 'This man,' he said, jabbing at the picture with a long index finger. 'Do you know this man?'

When Gibreel saw, staring out of the photograph, a young man of extreme beauty, with a strikingly aquiline nose and longish black hair, oiled, with a central parting, he knew that his instincts had been correct, that here, standing on a busy street corner watching the crowd in case he saw himself going by, was a Soul in search of its mislaid body, a spectre in desperate need of its lost physical casing – for it is known to archangels that the soul or ka cannot exist (once the golden cord of light linking it to the body is severed) for more than a night and a day. 'I can help you,' he promised, and the young soul looked at him in wild disbelief. Gibreel leaned forward, grasped the ka's face between his hands, and kissed it firmly upon the mouth, for the spirit that is kissed by an archangel regains, at once, its lost sense of direction, and is set upon the true and righteous path. – The lost soul, however, had a most surprising reaction to being favoured by an archangelic kiss. 'Sod you,' it shouted, 'I may be desperate, mate, but I'm not that desperate,' – after which, manifesting a solidity most unusual in a disembodied spirit, it struck the Archangel of the Lord a resounding blow upon the nose with the very fist in which its image was clasped; – with disorienting, and bloody, results.

When his vision cleared, the lost soul had gone but there, floating on her carpet a couple of feet off the ground, was Rekha Merchant, mocking his discomfiture. 'Not such a great start,' she snorted. 'Archangel my foot. Gibreel janab, you're off your head, take it from me. You played too many winged types for your own good. I wouldn't trust that Deity of yours either, if I were you,' she added in a more conspiratorial tone, though Gibreel suspected that her intentions remained satirical. 'He hinted as much himself, fudging the answer to your Oopar–Neechay question like he did.

This notion of separation of functions, light versus dark, evil versus good, may be straightforward enough in Islam – *O, children of Adam, let not the Devil seduce you, as he expelled your parents from the garden, pulling off from them their clothing that he might show them their shame* – but go back a bit and you see that it's a pretty recent fabrication. Amos, eighth century B C, asks: "Shall there be evil in a city and the Lord hath not done it?" Also Jahweh, quoted by Deutero-Isaiah two hundred years later, remarks: "I form the light, and create darkness; I make peace and create evil; I the Lord do all these things." It isn't until the Book of Chronicles, merely fourth century B C, that the word *shaitan* is used to mean a being, and not only an attribute of God.' This speech was one of which the 'real' Rekha would plainly have been incapable, coming as she did from a polytheistic tradition and never having evinced the faintest interest in comparative religion or, of all things, the Apocrypha. But the Rekha who had been pursuing him ever since he fell from *Bostan* was, Gibreel knew, not real in any objective, psychologically or corporeally consistent manner. – What, then, was she? It would be easy to imagine her as a thing of his own making – his own accomplice-adversary, his inner demon. That would account for her ease with the arcana. – But how had he himself come by such knowledge? Had he truly, in days gone by, possessed it and then lost it, as his memory now informed him? (He had a nagging notion of inaccuracy here, but when he tried to fix his thoughts upon his 'dark age', that is to say the period during which he had unaccountably come to disbelieve in his angelhood, he was faced with a thick bank of clouds, through which, peer and blink as he might, he could make out little more than shadows.) – Or could it be that the material now filling his thoughts, the echo, to give but a single example, of how his lieutenant-angels Ithuriel and Zephon had found the adversary *squat like a toad* by Eve's ear in Eden, using his wiles 'to reach/The organs of her fancy, and with them forge/Illusions as he list, phantasms and dreams', had in fact been planted in his head by that same ambiguous Creature, that Upstairs-Downstairs Thing, who had confronted him in Alleluia's boudoir, and awoken him from his long waking sleep? – Then Rekha, too, was perhaps an emissary of this God, an external, divine antagonist and not an inner, guilt-produced shade; one sent to wrestle with him and make him whole again.

His nose, leaking blood, began to throb painfully. He had never been able to tolerate pain. 'Always a cry-baby,' Rekha laughed in his face. Shaitan had understood more:

> *Lives there who loves his pain?*
> *Who would not, finding way, break loose from hell,*
> *Though thither doomed? Thou wouldst thyself, no doubt,*
> *And boldly venture to whatever place*
> *Farthest from pain, where thou mightst hope to change*
> *Torment with ease . . .*

He couldn't have put it better. A person who found himself in an inferno would do anything, rape, extortion, murder, felo de se, whatever it took to get out . . . he dabbed a handkerchief at his nose as Rekha, still present on her flying rug, and intuiting his ascent (descent?) into the realm of metaphysical speculation, attempted to get things back on to more familiar ground. 'You should have stuck with me,' she opined. 'You could have loved me, good and proper. I knew how to love. Not everybody has the capacity for it; I do, I mean did. Not like that self-centred blonde bombshell thinking secretly about having a child and not even mentioning same to you. Not like your God, either; it's not like the old days, when such Persons took proper interest.'

This needed contesting on several grounds. 'You were married, start to finish,' he replied. 'Ball-bearings. I was your side dish. Nor will I, who waited so long for Him to manifest Himself, now speak poorly of Him post facto, after the personal appearance. Finally, what's all this baby-talk? You'll go to any extreme, seems like.'

'You don't know what hell is,' she snapped back, dropping the mask of her imperturbability. 'But, buster, you sure will. If you'd ever said, I'd have thrown over that ball-bearings bore in two secs, but you kept mum. Now I'll see you down there: Neechayvala's Hotel.'

'You'd never have left your children,' he insisted. 'Poor fellows, you even threw them down first when you jumped.' That set her off. 'Don't you talk! To dare to talk! Mister, I'll cook your goose! I'll fry your heart and eat it up on toast! – And as to your Snow White princess, she is of the opinion that a child is a mother's property only, because men may come and men may go but she goes on forever, isn't it? You're only the seed, excuse me, she is the garden. Who asks a seed permission to plant? What do you know, damn fool Bombay boy messing with the modern ideas of mames.'

'And you,' he came back strongly. 'Did you, for example, ask their Daddyji's permission before you threw his kiddies off the roof?'

She vanished in fury and yellow smoke, with an explosion that made him stagger and knocked the hat off his head (it lay upturned on the pavement at his feet). She unleashed, too, an olfactory effect of such nauseous potency as to make him gag and retch. Emptily: for he was perfectly void of all foodstuffs and liquids, having partaken of no nourishment for many days. Ah, immortality, he thought: ah, noble release from the tyranny of the body. He noticed that there were two individuals watching him curiously, one a violent-looking youth in studs and leather, with a rainbow Mohican haircut and a streak of face-paint lightning zigzagging down his nose, the other a kindly middle-aged woman in a headscarf. Very well then: seize the day. 'Repent,' he cried passionately. 'For I am the Archangel of the Lord.'

'Poor bastard,' said the Mohican and threw a coin into Farishta's fallen hat. He walked on; the kindly, twinkling lady, however, leaned confidentially towards Gibreel and passed him a leaflet. 'You'll be interested in this.' He quickly identified it as a racist text demanding the 'repatriation' of the country's black citizenry. She took him, he deduced, for a white angel. So angels were not exempt from such categories, he wonderingly learned.

'Look at it this way,' the woman was saying, taking his silence for uncertainty – and revealing, by slipping into an over-articulated, over-loud mode of delivery, that she thought him not quite pukka, a Levantine angel, maybe, Cypriot or Greek, in need of her best talking-to-the-afflicted voice. 'If they came over and filled up wherever you come from, well! You wouldn't like *that*.'

Punched in the nose, taunted by phantoms, given alms instead of reverence, and in divers ways shewn the depths to which the denizens of the city had sunk, the intransigence of the evil manifest there, Gibreel became more determined than ever to commence the doing of good, to initiate the great work of rolling back the frontiers of the adversary's dominion. The atlas in his pocket was his master-plan. He would redeem the city square by square, from Hockley Farm in the north-west corner of the charted area to Chance Wood in the south-east; after which, perhaps, he would celebrate the conclusion of his labours by playing a round of golf at the aptly named course situated at the very edge of the map: Wildernesse.

And somewhere along the way the adversary himself would be waiting. Shaitan, Iblis, or whatever name he had adopted – and in point of fact that name was on the tip of Gibreel's tongue – just as the face of the adversary, horned and malevolent, was still somewhat out of focus . . . well, it would take shape soon enough, and the name would come back, Gibreel was sure of it, for were not his powers growing every day, was he not the one who, restored to his glory, would hurl the adversary down, once more, into the Darkest Deeps? – That name: what was it? Tch-something? Tchu Tché Tchin Tchow. No matter. All in good time.

But the city in its corruption refused to submit to the dominion of the cartographers, changing shape at will and without warning, making it impossible for Gibreel to approach his quest in the systematic manner he would have preferred. Some days he would turn a corner at the end of a grand colonnade built of human flesh and covered in skin that bled when scratched, and find himself in an uncharted wasteland, at whose distant rim he could see tall familiar buildings, Wren's dome, the high metallic spark-plug of the Telecom Tower, crumbling in the wind like sandcastles. He would stumble across bewildering and anonymous parks and emerge into the crowded streets of the West End, upon which, to the consternation of the motorists, acid had begun to drip from the sky, burning great holes in the surfaces of the roads. In this pandemonium of mirages he often heard laughter: the city was mocking his impotence, awaiting his surrender, his recognition that what existed here was beyond his powers to comprehend, let alone to change. He shouted curses at his still-faceless adversary, pleaded with the Deity for a further sign, feared that his energies might, in truth, never be equal to the task. In brief, he was becoming the most wretched and bedraggled of archangels, his garments filthy, his hair lank and greasy, his chin sprouting hair in uncontrollable tufts. It was in this sorry condition that he arrived at the Angel Underground.

It must have been early in the morning, because the station staff drifted up as he watched, to unlock and then roll back the metal grille of night. He followed them in, shuffling along, head low, hands deep in pockets (the street atlas had been discarded long ago); and raising his eyes at last, found himself looking into a face on the verge of dissolving into tears.

'Good morning,' he ventured, and the young woman in the ticket office responded bitterly, 'What's good about it, that's what I want to know,' and now her tears did come, plump, globular and plenteous. 'There, there, child,' he said, and she gave him a disbelieving look. 'You're no priest,' she opined. He answered, a little tentatively: 'I am the Angel, Gibreel.' She began to laugh, as abruptly as she had wept. 'Only angels roun here hang from the lamp-posts at Christmas. Illuminations. Only the Council swing them by their necks.' He was not to be put off. 'I am Gibreel,' he repeated, fixing her with his eye. 'Recite.' And, to her own emphatically expressed astonishment, *I cyaan believe I doin this, emptyin my heart to some tramp, I not like this, you know,* the ticket clerk began to speak.

Her name was Orphia Phillips, twenty years old, both parents alive and dependent on her, especially now that her fool sister Hyacinth had lost her job as a physiotherapist by 'gettin up to she nonsense'. The young man's name, for of course there was a young man, was Uriah Moseley. The station had recently installed two gleaming new elevators and Orphia and Uriah were their operators. During rush-hours, when both lifts were working, they had little time for conversation; but for the rest of the day, only one lift was used. Orphia took up her position at the ticket-collection point just along from the elevator-shaft, and Uri managed to spend a good deal of time down there with her, leaning against the door-jamb of his gleaming lift and picking his teeth with the silver toothpick his great-grandfather had liberated from some old-time plantation boss. It was true love. 'But I jus get carry away,' Orphia wailed at Gibreel. 'I always too hasty for sense.' One afternoon, during a lull, she had deserted her post and stepped up right in front of him as he leaned and picked teeth, and seeing the look in her eye he put away the pick. After that he came to work with a spring in his step; she, too, was in heaven as she descended each day into the bowels of the earth. Their kisses grew longer and more passionate. Sometimes she would not detach herself when the buzzer rang for the lift; Uriah would have to push her back, with a cry of, 'Cool off, girl, the public.' Uriah had a vocational attitude to his work. He spoke to her of his pride in his uniform, of his satisfaction at being in the public service, giving his life to society. She thought he sounded a shade pompous, and wanted to say, 'Uri, man, you jus a elevator boy here,' but intuiting that such realism would not be well received, she held her troublesome tongue, or, rather, pushed it into his mouth.

Their embraces in the tunnel became wars. Now he was trying

to get away, straightening his tunic, while she bit his ear and pushed her hand down inside his trousers. 'You crazy,' he said, but she, continuing, inquired: 'So? You vex?'

They were, inevitably, caught: a complaint was lodged by a kindly lady in headscarf and tweeds. They had been lucky to keep their jobs. Orphia had been 'grounded', deprived of elevator-shafts and boxed into the ticket booth. Worse still, her place had been taken by the station beauty, Rochelle Watkins. 'I know what going on,' she cried angrily. 'I see Rochelle expression when she come up, fixin up her hair an all o' dat.' Uriah, nowadays, avoided Orphia's eyes.

'Can't figure out how you get me to tell you me business,' she concluded, uncertainly. 'You not no angel. That is for sure.' But she was unable, try as she might, to break away from his trans-fixing gaze. 'I know,' he told her, 'what is in your heart.'

He reached in through the booth's window and took her unre-sisting hand. – Yes, this was it, the force of her desires filling him up, enabling him to translate them back to her, making action possible, allowing her to say and do what she most profoundly required; this was what he remembered, this quality of being joined to the one to whom he appeared, so that what followed was the product of their joining. At last, he thought, the archangelic functions return. – Inside the ticket booth, the clerk Orphia Phillips had her eyes closed, her body had slumped down in her chair, looking slow and heavy, and her lips were moving. – And his own, in unison with hers. – There. It was done.

At this moment the station manager, a little angry man with nine long hairs, fetched from ear-level, plastered across his bald-ness, burst like a cuckoo from his little door. 'What's your game?' he shouted at Gibreel. 'Get out of it before I call the police.' Gibreel stayed where he was. The station manager saw Orphia emerging from her trance and began to shriek. 'You, Phillips. Never saw the like. Anything in trousers, but this is ridiculous. All my born days. And nodding off on the job, the idea.' Orphia stood up, put on her raincoat, picked up her folding umbrella, emerged from ticket booth. 'Leaving public property unattended.

You get back in there this minute, or it's your job, sure as eggsis.'
Orphia headed for the spiral stairs and moved towards the lower
depths. Deprived of his employee, the manager swung round to
face Gibreel. 'Go on,' he said. 'Eff off. Go crawl back under your
stone.'

'I am waiting,' replied Gibreel with dignity, 'for the lift.'

When she reached the bottom of the stairs, Orphia Phillips
turning a corner saw Uriah Moseley leaning against the ticket-
collection booth in that way he had, and Rochelle Watkins simpering with delight. But Orphia knew what to do. 'You let
'Chelle feel you toothpick yet, Uri?' she sang out. 'She'd surely
love to hold it.'

They both straightened up, stung. Uriah began blustering:
'Don't be so common now, Orphia,' but her eyes stopped him in
his tracks. Then he began to walk towards her, dreamily, leaving
Rochelle flat. 'Thas right, Uri,' she said softly, never looking away
from him for an instant. 'Come along now. Come to momma.'
*Now walk backwards to the lift and just suck him right in there, and after
that it's up and away we go.* – But something was wrong here. He
wasn't walking any more. Rochelle Watkins was standing beside
him, too damn close, and he'd come to a halt. 'You tell her,
Uriah,' Rochelle said. 'Her stupid obeah don't signify down here.'
Uriah was putting an arm around Rochelle Watkins. This wasn't
the way she'd dreamed it, the way she'd suddenly been certain-
sure it would be, after that Gibreel took her hand, just like that, as
if they were *intended*; wee-yurd, she thought; what was happening
to her? She advanced. – 'Get her offa me, Uriah,' Rochelle
shouted. 'She mashin up me uniform and all.' – Now Uriah,
holding the struggling ticket clerk by both wrists, gave out the
news: 'I aks her to get marry!' – Whereupon the fight went out of
Orphia. Beaded plaits no longer whirled and clicked. 'So you out
of order, Orphia Phillips,' Uriah continued, puffing somewhat.
'And like the lady say, no obeah na change nutten.' Orphia, also
breathing heavily, her clothes disarranged, flopped down on the
floor with her back to the curved tunnel wall. The noise of a train
pulling in came up towards them; the affianced couple hurried to

their posts, tidying themselves up, leaving Orphia where she sat. 'Girl,' Uriah Moseley offered by way of farewell, 'you too damn outrageous for me.' Rochelle Watkins blew Uriah a kiss from her ticket-collection booth; he, lounging against his lift, picked his teeth. 'Home cooking,' Rochelle promised him. 'And no surprises.'

'You filthy bum,' Orphia Phillips screamed at Gibreel after walking up the two hundred and forty-seven steps of the spiral staircase of defeat. 'You no good devil bum. Who ask you to mash up me life so?'

Even the halo has gone out, like a broken bulb, and I don't know where's the store. Gibreel on a bench in the small park near the station meditated over the futility of his efforts to date. And found blasphemies surfacing once again: if the dabba had the wrong markings and so went to incorrect recipient, was the dabbawalla to blame? If special effect – travelling mat, or such – didn't work, and you saw the blue outline shimmering at the edge of the flying fellow, how to blame the actor? Bythesametoken, if his angeling was proving insufficient, whose fault, please, was this? His, personally, or some other Personage? – Children were playing in the garden of his doubting, among the midge-clouds and rosebushes and despair. Grandmother's footsteps, ghostbusters, tag. Ellowen deeowen, London. The fall of angels, Gibreel reflected, was not the same kettle as the Tumble of Woman and Man. In the case of human persons, the issue had been morality. Of the fruit of the tree of the knowledge of good and evil they shouldst not eat, and ate. Woman first, and at her suggestion man, acquired the verboten ethical standards, tastily apple-flavoured: the serpent brought them a value system. Enabling them, among other things, to judge the Deity Itself, making possible in good time all the awkward inquiries: why evil? Why suffering? Why death? – So, out they went. It didn't want Its pretty creatures getting above their station. – Children giggled in his face: *something straaange in the neighbourhood.* Armed with zapguns, they made as if to bust him like some common, lowdown spook. *Come away from there,* a woman commanded, a tightly groomed woman, white, a redhead, with a broad stripe of freckles across the middle of her face; her voice was full of distaste. *Did you hear me? Now!* – Whereas the angels' crash was a simple matter of power: a straightforward piece of celestial police work, punishment for rebellion, good and tough 'pour encourager les autres'. – Then how unconfident of Itself this Deity was, Who didn't want Its finest creations to know right from wrong; and Who reigned by terror, insisting upon the unqualified submission of even Its closest associates, packing off all dissidents to Its blazing Siberias, the gulag-infernos of Hell . . . he checked himself. These were satanic thoughts, put into his head by Iblis-Beelzebub-Shaitan. If the Entity were still punishing him for his earlier lapse of faith, this was no way to earn remission. He must simply continue until, purified, he felt his full potency restored. Emptying his mind, he sat in the gathering darkness and watched the children (now at some distance) play. *Ip-dip-sky-blue who's-there-not-you not-because-you're-dirty not-because-you're-clean,* and here, he was sure, one of the boys, a grave eleven-year-old with outsize eyes, stared straight at him: *my-mother-says you're-the-fairy-queen.*

Rekha Merchant materialized, all jewels and finery. 'Bachchas are making rude rhymes about you now. Angel of the Lord,' she gibed. 'Even that little ticket-girl back there, she isn't so impressed. Still doing badly, baba, looks like to me.'

On this occasion, however, the spirit of the suicide Rekha Merchant had not come merely to mock. To his astonishment she claimed that his many tribulations had been of her making: 'You imagine there is only your One Thing in charge?' she cried. 'Well, lover-boy, let me put you wise.' Her smart-alec Bombay English speared him with a sudden nostalgia for his lost city, but she wasn't waiting for him to regain his composure. 'Remember that I died for love of you, you creepo; this gives me rights. In particular, to be revenged upon you, by totally bungling up your

life. A man must suffer for causing a lover's leap; don't you think
so? That's the rule, anyway. For so long now I've turned you
inside out; now I'm just fed up. Don't forget how I was so good at
forgiving! You liked it also, na? Therefore I have come to say that
compromise solution is always possible. You want to discuss it, or
you prefer to go on being lost in this craziness, becoming not an
angel but a down-and-out hobo, a stupid joke?'

Gibreel asked: 'What compromise?'

'What else?' she replied, her manner transformed, all gentleness,
with a shine in her eyes. 'My farishta, a so small thing.'

If he would only say he loved her:

If he would only say it, and, once a week, when she came to lie
with him, show his love:

If on a night of his choice it could be as it was during the ball-
bearings-man's absences on business:

'Then I will terminate the insanities of the city, with which I
am persecuting you; nor will you be possessed, any longer, by this
crazy notion of changing, *redeeming* the city like something left in
a pawnshop; it'll all be calm-calm; you can even live with your
paleface mame and be the greatest film star in the world; how
could I be jealous, Gibreel, when I'm already dead, I don't want
you to say I'm as important as her, no, just a second-rank love will
do for me, a side-dish amour; the foot in the other boot. How
about it, Gibreel, just three-little-words, what do you say?'

Give me time.

'It isn't even as if I'm asking for something new, something you
haven't already agreed to, done, indulged in. Lying with a
phantom is not such a bad-bad thing. What about down at that
old Mrs Diamond's – in the boathouse, that night? Quite a
tamasha, you don't think so? So: who do you think put it on?
Listen: I can take for you any form you prefer; one of the advan-
tages of my condition. You wish her again, that boathouse mame
from the stone age? Hey presto. You want the mirror image of
your own mountain-climber sweaty tomboy iceberg? Also,
allakazoo, allakazam. Who do you think it was, waiting for you
after the old lady died?'

All that night he walked the city streets, which remained stable, banal, as if restored to the hegemony of natural laws; while Rekha – floating before him on her carpet like an artiste on a stage, just above head-height – serenaded him with the sweetest of love songs, accompanying herself on an old ivory-sided harmonium, singing everything from the gazals of Faiz Ahmed Faiz to the best old film music, such as the defiant air sung by the dancer Anarkali in the presence of the Grand Mughal Akbar in the fifties classic *Mughal-e-Azam*, – in which she declares and exults in her impossible, forbidden love for the Prince, Salim, – 'Pyaar kiya to darna kya?' – That is to say, more or less, *why be afraid of love?* and Gibreel, whom she had accosted in the garden of his doubt, felt the music attaching strings to his heart and leading him towards her, because what she asked was, just as she said, such a little thing, after all.

He reached the river; and another bench, cast-iron camels supporting the wooden slats, beneath Cleopatra's Needle. Sitting, he closed his eyes. Rekha sang Faiz:

> *Do not ask of me, my love,*
> *that love I once had for you . . .*
> *How lovely you are still, my love,*
> *but I am helpless too;*
> *for the world has other sorrows than love,*
> *and other pleasures too.*
> *Do not ask of me, my love,*
> *that love I once had for you.*

Gibreel saw a man behind his closed eyes: not Faiz, but another poet, well past his heyday, a decrepit sort of fellow. – Yes, that was his name: Baal. What was he doing here? What did he have to say for himself? – Because he was certainly trying to say something; his speech, thick and slurry, made understanding difficult . . . *Any new idea, Mahound, is asked two questions. The first is asked when it's weak: WHAT KIND OF AN IDEA ARE YOU? Are you the kind that compromises, does deals, accommodates itself to society, aims to find a niche, to survive; or are you the cussed, bloody-minded, ramrod-backed type of damnfool notion that would rather break than sway with the breeze? – The kind that will almost certainly, ninety-nine times out of a hundred, be smashed to bits; but, the hundredth time, will change the world.*

'What's the second question?' Gibreel asked aloud.

Answer the first one first.

Gibreel, opening his eyes at dawn, found Rekha unable to sing, silenced by expectations and uncertainties. He let her have it straight off. 'It's a trick. There is no God but God. You are neither the Entity nor Its adversary, but only some caterwauling mist. No compromises; I won't do deals with fogs.' He saw, then, the emeralds and brocades fall from her body, followed by the flesh, until only the skeleton remained, after which that, too, crumbled away; finally, there was a piteous, piercing shriek, as whatever was left of Rekha flew with vanquished fury into the sun.

And did not return: except at – or near – the end.

Convinced that he had passed a test, Gibreel realized that a great weight had lifted from him; his spirits grew lighter by the second, until by the time the sun was in the sky he was literally delirious with joy. Now it could really begin: the tyranny of his enemies, of Rekha and Alleluia Cone and all the women who wished to bind him in the chains of desires and songs, was broken for good; now he could feel light streaming out, once more, from the unseen point just behind his head; and his weight, too, began to diminish. – Yes, he was losing the last traces of his humanity, the gift of flight was being restored to him, as he became ethereal, woven of illumined air. – He could simply step, this minute, off this blackened parapet and soar away above the old grey river; – or leap from any of its bridges and never touch land again. So: it was time to show the city a great sight, for when it perceived the Archangel Gibreel standing in all his majesty upon the western horizon, bathed in the rays of the rising sun, then surely its people would be sore afraid and repent them of their sins.

He began to enlarge his person.

How astonishing, then, that of all the drivers streaming along the Embankment – it was, after all, rush–hour – not one should so much as look in his direction, or acknowledge him! This was in truth a people who had forgotten how to see. And because the relationship between men and angels is an ambiguous one – in which the angels, or mala'ikah, are both the controllers of nature and the intermediaries between the Deity and the human race; but at the same time, as the Quran clearly states, *we said unto the angels, be submissive unto Adam,* the point being to symbolize man's ability to master, through knowledge, the forces of nature which the angels represented – there really wasn't much that the ignored and infuriated malak Gibreel could do about it. Archangels could only speak when men chose to listen. What a bunch! Hadn't he warned the Over-Entity at the very beginning about this crew of criminals and evildoers? 'Wilt thou place in the earth such as make mischief in it and shed blood?' he had asked, and the Being, as usual, replied only that he knew better. Well, there they were, the masters of the earth, canned like tuna on wheels and blind as bats, their heads full of mischief and their newspapers of blood.

It really was incredible. Here appeared a celestial being, all radiance, effulgence and goodness, larger than Big Ben, capable of straddling the Thames colossus-style, and these little ants remained immersed in drive-time radio and quarrels with fellow-motorists. 'I am Gibreel,' he shouted in a voice that shook every building on the riverbank: nobody noticed. Not one person came running out of those quaking edifices to escape the earthquake. Blind, deaf and asleep.

He decided to force the issue.

The stream of traffic flowed past him. He took a mighty breath, lifted one gigantic foot, and stepped out to face the cars.

Gibreel Farishta was returned to Allie's doorstep, badly bruised, with many grazes on his arms and face, and jolted into sanity, by a tiny shining gentleman with an advanced stammer who

introduced himself with some difficulty as the film producer S.S.
Sisodia, 'known as Whiwhisky because I'm papa partial to a titi
tipple; mamadam, my caca card.' (When they knew each other
better, Sisodia would send Allie into convulsions of laughter by
rolling up his right trouser-leg, exposing the knee, and pro-
nouncing, while he held his enormous wraparound movie-man
glasses to his shin: 'Self pawpaw portrait.' He was longsighted to a
degree: 'Don't need help to see moomovies but real life gets too
damn cloclose up.') It was Sisodia's rented limo that hit Gibreel, a
slow-motion accident luckily, owing to traffic congestion; the
actor ended up on the bonnet, mouthing the oldest line in the
movies: *Where am I*, and Sisodia, seeing the legendary features of
the vanished demigod squashed up against the limousine's wind-
shield, was tempted to answer: *Baback where you bibi belong: on the
iska iska iscreen.* – 'No bobobones broken,' Sisodia told Allie. 'A
mimi miracle. He ista ista istepped right in fafa front of the
weewee wehicle.'

So you're back, Allie greeted Gibreel silently. *Seems this is where
you always land up after you fall.*

'Also Scotch-and-Sisodia,' the film producer reverted to the
question of his sobriquets. 'For hoohoo humorous reasons. My
fafavourite pup pup poison.'

'It is very kind of you to bring Gibreel home,' Allie belatedly
got the point. 'You must allow us to offer you a drink.'

'Sure! Sure!' Sisodia actually clapped his hands. 'For me, for
whowhole of heehee Hindi cinema, today is a baba banner day.'

'You have not heard perhaps the story of the paranoid schizo-
phrenic who, believing himself to be the Emperor Napoleon
Bonaparte, agreed to undergo a lie-detector test?' Alicja Cohen,
eating gefilte fish hungrily, waved one of Bloom's forks under
her daughter's nose. 'The question they asked him: are you Napoleon? And the answer he gave, smiling wickedly, no doubt: *No.*
So they watch the machine, which indicates with all the insight
of modern science that the lunatic is lying.' Blake again, Allie

thought. *Then I asked: does a firm perswasion that a thing is so, make it so? He* – i.e. Isaiah – *replied. All poets believe that it does. & in ages of imagination this firm perswasion removed mountains; but many are not capable of a firm perswasion of any thing.* 'Are you listening to me, young woman? I'm serious here. That gentleman you have in your bed: he requires not your nightly attentions – excuse me but I'll speak plainly, seeing I must – but, to be frank, a padded cell.'

'You'd do that, wouldn't you,' Allie hit back. 'You'd throw away the key. Maybe you'd even plug him in. Burn the devils out of his brain: strange how our prejudices never change.'

'Hmm,' Alicja ruminated, adopting her vaguest and most inno-cent expression in order to infuriate her daughter. 'What can it harm? Yes, maybe a little voltage, a little dose of the juice . . .'

'What he needs is what he's getting, mother. Proper medical supervision, plenty of rest, and something you maybe forgot about.' She dried suddenly, her tongue knotted, and it was in quite a different, low voice, staring at her untouched salad, that she got out the last word. 'Love.'

'Ah, the power of love,' Alicja patted her daughter's (at once withdrawn) hand. 'No, it's not what I forgot, Alleluia. It's what you just begun for the first time in your beautiful life to learn. And who do you pick?' She returned to the attack. 'An out-to-lunch! A ninety-pennies-in-the-pound! A butterflies-in-the-brainbox! I mean, *angels*, darling, I never heard the like. Men are always claiming special privileges, but this one is a first.'

'Mother . . .' Allie began, but Alicja's mood had changed again, and this time, when she spoke, Allie was not listening to the words, but hearing the pain they both revealed and concealed, the pain of a woman to whom history had most brutally happened, who had already lost a husband and seen one daughter precede her to what she once, with unforgettable black humour, referred to (she must have read the sports pages, by some chance, to come across the phrase) as an *early bath*. 'Allie, my baby,' Alicja Cohen said, 'we're going to have to take good care of you.'

One reason why Allie was able to spot that panic-anguish in her mother's face was her recent sighting of the same combination on

the features of Gibreel Farishta. After Sisodia returned him to her
care, it became plain that Gibreel had been shaken to the very
marrow, and there was a haunted look to him, a scarified popeyed
quality, that quite pierced her heart. He faced the fact of his
mental illness with courage, refusing to play it down or call it by a
false name, but his recognition of it had, understandably, cowed
him. No longer (for the present, anyway) the ebullient vulgarian
for whom she had conceived her 'grand passion', he became for
her, in this newly vulnerable incarnation, more lovable than ever.
She grew determined to lead him back to sanity, to stick it out; to
wait out the storm, and conquer the peak. And he was, for the
moment, the easiest and most malleable of patients, somewhat
dopey as a result of the heavy-duty medication he was being given
by the specialists at the Maudsley Hospital, sleeping long hours,
and acquiescing, when awake, in all her requests, without a
murmur of protest. In alert moments he filled in for her the full
background to his illness: the strange serial dreams, and before that
the near-fatal breakdown in India. 'I am no longer afraid of sleep,'
he told her. 'Because what's happened in my waking time is now
so much worse.' His greatest fear reminded her of Charles II's
terror, after his Restoration, of being sent 'on his travels' again:
'I'd give anything only to know it won't happen any more,' he
told her, meek as a lamb.

Lives there who loves his pain? 'It won't happen,' she reassured
him. 'You've got the best help there is.' He quizzed her about
money, and, when she tried to deflect the questions, insisted that
she withdraw the psychiatric fees from the small fortune stashed in
his money-belt. His spirits remained low. 'Doesn't matter what
you say,' he mumbled in response to her cheery optimisms. 'The
craziness is in here and it drives me wild to think it could get out
any minute, right now, and *he* would be in charge again.' He had
begun to characterize his 'possessed', 'angel' self as another person:
in the Beckettian formula, *Not I. He.* His very own Mr Hyde.
Allie attempted to argue against such descriptions. 'It isn't *he*, it's
you, and when you're well, it won't be you any more.'

It didn't work. For a time, however, it looked as though the treatment was going to. Gibreel seemed calmer, more in control; the serial dreams were still there – he would still speak, at night, verses in Arabic, a language he did not know: *tilk al-gharaniq al-'ula wa inna shafa'ata-hunna la-turtaja,* for example, which turned out to mean (Allie, woken by his sleeptalk, wrote it down phonetically and went with her scrap of paper to the Brickhall mosque, where her recitation made a mullah's hair stand on end under his turban): 'These are exalted females whose intercession is to be desired' – but he seemed able to think of these nightshows as separate from himself, which gave both Allie and the Maudsley psychiatrists the feeling that Gibreel was slowly reconstructing the boundary wall between dreams and reality, and was on the road to recovery; whereas in fact, as it turned out, this separation was related to, was the same phenomenon as, his splitting of his sense of himself into two entities, one of which he sought heroically to suppress, but which he also, by characterizing it as other than himself, preserved, nourished, and secretly made strong.

As for Allie, she lost, for a while, the prickly, *wrong* feeling of being stranded in a false milieu, an alien narrative; caring for Gibreel, investing in his brain, as she put it to herself, fighting to salvage him so that they could resume the great, exciting struggle of their love – because they would probably quarrel all the way to the grave, she mused tolerantly, they'd be two old codgers flapping feebly at one another with rolled-up newspapers as they sat upon the evening verandas of their lives – she felt more closely joined to him each day; rooted, so to speak, in his earth. It was some time since Maurice Wilson had been seen sitting among the chimneypots, calling her to her death.

Mr 'Whisky' Sisodia, that gleaming and charm-packed knee in spectacles, became a regular caller – three or four visits a week – during Gibreel's convalescence, invariably arriving with boxes full of goodies to eat. Gibreel had been literally fasting to death during his 'angel period', and the medical opinion was that starvation had contributed in no small degree to his hallucinations. 'So now we fafatten him up,' Sisodia smacked his palms together, and once the invalid's stomach was up to it, 'Whisky' plied him with delicacies: Chinese sweet-corn and chicken soup, Bombay-style bhel-puri from the new, chic but unfortunately named 'Pagal Khana' restaurant whose 'Crazy Food' (but the name could also be translated as *Madhouse*) had grown popular enough, especially among the younger set of British Asians, to rival even the long-standing pre-eminence of the Shaandaar Café, from which Sisodia, not wishing to show unseemly partisanship, also fetched eats – sweetmeats, samosas, chicken patties – for the increasingly voracious Gibreel. He brought, too, dishes made by his own hand, fish curries, raitas, sivayyan, khir, and doled out, along with the edibles, name-dropping accounts of celebrity dinner parties: how Pavarotti had loved Whisky's lassi, and O but that poor James Mason had just adored his spicy prawns. Vanessa, Amitabh, Dustin, Sridevi, Christopher Reeve were all invoked. 'One soosoo superstar should be aware of the tatastes of his pipi peers.' Sisodia was something of a legend himself, Allie learned from Gibreel. The most slippery and silver-tongued man in the business, he had made a string of 'quality' pictures on microscopic budgets, keeping going for over twenty years on pure charm and nonstop hustle. People on Sisodia projects got paid with the greatest difficulty, but somehow failed to mind. He had once quelled a cast revolt – over pay, inevitably – by whisking the entire unit off for a grand picnic in one of the most fabulous maharajah palaces in India, a place that was normally off limits to all but the high-born elite, the Gwaliors and Jaipurs and Kashmirs. Nobody ever knew how he fixed it, but most members of that unit had since signed up to work on further Sisodia ventures, the pay issue buried beneath the grandeur of such gestures. 'And if he's needed he is always there,' Gibreel added. 'When Charulata, a wonderful dancer-actress he'd often used, needed the cancer treatment, suddenly years of unpaid fees materialized overnight.'

These days, thanks to a string of surprise box-office hits based on old fables drawn from the *Katha-Sarit-Sagar* compendium – the 'Ocean of the Streams of Story', longer than the Arabian Nights and equally as fantasticated – Sisodia was no longer based exclusively in his tiny office on Bombay's Readymoney Terrace, but had apartments in London and New York, and Oscars in his toilets. The story was that he carried, in his wallet, a photograph of the Hong Kong-based kung-phooey producer Run Run Shaw, his supposed hero, whose name he was quite unable to say. 'Sometimes four Runs, sometimes a sixer,' Gibreel told Allie, who was happy to see him laugh. 'But I can't swear. It's only a media rumour.'

Allie was grateful for Sisodia's attentiveness. The famous producer appeared to have limitless time at his disposal, whereas Allie's schedule had just then grown very full. She had signed a promotional contract with a giant chain of freezer-food centres whose advertising agent, Mr Hal Valance, told Allie during a power breakfast – grapefruit, dry toast, decaf, all at Dorchester prices – that her *profile*, 'uniting as it does the positive parameters (for our client) of "coldness" and "cool", is right on line. Some stars end up being vampires, sucking attention away from the brand name, you understand, but this feels like real synergy.' So now there were freezer-mart openings to cut ribbons at, and sales conferences, and advertising shots with tubs of softscoop ice-cream; plus the regular meetings with the designers and manufacturers of her autograph lines of equipment and leisurewear; and, of course, her fitness programme. She had signed on for Mr Joshi's highly recommended martial arts course at the local sports centre, and continued, too, to force her legs to run five miles a day around the Fields, in spite of the soles-on-broken-glass pain. 'No pop problem,' Sisodia would send her off with a cheery wave. 'I will iss iss issit here-only until you return. To be with Gigibreel is for me a pip pip privilege.' She left him regaling Farishta with his inexhaustible anecdotes, opinions and general chitchat, and when she returned he would still be going strong. She came to identify several major themes; notably, his corpus of statements about The Trouble With The English. 'The trouble with the Engenglish is that their hiss hiss history happened overseas, so they dodo don't know what it means.' – 'The see secret of a dinner party in London is to ow ow outnumber the English. If they're

outnumbered they bebehave; otherwise, you're in trouble.' – 'Go
to the Ché Ché Chamber of Horrors and you'll see what's rah rah
wrong with the English. That's what they rereally like, caw
corpses in bubloodbaths, mad barbers, etc. etc. etera. Their pay
papers full of kinky sex and death. But they tell the whir world
they're reserved, ist ist istiff upper lip and so on, and we're ist ist
istupid enough to believe.' Gibreel listened to this collection of
prejudices with what seemed like complete assent, irritating Allie
profoundly. Were these generalizations really all they saw of England? 'No,' Sisodia conceded with a shameless smile. 'But it feels
googood to let this ist ist istuff out.'

By the time the Maudsley people felt able to recommend a
major reduction in Gibreel's dosages, Sisodia had become so much
a fixture at his bedside, a sort of unofficial, eccentric and amusing
layabout cousin, that when he sprung his trap Gibreel and Allie
were taken completely by surprise.

He had been in touch with colleagues in Bombay: the seven producers whom Gibreel had left in the lurch when he boarded Air
India's Flight 420, *Bostan*, 'All are eel, elated by the news of your
survival,' he informed Gibreel. 'Unf unf unfortunately, question
of breach of contract ararises.' Various other parties were also
interested in suing the renascent Farishta for plenty, in particular a
starlet named Pimple Billimoria, who alleged loss of earnings and
professional damage. 'Could um amount to curcrores,' Sisodia
said, looking lugubrious. Allie was angry. 'You stirred up this hor-
nets' nest,' she said. 'I should have known: you were too good to
be true.'

Sisodia became agitated. 'Damn damn damn.'

'Ladies present,' Gibreel, still a little drug-woozy, warned; but
Sisodia windmilled his arms, indicating that he was trying to force
words past his overexcited teeth. Finally: 'Damage limitation. My
intention. Not betrayal, you mumust not thithithink.'

To hear Sisodia tell it, nobody back in Bombay really wanted to sue Gibreel, to kill in court the goose that laid the golden eggs. All parties recognized that the old projects were no longer capable of being restarted: actors, directors, key crew members, even sound stages were otherwise committed. All parties further recognized that Gibreel's return from the dead was an item of a commercial value greater than any of the defunct films; the question was how to utilize it best, to the advantage of all concerned. His landing up in London also suggested the possibility of an international connection, maybe overseas funding, use of non-Indian locations, participation of stars 'from foreign', etc.: in short, it was time for Gibreel to emerge from retirement and face the cameras again. 'There is no chochoice,' Sisodia explained to Gibreel, who sat up in bed trying to clear his head. 'If you refuse, they will move against you *en bloc*, and not even your four four fortune could suffice. Bankruptcy, jajajail, funtoosh.'

Sisodia had talked himself into the hot seat: all the principals had agreed to grant him executive powers in the matter, and he had put together quite a package. The British-based entrepreneur Billy Battuta was eager to invest both in sterling and in 'blocked rupees', the non-repatriable profits made by various British film distributors in the Indian subcontinent, which Battuta had taken over in return for cash payments in negotiable currencies at a knockdown (37-point discount) rate. All the Indian producers would chip in, and Miss Pimple Billimoria, to guarantee her silence, was to be offered a showcase supporting role featuring at least two dance numbers. Filming would be spread between three continents – Europe, India, the North African coast. Gibreel got above-the-title billing, and three percentage points of producers' net profits . . . 'Ten,' Gibreel interrupted, 'against two of the gross.' His mind was obviously clearing. Sisodia didn't bat an eyelid. 'Ten against two,' he agreed. 'Pre-publicity campaign to be as fofollows . . .'

'But what's the project?' Allie Cone demanded. Mr 'Whisky' Sisodia beamed from ear to ear. 'Dear mamadam,' he said. 'He will play the archangel, Gibreel.'

The proposal was for a series of films, both historical and contemporary, each concentrating on one incident from the angel's long and illustrious career: a trilogy, at least. 'Don't tell me,' Allie said, mocking the small shining mogul. *'Gibreel in Jahilia, Gibreel Meets the Imam, Gibreel with the Butterfly Girl.'* Sisodia wasn't one bit embarrassed, but nodded proudly. 'Stostorylines, draft scenarios, cacasting options are already well in haha hand.' That was too much for Allie. 'It stinks,' she raged at him, and he retreated from her, a trembling and placatory knee, while she pursued him, until she was actually chasing him around the apartment, banging into the furniture, slamming doors. 'It exploits his sickness, has nothing to do with his present needs, and shows an utter contempt for his own wishes. He's retired; can't you people respect that? He doesn't want to be a star. And will you please stand still. I'm not going to eat you.'

He stopped running, but kept a cautious sofa between them. 'Please see that this is imp imp imp,' he cried, his stammer crippling his tongue on account of his anxiety. 'Can the moomoon retire? Also, excuse, there are his seven sig sig sig. *Signatures.* Committing him absolutely. Unless and until you decide to commit him to a papapa.' He gave up, sweating freely.

'A what?'

'Pagal Khana. Asylum. That would be another wwwway.'

Allie lifted a heavy brass inkwell in the shape of Mount Everest and prepared to hurl it. 'You really are a skunk,' she began, but then Gibreel was standing in the doorway, still rather pale, bony and hollow-eyed. 'Alleluia,' he said, 'I am thinking that maybe I want this. Maybe I need to go back to work.'

'Gibreel sahib! I can't tell you how delighted. A star is reborn.' Billy Battuta was a surprise: no longer the hair-gel-and-finger-rings society column shark, he was unshowily dressed in brass-buttoned blazer and blue jeans, and instead of the cocksure swagger Allie had expected there was an attractive, almost deferential reticence. He had grown a neat goatee beard which gave him a striking resemblance to the Christ-image on the Turin Shroud. Welcoming the three of them (Sisodia had picked them up in his limo, and the driver, Nigel, a sharp dresser from St Lucia, spent the journey telling Gibreel how many other pedestrians his lightning reflexes had saved from serious injury or death, punctuating these reminiscences with car-phone conversations in which mysterious deals involving amazing sums of money were discussed), Billy had shaken Allie's hand warmly, and then fallen upon Gibreel and hugged him in pure, infectious joy. His companion Mimi Mamoulian was rather less low-key. 'It's all fixed,' she announced. 'Fruit, starlets, paparazzi, talk-shows, rumours, little hints of scandal: everything a world figure requires. Flowers, personal security, zillion-pound contracts. Make yourselves at home.'

That was the general idea, Allie thought. Her initial opposition to the whole scheme had been overcome by Gibreel's own interest, which, in turn, prompted his doctors to go along with it, estimating that his restoration to his familiar milieu – *going home*, in a way – might indeed be beneficial. And Sisodia's purloining of the dream-narratives he'd heard at Gibreel's bedside could be seen as serendipitous: for once those stories were clearly placed in the artificial, fabricated world of the cinema, it ought to become easier for Gibreel to see them as fantasies, too. That Berlin Wall between the dreaming and waking state might well be more rapidly rebuilt as a result. The bottom line was that it was worth the try.

Things (being things) didn't work out quite as planned. Allie found herself resenting the extent to which Sisodia, Battuta and Mimi moved in on Gibreel's life, taking over his wardrobe and daily schedules, and moving him out of Allie's apartment, declaring that the time for a 'permanent liaison' was not yet ripe, 'imagewise'. After the stint at the Ritz, the movie star was given three rooms in Sisodia's cavernous, designer-chic flat in an old mansion block near Grosvenor Square, all Art Deco marbled floors and scumbling on the walls. Gibreel's own passive acceptance of these changes was, for Allie, the most infuriating aspect of all, and she began to comprehend the size of the step he'd taken when he left behind what was clearly second nature to him, and came hunting for her. Now that he was sinking back into that universe of armed bodyguards and maids with breakfast trays and giggles, would he dump her as dramatically as he had entered her life? Had she helped to engineer a reverse migration that would leave her high and dry? Gibreel stared out of newspapers, magazines, television sets, with many different women on his arm, grinning foolishly. She hated it, but he refused to notice. 'What are you worrying?' he dismissed her, while sinking into a leather sofa the size of a small pick-up truck. 'It's only photo opportunities: business, that's all.'

Worst of all: *he* got jealous. As he came off the heavy drugs, and as his work (as well as hers) began to force separations upon them, he began to be possessed, once again, by that irrational, out-of-control suspiciousness which had precipitated the ridiculous quarrel over the Brunel cartoons. Whenever they met he would put her through the mill, interrogating her minutely: where had she been, who had she seen, what did he do, did she lead him on? She felt as if she were suffocating. His mental illness, the new influences in his life, and now this nightly third-degree treatment: it was as though her real life, the one she wanted, the one she was hanging in there and fighting for, was being buried deeper and deeper under this avalanche of wrongnesses. *What about what I need,* she felt like screaming, *when do I get to set the terms?* Driven to the very edge of her self-control, she asked, as a last resort, her mother's advice. In her father's old study in the Moscow Road house – which Alicja had kept just the way Otto liked it, except that now the curtains were drawn back to let in what light England could come up with, and there were flower-vases at strategic points – Alicja at first offered little more than world-weariness. 'So a woman's life-plans are being smothered by a man's,' she said, not unkindly. 'So welcome to your gender. I see it's strange for you to be out of control.' And Allie confessed: she wanted to leave him, but found she couldn't. Not just because of guilt about abandoning a seriously unwell person; also because of 'grand passion', because of the word that still dried her tongue when she tried to say it. 'You want his child,' Alicja put her finger on it. At first Allie blazed: 'I want *my* child,' but then, subsiding abruptly, blowing her nose, she nodded dumbly, and was on the verge of tears.

'You want your head examining is what,' Alicja comforted her. How long since they had been like this in one another's arms? Too long. And maybe it would be the last time . . . Alicja hugged her daughter, said: 'So dry your eyes. Comes now the good news. Your affairs might be shot to ribbons, but your old mother is in better shape.'

There was an American college professor, a certain Boniek, big in genetic engineering. 'Now don't start, dear, you don't know anything, it's not all Frankenstein and geeps, it has many beneficial applications,' Alicja said with evident nervousness, and Allie, overcoming her surprise and her own red-rimmed unhappiness, burst into convulsive, liberating sobs of laughter; in which her mother joined. 'At your age,' Allie wept, 'you ought to be ashamed.' – 'Well, I'm not,' the future Mrs Boniek rejoined. 'A professor, and in Stanford, California, so he brings the sunshine also. I intend to spend many hours working on my tan.'

When she discovered (a report found by chance in a desk drawer at the Sisodia palazzo) that Gibreel had started having her followed, Allie did, at last, make the break. She scribbled a note – *This is killing me* – slipped it inside the report, which she placed on the desktop; and left without saying goodbye. Gibreel never rang her up. He was rehearsing, in those days, for his grand public reappearance at the latest in a successful series of stage song-and-dance shows featuring Indian movie stars and staged by one of Billy Battuta's companies at Earls Court. He was to be the unannounced, surprise top-of-the-bill show-stopper, and had been rehearsing dance routines with the show's chorus line for weeks: also reacquainting himself with the art of mouthing to playback music. Rumours of the identity of the Mystery Man or Dark Star were being carefully circulated and monitored by Battuta's promo men, and the Valance advertising agency had been hired to devise a series of 'teaser' radio commercials and a local 48-sheet poster campaign. Gibreel's arrival on the Earls Court stage – he was to be lowered from the flies surrounded by clouds of cardboard and smoke – was the intended climax to the English segment of his re-entry into his superstardom; next stop, Bombay. Deserted, as he called it, by Alleluia Cone, he once more 'refused to crawl'; and immersed himself in work.

The next thing that went wrong was that Billy Battuta got himself arrested in New York for his Satanic sting. Allie, reading about it in the Sunday papers, swallowed her pride and called Gibreel at the rehearsal rooms to warn him against consorting with such patently criminal elements. 'Battuta's a hood,' she insisted. 'His whole manner was a performance, a fake. He wanted to be sure he'd be a hit with the Manhattan dowagers, so he made us his tryout audience. That goatee! And a college blazer, for God's sake: how did we fall for it?' But Gibreel was cold and withdrawn; she had ditched him, in his book, and he wasn't about to take advice from deserters. Besides, Sisodia and the Battuta promo team had assured him – and he had grilled them about it all right – that Billy's problems had no relevance to the gala night (Filmmela, that was the name) because the financial arrangements remained solid, the monies for fees and guarantees had already been allocated, all the Bombay-based stars had confirmed, and would participate as planned. 'Plans fifilling up fast,' Sisodia promised. 'Shoshow must go on.'

The next thing that went wrong was inside Gibreel.

Sisodia's determination to keep people guessing about this Dark Star meant that Gibreel had to enter the Earls Court stage-door

dressed in a burqa. So that even his sex remained a mystery. He
was given the largest dressing-room – a black five-pointed star had
been stuck on the door – and was unceremoniously locked in by
the bespectacled genuform producer. In the dressing-room he
found his angel-costume, including a contraption that, when tied
around his forehead, would cause lightbulbs to glow behind him,
creating the illusion of a halo; and a closed-circuit television, on
which he would be able to watch the show – Mithun and Kimi
cavorting for the 'disco diwané' set; Jayapradha and Rekha (no
relation: the megastar, not a figment on a rug) submitting regally
to on-stage interviews, in which Jaya divulged her views on
polygamy while Rekha fantasized about alternative lives – 'If
I'd been born out of India, I'd have been a painter in Paris'; he-
man stunts from Vinod and Dharmendra; Sridevi getting her sari
wet – until it was time for him to take up his position on a winch-
operated 'chariot' high above the stage. There was a cordless telephone, on which Sisodia called to tell him that the house was
full – 'All sorts are here,' he triumphed, and proceeded to offer
Gibreel his technique of crowd analysis: you could tell the Pak-
istanis because they dressed up to the gills, the Indians because
they dressed down, and the Bangladeshis because they dressed
badly, 'all that pupurple and pink and gogo gold *gota* that they
like' – and which otherwise remained silent; and, finally, a large
gift-wrapped box, a little present from his thoughtful producer,
which turned out to contain Miss Pimple Billimoria wearing a
winsome expression and a quantity of gold ribbon. The movies
were in town.

The strange feeling began – that is, *returned* – when he was in the
'chariot', waiting to descend. He thought of himself as moving
along a route on which, any moment now, a choice would be
offered him, a choice – the thought formulated itself in his head
without any help from him – between two realities, this world
and another that was also right there, visible but unseen. He felt

slow, heavy, distanced from his own consciousness, and realized that he had not the faintest idea which path he would choose, which world he would enter. The doctors had been wrong, he now perceived, to treat him for schizophrenia; the splitting was not in him, but in the universe. As the chariot began its descent towards the immense, tidal roar that had begun to swell below him, he rehearsed his opening line – *My name is Gibreel Farishta, and I'm back* – and heard it, so to speak, in stereo, because it, too, belonged in both worlds, with a different meaning in each; – and now the lights hit him, he raised his arms high, he was returning wreathed in clouds, – and the crowd had recognized him, and his fellow-performers, too; people were rising from their seats, every man, woman and child in the auditorium, surging towards the stage, unstoppable, like a sea. – The first man to reach him had time to scream out *Remember me, Gibreel? With the six toes? Maslama, sir: John Maslama. I kept secret your presence among us; but yes, I have been speaking out about the coming of the Lord, I have gone before you, a voice crying in the wilderness, the crooked shall be made straight and the rough places plain* – but then he had been dragged away, and the security guards were around Gibreel, *they're out of control, it's a fucking riot, you'll have to* – but he wouldn't go, because he'd seen that at least half the crowd were wearing bizarre headgear, rubber horns to make them look like demons, as if they were badges of belonging and defiance; – and in that instant when he saw the adversary's sign he felt the universe fork and he stepped down the left-hand path.

The official version of what followed, and the one accepted by all the news media, was that Gibreel Farishta had been lifted out of the danger area in the same winch-operated chariot in which he'd descended, and from which he hadn't had time to emerge; – and that it would therefore have been easy for him to make his escape, from his isolated and unwatched place high above the mêlée. This version proved resilient enough to survive the 'revelation' in the *Voice* that the assistant stage manager in charge of the winch had not, repeat not, set it in motion after it landed; – that, in fact, the chariot remained grounded throughout the riot of the ecstatic film fans; – and that substantial sums of money had been paid to the backstage staff to persuade them to collude in the fabrication of a story which, because totally fictional, was realistic enough for the newspaper-buying public to believe. However, the rumour that Gibreel Farishta had actually levitated away from the Earls Court stage and vanished into the blue under his own steam spread rapidly through the city's Asian population, and was fed by many accounts of the halo that had been seen streaming out from a point just behind his head. Within days of the second disappearance of Gibreel Farishta, vendors of novelties in Brickhall, Wembley and Brixton were selling as many toy haloes (green fluorescent hoops were the most popular) as headbands to which had been affixed a pair of rubber horns.

He was hovering high over London! – Haha, they couldn't touch him now, the devils rushing upon him in that Pandemonium! – He looked down upon the city and saw the English. The trouble with the English was that they were English: damn cold fish! – Living underwater most of the year, in days the colour of night! – Well: he was here now, the great Transformer, and this time there'd be some changes made – the laws of nature are the laws of its transformation, and he was the very person to utilize the same! – Yes, indeed: this time, clarity.

He would show them – yes! – his *power*. – These powerless English! – Did they not think their history would return to haunt them? – 'The native is an oppressed person whose permanent dream is to become the persecutor' (Fanon). English women no longer bound him; the conspiracy stood exposed! – Then away with all fogs. He would make this land anew. He was the Archangel, Gibreel. – *And I'm back!*

The face of the adversary hung before him once again, sharpening, clarifying. Moony with a sardonic curl to the lips: but the name still eluded . . . *tcha*, like tea? *Shah*, a king? Or like a (royal? tea?) dance: *Shatchacha*. – Nearly there. – And the nature of the adversary: self-hating, constructing a false ego, auto-destructive.

Fanon again: 'In this way the individual' – the Fanonian *native* – 'accepts the disintegration ordained by God, bows down before the settler and his lot, and by a kind of interior restabilization acquires a stony calm.' – *I'll give him stony calm!* – Native and settler, that old dispute, continuing now upon these soggy streets, with reversed categories. – It occurred to him now that he was forever joined to the adversary, their arms locked around one another's bodies, mouth to mouth, head to tail, as when they fell to earth: when they *settled*. – As things begin so they continue. – Yes, he was coming closer. – Chichi? Sasa? – *My other, my love . . .*

. . . No! – He floated over parkland and cried out, frightening the birds. – No more of these England-induced ambiguities, these Biblical–Satanic confusions! – Clarity, clarity, at all costs clarity! – This Shaitan was no fallen angel. – Forget those son-of-the-morning fictions; this was no good boy gone bad, but pure evil. Truth was, he wasn't an angel at all! – 'He was of the djinn, so he transgressed.' – Quran 18:50, there it was as plain as the day. – How much more straightforward this version was! How much more practical, down-to-earth, comprehensible! – Iblis/Shaitan standing for the darkness, Gibreel for the light. – Out, out with these sentimentalities: *joining, locking together, love*. Seek and destroy: that was all.

. . . O most slippery, most devilish of cities! – In which such stark, imperative oppositions were drowned beneath an endless drizzle of greys. – How right he'd been, for instance, to banish those Satanico-Biblical doubts of his, – those concerning God's unwillingness to permit dissent among his lieutenants, – for as Iblis/Shaitan was no angel, so there had been no angelic dissidents for the Divinity to repress; – and those concerning forbidden fruit, and God's supposed denial of moral choice to his creations; – for nowhere in the entire Recitation was that Tree called (as the Bible had it) the root of the knowledge of good and evil. *It was simply a different Tree!* Shaitan, tempting the Edenic couple, called it only 'the Tree of Immortality' – and as he was a liar, so the truth (discovered by inversion) was that the banned fruit (apples were not specified) hung upon the Death-Tree, no less, the slayer of men's souls. – What remained now of that morality-fearing God? Where was He to be found? – Only down below, in English hearts. – Which he, Gibreel, had come to transform.

Abracadabra!

Hocus Pocus!

But where should he begin? – Well, then, the trouble with the English was their:

Their:

In a word, Gibreel solemnly pronounced, *their weather.*

Gibreel Farishta floating on his cloud formed the opinion that the moral fuzziness of the English was meteorologically induced. 'When the day is not warmer than the night,' he reasoned, 'when the light is not brighter than the dark, when the land is not drier than the sea, then clearly a people will lose the power to make distinctions, and commence to see everything – from political parties to sexual partners to religious beliefs – as much-the-same, nothing-to-choose, give-or-take. What folly! For truth is extreme, it is *so* and not *thus,* it is *him* and not *her;* a partisan matter, not a spectator sport. It is, in brief, *heated.* City,' he cried, and his voice rolled over the metropolis like thunder, 'I am going to tropicalize you.'

Gibreel enumerated the benefits of the proposed metamorphosis of London into a tropical city: increased moral definition, institution of a national siesta, development of vivid and expansive patterns of behaviour among the populace, higher-quality popular music, new birds in the trees (macaws, peacocks, cockatoos), new trees under the birds (coco-palms, tamarind, banyans with hanging beards). Improved street-life, outrageously coloured flowers (magenta, vermilion, neon-green), spider-monkeys in the oaks. A new mass market for domestic air-conditioning units, ceiling fans, anti-mosquito coils and sprays. A coir and copra industry. Increased appeal of London as a centre for conferences, etc.; better cricketers; higher emphasis on ball-control among professional footballers, the traditional and soulless English commitment to 'high workrate' having been rendered obsolete by the heat. Religious fervour, political ferment, renewal of interest in the intelligentsia. No more British reserve; hot-water bottles to be banished forever, replaced in the foetid nights by the making of slow and odorous love. Emergence of new social values: friends to commence dropping in on one another without making appointments, closure of old folks' homes, emphasis on the extended family. Spicier food; the use of water as well as paper in English toilets; the joy of running fully dressed through the first rains of the monsoon.

Disadvantages: cholera, typhoid, legionnaires' disease, cockroaches, dust, noise, a culture of excess.

Standing upon the horizon, spreading his arms to fill the sky, Gibreel cried: 'Let it be.'

Three things happened, fast.

The first was that, as the unimaginably colossal, elemental forces of the transformational process rushed out of his body (for was he not their *embodiment*?), he was temporarily overcome by a warm, spinning heaviness, a soporific churning (not at all unpleasant) that made him close, just for an instant, his eyes.

The second was that the moment his eyes were shut the horned and goaty features of Mr Saladin Chamcha appeared, on the screen of his mind, as sharp and well-defined as could be; accompanied, as if it were sub-titled there, by the adversary's name.

And the third thing was that Gibreel Farishta opened his eyes to find himself collapsed, once again, on Alleluia Cone's doorstep, begging her forgiveness, weeping *O God, it happened, it really happened again.*

She put him to bed; he found himself escaping into sleep, diving headlong into it, away from Proper London and towards Jahilia, because the real terror had crossed the broken boundary wall, and stalked his waking hours.

'A homing instinct: one crazy heading for another,' Alicja said when her daughter phoned with the news. 'You must be putting out a signal, some sort of bleeping thing.' As usual, she hid her concern beneath wisecracks. Finally she came out with it: 'This time be sensible, Alleluia, okay? This time the asylum.'

'We'll see, mother. He's asleep right now.'

'So he isn't going to wake up?' Alicja expostulated, then controlled herself. 'All right, I know, it's your life. Listen, isn't this weather something? They say it could last months: "blocked pattern", I heard on television, rain over Moscow, while here it's a tropical heatwave. I called Boniek at Stanford and told him: now we have weather in London, too.'

PART VI

RETURN TO JAHILIA

When Baal the poet saw a single teardrop the colour of blood emerging from the corner of the left eye of the statue of Al-Lat in the House of the Black Stone, he understood that the Prophet Mahound was on his way back to Jahilia after an exile of a quarter-century. He belched violently – an affliction of age, this, its coarseness seeming to correspond to the general thickening induced by the years, a thickening of the tongue as well as the body, a slow congealment of the blood, that had turned Baal at fifty into a figure quite unlike his quick young self. Sometimes he felt that the air itself had thickened, resisting him, so that even a shortish walk could leave him panting, with an ache in his arm and an irregularity in his chest . . . and Mahound must have changed, too, returning as he was in splendour and omnipotence to the place whence he fled empty-handed, without so much as a wife. Mahound at sixty-five. Our names meet, separate, and meet again, Baal thought, but the people going by the names do not remain the same. He left Al-Lat to emerge into bright sunlight, and heard from behind his back a little snickering laugh. He turned, weightily; nobody to be seen. The hem of a robe vanishing around a corner. These days, down-at-heel Baal often made strangers giggle in the street. 'Bastard!' he shouted at the top of his voice, scandalizing the other worshippers in the House. Baal, the decrepit poet, behaving badly again. He shrugged and headed for home.

The city of Jahilia was no longer built of sand. That is to say, the passage of the years, the sorcery of the desert winds, the petrifying moon, the forgetfulness of the people and the inevitability of progress had hardened the town, so that it had lost its old, shifting, provisional quality of a mirage in which men could live, and become a prosaic place, quotidian and (like its poets) poor. Mahound's arm had grown long; his power had encircled Jahilia, cutting off its life-blood, its pilgrims and caravans. The fairs of Jahilia, these days, were pitiful to behold.

Even the Grandee himself had acquired a threadbare look, his white hair as full of gaps as his teeth. His concubines were dying of old age, and he lacked the energy – or, so the rumours murmured in the desultory alleys of the city, the need – to replace them. Some days he forgot to shave, which added to his look of dilapidation and defeat. Only Hind was the same as ever.

She had always had something of a reputation as a witch, who could wish illnesses upon you if you failed to bow down before her litter as it passed, an occultist with the power of transforming men into desert snakes when she had had her fill of them, and then catching them by the tail and having them cooked in their skins for her evening meal. Now that she had reached sixty the legend of her necromancy was being given new substantiation by her extraordinary and unnatural failure to age. While all around her hardened into stagnation, while the old gangs of Sharks grew middle-aged and squatted on street corners playing cards and rolling dice, while the old knot-witches and contortionists starved to death in the gullies, while a generation grew up whose conservatism and unquestioning worship of the material world was born of their knowledge of the probability of unemployment and penury, while the great city lost its sense of itself and even the cult of the dead declined in popularity to the relief of the camels of Jahilia, whose dislike of being left with severed hamstrings on human graves was easy to comprehend . . . while Jahilia decayed, in short, Hind remained unwrinkled, her body as firm as any young woman's, her hair as black as crow feathers, her eyes sparkling like knives, her bearing still haughty, her voice still brooking no opposition. Hind, not Simbel, ruled the city now; or so she undeniably believed.

As the Grandee grew into a soft and pursy old age, Hind took to writing a series of admonitory and hortatory epistles or *bulls* to the people of the city. These were pasted up on every street in town. So it was that Hind and not Abu Simbel came to be thought of by Jahilians as the embodiment of the city, its living avatar, because they found in her physical unchangingness and in the unflinching resolve of her proclamations a description of themselves far more palatable than the picture they saw in the mirror of Simbel's crumbling face. Hind's posters were more influential than any poet's verses. She was still sexually voracious, and had slept with every writer in the city (though it was a long time since Baal had been allowed into her bed); now the writers were used up, discarded, and she was rampant. With sword as well as pen. She was Hind, who had joined the Jahilian army disguised as a man, using sorcery to deflect all spears and swords, seeking out her brothers' killer through the storm of war. Hind, who butchered the Prophet's uncle, and ate old Hamza's liver and his heart.

Who could resist her? For her eternal youth which was also theirs; for her ferocity which gave them the illusion of being invincible; and for her bulls, which were refusals of time, of history, of age, which sang the city's undimmed magnificence and defied the garbage and decrepitude of the streets, which insisted on greatness, on leadership, on immortality, on the status of Jahilians as custodians of the divine . . . for these writings the people forgave her her promiscuity, they turned a blind eye to the stories of Hind being weighed in emeralds on her birthday, they ignored rumours of orgies, they laughed when told of the size of her wardrobe, of the five hundred and eighty-one nightgowns made of gold leaf and the four hundred and twenty pairs of ruby slippers. The citizens of Jahilia dragged themselves through their increasingly dangerous streets, in which murder for small change was becoming commonplace, in which old women were being raped and ritually slaughtered, in which the riots of the starving were brutally put down by Hind's personal police force, the Manticorps; and in spite of the evidence of their eyes, stomachs and wallets, they believed what Hind whispered in their ears: Rule, Jahilia, glory of the world.

Not all of them, of course. Not, for example, Baal. Who looked away from public affairs and wrote poems of unrequited love.

Munching a white radish, he arrived home, passing beneath a dingy archway in a cracking wall. Here there was a small urinous courtyard littered with feathers, vegetable peelings, blood. There was no sign of human life: only flies, shadows, fear. These days it was necessary to be on one's guard. A sect of murderous hashashin roamed the city. Affluent persons were advised to approach their homes on the opposite side of the street, to make sure that the house was not being watched; when the coast was clear they would rush for the door and shut it behind them before any lurking criminal could push his way in. Baal did not bother with such precautions. Once he had been affluent, but that was a quarter of a century ago. Now there was no demand for satires – the general fear of Mahound had destroyed the market for insults and wit. And with the decline of the cult of the dead had come a sharp drop in orders for epitaphs and triumphal odes of revenge. Times were hard all around.

Dreaming of long-lost banquets, Baal climbed an unsteady wooden staircase to his small upstairs room. What did he have to steal? He wasn't worth the knife. Opening his door, he began to enter, when a push sent him tumbling to bloody his nose against the far wall. 'Don't kill me,' he squealed blindly. 'O God, don't murder me, for pity's sake, O.'

The other hand closed the door. Baal knew that no matter how loudly he screamed they would remain alone, sealed off from the world in that uncaring room. Nobody would come; he himself, hearing his neighbour shriek, would have pushed his cot against the door.

The intruder's hooded cloak concealed his face completely.

Baal mopped his bleeding nose, kneeling, shaking uncontrollably. 'I've got no money,' he implored. 'I've got nothing.' Now the stranger spoke: 'If a hungry dog looks for food, he does not look in the doghouse.' And then, after a pause: 'Baal. There's not much left of you. I had hoped for more.'

Now Baal felt oddly affronted as well as terrified. Was this some kind of demented fan, who would kill him because he no longer lived up to the power of his old work? Still trembling, he attempted self-deprecation. 'To meet a writer is, usually, to be disappointed,' he offered. The other ignored this remark. 'Mahound is coming,' he said.

This flat statement filled Baal with the most profound terror. 'What's that got to do with me?' he cried. 'What does he want? It was a long time ago – a lifetime – more than a lifetime. What does he want? Are you from, are you sent by him?'

'His memory is as long as his face,' the intruder said, pushing back his hood. 'No, I am not his messenger. You and I have something in common. We are both afraid of him.'

'I know you,' Baal said.

'Yes.'

'The way you speak. You're a foreigner.'

' "A revolution of water-carriers, immigrants and slaves," ' the stranger quoted. 'Your words.'

'You're the immigrant,' Baal remarked. 'The Persian. Sulaiman.' The Persian smiled his crooked smile. 'Salman,' he corrected. 'Not wise, but peaceful.'

'You were one of the closest to him,' Baal said, perplexed.

'The closer you are to a conjurer,' Salman bitterly replied, 'the easier to spot the trick.'

And Gibreel dreamed this:

At the oasis of Yathrib the followers of the new faith of Submission found themselves landless, and therefore poor. For many years they financed themselves by acts of brigandage, attacking the rich camel-trains on their way to and from Jahilia. Mahound had no time for scruples, Salman told Baal, no qualms about ends and

means. The faithful lived by lawlessness, but in those years
Mahound – or should one say the Archangel Gibreel? – should
one say Al-Lah? – became obsessed by law. Amid the palm-trees
of the oasis Gibreel appeared to the Prophet and found himself
spouting rules, rules, rules, until the faithful could scarcely bear the
prospect of any more revelation, Salman said, rules about every
damn thing, if a man farts let him turn his face to the wind, a rule
about which hand to use for the purpose of cleaning one's behind.
It was as if no aspect of human existence was to be left unregu-
lated, free. The revelation – the *recitation* – told the faithful how
much to eat, how deeply they should sleep, and which sexual
positions had received divine sanction, so that they learned that
sodomy and the missionary position were approved of by the
archangel, whereas the forbidden postures included all those in
which the female was on top. Gibreel further listed the permitted
and forbidden subjects of conversation, and earmarked the parts of
the body which could not be scratched no matter how unbearably
they might itch. He vetoed the consumption of prawns, those
bizarre other-worldly creatures which no member of the faithful
had ever seen, and required animals to be killed slowly, by
bleeding, so that by experiencing their deaths to the full they
might arrive at an understanding of the meaning of their lives, for
it is only at the moment of death that living creatures understand
that life has been real, and not a sort of dream. And Gibreel the
archangel specified the manner in which a man should be buried,
and how his property should be divided, so that Salman the Persian got to wondering what manner of God this was that sounded
so much like a businessman. This was when he had the idea that
destroyed his faith, because he recalled that of course Mahound
himself had been a businessman, and a damned successful one at
that, a person to whom organization and rules came naturally, so
how excessively convenient it was that he should have come
up with such a very businesslike archangel, who handed down
the management decisions of this highly corporate, if non-
corporeal, God.

After that Salman began to notice how useful and well timed

the angel's revelations tended to be, so that when the faithful were disputing Mahound's views on any subject, from the possibility of space travel to the permanence of Hell, the angel would turn up with an answer, and he always supported Mahound, stating beyond any shadow of a doubt that it was impossible that a man should ever walk upon the moon, and being equally positive on the transient nature of damnation: even the most evil of doers would eventually be cleansed by hellfire and find their way into the perfumed gardens, Gulistan and Bostan. It would have been different, Salman complained to Baal, if Mahound took up his positions after receiving the revelation from Gibreel; but no, he just laid down the law and the angel would confirm it afterwards; so I began to get a bad smell in my nose, and I thought, this must be the odour of those fabled and legendary unclean creatures, what's their name, prawns.

The fishy smell began to obsess Salman, who was the most highly educated of Mahound's intimates owing to the superior educational system then on offer in Persia. On account of his scholastic advancement Salman was made Mahound's official scribe, so that it fell to him to write down the endlessly proliferating rules. All those revelations of convenience, he told Baal, and the longer I did the job the worse it got. – For a time, however, his suspicions had to be shelved, because the armies of Jahilia marched on Yathrib, determined to swat the flies who were pestering their camel-trains and interfering with business. What followed is well known, no need for me to repeat, Salman said, but then his immodesty burst out of him and forced him to tell Baal how he personally had saved Yathrib from certain destruction, how he had preserved Mahound's neck with his idea of a ditch. Salman had persuaded the Prophet to have a huge trench dug all the way around the unwalled oasis settlement, making it too wide even for the fabled Arab horses of the famous Jahilian cavalry to leap across. A ditch: with sharpened stakes at the bottom. When the Jahilians saw this foul piece of unsportsmanlike hole-digging their sense of chivalry and honour obliged them to behave as if the ditch had not been dug, and to ride their horses at it, full-tilt. The flower of Jahilia's army, human as well as equine, ended up impaled on the pointed sticks of Salman's Persian deviousness, trust an immigrant not to play the game. – And after the defeat of Jahilia? Salman lamented to Baal: You'd have thought I'd have been a hero, I'm not a vain man but where were the public honours, where was the gratitude of Mahound, why didn't the archangel mention *me* in despatches? Nothing, not a syllable, it was as if the faithful thought of my ditch as a cheap trick, too, an outlandish thing, dishonouring, unfair; as if their manhood had been damaged by the thing, as though I'd hurt their pride by saving their skins. I kept my mouth shut and said nothing, but I lost a lot of friends after that, I can tell you, people hate you to do them a good turn.

In spite of the ditch of Yathrib, the faithful lost a good many men in the war against Jahilia. On their raiding sorties they lost as many lives as they claimed. And after the end of the war, hey presto, there was the Archangel Gibreel instructing the surviving males to marry the widowed women, lest by remarrying outside the faith they be lost to Submission. Oh, such a practical angel, Salman sneered to Baal. By now he had produced a bottle of toddy from the folds of his cloak and the two men were drinking steadily in the failing light. Salman grew ever more garrulous as the yellow liquid in the bottle went down; Baal couldn't recall when he'd last heard anyone talk up such a storm. O, those matter-of-fact revelations, Salman cried, we were even told it didn't matter if we were already married, we could have up to four marriages if we could afford it, well, you can imagine, the lads really went for that.

What finally finished Salman with Mahound: the question of the women; and of the Satanic verses. Listen, I'm no gossip, Salman drunkenly confided, but after his wife's death Mahound was no angel, you understand my meaning. But in Yathrib he almost met his match. Those women up there: they turned his beard half-white in a year. The point about our Prophet, my dear Baal, is that he didn't like his women to answer back, he went for mothers and daughters, think of his first wife and then Ayesha: too old and too young, his two loves. He didn't like to pick on someone his own size. But in Yathrib the women are different, you don't know, here in Jahilia you're used to ordering your females about but up there they won't put up with it. When a man gets married he goes to live with his wife's people! Imagine! Shocking, isn't it? And throughout the marriage the wife keeps her own tent. If she wants to get rid of her husband she turns the tent round to face in the opposite direction, so that when he comes to her he finds fabric where the door should be, and that's that, he's out, divorced, not a thing he can do about it. Well, our girls were beginning to go for that type of thing, getting who knows what sort of ideas in their heads, so at once, bang, out comes the rule book, the angel starts pouring out rules about what women mustn't do, he starts forcing them back into the docile attitudes the Prophet prefers, docile or maternal, walking three steps behind or sitting at home being wise and waxing their chins. How the women of Yathrib laughed at the faithful, I swear, but that man is a magician, nobody could resist his charm; the faithful women did as he ordered them. They Submitted: he was offering them Paradise, after all.

'Anyway,' Salman said near the bottom of the bottle, 'finally I decided to test him.'

One night the Persian scribe had a dream in which he was hovering above the figure of Mahound at the Prophet's cave on Mount Cone. At first Salman took this to be no more than a nostalgic reverie of the old days in Jahilia, but then it struck him that his point of view, in the dream, had been that of the archangel, and at that moment the memory of the incident of the Satanic verses came back to him as vividly as if the thing had happened the previous day. 'Maybe I hadn't dreamed of myself as Gibreel,' Salman recounted. 'Maybe I was Shaitan.' The realization of this possibility gave him his diabolic idea. After that, when he sat at the Prophet's feet, writing down rules rules rules, he began, surreptitiously, to change things.

'Little things at first. If Mahound recited a verse in which God was described as *all-hearing, all-knowing,* I would write, *all-knowing, all-wise.* Here's the point: Mahound did not notice the alterations. So there I was, actually writing the Book, or rewriting, anyway, polluting the word of God with my own profane language. But, good heavens, if my poor words could not be distinguished from the Revelation by God's own Messenger, then what did that mean? What did that say about the quality of the divine poetry? Look, I swear, I was shaken to my soul. It's one thing to be a smart bastard and have half-suspicions about funny business, but it's quite another thing to find out that you're right. Listen: I changed my life for that man. I left my country, crossed the world, settled among people who thought me a slimy foreign coward for saving their, who never appreciated what I, but never mind that. The truth is that what I expected when I made that first tiny change, *all-wise* instead of *all-hearing* – what I *wanted* – was to read it back to the Prophet, and he'd say, What's the matter with you, Salman, are you going deaf? And I'd say, Oops, O God, bit of a slip, how could I, and correct myself. But it didn't happen; and now I was writing the Revelation and nobody was noticing, and I didn't have the courage to own up. I was scared silly, I can tell you. Also: I was sadder than I have ever been. So I had to go on doing it. Maybe he'd just missed out once, I thought, anybody can make a mistake. So the next time I changed a bigger thing. He said *Christian*, I wrote down *Jew*. He'd notice that, surely; how could he not? But when I read him the chapter he nodded and thanked me politely, and I went out of his tent with tears in my eyes. After that I knew my days in Yathrib were numbered; but I had to go on doing it. I had to. There is no bitterness like that of a man who finds out he has been believing in a ghost. I would fall, I knew, but he would fall with me. So I went on with my devilment, changing verses, until one day I read my lines to him and saw him frown and shake his head as if to clear his mind, and then nod his approval slowly, but with a little doubt. I knew I'd reached the edge, and that the next time I rewrote the Book he'd know everything. That night I lay awake, holding his fate in my hands as well as my own. If I allowed myself to be destroyed I

could destroy him, too. I had to choose, on that awful night,
whether I preferred death with revenge to life without anything.
As you see, I chose: life. Before dawn I left Yathrib on my camel,
and made my way, suffering numerous misadventures I shall not
trouble to relate, back to Jahilia. And now Mahound is coming in
triumph; so I shall lose my life after all. And his power has grown
too great for me to unmake him now.'

Baal asked: 'Why are you sure he will kill you?'

Salman the Persian answered: 'It's his Word against mine.'

When Salman had slipped into unconsciousness on the floor, Baal
lay on his scratchy straw-filled mattress, feeling the steel ring of
pain around his forehead, the flutter of warning in his heart.
Often his tiredness with his life had made him wish not to grow
old, but, as Salman had said, to dream of a thing is very different
from being faced with the fact of it. For some time now he had
been conscious that the world was closing in around him. He
could no longer pretend that his eyes were what they ought to be,
and their dimness made his life even more shadowy, harder to
grasp. All this blurring and loss of detail: no wonder his poetry had
gone down the drain. His ears were getting to be unreliable, too.
At this rate he'd soon end up sealed off from everything by the
loss of his senses . . . but maybe he'd never get the chance.
Mahound was coming. Maybe he would never kiss another
woman. Mahound, Mahound. Why has this chatterbox drunk
come to me, he thought angrily. What do I have to do with his
treachery? Everyone knows why I wrote those satires years ago;
he must know. How the Grandee threatened and bullied. I can't
be held responsible. And anyway: who is he, that prancing
sneering boy-wonder, Baal of the cutting tongue? I don't recognize him. Look at me: heavy, dull, nearsighted, soon to be deaf.
Who do I threaten? Not a soul. He began to shake Salman: wake
up, I don't want to be associated with you, you'll get me into
trouble.

The Persian snored on, sitting splay-legged on the floor with
his back to the wall, his head hanging sideways like a doll's; Baal,
racked by headache, fell back on to his cot. His verses, he thought,
what had they been? *What kind of idea* damn it, he couldn't even
remember them properly *does Submission seem today* yes, something
like that, after all this time it was scarcely surprising *an idea that
runs away* that was the end anyhow. Mahound, any new idea is
asked two questions. When it's weak: will it compromise? We
know the answer to that one. And now, Mahound, on your
return to Jahilia, time for the second question: How do you
behave when you win? When your enemies are at your mercy
and your power has become absolute: what then? We have all
changed: all of us except Hind. Who seems, from what this
drunkard says, more like a woman of Yathrib than Jahilia. No
wonder the two of you didn't hit it off: she wouldn't be your
mother or your child.

As he drifted towards sleep, Baal surveyed his own uselessness,
his failed art. Now that he had abdicated all public platforms, his
verses were full of loss: of youth, beauty, love, health, innocence,
purpose, energy, certainty, hope. Loss of knowledge. Loss of
money. The loss of Hind. Figures walked away from him in his
odes, and the more passionately he called out to them the faster
they moved. The landscape of his poetry was still the desert, the
shifting dunes with the plumes of white sand blowing from their
peaks. Soft mountains, uncompleted journeys, the impermanence
of tents. How did one map a country that blew into a new form
every day? Such questions made his language too abstract, his
imagery too fluid, his metre too inconstant. It led him to create
chimeras of form, lionheaded goatbodied serpenttailed imposs-
ibilities whose shapes felt obliged to change the moment they
were set, so that the demotic forced its way into lines of classical
purity and images of love were constantly degraded by the intrusion of elements of farce. Nobody goes for that stuff, he thought
for the thousand and first time, and as unconsciousness arrived he
concluded, comfortingly: Nobody remembers me. Oblivion is

safety. Then his heart missed a beat and he came wide awake, frightened, cold. *Mahound, maybe I'll cheat you of your revenge.* He spent the night awake, listening to Salman's rolling, oceanic snores.

Gibreel dreamed campfires:

A famous and unexpected figure walks, one night, between the campfires of Mahound's army. Perhaps on account of the dark, – or it might be because of the improbability of his presence here, – it seems that the Grandee of Jahilia has regained, in this final moment of his power, some of the strength of his earlier days. He has come alone; and is led by Khalid the erstwhile water-carrier and the former slave Bilal to the quarters of Mahound.

Next, Gibreel dreamed the Grandee's return home:

The town is full of rumours and there's a crowd in front of the house. After a time the sound of Hind's voice lifted in rage can be clearly heard. Then at an upper balcony Hind shows herself and demands that the crowd tear her husband into small pieces. The Grandee appears beside her; and receives loud, humiliating smacks on both cheeks from his loving wife. Hind has discovered that in spite of all her efforts she has not been able to prevent the Grandee from surrendering the city to Mahound.

Moreover: Abu Simbel has embraced the faith.

Simbel in his defeat has lost much of his recent wispiness. He permits Hind to strike him, and then speaks calmly to the crowd. He says: Mahound has promised that anyone within the Grandee's walls will be spared. 'So come in, all of you, and bring your families, too.'

Hind speaks for the angry crowd. 'You old fool. How many citizens can fit inside a single house, even this one? You've done a deal to save your own neck. Let them rip you up and feed you to the ants.'

Still the Grandee is mild. 'Mahound also promises that all who are found at home, behind closed doors, will be safe. If you will not come into my home then go to your own; and wait.'

A third time his wife attempts to turn the crowd against him; this is a balcony scene of hatred instead of love. There can be no compromise with Mahound, she shouts, he is not to be trusted, the people must repudiate Abu Simbel and prepare to fight to the last man, the last woman. She herself is prepared to fight beside them and die for the freedom of Jahilia. 'Will you merely lie down before this false prophet, this Dajjal? Can honour be expected of a man who is preparing to storm the city of his birth? Can compromise be hoped for from the uncompromising, pity from the pitiless? We are the mighty of Jahilia, and our goddesses, glorious in battle, will prevail.' She commands them to fight in the name of Al-Lat. But the people begin to leave.

Husband and wife stand on their balcony, and the people see them plain. For so long the city has used these two as its mirrors; and because, of late, Jahilians have preferred Hind's images to the greying Grandee, they are suffering, now, from profound shock. A people that has remained convinced of its greatness and invulnerability, that has chosen to believe such a myth in the face of all the evidence, is a people in the grip of a kind of sleep, or madness. Now the Grandee has awakened them from that sleep; they stand disoriented, rubbing their eyes, unable to believe at first − if we are so mighty, how then have we fallen so fast, so utterly? − and then belief comes, and shows them how their confidence has been built on clouds, on the passion of Hind's proclamations and on very little else. They abandon her, and with her, hope. Plunging into despair, the people of Jahilia go home to lock their doors.

She screams at them, pleads, loosens her hair. 'Come to the House of the Black Stone! Come and make sacrifice to Lat!' But they have gone. And Hind and the Grandee are alone on their balcony, while throughout Jahilia a great silence falls, a great stillness begins, and Hind leans against the wall of her palace and closes her eyes.

It is the end. The Grandee murmurs softly: 'Not many of us have as much reason to be scared of Mahound as you. If you eat a man's favourite uncle's innards, raw, without so much as salt or garlic, don't be surprised if he treats you, in turn, like meat.' Then he leaves her, and goes down into the streets from which even the dogs have vanished, to unlock the city gates.

Gibreel dreamed a temple:

By the open gates of Jahilia stood the temple of Uzza. And Mahound spake unto Khalid who had been a carrier of water before, and now bore greater weights: 'Go thou and cleanse the place.' So Khalid with a force of men descended upon the temple, for Mahound was loth to enter the city while such abominations stood at its gates.

When the guardian of the temple, who was of the tribe of Shark, saw the approach of Khalid with a great host of warriors, he took up his sword and went to the idol of the goddess. After making his final prayers he hung his sword about her neck, saying, 'If thou be truly a goddess, Uzza, defend thyself and thy servant against the coming of Mahound.' Then Khalid entered the temple, and when the goddess did not move the guardian said, 'Now verily do I know that the God of Mahound is the true God, and this stone but a stone.' Then Khalid broke the temple and the idol and returned to Mahound in his tent. And the Prophet asked: 'What didst thou see?' Khalid spread his arms. 'Nothing,' said he. 'Then thou hast not destroyed her,' the Prophet cried. 'Go again, and complete thy work.' So Khalid returned to the fallen temple, and there an enormous woman, all black but for her long scarlet tongue, came running at him, naked from head to foot, her black hair flowing to her ankles from her head. Nearing him, she halted, and recited in her terrible voice of sulphur and hellfire: 'Have you heard of Lat, and Manat, and Uzza, the Third, the Other? They are the Exalted Birds . . .' But Khalid interrupted her, saying, 'Uzza, those are the Devil's verses, and you the Devil's daughter, a creature not to be worshipped, but denied.' So he drew his sword and cut her down.

And he returned to Mahound in his tent and said what he had

seen. And the Prophet said, 'Now may we come into Jahilia,' and they arose, and came into the city, and possessed it in the Name of the Most High, the Destroyer of Men.

How many idols in the House of the Black Stone? Don't forget: three hundred and sixty. Sun-god, eagle, rainbow. The colossus of Hubal. Three hundred and sixty wait for Mahound, knowing they are not to be spared. And are not: but let's not waste time there. Statues fall; stone breaks; what's to be done is done.

Mahound, after the cleansing of the House, sets up his tent on the old fairground. The people crowd around the tent, embracing the victorious faith. The Submission of Jahilia: this, too, is inevitable, and need not be lingered over.

While Jahilians bow before him, mumbling their life-saving sentences, *there is no God but Al-Lah,* Mahound whispers to Khalid. Somebody has not come to kneel before him; somebody long awaited. 'Salman,' the Prophet wishes to know. 'Has he been found?'

'Not yet. He's hiding; but it won't be long.'

There is a distraction. A veiled woman kneels before him, kissing his feet. 'You must stop,' he enjoins. 'It is only God who must be worshipped.' But what foot-kissery this is! Toe by toe, joint by joint, the woman licks, kisses, sucks. And Mahound, unnerved, repeats: 'Stop. This is incorrect.' Now, however, the woman is attending to the soles of his feet, cupping her hands beneath his heel . . . he kicks out, in his confusion, and catches her in the throat. She falls, coughs, then prostrates herself before him, and says firmly: 'There is no God but Al-Lah, and Mahound is his Prophet.' Mahound calms himself, apologizes, extends a hand. 'No harm will come to you,' he assures her. 'All who Submit are spared.' But there is a strange confusion in him, and now he understands why, understands the anger, the bitter irony in her overwhelming, excessive, sensual adoration of his feet. The woman throws off her veil: Hind.

'The wife of Abu Simbel,' she announces clearly, and a hush falls. 'Hind,' Mahound says. 'I had not forgotten.'

But, after a long instant, he nods. 'You have Submitted. And are welcome in my tents.'

The next day, amid the continuing conversions, Salman the Persian is dragged into the Prophet's presence. Khalid, holding him by the ear, holding a knife at his throat, brings the immigrant snivelling and whimpering to the takht. 'I found him, where else, with a whore, who was screeching at him because he didn't have the money to pay her. He stinks of alcohol.'

'Salman Farsi,' the Prophet begins to pronounce the sentence of death, but the prisoner begins to shriek the qalmah: 'La ilaha ilallah! La ilaha!'

Mahound shakes his head. 'Your blasphemy, Salman, can't be forgiven. Did you think I wouldn't work it out? To set your words against the Words of God.'

Scribe, ditch-digger, condemned man: unable to muster the smallest scrap of dignity, he blubbers whimpers pleads beats his breast abases himself repents. Khalid says: 'This noise is unbearable, Messenger. Can I not cut off his head?' At which the noise increases sharply. Salman swears renewed loyalty, begs some more, and then, with a gleam of desperate hope, makes an offer. 'I can show you where your true enemies are.' This earns him a few seconds. The Prophet inclines his head. Khalid pulls the kneeling Salman's head back by the hair: 'What enemies?' And Salman says a name. Mahound sinks deep into his cushions as memory returns.

'Baal,' he says, and repeats, twice: 'Baal, Baal.'

Much to Khalid's disappointment, Salman the Persian is not sentenced to death. Bilal intercedes for him, and the Prophet, his mind elsewhere, concedes: yes, yes, let the wretched fellow live. O generosity of Submission! Hind has been spared; and Salman; and in all of Jahilia not a door has been smashed down, not an old foe dragged out to have his gizzard slit like a chicken's in the dust. This is Mahound's answer to the second question: *What happens when you win?* But one name haunts Mahound, leaps around him, young, sharp, pointing a long painted finger, singing verses whose cruel brilliance ensures their painfulness. That night, when the

supplicants have gone, Khalid asks Mahound: 'You're still thinking about him?' The Messenger nods, but will not speak. Khalid
says: 'I made Salman take me to his room, a hovel, but he isn't
there, he's hiding out.' Again, the nod, but no speech. Khalid
presses on: 'You want me to dig him out? Wouldn't take much
doing. What d'you want done with him? This? This?' Khalid's
finger moves first across his neck and then, with a sharp jab, into
his navel. Mahound loses his temper. 'You're a fool,' he shouts at
the former water-carrier who is now his military chief of staff.
'Can't you ever work things out without my help?'

Khalid bows and goes. Mahound falls asleep: his old gift, his
way of dealing with bad moods.

But Khalid, Mahound's general, could not find Baal. In spite of
door-to-door searches, proclamations, turnings of stones, the poet
proved impossible to nab. And Mahound's lips remained closed,
would not part to allow his wishes to emerge. Finally, and not
without irritation, Khalid gave up the search. 'Just let that bastard
show his face, just once, any time,' he vowed in the Prophet's tent
of softnesses and shadows. 'I'll slice him so thin you'll be able to
see right through each piece.'

It seemed to Khalid that Mahound looked disappointed; but in
the low light of the tent it was impossible to be sure.

Jahilia settled down to its new life: the call to prayers five times a
day, no alcohol, the locking up of wives. Hind herself retired to
her quarters . . . but where was Baal?

Gibreel dreamed a curtain:

The Curtain, *Hijab*, was the name of the most popular brothel
in Jahilia, an enormous palazzo of date-palms in water-tinkling
courtyards, surrounded by chambers that interlocked in bewildering mosaic patterns, permeated by labyrinthine corridors which
had been deliberately decorated to look alike, each of them
bearing the same calligraphic invocations to Love, each carpeted

with identical rugs, each with a large stone urn positioned against
a wall. None of The Curtain's clients could ever find their way,
without help, either into the rooms of their favoured courtesan or
back again to the street. In this way the girls were protected from
unwanted guests and the business ensured payment before departure. Large Circassian eunuchs, dressed after the ludicrous fashion
of lamp-genies, escorted the visitors to their goals and back again,
sometimes with the help of balls of string. It was a soft windowless
universe of draperies, ruled over by the ancient and nameless
Madam of the Curtain whose guttural utterances from the secrecy
of a chair shrouded in black veils had acquired, over the years,
something of the oracular. Neither her staff nor her clients were
able to disobey that sibylline voice that was, in a way, the profane
antithesis of Mahound's sacred utterances in a larger, more easily
penetrable tent not so very far away. So that when the raddled
poet Baal prostrated himself before her and begged for help, her
decision to hide him and save his life as an act of nostalgia for the
beautiful, lively and wicked youth he had once been was accepted
without question; and when Khalid's guards arrived to search the
premises the eunuchs led them on a dizzy journey around that
overground catacomb of contradictions and irreconcilable routes,
until the soldiers' heads were spinning, and after looking inside
thirty-nine stone urns and finding nothing but unguents and
pickles they left, cursing heavily, never suspecting that there was a
fortieth corridor down which they had never been taken, a fortieth urn inside which there hid, like a thief, the quivering,
pajama-wetting poet whom they sought.

After that the Madam had the eunuchs dye the poet's skin until
it was blue-black, and his hair as well, and dressing him in the
pantaloons and turban of a djinn she ordered him to begin a body-
building course, since his lack of condition would certainly arouse
suspicions if he didn't tone up fast.

Baal's sojourn 'behind The Curtain' by no means deprived him
of information about events outside; quite the reverse, in fact,

because in the course of his eunuchly duties he stood guard outside the pleasure-chambers and heard the customers' gossip. The
absolute indiscretion of their tongues, induced by the gay abandon
of the whores' caresses and by the clients' knowledge that their
secrets would be kept, gave the eavesdropping poet, myopic and
hard of hearing as he was, a better insight into contemporary
affairs than he could possibly have gained if he'd still been free to
wander the newly puritanical streets of the town. The deafness
was a problem sometimes; it meant that there were gaps in his
knowledge, because the customers frequently lowered their voices
and whispered; but it also minimized the prurient element in his
listenings-in, since he was unable to hear the murmurings that
accompanied fornication, except, of course, at such moments
in which ecstatic clients or feigning workers raised their voices in
cries of real or synthetic joy.

What Baal learned at The Curtain:

From the disgruntled butcher Ibrahim came the news that in
spite of the new ban on pork the skin-deep converts of Jahilia
were flocking to his back door to buy the forbidden meat in
secret, 'sales are up,' he murmured while mounting his chosen
lady, 'black pork prices are high; but damn it, these new rules
have made my work tough. A pig is not an easy animal to
slaughter in secret, without noise,' and thereupon he began some
squealing of his own, for reasons, it is to be presumed, of pleasure
rather than pain. – And the grocer, Musa, confessed to another of
The Curtain's horizontal staff that the old habits were hard to
break, and when he was sure nobody was listening he still said a
prayer or two to 'my lifelong favourite, Manat, and sometimes,
what to do, Al-Lat as well; you can't beat a female goddess,
they've got attributes the boys can't match,' after which he,
too, fell upon the earthly imitations of these attributes with a will.
So it was that faded, fading Baal learned in his bitterness that no
imperium is absolute, no victory complete. And, slowly, the criticisms of Mahound began.

Baal had begun to change. The news of the destruction of the great temple of Al-Lat at Taif, which came to his ears punctuated by the grunts of the covert pig-sticker Ibrahim, had plunged him into a deep sadness, because even in the high days of his young cynicism his love of the goddess had been genuine, perhaps his only genuine emotion, and her fall revealed to him the hollowness of a life in which the only true love had been felt for a lump of stone that couldn't fight back. When the first, sharp edge of grief had been dulled, Baal became convinced that Al-Lat's fall meant that his own end was not far away. He lost that strange sense of safety that life at The Curtain had briefly inspired in him; but the returning knowledge of his impermanence, of certain discovery followed by equally certain death, did not, interestingly enough, make him afraid. After a lifetime of dedicated cowardice he found to his great surprise that the effect of the approach of death really did enable him to taste the sweetness of life, and he wondered at the paradox of having his eyes opened to such a truth in that house of costly lies. And what was the truth? It was that Al-Lat was dead – had never lived – but that didn't make Mahound a prophet. In sum, Baal had arrived at godlessness. He began, stumblingly, to move beyond the idea of gods and leaders and rules, and to perceive that his story was so mixed up with Mahound's that some great resolution was necessary. That this resolution would in all probability mean his death neither shocked nor bothered him overmuch; and when Musa the grocer grumbled one day about the twelve wives of the Prophet, *one rule for him, another for us,* Baal understood the form his final confrontation with Submission would have to take.

The girls of The Curtain – it was only by convention that they were referred to as 'girls', as the eldest was a woman well into her fifties, while the youngest, at fifteen, was more experienced than many fifty-year-olds – had grown fond of this shambling Baal, and in point of fact they enjoyed having a eunuch-who-wasn't, so that out of working hours they would tease him deliciously, flaunting their bodies before him, placing their breasts against his lips, twining their legs around his waist, kissing one another passionately just an inch away from his face, until the ashy writer was hopelessly aroused; whereupon they would laugh at his stiffness and mock him into blushing, quivering detumescence; or, very occasionally, and when he had given up all expectation of such a thing, they would depute one of their number to satisfy, free of charge, the lust they had awakened. In this way, like a myopic, blinking, tame bull, the poet passed his days, laying his head in women's laps, brooding on death and revenge, unable to say whether he was the most contented or the wretchedest man alive.

It was during one of these playful sessions at the end of a working day, when the girls were alone with their eunuchs and their wine, that Baal heard the youngest talking about her client, the grocer, Musa. 'That one!' she said. 'He's got a bee in his bonnet about the Prophet's wives. He's so annoyed about them that he gets excited just by mentioning their names. He tells me that I personally am the spitting image of Ayesha herself, and she's His Nibs's favourite, as all are aware. So there.'

The fifty-year-old courtesan butted in. 'Listen, those women in that harem, the men don't talk about anything else these days. No wonder Mahound secluded them, but it's only made things worse. People fantasize more about what they can't see.'

Especially in this town, Baal thought; above all in our Jahilia of the licentious ways, where until Mahound arrived with his rule book the women dressed brightly, and all the talk was of fucking and money, money and sex, and not just the talk, either.

He said to the youngest whore: 'Why don't you pretend for him?'

'Who?'

'Musa. If Ayesha gives him such a thrill, why not become his private and personal Ayesha?'

'God,' the girl said. 'If they heard you say that they'd boil your balls in butter.'

How many wives? Twelve, and one old lady, long dead. How many whores behind The Curtain? Twelve again; and, secret on

her black-tented throne, the ancient Madam, still defying death.
Where there is no belief, there is no blasphemy. Baal told the
Madam of his idea; she settled matters in her voice of a laryngitic
frog. 'It is very dangerous,' she pronounced, 'but it could be damn
good for business. We will go carefully; but we will go.'

The fifteen-year-old whispered something in the grocer's ear. At
once a light began to shine in his eyes. 'Tell me everything,' he
begged. 'Your childhood, your favourite toys, Solomon's-horses
and the rest, tell me how you played the tambourine and the
Prophet came to watch.' She told him, and then he asked about
her deflowering at the age of twelve, and she told him that, and
afterwards he paid double the normal fee, because 'it's been the
best time of my life'. 'We'll have to be careful of heart conditions,'
the Madam said to Baal.

When the news got around Jahilia that the whores of The Curtain
had each assumed the identity of one of Mahound's wives, the
clandestine excitement of the city's males was intense; yet, so
afraid were they of discovery, both because they would surely lose
their lives if Mahound or his lieutenants ever found out that they
had been involved in such irreverences, and because of their desire
that the new service at The Curtain be maintained, that the secret
was kept from the authorities. In those days Mahound had
returned with his wives to Yathrib, preferring the cool oasis climate of the north to Jahilia's heat. The city had been left in the
care of General Khalid, from whom things were easily concealed.
For a time Mahound had considered telling Khalid to have all the
brothels of Jahilia closed down, but Abu Simbel had advised him
against so precipitate an act. 'Jahilians are new converts,' he
pointed out. 'Take things slowly.' Mahound, most pragmatic of
Prophets, had agreed to a period of transition. So, in the Prophet's
absence, the men of Jahilia flocked to The Curtain, which experienced a three hundred per cent increase in business. For obvious

reasons it was not politic to form a queue in the street, and so on many days a line of men curled around the innermost courtyard of the brothel, rotating about its centrally positioned Fountain of Love much as pilgrims rotated for other reasons around the ancient Black Stone. All customers of The Curtain were issued with masks, and Baal, watching the circling masked figures from a high balcony, was satisfied. There were more ways than one of refusing to Submit.

In the months that followed, the staff of The Curtain warmed to the new task. The fifteen-year-old whore 'Ayesha' was the most popular with the paying public, just as her namesake was with Mahound, and like the Ayesha who was living chastely in her apartment in the harem quarters of the great mosque at Yathrib, this Jahilian Ayesha began to be jealous of her preeminent status of Best Beloved. She resented it when any of her 'sisters' seemed to be experiencing an increase in visitors, or receiving exceptionally generous tips. The oldest, fattest whore, who had taken the name of 'Sawdah', would tell her visitors – and she had plenty, many of the men of Jahilia seeking her out for her maternal and also grateful charms – the story of how Mahound had married her and Ayesha, on the same day, when Ayesha was just a child. 'In the two of us,' she would say, exciting men terribly, 'he found the two halves of his dead first wife: the child, and the mother, too.' The whore 'Hafsah' grew as hot-tempered as her namesake, and as the twelve entered into the spirit of their roles the alliances in the brothel came to mirror the political cliques at the Yathrib mosque; 'Ayesha' and 'Hafsah', for example, engaged in constant, petty rivalries against the two haughtiest whores, who had always been thought a bit stuck-up by the others and who had chosen for themselves the most aristocratic identities, becoming 'Umm Salamah the Makhzumite' and, snootiest of all, 'Ramlah', whose namesake, the eleventh wife of Mahound, was the daughter of Abu Simbel and Hind. And there was a 'Zainab bint Jahsh', and a 'Juwairiyah', named after the bride captured on a military expedition, and a 'Rehana the Jew', a 'Safia' and a 'Maimunah', and, most erotic of all the whores, who knew tricks she refused to teach to competitive 'Ayesha': the glamourous Egyptian, 'Mary the Copt'. Strangest of all was the whore who had taken the name of 'Zainab bint Khuzaimah', knowing that this wife of Mahound had recently died. The necrophilia of her lovers, who forbade her to make any movements, was one of the more unsavoury aspects of the new regime at The Curtain. But business was business, and this, too, was a need that the courtesans fulfilled.

By the end of the first year the twelve had grown so skilful in their roles that their previous selves began to fade away. Baal, more myopic and deafer by the month, saw the shapes of the girls moving past him, their edges blurred, their images somehow doubled, like shadows superimposed on shadows. The girls began to entertain new notions about Baal, too. In that age it was customary for a whore, on entering her profession, to take the kind of husband who wouldn't give her any trouble – a mountain, maybe, or a fountain, or a bush – so that she could adopt, for form's sake, the title of a married woman. At The Curtain, the rule was that all the girls married the Love Spout in the central courtyard, but now a kind of rebellion was brewing, and the day came when the prostitutes went together to the Madam to announce that now that they had begun to think of themselves as the wives of the Prophet they required a better grade of husband than some spurting stone, which was almost idolatrous, after all; and to say that they had decided that they would all become the brides of the bumbler, Baal. At first the Madam tried to talk them out of it, but when she saw that the girls meant business she conceded the point, and told them to send the writer in to see her. With many giggles and nudges the twelve courtesans escorted the shambling poet into the throne room. When Baal heard the plan his heart began to thump so erratically that he lost his balance and fell, and 'Ayesha' screamed in her fright: 'O God, we're going to be his widows before we even get to be his wives.'

But he recovered: his heart regained its composure. And, having no option, he agreed to the twelvefold proposal. The Madam then married them all off herself, and in that den of degeneracy, that anti-mosque, that labyrinth of profanity, Baal became the husband of the wives of the former businessman, Mahound.

His wives now made plain to him that they expected him to fulfil his husbandly duties in every particular, and worked out a rota system under which he could spend a day with each of the girls in turn (at The Curtain, day and night were inverted, the night being for business and the day for rest). No sooner had he embarked upon this arduous programme than they called a meeting at which he was told that he ought to start behaving a little more like the 'real' husband, that is, Mahound. 'Why can't you change your name like the rest of us?' bad-tempered 'Hafsah' demanded, but at this Baal drew the line. 'It may not be much to be proud of,' he insisted, 'but it's my name. What's more, I don't work with the clients here. There's no business reason for such a change.' 'Well, anyhow,' the voluptuous 'Mary the Copt' shrugged, 'name or no name, we want you to start acting like him.'

'I don't know much about,' Baal began to protest, but 'Ayesha', who really was the most attractive of them all, or so he had commenced to feel of late, made a delightful moue. 'Honestly, husband,' she cajoled him. 'It's not so tough. We just want you to, you know. Be the boss.'

It turned out that the whores of The Curtain were the most old-fashioned and conventional women in Jahilia. Their work, which could so easily have made them cynical and disillusioned (and they were, of course, capable of entertaining ferocious notions about their visitors), had turned them into dreamers instead. Sequestered from the outside world, they had conceived a fantasy of 'ordinary life' in which they wanted nothing more than to be the obedient, and – yes – submissive helpmeets of a man who was wise, loving and strong. That is to say: the years of enacting the fantasies of men had finally corrupted their dreams, so that even in their hearts of hearts they wished to turn themselves into the oldest male fantasy of all. The added spice of acting out the home life of the Prophet had got them all into a state of high excitement, and the bemused Baal discovered what it was to have twelve women competing for his favours, for the beneficence of his smile, as they washed his feet and dried them with their hair, as they oiled his body and danced for him, and in a thousand ways enacted the dream-marriage they had never really thought they would have.

It was irresistible. He began to find the confidence to order them about, to adjudicate between them, to punish them when he was angry. Once when their quarreling irritated him he forswore them all for a month. When he went to see 'Ayesha' after twenty-nine nights she teased him for not having been able to stay away. 'That month was only twenty-nine days long,' he replied. Once he was caught with 'Mary the Copt' by 'Hafsah', in 'Hafsah's' quarters and on 'Ayesha's' day. He begged 'Hafsah' not to tell 'Ayesha', with whom he had fallen in love; but she told her anyway and Baal had to stay away from 'Mary' of the fair skin and curly hair for quite a time after that. In short, he had fallen prey to the seductions of becoming the secret, profane mirror of Mahound; and he had begun, once again, to write.

The poetry that came was the sweetest he had ever written. Sometimes when he was with Ayesha he felt a slowness come over him, a heaviness, and he had to lie down. 'It's strange,' he told her. 'It is as if I see myself standing beside myself. And I can make him, the standing one, speak; then I get up and write down his verses.' These artistic slownesses of Baal were much admired by his wives. Once, tired, he dozed off in an armchair in the chambers of 'Umm Salamah the Makhzumite'. When he woke, hours later, his body ached, his neck and shoulders were full of knots, and he berated Umm Salamah: 'Why didn't you wake me?' She answered: 'I was afraid to, in case the verses were coming to you.' He shook his head. 'Don't worry about that. The only woman in whose company the verses come is "Ayesha", not you.'

Two years and a day after Baal began his life at The Curtain, one of Ayesha's clients recognized him in spite of the dyed skin,

pantaloons and body-building exercises. Baal was stationed outside
Ayesha's room when the client emerged, pointed right at him and
shouted: 'So this is where you got to!' Ayesha came running, her
eyes blazing with fear. But Baal said, 'It's all right. He won't make
any trouble.' He invited Salman the Persian to his own quarters
and uncorked a bottle of the sweet wine made with uncrushed
grapes which the Jahilians had begun to make when they found
out that it wasn't forbidden by what they had started disrespect-
fully calling the Rule Book.

'I came because I'm finally leaving this infernal city,' Salman
said, 'and I wanted one moment of pleasure out of it after all the
years of shit.' After Bilal had interceded for him in the name of
their old friendship the immigrant had found work as a letter-
writer and all-purpose scribe, sitting cross-legged by the roadside
in the main street of the financial district. His cynicism and despair
had been burnished by the sun. 'People write to tell lies,' he said,
drinking quickly. 'So a professional liar makes an excellent living.
My love letters and business correspondence became famous as the
best in town because of my gift for inventing beautiful falsehoods
that involved only the tiniest departure from the facts. As a result I
have managed to save enough for my trip home in just two years.
Home! The old country! I'm off tomorrow, and not a minute too
soon.'

As the bottle emptied Salman began once again to talk, as Baal
had known he would, about the source of all his ills, the Messenger and his message. He told Baal about a quarrel between
Mahound and Ayesha, recounting the rumour as if it were incon-
trovertible fact. 'That girl couldn't stomach it that her husband
wanted so many other women,' he said. 'He talked about neces-
sity, political alliances and so on, but she wasn't fooled. Who can
blame her? Finally he went into – what else – one of his trances,
and out he came with a message from the archangel. Gibreel had
recited verses giving him full divine support. God's own permission to fuck as many women as he liked. So there: what could
poor Ayesha say against the verses of God? You know what she

did say? This: "Your God certainly jumps to it when you need him to fix things up for you." Well! If it hadn't been Ayesha, who knows what he'd have done, but none of the others would have dared in the first place.' Baal let him run on without interruption. The sexual aspects of Submission exercised the Persian a good deal: 'Unhealthy,' he pronounced. 'All this segregation. No good will come of it.'

At length Baal did start arguing, and Salman was astonished to hear the poet taking Mahound's side: 'You can see his point of view,' Baal reasoned. 'If families offer him brides and he refuses he creates enemies, – and besides, he's a special man and one can see the argument for special dispensations, – and as for locking them up, well, what a dishonour it would be if anything bad happened to one of them! Listen, if you lived in here, you wouldn't think a little less sexual freedom was such a bad thing, – for the common people, I mean.'

'Your brain's gone,' Salman said flatly. 'You've been out of the sun too long. Or maybe that costume makes you talk like a clown.'

Baal was pretty tipsy by this time, and began some hot retort, but Salman raised an unsteady hand. 'Don't want to fight,' he said. 'Lemme tell you instead. Hottest story in town. Whoo-whoo! And it's relevant to whatch, whatchyou say.'

Salman's story: Ayesha and the Prophet had gone on an expedition to a far-flung village, and on the way back to Yathrib their party had camped in the dunes for the night. Camp was struck in the dark before the dawn. At the last moment Ayesha was obliged by a call of nature to rush out of sight into a hollow. While she was away her litter-bearers picked up her palanquin and marched off. She was a light woman, and, failing to notice much difference in the weight of that heavy palanquin, they assumed she was inside. Ayesha returned after relieving herself to find herself alone, and who knows what might have befallen her if a young man, a certain Safwan, had not chanced to pass by on his camel . . . Safwan brought Ayesha back to Yathrib safe and sound; at which

point tongues began to wag, not least in the harem, where opportunities to weaken Ayesha's power were eagerly seized by her
opponents. The two young people had been alone in the desert
for many hours, and it was hinted, more and more loudly, that
Safwan was a dashingly handsome fellow, and the Prophet was
much older than the young woman, after all, and might she not
therefore have been attracted to someone closer to her own age?
'Quite a scandal,' Salman commented, happily.

'What will Mahound do?' Baal wanted to know.

'O, he's done it,' Salman replied. 'Same as ever. He saw his pet,
the archangel, and then informed one and all that Gibreel had
exonerated Ayesha.' Salman spread his arms in worldly resigna-
tion. 'And this time, mister, the lady didn't complain about the
convenience of the verses.'

Salman the Persian left the next morning with a northbound
camel-train. When he left Baal at The Curtain, he embraced the
poet, kissed him on both cheeks and said: 'Maybe you're right.
Maybe it's better to keep out of the daylight. I hope it lasts.' Baal
replied: 'And I hope you find home, and that there is something
there to love.' Salman's face went blank. He opened his mouth,
shut it again, and left.

'Ayesha' came to Baal's room for reassurance. 'He won't spill
out the secret when he's drunk?' she asked, caressing Baal's hair.
'He gets through a lot of wine.'

Baal said: 'Nothing is ever going to be the same again.' Salman's
visit had wakened him from the dream into which he had slowly
subsided during his years at The Curtain, and he couldn't go back
to sleep.

'Of course it will,' Ayesha urged. 'It will. You'll see.'

Baal shook his head and made the only prophetic remark of his
life. 'Something big is going to happen,' he foretold. 'A man can't
hide behind skirts forever.'

The next day Mahound returned to Jahilia and soldiers came to inform the Madam of The Curtain that the period of transition was at an end. The brothels were to be closed, with immediate effect. Enough was enough. From behind her drapes, the Madam requested that the soldiers withdraw for an hour in the name of propriety to enable the guests to leave, and such was the inexperience of the officer in charge of the vice-squad that he agreed. The Madam sent her eunuchs to inform the girls and escort the clients out by a back door. 'Please apologize to them for the interruption,' she ordered the eunuchs, 'and say that in the circumstances, no charge will be made.'

They were her last words. When the alarmed girls, all talking at once, crowded into the throne room to see if the worst were really true, she made no answer to their terrified questions, are we out of work, how do we eat, will we go to jail, what's to become of us, – until 'Ayesha' screwed up her courage and did what none of them had ever dared attempt. When she threw back the black hangings they saw a dead woman who might have been fifty or a hundred and twenty-five years old, no more than three feet tall, looking like a big doll, curled up in a cushion-laden wickerwork chair, clutching the empty poison-bottle in her fist.

'Now that you've started,' Baal said, coming into the room, 'you may as well take all the curtains down. No point trying to keep the sun out any more.'

The young vice-squad officer, Umar, allowed himself to display a rather petulant bad temper when he found out about the suicide of the brothel-keeper. 'Well, if we can't hang the boss, we'll just have to make do with the workers,' he shouted, and ordered his men to place the 'tarts' under close arrest, a task the men performed with zeal. The women made a noise and kicked out at their captors, but the eunuchs stood and watched without twitching a muscle, because Umar had said to them: 'They want the cunts to be put on trial, but I've no instructions about you. So if you don't want to lose your heads as well as your balls, keep out of this.' Eunuchs failed to defend the women of The Curtain while soldiers wrestled them to the ground; and among the eunuchs was Baal, of the dyed skin and poetry. Just before the youngest 'cunt' or 'slit' was gagged, she yelled: 'Husband, for God's sake, help us, if you are a man.' The vice-squad captain was amused. 'Which of you is her husband?' he asked, staring carefully into each turban-topped face. 'Come on, own up. What's it like to watch the world with your wife?'

Baal fixed his gaze on infinity to avoid 'Ayesha's' glares as well as Umar's narrowed eyes. The officer stopped in front of him. 'Is it you?'

'Sir, you understand, it's just a term,' Baal lied. 'They like to joke, the girls. They call us their husbands because we, we . . .'

Without warning, Umar grabbed him by the genitals and squeezed. 'Because you can't be,' he said. 'Husbands, eh. Not bad.'

When the pain subsided, Baal saw that the women had gone. Umar gave the eunuchs a word of advice on his way out. 'Get lost,' he suggested. 'Tomorrow I may have orders about you. Not many people get lucky two days running.'

When the girls of The Curtain had been taken away, the eunuchs sat down and wept uncontrollably by the Fountain of Love. But Baal, full of shame, did not cry.

Gibreel dreamed the death of Baal:

The twelve whores realized, soon after their arrest, that they had grown so accustomed to their new names that they couldn't remember the old ones. They were too frightened to give their jailers their assumed titles, and as a result were unable to give any names at all. After a good deal of shouting and a good many threats the jailers gave in and registered them by numbers, as Curtain No. 1, Curtain No. 2 and so on. Their former clients, terrified of the consequences of letting slip the secret of what the whores had been up to, also remained silent, so that it is possible that nobody would have found out if the poet Baal had not started pasting his verses to the walls of the city jail.

Two days after the arrests, the jail was bursting with prostitutes and pimps, whose numbers had increased considerably during the two years in which Submission had introduced sexual segregation to Jahilia. It transpired that many Jahilian men were prepared to countenance the jeers of the town riff-raff, to say nothing of possible prosecution under the new immorality laws, in order to stand below the windows of the jail and serenade those painted ladies whom they had grown to love. The women inside were entirely unimpressed by these devotions, and gave no encouragement whatsoever to the suitors at their barred gates. On the third day, however, there appeared among these lovelorn fools a peculiarly woebegone fellow in turban and pantaloons, with dark skin that was beginning to look decidedly blotchy. Many passers-by sniggered at the look of him, but when he began to sing his verses the sniggering stopped at once. Jahilians had always been connoisseurs of the art of poetry, and the beauty of the odes being sung by the peculiar gent stopped them in their tracks. Baal sang his love poems, and the ache in them silenced the other versifiers, who allowed Baal to speak for them all. At the windows of the jail, it was possible to see for the first time the faces of the sequestered whores, who had been drawn there by the magic of the lines. When he finished his recital he went forward to nail his poetry to the wall. The guards at the gates, their eyes running with tears, made no move to stop him.

Every evening after that, the strange fellow would reappear and recite a new poem, and each set of verses sounded lovelier than the last. It was perhaps this surfeit of loveliness which prevented anybody from noticing, until the twelfth evening, when he completed his twelfth and final set of verses, each of which were dedicated to a different woman, that the names of his twelve 'wives' were the same as those of another group of twelve.

But on the twelfth day it was noticed, and at once the large crowd that had taken to gathering to hear Baal read changed its mood. Feelings of outrage replaced those of exaltation, and Baal was surrounded by angry men demanding to know the reasons for this oblique, this most byzantine of insults. At this point Baal took off his absurd turban. 'I am Baal,' he announced. 'I recognize no jurisdiction except that of my Muse; or, to be exact, my dozen Muses.'

Guards seized him.

The General, Khalid, had wanted to have Baal executed at once, but Mahound asked that the poet be brought to trial immediately following the whores. So when Baal's twelve wives, who had divorced stone to marry him, had been sentenced to death by stoning to punish them for the immorality of their lives, Baal stood face to face with the Prophet, mirror facing image, dark facing light. Khalid, sitting at Mahound's right hand, offered Baal a last chance to explain his vile deeds. The poet told the story of his stay at The Curtain, using the simplest language, concealing nothing, not even his final cowardice, for which everything he had done since had been an attempt at reparation. But now an unusual thing happened. The crowd packed into that tent of judgment, knowing that this was after all the famous satirist Baal, in his day the owner of the sharpest tongue and keenest wit in Jahilia, began (no matter how hard it tried not to) to laugh. The more honestly and simply Baal described his marriages to the twelve 'wives of the Prophet', the more uncontrollable became the horrified mirth of the audience. By the end of his speech the good folk of Jahilia were literally weeping with laughter, unable to restrain themselves even when soldiers with bullwhips and scimitars threatened them with instant death.

'I'm not kidding!' Baal screeched at the crowd, which hooted yelled slapped its thighs in response. 'It's no joke!' Ha ha ha. Until, at last, silence returned; the Prophet had risen to his feet.

'In the old days you mocked the Recitation,' Mahound said in the hush. 'Then, too, these people enjoyed your mockery. Now you return to dishonour my house, and it seems that once again you succeed in bringing the worst out of the people.'

Baal said, 'I've finished. Do what you want.'

So he was sentenced to be beheaded, within the hour, and as soldiers manhandled him out of the tent towards the killing ground, he shouted over his shoulder: 'Whores and writers, Mahound. We are the people you can't forgive.'

Mahound replied, 'Writers and whores. I see no difference here.'

Once upon a time there was a woman who did not change.

After the treachery of Abu Simbel handed Jahilia to Mahound on a plate and replaced the idea of the city's greatness with the reality of Mahound's, Hind sucked toes, recited the La-ilaha, and then retreated to a high tower of her palace, where news reached her of the destruction of the Al-Lat temple at Taif, and of all the statues of the goddess that were known to exist. She locked herself into her tower room with a collection of ancient books written in scripts which no other human being in Jahilia could decipher; and for two years and two months she remained there, studying her occult texts in secret, asking that a plate of simple food be left outside her door once a day and that her chamberpot be emptied at the same time. For two years and two months she saw no other living being. Then she entered her husband's bedroom at dawn, dressed in all her finery, with jewels glittering at her wrists, ankles, toes, ears and throat. 'Wake up,' she commanded, flinging back his curtains. 'It's a day for celebrations.' He saw that she hadn't aged by so much as a day since he last saw her; if anything, she looked younger than ever, which gave credence to the rumours which suggested that her witchcraft had persuaded time to run backwards for her within the confines of her tower room. 'What have we got to celebrate?' the former Grandee of Jahilia asked, coughing up his usual morning blood. Hind replied: 'I may not be able to reverse the flow of history, but revenge, at least, is sweet.'

Within an hour the news arrived that the Prophet, Mahound, had fallen into a fatal sickness, that he lay in Ayesha's bed with his head thumping as if it had been filled up with demons. Hind continued to make calm preparations for a banquet, sending servants to every corner of the city to invite guests. But of course nobody would come to a party on that day. In the evening Hind sat alone in the great hall of her home, amid the golden plates and crystal glasses of her revenge, eating a simple plate of couscous while surrounded by glistening, steaming, aromatic dishes of every imaginable type. Abu Simbel had refused to join her, calling her eating an obscenity. 'You ate his uncle's heart,' Simbel cried, 'and now you would eat his.' She laughed in his face. When the servants began to weep she dismissed them, too, and sat in solitary rejoicing while candles sent strange shadows across her absolute, uncompromising face.

Gibreel dreamed the death of Mahound:

For when the head of the Messenger began to ache as never before, he knew the time had come when he would be offered the Choice:

Since no Prophet may die before he has been shown Paradise, and afterward asked to choose between this world and the next:

So that as he lay with his head in his beloved Ayesha's lap, he closed his eyes, and life seemed to depart from him; but after a time he returned:

And he said unto Ayesha, 'I have been offered and made my Choice, and I have chosen the kingdom of God.'

Then she wept, knowing that he was speaking of his death; whereupon his eyes moved past her, and seemed to fix upon another figure in the room, even though when she, Ayesha, turned to look she saw only a lamp there, burning upon its stand:

'Who's there?' he called out. 'Is it Thou, Azraeel?'

But Ayesha heard a terrible, sweet voice, that was a woman's, make reply: 'No, Messenger of Al-Lah, it is not Azraeel.'

And the lamp blew out; and in the darkness Mahound asked: 'Is this sickness then thy doing, O Al-Lat?'

And she said: 'It is my revenge upon you, and I am satisfied. Let them cut a camel's hamstrings and set it on your grave.'

Then she went, and the lamp that had been snuffed out burst once more into a great and gentle light, and the Messenger murmured, 'Still, I thank Thee, Al-Lat, for this gift.'

Not long afterwards he died. Ayesha went out into the next

room, where the other wives and disciples were waiting with heavy hearts, and they began mightily to lament:

But Ayesha wiped her eyes, and said: 'If there be any here who worshipped the Messenger, let them grieve, for Mahound is dead; but if there be any here who worship God, then let them rejoice, for He is surely alive.'

It was the end of the dream.

PART VII

THE
ANGEL AZRAEEL

1

It all boiled down to love, reflected Saladin Chamcha in his den: love, the refractory bird of Meilhac and Halévy's libretto for *Carmen* – one of the prize specimens, this, in the Allegorical Aviary he'd assembled in lighter days, and which included among its winged metaphors the Sweet (of youth), the Yellow (more lucky than me), Khayyám–FitzGerald's adjectiveless Bird of Time (which has but a little way to fly, and lo! is on the Wing), and the Obscene; this last from a letter written by Henry James, Sr, to his sons . . . 'Every man who has reached even his intellectual teens begins to suspect that life is no farce; that it is not genteel comedy even; that it flowers and fructifies on the contrary out of the profoundest tragic depths of the essential dearth in which its subject's roots are plunged. The natural inheritance of everyone who is capable of spiritual life is an unsubdued forest where the wolf howls and the obscene bird of night chatters.' Take *that*, kids. – And in a separate but proximate glass display-case of the younger, happier Chamcha's fancy there fluttered a captive from a piece of hit-parade bubblegum music, the Bright Elusive Butterfly, which shared *l'amour* with the *oiseau rebelle*.

Love, a zone in which nobody desirous of compiling a human (as opposed to robotic, Skinnerian-android) body of experience could afford to shut down operations, did you down, no question about it, and very probably did you in as well. It even warned you in advance. 'Love is an infant of Bohemia,' sings Carmen, herself the very Idea of the Beloved, its perfect pattern, eternal and divine, 'and if I love you, look out for you.' You couldn't ask for fairer. For his own part, Saladin in his time had loved widely, and was now (he had come to believe) suffering Love's revenges upon the foolish lover. Of the things of the mind, he had most loved the protean, inexhaustible culture of the English-speaking peoples; had said, when courting Pamela, that *Othello*, 'just that one play', was worth the total output of any other dramatist in any other language, and though he was conscious of hyperbole, he didn't think the exaggeration very great. (Pamela, of course, made incessant efforts to betray her class and race, and so, predictably, professed herself horrified, bracketing Othello with Shylock and beating the racist Shakespeare over the head with the brace of them.) He had been striving, like the Bengali writer, Nirad Chaudhuri, before him – though without any of that impish, colonial intelligence's urge to be seen as an enfant terrible – to be worthy of the challenge represented by the phrase *Civis Britannicus sum*. Empire was no more, but still he knew 'all that was good and living within him' to have been 'made, shaped and quickened' by his encounter with this islet of sensibility, surrounded by the cool sense of the sea. – Of material things, he had given his love to this city, London, preferring it to the city of his birth or to any other; had been creeping up on it, stealthily, with mounting excitement, freezing into a statue when it looked in his direction, dreaming of being the one to possess it and so, in a sense, *become* it, as when in the game of grandmother's footsteps the child who touches the one who's *it* ('on it', today's young Londoners would say) takes over that cherished identity; as, also, in the myth of the Golden Bough. London, its conglomerate nature mirroring his own, its reticence also his; its gargoyles, the ghostly footfalls in its streets of Roman feet, the honks of its departing migrant geese. Its hospitality – yes! – in spite of immigration laws, and his own recent experience, he still insisted on the truth of that: an imperfect welcome, true, one capable of bigotry, but a real thing, nonetheless, as was attested by the existence in a South London borough of a pub in which no language but Ukrainian could be heard, and by the annual reunion, in Wembley, a stone's throw from the great stadium surrounded by imperial echoes – Empire Way, the Empire Pool – of more than a hundred delegates, all tracing their ancestry back to a single, small Goan village. – 'We Londoners can be proud of our hospitality,' he'd told Pamela, and she, giggling helplessly, took him to see the Buster Keaton movie of that name, in which the comedian, arriving at the end of an absurd railway line, gets a murderous reception. In those days they had enjoyed such oppositions, and after hot disputes had ended up in bed . . . He returned his wandering thoughts to the subject of the metropolis. Its – he repeated stubbornly to himself – long history as a refuge, a role it maintained in spite of the recalcitrant ingratitude of the refugees' children; and without any of the self-congratulatory huddled-masses rhetoric of the 'nation of immigrants' across the ocean, itself far from perfectly open-armed. Would the United States, with its are-you-now-have-you-ever-beens, have permitted Ho Chi Minh to cook in its hotel kitchens? What would its McCarran–Walter Act have to say about a latter-day Karl Marx, standing bushy-bearded at its gates, waiting to cross its yellow lines? O Proper London! Dull would he truly be of soul who did not prefer its faded splendours, its new hesitancies, to the hot certainties of that transatlantic New Rome with its Nazified architectural gigantism, which employed the oppressions of size to make its human occupants feel like worms . . . London, in spite of an increase in excrescences such as the NatWest Tower – a corporate logo extruded into the third dimension – preserved the human scale. *Viva! Zindabad!*

Pamela had always taken a caustic view of such rhapsodies. 'These are museum-values,' she used to tell him. 'Sanctified, hanging in golden frames on honorific walls.' She had never had any time for what endured. Change everything! Rip it up! He said: 'If you succeed you will make it impossible for anybody like you, in one or two generations' time, to come along.' She celebrated this vision of her own obsolescence. If she ended up like the dodo – a stuffed relic, *Class Traitor, 1980s* – that would, she said, certainly suggest an improvement in the world. He begged to differ, but by this time they had begun to embrace: which surely was an improvement, so he conceded the other point.

(One year, the government had introduced admission charges at museums, and groups of angry art-lovers picketed the temples of culture. When he saw this, Chamcha had wanted to get up a placard of his own and stage a one-man counter-protest. Didn't these people know what the stuff inside was *worth*? There they were, cheerfully rotting their lungs with cigarettes worth more per packet than the charges they were protesting against; what they were demonstrating to the world was the low value they placed upon their cultural heritage . . . Pamela put her foot down. 'Don't you dare,' she said. She held the then-correct view: that the museums were *too valuable* to charge for. So: 'Don't you dare,' and to his surprise he found he did not. He had not meant what he would have seemed to mean. He had meant that he would have given, maybe, in the right circumstances, his *life* for what was in those museums. So he could not take seriously these objections to a charge of a few pence. He quite saw, however, that this was an obscure and ill-defended position.)

– *And of human beings, Pamela, I loved you.* –

Culture, city, wife; and a fourth and final love, of which he had spoken to nobody: the love of a dream. In the old days the dream had recurred about once a month; a simple dream, set in a city park, along an avenue of mature elms, whose overarching branches turned the avenue into a green tunnel into which the sky and the sunlight were dripping, here and there, through the perfect imperfections in the canopy of leaves. In this sylvan secrecy, Saladin saw himself, accompanied by a small boy of about five, whom he was teaching to ride a bicycle. The boy, wobbling alarmingly at first, made heroic efforts to gain and maintain his balance, with the ferocity of one who wishes his father to be proud of him. The dream-Chamcha ran along behind his imagined son, holding the bike upright by gripping the parcel-rack over the rear wheel. Then he released it, and the boy (not knowing himself to be unsupported) kept going: balance came like a gift of flight, and the two of them were gliding down the avenue, Chamcha running, the boy pedalling harder and harder. 'You did it!' Saladin rejoiced, and the equally elated child shouted back: 'Look at me! See how quickly I learned! Aren't you pleased with me? Aren't you pleased?' It was a dream to weep at; for when he awoke, there was no bicycle and no child.

'What will you do now?' Mishal had asked him amid the wreckage of the Hot Wax nightclub, and he'd answered, too lightly: 'Me? I think I'll come back to life.' Easier said than done; it was life, after all, that had rewarded his love of a dream-child with childlessness; his love of a woman, with her estrangement from him and her insemination by his old college friend; his love of a city, by hurling him down towards it from Himalayan heights; and his love of a civilization, by having him bedevilled, humiliated, broken upon its wheel. Not quite broken, he reminded himself; he was whole again, and there was, too, the example of Niccolò Machiavelli to consider (a wronged man, his name, like that of Muhammad-Mahon-Mahound, a synonym for evil; whereas in fact his staunch republicanism had earned him the rack, upon which he survived, was it three turns of the wheel? – enough, at any rate, to make most men confess to raping their grandmothers, or anything else, just to make the pain go away; – yet he had confessed to nothing, having committed no crimes while serving the Florentine republic, that all-too-brief interruption in the power of the Medici family); if Niccolò could survive such tribulation and live to write that perhaps embittered, perhaps sardonic parody of the sycophantic mirror-of-princes literature then so much in vogue, *Il Principe*, following it with the magisterial *Discorsi*, then he, Chamcha, need certainly not permit himself the luxury of defeat. Resurrection it was, then; roll back that boulder from the cave's dark mouth, and to hell with the legal problems.

Mishal, Hanif Johnson and Pinkwalla – in whose eyes Chamcha's metamorphoses had made the actor a hero, through whom the magic of special-effects fantasy-movies *(Labyrinth,*

Legend, Howard the Duck) entered the Real – drove Saladin over to Pamela's place in the DJ's van; this time, though, he squashed himself into the cab along with the other three. It was early afternoon; Jumpy would still be at the sports centre. 'Good luck,' said Mishal, kissing him, and Pinkwalla asked if they should wait. 'No, thanks,' Saladin replied. 'When you've fallen from the sky, been abandoned by your friend, suffered police brutality, metamorphosed into a goat, lost your work as well as your wife, learned the power of hatred and regained human shape, what is there left to do but, as you would no doubt phrase it, demand your rights?' He waved goodbye. 'Good for you,' Mishal said, and they had gone. On the street corner the usual neighbourhood kids, with whom his relations had never been good, were bouncing a football off a lamp-post. One of them, an evil-looking piggy-eyed lout of nine or ten, pointed an imaginary video remote control at Chamcha and yelled: 'Fast forward!' His was a generation that believed in skipping life's boring, troublesome, unlikable bits, going fast-forward from one action-packed climax to the next. *Welcome home,* Saladin thought, and rang the doorbell.

Pamela, when she saw him, actually caught at her throat. 'I didn't think people did that any more,' he said. 'Not since *Dr Strangelove.'* Her pregnancy wasn't visible yet; he inquired after it, and she blushed, but confirmed that it was going well. 'So far so good.' She was naturally off balance; the offer of coffee in the kitchen came several beats too late (she 'stuck with' her whisky, drinking rapidly in spite of the baby); but in point of fact Chamcha felt *one down* (there had been a period in which he'd been an avid devotee of Stephen Potter's amusing little books) throughout this encounter. Pamela clearly felt that she ought to be the one in the bad position. She was the one who had wanted to break the marriage, who had denied him at least thrice; but he was as fumbling and abashed as she, so that they seemed to compete for the right to occupy the doghouse. The reason for Chamcha's discomfiture – and he had not, let's recall, arrived in this awkward spirit, but in feisty, pugnacious mood – was that he had realized, on seeing Pamela, with her too-bright brightness, her face like a saintly mask behind which who knows what worms feasted on rotting meat (he was alarmed by the hostile violence of the images arising from his unconscious), her shaven head under its absurd turban, her whisky breath, and the hard thing that had entered the little lines around her mouth, that he had quite simply fallen out of love, and would not want her back even should she want (which was improbable but not inconceivable) to return. The instant he became aware of this he commenced for some reason to feel guilty, and, as a result, at a conversational disadvantage. The white-haired dog was growling at him, too. He recalled that he'd never really cared for pets.

'I suppose,' she addressed her glass, sitting at the old pine table in the spacious kitchen, 'that what I did was unforgivable, huh?'

That little Americanizing *huh* was new: another of her infinite series of blows against her breeding? Or had she caught it from Jumpy, or some hip little acquaintance of his, like a disease? (The snarling violence again: down with it. Now that he no longer wanted her, it was entirely inappropriate to the situation.) 'I don't think I can say what I'm capable of forgiving,' he replied. 'That particular response seems to be out of my control; it either operates or it doesn't and I find out in due course. So let's say, for the moment, that the jury's out.' She didn't like that, she wanted him to defuse the situation so that they could enjoy their blasted coffee. Pamela had always made vile coffee: still, that wasn't his problem now. 'I'm moving back in,' he said. 'It's a big house and there's plenty of room. I'll take the den, and the rooms on the floor below, including the spare bathroom, so I'll be quite independent. I propose to use the kitchen very sparingly. I'm assuming that, as my body was never found, I'm still officially missing-presumed-dead, that you haven't gone to court to have me wiped off the slate. In which case it shouldn't take too long to resuscitate me, once I alert Bentine, Milligan and Sellers.' (Respectively, their lawyer, their accountant and Chamcha's agent.) Pamela listened dumbly, her posture informing him that she wouldn't be offering any counter-arguments, that whatever he wanted was okay: making amends with body language. 'After that,' he concluded, 'we sell up and you get your divorce.' He swept out, making an exit before he got the shakes, and made it to his den just before they hit him. Pamela, downstairs, would be weeping; he had never found crying easy, but he was a champion shaker. And now there was his heart, too: boom badoom doodoodoom.

To be born again, first you have to die.

Alone, he all at once remembered that he and Pamela had once disagreed, as they disagreed on everything, on a short-story they'd both read, whose theme was precisely the nature of the unforgivable. Title and author eluded him, but the story came back vividly. A man and a woman had been intimate friends (never lovers) for all their adult lives. On his twenty-first birthday (they were both poor at the time) she had given him, as a joke, the most horrible, cheap glass vase she could find, its colours a garish parody of Venetian gaiety. Twenty years later, when they were both successful and greying, she visited his home and quarrelled with him over his treatment of a mutual friend. In the course of the quarrel her eye fell upon the old vase, which he still kept in pride of place on his sitting-room mantelpiece, and, without pausing in her tirade, she swept it to the floor, smashing it beyond hope of repair. He never spoke to her again; when she died, half a century later, he refused to visit her deathbed or attend her funeral, even though messengers were sent to tell him that these were her dearest wishes. 'Tell her,' he said to the emissaries, 'that she never knew how much I valued what she broke.' The emissaries argued, pleaded, raged. If she had not known how much meaning he had invested in the trifle, how could she in all fairness be blamed? And had she not made countless attempts, over the years, to apologize and atone? And she was dying, for heaven's sake; could not this ancient, childish rift be healed at the last? They had lost a lifetime's friendship; could they not even say goodbye? 'No,' said the unforgiving man. – 'Really because of the vase? Or are you concealing some other, darker matter?' – 'It was the vase,' he answered, 'the vase, and nothing but.' Pamela thought the man petty and cruel, but Chamcha had even then appreciated the curious privacy, the inexplicable inwardness of the issue. 'Nobody can judge an internal injury,' he had said, 'by the size of the superficial wound, of the hole.'

Sunt lacrimae rerum, as the ex-teacher Sufyan would have said, and Saladin had ample opportunity in the next many days to contemplate the tears in things. He remained at first virtually immobile in his den, allowing it to grow back around him at its own pace, waiting for it to regain something of the solid comforting quality of its old self, as it had been before the altering of the universe. He watched a good deal of television with half an eye, channel-hopping compulsively, for he was a member of the remote-control culture of the present as much as the piggy boy on the street corner; he, too, could comprehend, or at least enter the illusion of comprehending, the composite video monster his button-pushing brought into being ... what a leveller this remote-control gizmo was, a Procrustean bed for the twentieth century; it chopped down the heavyweight and stretched out the slight until all the set's emissions, commercials, murders, game-shows, the thousand and one varying joys and terrors of the real and the imagined, acquired an equal weight; – and whereas the original Procrustes, citizen of what could now be termed a 'hands-on' culture, had to exercise both brain and brawn, he, Chamcha, could lounge back in his Parker-Knoll recliner chair and let his fingers do the chopping. It seemed to him, as he idled across the channels, that the box was full of freaks: there were mutants – 'Mutts' – on *Dr Who*, bizarre creatures who appeared to have been crossbred with different types of industrial machinery: forage harvesters, grabbers, donkeys, jackhammers, saws, and whose cruel priest-chieftains were called *Mutilasians*; children's television appeared to be extremely populated by humanoid robots and creatures with metamorphic bodies, while the adult programmes offered a continual parade of the misshapen human by-products of the newest notions in modern medicine, and its accomplices, modern disease and war. A hospital in Guyana had apparently preserved the body of a fully formed merman, complete with gills

and scales. Lycanthropy was on the increase in the Scottish High-
lands. The genetic possibility of centaurs was being seriously discussed. A sex-change operation was shown. – He was reminded of
an execrable piece of poetry which Jumpy Joshi had hesitantly
shown him at the Shaandaar B and B. Its name, 'I Sing the Body
Eclectic', was fully representative of the whole. – But the fellow
has a whole body, after all, Saladin thought bitterly. He made
Pamela's baby with no trouble at all: no broken sticks on his damn
chromosomes . . . he caught sight of himself in a rerun of an old
Aliens Show 'classic'. (In the fast-forward culture, classic status
could be achieved in as little as six months; sometimes even
overnight.) The effect of all this box-watching was to put a severe
dent in what remained of his idea of the normal, average quality of
the real; but there were also countervailing forces at work.

On *Gardeners' World* he was shown how to achieve something
called a 'chimeran graft' (the very same, as chance would have it,
that had been the pride of Otto Cone's garden); and although his
inattention caused him to miss the names of the two trees that had
been bred into one – Mulberry? Laburnum? Broom? – the
tree itself made him sit up and take notice. There it palpably was,
a chimera with roots, firmly planted in and growing vigorously
out of a piece of English earth: a tree, he thought, capable of
taking the metaphoric place of the one his father had chopped
down in a distant garden in another, incompatible world. If such a
tree were possible, then so was he; he, too, could cohere, send
down roots, survive. Amid all the televisual images of hybrid
tragedies – the uselessness of mermen, the failures of plastic
surgery, the Esperanto-like vacuity of much modern art, the
Coca-Colonization of the planet – he was given this one gift. It
was enough. He switched off the set.

Gradually, his animosity towards Gibreel lessened. Nor did
horns, goat-hoofs, etc. show any signs of manifesting themselves
anew. It seemed a cure was in progress. In point of fact, with the
passage of the days not only Gibreel, but everything which had
befallen Saladin of late that was irreconcilable with the prosiness of

everyday life came to seem somehow irrelevant, as even the most stubborn of nightmares will once you've splashed your face, brushed your teeth and had a strong, hot drink. He began to make journeys into the outside world – to those professional advisers, lawyer accountant agent, whom Pamela used to call 'the Goons', and when sitting in the panelled, book- and ledger-lined stability of those offices in which miracles could plainly never happen he took to speaking of his 'breakdown', – 'the shock of the accident', – and so on, explaining his disappearance as though he had never tumbled from the sky, singing 'Rule, Britannia' while Gibreel yowled an air from the movie *Shree 420*. He made a conscious effort to resume his old life of delicate sensibilities, taking himself off to concerts and art galleries and plays, and if his responses were rather dull; – if these pursuits singularly failed to send him home in the state of exaltation which was the return he expected from all high art; – then he insisted to himself that the thrill would soon return; he had had 'a bad experience', and needed a little time.

In his den, seated in the Parker-Knoll armchair, surrounded by his familiar objects – the china pierrots, the mirror in the shape of a cartoonist's heart, Eros holding up the globe of an antique lamp – he congratulated himself on being the sort of person who had found hatred impossible to sustain for long. Maybe, after all, love was more durable than hate; even if love changed, some shadow of it, some lasting shape, persisted. Towards Pamela, for example, he was now sure he felt nothing but the most altruistic affections. Hatred was perhaps like a finger-print upon the smooth glass of the sensitive soul; a mere grease-mark, which disappeared if left alone. Gibreel? Pooh! He was forgotten; he no longer existed. There; to surrender animosity was to become free.

Saladin's optimism grew, but the red tape surrounding his return to life proved more obstructive than he expected. The banks were taking their time about unblocking his accounts; he was obliged to borrow from Pamela. Nor was work easy to come by. His agent, Charlie Sellers, explained over the phone: 'Clients get funny. They start talking about zombies, they feel sort of unclean: as if they were robbing a grave.' Charlie, who still sounded in her early fifties like a disorganized and somewhat daffy young thing of the best county stock, gave the impression that she rather sympathized with the clients' point of view. 'Wait it out,' she advised. 'They'll come round. After all, it isn't as if you were Dracula, for heaven's sake.' Thank you, Charlie.

Yes: his obsessive loathing of Gibreel, his dream of exacting some cruel and appropriate revenge, – these were things of the past, aspects of a reality incompatible with his passionate desire to re-establish ordinary life. Not even the seditious, deconstructive imagery of television could deflect him. What he was rejecting was a portrait of himself and Gibreel as *monstrous*. Monstrous, indeed: the most absurd of ideas. There were real monsters in the world – mass-murdering dictators, child rapists. The Granny Ripper. (Here he was forced to admit that in spite of his old, high estimate of the Metropolitan Police, the arrest of Uhuru Simba was just too darned neat.) You only had to open the tabloids any day of the week to find crazed homosexual Irishmen stuffing babies' mouths with earth. Pamela, naturally, had been of the view that 'monster' was too – what? – *judgmental* a term for such persons; compassion, she said, required that we see them as casualties of the age. Compassion, he replied, demanded that we see their victims as the casualties. 'There's nothing to be done with you,' she had said in her most patrician voice. 'You actually do think in cheap debating points.'

And other monsters, too, no less real than the tabloid fiends: money, power, sex, death, love. Angels and devils – who needed them? 'Why demons, when man himself is a demon?' the Nobel Laureate Singer's 'last demon' asked from his attic in Tishevitz. To which Chamcha's sense of balance, his much-to-be-said-for-and-against reflex, wished to add: 'And why angels, when man is angelic too?' (If this wasn't true, how to explain, for instance, the Leonardo Cartoon? Was Mozart really Beelzebub in a powdered wig?) – But, it had to be conceded, and this was his original point, that the circumstances of the age required no diabolic explanations.

I'm saying nothing. Don't ask me to clear things up one way or the other; the time of revelations is long gone. The rules of Creation are pretty clear: you set things up, you make them thus and so, and then you let them roll. Where's the pleasure if you're always intervening to give hints, change the rules, fix the fights? Well, I've been pretty self-controlled up to this point and I don't plan to spoil things now. Don't think I haven't wanted to butt in; I have, plenty of times. And once, it's true, I did. I sat on Alleluia Cone's bed and spoke to the superstar, Gibreel. *Ooparvala or Neechayvala,* he wanted to know, and I didn't enlighten him; I certainly don't intend to blab to this confused Chamcha instead.

I'm leaving now. The man's going to sleep.

His reborn, fledgling, still-fallible optimism was hardest to maintain at night; because at night that otherworld of horns and hoofs was not so easily denied. There was the matter, too, of the two women who had started haunting his dreams. The first – it was hard to admit this, even to himself – was none other than the child-woman of the Shaandaar, his loyal ally in that nightmare time which he was now trying so mightily to conceal behind banalities and mists, the aficionada of the martial arts, Hanif Johnson's lover, Mishal Sufyan.

The second – whom he'd left in Bombay with the knife of his departure sticking in her heart, and who must still think him dead – was Zeeny Vakil.

His jumpiness of Jumpy Joshi when he learned that Saladin Chamcha had returned, in human form, to reoccupy the upper storeys of the house in Notting Hill, was frightful to behold, and incensed Pamela more than she could say. On the first night – she had decided not to tell him until they were safely in bed – he leaped, on hearing the news, a good three feet clear of the bed and stood on the pale blue carpet, stark naked and quaking with his thumb stuck in his mouth.

'Come back here and stop being foolish,' she commanded, but he shook his head wildly, and removed his thumb long enough to gibber: 'But if he's *here*! In this *house*! Then how can *I* . . . ?' – With which he snatched up his clothes in an untidy bundle, and fled from her presence; she heard thumps and crashes which suggested that his shoes, possibly accompanied by himself, had fallen down the stairs. 'Good,' she screamed after him. 'Chicken, break your neck.'

Some moments later, however, Saladin was visited by the purple-faced figure of his estranged and naked-headed wife, who spoke thickly through clamped teeth. 'J.J. is standing outside in the street. The damn fool says he can't come in unless you say it's okay with you.' She had, as usual, been drinking. Chamcha, greatly astonished, more or less blurted out: 'What about you, you want him to come in?' Which Pamela interpreted as his way of rubbing salt in the wound. Turning an even deeper shade of purple she nodded with humiliated ferocity. *Yes.*

So it was that on his first night home, Saladin Chamcha went outside – 'Hey, hombre! You're really *well*!' Jumpy greeted him in terror, making as if to slap palms, to conceal his fear – and persuaded his wife's lover to share her bed. Then he retreated upstairs, because Jumpy's mortification now prevented him from entering the house until Chamcha was safely out of the way.

'What a man!' Jumpy wept at Pamela. 'He's a *prince*, a *saint*!'

'If you don't pack it in,' Pamela Chamcha warned apoplectically, 'I'll set the fucking dog on you.'

Jumpy continued to find Chamcha's presence distracting, envisaging him (or so it appeared from his behaviour) as a minatory shade that needed to be constantly placated. When he cooked Pamela a meal (he had turned out, to her surprise and relief, to be quite a Mughlai chef) he insisted on asking Chamcha down to join them, and, when Saladin demurred, took him up a tray, explaining to Pamela that to do otherwise would be rude, and also provocative. 'Look what he permits under his own roof! He's a *giant*; least we can do is have good manners.' Pamela, with mounting rage, was obliged to put up with a series of such acts and their accompanying homilies. 'I'd never have believed you were so conventional,' she fumed, and Jumpy replied: 'It's just a question of respect.'

In the name of respect, Jumpy carried Chamcha cups of tea, newspapers and mail; he never failed, on arriving at the big house, to go upstairs for a visit of at least twenty minutes, the minimum time commensurate with his sense of politeness, while Pamela cooled her heels and knocked back bourbon three floors below. He brought Saladin little presents: propitiatory offerings of books, old theatre handbills, masks. When Pamela attempted to put her foot down, he argued against her with an innocent, but also mulish passion: 'We can't behave as if the man's invisible. He's here, isn't he? Then we must involve him in our lives.' Pamela replied sourly: 'Why don't you just ask him to come down and join us in bed?' To which Jumpy, seriously, replied: 'I didn't think you'd approve.'

In spite of his inability to relax and take for granted Chamcha's residence upstairs, something in Jumpy Joshi was eased by receiving, in this unusual way, his predecessor's blessings. Able to reconcile the imperatives of love and friendship, he cheered up a good deal, and found the idea of fatherhood growing on him. One night he dreamed a dream that made him weep, the next morning, in delighted anticipation: a simple dream, in which he was running down an avenue of overarching trees, helping a small boy to ride a bicycle. 'Aren't you pleased with me?' the boy cried in his elation. 'Look: aren't you pleased?'

Pamela and Jumpy had both become involved in the campaign mounted to protest against the arrest of Dr Uhuru Simba for the so-called Granny Ripper Murders. This, too, Jumpy went upstairs to discuss with Saladin. 'The whole thing's completely trumped-

up, based on circumstantial evidence and insinuations. Hanif
reckons he can drive a truck through the holes in the prosecution
case. It's just a straightforward malicious fit-up; the only question
is how far they'll go. They'll verbal him for sure. Maybe there will
even be witnesses saying they saw him do the slicing. Depends
how badly they want to get him. Pretty badly, I'd say; he's been a
loud voice around town for some while.' Chamcha recommended
caution. Recalling Mishal Sufyan's loathing for Simba, he said:
'The fellow has – has he not? – a record of violence towards
women . . .' Jumpy turned his palms outward. 'In his personal
life,' he owned, 'the guy's frankly a piece of shit. But that doesn't
mean he disembowels senior citizens; you don't have to be an
angel to be innocent. Unless, of course, you're black.' Chamcha
let this pass. 'The point is, this isn't personal, it's political,' Jumpy
emphasized, adding, as he got up to leave, 'Um, there's a public
meeting about it tomorrow. Pamela and I have to go; please, I
mean if you'd like, if you'd be interested, that is, come along if
you want.'

'You asked him to go with us?' Pamela was incredulous. She
had started to feel nauseous most of the time, and it did nothing
for her mood. 'You actually did that without consulting me?'
Jumpy looked crestfallen. 'Doesn't matter, anyhow,' she let him
off the hook. 'Catch *him* going to anything like *that*.'

In the morning, however, Saladin presented himself in the hall,
wearing a smart brown suit, a camel coat with a silk collar, and a
rather natty brown homburg hat. 'Where are you off to?' Pamela,
in turban, army-surplus leather jacket and tracksuit bottoms that
revealed the incipient thickening of her middle, wanted to know.
'Bloody Ascot?' 'I believe I was invited to a meeting,' Saladin
answered in his least combative manner, and Pamela freaked.
'You want to be careful,' she warned him. 'The way you look,
you'll probably get fucking mugged.'

What drew him back into the otherworld, into that undercity
whose existence he had so long denied? – What, or rather who,

forced him by the simple fact of its (her) existence, to emerge from that cocoon-den in which he was being – or so he believed – restored to his former self, and plunge once more into the per- ilous (because uncharted) waters of the world and of himself? 'I'll be able to fit in the meeting,' Jumpy Joshi had told Saladin, 'before my karate class.' – Where his star pupil waited: long, rainbow- haired and, Jumpy added, just past her eighteenth birthday. – Not knowing that Jumpy, too, was suffering some of the same illicit longings, Saladin crossed town to be nearer to Mishal Sufyan.

He had expected the meeting to be small, envisaging a back room somewhere full of suspicious types looking and talking like clones of Malcolm X (Chamcha could remember finding funny a TV comic's joke – 'Then there's the one about the black man who changed his name to Mr X and sued the *News of the World* for libel' – and provoking one of the worst quarrels of his marriage), with maybe a few angry-looking women as well; he had pictured much fist-clenching and righteousness. What he found was a large hall, the Brickhall Friends Meeting House, packed wall-to-wall with every conceivable sort of person – old, wide women and uniformed schoolchildren, Rastas and restaurant workers, the staff of the small Chinese supermarket in Plassey Street, soberly dressed gents as well as wild boys, whites as well as blacks; the mood of the crowd was far from the kind of evangelical hysteria he'd imag- ined; it was quiet, worried, wanting to know what could be done. There was a young black woman standing near him who gave his attire an amused once-over; he stared back at her, and she laughed: 'Okay, sorry, no offence.' She was wearing a lenticular badge, the sort that changed its message as you moved. At some angles it read, *Uhuru for the Simba;* at others, *Freedom for the Lion.* 'It's on account of the meaning of his chosen name,' she explained redundantly. 'In African.' Which language? Saladin wanted to know. She shrugged, and turned away to listen to the speakers. It was African: born, by the sound of her, in Lewisham or Deptford or New Cross, that was all she needed to know . . . Pamela hissed into his ear. 'I see you finally found somebody to feel superior to.' She could still read him like a book.

A minute woman in her middle seventies was led up on to the stage at the far end of the hall by a wiry man who, Chamcha was almost reassured to observe, really did look like an American Black Power leader, the young Stokely Carmichael, in fact – the same intense spectacles – and who was acting as a sort of compère. He turned out to be Dr Simba's kid brother Walcott Roberts, and the tiny lady was their mother, Antoinette. 'God knows how anything as big as Simba ever came out of her,' Jumpy whispered, and Pamela frowned angrily, out of a new feeling of solidarity with all pregnant women, past as well as present. When Antoinette Roberts spoke, however, her voice was big enough to fill the room on lung-power alone. She wanted to talk about her son's day in court, at the committal proceedings, and she was quite a performer. Hers was what Chamcha thought of as an educated voice; she spoke in the BBC accents of one who learned her English diction from the World Service, but there was gospel in there, too, and hellfire sermonizing. 'My son filled that dock,' she told the silent room. 'Lord, he filled it *up*. Sylvester – you will pardon me if I use the name I gave him, not meaning to belittle the warrior's name he took for himself, but only out of ingrained habit – Sylvester, he burst upwards from that dock like Leviathan from the waves. I want you to know how he spoke: he spoke loud, and he spoke clear. He spoke looking his adversary in the eye, and could that prosecutor stare him down? Never in a month of Sundays. And I want you to know what he said: "I stand here," my son declared, "because I have chosen to occupy the old and honourable role of the uppity nigger. I am here because I have not been willing to seem reasonable. I am here for my ingratitude." He was a colossus among the dwarfs. "Make no mistake," he said in that court, "we are here to change things. I concede at once that we shall ourselves be changed; African, Caribbean, Indian, Pakistani, Bangladeshi, Cypriot, Chinese, we are other than what we would have been if we had not crossed the oceans, if our mothers and fathers had not crossed the skies in search of work and dignity and a better life for their children. We have been made again: but I say that we shall also be the ones to remake this society, to shape it from the bottom to the top. We shall be the hewers of the dead wood and the gardeners of the new. It is our turn now." I wish you to think on what my son, Sylvester Roberts, Dr Uhuru Simba, said in the place of justice. Think on it while we decide what we must do.'

Her son Walcott helped her leave the stage amid cheers and chants; she nodded judiciously in the direction of the noise. Less charismatic speeches followed. Hanif Johnson, Simba's lawyer, made a series of suggestions – the visitors' gallery must be packed, the dispensers of justice must know that they were being watched; the court must be picketed, and a rota should be organized; there was the need for a financial appeal. Chamcha murmured to Jumpy: 'Nobody mentions his history of sexual aggression.' Jumpy shrugged. 'Some of the women he's attacked are in this room. Mishal, for example, is over there, look, in the corner by the stage. But this isn't the time or place for that. Simba's bull craziness is, you could say, a trouble in the family. What we have here is trouble with the Man.' In other circumstances, Saladin would have had a good deal to say in response to such a statement. – He would have objected, for one thing, that a man's record of violence could not be set aside so easily when he was accused of murder. – Also that he didn't like the use of such American terms as 'the Man' in the very different British situation, where there was no history of slavery; it sounded like an attempt to borrow the glamour of other, more dangerous struggles, a thing he also felt about the organizers' decision to punctuate the speeches with such meaning-loaded songs as *We Shall Overcome*, and even, for Pete's sake, *Nkosi Sikelel' iAfrika*. As if all causes were the same, all histories interchangeable. – But he said none of these things, because his head had begun to spin and his senses to reel, owing to his having been given, for the first time in his life, a stupefying premonition of his death.

– Hanif Johnson was finishing his speech. *As Dr Simba has written, newness will enter this society by collective, not individual,*

actions. He was quoting what Chamcha recognized as one of
Camus's most popular slogans. *The passage from speech to moral
action,* Hanif was saying, *has a name: to become human.* – And now a
pretty young British Asian woman with a slightly-too-bulbous
nose and a dirty, bluesy voice was launching into Bob Dylan's
song, *I Pity the Poor Immigrant.* Another false and imported note,
this: the song actually seemed rather hostile towards immigrants,
though there were lines that struck chords, about the immigrant's
visions shattering like glass, about how he was obliged to 'build his
town with blood'. Jumpy, with his versifying attempts to redefine
the old racist image of the rivers of blood, would appreciate that. –
All these things Saladin experienced and thought as if from a considerable distance. – What had happened? This: when Jumpy Joshi
pointed out Mishal Sufyan's presence at the Friends Meeting
House, Saladin Chamcha, looking in her direction, saw a blazing
fire burning in the centre of her forehead; and felt, in the same
moment, the beating, and the icy shadow, of a pair of gigantic
wings. – He experienced the kind of blurring associated with
double vision, seeming to look into two worlds at once; one was
the brightly lit, no-smoking-allowed meeting hall, but the other
was a world of phantoms, in which Azraeel, the exterminating
angel, was swooping towards him, and a girl's forehead could
burn with ominous flames. – *She's death to me, that's what it means,*
Chamcha thought in one of the two worlds, while in the other he
told himself not to be foolish; the room was full of people wearing
those inane tribal badges that had latterly grown so popular, green
neon haloes, devil-horns painted with fluorescent paint; Mishal
probably had on some piece of space-age junk jewellery. – But his
other self took over again, *she's off limits to you,* it said, *not all possibilities are open to us. The world is finite; our hopes spill over its rim.* –
Whereupon his heart got in on the act, bababoom, boomba,
dabadoom.

Now he was outside, with Jumpy fussing over him and even
Pamela showing concern. 'I'm the one with the bun in the oven,'
she said with a gruff remnant of affection. 'What business have
you got to pass out?' Jumpy insisted: 'You'd best come with me to

my class; just sit quietly, and afterwards I'll take you home.' – But Pamela wanted to know if a doctor was required. *No, no, I'll go with Jumpy, I'll be fine. It was just hot in there. Airless. My clothes too warm. A stupid thing. A nothing.*

There was an art cinema next to the Friends House, and he was leaning against a movie poster. The film was *Mephisto*, the story of an actor seduced into a collaboration with Nazism. In the poster, the actor – played by the German star Klaus Maria Brandauer – was dressed up as Mephistophilis, face white, body cloaked in black, arms upraised. Lines from *Faust* stood above his head:

– *Who art thou, then?*
– *Part of that Power, not understood,*
Which always wills the Bad, and always works the Good.

At the sports centre: he could scarcely bring himself to glance in Mishal's direction. (She too had left the Simba meeting in time to make the class.) – Although she was all over him, *you came back, I bet it was to see me, isn't that nice,* he could hardly speak a civil word, much less ask *were you wearing a luminous something in the middle of your,* because she wasn't now, kicking her legs and flexing her long body, resplendent in its black leotard. – Until, sensing the coldness in him, she backed off, all confusion and injured pride.

'Our other star hasn't turned up today,' Jumpy mentioned to Saladin during a break in the exercises. 'Miss Alleluia Cone, the one who climbed Everest. I was meaning to introduce you two. She knows, I mean, she's apparently with, Gibreel. Gibreel Farishta, the actor, your fellow-survivor of the crash.'

Things are closing in on me. Gibreel was drifting towards him, like India when, having come unstuck from the Gondwanaland proto-continent, it floated towards Laurasia. (His processes of mind, he recognized absently, were coming up with some pretty strange associations.) When they collided, the force would hurl up Himalayas. – What is a mountain? An obstacle; a transcendence; above all, an *effect*.

'Where are you going?' Jumpy was calling. 'I thought I was giving you a lift. Are you okay?'

I'm fine. I need to walk, that's all.

'Okay, but only if you're sure.'

Sure. Walk away fast, without catching Mishal's aggrieved eye. . . . In the street. Walk quickly, out of this wrong place, this underworld. – God: no escape. Here's a shop-front, a store selling musical instruments, trumpets saxophones oboes, what's the name? – *Fair Winds*, and here in the window is a cheaply printed handbill. Announcing the imminent return of, that's right, the Archangel Gibreel. His return and the salvation of the earth. *Walk. Walk away fast.*

. . . Hail this taxi. (His clothes inspire deference in the driver.) Climb in squire do you mind the radio. Some scientist who got caught in that hijacking and lost the half of his tongue. American. They rebuilt it, he says, with flesh taken from his posterior, excuse my French. Wouldn't fancy a mouthful of my own buttock meat myself but the poor bugger had no option did he. Funny bastard. Got some funny ideas.

Eugene Dumsday on the radio discussed the gaps in the fossil record with his new, buttocky tongue. *The Devil tried to silence me but the good Lord and American surgical techniques knew better.* These gaps were the creationist's main selling-point: if natural selection was the truth, where were all the random mutations that got deselected? Where were the monster-children, the deformed babies of evolution? The fossils were silent. No three-legged horses there. *No point arguing with these geezers,* the cabbie said. *I don't hold with God myself.* No point, one small part of Chamcha's consciousness agreed. No point suggesting that 'the fossil record' wasn't some sort of perfect filing cabinet. And evolution theory had come a long way since Darwin. It was now being argued that major changes in species happened not in the stumbling, hit-and-miss manner first envisaged, but in great, radical leaps. The history of life was not the bumbling progress – the very English, middle-class progress – Victorian thought had wanted it to be, but violent, a thing of dramatic, cumulative transformations: in the old formulation, more revolution than evolution. – I've heard enough, the cabbie said. Eugene Dumsday vanished from the ether, to be replaced by disco music. *Ave atque vale.*

What Saladin Chamcha understood that day was that he had been living in a state of phoney peace, that the change in him was irreversible. A new, dark world had opened up for him (or: within him) when he fell from the sky; no matter how assiduously he attempted to re-create his old existence, this was, he now saw, a fact that could not be unmade. He seemed to see a road before him, forking to left and right. Closing his eyes, settling back against taxicab upholstery, he chose the left-hand path.

2

The temperature continued to rise; and when the heatwave
reached its highest point, and stayed up there so long that the
whole city, its edifices, its waterways, its inhabitants, came perilously close to the boil, – then Mr Billy Battuta and his companion Mimi Mamoulian, recently returned to the metropolis
after a period as guests of the penal authority of New York,
announced their 'grand coming-out' party. Billy's business connections downtown had arranged for his case to be heard by a
well-disposed judge; his personal charm had persuaded every one
of the wealthy female 'marks' from whom he'd extracted such
generous amounts for the purpose of the re-purchase of his soul
from the Devil (including Mrs Struwelpeter) to sign a clemency
petition, in which the matrons stated their conviction that Mr
Battuta had honestly repented him of his error, and asked, in the
light of his vow to concentrate henceforth on his startlingly brilliant entrepreneurial career (whose social usefulness in terms of
wealth creation and the provision of employment to many persons, they suggested, should also be considered by the court in
mitigation of his offences), and his further vow to undergo a full
course of psychiatric treatment to help him overcome his weakness for criminal capers, – that the worthy judge settle upon some
lighter punishment than a prison sentence, 'the deterrent purpose

underlying such incarceration being better served here,' in the ladies' opinion, 'by a judgment of a more Christian sort'. Mimi, adjudged to be no more than Billy's love-duped underling, was given a suspended sentence; for Billy it was deportation, and a stiff fine, but even this was rendered considerably less severe by the judge's consent to Billy's attorney's plea that his client be allowed to leave the country voluntarily, without having the stigma of a deportation order stamped into his passport, a thing that would do great damage to his many business interests. Twenty-four hours after the judgment Billy and Mimi were back in London, whooping it up at Crockford's, and sending out fancy invitation cards to what promised to be *the* party of that strangely sweltering season. One of these cards found its way, with the assistance of Mr S. S. Sisodia, to the residence of Alleluia Cone and Gibreel Farishta; another arrived, a little belatedly, at Saladin Chamcha's den, slipped under the door by the solicitous Jumpy. (Mimi had called Pamela to invite her, adding, with her usual directness: 'Any notion where that husband of yours has gotten to?' – Which Pamela answered, with English awkwardness, *yes er but*. Mimi got the whole story out of her in less than half an hour, which wasn't bad, and concluded triumphantly: 'Sounds like your life is looking up, Pam. Bring 'em both; bring anyone. It's going to be quite a circus.')

The location for the party was another of Sisodia's inexplicable triumphs: the giant sound stage at the Shepperton film studios had been procured, apparently at no cost, and the guests would be able, therefore, to take their pleasures in the huge re-creation of Dickensian London that stood within. A musical adaptation of the great writer's last completed novel, renamed *Friend!*, with book and lyrics by the celebrated genius of the musical stage, Mr Jeremy Bentham, had proved a mammoth hit in the West End and on Broadway, in spite of the macabre nature of some of its scenes; now, accordingly, *The Chums*, as it was known in the business, was receiving the accolade of a big-budget movie production. 'The pipi PR people,' Sisodia told Gibreel on the phone, 'think that such a fufufuck, *function*, which is to be most ista ista istar ista ista istudded, will be good for their bibuild up cacampaign.'

The appointed night arrived: a night of dreadful heat.

Shepperton! – Pamela and Jumpy are already here, borne on the wings of Pamela's MG, when Chamcha, having disdained their company, arrives in one of the fleet of coaches the evening's hosts have made available to those guests wishing for whatever reason to be driven rather than to drive. – And someone else, too, – the one with whom our Saladin fell to earth, – has come; is wandering within. – Chamcha enters the arena; and is amazed. – Here London has been altered – no, *condensed*, – according to the imperatives of film. – Why, here's the Stucconia of the Veneerings, those bran-new, spick and span new people, lying shockingly adjacent to Portman Square, and the shady angle containing various Podsnaps. – And worse: behold the dustman's mounds of Boffin's Bower, supposedly in the near vicinity of Holloway, looming in this abridged metropolis over Fascination Fledgeby's rooms in the Albany, the West End's very heart! – But the guests are not disposed to grumble; the reborn city, even rearranged, still takes the breath away; most particularly in that part of the immense studio through which the river winds, the river with its fogs and Gaffer Hexam's boat, the ebbing Thames flowing beneath two bridges, one of iron, one of stone. – Upon its cobbled banks the guests' gay footsteps fall; and there sound mournful, misty, footfalls of ominous note. A dry ice pea-souper lifts across the set.

Society grandees, fashion models, film stars, corporation bigwigs, a brace of minor royal Personages, useful politicians and suchlike riff-raff perspire and mingle in these counterfeit streets with numbers of men and women as sweat-glistened as the 'real' guests and as counterfeit as the city: hired extras in period costume, as well as a selection of the movie's leading players. Chamcha, who realizes in the moment of sighting him that this encounter has been the whole purpose of his journey, – which fact he has succeeded in keeping from himself until this instant, – spots Gibreel in the increasingly riotous crowd.

Yes: there, on London Bridge Which Is Of Stone, without a doubt, Gibreel! – And that must be his Alleluia, his Icequeen Cone! – What a distant expression he seems to be wearing, how he lists a few degrees to the left; and how she seems to dote on him – how everyone adores him: for he is among the very greatest at the party, Battuta to his left, Sisodia at Allie's right, and all about a host of faces that would be recognized from Peru to Timbuctoo! – Chamcha struggles through the crowd, which grows ever more dense as he nears the bridge; – but he is resolved – Gibreel, he will reach Gibreel! – when with a clash of cymbals loud music strikes up, one of Mr Bentham's immortal, show-stopping tunes, and the crowd parts like the Red Sea before the children of Israel. – Chamcha, off-balance, staggers back, is crushed by the parting crowd against a fake half-timbered edifice – what else? – a Curiosity Shop; and, to save himself, retreats within, while a great singing throng of bosomy ladies in mobcaps and frilly blouses, accompanied by an over-sufficiency of stovepipe-hatted gents, comes rollicking down the riverside street, singing for all they're worth.

> *What kind of fellow is Our Mutual Friend?*
> *What does he intend?*
> *Is he the kind of fellow on whom we may depend?*
> *&c. &c. &c.*

'It's a funny thing,' a woman's voice says behind him, 'but when we were doing the show at the C—— Theatre, there was an outbreak of lust among the cast; quite unparalleled, in my experience. People started missing their cues because of the shenanigans in the wings.'

The speaker, he observes, is young, small, buxom, far from unattractive, damp from the heat, flushed with wine, and evidently in the grip of the libidinous fever of which she speaks. – The 'room' has little light, but he can make out the glint in her eye. 'We've got time,' she continues matter-of-factly. 'After this lot finish there's Mr Podsnap's solo.' Whereupon, arranging herself in an expert parody of the Marine Insurance agent's self-important posture, she launches into her own version of the scheduled musical Podsnappery:

> *Ours is a Copious Language,*
> *A Language Trying to Strangers;*
> *Ours is the Favoured Nation,*
> *Blest, and Safe from Dangers . . .*

Now, in Rex-Harrisonian speech-song, she addresses an invisible Foreigner. 'And How Do You Like London? – "Aynor-maymong rich?" – Enormously Rich, we say. Our English adverbs do Not terminate in Mong. – And Do You Find, Sir, Many Evidences of our British Constitution in the Streets of the World's Metropolis, London, Londres, London? – I would say,' she adds, still Podsnapping, 'that there is in the Englishman a combination of qualities, a modesty, an independence, a responsibility, a repose, which one would seek in vain among the Nations of the Earth.'

The creature has been approaching Chamcha while delivering herself of these lines; – unfastening, the while, her blouse; – and he, mongoose to her cobra, stands there transfixed; while she, exposing a shapely right breast, and offering it to him, points out that she has drawn upon it, – as an act of civic pride, – the map of London, no less, in red magic-marker, with the river all in blue. The metropolis summons him; – but he, giving an entirely Dickensian cry, pushes his way out of the Curiosity Shop into the madness of the street.

Gibreel is looking directly at him from London Bridge; their eyes – or so it seems to Chamcha – meet. Yes: Gibreel lifts, and waves, an unexcited arm.

What follows is tragedy. – Or, at the least the echo of tragedy, the full-blooded original being unavailable to modern men and women, so it's said. – A burlesque for our degraded, imitative times, in which clowns re-enact what was first done by heroes and by kings. – Well, then, so be it. – The question that's asked here remains as large as ever it was: which is, the nature of evil, how it's born, why it grows, how it takes unilateral possession of a many-sided human soul. Or, let's say: the enigma of Iago.

It's not unknown for literary-theatrical exegetes, defeated by the character, to ascribe his actions to 'motiveless malignity'. Evil is evil and will do evil, and that's that; the serpent's poison is his very definition. – Well, such shruggings-off will not pass muster here. My Chamcha may be no Ancient of Venice, my Allie no smothered Desdemona, Farishta no match for the Moor, but they will, at least, be costumed in such explanations as my understanding will allow. – And so, now, Gibreel waves in greeting; Chamcha approaches; the curtain rises on a darkening stage.

Let's observe, first, how isolated this Saladin is; his only willing companion an inebriated and cartographically bosomed stranger, he struggles alone through that partying throng in which all persons appear to be (and are not) one another's friends; – while there on London Bridge stands Farishta, beset by admirers, at the very centre of the crowd;

and, next, let us appreciate the effect on Chamcha, who loved England in the form of his lost English wife, – of the golden, pale and glacial presence by Farishta's side of Alleluia Cone; he snatches a glass from a passing waiter's tray, drinks the wine fast, takes another; and seems to see, in distant Allie, the entirety of his loss;

and in other ways, as well, Gibreel is fast becoming the sum of Saladin's defeats; – there with him now, at this very moment, is another traitor; mutton dressed as lamb, fifty plus and batting her eyelashes like an eighteen-year-old, is Chamcha's agent, the redoubtable Charlie Sellers; – you wouldn't liken *him* to a Transylvanian bloodsucker, would you, Charlie, the irate watcher inwardly cries; – and grabs another glass; – and sees, at its bottom, his own anonymity, the other's equal celebrity, and the great injustice of the division;

most especially – he bitterly reflects – because Gibreel, London's conqueror, can see no value in the world now falling at his feet! – why, the bastard always sneered at the place, Proper London, Vilayet, the English, Spoono, what cold fish they are, I swear; – Chamcha, moving inexorably towards him through the crowd, seems to see, *right now*, that same sneer upon Farishta's face, that scorn of an inverted Podsnap, for whom all things English are worthy of derision instead of praise; – O God, the cruelty of it, that he, Saladin, whose goal and crusade it was to make this town his own, should have to see it kneeling before his contemptuous rival! – so there is also this: that Chamcha longs to stand in Farishta's shoes, while his own footwear is of no interest whatsoever to Gibreel.

What is unforgivable?

Chamcha, looking upon Farishta's face for the first time since their rough parting in Rosa Diamond's hall, seeing the strange blankness in the other's eyes, recalls with overwhelming force the earlier blankness, Gibreel standing on the stairs and doing nothing while he, Chamcha, horned and captive, was dragged into the night; and feels the return of hatred, feels it filling him bottom-to-top with fresh green bile, *never mind about excuses*, it cries, *to hell with mitigations and what-could-he-have-dones; what's beyond forgiveness is beyond. You can't judge an internal injury by the size of the hole.*

So: Gibreel Farishta, put on trial by Chamcha, gets a rougher ride than Mimi and Billy in New York, and is declared guilty, for all perpetuity, of the Inexcusable Thing. From which what follows, follows. – But we may permit ourselves to speculate a while about the true nature of this Ultimate, this Inexpiable Offence. –

Is it really, can it be, simply his silence on Rosa's stairs? – Or are there deeper resentments here, gripes for which this so-called Primary Cause is, in truth, no more than a substitute, a front? – For are they not conjoined opposites, these two, each man the other's shadow? – One seeking to be transformed into the foreignness he admires, the other preferring, contemptuously, to transform; one, a hapless fellow who seems to be continually punished for uncommitted crimes, the other, called angelic by one and all, the type of man who gets away with everything. – We may describe Chamcha as being somewhat less than life-size; but loud, vulgar Gibreel is, without question, a good deal larger than life, a disparity which might easily inspire neo-Procrustean lusts in Chamcha: to stretch himself by cutting Farishta down to size.

What is unforgivable?

What if not the shivering nakedness of being *wholly known* to a person one does not trust? – And has not Gibreel seen Saladin Chamcha in circumstances – hijack, fall, arrest – in which the secrets of the self were utterly exposed?

Well, then. – Are we coming closer to it? Should we even say that these are two fundamentally different *types* of self? Might we not agree that Gibreel, for all his stage-name and performances; and in spite of born-again slogans, new beginnings, metamorphoses; – has wished to remain, to a large degree, *continuous* – that is, joined to and arising from his past; – that he chose neither near-fatal illness nor transmuting fall; that, in point of fact, he fears above all things the altered states in which his dreams leak into, and overwhelm, his waking self, making him that angelic Gibreel he has no desire to be; – so that his is still a self which, for our present purposes, we may describe as 'true' ... whereas Saladin Chamcha is a creature of *selected* discontinuities, a *willing* re-invention; his *preferred* revolt against history being what makes him, in our chosen idiom, 'false'? And might we then not go on to say that it is this falsity of self that makes possible in Chamcha a worse and deeper falsity – call this 'evil' – and that this is the truth, the door, that was opened in him by his fall? – While Gibreel, to follow the logic of our established terminology, is to be considered 'good' by virtue of *wishing to remain*, for all his vicissitudes, at bottom an untranslated man.

– But, and again but: this sounds, does it not, dangerously like an intentionalist fallacy? – Such distinctions, resting as they must on an idea of the self as being (ideally) homogeneous, non-hybrid, 'pure', – an utterly fantastic notion! – cannot, must not, suffice. No! Let's rather say an even harder thing: that evil may not be as far beneath our surfaces as we like to say it is. – That, in fact, we fall towards it *naturally*, that is, *not against our natures*. – And that Saladin Chamcha set out to destroy Gibreel Farishta because, finally, it proved so easy to do; the true appeal of evil being the seductive ease with which one may embark upon that road. (And, let us add in conclusion, the later impossibility of return.)

Saladin Chamcha, however, insists on a simpler line. 'It was his treason at Rosa Diamond's house; his silence, nothing more.'

He sets foot upon the counterfeit London Bridge. From a nearby red-and-white-striped puppeteer's booth, Mr Punch – whacking Judy – calls out to him: *That's the way to do it!* After which Gibreel, too, speaks a greeting, the enthusiasm of the words undone by the incongruous listlessness of the voice: 'Spoono, is it you. You bloody devil. There you are, big as life. Come here, you Salad baba, old Chumch.'

This happened:

The moment Saladin Chamcha got close enough to Allie Cone to be transfixed, and somewhat chilled, by her eyes, he felt his reborn animosity towards Gibreel extending itself to her, with her degree-zero go-to-hell look, her air of being privy to some great, secret mystery of the universe; also, her quality of what he would afterwards think of as *wilderness*, a hard, sparse thing, anti-social, self-contained, an essence. Why did it annoy him so much? Why, before she'd even opened her mouth, had he characterized her as part of the enemy?

Perhaps because he desired her; and desired, even more, what he took to be that inner certainty of hers; lacking which, he envied it, and sought to damage what he envied. If love is a yearning to be like (even to become) the beloved, then hatred, it must be said, can be engendered by the same ambition, when it cannot be fulfilled.

This happened: Chamcha invented an Allie, and became his fiction's antagonist . . . he showed none of this. He smiled, shook hands, was pleased to meet her; and embraced Gibreel. *I follow him to serve my turn upon him.* Allie, suspecting nothing, excused herself. The two of them must have so much to catch up on, she said; and, promising to return soon, departed: off, as she put it, to explore. He noticed that she hobbled slightly for a step or two; then paused, and strode off strongly. Among the things he did not know about her was her pain.

Not knowing that the Gibreel standing before him, remote of eye and perfunctory in his greeting, was under the most attentive medical supervision; – or that he was obliged to take, on a daily basis, certain drugs that dulled his senses, because of the very real possibility of a recurrence of his no-longer-nameless illness, that is to say, paranoid schizophrenia; – or that he had long been kept away, at Allie's absolute insistence, from the movie people whom she had come strongly to distrust, ever since his last rampage; – or that their presence at the Battuta–Mamoulian party was a thing to which she had been whole-heartedly opposed, acquiescing only after a terrible scene in which Gibreel had roared that he would be kept a prisoner no longer, and that he was determined to make a further effort to re-enter his 'real life'; – or that the effort of looking after a disturbed lover who was capable of seeing small bat-like imps hanging upside down in the refrigerator had worn Allie thin as a worn-out shirt, forcing upon her the roles of nurse, scapegoat and crutch – requiring her, in sum, to act against her own complex and troubled nature; – not knowing any of this, failing to comprehend that the Gibreel at whom he was looking, and believed he saw, Gibreel the embodiment of all the good fortune that the Fury-haunted Chamcha so signally lacked, was as much the creature of his fancy, as much a fiction, as his invented-resented Allie, that classic drop-dead blonde or femme fatale conjured up by his envious, tormented, Oresteian imagination, – Saladin in his ignorance nevertheless penetrated, by the merest chance, the chink in Gibreel's (admittedly somewhat quixotic) armour, and understood how his hated Other might most swiftly be unmade.

Gibreel's banal question made the opening. Limited by sedatives to small-talk, he asked vaguely: 'And how, tell me, is your goodwife?' At which Chamcha, his tongue loosened by alcohol, blurted out: 'How? Knocked up. Enceinte. Great with fucking child.' Soporific Gibreel missed the violence in this speech, beamed absently, placed an arm around Saladin's shoulders. 'Shabash, mubarak,' he offered congratulations. 'Spoono! Damn speedy work.'

'Congratulate her lover,' Saladin thickly raged. 'My old friend, Jumpy Joshi. Now there, I admit it, is a man. Women go wild, it seems. God knows why. They want his goddamn babies and they don't even wait to ask his leave.'

'For instance who?' Gibreel yelled, making heads turn and Chamcha recoil in surprise. 'Who who who?' he hooted, causing tipsy giggles. Saladin Chamcha laughed, too: but without pleasure. 'I'll tell you who for instance. My wife for instance, that's who. That is no lady, mister Farishta, Gibreel. Pamela, my no-lady wife.'

At this very moment, as luck would have it, – while Saladin in his cups was quite ignorant of the effect his words were having on Gibreel, – for whom two images had explosively combined, the first being his sudden memory of Rekha Merchant on a flying carpet warning him of Allie's secret wish to have a baby without informing the father, *who asks the seed for permission to plant*, and the second being an envisioning of the body of the martial arts instructor conjoined in high-kicking carnality with the same Miss Alleluia Cone, – the figure of Jumpy Joshi was seen crossing 'Southwark Bridge' in a state of some agitation, – hunting, in fact, for Pamela, from whom he had become separated during the same rush of singing Dickensians which had pushed Saladin towards the metropolitan breasts of the young woman in the Curiosity Shop. 'Talk of the devil,' Saladin pointed. 'There the bastard goes.' He turned towards Gibreel: but Gibreel had gone.

Allie Cone reappeared, angry, frantic. 'Where is he? Jesus! Can't I even leave him for a fucking *second*? Couldn't you have kept your sodding *eyes* on him?'

'Why, what's the matter – ?' But now Allie had plunged into the crowd, so that when Chamcha saw Gibreel crossing 'Southwark Bridge' she was out of earshot. – And here was Pamela, demanding: 'Have you seen Jumpy?' – And he pointed, 'That way,' whereupon she, too, vanished without a word of courtesy; and now Jumpy was seen, crossing 'Southwark Bridge' in the opposite direction, curly hair wilder than ever, coathanger shoulders hunched inside the greatcoat he had refused to remove, eyes searching, thumb homing in on mouth; – and, a little later, Gibreel headed across the simulacrum of that bridge Which Is Of Iron, going the same way as Jumpy went.

In short, events had begun to border on the farcical; but when, some minutes later, the actor playing the role of 'Gaffer Hexam', who kept watch over that stretch of the Dickensian Thames for floating corpses, to relieve them of their valuables before handing them over to the police, – came rowing rapidly down the studio river with his stipulated ragged, grizzled hair standing straight up on end, the farce was instantly terminated; for there in his disreputable boat lay the insensate body of Jumpy Joshi in his waterlogged greatcoat. 'Knocked cold,' the boatman cried, pointing to the huge lump rising up at the back of Jumpy's skull, 'and being unconscious in the water it's a miracle he never drowned.'

One week after that, in response to an impassioned telephone call from Allie Cone, who had tracked him down via Sisodia, Battuta and finally Mimi, and who appeared to have defrosted quite a bit, Saladin Chamcha found himself in the passenger seat of a three-

year-old silver Citroën station wagon which the future Alicja
Boniek had presented to her daughter before leaving for an
extended Californian stay. Allie had met him at Carlisle station,
repeating her earlier telephonic apologies – 'I'd no right to speak
to you like that; you knew nothing, I mean about his, well, thank
heavens nobody saw the attack, and it seems to have been hushed
up, but that poor man, an oar on the head from behind, it's too
bad; the point is, we've taken a place up north, friends of mine are
away, it just seemed best to get out of range of human beings, and,
well, he's been asking for you; you could really help him, I think,
and to be frank I could do with the help myself,' which left
Saladin little the wiser but consumed by curiosity – and now Scot-
land was rushing past the Citroën windows at alarming speed: an
edge of Hadrian's Wall, the old elopers' haven Gretna Green,
and then inland towards the Southern Uplands; Ecclefechan,
Lockerbie, Beattock, Elvanfoot. Chamcha tended to think of all
non-metropolitan locales as the deeps of interstellar space, and
journeys into them as fraught with peril: for to break down in
such emptiness would surely be to die alone and undiscovered. He
had noted warily that one of the Citroën's headlamps was broken,
that the fuel gauge was in the red (it turned out to be broken,
too), the daylight was failing, and Allie was driving as if the A74
were the track at Silverstone on a sunny day. 'He can't get far
without transport, but you never know,' she explained grimly.
'Three days ago he stole the car keys and they found him heading
the wrong way up an exit road on the M6, shouting about
damnation. *Prepare for the vengeance of the Lord,* he told the
motorway cops, *for I shall soon summon my lieutenant, Azraeel.* They
wrote it all down in their little books.' Chamcha, his heart still
filled with his own vengeful lusts, affected sympathy and shock.
'And Jumpy?' he inquired. Allie took both hands off the wheel
and spread them in an I-give-up gesture, while the car wobbled
terrifyingly across the bendy road. 'The doctors say the possessive
jealousy could be part of the same thing; at least, it can set the
madness off, like a fuse.'

She was glad of the chance to talk; and Chamcha lent her a willing ear. If she trusted him, it was because Gibreel did, too; he had no intention of demanding that trust. *Once he betrayed my trust; now let him, for a time, have confidence in me.* He was a tyro puppeteer; it was necessary to study the strings, to find out what was connected to what . . . 'I can't help it,' Allie was saying. 'I feel in some obscure way to blame for him. Our life isn't working out and it's my fault. My mother gets angry when I talk like this.' Alicja, on the verge of catching the plane west, berated her daughter at Terminal Three. 'I don't understand where you get these notions from,' she cried amid backpackers, briefcases and weeping Asian mums. 'You could say your father's life didn't go according to plan, either. So he should be blamed for the camps? Study history, Alleluia. In this century history stopped paying attention to the old psychological orientation of reality. I mean, these days, character isn't destiny any more. Economics is destiny. Ideology is destiny. Bombs are destiny. What does a famine, a gas chamber, a grenade care how you lived your life? Crisis comes, death comes, and your pathetic individual self doesn't have a thing to do with it, only to suffer the effects. This Gibreel of yours: maybe he's how history happens to you.' She had returned, without warning, to the grand style of wardrobe preferred by Otto Cone, and, it seemed, to an oratorical manner that suited the big black hats and frilly suits. 'Enjoy California, Mother,' Allie said sharply. 'One of us is happy,' Alicja said. 'Why shouldn't it be me?' And before her daughter could answer, she swept off past the passengers-only barrier, flourishing passport, boarding-pass, ticket, heading for the duty-free bottles of *Opium* and Gordon's Gin, which were on sale beneath an illuminated sign reading SAY HELLO TO THE GOOD BUYS.

In the last light, the road rounded a spur of treeless, heather-covered hills. Long ago, in another country, another twilight, Chamcha had rounded another such spur and come into sight of the remains of Persepolis. Now, however, he was heading for a human ruin; not to admire, and maybe even (for the decision to do evil is never finally taken until the very instant of the deed;

there is always a last chance to withdraw) to vandalize. To scrawl his name in Gibreel's flesh: *Saladin woz ear*. 'Why stay with him?' he asked Allie, and to his surprise she blushed. 'Why not spare yourself the pain?'

'I don't really know you, not at all, really,' she began, then paused and made a choice. 'I'm not proud of the answer, but it's the truth,' she said. 'It's the sex. We're unbelievable together, perfect, like nothing I've known. Dream lovers. He just seems to, to *know*. To know *me*.' She fell silent; the night hid her face. Chamcha's bitterness surged up again. Dream lovers were all around him; he, dreamless, could only watch. He gritted angry teeth; and bit, by mistake, his tongue.

Gibreel and Allie had holed up in Durisdeer, a village so small it didn't have a pub, and were living in a deconsecrated Free-kirk converted – the quasi-religious term sounded strange to Chamcha – by an architect friend of Allie's who had made a fortune out of such metamorphoses of the sacred into the profane. It struck Saladin as a gloomy sort of place, for all its white walls, recessed spotlights and wall-to-wall shag-pile carpeting. There were gravestones in the garden. As a retreat for a man suffering from paranoid delusions of being the chief archangel of God, Chamcha reflected, it wouldn't have been his own first choice. The Freekirk was set a little apart from the dozen or so other stone-and-tile houses that made up the community: isolated even within this isolation. Gibreel was standing at the door, a shadow against the illuminated hallway, when the car pulled up. 'You got here,' he shouted. 'Yaar, too good. Welcome to bloody jail.'

The drugs made Gibreel clumsy. As the three of them sat around the pitch-pine kitchen table beneath the gentrified pull-down dimmer-switched lighting, he twice knocked over his coffee-cup (he was ostentatiously off booze; Allie, pouring two generous shots of Scotch, kept Chamcha company), and, cursing, stumbled about the kitchen for paper-towels to mop up the mess. 'When I get sick of being this way I just cut down without telling her,' he confessed. 'And then the shit starts happening. I swear to you, Spoono, I can't bear the bloody idea that it will never stop, that the only choice is drugs or bugs in the brain. I can't bloody bear it. I swear, yaar, if I thought that was it, then, bas, I don't know, I'd, I don't know what.'

'Shut your face,' Allie softly said. But he shouted out: 'Spoono, I even hit her, do you know that? Bloody hell. One day I thought she was some rakshasa type of demon and I just went for her. Do you know how strong it is, the strength of madness?'

'Fortunately for me I'd been going to – oops, eek – those self-defence classes,' Allie grinned. 'He's exaggerating to save face. Actually he was the one who ended up banging his head on the floor.' – 'Right here,' Gibreel sheepishly assented. The kitchen floor was made of large flagstones. 'Painful,' Chamcha hazarded. 'Damn right,' Gibreel roared, strangely cheerful now. 'Knocked me bilkul cold.'

The Freekirk's interior had been divided into a large two-storey (in estate agent's jargon, 'double volume') reception-room – the former hall of congregation – and a more conventional half, with kitchen and utilities downstairs and bedrooms and bathroom above. Unable for some reason to sleep, Chamcha wandered at midnight into the great (and cold: the heatwave might be continuing in the south of England, but there wasn't a ripple of it up here, where the climate was autumnal and chill) living-room, and wandered among the ghost-voices of banished preachers while Gibreel and Allie made high-volume love. *Like Pamela.* He tried to think of Mishal, of Zeeny Vakil, but it didn't work. Stuffing his fingers in his ears, he fought against the sound effects of the copulation of Farishta and Alleluia Cone.

Theirs had been a high-risk conjoining from the start, he reflected: first, Gibreel's dramatic abandonment of career and rush across the earth, and now, Allie's uncompromising determination to *see it through*, to defeat in him this mad, angelic divinity and restore the humanity she loved. No compromises for them; they were going for broke. Whereas he, Saladin, had declared himself content to live under the same roof as his wife and her lover boy. Which was the better way? Captain Ahab drowned, he reminded himself; it was the trimmer, Ishmael, who survived.

⤝⤞

In the morning Gibreel ordered an ascent of the local 'Top'. But Allie declined, although it was plain to Chamcha that her return to the countryside had caused her to glow with joy. 'Bloody flat-foot mame,' Gibreel cursed her lovingly. 'Come on, Salad. Us damn city slickers can show the Everest conqueror how to climb. What a bloody upside-down life, yaar. We go mountain-climbing while she sits here and makes business calls.' Saladin's thoughts were racing: he understood, now, that strange hobble at Shepperton; understood, too, that this secluded haven would have to be temporary – that Allie, by coming here, was sacrificing her own life, and wouldn't be able to go on doing so indefinitely. What should he do? Anything? Nothing? – If revenge was to be taken, when and how? 'Get these boots on,' Gibreel commanded. 'You think the rain will hold off all fucking day?'

It didn't. By the time they reached the stone cairn at the summit of Gibreel's chosen climb, they were enveloped in a fine drizzle. 'Damn good show,' Gibreel panted. 'Look: there she is, down there, sitting back like the Grand Panjandrum.' He pointed down at the Freekirk. Chamcha, his heart pounding, was feeling foolish. He must start behaving like a man with a ticker problem. Where was the glory in dying of heart failure on this nothing of a Top, for nothing, in the rain? Then Gibreel got out his field-glasses and started scanning the valley. There were hardly any moving figures to be seen – two or three men and dogs, some sheep, no more. Gibreel tracked the men with his binoculars. 'Now that we're alone,' he suddenly said, 'I can tell you why we really came away to this damn empty hole. It's because of her. Yes, yes; don't be fooled by my act! It's all her bloody beauty. Men, Spoono: they chase her like goddamn flies. I swear! I see them, slobbering and grabbing. It isn't right. She is a very private person, the most private person in the world. We have to protect her from lust.'

This speech took Saladin by surprise. You poor bastard, he thought, you really are going off your wretched head at a rate of knots. And, hard on the heels of this thought, a second sentence appeared, as if by magic, in his head: *Don't imagine that means I'll let you off.*

On the drive back to the Carlisle railway station, Chamcha mentioned the depopulation of the countryside. 'There's no work,' Allie said. 'So it's empty. Gibreel says he can't get used to the idea that all this space indicates poverty: says it looks like luxury to him, after India's crowds.' – 'And your work?' Chamcha asked. 'What about that?' She smiled at him, the ice-maiden façade long gone. 'You're a nice man to ask. I keep thinking, one day it'll be my life in the middle, taking first place. Or, well, although I find it hard to use the first person plural: our life. That sounds better, right?'

'Don't let him cut you off,' Saladin advised. 'From Jumpy, from your own worlds, whatever.' This was the moment at which his campaign could truly be said to have begun; when he set a foot upon that effortless, seductive road on which there was only one way to go. 'You're right,' Allie was saying. 'God, if he only knew. His precious Sisodia, for example: it's not just seven-foot starlets he goes for, though he sure as hell likes those.' – 'He made a pass,' Chamcha guessed; and, simultaneously, filed the information away for possible later use. 'He's totally shameless,' Allie laughed. 'It was right under Gibreel's nose. He doesn't mind rejection, though: he just bows, and murmurs *no offoffoffence*, and that's that. Can you imagine if I told Gibreel?'

Chamcha at the railway station wished Allie luck. 'We'll have to be in London for a couple of weeks,' she said through the car window. 'I've got meetings. Maybe you and Gibreel can get together then; this has really done him good.'

'Call any time,' he waved goodbye, and watched the Citroën until it was out of sight.

That Allie Cone, the third point of a triangle of fictions – for had not Gibreel and Allie come together very largely by imagining, out of their own needs, an 'Allie' and a 'Gibreel' with whom each could fall in love; and was not Chamcha now imposing on them the requirements of his own troubled and disappointed heart? – was to be the unwitting, innocent agent of Chamcha's revenge, became even plainer to the plotter, Saladin, when he found that Gibreel, with whom he had arranged to spend an equatorial London afternoon, wanted nothing so much as to describe in embarrassing detail the carnal ecstasy of sharing Allie's bed. What manner of people were these, Saladin wondered with distaste, who enjoyed inflicting their intimacies on non-participating others? As Gibreel (with something like relish) described positions, love-bites, the secret vocabularies of desire, they strolled in Brickhall Fields among schoolgirls and roller-skating infants and fathers throwing boomerangs and frisbees incompetently at scornful sons, and picked their way through broiling horizontal secretarial flesh; and Gibreel interrupted his erotic rhapsody to mention, madly, that 'I sometimes look at these pink people and instead of skin, Spoono, what I see is rotting meat; I smell their putrefaction here,' he tapped his nostrils fervently, as if revealing a mystery, 'in my *nose*.' Then once again to Allie's inner thighs, her cloudy eyes, the perfect valley of her lower back, the little cries she liked to make. This was a man in imminent danger of coming apart at the seams. The wild energy, the manic particularity of his descriptions suggested to Chamcha that he'd been cutting down on his dosages again, that he was rolling upwards towards the crest of a deranged high, that condition of febrile excitement that was like blind drunkenness in one respect (according to Allie), namely that Gibreel could remember nothing of what he said or did when, as was inevitable, he came down to earth. – On and on went the descriptions, the unusual length of her nipples, her dislike of having her navel interfered with, the sensitivity of her toes. Chamcha told himself that, madness or no madness, what all this sex-talk revealed (because there had been Allie in the Citroën too) was the *weakness* of their so-called 'grand passion' – a term which Allie had only half-jokingly employed – because, in a phrase, there was nothing else about it that was any good; there was

simply no other aspect of their togetherness *to* rhapsodize about. –
At the same time, however, he felt himself becoming aroused.
He began to see himself standing outside her window, while she
stood there naked like an actress on a screen, and a man's hands
caressed her in a thousand ways, bringing her closer and closer to
ecstasy; he came to see himself as that pair of hands, he could
almost feel her coolness, her responses, almost hear her cries. – He
controlled himself. His desire disgusted him. She was unattainable;
this was pure voyeurism, and he would not succumb to it. – But
the desire Gibreel's revelations had aroused would not go away.

Gibreel's sexual obsession, Chamcha reminded himself, actually
made things easier. 'She's certainly a very attractive woman,' he
murmured by way of an experiment, and was gratified to receive a
furious, strung-out glare in return. After which Gibreel, making a
show of controlling himself, put his arm around Saladin and
boomed: 'Apologies, Spoono, I'm a bad-tempered bugger where
she's concerned. But you and me! We're bhai-bhai! Been through
the worst and come out smiling; come on now, enough of this
little nowhere park. Let's hit town.'

There is the moment before evil; then the moment of; then the
time after, when the step has been taken, and each subsequent
stride becomes progressively easier. 'Fine with me,' Chamcha
replied. 'It's good to see you looking so well.'

A boy of six or seven cycled past them on a BMX bike.
Chamcha, turning his head to follow the boy's progress, saw that
he was moving smoothly away down an avenue of overarching
trees, through which the hot sunlight managed here and there to
drip. The shock of discovering the location of his dream disoriented Chamcha briefly, and left him with a bad taste in his mouth:
the sour flavour of might-have-beens. Gibreel hailed a taxi; and
requested Trafalgar Square.

O, he was in a high good humour that day, rubbishing London
and the English with much of his old brio. Where Chamcha saw
attractively faded grandeur, Gibreel saw a wreck, a Crusoe-city,
marooned on the island of its past, and trying, with the help of a
Man-Friday underclass, to keep up appearances. Under the gaze of

stone lions he chased pigeons, shouting: 'I swear, Spoono, back home these fatties wouldn't last one day; let's take one home for dinner.' Chamcha's Englished soul cringed for shame. Later, in Covent Garden, he described for Gibreel's benefit the day the old fruit and vegetable market moved to Nine Elms. The authorities, worried about rats, had sealed the sewers and killed tens of thousands; but hundreds more survived. 'That day, starving rats swarmed out on to the pavements,' he recalled. 'All the way down the Strand and over Waterloo Bridge, in and out of the shops, desperate for food.' Gibreel snorted. 'Now I know this is a sinking ship,' he cried, and Chamcha felt furious at having given him the opening. 'Even the bloody rats are off.' And, after a pause: 'What they needed was a pied piper, no? Leading them to destruction with a tune.'

When he wasn't insulting the English or describing Allie's body from the roots of her hair to the soft triangle of 'the love-place, the goddamn yoni,' he seemed to wish to make lists: what were Spoono's ten favourite books, he wanted to know; also movies, female film stars, food. Chamcha offered conventional cosmopolitan answers. His movie-list included *Potemkin*, *Kane*, *Otto e Mezzo*, *The Seven Samurai*, *Alphaville*, *El Angel Exterminador*. 'You've been brainwashed,' Gibreel scoffed. 'All this Western art-house crap.' His top ten of everything came from 'back home', and was aggressively lowbrow. *Mother India*, *Mr India*, *Shree Charsawbees*: no Ray, no Mrinal Sen, no Aravindan or Ghatak. 'Your head's so full of junk,' he advised Saladin, 'you forgot everything worth knowing.'

His mounting excitement, his babbling determination to turn the world into a cluster of hit parades, his fierce walking pace – they must have walked twenty miles by the end of their travels – suggested to Chamcha that it wouldn't take much, now, to push him over the edge. *It seems I turned out to be a confidence man, too, Mimi. The art of the assassin is to draw the victim close; makes him easier to knife.* 'I'm getting hungry,' Gibreel imperiously announced. 'Take me to one of your top-ten eateries.'

In the taxicab, Gibreel needled Chamcha, who had not

informed him of the destination. 'Some Frenchy joint, na? Or
Japanese, with raw fishes and octopuses. God, why I trust your
taste.'

They arrived at the Shaandaar Café.

Jumpy wasn't there.

Nor, apparently, had Mishal Sufyan patched things up with her
mother; Mishal and Hanif were absent, and neither Anahita nor
her mother gave Chamcha a greeting that could be described as
warm. Only Haji Sufyan was welcoming: 'Come, come, sit;
you're looking good.' The café was oddly empty, and even
Gibreel's presence failed to create much of a stir. It took Chamcha
a few seconds to understand what was up; then he saw the quartet
of white youths sitting at a corner table, spoiling for a fight.

The young Bengali waiter (whom Hind had been obliged to
employ after her elder daughter's departure) came over and took
their order – aubergines, sikh kababs, rice – while staring angrily
in the direction of the troublesome quartet, who were, as Saladin
now perceived, very drunk indeed. The waiter, Amin, was as
annoyed with Sufyan as the drunks. 'Should never have let them
sit,' he mumbled to Chamcha and Gibreel. 'Now I'm obliged to
serve. It's okay for the seth; he's not the front line, see.'

The drunks got their food at the same time as Chamcha and
Gibreel. When they started complaining about the cooking, the
atmosphere in the room grew even more highly charged. Finally
they stood up. 'We're not eating this shit, you cunts,' yelled the
leader, a tiny, runty fellow with sandy hair, a pale thin face, and
spots. 'It's *shit*. You can go fuck yourselves, fucking cunts.' His
three companions, giggling and swearing, left the café. The leader
lingered for a moment. 'Enjoying your food?' he screamed at
Chamcha and Gibreel. 'It's fucking shit. Is that what you eat at
home, is it? Cunts.' Gibreel was wearing an expression that said,
loud and clear: so this is what the British, that great nation of con-
querors, have become in the end. He did not respond. The little
rat-faced speaker came over. 'I asked you a fucking question,' he

said. 'I said. Are you fucking enjoying your fucking *shit dinner?*'
And Saladin Chamcha, perhaps out of his annoyance that Gibreel
had not been confronted by the man he'd all but killed – catching
him off guard from behind, the coward's way – found himself
answering: 'We would be, if it wasn't for you.' Ratboy, swaying
on his feet, digested this information; and then did a very
surprising thing. Taking a deep breath, he drew himself up to his
full five foot five; then leaned forward, and spat violently and
copiously all over the food.

'Baba, if that's in your top ten,' Gibreel said in the taxi home,
'don't take me to the places you don't like so much.'

' "Minnamin, Gut mag alkan, Pern dirstan," ' Chamcha replied. 'It means, "My darling, God makes hungry, the Devil
thirsty." Nabokov.'

'Him again,' Gibreel complained. 'What bloody language?'

'He made it up. It's what Kinbote's Zemblan nurse tells him as
a child. In *Pale Fire.*'

'*Perndirstan,*' Farishta repeated. 'Sounds like a country: Hell,
maybe. I give up, anyway. How are you supposed to read a man
who writes in a made-up lingo of his own?'

They were almost back at Allie's flat overlooking Brickhall
Fields. 'The playwright Strindberg,' Chamcha said, absently, as if
following some profound train of thought, 'after two unhappy
marriages, wedded a famous and lovely twenty-year-old actress
called Harriet Bosse. In the *Dream* she was a great Puck. He wrote
for her, too: the part of Eleanora in *Easter.* An "angel of peace".
The young men went crazy for her, and Strindberg, well, he got
so jealous he almost lost his mind. He tried to keep her locked up
at home, far from the eyes of men. She wanted to travel; he
brought her travel books. It was like the old Cliff Richard
song: *Gonna lock her up in a trunk/so no big hunk/can steal her away
from me.*'

Farishta's heavy head nodded in recognition. He had fallen into
a kind of reverie. 'What happened?' he inquired as they reached
their destination. 'She left him,' Chamcha innocently declared.
'She said she could not reconcile him with the human race.'

Alleluia Cone read, as she walked home from the Tube, her mother's deliriously happy letter from Stanford, Calif. 'If people tell you happiness is unattainable,' Alicja wrote in large, looping, back-leaning, left-handed letters, 'kindly point them in my direction. I'll put them straight. I found it twice, the first time with your father, as you know, the second with this kind, broad man whose face is the exact colour of the oranges that grow all over these parts. Contentment, Allie. It beats excitement. Try it, you'll like it.' When she looked up, Allie saw Maurice Wilson's ghost sitting atop a large copper beech-tree in his usual woollen attire – tam-o'-shanter, diamond-pattern Pringle jersey, plus-fours – looking uncomfortably overdressed in the heat. 'I've no time for you now,' she told him, and he shrugged. *I can wait.* Her feet were bad again. She set her jaw and marched on.

Saladin Chamcha, concealed behind the very copper beech from which Maurice Wilson's ghost was surveying Allie's painful progress, observed Gibreel Farishta bursting out of the front door of the block of flats in which he'd been waiting impatiently for her return; observed him red-eyed and raving. The demons of jealousy were sitting on his shoulders, and he was screaming out the same old song, wherethehell whothe whatthe dontthinkyoucanpullthewool howdareyou bitchbitchbitch. It appeared that Strindberg had succeeded where Jumpy (because absent) had failed.

The watcher in the upper branches dematerialized; the other, with a satisfied nod, strolled away down an avenue of shady, spreading trees.

The telephone calls which now began to be received, first at their London residence and subsequently at a remote address in Dumfries and Galloway, by both Allie and Gibreel, were not too frequent; then again, they could not be termed infrequent. Nor were there too many voices to be plausible; then again, there were quite enough. These were not brief calls, such as those made by heavy breathers and other abusers of the telephone network, but, conversely, they never lasted long enough for the police, eavesdropping, to track them to their source. Nor did the whole unsavoury episode last very long – a mere matter of three and a half weeks, after which the callers desisted forever; but it might also be mentioned that it went on exactly as long as it needed to, that is, until it had driven Gibreel Farishta to do to Allie Cone what he had previously done to Saladin – namely, the Unforgivable Thing.

It should be said that nobody, not Allie, not Gibreel, not even the professional phone-tappers they brought in, ever suspected the calls of being a single man's work; but for Saladin Chamcha, once renowned (if only in somewhat specialist circles) as the Man of a Thousand Voices, such a deception was a simple matter, entirely lacking in effort or risk. In all, he was obliged to select (from his thousand voices and a voice) a total of no more than thirty-nine.

When Allie answered, she heard unknown men murmuring intimate secrets in her ear, strangers who seemed to know her body's most remote recesses, faceless beings who gave evidence of having learned, by experience, her choicest preferences among the myriad forms of love; and once the attempts at tracing the calls had begun her humiliation grew, because now she was unable simply to replace the receiver, but had to stand and listen, hot in the face and cold along the spine, making attempts (which didn't work) actually to prolong the calls.

Gibreel also got his share of voices: superb Byronic aristocrats boasting of having 'conquered Everest', sneering guttersnipes, unctuous best-friend voices mingling warning and mock-commiseration, *a word to the wise, how stupid can you, don't you know yet what she's, anything in trousers, you poor moron, take it from a pal.* But one voice stood out from the rest, the high soulful voice of a poet, one of the first voices Gibreel heard and the one that got deepest under his skin; a voice that spoke exclusively in rhyme, reciting doggerel verses of an understated naïvety, even innocence, which contrasted so greatly with the masturbatory coarseness of most of the other callers that Gibreel soon came to think of it as the most insidiously menacing of all.

> *I like coffee, I like tea,*
> *I like things you do with me.*

Tell her that, the voice swooned, and rang off. Another day it returned with another jingle:

> *I like butter, I like toast,*
> *You're the one I love the most.*

Give her that message, too; if you'd be so kind. There was something demonic, Gibreel decided, something profoundly immoral about cloaking corruption in this greetings-card tum-ti-tum.

> *Rosy apple, lemon tart,*
> *Here's the name of my sweetheart.*

A . . . l . . . l . . . Gibreel, in disgust and fear, banged down the receiver; and trembled. After that the versifier stopped calling for a while; but his was the voice Gibreel started waiting for, dreading its reappearance, having perhaps accepted, at some level deeper than consciousness, that this infernal, childlike evil was what would finish him off for good.

But O how easy it all turned out to be! How comfortably evil lodged in those supple, infinitely flexible vocal cords, those puppetmaster's strings! How surely it stepped out along the high wires of the telephone system, poised as a barefoot acrobat; how confidently it entered the victims' presence, as certain of its effect as a handsome man in a perfectly tailored suit! And how carefully it bided its time, sending forth every voice but the voice that would deliver the coup de grâce – for Saladin, too, had understood the doggerel's special potency – deep voices and squeaky voices, slow ones, quick ones, sad and cheerful, aggression-laden and shy. One by one, they dripped into Gibreel's ears, weakening his hold on the real world, drawing him little by little into their deceitful web, so that little by little their obscene, invented women began to coat the real woman like a viscous, green film, and in spite of his protestations to the contrary he started slipping away from her; and then it was time for the return of the little, satanic verses that made him mad.

> *Roses are red, violets are blue,*
> *Sugar never tasted sweet as you.*

Pass it on. He returned as innocent as ever, giving birth to a turmoil of butterflies in Gibreel's knotting stomach. After that the rhymes came thick and fast. They could have the smuttiness of the school playground:

> *When she's down at Waterloo*
> *She don't wear no yes she do*
> *When she's up at Leicester Square*
> *She don't wear no underwear;*

or, once or twice, the rhythm of a cheerleader's chant.

> *Knickerknacker, firecracker,*
> *Sis! Boom! Bah!*
> *Alleluia! Alleluia!*
> *Rah! Rah! Rah!*

And lastly, when they had returned to London, and Allie was absent at the ceremonial opening of a freezer food mart in Hounslow, the last rhyme.

Violets are blue, roses are red,
I've got her right here in my bed.

Goodbye, sucker.

Dialling tone.

Alleluia Cone returned to find Gibreel gone, and in the vandal-
ized silence of her apartment she determined that this time she
would not have him back, no matter in what sorry condition or
how wheedlingly he came crawling to her, pleading for forgiveness and for love; because before he left he had wrought a terrible
vengeance upon her, destroying every one of the surrogate
Himalayas she had collected over the years, thawing the ice-
Everest she kept in her freezer, pulling down and ripping to shreds
the parachute-silk peaks that rose above her bed, and hacking to
pieces (he'd used the small axe she kept with the fire extinguisher
in the broom cupboard) the priceless whittled memento of her
conquest of Chomolungma, given her by Pemba the sherpa, as a
warning as well as a commemoration. *To Ali Bibi. We were luck.*
Not to try again.

She flung open sash windows and screamed abuse at the innocent Fields beneath. 'Die slowly! Burn in hell!'

Then, weeping, she rang Saladin Chamcha to tell him the
bad news.

Mr John Maslama, owner of the Hot Wax nightclub, the record
chain of the same name, and of 'Fair Winds', the legendary store
where you could get yourself the finest horns – clarinets, saxophones, trombones – that a person could find to blow in the
whole of London town, was a busy man, so he would always
ascribe to the intervention of Divine Providence the happy
chance that caused him to be present in the trumpet store when

the Archangel of God walked in with thunder and lightning sitting like laurels upon his noble brow. Being a practical businessman, Mr. Maslama had up to this point concealed from his employees his extracurricular work as the chief herald of the returned Celestial and Semi-Godlike Being, sticking posters in his shop-windows only when he was sure he was unobserved, neglecting to sign the display advertisements he bought in newspapers and magazines at considerable personal expense, proclaiming the imminent Glory of the Coming of the Lord. He issued press releases through a public relations subsidiary of the Valance agency, asking that his own anonymity be guarded carefully. 'Our client is in a position to state,' these releases – which enjoyed, for a time, an amused vogue among Fleet Street diarists – cryptically announced, 'that his eyes have seen the Glory referred to above. Gibreel is among us at this moment, somewhere in the inner city of London – probably in Camden, Brickhall, Tower Hamlets or Hackney – and he will reveal himself soon, perhaps within days or weeks.' – All of this was obscure to the three tall, languid, male attendants in the Fair Winds store (Maslama refused to employ women sales assistants here; 'my motto,' he was fond of saying, 'is that nobody trusts a female to help him with his horn'); which was why none of them could believe their eyes when their hard-nosed employer suddenly underwent a complete change of personality, and rushed over to this wild, unshaven stranger as if he were God Almighty – with his two-tone patent leather shoes, Armani suit and slicked down Robert de Niro hair above proliferating eyebrows, Maslama didn't look the crawling type, but that's what he was *doing*, all right, on his goddamn *belly*, pushing his staff aside, *I'll attend to the gentleman myself,* bowing and scraping, walking backwards, would you believe? – Anyway, the stranger had this *fat money-belt* under his shirt and started hauling out numbers of high-denomination notes; he pointed at a trumpet on a high shelf, *that's the one*, just like that, hardly looked at it, and Mr Maslama was up the ladder *pronto*, I'll-get-it-I-said-I'll-*get*-it, and now the truly amazing part, he tried to refuse payment, Maslama!, it was no no *sir* no charge *sir*, but the stranger paid anyway, stuffing the notes into Maslama's upper jacket-pocket as if he were some sort of *bellhop*, you had to be there, and last of all the customer turns to the whole store and yells at the top of his voice, *I am the right hand of God.* – Straight up, you wouldn't credit it, the bloody day of judgment was at hand. – Maslama was right out of it after that, well shaken he was, he actually fell to his actual *knees.* – Then the stranger held the trumpet up over his head and shouted *I name this trumpet Azraeel, the Last Trump, the Exterminator of Men!* – and we just stood there, I tell you, turned to stone, because all around the fucking insane, *certifiable* bastard's head there was this bright *glow*, you know?, streaming out, like, from a point behind his head.

A halo.

Say what you like, the three shop-attendants afterwards repeated to anyone who would listen, *say what you like, but we saw what we saw.*

3

The death of Dr Uhuru Simba, formerly Sylvester Roberts, while in custody awaiting trial, was described by the Brickhall constabulary's community liaison officer, a certain Inspector Stephen Kinch, as 'a million-to-one shot'. It appeared that Dr Simba had been experiencing a nightmare so terrifying that it had caused him to scream piercingly in his sleep, attracting the immediate attention of the two duty officers. These gentlemen, rushing to his cell, arrived in time to see the still-sleeping form of the gigantic man literally lift off its bunk under the malign influence of the dream and plunge to the floor. A loud snap was heard by both officers; it was the sound of Dr Uhuru Simba's neck breaking. Death had been instantaneous.

The dead man's minuscule mother, Antoinette Roberts, standing in a cheap black hat and dress on the back of her younger son's pick-up truck, the veil of mourning pushed defiantly back off her face, was not slow to seize upon Inspector Kinch's words and hurl them back into his florid, loose-chinned, impotent face, whose hangdog expression bore witness to the humiliation of being referred to by his brother officers as *niggerjimmy* and, worse, *mushroom*, meaning that he was kept permanently in the dark, and from time to time – for example in the present regrettable circumstances – people threw shit all over him. 'I want you to under-

464

stand,' Mrs Roberts declaimed to the sizeable crowd that had gathered angrily outside the High Street police station, 'that these people are gambling with our lives. They are laying odds on our chances of survival. I want you all to consider what that means in terms of their respect for us as human beings.' And Hanif Johnson, as Uhuru Simba's solicitor, added his own clarification from Walcott Roberts's pick-up truck, pointing out that his client's alleged fatal plunge had been from the lower of the two bunks in his cell; that in an age of extreme overcrowding in the country's lock-ups it was unusual, to say the least, that the other bunk should have been unoccupied, ensuring that there were no witnesses to the death except for prison officers; and that a nightmare was by no means the only possible explanation for the screams of a black man in the hands of the custodial authorities. In his concluding remarks, afterwards termed 'inflammatory and unprofessional' by Inspector Kinch, Hanif linked the community liaison officer's words to those of the notorious racist John Kingsley Read, who had once responded to news of a black man's death with the slogan, 'One down; one million to go.' The crowd murmured and bubbled; it was a hot and malicious day. 'Stay hot,' Simba's brother Walcott cried out to the assembly. 'Don't anybody cool off. Maintain your rage.'

As Simba had in effect already been tried and convicted in what he had once called the 'rainbow press – red as rags, yellow as streaks, blue as movies, green as slime', his end struck many white people as rough justice, a murderous monster's retributive fall. But in another court, silent and black, he had received an entirely more favourable judgment, and these differing estimations of the deceased moved, in the aftermath of his death, on to the city streets, and fermented in the unending tropical heat. The 'rainbow press' was full of Simba's support for Qazhafi, Khomeini, Louis Farrakhan; while in the streets of Brickhall, young men and women maintained, and fanned, the slow flame of their anger, a shadow-flame, but one capable of blotting out the light.

Two nights later, behind the Charringtons Brewery in Tower Hamlets, the 'Granny Ripper' struck again. And the night after that, an old woman was murdered near the adventure playground in Victoria Park, Hackney; once again, the Ripper's hideous 'signature' – the ritual arrangement of the internal organs around the victim's body, whose precise configuration had never been made public – had been added to the crime. When Inspector Kinch, looking somewhat ragged at the edges, appeared on television to propound the extraordinary theory that a 'copycat killer' had somehow discovered the trademark which had been so carefully concealed for so long, and had therefore taken up the mantle which the late Uhuru Simba had let drop, – then the Commissioner of Police also deemed it wise, as a precautionary measure, to quadruple the police presence on the streets of Brickhall, and to hold such large numbers of police in reserve that it proved necessary to cancel the capital's football programme for the weekend. And, in truth, tempers were fraying all over Uhuru Simba's old patch; Hanif Johnson issued a statement to the effect that the increased police presence was 'provocative and incendiary', and at the Shaandaar and the Pagal Khana there began to assemble groups of young blacks and Asians determined to confront the cruising panda cars. At the Hot Wax, the effigy chosen for *meltdown* was none other than the perspiring and already deliquescent figure of the community liaison officer. And the temperature continued, inexorably, to rise.

Violent incidents began to occur more frequently: attacks on black families on council estates, harassment of black schoolchildren on their way home, brawls in pubs. At the Pagal Khana a rat-faced youth and three of his cronies spat over many people's food; as a result of the ensuing affray three Bengali waiters were charged with assault and the causing of actual bodily harm; the expectorating quartet was not, however, detained. Stories of police brutality, of black youths hauled swiftly into unmarked cars and vans belonging to the special patrol groups and flung out, equally discreetly, covered in cuts and bruises, spread throughout the communities. Self-defence patrols of young Sikh, Bengali and Afro-Caribbean males – described by their political opponents as *vigilante groups* – began to roam the borough, on foot and in old

Ford Zodiacs and Cortinas, determined not to 'take it lying down'. Hanif Johnson told his live-in lover, Mishal Sufyan, that in his opinion one more Ripper killing would light the fuse. 'That killer's not just crowing about being free,' he said. 'He's laughing about Simba's death as well, and that's what the people can't stomach.'

Down these simmering streets, one unseasonally humid night, came Gibreel Farishta, blowing his golden horn.

At eight o'clock that evening, a Saturday, Pamela Chamcha stood with Jumpy Joshi – who had refused to let her go unaccompanied – next to the Photo-Me machine in a corner of the main concourse of Euston station, feeling ridiculously conspiratorial. At eight-fifteen she was approached by a wiry young man who seemed taller than she remembered him; following him without a word, she and Jumpy got into his battered blue pick-up truck and were driven to a tiny flat above an off-licence in Railton Road, Brixton, where Walcott Roberts introduced them to his mother, Antoinette. The three men whom Pamela afterwards thought of as Haitians for what she recognized to be stereotypical reasons were not introduced. 'Have a glass of ginger wine,' Antoinette Roberts commanded. 'Good for the baby, too.'

When Walcott had done the honours Mrs Roberts, looking lost in a voluminous and threadbare armchair (her surprisingly pale legs, matchstick-thin, emerging from beneath her black dress to end in mutinous, pink ankle-socks and sensible lace-ups, failed by some distance to reach the floor), got to business. 'These gentlemen were colleagues of my boy,' she said. 'It turns out that the probable reason for his murder was the work he was doing on a subject which I am told is also of interest to you. We believe the time has come to work more formally, through the channels you represent.' Here one of the three silent 'Haitians' handed Pamela a red plastic briefcase. 'It contains,' Mrs Roberts mildly explained, 'extensive evidence of the existence of witches' covens throughout the Metropolitan Police.'

Walcott stood up. 'We should go now,' he said firmly. 'Please.' Pamela and Jumpy rose. Mrs Roberts nodded vaguely, absently, cracking the joints of her loose-skinned hands. 'Goodbye,' Pamela said, and offered conventional regrets. 'Girl, don't waste breath,' Mrs Roberts broke in. 'Just nail me those warlocks. Nail them through the *heart.*'

Walcott Roberts dropped them in Notting Hill at ten. Jumpy was coughing badly and complaining of the pains in the head that had recurred a number of times since his injuries at Shepperton, but when Pamela admitted to being nervous at possessing the only copy of the explosive documents in the plastic briefcase, Jumpy once again insisted on accompanying her to the Brickhall community relations council's offices, where she planned to make photocopies to distribute to a number of trusted friends and colleagues. So it was that at ten-fifteen they were in Pamela's beloved MG, heading east across the city, into the gathering storm. An old, blue Mercedes panel van followed them, as it had followed Walcott's pick-up truck; that is, without being noticed.

Fifteen minutes earlier, a patrol group of seven large young Sikhs jammed into a Vauxhall Cavalier had been driving over the Malaya Crescent canal bridge in southern Brickhall. Hearing a cry from the towpath under the bridge, and hurrying to the scene, they found a bland, pale man of medium height and build, fair hair flopping forward over hazel eyes, leaping to his feet, scalpel in hand, and rushing away from the body of an old woman whose blue wig had fallen off and lay floating like a jellyfish in the canal. The young Sikhs easily caught up with and overpowered the running man.

By eleven pm the news of the mass murderer's capture had penetrated every cranny of the borough, accompanied by a slew of rumours: the police had been reluctant to charge the maniac, the patrol members had been detained for questioning, a cover-up was being planned. Crowds began to gather on street corners, and as the pubs emptied a series of fights broke out. There was some damage to property: three cars had their windows smashed, a video store was looted, a few bricks were thrown. It was at this point, at half-past eleven on a Saturday night, with the clubs and dance-halls beginning to yield up their excited, highly charged populations, that the divisional superintendent of police, in consultation with higher authority, declared that riot conditions now existed in central Brickhall, and unleashed the full might of the Metropolitan Police against the 'rioters'.

Also at this point, Saladin Chamcha, who had been dining with Allie Cone at her apartment overlooking Brickhall Fields, keeping up appearances, sympathizing, murmuring encouraging insincerities, emerged into the night; found a *testudo* of helmeted men with plastic shields at the ready moving towards him across the Fields at a steady, inexorable trot; witnessed the arrival overhead of giant, locust-swarming helicopters from which light was falling like heavy rain; saw the advance of the water cannons; and, obeying an irresistible primal reflex, turned tail and ran, not knowing that he was going the wrong way, running full speed in the direction of the Shaandaar.

Television cameras arrive just in time for the raid on Club Hot Wax.

This is what a television camera sees: less gifted than the human eye, its night vision is limited to what klieg lights will show. A helicopter hovers over the nightclub, urinating light in long golden streams; the camera understands this image. The machine of state bearing down upon its enemies. – And now there's a camera in the sky; a news editor somewhere has sanctioned the cost of aerial photography, and from another helicopter a news team is *shooting down*. No attempt is made to chase this helicopter away. The noise of rotor blades drowns the noise of the crowd. In this respect, again, video recording equipment is less sensitive than, in this case, the human ear.

– Cut. – A man lit by a sun-gun speaks rapidly into a microphone. Behind them there is a disorderment of shadows. But between the reporter and the disordered shadow-lands there stands a wall: men in riot helmets, carrying shields. The reporter speaks gravely; petrolbombs plasticbullets policeinjuries water-cannon looting, confining himself, of course, to facts. But the camera sees what he does not say. A camera is a thing easily broken or purloined; its fragility makes it fastidious. A camera requires law, order, the thin blue line. Seeking to preserve itself, it remains behind the shielding wall, observing the shadow-lands from afar, and of course from above: that is, it chooses sides.

– Cut. – Sun-guns illuminate a new face, saggy-jowled, flushed. This face is named: sub-titled words appear across his tunic. *Inspector Stephen Kinch.* The camera sees him for what he is: a good man in an impossible job. A father, a man who likes his pint. He speaks: cannot-tolerate-no-go-areas better-protection-required-for-policemen see-the-plastic-riot-shields-catching-fire. He refers to organized crime, political agitators, bomb-factories, drugs. 'We understand some of these kids may feel they have grievances but we will not and cannot be the whipping boys of society.' Embold-ened by the lights and the patient, silent lenses, he goes further. These kids don't know how lucky they are, he suggests. They should consult their kith and kin. Africa, Asia, the Caribbean: now those are places with real problems. Those are places where people might have grievances worth respecting. Things aren't so bad here, not by a long chalk; no slaughters here, no torture, no military coups. People should value what they've got before they lose it. Ours always was a peaceful land, he says. Our industrious island race. – Behind him, the camera sees stretchers, ambulances, pain. – It sees strange humanoid shapes being hauled up from the bowels of the Club Hot Wax, and recognizes the effigies of the mighty. Inspector Kinch explains. They cook them in an oven down there, they call it fun, I wouldn't call it that myself. – The camera observes the wax models with distaste. – Is there not something *witchy* about them, something cannibalistic, an unwholesome smell? Have *black arts* been practised here? – The camera sees broken windows. It sees something burning in the middle distance: a car, a shop. It cannot understand, or demon-

strate, what any of this achieves. These people are burning their
own streets.

– Cut. – Here is a brightly lit video store. Several sets have been
left on in the windows; the camera, most delirious of narcissists,
watches TV, creating, for an instant, an infinite recession of television sets, diminishing to a point. – Cut. – Here is a serious head
bathed in light: a studio discussion. The head is talking about *outlaws*. Billy the Kid, Ned Kelly: these were men who stood *for* as
well as *against*. Modern mass-murderers, lacking this heroic
dimension, are no more than sick, damaged beings, utterly blank
as personalities, their crimes distinguished by an attention to procedure, to methodology – let's say *ritual* – driven, perhaps, by the
nonentity's longing to be noticed, to rise out of the ruck and
become, for a moment, a star. – Or by a kind of transposed death-
wish: to kill the beloved and so destroy the self. – *Which is the
Granny Ripper?* a questioner asks. *And what about Jack?* – The true
outlaw, the head insists, is a dark mirror-image of the hero. –
These rioters, perhaps? comes the challenge. *Aren't you in danger of
glamorizing, of 'legitimizing'?* – The head shakes, laments the mate-
rialism of modern youth. Looting video stores is not what the
head has been talking about. – *But what about the old-timers, then?
Butch Cassidy, the James brothers, Captain Moonlight, the Kelly gang.
They all robbed – did they not?* – *banks.* – Cut. – Later that night, the
camera will return to this shop-window. The television sets will
be missing.

– From the air, the camera watches the entrance to Club Hot
Wax. Now the police have finished with wax effigies and are
bringing out real human beings. The camera homes in on the
arrested persons: a tall albino man; a man in an Armani suit,
looking like a dark mirror-image of de Niro; a young girl of –
what? – fourteen, fifteen? – a sullen young man of twenty or
thereabouts. No names are titled; the camera does not know these
faces. Gradually, however, the *facts* emerge. The club DJ, Sewsunker Ram, known as 'Pinkwalla', and its proprietor, Mr John
Maslama, are to be charged with running a large-scale narcotics
operation – crack, brown sugar, hashish, cocaine. The man

arrested with them, an employee at Maslama's nearby 'Fair Winds' music store, is the registered owner of a van in which an unspeci- fied quantity of 'hard drugs' has been discovered; also numbers of 'hot' video recorders. The young girl's name is Anahita Sufyan; she is under-age, is said to have been drinking heavily, and, it is hinted, having sex with at least one of the three arrested men. She is further reported to have a history of truancy and association with known criminal types: a delinquent, clearly. – An illumi- nated journalist will offer the nation these titbits many hours after the event, but the news is already running wild in the streets: Pinkwalla! – And the *Wax*: they smashed the place up – *totalled* it! – Now it's *war*.

This happens, however – as does a great deal else – in places which the camera cannot see.

Gibreel:

moves as if through a dream, because after days of wandering the city without eating or sleeping, with the trumpet named Azraeel tucked safely in a pocket of his greatcoat, he no longer recognizes the distinction between the waking and dreaming states; – he understands now something of what omnipresence must be like, because he is moving through several stories at once, there is a Gibreel who mourns his betrayal by Alleluia Cone, and a Gibreel hovering over the death-bed of a Prophet, and a Gibreel watching in secret over the progress of a pilgrimage to the sea, waiting for the moment at which he will reveal himself, and a Gibreel who feels, more powerfully every day, the will of the adversary, drawing him ever closer, leading him towards their final embrace: the subtle, deceiving adversary, who has taken the face of his friend, of Saladin his truest friend, in order to lull him into lowering his guard. And there is a Gibreel who walks down the streets of London, trying to understand the will of God.

Is he to be the agent of God's wrath?

Or of his love?

Is he vengeance or forgiveness? Should the fatal trumpet remain in his pocket, or should he take it out and blow?

(I'm giving him no instructions. I, too, am interested in his choices – in the result of his wrestling match. Character *vs* destiny: a free-style bout. Two falls, two submissions or a knockout will decide.)

Wrestling, through his many stories, he proceeds.

There are times when he aches for her, Alleluia, her very name an exaltation; but then he remembers the diabolic verses, and turns his thoughts away. The horn in his pocket demands to be blown; but he restrains himself. Now is not the time. Searching for clues – *what is to be done?* – he stalks the city streets.

Somewhere he sees a television set through an evening window. There is a woman's head on the screen, a famous 'presenter', being interviewed by an equally famous, twinkling Irish 'host'. – What would be the worst thing you could imagine? – Oh, I think, I'm sure, it would be, oh, *yes*: to be alone on Christmas Eve. You'd really have to face yourself, wouldn't you, you'd look into a harsh mirror and ask yourself, *is this all there is?* – Gibreel, alone, not knowing the date, walks on. In the mirror, the adversary approaches at the same pace as his own, beckoning, stretching out his arms.

The city sends him messages. Here, it says, is where the Dutch king decided to live when he came over three centuries ago. In those days this was out of town, a village, set in green English fields. But when the King arrived to set up house, London squares sprang up amid the fields, red-brick buildings with Dutch crenellations rising against the sky, so that his courtiers might have places in which to reside. Not all migrants are powerless, the still-standing edifices whisper. They impose their needs on their new earth, bringing their own coherence to the new-found land, imagining it afresh. But look out, the city warns. Incoherence, too, must have its day. Riding in the parkland in which he'd chosen to live – which he'd *civilized* – William III was thrown by his horse, fell hard against the recalcitrant ground, and broke his royal neck.

Some days he finds himself among walking corpses, great crowds of the dead, all of them refusing to admit they're done for, corpses mutinously continuing to behave like living people, shopping, catching buses, flirting, going home to make love, smoking cigarettes. *But you're dead*, he shouts at them. *Zombies, get into your graves.* They ignore him, or laugh, or look embarrassed, or menace him with their fists. He falls silent, and hurries on.

The city becomes vague, amorphous. It is becoming impossible to describe the world. Pilgrimage, prophet, adversary merge, fade into mists, emerge. As does she: Allie, Al-Lat. *She is the exalted bird. Greatly to be desired.* He remembers now: she told him, long ago, about Jumpy's poetry. *He's trying to make a collection. A book.* The thumb-sucking artist with his infernal views. A book is a product of a pact with the Devil that inverts the Faustian contract, he'd told Allie. Dr Faustus sacrificed eternity in return for two dozen years of power; the writer agrees to the ruination of his life, and gains (but only if he's lucky) maybe not eternity, but posterity, at least. Either way (this was Jumpy's point) it's the Devil who wins.

What does a poet write? Verses. What jingle-jangles in Gibreel's brain? Verses. What broke his heart? Verses and again verses.

The trumpet, Azraeel, calls out from a greatcoat pocket: *Pick me up! Yesyesyes: the Trump. To hell with it all, the whole sorry mess: just puff up your cheeks and rooty-toot-toot. Come on, it's party time.*

How hot it is: steamy, close, intolerable. This is no Proper London: not this improper city. Airstrip One, Mahagonny, Alphaville. He wanders through a confusion of languages. Babel: a contraction of the Assyrian 'babilu'. 'The gate of God.' Babylondon.

Where's this?

– Yes. – He meanders, one night, behind the cathedrals of the Industrial Revolution, the railway termini of north London.

Anonymous King's Cross, the bat-like menace of the St Pancras tower, the red-and-black gas-holders inflating and deflating like giant iron lungs. Where once in battle Queen Boudicca fell, Gibreel Farishta wrestles with himself.

The Goodsway: – but O what succulent goods lounge in door-ways and under tungsten lamps, what delicacies are on offer in that way! – Swinging handbags, calling out, silver-skirted, wearing fish-net tights: these are not only young goods (average age thir-teen to fifteen) but also cheap. They have short, identical histories: all have babies stashed away somewhere, all have been thrown out of their homes by irate, puritanical parents, none of them are white. Pimps with knives take ninety per cent of their earnings. Goods are only goods, after all, especially when they're trash.

– Gibreel Farishta in the Goodsway is hailed from shadows and lamps; and quickens, at first, his pace. *What's this to do with me? Bloody pussies-galore.* But then he slows and stops, hearing some-thing else calling to him from lamps and shadows, some need, some wordless plea, hidden just under the tinny voices of ten-pound tarts. His footsteps slow down, then halt. He is held by their desires. *For what?* They are moving towards him now, drawn to him like fishes on unseen hooks. As they near him their walks change, their hips lose their swagger, their faces start looking their age, in spite of all the make-up. When they reach him, they kneel. *Who do you say that I am?* he asks, and wants to add: *I know your names. I met you once before, elsewhere, behind a curtain. Twelve of you then as now. Ayesha, Hafsah, Ramlah, Sawdah, Zainab, Zainab, Maimunah, Safia, Juwairiyah, Umm Salamah the Makhzumite, Rehana the Jew, and the beautiful Mary the Copt.* Silently, they remain on their knees. Their wishes are made known to him without words. *What is an archangel but a puppet? Kathputli, mario-nette. The faithful bend us to their will. We are forces of nature and they, our masters. Mistresses, too.* The heaviness in his limbs, the heat, and in his ears a buzzing like bees on summer afternoons. It would be easy to faint.

He does not faint.

He stands among the kneeling children, waiting for the pimps.

And when they come, he at last takes out, and presses to his lips, his unquiet horn: the exterminator, Azraeel.

After the stream of fire has emerged from the mouth of his golden trumpet and consumed the approaching men, wrapping them in a cocoon of flame, unmaking them so completely that not even their shoes remain sizzling on the sidewalk, Gibreel understands.

He is walking again, leaving behind him the gratitude of the whores, heading in the direction of the borough of Brickhall, Azraeel once more in his capacious pocket. Things are becoming clear.

He is the Archangel Gibreel, the angel of the Recitation, with the power of revelation in his hands. He can reach into the breasts of men and women, pick out the desires of their inmost hearts, and make them real. He is the quencher of desires, the slaker of lusts, the fulfiller of dreams. He is the genie of the lamp, and his master is the Roc.

What desires, what imperatives are in the midnight air? He breathes them in. – And nods, so be it, yes. – Let it be fire. This is a city that has cleansed itself in flame, purged itself by burning down to the ground.

Fire, falling fire. 'This is the judgment of God in his wrath,' Gibreel Farishta proclaims to the riotous night, 'that men be granted their heart's desires, and that they be by them consumed.'

Low-cost high-rise housing enfolds him. *Nigger eat white man's shit,* suggest the unoriginal walls. The buildings have names: 'Isandhlwana', 'Rorke's Drift'. But a revisionist enterprise is underway, for two of the four towers have been renamed, and bear, now, the names 'Mandela' and 'Toussaint l'Ouverture'. – The towers stand up on stilts, and in the concrete formlessness beneath and between them there is the howling of a perpetual wind, and the eddying of debris: derelict kitchen units, deflated bicycle tyres, shards of broken doors, dolls' legs, vegetable refuse extracted from plastic disposal bags by hungry cats and dogs, fast-food packets, rolling cans, shattered job prospects, abandoned hopes, lost illusions, expended angers, accumulated bitterness, vomited fear, and a rusting bath. He stands motionless while small groups of residents rush past in different directions. Some (not all) are carrying weapons. Clubs, bottles, knives. All of the groups contain white youngsters as well as black. He raises his trumpet to his lips and begins to play.

Little buds of flame spring up on the concrete, fuelled by the discarded heaps of possessions and dreams. There is a little, rotting pile of envy: it burns greenly in the night. The fires are every colour of the rainbow, and not all of them need fuel. He blows the little fire-flowers out of his horn and they dance upon the concrete, needing neither combustible materials nor roots. Here, a pink one! There, what would be nice?, I know: a silver rose. – And now the buds are blossoming into bushes, they are climbing like creepers up the sides of the towers, they reach out towards their neighbours, forming hedges of multicoloured flame. It is like watching a luminous garden, its growth accelerated many thousands of times, a garden blossoming, flourishing, becoming overgrown, tangled, becoming impenetrable, a garden of dense intertwined chimeras, rivalling in its own incandescent fashion the thornwood that sprang up around the palace of the sleeping beauty in another fairy-tale, long ago.

But here, there is no beauty, sleeping within. There is Gibreel Farishta, walking in a world of fire. In the High Street he sees houses built of flame, with walls of fire, and flames like gathered curtains hanging at the windows. – And there are men and women with fiery skins strolling, running, milling around him, dressed in coats of fire. The street has become red hot, molten, a river the colour of blood. – All, all is ablaze as he toots his merry horn, *giving the people what they want,* the hair and teeth of the citizenry are smoking and red, glass burns, and birds fly overhead on blazing wings.

The adversary is very close. The adversary is a magnet, is a whirlpool's eye, is the irresistible centre of a black hole, his gravitational force creating an event horizon from which neither Gibreel, nor light, can escape. *This way,* the adversary calls. *I'm over here.*

Not a palace, but only a café. And in the rooms above, a bed and breakfast joint. No sleeping princess, but a disappointed woman, overpowered by smoke, lies unconscious here; and beside her, on the floor beside their bed, and likewise unconscious, her husband, the Mecca-returned ex-schoolteacher, Sufyan. – While, elsewhere in the burning Shaandaar, faceless persons stand at windows waving piteously for help, being unable (no mouths) to scream.

The adversary: there he blows!

Silhouetted against the backdrop of the ignited Shaandaar Café, see, that's the very fellow!

Azraeel leaps unbidden into Farishta's hand.

Even an archangel may experience a revelation, and when Gibreel catches, for the most fleeting of instants, Saladin Chamcha's eye, – then in that fractional and infinite moment the veils are ripped away from his sight, – he sees himself walking with Chamcha in Brickhall Fields, lost in a rhapsody, revealing the most intimate secrets of his lovemaking with Alleluia Cone, – those same secrets which afterwards were whispered into telephones by a host of evil voices, – beneath all of which Gibreel now discerns the unifying talent of the adversary, who could be guttural and high, who insulted and ingratiated, who was both insistent and shy, who was prosaic, – yes! – and versifying, too. – And now, at last, Gibreel Farishta recognizes for the first time that the adversary has not simply adopted Chamcha's features as a disguise; – nor is this any case of paranormal possession, of body-snatching by an invader up from Hell; that, in short, the evil is not external to Saladin, but springs from some recess of his own true nature, that it has been spreading through his selfhood like a cancer, erasing what was good in him, wiping out his spirit, – and doing so with many deceptive feints and dodges, seeming at times to recede; while, in fact, during the illusion of remission, under cover of it, so to speak, it continued perniciously to spread; – and now, no doubt, it has filled him up; now there is nothing left of Saladin but this, the dark fire of evil in his soul, consuming him as wholly as the other fire, multicoloured and engulfing, is devouring the screaming city. Truly these are 'most horrid, malicious, bloody flames, not like the fine flame of an ordinary fire'.

The fire is an arch across the sky. Saladin Chamcha, the adversary, who is also *Spoono, my old Chumch*, has disappeared into the doorway of the Shaandaar Café. This is the maw of the black hole; the horizon closes around it, all other possibilities fade, the universe shrinks to this solitary and irresistible point. Blowing a great blast on his trumpet, Gibreel plunges through the open door.

The building occupied by the Brickhall community relations council was a single-storey monster in purple brick with bullet-proof windows, a bunker-like creation of the 1960s, when such lines were considered sleek. It was not an easy building to enter; the door had been fitted with an entryphone and opened on to a narrow alley down one side of the building which ended at a second, also security-locked, door. There was also a burglar alarm.

This alarm, it afterwards transpired, had been switched off, probably by the two persons, one male, one female, who had effected an entry with the assistance of a key. It was officially suggested that these persons had been bent on an act of sabotage, an 'inside job', since one of them, the dead woman, had in fact been an employee of the organization whose offices these were. The reasons for the crime remained obscure, and as the miscreants had perished in the blaze, it was unlikely that they would ever come to light. An 'own goal' remained, however, the most probable explanation.

A tragic affair; the dead woman had been heavily pregnant.

Inspector Stephen Kinch, issuing the statement in which these facts were stated, made a 'linkage' between the fire at the Brickhall CRC and that at the Shaandaar Café, where the second dead

person, the male, had been a semi-permanent resident. It was possible that the man had been the real firebug and the woman, who
was his mistress although married to and still cohabiting with
another man, had been no more than his dupe. Political motives –
both parties were well known for their radical views – could not
be discounted, though such was the muddiness of the water in the
far-left groupuscules they frequented that it would be hard ever to
get a clear picture of what such motives might have been. It was
also possible that the two crimes, even if committed by the same
man, could have had different motivations. Possibly the man was
simply the hired criminal, burning down the Shaandaar for the
insurance money at the behest of the now-deceased owners, and
torching the CRC at the behest of his lover, perhaps on account
of some intra-office vendetta?

That the burning of the CRC was an act of arson was beyond
doubt. Quantities of petrol had been poured over desks, papers,
curtains. 'Many people do not understand how quickly a petrol
fire spreads,' Inspector Kinch stated to scribbling journalists. The
corpses, which had been so badly burned that dental records had
been required for identification purposes, had been found in the
photocopying room. 'That's all we have.' The end.

I have more.

I have certain questions, anyhow. – About, for instance, an
unmarked blue Mercedes panel van, which followed Walcott
Roberts's pick-up truck, and then Pamela Chamcha's MG. –
About the men who emerged from this van, their faces behind
Hallowe'en masks, and forced their way into the CRC offices just
as Pamela unlocked the outer door. – About what really happened
inside those offices, because purple brick and bulletproof glass
cannot easily be penetrated by the human eye. – And about,
finally, the whereabouts of a red plastic briefcase, and the documents it contains.

Inspector Kinch? Are you there?

No. He's gone. He has no answers for me.

❦

Here is Mr Saladin Chamcha, in the camel coat with the silk collar, running down the High Street like some cheap crook. – The same, terrible Mr Chamcha who has just spent his evening in the company of a distraught Alleluia Cone, without feeling a flicker of remorse. – 'I look down towards his feet,' Othello said of Iago, 'but that's a fable.' Nor is Chamcha fabulous any more; his humanity is sufficient form and explanation for his deed. He has destroyed what he is not and cannot be; has taken revenge, returning treason for treason; and has done so by exploiting his enemy's weakness, bruising his unprotected heel. – There is satisfaction in this. – Still, here is Mr Chamcha, running. The world is full of anger and event. Things hang in the balance. A building burns.

Boomba, pounds his heart. *Doomba, boomba, dadoom.*

Now he sees the Shaandaar, on fire; and comes to a skidding halt. He has a constricted chest; – *badoomba!* – and there's a pain in his left arm. He doesn't notice; is staring at the burning building.

And sees Gibreel Farishta.

And turns; and runs inside.

'Mishal! Sufyan! Hind!' cries evil Mr Chamcha. The ground floor is not as yet ablaze. He flings open the door to the stairs, and a scalding, pestilential wind drives him back. *Dragon's breath,* he thinks. The landing is on fire; the flames reach in sheets from floor to ceiling. No possibility of advance.

'Anybody?' screams Saladin Chamcha. 'Is anybody there?' But the dragon roars louder than he can shout.

Something invisible kicks him in the chest, sends him toppling backwards, on to the café floor, amid the empty tables. *Doom,* sings his heart. *Take this. And this.*

There is a noise above his head like the scurrying of a billion rats, spectral rodents following a ghostly piper. He looks up: the ceiling is on fire. He finds he cannot stand. As he watches, a section of the ceiling detaches itself, and he sees the segment of beam falling towards him. He crosses his arms in feeble self-defence.

The beam pins him to the floor, breaking both his arms. His chest is full of pain. The world recedes. Breathing is hard. He can't speak. He is the Man of a Thousand Voices, and there isn't one left.

Gibreel Farishta, holding Azraeel, enters the Shaandaar Café.

What happens when you win?

When your enemies are at your mercy: how will you act then? Compromise is the temptation of the weak; this is the test for the strong. – 'Spoono,' Gibreel nods at the fallen man. 'You really fooled me, mister; seriously, you're quite a guy.' – And Chamcha, seeing what's in Gibreel's eyes, cannot deny the knowledge he sees there. 'Wha,' he begins, and gives up. *What are you going to do?* Fire is falling all around them now: a sizzle of golden rain. 'Why'd you do it?' Gibreel asks, then dismisses the question with a wave of the hand. 'Damnfool thing to be asking. Might as well inquire, what possessed you to rush in here? Damnfool thing to do. People, eh, Spoono? Crazy bastards, that's all.'

Now there are pools of fire all around them. Soon they will be encircled, marooned in a temporary island amid this lethal sea. Chamcha is kicked a second time in the chest, and jerks violently. Facing three deaths – by fire, by 'natural causes', and by Gibreel – he strains desperately, trying to speak, but only croaks emerge. 'Fa. Gur. Mmm.' *Forgive me.* 'Ha. Pa.' *Have pity.* The café tables are burning. More beams fall from above. Gibreel seems to have fallen into a trance. He repeats, vaguely: 'Bloody damnfool things.'

Is it possible that evil is never total, that its victory, no matter how overwhelming, is never absolute?

Consider this fallen man. He sought without remorse to shatter the mind of a fellow human being; and exploited, to do so, an entirely blameless woman, at least partly owing to his own impossible and voyeuristic desire for her. Yet this same man has risked death, with scarcely any hesitation, in a foolhardy rescue attempt.

What does this mean?

The fire has closed around the two men, and smoke is every-

where. It can only be a matter of seconds before they are overcome. There are more urgent questions to answer than the *damnfool* ones above.

What choice will Farishta make?

Does he have a choice?

Gibreel lets fall his trumpet; stoops; frees Saladin from the prison
of the fallen beam; and lifts him in his arms. Chamcha, with
broken ribs as well as arms, groans feebly, sounding like the creationist Dumsday before he got a new tongue of choicest rump.
'Ta. La.' *It's too late.* A little lick of fire catches at the hem of his
coat. Acrid black smoke fills all available space, creeping behind
his eyes, deafening his ears, clogging his nose and lungs. – Now,
however, Gibreel Farishta begins softly to exhale, a long, continuous exhalation of extraordinary duration, and as his breath
blows towards the door it slices through the smoke and fire like a
knife; – and Saladin Chamcha, gasping and fainting, with a mule
inside his chest, seems to see – but will ever afterwards be unsure
if it was truly so – the fire parting before them like the red sea it
has become, and the smoke dividing also, like a curtain or a veil;
until there lies before them a clear pathway to the door; – whereupon Gibreel Farishta steps quickly forward, bearing Saladin along
the path of forgiveness into the hot night air; so that on a night
when the city is at war, a night heavy with enmity and rage, there
is this small redeeming victory for love.

Conclusions.

Mishal Sufyan is outside the Shaandaar when they emerge,
weeping for her parents, being comforted by Hanif. – It is
Gibreel's turn to collapse; still carrying Saladin, he passes out at
Mishal's feet.

Now Mishal and Hanif are in an ambulance with the two
unconscious men, and while Chamcha has an oxygen mask over
his nose and mouth Gibreel, suffering nothing worse than exhaustion, is talking in his sleep: a delirious babble about a magic

trumpet and the fire that he blew, like music, from its mouth. – And Mishal, who remembers Chamcha as a devil, and has come to accept the possibility of many things, wonders: 'Do you think – ?' – But Hanif is definite, firm. 'Not a chance. This is Gibreel Farishta, the actor, don't you recognize? Poor guy's just playing out some movie scene.' Mishal won't let it go. 'But, Hanif,' – and he becomes emphatic. Speaking gently, because she has just been orphaned, after all, he absolutely insists. 'What has happened here in Brickhall tonight is a socio-political phenomenon. Let's not fall into the trap of some damn mysticism. We're talking about history: an event in the history of Britain. About the process of change.'

At once Gibreel's voice changes, and his subject-matter also. He mentions *pilgrims*, and a *dead baby*, and *like in 'The Ten Commandments'*, and a *decaying mansion*, and a *tree*; because in the aftermath of the purifying fire he is dreaming, for the very last time, one of his serial dreams; – and Hanif says: 'Listen, Mishu, darling. Just make-believe, that's all.' He puts his arm around her, kisses her cheek, holding her fast. *Stay with me. The world is real. We have to live in it; we have to live here, to live on.*

Just then Gibreel Farishta, still asleep, shouts at the top of his voice.

'Mishal! Come back! Nothing's happening! Mishal, for pity's sake; turn around, come back, come back.'

PART VIII

❧

THE
PARTING OF THE
ARABIAN SEA

❧

It had been the habit of Srinivas the toy merchant to threaten his wife and children, from time to time, that one day, when the material world had lost its savour, he would drop everything, including his name, and turn sanyasi, wandering from village to village with a begging bowl and a stick. Mrs Srinivas treated these threats tolerantly, knowing that her gelatinous and good-humoured husband liked to be thought of as a devout man, but also a bit of an adventurer (had he not insisted on that absurd and scarifying flight into the Grand Canyon in Amrika years ago?); the idea of becoming a mendicant holy man satisfied both needs. Yet, when she saw his ample posterior so comfortably ensconced in an armchair on their front porch, looking out at the world through stout wire netting, – or when she watched him playing with their youngest daughter, five-year-old Minoo, – or when she observed that his appetite, far from diminishing to begging-bowl proportions, was increasing contentedly with the passing years – then Mrs Srinivas puckered up her lips, adopted the insouciant expression of a film beauty (though she was as plump and wobbling as her spouse) and went whistling indoors. As a result, when she found his chair empty, with his glass of lime-juice unfinished on one of its arms, it took her completely by surprise.

To tell the truth, Srinivas himself could never properly explain what made him leave the comfort of his morning porch and stroll across to watch the arrival of the villagers of Titlipur. The urchin boys who knew everything an hour before it happened had been shouting in the street about an improbable procession of people coming with bags and baggage down the potato track towards the grand trunk road, led by a girl with silver hair, with great exclamations of butterflies over their heads, and, bringing up the rear, Mirza Saeed Akhtar in his olive-green Mercedes-Benz station wagon, looking like a mango-stone had got stuck in his throat.

For all its potato silos and famous toy factories, Chatnapatna was not such a big place that the arrival of one hundred and fifty persons could pass unnoticed. Just before the procession arrived Srinivas had received a deputation from his factory workers, asking for permission to close down operations for a couple of hours so that they could witness the great event. Knowing they would probably take the time off anyway, he agreed. But he himself remained, for a time, stubbornly planted on his porch, trying to pretend that the butterflies of excitement had not begun to stir in his capacious stomach. Later, he would confide to Mishal Akhtar: 'It was a presentiment. What to say? I knew you-all were not here for refreshments only. She had come for me.'

Titlipur arrived in Chatnapatna in a consternation of howling babies, shouting children, creaking oldsters, and sour jokes from the Osman of the boom-boom bullock for whom Srinivas did not care one jot. Then the urchins informed the toy king that among the travellers were the wife and mother-in-law of the zamindar Mirza Saeed, and they were on foot like the peasants, wearing simple kurta-pajamas and no jewels at all. This was the point at which Srinivas lumbered over to the roadside canteen around which the Titlipur pilgrims were crowding while potato bhurta and parathas were handed round. He arrived at the same time as the Chatnapatna police jeep. The Inspector was standing on the passenger seat, shouting through a megaphone that he intended to take strong action against this 'communal' march if it was not disbanded at once. Hindu–Muslim business, Srinivas thought; bad, bad.

The police were treating the pilgrimage as some kind of sectarian demonstration, but when Mirza Saeed Akhtar stepped forward and told the Inspector the truth the officer became confused.
Sri Srinivas, a Brahmin, was obviously not a man who had ever
considered making a pilgrimage to Mecca, but he was impressed
nevertheless. He pushed up through the crowd to hear what the
zamindar was saying: 'And it is the purpose of these good people
to walk to the Arabian Sea, believing as they do that the waters
will part for them.' Mirza Saeed's voice sounded weak, and the
Inspector, Chatnapatna's Station Head Officer, was unconvinced.
'Are you serious, ji?' Mirza Saeed said: 'Not me. *They*, but, are
serious as hell. I'm planning to change their minds before anything crazy happens.' The SHO, all straps, moustachioes and self-
importance, shook his head. 'But, see here, sir, how can I permit
so many individuals to congregate on the street? Tempers can be
inflamed; incident is possible.' Just then the crowd of pilgrims
parted and Srinivas saw for the first time the fantastic figure of the
girl dressed entirely in butterflies, with snowy hair flowing down
as far as her ankles. 'Arré deo,' he shouted, 'Ayesha, is it you?'
And added, foolishly: 'Then where are my Family Planning dolls?'
His outburst was ignored; everybody was watching Ayesha as
she approached the puff-chested SHO. She said nothing, but
smiled and nodded, and the fellow seemed to grow twenty years
younger, until in the manner of a boy of ten or eleven he said,
'Okay okay, mausi. Sorry, ma. No offence. I beg your pardon,
please.' That was the end of the police trouble. Later that day, in
the afternoon heat, a group of town youths known to have RSS
and Vishwa Hindu Parishad connections began throwing stones
from nearby rooftops; whereupon the Station Head Officer had
them arrested and in jail in two minutes flat.

'Ayesha, daughter,' Srinivas said aloud to the empty air, 'what
the hell happened to you?'

During the heat of the day the pilgrims rested in whatever
shade they could find. Srinivas wandered among them in a kind of
daze, filled up with emotion, realizing that a great turning-point
in his life had unaccountably arrived. His eyes kept searching out

the transformed figure of Ayesha the seer, who was resting in the shade of a pipal-tree in the company of Mishal Akhtar, her mother Mrs Qureishi, and the lovesick Osman with his bullock. Eventually Srinivas bumped into the zamindar Mirza Saeed, who was stretched out on the back seat of his Mercedes-Benz, unsleeping, a man in torment. Srinivas spoke to him with a humbleness born of his wonderment. 'Sethji, you don't believe in the girl?'

'Srinivas,' Mirza Saeed sat up to reply, 'we are modern men. We know, for instance, that old people die on long journeys, that God does not cure cancer, and that oceans do not part. We have to stop this idiocy. Come with me. Plenty of room in the car. Maybe you can help to talk them out of it; that Ayesha, she's grateful to you, perhaps she'll listen.'

'To come in the car?' Srinivas felt helpless, as though mighty hands were gripping his limbs. 'There is my business, but.'

'This is a suicide mission for many of our people,' Mirza Saeed urged him. 'I need help. Naturally I could pay.'

'Money is no object,' Srinivas retreated, affronted. 'Excuse, please, Sethji. I must consider.'

'Don't you see?' Mirza Saeed shouted after him. 'We are not communal people, you and I. Hindu–Muslim bhai-bhai! We can open up a secular front against this mumbo-jumbo.'

Srinivas turned back. 'But I am not an unbeliever,' he protested. 'The picture of goddess Lakshmi is always on my wall.'

'Wealth is an excellent goddess for a businessman,' Mirza Saeed said.

'And in my heart,' Srinivas added. Mirza Saeed lost his temper. 'But goddesses, I swear. Even your own philosophers admit that these are abstract concepts only. Embodiments of shakti which is itself an abstract notion: the dynamic power of the gods.'

The toy merchant was looking down at Ayesha as she slept under her quilt of butterflies. 'I am no philosopher, Sethji,' he said. And did not say that his heart had leapt into his mouth because he had realized that the sleeping girl and the goddess in the calendar on his factory wall had the identical, same-to-same, face.

When the pilgrimage left town, Srinivas accompanied it, turning a deaf ear to the entreaties of his wild-haired wife who picked up Minoo and shook her in her husband's face. He explained to Ayesha that while he did not wish to visit Mecca he had been seized by a longing to walk with her a while, perhaps even as far as the sea.

As he took his place among the Titlipur villagers and fell into step with the man next to him, he observed with a mixture of incomprehension and awe that infinite butterfly swarm over their heads, like a gigantic umbrella shading the pilgrims from the sun. It was as if the butterflies of Titlipur had taken over the functions of the great tree. Next he gave a little cry of fear, astonishment and pleasure, because a few dozen of those chameleon-winged creatures had settled on his shoulders and turned, upon the instant, the exact shade of scarlet of his shirt. Now he recognized the man at his side as the Sarpanch, Muhammad Din, who had chosen not to walk at the front. He and his wife Khadija strode contentedly forward in spite of their advanced years, and when he saw the lepidopteral blessing that had descended on the toy merchant, Muhammad Din reached out and grasped him by the hand.

It was becoming clear that the rains would fail. Lines of bony cattle migrated across the landscape, searching for a drink. *Love is Water*, someone had written in whitewash on the brick wall of a scooter factory. On the road they met other families heading south with their lives bundled up on the backs of dying donkeys, and these, too, were heading hopefully towards water. 'But not bloody salt water,' Mirza Saeed shouted at the Titlipur pilgrims. 'And not to see it divide itself in two! They want to stay alive, but you crazies want to die.' Vultures herded together by the roadside and watched the pilgrims pass.

Mirza Saeed spent the first weeks of the pilgrimage to the Arabian Sea in a state of permanent, hysterical agitation. Most of the

walking was done in the mornings and late afternoons, and at
these times Saeed would often leap out of his station wagon to
plead with his dying wife. 'Come to your senses, Mishu. You're a
sick woman. Come and lie down at least, let me press your feet a
while.' But she refused, and her mother shooed him away. 'See,
Saeed, you're in such a negative mood, it gets depressing. Go and
drink your Coke-shoke in your AC vehicle and leave us yatris in
peace.' After the first week the Air Conditioned vehicle lost its
driver. Mirza Saeed's chauffeur resigned and joined the foot-
pilgrims; the zamindar was obliged to get behind the wheel himself. After that, when his anxiety overcame him, it was necessary
to stop the car, park, and then rush madly back and forth among
the pilgrims, threatening, entreating, offering bribes. At least once
a day he cursed Ayesha to her face for ruining his life, but he
could never keep up the abuse because every time he looked at
her he desired her so much that he felt ashamed. The cancer had
begun to turn Mishal's skin grey, and Mrs Qureishi, too, was
beginning to fray at the edges; her society chappals had disinte-
grated and she was suffering from frightful foot-blisters that looked
like little water-balloons. When Saeed offered her the comfort of
the car, however, she continued to refuse point-blank. The spell
that Ayesha had placed upon the pilgrims was still holding firm. –
And at the end of these sorties into the heart of the pilgrimage
Mirza Saeed, sweating and giddy from the heat and his growing
despair, would realize that the marchers had left his car some way
behind, and he would have to totter back to it by himself, sunk in
gloom. One day he got back to the station wagon to find that an
empty coconut-shell thrown from the window of a passing bus
had smashed his laminated windscreen, which looked, now, like a
spider's web full of diamond flies. He had to knock all the pieces
out, and the glass diamonds seemed to be mocking him as they fell
on to the road and into the car, they seemed to speak of the tran-
sience and worthlessness of earthly possessions, but a secular man
lives in the world of things and Mirza Saeed did not intend to be
broken as easily as a windscreen. At night he would go to lie
beside his wife on a bedroll under the stars by the side of the grand

trunk road. When he told her about the accident she offered him cold comfort. 'It's a sign,' she said. 'Abandon the station wagon and join the rest of us at last.'

'Abandon a Mercedes-Benz?' Saeed yelped in genuine horror.

'So what?' Mishal replied in her grey, exhausted voice. 'You keep talking about ruination. Then what difference is a Mercedes going to make?'

'You don't understand,' Saeed wept. 'Nobody understands me.'

Gibreel dreamed a drought:

The land browned under the rainless skies. The corpses of buses and ancient monuments rotting in the fields beside the crops. Mirza Saeed saw, through his shattered windscreen, the onset of calamity: the wild donkeys fucking wearily and dropping dead, while still conjoined, in the middle of the road, the trees standing on roots exposed by soil erosion and looking like huge wooden claws scrabbling for water in the earth, the destitute farmers being obliged to work for the state as manual labourers, digging a reservoir by the trunk road, an empty container for the rain that wouldn't fall. Wretched roadside lives: a woman with a bundle heading for a tent of stick and rag, a girl condemned to scour, each day, this pot, this pan, in her patch of filthy dust. 'Are such lives really worth as much as ours?' Mirza Saeed Akhtar asked himself. 'As much as mine? As Mishal's? How little they have experienced, how little they have on which to feed the soul.' A man in a dhoti and loose yellow pugri stood like a bird on top of a milestone, perched there with one foot on the opposite knee, one hand under the opposite elbow, smoking a biri. As Mirza Saeed Akhtar passed him he spat, and caught the zamindar full in the face.

The pilgrimage advanced slowly, three hours' walking in the mornings, three more after the heat, walking at the pace of the slowest pilgrim, subject to infinite delays, the sickness of children, the harassment of the authorities, a wheel coming off one of the bullock carts; two miles a day at best, one hundred and fifty miles to the sea, a journey of approximately eleven weeks. The first death happened on the eighteenth day. Khadija, the tactless old

lady who had been for half a century the contented and con-
tenting spouse of Sarpanch Muhammad Din, saw an archangel in a
dream. 'Gibreel,' she whispered, 'is it you?'

'No,' the apparition replied. 'It's I, Azraeel, the one with the
lousy job. Excuse the disappointment.'

The next morning she continued with the pilgrimage, saying
nothing to her husband about her vision. After two hours they
neared the ruin of one of the Mughal milepost inns that had, in
times long gone, been built at five-mile intervals along the
highway. When Khadija saw the ruin she knew nothing of its past,
of the wayfarers robbed in their sleep and so on, but she understood its present well enough. 'I have to go in there and lie down,'
she said to the Sarpanch, who protested: 'But, the march!' 'Never
mind that,' she said gently. 'You can catch them up later.'

She lay down in the rubble of the old ruin with her head on a
smooth stone which the Sarpanch found for her. The old man
wept, but that didn't do any good, and she was dead within a
minute. He ran back to the march and confronted Ayesha angrily.
'I should never have listened to you,' he told her. 'And now you
have killed my wife.'

The march stopped. Mirza Saeed Akhtar, spotting an opportunity, insisted loudly that Khadija be taken to a proper Muslim
burial ground. But Ayesha objected. 'We are ordered by the
archangel to go directly to the sea, without returns or detours.'
Mirza Saeed appealed to the pilgrims. 'She is your Sarpanch's
beloved wife,' he shouted. 'Will you dump her in a hole by the
side of the road?'

When the Titlipur villagers agreed that Khadija should be
buried at once, Saeed could not believe his ears. He realized that
their determination was even greater than he had suspected: even
the bereaved Sarpanch acquiesced. Khadija was buried in the
corner of a barren field behind the ruined way-station of the past.

The next day, however, Mirza Saeed noticed that the Sarpanch
had come unstuck from the pilgrimage, and was mooching along
disconsolately, a little distance apart from the rest, sniffing the
bougainvillaea bushes. Saeed jumped out of the Mercedes and

rushed off to Ayesha, to make another scene. 'You monster!' he shouted. 'Monster without a heart! Why did you bring the old woman here to die?' She ignored him, but on his way back to the station wagon the Sarpanch came over and said: 'We were poor people. We knew we could never hope to go to Mecca Sharif, until she persuaded. She persuaded, and now see the outcome of her deeds.'

Ayesha the kahin asked to speak to the Sarpanch, but gave him not a single word of consolation. 'Harden your faith,' she scolded him. 'She who dies on the great pilgrimage is assured of a home in Paradise. Your wife is sitting now among the angels and the flowers; what is there for you to regret?'

That evening the Sarpanch Muhammad Din approached Mirza Saeed as he sat by a small campfire. 'Excuse, Sethji,' he said, 'but is it possible that I ride, as you once offered, in your motor-car?'

Unwilling wholly to abandon the project for which his wife had died, unable to maintain any longer the absolute belief which the enterprise required, Muhammad Din entered the station wagon of scepticism. 'My first convert,' Mirza Saeed rejoiced.

By the fourth week the defection of Sarpanch Muhammad Din had begun to have its effect. He sat on the back seat of the Mercedes as if he were the zamindar and Mirza Saeed the chauffeur, and little by little the leather upholstery and the air-conditioning unit and the whisky-soda cabinet and the electrically operated mirror-glass windows began to teach him hauteur; his nose tilted into the air and he acquired the supercilious expression of a man who can see without being seen. Mirza Saeed in the driver's seat felt his eyes and nose filling up with the dust that came in through the hole where the windscreen used to be, but in spite of such discomforts he was feeling better than before. Now, at the end of each day, a cluster of pilgrims would congregate around the Mercedes-Benz with its gleaming star, and Mirza Saeed would try and talk sense into them while they watched

Sarpanch Muhammad Din raise and lower the mirror-glass rear windows, so that they saw, alternately, his features and their own. The Sarpanch's presence in the Mercedes lent new authority to Mirza Saeed's words.

Ayesha didn't try to call the villagers away, and so far her confidence had been justified; there had been no further defections to the camp of the faithless. But Saeed saw her casting numerous glances in his direction and whether she was a visionary or not Mirza Saeed would have bet good money that those were the bad-tempered glances of a young girl who was no longer sure of getting her own way.

Then she disappeared.

She went off during an afternoon siesta and did not reappear for a day and a half, by which time there was pandemonium among the pilgrims – she always knew how to whip up an audience's feelings, Saeed conceded; then she sauntered back up to them across the dust-clouded landscape, and this time her silver hair was streaked with gold, and her eyebrows, too, were golden. She summoned the villagers to her and told them that the archangel was displeased that the people of Titlipur had been filled up with doubts just because of the ascent of a martyr to Paradise. She warned that he was seriously thinking of withdrawing his offer to part the waters, 'so that all you'll get at the Arabian Sea is a salt-water bath, and then it's back to your deserted potato fields on which no rain will ever fall again.' The villagers were appalled. 'No, it can't be,' they pleaded. 'Bibiji, forgive us.' It was the first time they had used the name of the longago saint to describe the girl who was leading them with an absolutism that had begun to frighten them as much as it impressed. After her speech the Sarpanch and Mirza Saeed were left alone in the station wagon. 'Second round to the archangel,' Mirza Saeed thought.

By the fifth week the health of most of the older pilgrims had deteriorated sharply, food supplies were running low, water was hard to find, and the children's tear ducts were dry. The vulture herds were never far away.

As the pilgrims left behind the rural areas and came towards more densely populated zones, the level of harassment increased. The long-distance buses and trucks often refused to deviate and the pedestrians had to leap, screaming and tumbling over each other, out of their way. Cyclists, families of six on Rajdoot motor-scooters, petty shop-keepers hurled abuse. 'Crazies! Hicks! Muslims!' Often they were obliged to keep marching for an entire night because the authorities in this or that small town didn't want such riff-raff sleeping on their pavements. More deaths became inevitable.

Then the bullock of the convert, Osman, fell to its knees amid the bicycles and camel-dung of a nameless little town. 'Get up, idiot,' he yelled at it impotently. 'What do you think you're doing, dying on me in front of the fruit-stalls of strangers?' The bullock nodded, twice for yes, and expired.

Butterflies covered the corpse, adopting the colour of its grey hide, its horn-cones and bells. The inconsolable Osman ran to Ayesha (who had put on a dirty sari as a concession to urban prudery, even though butterfly clouds still trailed off her like glory). 'Do bullocks go to Heaven?' he asked in a piteous voice; she shrugged. 'Bullocks have no souls,' she said coolly, 'and it is souls we march to save.' Osman looked at her and realized he no longer loved her. 'You've become a demon,' he told her in disgust.

'I am nothing,' Ayesha said. 'I am a messenger.'

'Then tell me why your God is so anxious to destroy the innocent,' Osman raged. 'What's he afraid of? Is he so unconfident that he needs us to die to prove our love?'

As though in response to such blasphemy, Ayesha imposed even stricter disciplinary measures, insisting that all pilgrims say all five prayers, and decreeing that Fridays would be days of fasting. By the end of the sixth week she had forced the marchers to leave four more bodies where they fell: two old men, one old woman, and one six-year-old girl. The pilgrims marched on, turning their backs on the dead; behind them, however, Mirza Saeed Akhtar gathered up the bodies and made sure they received a decent burial. In this he was assisted by the Sarpanch, Muhammad Din, and the former untouchable, Osman. On such days they would fall quite a way behind the march, but a Mercedes-Benz station wagon doesn't take long to catch up with over a hundred and forty men, women and children walking wearily towards the sea.

The dead grew in number, and the groups of unsettled pilgrims around the Mercedes got larger night by night. Mirza Saeed began to tell them stories. He told them about lemmings, and how the enchantress Circe turned men into pigs; he told, too, the story of a pipe-player who lured a town's children into a mountain-crack. When he had told this tale in their own language he recited verses in English, so that they could listen to the music of the poetry even though they didn't understand the words. 'Hamelin town's in Brunswick,' he began. 'Near famous Hanover City. The River Weser, deep and wide, washes its walls on the southern side . . .'

Now he had the satisfaction of seeing the girl Ayesha advance, looking furious, while the butterflies glowed like the campfire behind her, making it appear as though flames were streaming from her body.

'Those who listen to the Devil's verses, spoken in the Devil's tongue,' she cried, 'will go to the Devil in the end.'

'It's a choice, then,' Mirza Saeed answered her, 'between the devil and the deep blue sea.'

Eight weeks had passed, and relations between Mirza Saeed and his wife Mishal had so deteriorated that they were no longer on speaking terms. By now, and in spite of the cancer that had turned her as grey as funeral ash, Mishal had become Ayesha's chief lieutenant and most devoted disciple. The doubts of other marchers had only strengthened her own faith, and for these doubts she unequivocally blamed her husband.

'Also,' she had rebuked him in their last conversation, 'there is no warmth in you any more. I feel afraid to approach.'

'No warmth?' he yelled. 'How can you say it? No warmth? For whom did I come running on this damnfool pilgrimage? To look after whom? Because I love whom? Because I am so worried about, so sad about, so filled with misery about whom? No warmth? Are you a stranger? How can you say such a thing?'

'Listen to yourself,' she said in a voice which had begun to fade into a kind of smokiness, an opacity. 'Always anger. Cold anger, icy, like a fort.'

'This isn't anger,' he bellowed. 'This is anxiety, unhappiness, wretchedness, injury, pain. Where can you hear anger?'

'I hear it,' she said. 'Everyone can hear, for miles around.'

'Come with me,' he begged her. 'I'll take you to the top clinics in Europe, Canada, the USA. Trust in Western technology. They can do marvels. You always liked gadgets, too.'

'I am going on a pilgrimage to Mecca,' she said, and turned away.

'You damn stupid bitch,' he roared at her back. 'Just because you're going to die doesn't mean you have to take all these people with you.' But she walked away across the roadside camp-site, never looking back; and now that he'd proved her point by losing control and speaking the unspeakable he fell to his knees and wept. After that quarrel Mishal refused to sleep beside him any more. She and her mother rolled out their bedding next to the butterfly-shrouded prophetess of their Meccan quest.

By day, Mishal worked ceaselessly among the pilgrims, reassuring them, bolstering their faith, gathering them together beneath the wing of her gentleness. Ayesha had started retreating deeper and deeper into silence, and Mishal Akhtar became, to all intents and purposes, the leader of the pilgrims. But there was one pilgrim over whom she lost her grip: Mrs Qureishi, her mother, the wife of the director of the state bank.

The arrival of Mr Qureishi, Mishal's father, was quite an event. The pilgrims had stopped in the shade of a line of plane-trees and were busy gathering brushwood and scouring cookpots when the motorcade was sighted. At once Mrs Qureishi, who was twenty-five pounds lighter than she had been at the beginning of the walk, leaped squeakily to her feet and tried frantically to brush the dirt off her clothes and to put her hair in order. Mishal saw her mother fumbling feebly with a molten lipstick and asked, 'What's bugging you, ma? Relax, na.'

Her mother pointed feebly at the approaching cars. Moments later the tall, severe figure of the great banker was standing over them. 'If I had not seen it I would not have believed,' he said. 'They told me, but I pooh-poohed. Therefore it took me this long to find out. To vanish from Peristan without a word: now what in tarnation?'

Mrs Qureishi shook helplessly under her husband's eyes, beginning to cry, feeling the calluses on her feet and the fatigue that had sunk into every pore of her body. 'O God, I don't know, I am sorry,' she said. 'God knows what came over.'

'Don't you know I occupy a delicate post?' Mr Qureishi cried. 'Public confidence is of essence. How does it look then that my wife gallivants with bhangis?'

Mishal, embracing her mother, told her father to stop bullying. Mr Qureishi saw for the first time that his daughter had the mark of death on her forehead and deflated instantly like an inner tube. Mishal told him about the cancer, and the promise of the seer Ayesha that a miracle would occur in Mecca, and she would be completely cured.

'Then let me fly you to Mecca, pronto,' her father pleaded. 'Why walk if you can go by Airbus?'

But Mishal was adamant. 'You should go away,' she told her father. 'Only the faithful can make this thing come about. Mummy will look after me.'

Mr Qureishi in his limousine helplessly joined Mirza Saeed at the rear of the procession, constantly sending one of the two ser-

vants who had accompanied him on motor-scooters to ask Mishal
if she would like food, medicine, Thums Up, anything at all.
Mishal turned down all his offers, and after three days – because
banking is banking – Mr Qureishi departed for the city, leaving
behind one of the motor-scooter chaprassis to serve the women.
'He is yours to command,' he told them. 'Don't be stupid now.
Make this as easy as you can.'

The day after Mr Qureishi's departure, the chaprassi Gul
Muhammad ditched his scooter and joined the foot-pilgrims,
knotting a handkerchief around his head to indicate his devotion.
Ayesha said nothing, but when she saw the scooter-wallah join the
pilgrimage she grinned an impish grin that reminded Mirza Saeed
that she was, after all, not only a figure out of a dream, but also a
flesh-and-blood young girl.

Mrs Qureishi began to complain. The brief contact with her
old life had broken her resolve, and now that it was too late she
had started thinking constantly about parties and soft cushions and
glasses of iced fresh lime soda. It suddenly seemed wholly unreasonable to her that a person of her breeding should be asked to go
barefoot like a common sweeper. She presented herself to Mirza
Saeed with a sheepish expression on her face.

'Saeed, son, do you hate me completely?' she wheedled, her
plump features arranging themselves in a parody of coquettishness.

Saeed was appalled by her grimace. 'Of course not,' he managed to say.

'But you do, you loathe me, and my cause is hopeless,' she
flirted.

'Ammaji,' Saeed gulped, 'what are you saying?'

'Because I have from time to time spoken roughly to you.'

'Please forget it,' Saeed said, bemused by her performance, but
she would not. 'You must know it was all for love, isn't it? Love,'
said Mrs. Qureishi, 'it is a many-splendoured thing.'

'Makes the world go round,' Mirza Saeed agreed, trying to
enter into the spirit of the conversation.

'Love conquers all,' Mrs Qureishi confirmed. 'It has conquered my anger. This I must demonstrate to you by riding with you in your motor.'

Mirza Saeed bowed. 'It is yours, Ammaji.'

'Then you will ask those two village men to sit in front with you. Ladies must be protected, isn't it?'

'It is,' he replied.

The story of the village that was walking to the sea had spread all over the country, and in the ninth week the pilgrims were being pestered by journalists, local politicos in search of votes, businessmen who offered to sponsor the march if the yatris would only consent to wear sandwich boards advertising various goods and services, foreign tourists looking for the mysteries of the East, nostalgic Gandhians, and the kind of human vultures who go to motor-car races to watch the crashes. When they saw the host of chameleon butterflies and the way they both clothed the girl Ayesha and provided her with her only solid food, these visitors were amazed, and retreated with confounded expectations, that is to say with a hole in their pictures of the world that they could not paper over. Photographs of Ayesha were appearing in all the papers, and the pilgrims even passed advertising hoardings on which the lepidopteral beauty had been painted three times as large as life, beside slogans reading *Our cloths also are as delicate as a butterfly's wing,* or suchlike. Then more alarming news reached them. Certain religious extremist groupings had issued statements denouncing the 'Ayesha Haj' as an attempt to 'hijack' public attention and to 'incite communal sentiment'. Leaflets were being distributed – Mishal picked them up off the road – in which it was claimed that 'Padyatra, or foot-pilgrimage, is an ancient, pre-Islamic tradition of national culture, not imported property of Mughal immigrants.' Also: 'Purloining of this tradition by so-called Ayesha Bibiji is flagrant and deliberate inflammation of already sensitive situation.'

'There will be no trouble,' the kahin broke her silence to announce.

Gibreel dreamed a suburb:

As the Ayesha Haj neared Sarang, the outermost suburb of the great metropolis on the Arabian Sea towards which the visionary girl was leading them, journalists, politicos and police officers redoubled their visits. At first the policemen threatened to disband the march forcibly; the politicians, however, advised that this would look very like a sectarian act and could lead to outbreaks of communal violence from top to bottom of the country. Eventually the police chiefs agreed to permit the march, but groused menacingly about being 'unable to guarantee safe passages' for the pilgrims. Mishal Akhtar said: 'We are going on.'

The suburb of Sarang owed its relative affluence to the presence of substantial coal deposits nearby. It turned out that the coal-miners of Sarang, men whose lives were spent boring pathways through the earth – 'parting' it, one might say – could not stomach the notion that a girl could do the same, with a wave of her hand, for the sea. Cadres of certain communalist groupings had been at work, inciting the miners to violence, and as a result of the activities of these agents provocateurs a mob was forming, carrying banners demanding: NO ISLAMIC PADYATRA! BUTTERFLY WITCH, GO HOME.

On the night before they were due to enter Sarang, Mirza Saeed made another futile appeal to the pilgrims. 'Give up,' he implored uselessly. 'Tomorrow we will all be killed.' Ayesha whispered in Mishal's ear, and she spoke up: 'Better a martyr than a coward. Are there any cowards here?'

There was one. Sri Srinivas, explorer of the Grand Canyon, proprietor of a Toy Univas, whose motto was creativity and sincerity, sided with Mirza Saeed. As a devout follower of the goddess Lakshmi, whose face was so perplexingly also Ayesha's, he felt unable to participate in the coming hostilities on either side. 'I am a weak fellow,' he confessed to Saeed. 'I have loved Miss Ayesha, and a man should fight for what he loves; but, what to do, I require neutral status.' Srinivas was the fifth member of the renegade society in the Mercedes-Benz, and now Mrs Qureishi had no option but to share the back seat with a common man. Srinivas greeted her unhappily, and, seeing her bounce grumpily along the seat away from him, attempted to placate. 'Please to accept a token of my esteem.' – And produced, from an inside pocket, a Family Planning doll.

That night the deserters remained in the station wagon while the faithful prayed in the open air. They had been allowed to camp in a disused goods train marshalling yard, guarded by military police. Mirza Saeed couldn't sleep. He was thinking about something Srinivas had said to him, about being a Gandhian in his head, 'but I'm too weak to put such notions into practice. Excuse me, but it's true. I was not cut out for suffering, Sethji. I should have stayed with wife and kiddies and cut out this adventure disease that has made me land up in such a place.'

In my family, too, Mirza Saeed in his insomnia answered the sleeping toy merchant, we have suffered from a kind of disease: one of detachment, of being unable to connect ourselves to things, events, feelings. Most people define themselves by their work, or where they come from, or suchlike; we have lived too far inside our heads. It makes actuality damn hard to handle.

Which was to say that he found it hard to believe that all this was really happening; but it was.

When the Ayesha Pilgrims were ready to set off the next morning, the huge clouds of butterflies that had travelled with them all the way from Titlipur suddenly broke up and vanished from view, revealing that the sky was filling up with other, more prosaic clouds. Even the creatures that had been clothing Ayesha – the elite corps, so to speak – decamped, and she had to lead the procession dressed in the mundanity of an old cotton sari with a block-printed hem of leaves. The disappearance of the miracle that had seemed to validate their pilgrimage depressed all the marchers; so that in spite of all Mishal Akhtar's exhortations they

were unable to sing as they moved forwards, deprived of the
benediction of the butterflies, to meet their fate.

The No Islamic Padyatra street mob had prepared a welcome for
Ayesha in a street lined on both sides with the shacks of bicycle
repairers. They had blocked the pilgrims' routes with dead
bicycles, and waited behind this barricade of broken wheels, bent
handlebars and silenced bells as the Ayesha Haj entered the
northern sector of the street. Ayesha walked towards the mob as if
it did not exist, and when she reached the last crossroads, beyond
which the clubs and knives of the enemy awaited her, there was a
thunderclap like the trumpet of doom and an ocean fell down out
of the sky. The drought had broken too late to save the crops;
afterwards many of the pilgrims believed that God had been saving
up the water for just this purpose, letting it build up in the sky
until it was as endless as the sea, sacrificing the year's harvest in
order to save his prophetess and her people.

The stunning force of the downpour unnerved both pilgrims
and assailants. In the confusion of the flood a second doom-
trumpet was heard. This was, in point of fact, the horn of Mirza
Saeed's Mercedes-Benz station wagon, which he had driven at
high speed through the suffocating side gullies of the suburb,
bringing down racks of shirts hanging on rails, and pumpkin bar-
rows, and trays of cheap plastic notions, until he reached the street
of basket-workers that intersected the street of bicycle repairers
just to the north of the barricade. Here he accelerated as hard as he
could and charged towards the crossroads, scattering pedestrians
and wickerwork stools in all directions. He reached the crossroads
immediately after the sea fell out of the sky, and braked violently.
Sri Srinivas and Osman leaped out, seized Mishal Akhtar and the
prophetess Ayesha, and hauled them into the Mercedes in a flurry
of legs, sputum and abuse. Saeed accelerated away from the scene
before anybody had managed to get the blinding water out of
their eyes.

Inside the car: bodies heaped in an angry jumble. Mishal Akhtar shouted abuse at her husband from the bottom of the pile: 'Saboteur! Traitor! Scum from somewhere! Mule!' – To which Saeed sarcastically replied, 'Martyrdom is too easy, Mishal. Don't you want to watch the ocean open, like a flower?'

And Mrs Qureishi, sticking her head out through Osman's inverted legs, added in a pink-faced gasp: 'Okay, come on, Mishu, quit. We meant well.'

Gibreel dreamed a flood:

When the rains came, the miners of Sarang had been waiting for the pilgrims with their pickaxes in their hands, but when the bicycle barricade was swept away they could not avoid the idea that God had taken Ayesha's side. The town's drainage system surrendered instantly to the overwhelming assault of the water, and the miners were soon standing in a muddy flood that reached as high as their waists. Some of them tried to move towards the pilgrims, who also continued to make efforts to advance. But now the rainstorm redoubled its force, and then doubled it again, falling from the sky in thick slabs through which it was getting difficult to breathe, as though the earth were being engulfed, and the firmament above were reuniting with the firmament below.

Gibreel, dreaming, found his vision obscured by water.

The rain stopped, and a watery sun shone down on a Venetian scene of devastation. The roads of Sarang were now canals, along which there journeyed all manner of flotsam. Where only recently scooter-rickshaws, camel-carts and repaired bicycles had gone, there now floated newspapers, flowers, bangles, watermelons, umbrellas, chappals, sunglasses, baskets, excrement, medicine bottles, playing cards, dupattas, pancakes, lamps. The water had an odd, reddish tint that made the sodden populace imagine that the street was flowing with blood. There was no trace of bully-boy miners or of Ayesha Pilgrims. A dog swam across the intersection by the collapsed bicycle barricade, and all around there lay the damp silence of the flood, whose waters lapped at marooned buses, while children stared from the roofs of deliquescent gullies, too shocked to come out and play.

Then the butterflies returned.

From nowhere, as if they had been hiding behind the sun; and to celebrate the end of the rain they had all taken the colour of sunlight. The arrival of this immense carpet of light in the sky utterly bewildered the people of Sarang, who were already reeling in the aftermath of the storm; fearing the apocalypse, they hid indoors and closed their shutters. On a nearby hillside, however, Mirza Saeed Akhtar and his party observed the miracle's return and were filled, all of them, even the zamindar, with a kind of awe.

Mirza Saeed had driven hell-for-leather, in spite of being half-blinded by the rain which poured through the smashed windscreen, until on a road that led up and around the bend of a hill he came to a halt at the gates of the No. 1 Sarang Coalfield. The pit-heads were dimly visible through the rain. 'Brainbox,' Mishal Akhtar cursed him weakly. 'Those bums are waiting for us back there, and you drive us up here to see their pals. Tip-top notion, Saeed. Extra fine.'

But they had no more trouble from miners. That was the day of the mining disaster that left fifteen thousand pitmen buried alive beneath the Sarangi hill. Saeed, Mishal, the Sarpanch, Osman, Mrs Qureishi, Srinivas and Ayesha stood exhausted and soaked to the skin by the roadside as ambulances, fire-engines, salvage operators and pit bosses arrived in large quantities and left, much later, shaking their heads. The Sarpanch caught his earlobes between thumbs and forefingers. 'Life is pain,' he said. 'Life is pain and loss; it is a coin of no value, worth even less than a kauri or a dam.'

Osman of the dead bullock, who, like the Sarpanch, had lost a dearly loved companion during the pilgrimage, also wept. Mrs Qureishi attempted to look on the bright side: 'Main thing is that we're okay,' but this got no response. Then Ayesha closed her eyes and recited in the sing-song voice of prophecy, 'It is a judgment upon them for the bad attempt they made.'

Mirza Saeed was angry. 'They weren't at the bloody barricade,' he shouted. 'They were working under the goddamned ground.'

'They dug their own graves,' Ayesha replied.

This was when they sighted the returning butterflies. Saeed watched the golden cloud in disbelief, as it first gathered and then sent out streams of winged light in every direction. Ayesha wanted to return to the crossroads. Saeed objected: 'It's flooded down there. Our only chance is to drive down the opposite side of this hill and come out the other side of town.' But Ayesha and Mishal had already started back; the prophetess was supporting the other, ashen woman, holding her around the waist.

'Mishal, for God's sake,' Mirza Saeed called after his wife. 'For the love of God. What will I do with the motor-car?'

But she went on down the hill, towards the flood, leaning heavily on Ayesha the seer, without looking round.

This was how Mirza Saeed Akhtar came to abandon his beloved Mercedes-Benz station wagon near the entrance to the drowned mines of Sarang, and join in the foot-pilgrimage to the Arabian Sea.

The seven bedraggled travellers stood thigh-deep in water at the intersection of the street of bicycle repairers and the alley of the basket-weavers. Slowly, slowly, the water had begun to go down. 'Face it,' Mirza Saeed argued. 'The pilgrimage is finished. The villagers are who knows where, maybe drowned, possibly murdered, certainly lost. There's nobody left to follow you but us.' He stuck his face into Ayesha's. 'So forget it, sister; you're sunk.'

'Look,' Mishal said.

From all sides, out of little tinkers' gullies, the villagers of Titlipur were returning to the place of their dispersal. They were all coated from neck to ankles in golden butterflies, and long lines of the little creatures went before them, like ropes drawing them to safety out of a well. The people of Sarang watched in terror from their windows, and as the waters of retribution receded, the Ayesha Haj re-formed in the middle of the road.

'I don't believe it,' said Mirza Saeed.

But it was true. Every single member of the pilgrimage had been tracked down by the butterflies and brought back to the main road. And stranger claims were later made: that when the creatures had settled on a broken ankle the injury had healed, or that an open wound had closed as if by magic. Many marchers said they had awoken from unconsciousness to find the butterflies fluttering about their lips. Some even believed that they had been dead, drowned, and that the butterflies had brought them back to life.

'Don't be stupid,' Mirza Saeed cried. 'The storm saved you; it washed away your enemies, so it's not surprising few of you are hurt. Let's be scientific, please.'

'Use your eyes, Saeed,' Mishal told him, indicating the presence before them of over a hundred men, women and children enveloped in glowing butterflies. 'What does your science say about this?'

In the last days of the pilgrimage, the city was all around them. Officers from the Municipal Corporation met with Mishal and Ayesha and planned a route through the metropolis. On this route were mosques in which the pilgrims could sleep without clogging up the streets. Excitement in the city was intense: each day, when the pilgrims set off towards their next resting-place, they were watched by enormous crowds, some sneering and hostile, but many bringing presents of sweetmeats, medicines and food.

Mirza Saeed, worn-out and filthy, was in a state of deep frustration on account of his failure to convince more than a handful of the pilgrims that it was better to put one's trust in reason than in miracles. Miracles had been doing pretty well for them, the Titlipur villagers pointed out, reasonably enough. 'Those blasted butterflies,' Saeed muttered to the Sarpanch. 'Without them, we'd have a chance.'

'But they have been with us from the start,' the Sarpanch replied with a shrug.

Mishal Akhtar was clearly close to death; she had begun to smell of it, and had turned a chalky white colour that frightened Saeed badly. But Mishal wouldn't let him come near her. She had ostracized her mother, too, and when her father took time off from banking to visit her on the pilgrimage's first night in a city mosque, she told him to buzz off. 'Things have come to the point,' she announced, 'where only the pure can be with the pure.' When Mirza Saeed heard the diction of Ayesha the prophetess emerging from his wife's mouth he lost all but the tiniest speck of hope.

Friday came, and Ayesha agreed that the pilgrimage could halt for a day to participate in the Friday prayers. Mirza Saeed, who had forgotten almost all the Arabic verses that had once been stuffed into him by rote, and could scarcely remember when to stand with his hands held in front of him like a book, when to genuflect, when to press his forehead to the ground, stumbled through the ceremony with growing self-disgust. At the end of the prayers, however, something happened that stopped the Ayesha Haj in its tracks.

As the pilgrims watched the congregation leaving the courtyard of the mosque, a commotion began outside the main gate. Mirza Saeed went to investigate. 'What's the hoo-hah?' he asked as he struggled through the crowd on the mosque steps; then he saw the basket sitting on the bottom step. – And heard, rising from the basket, the baby's cry.

The foundling was perhaps two weeks old, clearly illegitimate, and it was equally plain that its options in life were limited. The crowd was in a doubtful, confused mood. Then the mosque's Imam appeared at the head of the flight of steps, and beside him was Ayesha the seer, whose fame had spread throughout the city.

The crowd parted like the sea, and Ayesha and the Imam came

down to the basket. The Imam examined the baby briefly; rose; and turned to address the crowd.

'This child was born in devilment,' he said. 'It is the Devil's child.' He was a young man.

The mood of the crowd shifted towards anger. Mirza Saeed Akhtar shouted out: 'You, Ayesha, kahin. What do you say?'

'Everything will be asked of us,' she replied.

The crowd, needing no clearer invitation, stoned the baby to death.

After that the Ayesha Pilgrims refused to move on. The death of the foundling had created an atmosphere of mutiny among the weary villagers, none of whom had lifted or thrown a stone. Mishal, snow-white now, was too enfeebled by her illness to rally the marchers; Ayesha, as ever, refused to dispute. 'If you turn your backs on God,' she warned the villagers, 'don't be surprised when he does the same to you.'

The pilgrims were squatting in a group in a corner of the large mosque, which was painted lime-green on the outside and bright blue within, and lit, when necessary, by multicoloured neon 'tube lights'. After Ayesha's warning they turned their backs on her and huddled closer together, although the weather was warm and humid enough. Mirza Saeed, spotting his opportunity, decided to challenge Ayesha directly once again. 'Tell me,' he asked sweetly, 'how exactly does the angel give you all this information? You never tell us his precise words, only your interpretations of them. Why such indirection? Why not simply quote?'

'He speaks to me,' Ayesha answered, 'in clear and memorable forms.'

Mirza Saeed, full of the bitter energy of his desire for her, and the pain of his estrangement from his dying wife, and the memory of the tribulations of the march, smelled in her reticence the weakness he had been probing for. 'Kindly be more specific,' he insisted. 'Or why should anyone believe? What are these forms?'

'The archangel sings to me,' she admitted, 'to the tunes of popular hit songs.'

Mirza Saeed Akhtar clapped his hands delightedly and began to laugh the loud, echoing laughter of revenge, and Osman the bullock-boy joined in, beating on his dholki and prancing around the squatting villagers, singing the latest filmi ganas and making nautch-girl eyes. 'Ho ji!' he carolled. 'This is how Gibreel recites, ho ji! Ho ji!'

And one after the other, pilgrim after pilgrim rose and joined in the dance of the circling drummer, dancing their disillusion and disgust in the courtyard of the mosque, until the Imam came running to shriek at the ungodliness of their deeds.

Night fell. The villagers of Titlipur were grouped around their Sarpanch, Muhammad Din, and serious talks about returning to Titlipur were under way. Perhaps a little of the harvest could be saved. Mishal Akhtar lay dying with her head in her mother's lap, racked by pain, with a single tear emerging from her left eye. And in a far corner of the courtyard of the greenblue mosque with its technicolour tube-lighting, the visionary and the zamindar sat alone and talked. A moon – new, horned, cold – shone down.

'You're a clever man,' Ayesha said. 'You knew how to take your chance.'

This was when Mirza Saeed made his offer of a compromise. 'My wife is dying,' he said. 'And she wants very much to go to Mecca Sharif. So we have interests in common, you and I.'

Ayesha listened. Saeed pressed on: 'Ayesha, I'm not a bad man. Let me tell you, I've been damn impressed by many things on this walk; *damn* impressed. You have given these people a profound spiritual experience, no question. Don't think we modern types lack a spiritual dimension.'

'The people have left me,' Ayesha said.

'The people are confused,' Saeed replied. 'Point is, if you actually take them to the sea and then nothing happens, my God, they really could turn against you. So here's the deal. I gave a tinkle to

Mishal's papa and he agreed to underwrite half the cost. We propose to fly you and Mishal, and let's say ten – twelve! – of the villagers, to Mecca, within forty-eight hours, personally. Reservations are available. We leave it to you to select the individuals best suited to the trip. Then, truly, you will have performed a miracle for some instead of for none. And in my view the pilgrimage itself has been a miracle, in a way. So you will have done very much.'

He held his breath.

'I must think,' Ayesha said.

'Think, think,' Saeed encouraged her happily. 'Ask your archangel. If he agrees, it must be right.'

Mirza Saeed Akhtar knew that when Ayesha announced that the Archangel Gibreel had accepted his offer her power would be destroyed forever, because the villagers would perceive her fraudulence and her desperation, too. – But how could she turn him down? – What choice did she really have? 'Revenge is sweet,' he told himself. Once the woman was discredited, he would certainly take Mishal to Mecca, if that were still her wish.

The butterflies of Titlipur had not entered the mosque. They lined its exterior walls and onion dome, glowing greenly in the dark.

Ayesha in the night: stalking the shadows, lying down, rising to go on the prowl again. There was an uncertainty about her; then the slowness came, and she seemed to dissolve into the shadows of the mosque. She returned at dawn.

After the morning prayer she asked the pilgrims if she might address them; and they, doubtfully, agreed.

'Last night the angel did not sing,' she said. 'He told me, instead, about doubt, and how the Devil makes use of it. I said, but they doubt me, what can I do? He answered: only proof can silence doubt.'

She had their full attention. Next she told them what Mirza Saeed had suggested in the night. 'He told me to go and ask my angel, but I know better,' she cried. 'How could I choose between you? It is all of us, or none.'

'Why should we follow you,' the Sarpanch asked, 'after all the dying, the baby, and all?'

'Because when the waters part, you will be saved. You will enter into the Glory of the Most High.'

'What waters?' Mirza Saeed yelled. 'How will they divide?'

'Follow me,' Ayesha concluded, 'and judge me by their parting.'

His offer had contained an old question: *What kind of idea are you?* And she, in turn, had offered him an old answer. *I was tempted, but am renewed; am uncompromising; absolute; pure.*

The tide was in when the Ayesha Pilgrimage marched down an alley beside the Holiday Inn, whose windows were full of the mistresses of film stars using their new Polaroid cameras, – when the pilgrims felt the city's asphalt turn gritty and soften into sand, – when they found themselves walking through a thick mulch of rotting coconuts abandoned cigarette packets pony turds non-degradable bottles fruit peelings jellyfish and paper, – on to the mid-brown sand overhung by high leaning coco-palms and the balconies of luxury sea-view apartment blocks, – past the teams of young men whose muscles were so well-honed that they looked like deformities, and who were performing gymnastic contortions of all sorts, in unison, like a murderous army of ballet dancers, – and through the beachcombers, clubmen and families who had come to take the air or make business contacts or scavenge a living from the sand, – and gazed, for the first time in their lives, upon the Arabian Sea.

Mirza Saeed saw Mishal, who was being supported by two of the village men, because she was no longer strong enough to stand up by herself. Ayesha was beside her, and Saeed had the idea that the prophetess had somehow stepped out of the dying woman, that all the brightness of Mishal had hopped out of her body and taken this mythological shape, leaving a husk behind to die. Then he was angry with himself for allowing Ayesha's supernaturalism to infect him, too.

The villagers of Titlipur had agreed to follow Ayesha after a long discussion in which they had asked her not to take part. Their common sense told them that it would be foolish to turn back when they had come so far and were in sight of their first goal; but the new doubts in their minds sapped their strength. It was as if they were emerging from some Shangri-La of Ayesha's making, because now that they were simply walking behind her rather than following her in the true sense, they seemed to age and sicken with every step they took. By the time they saw the sea they were a lame, tottering, rheumy, feverish, red-eyed bunch, and Mirza Saeed wondered how many of them would manage the final few yards to the water's edge.

The butterflies were with them, high over their heads.

'What now, Ayesha?' Saeed called out to her, filled with the horrible notion that his beloved wife might die here under the hoofs of ponies for rent and beneath the eyes of sugarcane-juice vendors. 'You have brought us all to the edges of extinction, but here is an unquestionable fact: the sea. Where is your angel now?'

She climbed up, with the villagers' help, on to an unused thela lying next to a soft-drink stall, and didn't answer Saeed until she could look down at him from her new perch. 'Gibreel says the sea is like our souls. When we open them, we can move through into wisdom. If we can open our hearts, we can open the sea.'

'Partition was quite a disaster here on land,' he taunted her. 'Quite a few guys died, you might remember. You think it will be different in the water?'

'Shh,' said Ayesha suddenly. 'The angel's almost here.'

It was, on the face of it, surprising that after all the attention the march had received the crowd at the beach was no better than moderate; but the authorities had taken many precautions, closing roads, diverting traffic; so there were perhaps two hundred gawpers on the beach. Nothing to worry about.

What *was* strange was that the spectators did not see the butterflies, or what they did next. But Mirza Saeed clearly observed the great glowing cloud fly out over the sea; pause; hover; and form itself into the shape of a colossal being, a radiant giant constructed wholly of tiny beating wings, stretching from horizon to horizon, filling the sky.

'The angel!' Ayesha called to the pilgrims. 'Now you see! He's been with us all the way. Do you believe me now?' Mirza Saeed saw absolute faith return to the pilgrims. 'Yes,' they wept, begging her forgiveness. 'Gibreel! Gibreel! Ya Allah.'

Mirza Saeed made his last effort. 'Clouds take many shapes,' he shouted. 'Elephants, film stars, anything. Look, it's changing even now.' But nobody paid any attention to him; they were watching, full of amazement, as the butterflies dived into the sea.

The villagers were shouting and dancing for joy. 'The parting! The parting!' they cried. Bystanders called out to Mirza Saeed: 'Hey, mister, what are they getting so fired up about? We can't see anything going on.'

Ayesha had begun to walk towards the water, and Mishal was being dragged along by her two helpers. Saeed ran to her and began to struggle with the village men. 'Let go of my wife. At once! Damn you! I am your zamindar. Release her; remove your filthy hands!' But Mishal whispered: 'They won't. Go away, Saeed. You are closed. The sea only opens for those who are open.'

'Mishal!' he screamed, but her feet were already wet.

Once Ayesha had entered the water the villagers began to run. Those who could not leapt upon the backs of those who could. Holding their babies, the mothers of Titlipur rushed into the sea; grandsons bore their grandmothers on their shoulders and rushed into the waves. Within minutes the entire village was in the water, splashing about, falling over, getting up, moving steadily forwards, towards the horizon, never looking back to shore. Mirza Saeed was in the water, too. 'Come back,' he beseeched his wife. 'Nothing is happening; come back.'

At the water's edge stood Mrs Qureishi, Osman, the Sarpanch, Sri Srinivas. Mishal's mother was sobbing operatically: 'O my baby, my baby. What will become?' Osman said: 'When it becomes clear that miracles don't happen, they will turn back.' 'And the butterflies?' Srinivas asked him, querulously. 'What were they? An accident?'

It dawned on them that the villagers were not coming back. 'They must be nearly out of their depth,' the Sarpanch said. 'How many of them can swim?' asked blubbering Mrs Qureishi. 'Swim?' shouted Srinivas. 'Since when can village folk swim?' They were all screaming at one another as if they were miles apart, jumping from foot to foot, their bodies willing them to enter the water, to do something. They looked as if they were dancing on a fire. The incharge of the police squad that had been sent down for crowd control purposes came up as Saeed came running out of the water.

'What is befalling?' the officer asked. 'What is the agitation?'

'Stop them,' Mirza Saeed panted, pointing out to sea.

'Are they miscreants?' the policeman asked.

'They are going to die,' Saeed replied.

It was too late. The villagers, whose heads could be seen bobbing about in the distance, had reached the edge of the under-water shelf. Almost all together, making no visible attempt to save themselves, they dropped beneath the water's surface. In moments, every one of the Ayesha Pilgrims had sunk out of sight.

None of them reappeared. Not a single gasping head or thrashing arm.

Saeed, Osman, Srinivas, the Sarpanch, and even fat Mrs Qureishi ran into the water, shrieking: 'God have mercy; come on, everybody, help.'

Human beings in danger of drowning struggle against the water. It is against human nature simply to walk forwards meekly until the sea swallows you up. But Ayesha, Mishal Akhtar and the villagers of Titlipur subsided below sea-level; and were never seen again.

Mrs Qureishi was pulled to shore by policemen, her face blue, her lungs full of water, and needed the kiss of life. Osman, Srinivas and the Sarpanch were dragged out soon afterwards. Only Mirza Saeed Akhtar continued to dive, further and further out to sea,

staying under for longer and longer periods; until he, too, was rescued from the Arabian Sea, spent, sick and fainting. The pilgrimage was over.

Mirza Saeed awoke in a hospital ward to find a CID man by his
bedside. The authorities were considering the feasibility of
charging the survivors of the Ayesha expedition with attempted
illegal emigration, and detectives had been instructed to get down
their stories before they had had a chance to confer.

This was the testimony of the Sarpanch of Titlipur, Muhammad
Din: 'Just when my strength had failed and I thought I would
surely die there in the water, I saw it with my own eyes; I saw the
sea divide, like hair being combed; and they were all there, far
away, walking away from me. She was there also, my wife,
Khadija, whom I loved.'

This is what Osman the bullock-boy told the detectives, who
had been badly shaken by the Sarpanch's deposition: 'At first I was
in great fear of drowning myself. Still, I was searching searching,
mainly for her, Ayesha, whom I knew from before her alteration.
And just at the last, I saw it happen, the marvellous thing. The
water opened, and I saw them go along the ocean-floor, among
the dying fish.'

Sri Srinivas, too, swore by the goddess Lakshmi that he had seen
the parting of the Arabian Sea; and by the time the detectives got
to Mrs Qureishi, they were utterly unnerved, because they knew
that it was impossible for the men to have cooked up the story
together. Mishal's mother, the wife of the great banker, told the
same story in her own words. 'Believe don't believe,' she finished
emphatically, 'but what my eyes have seen my tongue repeats.'

Goosepimply CID men attempted the third degree: 'Listen,
Sarpanch, don't shit from your mouth. So many were there,
nobody saw these things. Already the drowned bodies are floating
to shore, swollen like balloons and stinking like hell. If you go on
lying we will take you and stick your nose in the truth.'

'You can show me whatever you want,' Sarpanch Muhammad
Din told interrogators. 'But I still saw what I saw.'

'And you?' the CID men assembled, once he awoke, to ask Mirza Saeed Akhtar. 'What did you see at the beach?'

'How can you ask?' he protested. 'My wife has drowned. Don't come hammering with your questions.'

When he found out that he was the only survivor of the Ayesha Haj not to have witnessed the parting of the waves – Sri Srinivas was the one who told him what the others saw, adding mournfully: 'It is our shame that we were not thought worthy to accompany. On us, Sethji, the waters closed, they slammed in our faces like the gates of Paradise' – Mirza Saeed broke down and wept for a week and a day, the dry sobs continuing to shake his body long after his tear ducts had run out of salt.

Then he went home.

Moths had eaten the punkahs of Peristan and the library had been consumed by a billion hungry worms. When he turned on the taps, snakes oozed out instead of water, and creepers had twined themselves around the four-poster bed in which Viceroys had once slept. It was as if time had accelerated in his absence, and centuries had somehow elapsed instead of months, so that when he touched the giant Persian carpet rolled up in the ballroom it crumbled under his hand, and the baths were full of frogs with scarlet eyes. At night there were jackals howling on the wind. The great tree was dead, or close to death, and the fields were barren as the desert; the gardens of Peristan, in which, long ago, he first saw a beautiful young girl, had long ago yellowed into ugliness. Vultures were the only birds in the sky.

He pulled a rocking-chair out on to his veranda, sat down, and rocked himself gently to sleep.

Once, only once, he visited the tree. The village had crumbled into dust; landless peasants and looters had tried to seize the abandoned land, but the drought had driven them away. There had been no rain here. Mirza Saeed returned to Peristan and padlocked the rusty gates. He was not interested in the fate of his fellow-survivors; he went to the telephone and ripped it out of the wall.

After an uncounted passage of days it occurred to him that he was starving to death, because he could smell his body reeking of nail-varnish remover; but as he felt neither hungry nor thirsty, he decided there was no point bothering to find food. For what? Much better to rock in this chair, and not think, not think, not think.

On the last night of his life he heard a noise like a giant crushing a forest beneath his feet, and smelled a stench like the giant's fart, and he realized that the tree was burning. He got out of his chair and staggered dizzily down to the garden to watch the fire, whose flames were consuming histories, memories, genealogies, purifying the earth, and coming towards him to set him free; – because the wind was blowing the fire towards the grounds of the mansion, so soon enough, soon enough, it would be his turn. He saw the tree explode into a thousand fragments, and the trunk crack, like a heart; then he turned away and reeled towards the place in the garden where Ayesha had first caught his eye; – and now he felt a slowness come upon him, a great heaviness, and he lay down on the withered dust. Before his eyes closed he felt something brushing at his lips, and saw the little cluster of butter-flies struggling to enter his mouth. Then the sea poured over him, and he was in the water beside Ayesha, who had stepped miracu-lously out of his wife's body . . . 'Open,' she was crying. 'Open wide!' Tentacles of light were flowing from her navel and he chopped at them, chopped, using the side of his hand. 'Open,' she screamed. 'You've come this far, now do the rest.' – How could he hear her voice? – They were under water, lost in the roaring of the sea, but he could hear her clearly, they could all hear her, that voice like a bell. 'Open,' she said. He closed.

He was a fortress with clanging gates. – He was drowning. –

She was drowning, too. He saw the water fill her mouth, heard it begin to gurgle into her lungs. Then something within him refused that, made a different choice, and at the instant that his heart broke, he opened.

His body split apart from his adam's-apple to his groin, so that she could reach deep within him, and now she was open, they all were, and at the moment of their opening the waters parted, and they walked to Mecca across the bed of the Arabian Sea.

PART IX

A
WONDERFUL
LAMP

1

Eighteen months after his heart attack, Saladin Chamcha took to the air again in response to the telegraphed news that his father was in the terminal stages of multiple myeloma, a systemic cancer of the bone marrow that was 'one hundred per cent fatal', as Chamcha's GP unsentimentally put it when he telephoned her to check. There had been no real contact between father and son since Changez Chamchawala sent Saladin the proceeds from his felled walnut-tree all those eternities ago. Saladin had sent a brief note reporting that he had survived the *Bostan* disaster, and had been sent an even terser missive in return: 'Rec.'d yr. communication. This information already to hand.' When the bad news telegram arrived, however – the signatory was the unknown second wife, Nasreen II, and the tone was pretty unvarnished: FATHER GOING FAST + IF DESIROUS OF SEEING BETTER MOVE IT + N CHAMCHAWALA (MRS) – he discovered to his surprise that after a lifetime of tangled relationships with his father, after long years of crossed wires and 'irrevocable sunderings', he was once again capable of an uncomplicated reaction. Simply, overwhelmingly, it was imperative that he reach Bombay before Changez left it for good.

He spent the best part of a day first standing in the visa queue at the consular section of India House, and then trying to persuade a jaded official of the urgency of his application. He had stupidly forgotten to bring the telegram, and was told, as a result, that 'it is issue of proof. You see, anybody could come and tell that their father is dying, isn't it? In order to expedite.' Chamcha fought to restrain his anger, but finally burst. 'Do I look like a Khalistan zealot to you?' The official shrugged. 'I'll tell you who I am,' Chamcha bellowed, incensed by that shrug, 'I'm the poor bastard who got blown up by terrorists, fell thirty thousand feet out of the sky because of terrorists, and now because of those same terrorists I have to be insulted by pen-pushers like you.' His visa application, placed firmly at the bottom of a large pile by his adversary, was not granted until three days later. The first available flight was thirty-six hours after that: and it was an Air India 747, and its name was *Gulistan*.

Gulistan and Bostan, the twin gardens of Paradise – one blew apart, and then there was one . . . Chamcha, moving down one of the drains through which Terminal Three dripped passengers into aircraft, saw the name painted next to the 747's open door, and turned a couple of shades paler. Then he heard the sari-clad Indian stewardess greeting him in an unmistakably Canadian accent, and lost his nerve, spinning away from the plane in a reflex of straightforward terror. As he stood there, facing the irritable throng of passengers waiting to board, he was conscious of how absurd he must look, with his brown leather holdall in one hand, two zippered suit-hanger bags in the other, and his eyes out on stalks; but for a long moment he was entirely unable to move. The crowd grew restive; *if this is an artery,* he found himself thinking, *then I'm the blasted clot.* 'I used to chichi chicken out also,' said a cheerful voice. 'But now I've got the titrick. I fafa flap my hands during tatake-off and the plane always mama makes it into the isk isk isky.'

'Today the top gogo goddess is absolutely Lakshmi,' Sisodia confided over whisky once they were safely aloft. (He had been as good as his word, flapping his arms wildly as *Gulistan* rushed down the runway, and afterwards settled back contentedly in his seat, beaming modestly. 'Wowoworks every time.' They were both travelling in the 747's upper deck, reserved for business class non-smokers, and Sisodia had moved into the empty seat next to Chamcha like air filling a vacuum. 'Call me Whisky,' he insisted. 'What lie lie line are you in? How mum much do you earn? How long you bibi been away? You know any women in town, or you want heh heh help?') Chamcha closed his eyes and fixed his thoughts on his father. The saddest thing, he realized, was that he could not remember a single happy day with Changez in his entire life as a man. And the most gladdening thing was the discovery that even the unforgivable crime of being one's father could be forgiven, after all, in the end. *Hang on,* he pleaded silently. *I'm coming as fast as I can.* 'In these hihighly material times,' Sisodia explained, 'who else but goddess of wewealth? In Bombay the young businessmen are hoho holding all night poopoo pooja parties. Statue of Lakshmi presides, with hands tuturned out, and lightbulbs running down her fifi fingers, lighting in sequence, you get me, as if the wealth is paw paw pouring down her palms.' On the cabin's movie screen a stewardess was demonstrating the various safety procedures. In a corner of the screen an inset male figure translated her into sign language. This was progress, Chamcha recognized. Film instead of human beings, a small increase in sophistication (the signing) and a large increase in cost. High technology at the service, ostensibly, of safety; while in reality air travel got daily more dangerous, the world's stock of aircraft was ageing and nobody could afford to renew it. Bits fell off planes every day, or so it seemed, and collisions and near-misses were also on the up. So the film was a kind of lie, because by existing it said: *Observe the lengths we'll go to for your security. We'll even make you a movie about it.* Style instead of substance, the image instead of the reality . . . 'I'm planning a big bubudget picture about her,' Sisodia said. 'This is in strictest coco confidence. Maybe a Sridevi weewee wehicle, I hohope so. Now that Gibreel's comeback is flaw flaw flopping, she is number one supreme.'

Chamcha had heard that Gibreel Farishta had hit the comeback trail. His first film, *The Parting of the Arabian Sea,* had bombed badly; the special effects looked home-made, the girl in the central Ayesha role, a certain Pimple Billimoria, had been woefully inadequate, and Gibreel's own portrayal of the archangel had struck many critics as narcissistic and megalomaniac. The days when he could do no wrong were gone; his second feature, *Mahound,* had hit every imaginable religious reef, and sunk without trace. 'You see, he chochose to go with other producers,' Sisodia lamented. 'The greegreed of the ista ista istar. With me the if if effects always work and the good tataste also you can take for gug, grunt, granted.' Saladin Chamcha closed his eyes and leaned back in his seat. He had drunk his whisky too fast on account of his fear of flying, and his head had begun to spin. Sisodia appeared not to recall his past connection to Farishta, which was fine. That was where the connection belonged: in the past. 'Shh shh Sridevi as Lakshmi,' Sisodia sang out, not very confidentially. 'Now that is sosolid gold. You are an ack actor. You should work back hohome. Call me. Maybe we can do bubusiness. This picture: solid pap pap *platinum.*'

Chamcha's head whirled. What strange meanings words were taking on. Only a few days ago that *back home* would have rung false. But now his father was dying and old emotions were sending tentacles out to grasp him. Maybe his tongue was twisting again, sending his accent East along with the rest of him. He hardly dared open his mouth.

Almost twenty years earlier, when the young and newly renamed Saladin was scratching a living on the margins of the London theatre, in order to maintain a safe distance from his father; and when Changez was retreating in other ways, becoming both reclusive and religious; back then, one day, out of the blue, the father had written to the son, offering him a house. The property was a rambling mansion in the hill-station of Solan. 'The first property I ever owned,' Changez wrote, 'and so it is the first I am gifting to you.' Saladin's instant reaction was to see the offer as a snare, a way of rejoining him to *home,* to the webs of his father's power; and when he learned that the Solan property had long ago been requisitioned by the Indian Government in return for a peppercorn rent, and that it had for many years been occupied by a boys' school, the gift stood revealed as a delusion as well. What did Chamcha care if the school were willing to treat him, on any visits he cared to make, as a visiting Head of State, putting on march-pasts and gymnastic displays? That sort of thing appealed to Changez's enormous vanity, but Chamcha wanted none of it. The point was, the school wasn't budging; the gift was useless, and probably an administrative headache as well. He wrote to his father refusing the offer. It was the last time Changez Chamchawala tried to give him anything. *Home* receded from the prodigal son.

'I never forget a faface,' Sisodia was saying. 'You're mimi Mimi's friend. The *Bostan* susurvivor. Knew it the moment I saw you papa panic at the gaga gate. Hope you're not feefeeling too baba bad.' Saladin, his heart sinking, shook his head, no, I'm fine, honestly. Sisodia, gleaming, knee-like, winked hideously at a passing stewardess and summoned more whisky. 'Such a shashame about Gibreel and his lady,' Sisodia went on. 'Such a nice name that she had, alla alla Alleluia. What a temper on that boy, what a jeajealous tata type. Hard for a momodern gaga girl. They bus bust up.' Saladin retreated, once again, into a pretence of sleep. *I have only just recovered from the past. Go, go away.*

He had formally declared his recovery complete only five weeks earlier, at the wedding of Mishal Sufyan and Hanif Johnson. After the death of her parents in the Shaandaar fire Mishal had been assailed by a terrible, illogical guilt that caused her mother to appear to her in dreams and admonish her: 'If only you'd passed the fire extinguisher when I asked. If only you'd blown a little harder. But you never listen to what I say and your lungs are so cigarette-rotten that you could not blow out one candle let alone a burning house.' Under the severe eye of her mother's ghost Mishal moved out of Hanif's apartment, took a room in a place with three other women, applied for and got Jumpy Joshi's old job at the sports centre, and fought the insurance companies until they paid up. Only when the Shaandaar was ready to reopen under her management did Hind Sufyan's ghost agree that it was time to be off to the after-life; whereupon Mishal telephoned Hanif and asked him to marry her. He was too surprised to reply, and had to pass the telephone to a colleague who explained that the cat had got Mr Johnson's tongue, and accepted Mishal's offer on the dumbstruck lawyer's behalf. So everybody was recovering from the tragedy; even Anahita, who had been obliged to live with a stiflingly old-fashioned aunt, managed to look pleased at the wedding, perhaps because Mishal had promised her her own rooms in the renovated Shaandaar Hotel. Mishal had asked Saladin to be her chief witness in recognition of his attempt to save her parents' life, and on their way to the registry office in Pinkwalla's van (all charges against the DJ and his boss, John Maslama, had been dropped for lack of evidence) Chamcha told the bride: 'Today feels like a new start for me, too; perhaps for all of us.' In his own case there had been by-pass surgery, and the difficulty of coming to terms with so many deaths, and nightmare visions of being metamorphosed once more into some sort of sulphurous, cloven-hoof demon. He was also, for a time, professionally crippled by a shame so profound that, when clients finally did begin to book him once more and ask for one of his voices, for example the voice of a frozen pea or a glove-puppet packet of sausages, he felt the memory of his telephonic crimes welling up in his throat and strangling the impersonations at birth. At Mishal's wedding, however, he suddenly felt free. It was quite a ceremony, largely because the young couple could not refrain from kissing one another throughout the procedure, and had to be urged by the registrar (a pleasant young woman who also exhorted the guests not to drink too much that day if they planned to drive) to hurry up and get through the words before it was time for the next wedding party to arrive. Afterwards at the Shaandaar the kissing continued, the kisses becoming gradually longer and more explicit, until finally the guests had the feeling that they were intruding on a private moment, and slipped quietly away leaving Hanif and Mishal to enjoy a passion so engulfing that they did not even notice their friends' departure; they remained oblivious, too, of the small crowd of children that gathered outside the windows of the Shaandaar Café to watch them. Chamcha, the last guest to leave, did the newlyweds the favour of pulling down the blinds, much to the children's annoyance; and strolled off down the rebuilt High Street feeling so light on his feet that he actually gave a kind of embarrassed skip.

Nothing is forever, he thought beyond closed eyelids somewhere over Asia Minor. Maybe unhappiness is the continuum through which a human life moves, and joy just a series of blips, of islands in the stream. Or if not unhappiness, then at least melancholy . . . These broodings were interrupted by a lusty snore from the seat beside him. Mr Sisodia, whisky-glass in hand, was asleep.

The producer was evidently a hit with the stewardesses. They fussed around his sleeping person, detaching the glass from his fingers and removing it to a place of safety, spreading a blanket over his lower half, and trilling admiringly over his snoring head: 'Doesn't he look poochie? Just a little cuteso, I swear!' Chamcha was reminded unexpectedly of the society ladies of Bombay patting him on the head during his mother's little soirées, and fought back tears of surprise. Sisodia actually looked faintly obscene; he had removed his spectacles before falling asleep, and their absence gave him an oddly naked appearance. To Chamcha's eyes he resembled nothing so much as an outsize Shiva lingam. Maybe that accounted for his popularity with the ladies.

Flicking through the magazines and newspapers he was offered by the stewardesses, Saladin chanced upon an old acquaintance in trouble. Hal Valance's sanitized *Aliens Show* had flopped badly in the United States and was being taken off the air. Worse still, his advertising agency and its subsidiaries had been swallowed by an American leviathan, and it was probable that Hal was on the way out, conquered by the transatlantic dragon he had set out to tame. It was hard to feel sorry for Valance, unemployed and down to his last few millions, abandoned by his beloved Mrs Torture and her pals, relegated to the limbo reserved for fallen favourites, along with busted entrepreneur-boffins and insider-dealing financiers and renegade ex-ministers; but Chamcha, flying to his father's deathbed, was in so heightened an emotional condition that he managed a valedictory lump in the throat even for wicked Hal. *At whose pool table,* he wondered vaguely, *is Baby playing now?*

In India, the war between men and women showed no sign of abating. In the *Indian Express* he read an account of the latest 'bride suicide'. *The husband, Prajapati, is absconding.* On the next page, in the weekly small-ad marriage market, the parents of young men still demanded, and the parents of young women proudly offered, brides of 'wheatish' complexions. Chamcha remembered Zeeny's friend, the poet Bhupen Gandhi, speaking of such things with passionate bitterness. 'How to accuse others of being prejudiced when our own hands are so dirty?' he had declaimed. 'Many of you in Britain speak of victimization. Well. I have not been there, I don't know your situation, but in my personal experience I have never been able to feel comfortable about being described as a victim. In class terms, obviously, I am not. Even speaking culturally, you find here all the bigotries, all the procedures associated with oppressor groups. So while many Indians are undoubtedly oppressed, I don't think any of *us* are entitled to lay claim to such a glamorous position.'

'Trouble with Bhupen's radical critiques,' Zeeny had remarked, 'is that reactionaries like Salad baba here just love to lap them up.'

An armaments scandal was raging; had the Indian government paid kickbacks to middlemen, and then gone in for a cover-up? Vast sums of money were involved, the Prime Minister's credibility had been weakened, but Chamcha couldn't be bothered with any of it. He was staring at the fuzzy photograph, on an inside page, of indistinct, bloated shapes floating down-river in large numbers. In a north Indian town there had been a massacre of Muslims, and their corpses had been dumped in the water, where they awaited the ministrations of some twentieth-century Gaffer Hexam. There were hundreds of bodies, swollen and rancid; the stench seemed to rise off the page. And in Kashmir a once-popular Chief Minister who had 'made an accommodation' with the Congress-I had shoes hurled at him during the Eid prayers by irate groups of Islamic fundamentalists. Communalism, sectarian tension, was omnipresent: as if the gods were going to war. In the eternal struggle between the world's beauty and its cruelty, cruelty was gaining ground by the day. Sisodia's voice intruded on these morose thoughts. The producer had woken up to see the photograph from Meerut staring up from Chamcha's fold-out table. 'Fact is,' he said without any of his usual bonhomie, 'religious fafaith, which encodes the highest ass ass aspirations of human race, is now, in our cocountry, the servant of lowest instincts, and gogo God is the creature of evil.'

KNOWN HISTORY SHEETERS RESPONSIBLE FOR KILLINGS, a government spokesman alleged, but 'progressive elements' rejected this analysis. CITY CONSTABULARY CONTAMINATED BY COMMUNAL AGITATORS, the counter-argument suggested. HINDU NATIONALISTS RUN AMUCK. A political fortnightly contained a photograph of signboards that had been mounted outside the Juma Masjid in Old Delhi. The Imam, a loose-bellied man with cynical eyes, who could be found most mornings in his 'garden' – a red-earth-and-rubble waste land in the shadow of the mosque – counting rupees donated by the faithful and rolling up each note individually, so that he seemed to be holding a handful of thin beedi-like cigarettes – and who was no stranger to communalist politics himself, was apparently determined that the Meerut horror should be turned to good account. *Quench the Fire under our Breast,* the signboards cried. *Salute with Reverence those who met Martyrdom from the Bullets of the Polis.* Also: *Alas! Alas! Alas! Awak the Prime Minister!* And finally, the call to action: *Bandh will be observed,* and the date of the strike.

'Bad days,' Sisodia went on. "For the moomoo movies also TV and economics have Delhi Delhi deleterious effects.' Then he cheered up as stewardesses approached. 'I will confess to being a mem member of the mile high cluck cluck club," he said gaily within the attendants' hearing. 'And you? Should I see what I can ficfic fix?'

O, the dissociations of which the human mind is capable, marvelled Saladin gloomily. O, the conflicting selves jostling and joggling within these bags of skin. No wonder we are unable to remain focused on anything for very long; no wonder we invent remote-control channel-hopping devices. If we turned these instruments upon ourselves we'd discover more channels than a cable or satellite mogul ever dreamed of . . . He himself had found his thoughts straying, no matter how hard he tried to fix them on his father, towards the question of Miss Zeenat Vakil. He had wired ahead, informing her of his arrival; would she meet the flight? What might or might not happen between them? Had he, by leaving her, by not returning, by losing touch for a time, done the Unforgivable Thing? Was she – he thought, and was shocked by the realization that it had simply not occurred to him earlier – married? In love? Involved? And as for himself: what did he really want? *I'll know when I see her,* he thought. The future, even when it was only a question-shrouded glimmer, would not be eclipsed by the past; even when death moved towards the centre of the stage, life went on fighting for equal rights.

The flight passed without incident.

Zeenat Vakil was not waiting at the airport.

'Come along,' Sisodia waved. 'My car has come to pipi pick, so please to lelet me drop.'

Thirty-five minutes later Saladin Chamcha was at Scandal Point, standing at the gates of childhood with holdall and suit-bags, looking at the imported video-controlled entry system. Anti-narcotics slogans had been painted on the perimeter wall: DREAMS ALL DROWN/WHEN SUGAR IS BROWN. And: FUTURE IS BLACK/ WHEN SUGAR IS BROWN. Courage, my old, he braced himself; and rang as directed, once, firmly, for attention.

In the luxuriant garden the stump of the felled walnut-tree caught his unquiet eye. They probably used it as a picnic table now, he mused bitterly. His father had always had a gift for the melo-dramatic, self-pitying gesture, and to eat his lunch off a surface which packed such an emotional wallop – with, no doubt, many profound sighs between the large mouthfuls – would be right in character. Was he going to camp up his death, too, Saladin wondered. What a grandstand play for sympathy the old bastard could make now! Anyone in the vicinity of a dying man was utterly at his mercy. Punches delivered from a deathbed left bruises that never faded.

His stepmother emerged from the dying man's marbled mansion to greet Chamcha without a hint of rancour. 'Salahuddin. Good you came. It will lift his spirit, and now it is his spirit that he must fight with, because his body is more or less kaput.' She was perhaps six or seven years younger than Saladin's mother would have been, but out of the same birdlike mould. His large, expansive father had been remarkably consistent in these matters at least. 'How long does he have?' Saladin asked. Nasreen was as undeceived as her telegram had suggested. 'It could be any day.' The myeloma was present throughout Changez's 'long bones' – the cancer had brought its own vocabulary to the house; one no longer spoke of *arms and legs* – and in his skull. Cancerous cells had even been detected in the blood around the bones. 'We should have spotted it,' Nasreen said, and Saladin began to feel the old lady's power, the force of will with which she was reining in her feelings. 'His pronounced weight-loss these past two years. Also he has complained of aches and pains, for instance in the knees. You know how it is. With an old man, you blame his age, you don't imagine that a vile, hideous disease.' She stopped, needing to control her voice. Kasturba, the ex-ayah, had come out to join them in the garden. It turned out that her husband Vallabh had died almost a year earlier, of old age, in his sleep: a kinder death than the one now eating its way out of the body of his employer, the seducer of his wife. Kasturba was still dressing in Nasreen I's old, loud saris: today she had chosen one of the dizziest of the Op-Art black-and-white prints. She, too, greeted Saladin warmly: hugs kisses tears. 'As for me,' she sobbed, 'I will never stop praying for a miracle while there is one breath left in his poor lungs.'

Nasreen II embraced Kasturba; each woman rested her head on

the other's shoulder. The intimacy between the two women was spontaneous and untarnished by resentments; as if the proximity of death had washed away the quarrels and jealousies of life. The two old ladies comforted one another in the garden, each consoling the other for the imminent loss of the most precious of things: love. Or, rather: the beloved. 'Come on,' Nasreen finally said to Saladin. 'He should see you, pronto.'

'Does he know?' Saladin asked. Nasreen answered evasively. 'He is an intelligent man. He keeps asking, where has all the blood gone? He says, there are only two illnesses in which the blood vanishes like this. One is tuberculosis.' But, Saladin pressed, he never actually speaks the word? Nasreen lowered her head. The word had not been spoken, either by Changez or in his presence. 'Shouldn't he know?' Chamcha asked. 'Doesn't a man have the right to prepare for his death?' He saw Nasreen's eyes blaze for an instant. *Who do you think you are to tell us our duty. You have sacrificed all rights.* Then they faded, and when she spoke her voice was level, unemotional, low. 'Maybe you're correct.' But Kasturba wailed: 'No! How to tell him, poor man? It will break his heart.'

The cancer had thickened Changez's blood to the point at which his heart was having the greatest difficulty pumping it round his body. It had also polluted the bloodstream with alien bodies, platelets, that would attack any blood with which he was transfused, even blood of his own type. *So, even in this small way, I can't help him*, Saladin understood. Changez could easily die of these side-effects before the cancer did for him. If he did die from the cancer, the end would take the form either of pneumonia or of kidney failure; the doctors, knowing they could do nothing for him, had sent him home to wait for it. 'Because myeloma is systemic, chemotherapy and radiation treatment are not used,' Nasreen explained. 'Only medicament is the drug Melphalan, which can in some cases prolong life, even for years. However, we are informed he is in the category which will not respond to Melphalan tablets.' *But he has not been told*, Saladin's inner voices insisted. *And that's wrong, wrong, wrong.* 'Still, a miracle has happened,' Kasturba cried. 'The doctors told that normally this is one of the most painful cancers; but your father is in no pain. If one prays, then sometimes a kindness is granted.' It was on account of the freak absence of pain that the cancer had taken so long to diagnose; it had been spreading in Changez's body for at least two years. 'I must see him now,' Saladin gently asked. A bearer had taken his holdall and suit-bags indoors while they spoke; now, at last, he followed his garments indoors.

The interior of the house was unchanged – the generosity of the second Nasreen towards the memory of the first seemed boundless, at least during these days, the last on earth of their mutual spouse – except that Nasreen II had moved in her collection of stuffed birds (hoopoes and rare parrots under glass bell-jars, a full-grown King Penguin in the marble-and-mosaic hall, its beak swarming with tiny red ants) and her cases of impaled butterflies. Saladin moved past this colorful gallery of dead wings towards his father's study – Changez had insisted on vacating his bedroom and having a bed moved downstairs into that wood-panelled retreat full of rotting books, so that people didn't have to run up and down all day to look after him – and came, at last, to death's door.

Early in life Changez Chamchawala had acquired the disconcerting knack of sleeping with his eyes wide open, 'staying on guard', as he liked to say. Now, as Saladin quietly entered the room, the effect of those open grey eyes staring blindly at the ceiling was positively unnerving. For a moment Saladin thought he was too late; that Changez had died while he'd been chatting in the garden. Then the man on the bed emitted a series of small coughs, turned his head, and extended an uncertain arm. Saladin Chamcha went towards his father and bowed his head beneath the old man's caressing palm.

To fall in love with one's father after the long angry decades was a serene and beautiful feeling; a renewing, life-giving thing, Saladin wanted to say, but did not, because it sounded vampirish; as if by sucking this new life out of his father he was making room, in

Changez's body, for death. Although he kept it quiet, however, Saladin felt hourly closer to many old, rejected selves, many alternative Saladins – or rather Salahuddins – which had split off from himself as he made his various life choices, but which had apparently continued to exist, perhaps in the parallel universes of quantum theory. Cancer had stripped Changez Chamchawala literally to the bone; his cheeks had collapsed into the hollows of the skull, and he had to place a foam-rubber pillow under his buttocks because of the atrophying of his flesh. But it had also stripped him of his faults, of all that had been domineering, tyrannical and cruel in him, so that the mischievous, loving and brilliant man beneath lay exposed, once again, for all to see. *If only he could have been this person all his life,* Saladin (who had begun to find the sound of his full, un-Englished name pleasing for the first time in twenty years) found himself wishing. How hard it was to find one's father just when one had no choice but to say goodbye.

On the morning of his return Salahuddin Chamchawala was asked by his father to give him a shave. 'These old women of mine don't know which side of a Philishave is the business end.' Changez's skin hung off his face in soft, leathery jowls, and his hair (when Salahuddin emptied the machine) looked like ashes. Salahuddin could not remember when he had last touched his father's face this way, gently drawing the skin tight as the cordless shaver moved across it, and then stroking it to make sure it felt smooth. When he had finished he continued for a moment to run his fingers along Changez's cheeks. 'Look at the old man,' Nasreen said to Kasturba as they entered the room, 'he can't take his eyes off his boy.' Changez Chamchawala grinned an exhausted grin, revealing a mouth full of shattered teeth, flecked with spittle and crumbs.

When his father fell asleep again, after being forced by Kasturba and Nasreen to drink a small quantity of water, and gazed up at – what? – with his open, dreaming eyes, which could see into three worlds at once, the actual world of his study, the visionary world of dreams, and the approaching after-life as well (or so Salahuddin, in a fanciful moment, found himself imagining); – then the son went to Changez's old bedroom for a rest. Grotesque heads in painted terracotta glowered down at him from the walls: a horned demon; a leering Arab with a falcon on his shoulder; a bald man rolling his eyes upwards and putting his tongue out in panic as a huge black fly settled on his eyebrow. Unable to sleep beneath these figures, which he had known all his life and also hated, because he had come to see them as portraits of Changez, he moved finally to a different, neutral room.

Waking up in the early evening, he went downstairs to find the two old women outside Changez's room, trying to work out the details of his medication. Apart from the daily Melphalan tablet, he had been prescribed a whole battery of drugs in an attempt to combat the cancer's pernicious side-effects: anaemia, the strain on the heart, and so on. Isosorbide dinitrate, two tablets, four times a day; Furosemide, one tablet, three times; Prednisolone, six tablets, twice daily . . . 'I'll do this,' he told the relieved old women. 'At least it is one thing I can do.' Agarol for his constipation, Spironolactone for goodness knew what, and a zyloric, Allopurinol: he suddenly remembered, crazily, an antique theatre review in which the English critic, Kenneth Tynan, had imagined the polysyllabic characters in Marlowe's *Tamburlaine the Great* as 'a horde of pills and wonder drugs bent on decimating one another':

> *Beard'st thou me here, thou bold Barbiturate?*
> *Sirrah, thy grandam's dead – old Nembutal.*
> *The spangled stars shall weep for Nembutal . . .*
> *Is it not passing brave to be a king,*
> *Aureomycin and Formaldehyde,*
> *Is it not passing brave to be a king*
> *And ride in triumph through Amphetamine?*

The things one's memory threw up! But perhaps this pharmaceutical *Tamburlaine* was not such a bad eulogy for the fallen monarch lying here in his bookwormed study, staring into three worlds, waiting for the end. 'Come on, Abba,' he marched cheerily into the presence. 'Time to save your life.'

Still in its place, on a shelf in Changez's study: a certain copper-and-brass lamp, reputed to have the power of wish fulfilment, but as yet (because never rubbed) untested. Somewhat tarnished now, it looked down upon its dying owner; and was observed, in its turn, by his only son. Who was sorely tempted, for an instant, to get it down, rub three times, and ask the turbanned djinni for a magic spell . . . however, Salahuddin left the lamp where it was. There was no place for djinns or ghouls or afreets here; no spooks or fancies could be permitted. No magic formulae; just the impotence of the pills. 'Here's the medicine man,' Salahuddin sang out, rattling the little bottles, rousing his father from sleep. 'Medicine,' Changez grimaced childishly. 'Eek, bhaak, thoo.'

That night, Salahuddin forced Nasreen and Kasturba to sleep comfortably in their own beds while he kept watch over Changez from a mattress on the floor. After his midnight dose of Isosorbide, the dying man slept for three hours, and then needed to go to the toilet. Salahuddin virtually lifted him to his feet, and was astonished at Changez's lightness. This had always been a weighty man, but now he was a living lunch for the advancing cancer cells . . . in the toilet, Changez refused all help. 'He won't let you do one thing,' Kasturba had complained lovingly. 'Such a shy fellow that he is.' On his way back to bed he leaned lightly on Salahuddin's arm, and shuffled along flat-footed in old, worn bedroom slippers, his remaining hairs sticking out at comical angles, his head stuck beakily forward on its scrawny, fragile neck. Salahuddin suddenly longed to pick the old man up, to cradle him in his arms and sing soft, comforting songs. Instead, he blurted out, at this least appropriate of moments, an appeal for reconciliation. 'Abba, I came because I didn't want there to be trouble between us any more . . .' *Fucking idiot. The Devil damn thee black, thou cream-fac'd loon. In the middle of the bloody night! And if he hasn't*

guessed he's dying, that little deathbed speech will certainly have let him know. Changez continued to shuffle along; his grip on his son's arm tightened very slightly. 'That doesn't matter any more,' he said. 'It's forgotten, whatever it was.'

In the morning, Nasreen and Kasturba arrived in clean saris, looking rested and complaining, 'It was so terrible sleeping away from him that we didn't sleep one wink.' They fell upon Changez, and so tender were their caresses that Salahuddin had the same sense of spying on a private moment that he'd had at the wedding of Mishal Sufyan. He left the room quietly while the three lovers embraced, kissed and wept.

Death, the great fact, wove its spell around the house on Scandal Point. Salahuddin surrendered to it like everyone else, even Changez, who, on that second day, often smiled his old crooked smile, the one that said *I know what's up, I'll go along with it, just don't think I'm fooled*. Kasturba and Nasreen fussed over him constantly, brushing his hair, coaxing him to eat and drink. His tongue had grown fat in his mouth, slurring his speech slightly, making it hard to swallow; he refused anything at all fibrous or stringy, even the chicken breasts he had loved all his life. A mouthful of soup, puréed potatoes, a taste of custard. Baby food. When he sat up in bed Salahuddin sat behind him; Changez leaned against his son's body while he ate.

'Open the house,' Changez commanded that morning. 'I want to see some smiling faces here, instead of your three glum mugs.' So, after a long time, people came: young and old, half-forgotten cousins, uncles, aunts; a few comrades from the old days of the nationalist movement, poker-backed gentlemen with silver hair, achkan jackets and monocles; employees of the various foundations and philanthropical enterprises set up by Changez years ago; rival manufacturers of agricultural sprays and artificial dung. A real bag of allsorts, Salahuddin thought; but marvelled, also, at how beautifully everyone behaved in the presence of the dying man: the young spoke to him intimately about their lives, as if reassuring him that life itself was invincible, offering him the rich consolation of being a member of the great procession of the human race, – while the old evoked the past, so that he knew nothing was forgotten, nothing lost; that in spite of the years of self-imposed sequestration he remained joined to the world. Death brought out the best in people; it was good to be shown – Salahuddin realized – that this, too, was what human beings were like: considerate, loving, even noble. We are still capable of exaltation, he thought in celebratory mood; in spite of everything, we can still transcend. A pretty young woman – it occurred to Salahuddin that she was probably his niece, and he felt ashamed that he didn't know her name – was taking Polaroid snapshots of Changez with his visitors, and the sick man was enjoying himself hugely, pulling faces, then kissing the many proffered cheeks with a light in his eyes that Salahuddin identified as nostalgia. 'It's like a birthday party,' he thought. Or: like Finnegan's wake. The dead man refusing to lie down and let the living have all the fun.

'We have to tell him,' Salahuddin insisted when the visitors had left. Nasreen bowed her head; and nodded. Kasturba burst into tears.

They told him the next morning, having asked the specialist to attend to answer any questions Changez might have. The specialist, Panikkar (a name the English would mispronounce and giggle over, Salahuddin thought, like the Muslim 'Fakhar'), arrived at ten, shining with self-esteem. 'I should tell him,' he said, taking control. 'Most patients feel ashamed to let their loved ones see their fear.' 'The hell you will,' Salahuddin said with a vehemence that took him by surprise. 'Well, in that case,' Panikkar shrugged, making as if to leave; which won the argument, because now Nasreen and Kasturba pleaded with Salahuddin: 'Please, let's not fight.' Salahuddin, defeated, ushered the doctor into his father's presence; and shut the study door.

'I have a cancer,' Changez Chamchawala said to Nasreen, Kasturba and Salahuddin after Panikkar's departure. He spoke clearly, enunciating the word with defiant, exaggerated care. 'It is very far advanced. I am not surprised. I said to Panikkar: "This is what I told you the very first day. Where else could all the blood have gone?" ' – Outside the study, Kasturba said to Salahuddin: 'Since you came, there was a light in his eye. Yesterday, with all the people, how happy he was! But now his eye is dim. Now he won't fight.'

That afternoon Salahuddin found himself alone with his father while the two women napped. He discovered that he, who had been so determined to have everything out in the open, to say the word, was now awkward and inarticulate, not knowing how to speak. But Changez had something to say.

'I want you to know,' he said to his son, 'that I have no problem about this thing at all. A man must die of something, and it is not as though I were dying young. I have no illusions; I know I am not going anywhere after this. It's the end. That's okay. The only thing I'm afraid of is pain, because when there is pain a man loses his dignity. I don't want that to happen.' Salahuddin was awestruck. *First one falls in love with one's father all over again, and then one learns to look up to him, too.* 'The doctors say you're a case in a million,' he replied truthfully. 'It looks like you have been spared the pain.' Something in Changez relaxed at that, and Salahuddin realized how afraid the old man had been, how much he'd needed to be told . . . 'Bas,' Changez Chamchawala said gruffly. 'Then I'm ready. And by the way: you get the lamp, after all.'

An hour later the diarrhoea began: a thin black trickle. Nasreen's anguished phone calls to the emergency room of the Breach Candy Hospital established that Panikkar was unavailable. 'Take him off the Agarol at once,' the duty doctor ordered, and prescribed Imodium instead. It didn't help. At seven pm the risk of dehydration was growing, and Changez was too weak to sit up for his food. He had virtually no appetite, but Kasturba managed to spoon-feed him a few drops of semolina with skinned apricots. 'Yum, yum,' he said ironically, smiling his crooked smile.

He fell asleep, but by one o'clock had been up and down three times. 'For God's sake,' Salahuddin shouted down the telephone, 'give me Panikkar's home number.' But that was against hospital procedure. 'You must judge,' said the duty doctor, 'if the time has come to bring him down.' Bitch, Salahuddin Chamchawala mouthed. 'Thanks a lot.'

At three o'clock Changez was so weak that Salahuddin more or less carried him to the toilet. 'Get the car out,' he shouted at Nasreen and Kasturba. 'We're going to the hospital. Now.' The proof of Changez's decline was that, this last time, he permitted his son to help him out. 'Black shit is bad,' he said, panting for breath. His lungs had filled up alarmingly; the breath was like bubbles pushing through glue. 'Some cancers are slow, but I think this is very fast. Deterioration is very rapid.' And Salahuddin, the apostle of truth, told comforting lies: *Abba, don't worry. You'll be fine.* Changez Chamchawala shook his head. 'I'm going, son,' he said. His chest heaved; Salahuddin grabbed a large plastic mug and held it under Changez's mouth. The dying man vomited up more than a pint of phlegm mixed up with blood: and after that was too weak to talk. This time Salahuddin did have to carry him, to the back seat of the Mercedes, where he sat between Nasreen and Kasturba while Salahuddin drove at top speed to Breach Candy Hospital, half a mile down the road. 'Shall I open the window, Abba?' he asked at one point, and Changez shook his head and bubbled: 'No.' Much later, Salahuddin realized this had been his father's last word.

The emergency ward. Running feet, orderlies, wheelchair, Changez being heaved on to a bed, curtains. A young doctor, doing what had to be done, very quickly but without the appearance of speed. *I like him,* Salahuddin thought. Then the doctor looked him in the eye and said: 'I don't think he's going to make it.' It felt like being punched in the stomach. Salahuddin realized he'd been clinging on to a futile hope, *they'll fix him and we'll take him home; this isn't 'it',* and his instant reaction to the doctor's words was rage. *You're the mechanic. Don't tell me the car won't start; mend the damn thing.* Changez was flat out, drowning in his lungs. 'We can't get at his chest in this kurta; may we . . .' *Cut it off. Do what you have to do.* Drips, the blip of a weakening heartbeat on a screen, helplessness. The young doctor murmuring: 'It won't be long now, so . . .' At which, Salahuddin Chamchawala did a crass thing. He turned to Nasreen and Kasturba and said: 'Come quickly now. Come and say goodbye.' 'For God's sake!' the doctor exploded . . . the women did not weep, but came up to Changez and took a hand each. Salahuddin blushed for shame. He would never know if his father heard the death-sentence dripping from the lips of his son.

Now Salahuddin found better words, his Urdu returning to him after a long absence. *We're all beside you, Abba. We all love you very much.* Changez could not speak, but that was, – was it not? – yes, it must have been – a little nod of recognition. *He heard me.* Then all of a sudden Changez Chamchawala left his face; he was still alive, but he had gone somewhere else, had turned inwards to look at whatever there was to see. *He is teaching me how to die,* Salahuddin thought. *He does not avert his eyes, but looks death right in the face.* At no point in his dying did Changez Chamchawala speak the name of God.

'Please,' the doctor said, 'go outside the curtain now and let us make our effort.' Salahuddin took the two women a few steps away; and now, when a curtain hid Changez from their sight, they wept. 'He swore he would never leave me,' Nasreen sobbed, her iron control broken at last, 'and he has gone away.' Salahuddin went to watch through a crack in the curtain; – and saw the voltage being pumped into his father's body, the sudden green jaggedness of the pulse on the monitor screen; saw doctor and nurses pounding his father's chest; saw defeat.

The last thing he had seen in his father's face, just before the medical staff's final, useless effort, was the dawning of a terror so profound that it chilled Salahuddin to the bone. What had he seen? What was it that waited for him, for all of us, that brought such fear to a brave man's eyes? – Now, when it was over, he returned to Changez's bedside; and saw his father's mouth curved upwards, in a smile.

He caressed those sweet cheeks. *I didn't shave him today. He died with stubble on his chin.* How cold his face was already; but the brain, the brain retained a little warmth. They had stuffed cotton-wool into his nostrils. *But suppose there's been a mistake? What if he wants to breathe?* Nasreen Chamchawala was beside him. 'Let's take your father home,' she said.

Changez Chamchawala returned home in an ambulance, lying in an aluminum tray on the floor between the two women who had loved him, while Salahuddin followed in the car. Ambulance men laid him to rest in his study; Nasreen turned the air-conditioner up high. This was, after all, a tropical death, and the sun would be up soon.

What did he see? Salahuddin kept thinking. *Why the horror? And, whence that final smile?*

People came again. Uncles, cousins, friends took charge, arranging everything. Nasreen and Kasturba sat on white sheets on the floor of the room in which, once upon a time, Saladin and Zeeny had visited the ogre, Changez; women sat with them to mourn, many of them reciting the qalmah over and over, with the help of counting beads. Salahuddin was irritated by this; but lacked the will to tell them to stop. – Then the mullah came, and sewed Changez's winding-sheet, and it was time to wash the body; and even though there were many men present, and there was no need for him to help, Salahuddin insisted. *If he could look his death in the eye, then I can do it, too.* – And when his father was being washed, his body rolled this way and that at the mullah's command, the flesh bruised and slabby, the appendix scar long and brown, Salahuddin recalled the only other time in his life when he'd seen his physically demure father naked: he'd been nine years old, blundering into a bathroom where Changez was taking a shower, and the sight of his father's penis was a shock he'd never forgotten. That thick squat organ, like a club. O the power of it; and the insignificance of his own . . . 'His eyes won't close,' the mullah complained. 'You should have done it before.' He was a stocky, pragmatic fellow, this mullah with his moustacheless beard. He treated the dead body as a commonplace thing, needing washing the way a car does, or a window, or a dish. 'You are from London? Proper London? – I was there many years. I was doorman at Claridge's Hotel.' *Oh? Really? How interesting.* The man wanted to make small-talk! Salahuddin was appalled. *That's my father, don't you understand?* 'These garments,' the mullah asked, indicating Changez's last kurta-pajama outfit, the one which the hospital staff had cut open to get at his chest. 'You have need of them?' *No, no. Take them. Please.* 'You are very kind.' Small pieces of black cloth were being stuffed into Changez's mouth and under his eyelids. 'This cloth has been to Mecca,' the mullah said. *Get it out!* 'I don't understand. It is holy fabric.' *You heard me: out, out.* 'May God have mercy on your soul.'

And:

The bier, strewn with flowers, like an outsize baby's cot.

The body, wrapped in white, with sandalwood shavings, for fragrance, scattered all about it.

More flowers, and a green silken covering with Quranic verses embroidered upon it in gold.

The ambulance, with the bier resting in it, awaiting the widows' permission to depart.

The last farewells of women.

The graveyard. Male mourners rushing to lift the bier on their shoulders trample Salahuddin's foot, ripping off a segment of the nail on his big toe.

Among the mourners, an estranged old friend of Changez's, here in spite of double pneumonia; – and another old gentleman, weeping copiously, who will die himself the very next day; – and all sorts, the walking records of a dead man's life.

The grave. Salahuddin climbs down into it, stands at the head end, the gravedigger at the foot. Changez Chamchawala is lowered down. *The weight of my father's head, lying in my hand. I laid it down; to rest.*

The world, somebody wrote, is the place we prove real by dying in it.

Waiting for him when he returned from the graveyard: a copper-and-brass lamp, his renewed inheritance. He went into Changez's study and closed the door. There were his old slippers by the bed: he had become, as he'd foretold, 'a pair of emptied shoes'. The bedclothes still bore the imprint of his father's body; the room was full of sickly perfume: sandalwood, camphor, cloves. He took the lamp from its shelf and sat at Changez's desk. Taking a handkerchief from his pocket, he rubbed briskly: once, twice, thrice.

The lights all went on at once.

Zeenat Vakil entered the room.

'O God, I'm sorry, maybe you wanted them off, but with the blinds closed it was just so sad.' Waving her arms, speaking loudly in her beautiful croak of a voice, her hair woven, for once, into a waist-length ponytail, here she was, his very own djinn. 'I feel so bad I didn't come before, I was just trying to hurt you, what a time to choose, so bloody self-indulgent, yaar, it's good to see you, you poor orphaned goose.'

She was the same as ever, immersed in life up to her neck, combining occasional art lectures at the university with her medical practice and her political activities. 'I was at the goddamn hospital when you came, you know? I was right there, but I didn't know about your dad until it was over, and even then I didn't come to give you a hug, what a bitch, if you want to throw me out I will have no complaints.' This was a generous woman, the most generous he'd known. *When you see her, you'll know,* he had promised himself, and it turned out to be true. 'I love you,' he heard himself saying, stopping her in her tracks. 'Okay, I won't hold you to that,' she finally said, looking hugely pleased. 'Balance of your mind is obviously disturbed. Lucky for you you aren't in one of our great public hospitals; they put the loonies next to the heroin addicts, and there's so much drug traffic in the wards that the poor schizos end up with bad habits. – Anyway, if you say it again after forty days, watch out, because maybe then I'll take it seriously. Just now it could be a disease.'

Undefeated (and, it appeared, unattached), Zeeny's re-entry into his life completed the process of renewal, of regeneration, that had been the most surprising and paradoxical product of his father's terminal illness. His old English life, its bizarreries, its evils, now seemed very remote, even irrelevant, like his truncated stage-name. 'About time,' Zeeny approved when he told her of his return to *Salahuddin*. 'Now you can stop acting at last.' Yes, this looked like the start of a new phase, in which the world would be solid and real, and in which there was no longer the broad figure of a parent standing between himself and the inevitability of the grave. An orphaned life, like Muhammad's; like everyone's. A life illuminated by a strangely radiant death, which continued to glow, in his mind's eye, like a sort of magic lamp.

I must think of myself, from now on, as living perpetually in the first instant of the future, he resolved a few days later, in Zeeny's apart-ment on Sophia College Lane, while recovering in her bed from the toothy enthusiasms of her lovemaking. (She had invited him home shyly, as if she were removing a veil after long conceal-ment.) But a history is not so easily shaken off; he was also living, after all, in the *present moment of the past*, and his old life was about to surge around him once again, to complete its final act.

He became aware that he was a rich man. Under the terms of Changez's will, the dead tycoon's vast fortune and myriad business interests were to be supervised by a group of distinguished trustees, the income being divided equally between three parties: Changez's second wife Nasreen, Kasturba, whom he referred to in the document as 'in every true sense, my third', and his son, Salahuddin. After the deaths of the two women, however, the trust could be dissolved whenever Salahuddin chose: he inherited, in short, the lot. 'On the condition,' Changez Chamchawala had mischievously stipulated, 'that the scoundrel accepts the gift he previously spurned, viz., the requisitioned schoolhouse situated at Solan, Himachal Pradesh.' Changez might have chopped down a walnut-tree, but he had never attempted to cut Salahuddin out of his will. – The houses at Pali Hill and Scandal Point were excluded from these provisions, however. The former passed to Nasreen Chamchawala outright; the latter became, with imme-diate effect, the sole property of Kasturbabai, who quickly announced her intention of selling the old house to property developers. The site was worth crores, and Kasturba was wholly unsentimental about real estate. Salahuddin protested vehemently, and was slapped down hard. 'I have lived my whole life here,' she informed him. 'It is therefore for me only to say.' Nasreen Chamchawala was entirely indifferent to the fate of the old place. 'One more high-rise, one less piece of old Bombay,' she shrugged. 'What's the difference? Cities change.' She was already preparing to move back to Pali Hill, taking the cases of butterflies off the walls, assembling her stuffed birds in the hall. 'Let it go,' Zeenat Vakil said. 'You couldn't live in that museum, anyway.'

She was right, of course; no sooner had he resolved to set his face towards the future than he started mooning around and regretting childhood's end. 'I'm off to meet George and Bhupen, you remember,' she said. 'Why don't you come along? You need to start plugging into the town.' George Miranda had just completed a documentary film about communalism, interviewing Hindus and Muslims of all shades of opinion. Fundamentalists of both religions had instantly sought injunctions banning the film from being shown, and, although the Bombay courts had rejected this request, the case had gone up to the Supreme Court. George, even more stubbly of chin, lank of hair and sprawling of stomach than Salahuddin remembered, drank rum in a Dhobi Talao boozer and thumped the table with pessimistic fists. 'This is the Supreme Court of Shah Bano fame,' he cried, referring to the notorious case in which, under pressure from Islamic extremists, the Court had ruled that alimony payments were contrary to the will of Allah, thus making India's laws even more reactionary than, for example, Pakistan's. 'So I don't have much hope.' He twisted, disconsolately, the waxy points of his moustache. His new girlfriend, a tall, thin Bengali woman with cropped hair that reminded Salahuddin a little of Mishal Sufyan, chose this moment to attack Bhupen Gandhi for having published a volume of poems about his visit to the 'little temple town' of Gagari in the Western Ghats. The poems had been criticized by the Hindu right; one eminent South Indian professor had announced that Bhupen had 'forfeited his right to be called an Indian poet', but in the opinion of the young woman, Swatilekha, Bhupen had been seduced by religion into a dangerous ambiguity. Grey hair flopping earnestly, moon-face shining, Bhupen defended himself. 'I have said that the only crop of Gagari is the stone gods being quarried from the hills. I have spoken of herds of legends, with sacred cowbells tinkling, grazing on the hillsides. These are not ambiguous images.' Swatilekha wasn't convinced. 'These days,' she insisted, 'our positions must be stated with crystal clarity. All metaphors are capable of misinterpretation.' She offered her theory. Society was orchestrated by what she called *grand narratives*: history, economics, ethics. In India, the development of a corrupt and closed state apparatus had 'excluded the masses of the people from the ethical project'. As a result, they sought ethical satisfactions in the oldest of the grand narratives, that is, religious faith. 'But these narratives are being manipulated by the theocracy and various political elements in an entirely retrogressive way.' Bhupen said: 'We can't deny the ubiquity of faith. If we write in such a way as to pre-judge such belief as in some way deluded or false, then are we not guilty of elitism, of imposing our world-view on the masses?' Swatilekha was scornful. 'Battle lines are being drawn up in India today,' she cried. 'Secular versus religious, the light versus the dark. Better you choose which side you are on.'

Bhupen got up, angrily, to go. Zeeny pacified him: 'We can't afford schisms. There's planning to be done.' He sat down again, and Swatilekha kissed him on the cheek. 'I'm sorry,' she said. 'Too much college education, George always says. In fact, I loved the poems. I was only arguing a case.' Bhupen, mollified, pretended to punch her on the nose; the crisis passed.

They had met, Salahuddin now gathered, to discuss their part in a remarkable political demonstration: the formation of a human chain, stretching from the Gateway of India to the outermost northern suburbs of the city, in support of 'national integration'. The Communist Party of India (Marxist) had recently organized just such a human chain in Kerala, with great success. 'But,' George Miranda argued, 'here in Bombay it will be totally another matter. In Kerala the CP(M) is in power. Here, with these Shiv Sena bastards in control, we can expect every type of harassment, from police obstructionism to out-and-out assaults by mobs on segments of the chain – especially when it passes, as it will have to, through the Sena's fortresses, in Mazagaon, etc.' In spite of these dangers, Zeeny explained to Salahuddin, such public demonstrations were essential. As communal violence escalated – and Meerut was only the latest in a long line of murderous incidents – it was imperative that the forces of disintegration weren't permitted to have things all their own way. 'We must show that there are also counterforces at work.' Salahuddin was somewhat bemused at the rapidity with which, once again, his life had begun to change. *Me, taking part in a CP(M) event. Wonders will never cease; I really must be in love.*

Once they had settled matters – how many friends each of them might manage to bring along, where to assemble, what to carry in the way of food, drink and first-aid equipment – they relaxed, drank down the cheap, dark rum, and chattered inconsequentially, and that was when Salahuddin heard, for the first time, the rumours about the odd behaviour of the film star Gibreel Farishta that had started circulating in the city, and felt his old life prick him like a hidden thorn; – heard the past, like a distant trumpet, ringing in his ears.

The Gibreel Farishta who returned to Bombay from London to pick up the threads of his film career was not, by general consensus, the old, irresistible Gibreel. 'Guy seems hell-bent on a suicide course,' George Miranda, who knew all the filmi gossip, declared. 'Who knows why? They say because he was unlucky in love he's gone a little wild.' Salahuddin kept his mouth shut, but felt his face heating up. Allie Cone had refused to have Gibreel back after the fires of Brickhall. In the matter of forgiveness, Salahuddin reflected, nobody had thought to consult the entirely innocent and greatly injured Alleluia; *once again, we made her life peripheral to our own. No wonder she's still hopping mad.* Gibreel had told Salahuddin, in a final

and somewhat strained telephone call, that he was returning to
Bombay 'in the hope that I never have to see her, or you, or this
damn cold city, again in what remains of my life'. And now here he
was, by all accounts, shipwrecking himself again, and on home
ground, too. 'He's making some weird movies,' George went on.
'And this time he's had to put in his own cash. After the two flops,
producers have been pulling out fast. So if this one goes down, he's
broke, done for, *funtoosh.*' Gibreel had embarked on a modern-dress
remake of the Ramayana story in which the heroes and heroines
had become corrupt and evil instead of pure and free from sin. Here
was a lecherous, drunken Rama and a flighty Sita; while Ravana,
the demon-king, was depicted as an upright and honest man.
'Gibreel is playing Ravana,' George explained in fascinated horror.
'Looks like he's trying deliberately to set up a final confrontation
with religious sectarians, knowing he can't win, that he'll be broken
into bits.' Several members of the cast had already walked off the
production, and given lurid interviews accusing Gibreel of 'blasphemy', 'satanism' and other misdemeanours. His most recent mistress, Pimple Billimoria, was seen on the cover of *Ciné-Blitz*, saying:
'It was like kissing the Devil.' Gibreel's old problem of sulphurous
halitosis had evidently returned with a vengeance.

His erratic behaviour had been causing tongues to wag even
more than his choice of subjects to film. 'Some days he's sweetness
and light,' George said. 'On others, he comes to work like lord
god almighty and actually insists that people get down and kneel.
Personally I don't believe the film will be finished unless and until
he sorts out his mental health which, I genuinely feel, is affected.
First the illness, then the plane crash, then the unhappy love affair:
you can understand the guy's problems.' And there were worse
rumours: his tax affairs were under investigation; police officers
had visited him to ask questions about the death of Rekha Merchant, and Rekha's husband, the ball-bearings king, had threatened to 'break every bone in the bastard's body', so that for a few
days Gibreel had to be accompanied by bodyguards when he used
the Everest Vilas lifts; and worst of all were the suggestions of his
nocturnal visits to the city's red-light district where, it was hinted,

he had frequented certain Foras Road establishments until the dadas threw him out because the women were getting hurt. 'They say some of them were very badly damaged,' George said. 'That big hush-money had to be paid. I don't know. People say any damn thing. That Pimple of course jumped right on the bandwagon. *The Man that Hates Women*. She's making herself a femme fatale star out of all this. But there is something badly wrong with Farishta. You know the fellow, I hear,' George finished, looking at Salahuddin; who blushed.

'Not very well. Just because of the plane crash and so on.' He was in turmoil. It seemed Gibreel had not managed to escape from his inner demons. He, Salahuddin, had believed – naïvely, it now turned out – that the events of the Brickhall fire, when Gibreel saved his life, had in some way cleansed them both, had driven those devils out into the consuming flames; that, in fact, love had shown that it could exert a humanizing power as great as that of hatred; that virtue could transform men as well as vice. But nothing was forever; no cure, it appeared, was complete.

'The film industry is full of wackos,' Swatilekha was telling George, affectionately. 'Just look at you, mister.' But Bhupen grew serious. 'I always saw Gibreel as a positive force,' he said. 'An actor from a minority playing roles from many religions, and being accepted. If he has fallen out of favour, it's a bad sign.'

Two days later, Salahuddin Chamchawala read in his Sunday papers that an international team of mountaineers, on their way to attempt an ascent of the Hidden Peak, had arrived in Bombay; and when he saw that among the team was the famed 'Queen of Everest', Miss Alleluia Cone, he had a strange sense of being haunted, a feeling that the shades of his imagination were stepping out into the real world, that destiny was acquiring the slow, fatal logic of a dream. 'Now I know what a ghost is,' he thought. 'Unfinished business, that's what.'

Allie's presence in Bombay came, in the next two days, to preoccupy him more and more. His mind insisted on making strange connections, between, for example, the evident recovery of her feet and the end of her affair with Gibreel: as if he had been crippling her with his jealous love. His rational mind knew that, in fact, her problem with the fallen arches had preceded her relationship with Gibreel, but he had entered an oddly dreamy mood, and seemed impervious to logic. What was she really doing here? Why had she really come? Some terrible doom, he became convinced, was in store.

Zeeny, her medical surgeries, college lectures and work for the human-chain demonstration leaving her no time, at present, for Salahuddin and his moods, mistakenly saw his introverted silence as expressive of doubts – about his return to Bombay, about being dragged into political activity of a type that had always been abhorrent to him, about her. To disguise her fears, she spoke to him in the form of a lecture. 'If you're serious about shaking off your foreignness, Salad baba, then don't fall into some kind of rootless limbo instead. Okay? We're all here. We're right in front of you. You should really try and make an adult acquaintance with this place, this time. Try and embrace this city, as it is, not some childhood memory that makes you both nostalgic and sick. Draw it close. The actually existing place. Make its faults your own. Become its creature; belong.' He nodded, absently; and she, thinking he was preparing to leave her once again, stormed out in a rage that left him utterly perplexed.

Should he telephone Allie? Had Gibreel told her about the voices?

Should he try to see Gibreel?

Something is about to happen, his inner voice warned. *It's going to happen, and you don't know what it is, and you can't do a damn thing about it. Oh yes: it's something bad.*

It happened on the day of the demonstration, which, against all the odds, was a pretty fair success. A few minor skirmishes were reported from the Mazagaon district, but the event was, in general, an orderly one. CP(M) observers reported an unbroken chain of men and women linking hands from top to bottom of the city, and Salahuddin, standing between Zeeny and Bhupen on Muhammad Ali Road, could not deny the power of the image. Many people in the chain were in tears. The order to join hands had been given by the organizers – Swatilekha prominent among them, riding on the back of a jeep, megaphone in hand – at eight am precisely; one hour later, as the city's rush-hour traffic reached its blaring peak, the crowd began to disperse. However, in spite of the thousands involved in the event, in spite of its peaceful nature and positive message, the formation of the human chain was not reported on the Doordarshan television news. Nor did All-India Radio carry the story. The majority of the (government-supporting) 'language press' also omitted any mentions . . . one English-language daily, and one Sunday paper, carried the story; that was all. Zeeny, recalling the treatment of the Kerala chain, had forecast this deafening silence as she and Salahuddin walked home. 'It's a Communist show,' she explained. 'So, officially, it's a non-event.'

What grabbed the evening paper headlines?

What screamed at readers in inch-high letters, while the human chain was not permitted so much as a small-print whisper?

EVEREST QUEEN, FILM MOGUL PERISH
DOUBLE TRAGEDY ON MALABAR HILL –
GIBREEL FARISHTA VANISHES
CURSE OF EVEREST VILAS STRIKES AGAIN

The body of the respected movie producer, S. S. Sisodia, had been discovered by domestic staff, lying in the centre of the living-room rug in the apartment of the celebrated actor Mr Gibreel Farishta, with a hole through the heart. Miss Alleluia Cone, in what was believed to be a 'related incident', had fallen to her death from the roof of the skyscraper, from which, a couple of years previously, Mrs Rekha Merchant had hurled her children and herself towards the concrete below.

The morning papers were less equivocal about Farishta's latest role. FARISHTA, UNDER SUSPICION, ABSCONDS.

'I'm going back to Scandal Point,' Salahuddin told Zeeny, who, misunderstanding this withdrawal into an inner chamber of the spirit, flared up, 'Mister, you'd better make up your mind.' Leaving, he did not know how to reassure her; how to explain his overwhelming feeling of guilt, of *responsibility*: how to tell her that these killings were the dark flowers of seeds he had planted long ago? 'I just need to think,' he said, weakly, confirming her suspicions. 'Just a day or two.'

'Salad baba,' she said harshly, 'I've got to hand it to you, man. Your timing: really great.'

On the night after his participation in the making of the human chain, Salahuddin Chamchawala was looking out of the window of his childhood bedroom at the nocturnal patterns of the Arabian Sea, when Kasturba knocked urgently on his door. 'A man is here to see you,' she said, almost hissing the words, plainly scared. Salahuddin had seen nobody coming through the gate. 'From the servants' entrance,' Kasturba said in response to his inquiry. 'And, baba, listen, it is that Gibreel. Gibreel Farishta, who the papers say . . .' her voice trailed off and she chewed, fretfully, at the nails on her left hand.

'Where is he?'

'What to do, I was afraid,' Kasturba cried. 'I told him, in your father's study, he is waiting there only. But maybe it is better you don't go. Should I call the police? Baapu ré, that such a thing.'

No. Don't call. I'll go see what he wants.

Gibreel was sitting on Changez's bed with the old lamp in his hands. He was wearing a dirty white kurta-pajama outfit and looked like a man who had been sleeping rough. His eyes were unfocused, lightless, dead. 'Spoono,' he said wearily, waving the lamp in the direction of an armchair. 'Make yourself at home.'

'You look awful,' Salahuddin ventured, eliciting from the other man a distant, cynical, unfamiliar smile. 'Sit down and shut up, Spoono,' Gibreel Farishta said. 'I'm here to tell you a story.'

It was you, then, Salahuddin understood. *You really did it: you murdered them both.* But Gibreel had closed his eyes, put his fingertips together and embarked upon his story, – which was also the end of many stories, – thus:

Kan ma kan
Fi qadim azzaman . . .

It was so   it was not   in a time long forgot
Well, anyway   goes something like this
I can't be sure   because when they came to call I wasn't myself   no yaar   not myself at all   some days are hard   how to tell you what sickness is like   something like this   but I can't be sure
Always one part of me is standing outside   screaming   no please don't no   but it does no good   you see   when the sickness comes
I am the angel   the god damned angel of god   and these days it's the avenging angel   Gibreel the avenger   always vengeance   why
I can't be sure   something like this   for the crime of being human
especially female   but not exclusively   people must pay
Something like that
So he brought her along   he meant no harm   I know that now   he just wanted us to be together   caca can't you see he said   she isn't ohoh over you   not by a longshot   and you he said   still crazy fofor her   everyone knows   all he wanted was for us to be   to be   to be
But I heard verses
You get me Spoono
V e r s e s
Rosy apple lemon tart   Sis boom bah

/

I like coffee I like tea

Violets are blue   roses are red   remember me   when I am
dead dead dead

That type of thing

Couldn't get them out of my nut   and she changed in front
of my eyes   I called her names   whore   like that   and him I
knew about him

Sisodia   lecher from somewhere   I knew what they were
up to

laughing at me   in my own home   something like that

I like butter I like toast

Verses Spoono who do you think makes such damn things up

So I called down the wrath of God   I pointed my finger   I
shot him in the heart   but she   bitch I thought bitch   cool
as ice

stood and waited   just waited   and then I don't know   I
can't be sure   we weren't alone

Something like this

Rekha was there   floating on her carpet   you remember her
Spoono

you remember Rekha on her carpet   when we fell   and
someone else mad looking guy   Scottish get-up   *gora* type

didn't catch the name

She saw them or she didn't see them   I can't be sure   she just
stood there

It was Rekha's idea   take her upstairs   summit of Everest
once you've been there   the only way is down

I pointed my finger at her   we went up

I didn't push her

Rekha pushed her

I wouldn't have pushed her

Spoono

Understand me Spoono

Bloody hell

I loved that girl.

Salahuddin was thinking how Sisodia, with his remarkable gift for the chance encounter (Gibreel stepping out in front of London traffic, Salahuddin himself panicking before an open aircraft door, and now, it seemed, Alleluia Cone in her hotel lobby) had finally bumped accidentally into death; – and thinking, too, about Allie, less lucky a faller than himself, making (instead of her longed-for solo ascent of Everest) this ignominiously fatal descent, – and about how he was going to die for his verses, but could not find it in himself to call the death-sentence unjust.

There was a knocking at the door. *Open, please. Police.* Kasturba had called them, after all.

Gibreel took the lid off the wonderful lamp of Changez Chamchawala and let it fall clattering to the floor.

He's hidden a gun inside, Salahuddin realized. 'Watch out,' he shouted. 'There's an armed man in here.' The knocking stopped, and now Gibreel rubbed his hand along the side of the magic lamp: once, twice, thrice.

The revolver jumped up, into his other hand.

A fearsome jinnee of monstrous stature appeared, Salahuddin remembered. *'What is your wish? I am the slave of him who holds the lamp.'* What a limiting thing is a weapon, Salahuddin thought, feeling oddly detached from events. – Like Gibreel when the sickness came. – Yes, indeed; a most confining manner of thing. – For how few the choices were, now that Gibreel was the *armed man* and he, the *unarmed*; how the universe had shrunk! The true djinns of old had the power to open the gates of the Infinite, to make all things possible, to render all wonders capable of being attained; how banal, in comparison, was this modern spook, this degraded descendant of mighty ancestors, this feeble slave of a twentieth-century lamp.

"I told you a long time back,' Gibreel Farishta quietly said, 'that if I thought the sickness would never leave me, that it would always return, I would not be able to bear up to it.' Then, very quickly, before Salahuddin could move a finger, Gibreel put the barrel of the gun into his own mouth; and pulled the trigger; and was free.

He stood at the window of his childhood and looked out at the Arabian Sea. The moon was almost full; moonlight, stretching from the rocks of Scandal Point out to the far horizon, created the illusion of a silver pathway, like a parting in the water's shining hair, like a road to miraculous lands. He shook his head; could no longer believe in fairy-tales. Childhood was over, and the view from this window was no more than an old and sentimental echo. To the devil with it! Let the bulldozers come. If the old refused to die, the new could not be born.

'Come along,' Zeenat Vakil's voice said at his shoulder. It seemed that in spite of all his wrong-doing, weakness, guilt – in spite of his humanity – he was getting another chance. There was no accounting for one's good fortune, that was plain. There it simply was, taking his elbow in its hand. 'My place,' Zeeny offered. 'Let's get the hell out of here.'

'I'm coming,' he answered her, and turned away from the view.

ACKNOWLEDGEMENTS

The quotations from the Quran in this book are composites of the English versions of N. J. Dawood in the Penguin edition and of Maulana Muhammad Ali (Lahore, 1973), with a few touches of my own; that from Faiz Ahmad Faiz is a variant of the translation by Mahmood Jamal in the *Penguin Book of Modern Urdu Poetry*. For the description of the Manticore, I'm indebted to Jorge Luis Borges' *Book of Imaginary Beings*, while the material on Argentina derives, in part, from the writings of W. H. Hudson, especially *Far Away and Long Ago*. I should like to thank Pauline Melville for untangling my plaits from my dreadlocks; and to confess that the 'Gagari' poems of 'Bhupen Gandhi' are, in fact, echoes of Arun Kolatkar's collection *Jejuri*. The verses from 'Living Doll' are by Lionel Bart (© 1959 Peter Maurice Music Co. Ltd., all rights for the U.S. and Canada administered by Colgems-EMI Music, Inc.) and those by Kenneth Tynan in the novel's final section have been taken from *Tynan Right and Left* (copyright © Kenneth Tynan, 1967).

The identities of many of the authors from whom I've learned will, I hope, be clear from the text; others must remain anonymous, but I thank them, too.